FLINX OF THE COMMONWEALTH

FLINX OF THE COMMONWEALTH

**For Love of Mother-Not
The Tar-Aiym Krang
Orphan Star**

ALAN DEAN FOSTER

SCIENCE
FICTION

Contents

FOR LOVE OF MOTHER-NOT

For Michael and Audrey and Alexa Whelan;
good neighbors . . .

1

"Now there's a scrawny, worthless-looking little runt," Mother Mastiff thought. She cuddled the bag of woodcarvings a little closer to her waist, making certain it was protected from the rain by a flap of her slickertic. The steady drizzle that characterized Drallar's autumn weather fled from the water-resistant material.

Offworlders were hard pressed to distinguish any difference in the city's seasons. In the summer, the rain was warm; in autumn and winter, it was cooler. Springtime saw it give way to a steady, cloying fog. So rare was the appearance of the sun through the near-perpetual cloud cover that when it did peep through, the authorities were wont to call a public holiday.

It was not really a slave market Mother Mastiff was trudging past. That was an archaic term, employed only by cynics. It was merely the place where labor-income adjustments were formalized.

Drallar was the largest city on the world of Moth, its only true metropolis, and it was not a particularly wealthy one. By keeping taxes low, it had attracted a good number of offworld businesses and trading concerns to a well-situated but mostly inhospitable planet. It compensated by largely doing away with such annoying commercial aggravations as tariffs and regulations. While this resulted in considerable prosperity for some, it left the city government at a loss for general revenue.

Among the numerous areas that were rarely self-supporting was that involving care of the impoverished. In cases in which indigence was total and an individual was isolated by circumstance, it was deemed reasonable to allow a wealthier citizen to take over responsibility from the government. This thinned the welfare rolls and kept the bureaucracy content, while providing better care for the individual involved—or so the officials insisted—than he or she could receive from underfunded and impersonal government agencies.

The United Church, spiritual arm of the Commonwealth, frowned on such one-sided economic policies. But the Commonwealth did not like to interfere with domestic policies, and Drallarian officials hastened to assure the occasional visiting padre or counselor that legal safeguards prevented abuse of "adopted" individuals.

So it was that Mother Mastiff found herself leaning on her cane, clutching the bag of artwork, and staring at the covered dispersement platform while she tried to catch her breath. One curious attendee moved too close, crowding her. He glowered when she jabbed him in the foot with her cane but moved aside, not daring to confront her.

Standing motionless on the platform within the Circle of Compensation was a thin, solemn boy of eight or nine years. His red hair was slicked down from the rain and contrasted sharply with his dark skin. Wide, innocent eyes, so big they seemed to wrap around the sides of his face, stared out across the rain-dampened assembly. He kept his hands clasped behind his back. Only those eyes moved, their gaze flicking like an insect over the upturned faces of the crowd. The majority of the milling, would-be purchasers were indifferent to his presence.

To the boy's right stood a tall, slim representative of the government who ran the official sale—an assignment of responsibility, they called it—for the welfare bureau. Across from her a large readout listed the boy's vital statistics, which Mother Mastiff eyed casually.

Height and weight matched what she could see. Color of hair, eyes, and skin she had already noted. Living relatives, assigned or otherwise—a blank there. Personal history—another blank. A child of accident and calamity, she thought, thrown like so many others on the untender mercies of government care. Yes, he certainly would be better off under the wing of a private individual, by the looks of him. He might at least receive some decent food.

And yet there was something more to him, something that set him apart from the listless procession of orphans who paraded across that rain-swept platform, season after season. Mother Mastiff sensed something lurking behind those wide, mournful eyes—a maturity well beyond his years, a greater intensity to his stare than was to be expected from a child in his position. That stare continued to rove over the crowd, probing, searching. There was more of the hunter about the boy than the hunted.

The rain continued to fall. What activity there was among the watchers was concentrated on the back right corner of the platform, where a modestly attractive girl of about sixteen was next in line for consignment. Mother Mastiff let out a derisive snort. Government assurances or not, you couldn't tell her that those pushing, shoving snots in the front row didn't have something on their minds beyond an innocently altruistic concern for the girl's future. Oh, no!

The ever-shifting cluster of potential benefactors formed an island around which eddied the greater population of the marketplace. The marketplace itself was concentrated into a ring of stalls and shops and restaurants and dives that encircled the city center. The result was just modern enough to function and sufficiently unsophisticated to attract those intrigued by the mysterious.

It held no mysteries for Mother Mastiff. The marketplace of Drallar was her home. Ninety years she had spent battling that endless river of humanity and aliens, sometimes being sucked down, sometimes rising above the flow, but never in danger of drowning.

Now she had a shop—small, but her own. She bargained for objets d'art, traded knicknacks, electronics, and handicrafts, and managed to make just enough to keep herself clear of such places as the platform on which the boy was standing. She put herself in his place and shuddered. A ninety-year-old woman would not bring much of a price.

There was an awkwardly patched rip at the neck of her slickertic, and rain was beginning to find its way through the widening gap. The pouch of salables she clutched to her thin waist wasn't growing any lighter. Mother Mastiff had other business to transact, and she wanted to be back home before dark. As the sun of Moth set, the murky daylight of Drallar would fade to a slimy darkness, and things less than courteous would emerge from the slums that impinged on the marketplace. Only the careless and the cocky wandered abroad at such times, and Mother Mastiff was neither.

As the boy's eyes roved over the audience, they eventually reached her own—and stopped. Suddenly, Mother Mastiff felt queasy, unsteady. Her hand went to her stomach. Too much grease in the morning's breakfast, she thought. The eyes had already moved on. Since she had turned eighty-five, she had had to watch her diet. But, as she had told a friend, "I'd rather die of indigestion and on a full stomach than waste away eating pills and concentrates."

"One side there," she abruptly found herself saying, not sure what she was doing or why. "One side." She broke a path through the crowd, poking one observer in the ribs with her cane, disturb-

ing an ornithorpe's ornate arrangement of tail feathers, and generating a chirp of indignation from an overweight matron. She
worked her way down to the open area directly in front of the platform. The boy took no notice of her; his eyes continued to scan the
uncaring crowd.

"Please, ladies and gentlebeings," the official on the platform
pleaded, "won't one of you give this healthy, honest boy a home?
Your government requests it of you; civilization demands it of you.
You have a chance today to do two good turns at once; one for your
king and the other for this unfortunate youth."

"I'd like to give the king a good turn, all right," said a voice from
the milling crowd, "right where it would do him the most good."

The official shot the heckler an angry glare but said nothing.

"What's the minimum asking?" Be that *my* voice? Mother
Mastiff thought in wonderment.

"A mere fifty credits, madam, to satisfy department obligations
and the boy is yours. To watch over and care for." She hesitated,
then added, "If you think you can handle as active a youngster as
this one."

"I've handled plenty of youngsters in my time," Mother Mastiff
returned curtly. Knowing hoots sounded from the amused assembly. She studied the boy, who was looking down at her again. The
queasiness that had roiled in her stomach the first time their eyes
had met did not reoccur. Grease, she mused, have to cut down on
the cooking grease.

"Fifty credits, then," she said.

"Sixty." The deep voice that boomed from somewhere to the rear
of the crowd came as an unexpected interruption to her thoughts.

"Seventy," Mother Mastiff automatically responded. The official
on the platform quickly gazed back into the crowd.

"Eighty," the unseen competitor sounded.

She hadn't counted on competition. It was one thing to do a
child a good turn at reasonable cost to herself, quite another to saddle herself with an unconscionable expense.

"Ninety—curse you," she said. She turned and tried to locate her
opponent but could not see over the heads of the crowd. The voice
bidding against her was male, powerful, piercing. What the devil
would the owner of such a voice want with a child like this? she
thought.

"Ninety-five," it countered.

"Thank you, thank you. To you both, the government says." The
official's tone and expression had brightened perceptibly. The

lively and utterly unexpected bidding for the redheaded brat had alleviated her boredom as well as her concern. She would be able to show her boss a better than usual daily account sheet. "The bid is against you, madam."

"Damn the bid," Mother Mastiff muttered. She started to turn away, but something held her back. She was as good a judge of people as she was of the stock she sold to them, and there was something particular about this boy—though she couldn't say precisely what, which struck her as unusual. There was always profit in the unusual. Besides, that mournful stare was preying unashamedly on a part of her she usually kept buried.

"Oh, hell, one hundred, then, and be damned with it!" She barely managed to squeeze the figure out. Her mind was in a whirl. What was she doing there, neglecting her regular business, getting thoroughly soaked and bidding for an orphaned child? Surely at ninety her maternal instinct wasn't being aroused. She had never felt the least maternal instinct in her life, thank goodness.

She waited for the expected rumble of "one hundred and five," but instead heard a commotion toward the back of the crowd. She craned her neck, trying to see, cursing the genes that had left her so short. There were shouts, then yells of outrage and loud cursing from a dozen different throats. To the left, past the shielding bulk of the ornithorpe behind her, she could just make out the bright purple flash of uniformed gendarmes, their slickertics glaring in the dim light. This group seemed to be moving with more than usual energy.

She turned and fought her way forward and to the right, where a series of steps led to the platform. Halfway up the stairs, she squinted back into the crowd. The purple 'tics were just merging into the first wall of office and shop complexes. Ahead of them a massive human shape bobbed and dipped as it retreated from the pursuing police.

Mother Mastiff permitted herself a knowing nod. There were those who might want a young boy for other than humanitarian purposes. Some of them had criminal dossiers on file that stretched as far back as her lifeline. Obviously someone in the crowd, a salaried informer, perhaps, had recognized the individual bidding against her and had notified the authorities, who had responded with commendable speed.

"One hundred credits, then," the disappointed official announced from the platform. "Do I hear any more?" Naturally, she would not, but she played out the game for appearance's sake. A moment passed in silence. She shrugged, glanced over to where Mother Mastiff still stood on the stairway. "He's yours, old woman." Not "madam" any longer, Mother Mastiff thought sardonically. "Pay up, and mind the regulations, now."

"I've been dealing with the regulations of this government since long before ye were born, woman." She mounted the last few steps and, ignoring the official and the boy, strode back toward the Processing Office.

Inside, a bored clerk glanced up at her, noted the transaction-complete record as it was passed to his desk-top computer terminal, and asked matter-of-factly, "Name?"

"Mastiff," the visitor replied, leaning on her cane.

"That the last name?"

"First and last."

"Mastiff Mastiff?" The clerk gave her a sour look.

"Just *Mastiff*," the old woman said.

"The government prefers multiple names."

"Ye know what the government can do with its preferences."

The clerk sighed. He tapped the terminal's keys. "Age?"

"None of your business." She gave it a moment's thought and added, "Put down *old*."

The clerk did so, shaking his head dolefully. "Income?"

"Sufficient."

"Now look here, you," the clerk began exasperated, "in such matters as the acquisition of responsibility for welfared individuals, the city government requires certain specifics."

"The city government can shove its specifics in after its preferences." Mother Mastiff gestured toward the platform with her cane, a wide, sweeping gesture that the clerk had the presence of mind to duck. "The bidding is over. The other bidder has taken his leave. Hastily. Now I can take my money and go home, or I can contribute to the government's balance of payments and to your salary. Which is it to be?"

"Oh, all right," the clerk agreed petulantly. He completed his entries and punched a key. A seemingly endless form spat from the printout slot. Folded, it was about half a centimeter thick. "Read these."

Mother Mastiff hefted the sheaf of forms. "What are they?"

"Regulations regarding your new charge. The boy is yours to raise, not to mistreat. Should you ever be detected in violation of the instructions and laws therein stated"—he gestured at the wad—"he can be recovered from you with forfeiture of the acquisition fee. In addition, you must familiarize yourself with—" He broke off the lecture as the boy in question was escorted into the room by another official.

The youngster glanced at the clerk, then up at Mother Mastiff. Then, as if he'd performed similar rituals on previous occasions, he walked quietly up to her, took her left hand, and put his right hand in it. The wide, seemingly guileless eyes of a child gazed up at her face. They were bright green, she noted absently.

The clerk was about to continue, then found something unexpected lodged in his throat and turned his attention instead back to his desk top. "That's all. The two of you can go."

Mother Mastiff harrumphed as if she had won a victory and led the boy out onto the streets of Drallar. They had supplied him with that one vital piece of clothing, a small blue slickertic of his own. He pulled the cheap plastic tighter over his head as they reached the first intersection.

"Well, boy, 'tis done. Devil come take me and tell me if I know why I did it, but I expect that I'm stuck with ye now. And ye with me, of course. Do you have anything at the dorm we should go to recover?"

He shook his head slowly. Quiet sort, she thought. That was all to the good. Maybe he wouldn't be a quick squaller. She still wondered what had prompted her sudden and uncharacteristic outburst of generosity. The boy's hand was warm in her gnarled old palm. That palm usually enfolded a credcard for processing other people's money or artwork to be studied with an eye toward purchase and even, on occasion, a knife employed for something more radical than the preparation of food, but never before the hand of a small child. It was a peculiar sensation.

They worked their way through crowds hurrying to beat the onset of night, avoiding the drainage channels that ran down the center of each street. Thick aromas drifted from the dozens of food stalls and restaurants that fringed the avenue they were walking. Still the boy said not a word. Finally, tired of the way his face would turn toward any place from which steam and smells rose, Mother Mastiff halted before one establishment with which she was familiar. They were nearly home, anyway.

"You hungry, boy?"

He nodded slowly, just once.

"Stupid of me. I can go all day without food and not give it a second thought. I forget sometimes that others have not that tolerance in their bellies." She nodded toward the doorway. "Well, what are ye waiting for?"

She followed him into the restaurant, then led the way to a quiet booth set against the wall. A circular console rose from the center of the table. She studied the menu imprinted on its flank, compared it with the stature of the child seated expectantly next to her, then punched several buttons set alongside the menu.

Before too long, the console sank into the table, then reappeared a moment later stacked with food; a thick, pungent stew dimpled with vegetables, long stalks of some beige tuber, and a mass of multistriped bread.

"Go ahead," she said when the boy hesitated, admiring his reserve and table manners. "I'm not too hungry, and I never eat very much."

She watched him while he devoured the food, sometimes picking at the colorful bread to assuage what little hunger she felt herself, barely acknowledging the occasional greeting from a passing acquaintance or friend. When the bottom of the stew bowl had been licked to a fine polish and the last scrap of bread had vanished, she asked, "Still hungry?"

He hesitated, measuring her, then gave her a half nod. "I'm not surprised," she replied, "but I don't want ye to have any more tonight. You've just downed enough to fill a grown man. Any more on top of what you've already had and you'd end up wasting it all. Tomorrow morning, okay?" He nodded slowly, understanding.

"And one more thing, boy. Can ye talk?"

"Yes." His voice was lower than anticipated, unafraid and, she thought, tinged with thankfulness.

"I can talk pretty good," he added without further prompting, surprising her. "I've been told that for my age I'm a very good talker."

"That's nice. I was starting to worry." She slid from her seat, using her cane to help her stand, and took his hand once again. "It's not too far now."

"Not too far to where?"

"To where I live. To where ye will live from now on." They exited the restaurant and were enveloped by the wet night.

"What's your name?" He spoke without looking up at her, preferring instead to study the dim storefronts and isolated, illuminated shops. The intensity of his inspection seemed unnatural.

"Mastiff," she told him, then grinned. " 'Tis not my real name, boy, but one that someone laid upon me many years ago. For bet-

ter or worse, it's stuck longer with me than any man. 'Tis the name
of a dog of exceptional ferocity and ugliness."

"I don't think you're ugly," the boy replied. "I think you're beautiful."

She studied his open, little-boy expression. Dim-witted, dim-
sighted, or maybe just very smart, she thought.

"Can I call you Mother?" he asked hopefully, further confusing
her. "You are my mother now, aren't you?"

"Sort of, I expect. Don't ask me why."

"I won't cause you any trouble." His voice was suddenly concerned, almost frightened. "I've never caused anyone any trouble,
honest. I just want to be left alone."

Now what would prompt a desperate confession like that? she
wondered. She decided not to pursue the matter. "I've no demands
to make on ye," she assured him. "I'm a simple old woman, and I
live a simple life. It pleases me. It had best please ye as well."

"It sounds nice," he admitted agreeably. "I'll do my best to help
you any way I can."

"Devil knows there's plenty to do in the shop. I'm not quite as
flexible as I used to be." She chuckled aloud. "Get tired before
midnight now. You know, I actually need a full four hours' sleep?
Yes, I think ye can be of service. You'd best be. Ye cost enough."

"I'm sorry," he said, abruptly downcast.

"Stop that. I'll have none of that in my home."

"I mean, I'm sorry that I upset you."

She let out a wheeze of frustration, knelt and supported herself
with both hands locked to the shaft of the cane. It brought her
down to his eye level. He stood there and gazed solemnly back at
her.

"Now ye listen to me, boy. I'm no government agent. I don't
have the vaguest notion what possessed me to take charge of ye,
but 'tis done. I will not beat you unless you deserve it. I'll see to it
that you're well fed and reasonably warm. In return, I demand that
ye don't go about braying stupid things like 'I'm sorry.' Be that a
deal?"

He didn't have to think it over very long. "It's a deal—Mother."

"That's settled, then." She shook his hand. The gesture brought
forth a new phenomenon: his first smile. It made his tiny, lightly
freckled face seem to glow, and suddenly the night seemed less
chilly.

"Let's hurry," she said, struggling erect again. "I don't like being out this late, and you're not much the bodyguard. Never will be, by the looks of ye, though that's no fault of yours."

"Why is it so important to be home when it's dark?" he asked, and then added uncertainly, "Is that a stupid question?"

"No, boy." She smiled down at him as she hobbled up the street. "That's a smart question. It's important to be safe at home after dark because the dead tend to multiply in direct ratio to the absence of light. Though if you're cautious and never grow overconfident and learn the ways of it, you'll find that the darkness can be your friend as well as your enemy."

"I thought so," he said firmly. "I've thought so for"—his face screwed up as he concentrated hard on something—"for as long as I can remember."

"Oh?" She was still smiling at him. "And what makes you think that it's so besides the fact I just told it to ye?"

"Because," he replied, "most of the times I can ever remember being happy were in the dark."

She pondered that as they turned the corner. The rain had lessened considerably, giving way to the mist that passed for normal air in the city. It didn't trouble her lungs, but she worried about the boy. The one thing she didn't need was a sick child. He had cost her enough already.

Her stall-home was one of many scattered through the seemingly endless marketplace. Stout shutters protected the nondescript façade, which occupied ten meters at the far end of a side street. She pressed her palm to the door lock. The sensitized plastic glowed brightly for an instant, beeped twice, and then the door opened for them.

Once inside, she shoved the door shut behind them, then automatically turned to inspect her stock to make certain nothing had disappeared in her absence. There were racks of copper and silver wares, rare carved hardwoods for which Moth was justly renowned, well-crafted eating and drinking utensils, including many clearly designed for non-humans, cheap models of Moth itself with interrupted rings of flashy floatglitter, and various items of uncertain purpose.

Through this farrago of color and shape, the boy wandered. His eyes drank in everything, but he asked no questions, which she thought unusual.

It was in the nature of children to inquire about everything. But then, this was no ordinary child.

Toward the rear of the shop front a silver box stood on a dais. Its touch-sensitive controls connected the shop directly to the central bank of Drallar and enabled Mother Mastiff to process financial transactions for all customers, whether they came from up the street or halfway across the Commonwealth. A universal credcard allowed access to its owner's total wealth. Banks stored information; all hard currency was in general circulation.

Past the dais and the door it fronted were four rooms: a small storage chamber, a bathroom, a kitchen-dining area, and a bedroom. Mother Mastiff studied the arrangement for several minutes, then set about clearing the storage room. Ancient and long-unsold items were shoveled out onto the floor, together with cleaning equipment, clothing, canned goods, and other items. Somehow she would find room for them elsewhere.

Propped up against the far wall was a sturdy old cot. She touched a button on its side, and the device sprang to life, skittering about as it arranged itself on springy legs. Further excavation revealed a bag of support oil, which she plugged into the mattress. It was full and warm in minutes. Finally, she covered the cot with a thin thermosensitive blanket.

"This'll be your room," she told him. " 'Tis no palace, but 'tis yours. I know the importance of having something ye can call your own. Ye can fix up this bower however ye like."

The boy eyed her as if she had just bestowed all the treasures of Terra on him. "Thank you, Mother," he said softly. "It's wonderful."

"I sell things," she said, turning away from that radiant face. She gestured toward the storeroom out front. "The things ye saw on our way in."

"I guessed that. Do you make much money?"

"Now *ye* sound like the government agent back there at the platform." She smiled to show him she was teasing. "I get by. I'd much like to have a larger place than this, but at this point in my life"— she leaned her cane up against her bed as she strolled into the larger room—"it seems not likely I ever will. It does not bother me. I've had a good, full life and am content. You'll soon discover that my growls and barks are mostly show. Though not always." She patted him on the head and pointed toward the compact kitchen.

"Would ye like something hot to drink before we retire?"

"Yes, very much." Carefully, he took off his slickertic, which was dry by then. He hung it on a wall hook in his bedroom.

"We'll have to get ye some new clothes," she commented, watching him from the kitchen.

"These are okay."

"Maybe they are for ye, but they're not for me." She pinched her nose by way of explanation.

"Oh. I understand."

"Now what would ye like to drink?"

His face brightened once again. "Tea. What kinds of tea do you have?"

"What kinds of tea do ye like?"

"All kinds."

"Then I'll choose ye one." She found the cylinder and depressed the main switch on its side as she filled it with water from the tap. Then she searched her store of foodstuffs.

"This is Anar Black," she told him, "all the way from Rhyinpine. Quite a journey for dead leaves to make. I think 'tis milder than Anar White, which comes from the same world but grows further down the mountain sides. I have some local honey if ye like your drink sweet. Expensive, it is. Moth's flowers are scarce save where they're grown in hothouses. This world belongs to the fungi and the trees; the bees, poor things, have a hard time of it, even those who've grown woolly coats thick enough to keep the damp and cold out. If honey's too thick for ye, I've other sweeteners."

Hearing no reply, she turned to find him lying still on the floor, a tawny, curled-up smudge of red hair and dirty old clothes. His hands were bunched beneath his cheek, cushioning his head.

She shook her head and pushed the cylinder's *off* button. The pot sighed and ceased boiling. Bending, she got her wiry arms beneath him and lifted. Somehow she wrestled him onto the cot without waking him. Her hands pulled the thermal blanket up to his chin. It was programmed and would warm him quickly.

She stood there awhile, amazed at how much pleasure could be gained from so simple an activity as watching a child sleep. Then, still wondering what had come over her, she left him and made her way across to her own room, slowly removing her clothes as she walked. Before long, the last light in the rear of the little shop winked out, joining its neighbors in nightfall. Then there was only the light wind and the hiss of moisture evaporating from warm walls to break the silence of the mist-shrouded dark.

2

The boy ate as if the previous night's dinner had been no more substantial than a distant dream. She cooked him two full breakfasts and watched as he finished every bite. When the last pachnack was gone, and the final piece of bread wolfed down, she took him into the shop.

He watched intently as she entered the combination to the metal shutters. As they rose, they admitted a world entirely different from the empty night. One moment he was staring at the dully reflective line of metal strips. The next brought home to him all the noise, the confusion, and bustle and sights and smells of the great Drallarian marketplace; they flooded the stall, overwhelming him with their diversity and brilliance. Mother Mastiff was not a late sleeper—which was good, for the crowd would rise in tandem with the hidden sun. Not that the marketplace was ever completely deserted. There were always a few merchants whose wares benefited from the mask of night.

The boy could tell it was daytime because it had grown less dark. But the sun did not shine; it illuminated the raindrops. The morning had dawned warm, a good sign, and the moisture was still more mist than rain. A good day for business.

Mother Mastiff showed the boy around the shop, describing various items and reciting their prices and the reasons behind such pricing. She hoped to someday entrust the operation of the business to him. That would be better than having to close up every time she needed to rest or travel elsewhere. The sooner he learned, the better, especially considering the way he ate.

"I'll do everything I can, Mother," he assured her when she had concluded the brief tour.

"I know ye will, boy." She plopped down into her favorite chair, an overupholstered monstrosity covered with gemmac fur. The skins were worn down next to nothing, and the chair retained little value, but it was too comfortable for her to part with. She watched as the boy turned to stare at the passing crowd. How quiet he is, she thought. Quiet and intense. She let him study the passersby for a while before beckoning him closer.

"We've overlooked several things in the rush of the night, boy. One in particular."

"What's that?" he asked.

"I can't keep calling ye 'boy.' Have ye a name?"

"They call me Flinx."

"Be that your last name or your first?"

He shook his head slowly, his expression unhappy. "Mother, I don't know. It's what they called me."

"What 'they' called ye. Who be 'they'? Your"—she hesitated—"mother? Your father?"

Again, the slow sad shake of the head, red curls dancing. "I don't have a mother or a father. It's what the people called me."

"What people?"

"The people who watched over me and the other children."

Now that was strange. She frowned. "Other children? Ye have brothers and sisters, then?"

"I don't"—he strained to remember—"I don't *think* so. Maybe they were. I don't know. They were just the other children. I remember them from the early time. It was a strange time."

"What was so strange about it?"

"I was happy."

She nodded once, as though she understood. "So. Ye remember an early time when you were happy and there were lots of other children living with you."

He nodded vigorously. "Boys and girls both. And we had everything we could want, everything we asked for. All kinds of good food and toys to play with and . . ."

A wealthy family brought to ruin, perhaps. She let him ramble on about the early time, the happy time, a while longer. What catastrophe had overtaken the boy in infancy?

"How big was this family?" she asked. "We'll call it your family for now. How many other boys and girls were there?"

"I don't remember exactly. Lots."

"Can you count?"

"Oh, sure," he said proudly. "Two, three, four, five, and lots more than that."

Sounded like more than just a family, though an extended family could not be ruled out, she knew. "Do ye remember what happened to them, and to you? Ye were all happy, and ye had lots of friends, and then something happened."

"The bad people came," he whispered, his expression turning down. "Very bad people. They broke into where we lived. The peo-

ple who watched us and fed us and gave us toys fought the bad
people. There was lots of noise and guns going off and—and people fell down all around me. Good people and bad people both. I
stood and cried until somebody picked me up and carried me away.
They carried me down lots of halls and dark places, and I remember getting into some kind of a—car?"

She nodded approvingly. "Probably. Go on, boy."

"I was moved around a lot. That was the end of the happy time."

"What happened after that?" she prompted him.

"I'm not sure," he said slowly. "It's so hard to remember."

"I know 'tis painful for ye, Flinx. I need to know all about ye that
I can, so I can help ye as best as I'm able."

"If I tell you," he asked uncertainly, "you won't let the bad people come and take me away?"

"No," she said, her voice suddenly soft. "No, I won't let them
come and take ye away, Flinx. I won't let *anyone* come and take ye
away. Ever. I promise ye that."

He moved a little nearer and sat down on the extended leg support of the big chair. He had his eyes closed as he concentrated.

"I remember never staying in one place for very long at a time.
The people, the good people who took care of me and fed me, they
kept the bad people away. They were always upset about something, and they yelled at me a lot more than before."

"Were they mad at ye?"

"I don't think so. Not really." He licked his lips. "I think they
were scared, Mother. I know I was, but I think they were, also. And
then"—a look of confusion stole over his face—"I went to sleep.
For a *long* time. Only, it wasn't really a sleep. It was like I was
asleep and yet like I wasn't." He opened his eyes and looked up at
her. "Do you understand that, Mother? I don't."

"No, I'm not sure I do, boy." Her mind worked. Now who, she
wondered, would take the time and trouble to sedate a child for a
long period of time? And why bother?

"Then some more bad people suddenly showed up, I think," he
went on. "I didn't see them this time. But some of the people who
watched me died or went away. Then there was just me and one
man and one lady, and then they were gone, too."

"Your mother and father?"

"No, I don't think so," he told her. "Anyway, they never called
themselves that. They were just two of the good people. Then some
other people came and found me. People I'd never seen before.
They took me away with them."

"Were they good people or bad people?"

"I don't think they were either," the boy replied carefully. "I think they were kind of in-between people. I think maybe they were sorry for me. They tried to be nice, but"—he shrugged—"they were just in-between people. They moved me around a lot again, and there were different places and lots of new children I didn't know, and then there was yesterday, and you bought me. Right?"

She put a hand to her mouth and coughed. "I didn't buy ye, actually. I agreed to take responsibility for ye."

"But you paid the government money for me, didn't you? I was told that was what was going to happen to me."

"It was only to pay off the debt the government incurred for taking care of ye," she explained to him. "I don't actually own ye. I would never do that."

"Oh," he said quietly. "That's nice. I'm glad." He waited a moment, watching her, then added, "That's everything I can remember."

"Ye did fine." She leaned forward and pointed to her right, up the street. The chair groaned. "If ye walk six stalls that way, ye'll find a very small shop run by a mur man. His name be Cheneth. Go up to him and tell him who ye be and where ye came from. And ye can buy from him"—she thought a moment, not wishing to overdo things—"a half credit's worth of whatever ye see in his shop."

"What kind of shop is it?" he asked excitedly.

"Candy," she said, enjoying the light that came into his face. "Ye remember what candy is, don't ye? I can see by the expression on your face that ye do." She could also tell by the speed with which he took off up the street. He was back before long, those deep emerald eyes shining from his dark face. "Thank you, Mother."

"Go on, go on, move to one side! You're blocking my—our—view of the customers. Wander about, learn the ins and outs of where ye live now."

He vanished like a ray of sunshine, his red hair disappearing into the crowd.

Expensive, she thought to herself. That boy's going to be expensive to raise. How by the ringaps did I ever let myself fall into this? She grumbled silently for another several minutes until a potential customer appeared.

Flinx learned rapidly. He was undemonstrative, highly adaptable, and so quiet she hardly knew when he was around. Soon he was amazing her with his knowledge of the layout and workings of the marketplace and even the greater city beyond. He worked constantly on expanding his store of information, badgering shopkeepers with persistent questions, refusing to take "I don't know" for an answer.

Mother Mastiff put no restrictions on him. No one had ever told her it was improper to give an eight-year-old the run of a city as wild as Drallar. Never having raised a child before, she could always plead ignorance, and since he returned dutifully every night, unscathed and unharmed, she saw no reason to alter the practice despite the clucking disapproval of some of her neighbors.

"That's no way to handle a boy of an age that tender," they admonished her. "If you're not careful, you'll lose him. One night, he won't come home from these solo forays."

"A boy he is, tender he's not," she would reply. "Sharp he be, and not just for his age. I don't worry about him. I haven't the time, for one thing. No matter what happens to him, he's better off than he was under government care."

"He won't be better off if he ends up lying dead in a gutter somewhere," they warned her.

"He won't," she would reply confidently.

"You'll be sorry," they said. "You wait and see."

"I've been waiting and seeing going on ninety years" was her standard reply, "and I haven't been surprised yet. I don't expect this boy to break that record."

But she was wrong.

It was midafternoon. The morning mist had developed into a heavy rain. She was debating whether or not to send the boy out for some food or to wait. Half a dozen people were wandering through the shop, waiting for the downpour to let up—an unusually large number for any day.

After a while, Flinx wandered over and tugged shyly at her billowing skirt. "Mother Mastiff?"

"What is it, boy? Don't bother me now." She turned back to the customer who was inspecting antique jewelry that graced a locked display case near the rear of the stall. It was rare that she sold a piece of the expensive stuff. When she did, the profit was considerable.

The boy persisted, and she snapped at him. "I told ye, Flinx, not now!"

"It's very important, Mother."

She let out a sigh of exasperation and looked apologetically at the outworlder. "Excuse me a moment, good sir. Children, ye know."

The man smiled absently, thoroughly engrossed in a necklace that shone with odd pieces of metal and worn wood.

"What is it, Flinx?" she demanded, upset with him. "This better be important. You know how I don't like to be disturbed when I'm in the middle of—"

He interrupted her by pointing to the far end of the shop. "See that man over there?"

She looked up, past him. The man in question was bald and sported a well-trimmed beard and earrings. Instead of the light slickertic favored by the inhabitants of Moth, he wore a heavy off-world overcoat of black material. His features were slighter than his height warranted, and his mouth was almost delicate. Other than the earrings he showed no jewelry. His boots further marked him as an offworld visitor—they were relatively clean.

"I see him. What about him?"

"He's been stealing jewelry from the end case."

Mother Mastiff frowned. "Are you sure, boy?" Her tone was anxious. "He's an offworlder, and by the looks of him, a reasonably substantial one at that. If we accuse him falsely—"

"I'm positive, Mother."

"You saw him steal?"

"No, I didn't exactly *see* him."

"Then what the devil"—she wondered in a low, accusatory voice—"are ye talking about?"

"Go look at the case," he urged her.

She hesitated, then shrugged mentally. "No harm in that, I expect." Now whatever had gotten into the boy? She strolled toward the case, affecting an air of unconcern. As she drew near, the outworlder turned and walked away, apparently unperturbed by her approach. He hardly acted like a nervous thief about to be caught in the act.

Then she was bending over the case. Sure enough, the lock had been professionally picked. At least four rings, among the most valuable items in her modest stock, were missing. She hesitated only briefly before glancing down at Flinx.

"You're positive it was him, ye say?"

He nodded energetically.

Mother Mastiff put two fingers to her lips and let out a piercing whistle. Almost instantly, a half-dozen neighboring shopkeepers appeared. Still the bald man showed no hint of panic, simply stared curiously, along with the others in the store at the abrupt arrivals. The rain continued to pelt the street. Mother Mastiff raised a hand, pointed directly at the bald man, and said, "Restrain that thief!"

The man's eyes widened in surprise, but he made no move toward retreat. Immediately, several angry shopkeepers had him firmly by the arms. At least two of them were armed.

The bald man stood it for a moment or two, then angrily shook off his captors. His accent, when he spoke, marked him as a visitor from one of the softer worlds, like New Riviera or Centaurus B. "Now just a moment! What is going on here? I warn you, the next person who puts hands on me will suffer for it!"

"Don't threaten us, citizen," said Aljean, the accomplished clothier whose big shop dominated the far corner. "We'll settle this matter quick, and without the attention of police. We don't much like police on this street."

"I sympathize with you there," the man said, straightening his overcoat where he had been roughly handled. "I'm not especially fond of them myself." After a pause, he added in shock, "Surely that woman does not mean to imply that *I*—"

"That's what she's implyin', for sure," said one of the men flanking him. "If you've nothin' to fear, then you've no reason not to gift us a moment of your time."

"Certainly not. I don't see why—" The outworlder studied their expressions a moment, then shrugged. "Oh, well, if it will settle this foolishness."

"It'll settle it," another man said from behind a pistol.

"Very well. And I'll thank you to keep that weapon pointed away from me, please. Surely you don't need the succor of technology in addition to superior numbers?"

The shopkeeper hesitated and then turned the muzzle of his gun downward. But he did not put it away.

Mother Mastiff stared at the man for a moment, then looked expectantly down at Flinx. "Well? Did ye see where he put the rings?"

Flinx was gazing steadily at the bald man, those green eyes unwinking. "No, I didn't, Mother. But he took them. I'm sure of it."

"Right, then." Her attention went back to the offworlder. "Sir, I must ask ye to consent to a brief body search."

"This is most undignified," he complained. "I shall lodge a complaint with my tourist office."

"I'm sorry," she told him, "but if you've nothing to hide, it's best that we're assured of it."

"Oh, very well. Please hurry and get it over with. I have other places to go today. I'm on holiday, you know."

Acting uncertainly now, two of the men who had responded to Mother Mastiff's whistle searched the visitor. They did a thorough job of it, working him over with the experience of those who had dealt with thieves before. They searched everything from the lining of his overcoat to the heels of his boots. When they had finished, they gazed helplessly over at Mother Mastiff and shook their heads.

"Empty he is," they assured her. "Nothing on him."

"What's missing, Mother?" Aljean asked gently.

"Kill rings," she explained. "The only four kill rings in my stock. Took me years to accumulate them, and I wouldn't know how to go about replacing them. Search him again." She nodded at the bald man. "They're not very big and would be easy enough to hide."

They complied, paying particular attention this time to the thick metal belt buckle the man wore. It revealed a hidden compartment containing the man's credcard and little else. No rings.

When the second search proved equally fruitless, Mother Mastiff gazed sternly down at her charge. "Well, Flinx, what have ye to say for yourself?"

"He *did* take them, he did," the boy insisted, almost crying. "I know he did." He was still staring at the bald man. Suddenly, his eyes widened. "He *swallowed* them."

"Swallowed—now just a minute," the visitor began. "This is getting ugly. Am I to wait here, accused by a mischievous child?" He shook an angry finger at Flinx, who did not flinch or break his cold, green stare.

"He took them," the boy repeated, "and swallowed them."

"Did you see me take these rings?" the bald man demanded.

"No," Flinx admitted, "I didn't. But you took them. You know you did. They're inside you."

"Charming, the experiences one has on the slumworlds," the man said sarcastically. "Really, though, this exercise has ceased to be entertaining. I must go. My tour allots me only two days in this *wonderful* city, and I wouldn't want to waste any more time observing quaint local customs. Out of the kindness of my nature, I will not call upon the gendarmes to arrest you all. One side, please." He shoved past the uncertain shopkeepers and walked easily out into the rain.

Mother Mastiff eyed the man's retreating back. Her friends and fellow merchants watched her expectantly, helplessly. She looked down at the boy. Flinx had stopped crying. His voice was calm and unemotional as he gazed back up at her.

"He took them, Mother, and he's walking away with them *right now.*"

She could not explain what motivated her as she calmly told Aljean, "Call a gendarme, then."

The bald man heard that, stopped, and turned back to face them through the now gentle rain. "Really, old woman, if you think I'm going to wait—"

"Aljean," Mother Mastiff said, "Cheneth?" The two shopkeepers exchanged a glance, then jogged out to bring the bald man back— if false restraint charges were filed, they would be against Mother Mastiff and not them.

"I'm sorry, sir," Cheneth, the candy man, said as he gestured with his pistol, "but we're going to have to ask you to wait until the authorities arrive."

"And then what? Are they going to haul a free citizen to the magistrate because a child demands it?"

"A simple body scan should be sufficient," Mother Mastiff said as the three re-entered the shop. "Surely you've no reason to object to that?"

"Of course I'd object to it!" the visitor responded. "They have no reason or right to—"

"My, but you're suddenly arguing a lot for someone with nothing to worry about," Aljean, the clothier, observed. She was forty-two years old and had run her way through four husbands. She was very adept at spotting lies, and she was suddenly less convinced of this visitor's innocence. "Of course, if perhaps you realize now that you've somehow made a bit of mistake and that we quaint locals aren't quite the simpletons you believe us to be, and if you'd rather avoid the inconvenience of a scan, not to mention official attention, you'll learn that we're agreeably forgiving here if you'll just return to Mother Mastiff what you've taken."

"I haven't taken a damn—" the bald man started to say.

"The jails of Drallar are very, very uncomfortable," Aljean continued briskly. "Our government resents spending money on public needs. They especially scrimp when it comes to the comfort of wrongdoers. You being an offworlder now, I don't think you'd take well to half a year of unfiltered underground dampness. Mold will sprout in your lungs, and your eyelids will mildew."

All of a sudden, the man seemed to slump in on himself. He glared down at Flinx, who stared quietly back at him.

"I don't know how the hell you saw me, boy. I swear, no one saw me! No one!"

"I'll be blessed over," Cheneth murmured, his jaw dropping as he looked from the thief to the boy who had caught him. "Then you did take the rings!"

"Ay. Call off the authorities," he said to Aljean "You've said it would be enough if I gave back the rings. I agree."

Mother Mastiff nodded slowly. "I agree, also, provided that ye promise never to show your reflective crown in this part of this marketplace ever again."

"My word on it, as a professional," the man promised quickly. "I did not lie when I said that I was on holiday." He gave them a twisted smile. "I like to make my holidays self-supporting."

Mother Mastiff did not smile back. She held out a hand. "My kill rings, if ye please."

The man's smile twisted even further. "Soon enough. But first I will need certain edibles. There are several fruits which will suffice, or certain standard medications. I will also need clean cloths and disinfectant. The boy is right, you see. I did swallow them. Provide what I need and in an hour or so you will have your cursed rings back."

And forty minutes later she did.

After the thief and the little group of admiring shopkeepers had gone their respective ways, Mother Mastiff took her charge aside and confronted him with the question no one else had thought to ask.

"Now, boy, ye say ye didn't see him swallow the rings?"

"No, I didn't, Mother." Now that the crowd had dispersed and he had been vindicated, his shyness returned.

"Then how the ringap did ye know?"

Flinx hesitated.

"Come now, boy, out with it. Ye can tell me," she said in a coaxing tone. "I'm your mother now, remember. The only one you've got. I've been fair and straightforward with ye. Now 'tis your turn to do the same with me."

"You're sure?" He was fighting with himself, she saw. "You're sure you're not just being nice to me to fool me? You're not one of the bad people?"

That was a funny thing for him to bring up, she thought. "Of course I'm not one of them. Do I look like a bad people?"

"N-n-no," he admitted. "But it's hard to tell, sometimes."

"You've lived with me for some time now, boy. Ye know me bet-ter than that." Her voice became gentle again. "Come now. Fair is fair. So stop lying to me by insisting you didn't see him swallow those rings."

"I didn't," he said belligerently, "and I'm not lying. The man was—he was starting to walk away from the case, and he was un-comfortable. He was, he felt—what's the word? He felt guilty."

"Now how do ye know that?"

"Because," he murmured, not looking at her but staring out at the street where strange people scurried back and forth in the re-turning mist, "because I felt it." He put his small hand to his fore-head and rubbed gently. "Here."

Great Ganwrath of the Flood, Mother Mastiff thought sharply. The boy's a Talent. "You mean," she asked again, "you read his mind?"

"No," he corrected her. "It's not like that. It's just—it's a feeling I get sometimes."

"Do ye get this feeling whenever ye look at someone who's been guilty?"

"It's not only guilty," he explained, "it's all kinds of feelings. People—it's like a fire. You can feel heat from a fire." She nodded slowly. "Well, I can feel certain things from people's heads. Happiness or fear or hate and lots of other things I'm not sure about. Like when a man and a woman are together."

"Can ye do this whenever ye wish?" she asked.

"No. Hardly ever. Lots of times I can't feel a thing. It's clean then and doesn't jump in on me, and I can relax. Then there's other times when the feeling will just be there—in here," he added, tap-ping his forehead again. "I was looking toward that man, and the guilt and worry poured out of him like a fire, especially whenever he looked at the jewel case. He was worried, too, about being dis-covered somehow and being caught, and a lot of other things, too. He was thinking, was throwing out thoughts of lots of quick money. Money he was going to get unfairly."

"Emotions," she mused aloud, "all emotions." She began to chuckle softly. She had heard of such things before. The boy was an empathic telepath, though a crude one. He could read other people's emotions, though not their actual thoughts.

"It's all right, Flinx," she assured him. She put out a hand and gave his hair a playful tousle. "Ye did right well. Ye saved me, saved us both, a lot of money." She looked over at the small leatherine purse that now held the four recovered and cleansed rings. They still smelled of disinfectant.

"No wonder that thief couldn't figure out how you'd spotted him. Ye really didn't see him take the rings."

"No, Mother. I wasn't even sure what he'd taken."

"Ye just felt the reaction in his mind?"

"I guess," he said. "I—I don't know how it happens, but I know that most people can't do it, can they?"

"No," she said gently, "most other people can't. And sometimes they become very upset if they think there's someone around like ye who can."

Flinx nodded solemnly. "Like the bad people?"

"Maybe," she said, considering that possibility. "Maybe like the bad people, yes. Ye can't control the power, you're sure?"

"I'm sure. I've tried. Sometimes it's just there, a burning inside my head. But most of the time it's not."

She nodded. "That's too bad, too bad. Ye have what's called a Talent, Flinx."

"A Talent." He considered that a moment, then asked uncertainly, "Is it a good thing?"

"It can be. It can also be a dangerous thing, Flinx. We must make a secret of it, your secret and mine. Don't ever tell anyone else about it."

"I won't," he murmured, then added energetically, "I promise. Then you're not mad at me?"

"Mad?" She let out a long, rolling cackle. "Now how could I be mad with ye, boy? I've regained my jewelry, and you've gained quite a bit of respect among our neighbors. In the marketplace, that can be a tradable commodity, as ye may discover someday. They think you've a sharp eye and a sharper tongue. The reality be something more, though I wouldn't argue ye can cut words with the best of them. Keep your Talent to yourself. Remember, our secret."

"Our secret," he repeated solemnly.

"Can ye do anything else?" she asked him, trying not to sound eager. "Anything besides feeling what others be feeling?"

"I don't think so. Though sometimes it feels like—I don't know. It burns, and it makes me afraid. I don't know how it happens to me, or why."

"Don't trouble yourself about it, boy." She didn't press the matter when she saw how it upset him. "There's nothing to be afraid of." She drew him close, held him next to her thin, warm frame.

"Ye utilize your mind and everything else ye own. That's what it all's been given to ye for. A Talent be no different from any other ability. If there be anything else ye want to try with yourself, ye go ahead and try it. 'Tis your body and brain and none other's."

3

The couple came from Burley. Mother Mastiff could tell that by their rough accents and by the inordinate amount of gleaming metal jewelry they wore. They were handicraft hunting. The intricately worked burl of black caulderwood in Mother Mastiff's shop caught their attention immediately. It had been finely carved to show a panoramic view of a thoruped colony, one of many that infested Moth's northern-hemisphere continents. The carving ran the entire width of the burl, nearly two meters from end to end. It was a half meter thick and had been polished to a fine ebony glow.

It was a spectacular piece of work. Ordinarily, Mother Mastiff would not have considered parting with it, for it was the kind of showpiece that brought passersby into the stall. But this couple wanted it desperately, and only the impossibly high price seemed to be holding them back.

Flinx wandered in off the street, picked at a pile of small bracelets, and watched while the man and woman argued. Quite suddenly, they reached a decision: they had to have the piece. It would complete their recreation room, and they would be the envy of all their friends. Hang the shipping cost, the insurance, and the price! They'd take it. And they did, though the amount on their credcard barely covered it. Two men came later that afternoon to pick up the object and deliver it to the hotel where the visitors were staying.

Later that night, after the shop had closed, after supper, Mother Mastiff said casually, "You know, boy, that couple who bought the caulderwood carving today?"

"Yes, Mother?"

"They must have been in and out of the shop half a dozen times before they made up their minds."

"That's interesting," Flinx said absently. He was seated in a corner studying a chip on his portable viewer. He was very diligent about that. She never thought of sending him to a formal school—rental chips had been good enough for her as a child, and they'd damn well be good enough for him.

"Yes," she continued. "They barely had the money for it. I pressed them. I backed off, I did everything I could think of to convince them of its worth once I saw that they were really serious about buying the thing. Every time, no matter what I said, they left the shop and went off arguing between themselves.

"Then ye put in an appearance and stood there and watched them, and lo-de-do-de, sudden-like, their sales resistance just crumpled up and went aflight. Be that not interesting?"

"Not really," he replied. "Doesn't that happen lots of times?"

"Not with an item as expensive as the caulderwood, it doesn't. It hardly ever happens that way. Now I don't suppose ye had anything to do with the sudden change of heart on the part of those two? 'Tis not likely ye sensed their hesitation and maybe did something to help them along?"

"Of course not, Mother." He looked away from his viewer in surprise. "I can't do anything like that."

"Oh," she murmured, disappointed. "Ye wouldn't be lying to me now, would ye, boy?"

He shook his head violently. "Why would I do a thing like that? I'm just happy you made so much money on the sale. I'm always glad when you make money."

"Well, that be one thing we have in common, anyway," she said gruffly. "That's enough viewing for one night. You'll strain your young eyes. Be to bed, Flinx."

"All right, Mother." He walked over and bestowed the obligatory peck on her cheek before scurrying off to his own room. "G'night."

"Good night, boy."

She stayed awake in her own bedroom for a while, watching one of the rented entertainment chips on her own viewer.

The show had been recorded on Evoria and benefited from the exotic location and the presence of thranx performers. It was late when she finally shut it off and readied herself for sleep. A quick shower, half an hour brushing out her hair, and she was able to slide with a sigh beneath the thermal blanket.

As she lay in the dark, waiting for sleep, a sudden disquieting thought stole into her mind. Why *would* the boy lie to her about such a possible ability?

He might do it, she thought, because if he could convince one couple to make an unwanted purchase, he probably could do it to others. And if he could do it to others, what about this past autumn when she had been hurrying past the government auction platform on her way across town, and something had brought her to a puzzling halt. Wasn't it possible that the purchase she had made then—the unwanted, inexplicable-to-this-day purchase that she had never looked at too closely—had been helped along its way by the mental nudging of the purchased? Why had she bought him? None of her friends could quite understand it either.

Disturbed, she slipped out of the bed and walked across the resting and eating space to the boy's room. A glance inside revealed him sleeping soundly beneath his cover, as innocent-looking a child as one could hope to set eyes upon. But now something else was there, too, something unseen and unpredictable that she could never be certain about. Never again would she be able to relax completely in the boy's presence.

Already she had forgotten her initial regrets and had begun to extend to him the love she had never before been able to give to his like. He was an endearing little twit and had been more than helpful around the shop. It was good to have such company in her old age. But for a while now, just for a while, she would pat and reassure him with one hand and keep the other close by a weapon. At least until she could be sure in her own mind that it still was her own mind she could be sure of.

Silly old fool, she thought as she turned back toward her own room. You've praised him for having a Talent, and now you're worried about it. You can't have it both ways. Besides, what need to fear a Talent its owner could not control? That confession of the boy's seemed truthful enough, to judge by his distress and bewilderment.

She was feeling easier by the time she slipped into her bed the second time. No, there was no reason to worry. It was interesting, his Talent, but if he couldn't control it, well, no need to be concerned.

Clearly, anyone unable to master such an ability would never amount to much, anyway.

"Haithness, Cruachan, come here!"

The woman seated before the computer screen had spent still another morning poring through reams of abstract data. She was trying to put together a chemical puzzle of considerable complexity. But that morning, as happens on rare occasions, an especially vital piece of the puzzle had unexpectedly fallen into place. Instead of a morass of figures and undisciplined graphics, the screen now beamed out an image of perfect symmetry.

The man who hurried over from the center of the room to glance over her shoulder was tall, the lines striping his face impressive. The dark-haired woman who joined him in staring at the screen was equally imposing.

The chamber in which the three of them worked was situated in a small, nondescript office building located in an unimportant city on a backwater world. For all that the equipment they hovered over had a cobbled-together appearance, most of it was still of a type requiring enormous expertise to operate and great expense to fund.

Both the knowledge and the money came from scattered, seemingly unrelated locations throughout the Commonwealth. To the men and women who practically lived in the room, isolation was their honored burden, obscurity their most potent weapon. For they were members of a uniquely despised and persecuted minority, at war with the tenets of civilized society. Truly were their hearts pure and their purposes of noble mien—it was just their methodology that the rest of civilization questioned.

The three staring intently at the computer screen certainly did not look like candidates for such special attention. The tall man, Cruachan, had the look of a kindly grandfather; the Oriental lady seated before the console would have seemed more at home in an ancient era, clad in flowing silks and wooden shoes. Only the tall black woman standing opposite Cruachan showed some of her inner hardness in her face.

That hardness and cold resolve lived in each of them, however, fostered and intensified by two decades of persecution. They saw themselves as men and women apart from the common herd. Their aim was nothing less than the improvement of mankind in spite of itself. That their methods might result in damage to the innocent was something they had known from the beginning. They had put that and other conventionally moral beliefs aside, believing that such sacrifices were necessary that the majority might benefit. They called their group the Meliorare Society, an innocent-sounding name drawn to mask the intention of improving humanity via the artificial manipulation of genetic material.

Their troubles began when several of their less successful experiments came to light, whereupon the outcry over the revelations had been enormous. Now they were compelled to work in scattered outposts instead of in a single research installation, always barely a jump ahead of pursuing government authorities. They were looked down upon and viewed with horror by the general populace.

Many of their associates had already vanished, having been discovered and taken into custody by the relentless minions of an ignorant officialdom: martyrs to science, the survivors knew—inhuman monsters, according to the media reports.

Of course, the aims of the Meliorare Society were dangerous! Improvement—change—was always viewed as dangerous by the shortsighted. The members had steeled themselves to that way of thinking, and it no longer affected them. What mattered were results, not the opinions of the ignorant masses.

So they did not fear dying, did not fear the even more horrible punishment of selective mindwipe, because they believed in the rightness of their cause. If only one of their experiments turned out successfully, it would vindicate the work propounded on Terra some forty years earlier by the Society's founder. Then they would be able to re-emerge into the scientific community that had disowned them. They would be able to point with pride to a mature, noticeably improved human being.

The air of excitement that pervaded the room was restrained but clearly felt as they gathered around the computer screen.

"This had better live up to its readout, Nyassa-lee," Cruachan warned. "I have half a volume of information to process from the Cannachanna system, and as you know, we're likely going to have to abandon this place and move on within the month. That means reset, breakdown of equipment, and all the difficulties moving entails."

"You know me better than that, Cruachan," said the woman seated in the chair. There was no feeling of triumph in what she had just done; they had progressed beyond such trivialities. "I've been feeding and cross-correlating records on dispersal and individual subject characteristics for months now. It's finally paid off. I've located Number Twelve."

The tall black woman leaned closer to the screen. "Number Twelve—that sticks in the mind. Male, wasn't it?"

Nyassa-lee nodded and indicated the screen. "Here, I'll run the relevants back for you."

They refamiliarized themselves with the details of the case in question. It had been eight years since case interdiction. In the eight years since, they had encountered a number of other subjects. Most of them had grown into normal childhood. A few had even displayed tiny flashes of promise, but nothing worth a full-scale follow-up.

Then there had been those whose minds and bodies had been

horribly distorted and twisted by the original surgical manipulations, for which they each shared the blame. Unfortunate failures such as those had been made public by the government and had raised such an emotional outcry among the scientifically unsophisticated public that the government had been able to legalize its witch hunt against the Society.

Most of the subject children had been recovered by the government, raised in special homes, and restored to normality. Where possible, the genetic alterations performed by the Society's surgeons had been corrected to enable all the children to live a normal life.

If we cannot improve upon the normal, thought Haithness, then we do not deserve to explore and master the universe. Nature helps those who help themselves. Why should we not employ our learning and knowledge to give evolution a boost?

From the far corner of the darkened room, a man called out. "Brora reports that a government shuttle has landed at Calaroom shuttleport."

"Could be the usual load of agricultural specialists," Cruachan said thoughtfully.

"Possible," agreed the individual manning the communications console, "but can we afford that risk?"

"I hate to order evacuation on such slim evidence. Any word on how many passengers?"

"Hard to say," the man ventured, listening intently to his receiver. "Brora says at least a dozen he doesn't recognize."

"That's a lot of agricultural specialists, Cruachan," Haithness pointed out.

"It is." He called across to the communications specialist. "Tell Brora to pull back and prepare for departure. We can't take chances. Push evac time from a month to tonight."

"Tonight?" The voice of the communicator had a dubious ring. "I won't have half the equipment broken down by then."

"New communications equipment we can buy," Cruachan reminded him. "Replacements for ourselves are not available."

The man at the com console nodded and turned back to his station, speaking softly and hurriedly into the pickup. Cruachan returned his attention to the computer screen.

Information emerged. NUMBER TWELVE. MALE. PHYSICALLY UNDISTINGUISHED AS A CHILD. Next were descriptions of cerebral index and figures for cortical energy displacement.

Oh, yes; Cruachan remembered now. Unpredictable, that

Number Twelve. Patterns in brain activity suggesting paranormal activity but nothing concrete. Particularly fascinating had been the amount of activity emerging from the left side of the cerebrum, usually detected only in females. That by itself was not reason enough for excitement, but there were also continuous signs of functioning in at least two sections of brain that were not normally active, the "dead" areas of the mind. That activity, like the child himself, had also been unpredictable.

And yet, despite such encouraging evidence, the case history of Number Twelve was devoid of the usual promising developments. No hint of telepathy, psychokinesis, pyrokinesis, dual displacement, or any of the other multitude of abilities the Society had hoped to bring to full flower in its experimental children.

Still, Number Twelve at least exhibited a possible something.

"Well, this one certainly shows more promise than the last dozen or so," Haithness had to admit. "It's been so long since we had contact with him, I'd nearly forgotten those activity readings. We need to get to this one as quickly as possible. Where's he situated?"

Nyassa-lee tapped keys below the readout, bringing forth answers. "Where in the Commonwealth is that?" Haithness grumbled.

"Trading world," Cruachan put in, thinking hard. "Centrally located but unimportant in and of itself. A stopover world, low in native population."

"You won't mind going there once you've seen this," Nyassa-lee assured them both. Her fingers moved delicately over the keyboard a second time, and fresh information glowed on screen. "This is recent, from the local operative who relocated the subject. It appears that the child has definitely displayed one Talent, possibly two. Furthermore, he has done so in public and apparently without any specialized training."

"Without training," Cruachan whispered. "Remarkable, if true."

Nyassa-lee tapped the screen. "This operative has been reliable in the past and particularly noteworthy for the accuracy of his observations. The Talent in question is a telepathic variant of some sort. The operative is not a scientifically trained observer, of course, and he is even less certain of the second one, though its potential value may be even greater."

"What is it?" Haithness asked.

"I've been hard put to find a name for it. Basically, it seems that the child may be an emolterator."

The other woman looked confused. "I don't remember that on the list of possible Talents."

"It wasn't there. It's an original. Original with this child, it seems," Cruachan said. Nyassa-lee nodded. "It means that he may be able to influence the actions of others. Not mind control, nothing as strong as that. It would be more subtle. One possessing such an ability would have to utilize it very carefully. If this report is true . . ." His voice and thoughts drifted for a moment as he studied the readout.

"It seems the child's Talents have gone unnoticed by the authorities and that he has developed naturally. All without even the most rudimentary training. The signs certainly point to powerful potentials waiting to be unlocked."

"Either the child has grown up unaware of these Talents," Nyassa-lee said, studying new information as it appeared on the screen, "or else he is precociously clever."

"It may be just natural caution," Haithness put in. "It will be interesting to find out which is the case."

"Which we will do," Cruachan said firmly. "It's been a long time since we've had a subject as promising as this one come back to us. He could be the one we've searched for all these years."

"It had better not be a repeat of the last time we located a subject with these figures," Haithness cautioned, then indicated the new figures materializing on the screen. "Look at those neurological potentials. Remember the only other child who showed numbers like that?"

"Of course, I remember," Cruachan said irritably. "We won't lose this one the way we lost that girl—what the devil was the little monster's name?"

"Mahnahmi," Nyassa-lee reminded him. "Yes, if this boy's anything like that one, we're going to have to be extremely careful. I couldn't take a repeat of that experience."

"Neither could I, frankly," Cruachan admitted. "Our mistake was in trying to regain control over her directly. End result: the girl vanishes again, and two more of the Society go to a premature end. And we're still not sure how she accomplished it."

"We'll run across her again someday, when our methods are improved," Haithness said coolly. "Then we'll deal with her properly."

"I'm not sure I'd want to chance it." Nyassa-lee looked back at the screen. "Meanwhile, it would be good to keep in mind the fact that the potential of this Number Twelve theoretically exceeds even that of the girl."

"True," Cruachan admitted, studying the figures, "but it's clear that his development has been much slower. We should have plenty of time to cope with any maturing Talent and make certain it is safely contained, for the child's benefit as well as our own, of course."

"Of course," Haithness agreed calmly. "I am curious to know how you propose to accomplish that. You know how volatile a Talent can become if stressed."

"Yes, the girl gave us an impressive demonstration of that, didn't she?" Nyassa-lee's fingers brought forth fresh information from the console.

Another call sounded from across the room. "Brora says he's now convinced that the new arrivals at the port have nothing to do with the agricultural station. They have not stopped by the Agri section of government house; they are gathering instead in the subterranean quarter."

"Tell Brora to speed things up," Cruachan replied. "I definitely want the installation broken down by midnight."

"Yes, sir," the communicator responded briskly.

"You didn't answer my question," Haithness reminded the tall man. "How are we going to handle this one? If we try direct control as we did with the girl, we risk the same consequences. There is no way of predicting how a subject may react."

"Remember that the girl was still in infancy when we encountered her. We wrongly mistook her age for harmlessness. There was no reason to appeal to in her case—she was too young. I never expected that to work against us."

"It doesn't matter. The important thing is that he is still unskilled in the use of his Talent. That is also what makes him dangerous." Haithness indicated the figures on the screen. "Look at those. Undisciplined or not, we must handle this Number Twelve with extreme caution. We need a check of some kind, something strong enough to mute any juvenile emotional reactions."

Nyassa-lee glanced back and up at her colleague. "But we cannot wait."

"I agree with you there. This may be our last chance to gain control and direction over a subject with such potential. We don't want to waste our chance."

"I am aware of the considerations and risks," Cruachan assured them both. "I do not intend that we should try, as we did with the girl, to gain control directly. Instead, we will try to obtain control over someone who exercises control over the subject. Is there anyone who fits the requisite pattern?"

Nyassa-lee turned back to her keyboard. There was a pause before she replied, "One. It appears that the subject was purchased from government control by an elderly woman. She has raised the boy as her own."

"Surrogate mother," Haithness murmured. "That's good. It is virtually made to order. We could not hope for a stronger emotional bond."

There was no warmth in the voice of Haithness. Only one thing mattered to her: the success of the experiment. Time was running out for the Society, she knew; they had no way of knowing when the authorities might close in on them forever. They needed a success *now,* and this boy might be their last chance.

"I see one possible drawback," Cruachan said while pondering the information glowing on the screen. "The woman in question, the surrogate mother, is of an advanced age, though apparently healthy." He nudged Nyassa-lee, who obediently made room for him on the edge of the chair.

Cruachan fingered controls and frowned when the information he sought did not appear on the screen. "No detailed medical information on her. It could be difficult."

Haithness shrugged indifferently. "It does not matter what her condition is. We have to proceed regardless."

"I know, I know," Cruachan replied impatiently. "Our course is set, then. We will not go from here to Loser's World in hopes of relocating subject Number Fifty-six. Instead, we will establish standard mobile operations aboard the ship. Once we are certain we have escaped pursuit, we will plot course for this Moth. Then we should have enough time to proceed as planned."

"It will be necessary to isolate the subject from the mother." Haithness was thinking out loud. "Given the nature of the subject's observed Talents, if our information is accurate, it may be that within a limited geographical area he might be able to trace our activities. We will naturally need an uninterrupted period with the surrogate," she hesitated only briefly, "to persuade her to cooperate with us." A thin smile did little to alter her expression.

Cruachan nodded. "That should not be difficult to arrange. Fortunately for us, Moth is lightly populated. Technology is not unknown, but the level varies widely according to location. We should be able to establish ourselves and the necessary equipment at a sufficient distance from the metropolis where the subject and his parent are living to ensure our privacy and standard security."

The communicator turned from his instrumentation and interrupted them without hesitation. "Brora reports that at least half of the newly arrived agricultural experts are armed."

"That's that, then," Cruachan murmured with a resigned sigh. Another hurried move, another dash to still another strange world.

"Nyassa-lee, make certain that this information is transferred to ship storage. Haithness, you—"

"I know what needs to be done, Cruachan." She turned from him and calmly began transferring data from main storage to a portacube.

The communicator leaned back in his chair and frowned at his instruments. "I won't have time to break down much and move it out to the shuttle."

"It doesn't matter, Osteen," Cruachan assured him. "We have some duplicate equipment already aboard. I don't like abandoning more than we have to any more than you do." He indicated the expensive electronics with which the room had been paneled. "But we don't have a choice now. Regardless, something promising, truly promising, has come to our notice. After all these years, it appears that we have relocated one of the most promising of all the subject children."

"That's good news indeed, sir." Osteen was one of the few young men in the Meliorare Society. Cruachan would have preferred a man with more vision as prime communicator, but such individuals were scarce. Osteen at least was loyal and efficient. It was not his fault that he was intellectually inferior to the Society's original membership. But then, such a collection of visionary minds was not likely to join together again in Cruachan's lifetime, he knew.

Unless . . . unless the Society could put forth a shining testament to their noble ideals in the person of a single successful subject. This boy, perhaps, might be their vindication. They had to get to him quickly. During the past several years, they had had less and less time in which to work as the Commonwealth closed in on the remnants of the Society. Their survival rate did not bode well for the future: natural attrition was beginning to damage the cause as much as government interference.

The three of them, along with the sharp-eyed Brora, who had

sounded the latest warning, represented the largest surviving group from the original membership. The trust of all who had perished devolved upon them, Cruachan thought. They must not fail with this boy.

And he must not fail them.

4

Loneliness had never bothered Flinx before. He knew what it was, of course—the condition had been with him all his short life. In the past, he'd always been able to distance himself from its pain, but this feeling—this empty aloneness—was different from any loneliness he'd ever experienced before. It was a physical reality, stabbing at him, creating an ache in a mysterious, new part of his brain. It was different not only from his own loneliness but from the aloneness he'd occasionally sensed in others via his unpredictable Talent. In fact, the experience was so radically new that he had nothing to compare it with. Yet it *was* loneliness; of that he was certain. Loneliness and something else equally intense and recognizable: hunger. A gnawing, persistent desire for food.

The feelings were so bright and uncomplicated that Flinx couldn't help but wonder at their source. They beat insistently on his mind, refusing to fade away. Never before had such emotions been so open to him, so clear and strong. Normally, they would begin to fade, but these grew not weaker but stronger—and he did not have to strain to hold them at bay. They kept hammering at him until his mind finally gave in and woke him up.

Flinx rubbed at his eyes. It was pouring outside the shop, and the narrow window over the bed admitted the dim light of Moth's multiple moons, which somehow seeped through the nearly unbroken cloud cover. Flinx had rarely seen the bright rust-red moon called Flame or its smaller companions, but he'd spent his years of study well, and he knew where the light came from.

Slipping silently from the bed, he stood up and pulled on pants and shirt. A glow light bathed the kitchen and dining area in soft yellow. Across the way, ragged snores came from the vicinity of Mother Mastiff's bedroom. The loneliness he sensed was not hers.

The feeling persisted into wakefulness. Not a dream, then, which had been his first thought. The back of his head hurt with the strength of it, but though the actual pain was beginning to fade, the emotion was still as strong as it had been in sleep.

He did not wake Mother Mastiff as he inspected the rest of the kitchen area, the bathroom, and the single narrow closet. Quietly, he opened the front door and slipped out into the stall. The shutters were locked tight, keeping out weather and intruders alike. The familiar snoring provided a comforting background to his prowling.

Flinx had grown into a lithe young man of slightly less than average height and mildly attractive appearance. His hair was red as ever, but his dark skin now hid any suggestion of freckles. He moved with a gracefulness and silence that many of the older, more experienced marketplace thieves might have envied. Indeed, he could walk across a room paved with broken glass and metal without making a sound. It was a technique he had picked up from some of Drallar's less reputable citizens, much to Mother Mastiff's chagrin. All a part of his education, he had assured her. The thieves had a word for it: "skeoding," meaning to walk like a shadow. Only Flinx's brighter than normal hair made the professional purloiners cluck their tongues in disapproval. They would have welcomed him into their company, had he been of a mind to make thievery his profession. But Flinx would steal only if absolutely necessary, and then only from those who could afford it.

"I only want to use my ability to supplement my income," he had told the old master who had inquired about his future intentions, "and Mother Mastiff's, of course."

The master had laughed, showing broken teeth. "I understand, boy. I've been supplementin' my income in that manner goin' on fifty years now." He and his colleagues could not believe that one who showed such skill at relieving others of their possessions would not desire to make a career of it, especially since the youth's other prospects appeared dim.

"Yer goin' into the Church, I suppose?" one of the other thieves had taunted him, "t'become a Counselor First?"

"I don't think the spiritual life is for me," Flinx had replied. They all had a good laugh at that.

As he quietly opened the lock on the outside door, he thought back to what he had learned those past few years. A wise man did not move around Drallar late at night, particularly on so wet and dark a one. But he couldn't go back to sleep without locating the source of the feelings that battered at him. Loneliness and hunger, hunger and loneliness, filled his mind with restlessness. Who could possibly be broadcasting twin deprivations of such power?

The open doorway revealed a wall of rain. The angled street carried the water away to Drallar's efficient underground drainage system. Flinx stood in the gap for a long moment, watching. Suddenly an intense burst of emptiness made him wince. That decided him. He could no more ignore that hot pleading than he could leave an unstamped credcard lying orphaned in the street.

"That curiosity of yours will get ye into real trouble someday, boy," Mother Mastiff had told him on more than one occasion. "Mark me word."

Well, he had marked her word. Marked it and filed it. He turned away from the door and skeoded back to his little room. It was early summer, and the rain outside was relatively warm. Disdaining an underjacket, he took a slickertic from its wall hook and donned it; thus suitably shielded from the rain, he made his way back to the stall, out into the street, and closed the main door softly behind him.

A few lights like hibernating will-o'-the-wisps glowed faintly from behind unshuttered shop fronts on the main avenue where the idling wealthy night-cavorted in relative safety. On the side street where Mother Mastiff plied her trade, only a rare flicker of illumination emerged from behind locked shutters and windows.

As water cascaded off his shoulders, Flinx stood there and searched his mind. Something sent him off to his right. There was a narrow gap between Mother Mastiff's shop and that of old lady Marquin, who was on vacation in the south, and by turning sideways, he could just squeeze through.

Then he was standing in the service alleyway that ran behind the shops and a large office building. His eyes roved over a lunar landscape of uncollected garbage and refuse: old plastic packing crates, metal storage barrels, honeycomb containers for breakables, and other indifferently disposed of detritus. A couple of fleurms scurried away from his boots. Flinx watched them warily. He was not squeamish where the omnipresent fleurms were concerned, but he had a healthy respect for them. The critters were covered in a thick, silvery fur, and their little mouths were full of fine teeth. Each animal was as big around as Flinx's thumb and as long as his forearm. They were not really worms but legless mammals that did very well in the refuse piles and composting garbage that filled the alleys of Drallar to overflowing. He had heard horror stories of old men and women who had fallen into a drunken stupor in such places—only their exposed bones remained for the finding.

Flinx, however, was not drunk. The fleurms could inflict nasty bites, but they were shy creatures, nearly blind, and greatly preferred to relinquish the right of way when given the choice.

If it was dark on the street in front of the shop, it was positively stygian in the alley. To the east, far up the straightaway, he could make out a light and hear intermittent laughter. An odd night for a party. But the glow gave him a reference point, even if it was too far off to shed any light on his search.

The continuing surge of loneliness that he felt did not come from that distant celebration, nor did it rise from the heavily shuttered and barred doorways that opened onto the alley. The emotions Flinx was absorbing came from somewhere very near.

He moved forward, picking his way between the piles of debris, taking his time so as to give the fleurms and the red-blue carrion bugs time to scurry from his path.

All at once something struck with unexpected force at his receptive mind. The mental blow sent him to his knees. Somewhere a man was beating his wife. No unique circumstance, that, but Flinx felt it from the other side of the city. The woman was frightened and angry. She was reaching for the tiny dart gun she kept hidden in her bedroom dresser and was pointing its minuscule barrel at the man. Then it was the husband's turn to be frightened. He was pleading with her, not in words that Flinx could hear but via an emotional avalanche that ended in an abrupt, nonverbal scream of shock. Then came the emptiness that Flinx had grown to recognize as death.

He heard laughter, not from the party up the alley but from one of the lofty crystal towers that reared above the wealthy inurbs where the traders and transspatial merchants made their homes. And there was plotting afoot; someone was going to be cheated.

Far beyond the city boundaries in the forest to the west: happiness and rejoicing, accompanied by a new liquid sensation of emergence. A baby was born.

Very near, perhaps in one of the shops on Mother Mastiff's own street, an argument was raging. It involved accounts and falsification, waves of acrimonious resentment passing between short-term partners. Then the private grumblings of someone unknown and far away across the city center, someone plotting to kill, and kill more than one time, but plotting only—the kind of fantasizing that fills spare moments of every human brain, be it healthy or sick.

Then all the sensations were gone, all of them, the joyful and the doomed, the debaters and lovers and ineffectual dreamers. There was only the rain.

Blinking, he staggered to his feet and stood swaying unsteadily on the slope of the alley. Rain spattered off his slickertic, wove its way down the walls of the shops and the office building, to gurgle down the central drains. Flinx found himself staring blankly up the alley toward the distant point of light that marked the location of the party. Abruptly, the emotions of everyone at the party were sharp in his mind; only now he felt no pain. There was only a calm clarity and assurance.

He could see this woman anxiously yet uncertainly trying to tempt that man, see another criticizing the furniture, still another wondering how he could possibly live through the next day, feel laughter, fear, pleasure, lust, admiration, envy: the whole gamut of human emotions. They began to surge toward him like the storm he had just weathered, threatening the pain again, threatening to overwhelm him—

STOP IT, he ordered himself. Stop it—easy.

By careful manipulation of a piece of his mind he hadn't even been aware existed before, he discovered he was able to control the intensity of the emotions that threatened to drown him—not all of which had been human, either. He had felt at least two that were bizarre, yet recognizable enough for him to identify. They were the feelings of a mated pair of ornithorpes. It was the first time he had sensed anything from a nonhuman.

Slowly, he found he was able to regulate the assault, to damp it down to where he could manage it, sort out the individual feelings, choose, analyze—and then they were gone as suddenly as they had struck, along with all the rest of the blaze of emotion he had sucked in from around the city.

Hesitantly, he tried to focus his mind and bring back the sensations. It was as before. Try as he might, his mind stayed empty of any feelings save his own. His own—and one other. The loneliness was still there, nagging at him. The feeling was less demanding now, almost hesitant. The hunger was there, too.

Flinx took a step forward, another, a third—and something alive quickly scuttled out of his path, shoving aside empty containers and cans, plastic and metal clinking in the damp alley. He strained to see through the dimness, wishing now that he had had the presence of mind to bring a portable light from the shop. He took a cautious step toward the pile, ready to jump up and clear should the fleurms or whatever prove unexpectedly aggressive.

It was not a fleurm. For one thing, it was too long: nearly a meter. It was thicker, too, though not by much. He thought of the snakelike creatures that roamed the temperate forests to the south of Drallar. Some of them were poisonous. Occasionally, they and other forest predators made their way into the city under cover of rain and darkness to hunt out the small creatures that infested the urban trash heaps. It was rare, but not unheard of, that a citizen encountered such an intruder.

Flinx leaned close to the pile, and as he did so the hunger faded. Simultaneously, the feeling of loneliness intensified; the strength of it almost sent him reeling back against the shop wall. He was certain it came from the snakelike unknown.

The bump of curiosity—which Mother Mastiff was at such pains to warn him about—quickly overcame his natural caution. All he felt was amazement that such powerful mental projections could arise from so lowly a creature. Furthermore, there was no anger in the animal, no rudimentary danger signals. Only that persistent loneliness and the fleeting sense of hunger.

The creature moved again. He could see the bright, flashing red eyes even in the alley's faint light. Not a true reptile, he was sure. A cold-blooded creature would have been reduced to lethargy by the cool night air. This thing moved too rapidly.

Flinx took a step back, away from the pile. The creature was emerging. It slithered onto the wet pavement and then did something he did not expect. Snakes were not supposed to fly.

The pleated wings were blue and pink, bright enough for him to identify even in the darkness. No, the snake-thing certainly was not lethargic, for its wings moved in a blur, giving the creature the sound and appearance of a gigantic bee. It found a place on his shoulder in a single, darting movement. Flinx felt thin, muscular coils settle almost familiarly around his shoulder. The whole thing had happened too fast for him to dodge.

But the creature's intent was not to harm. It simply sat, resting against his warmth, and made no move to attack. The speed of the approach had paralyzed Flinx, but only for a moment. For as soon as it had settled against him, all that vast loneliness, every iota of that burning need had fled from the snake. At the same time, Flinx experienced a clarity within his own mind that he had never felt before. Whatever the creature was, wherever it had come from, it not only had the ability to make itself at home, it seemed to make its new host feel comfortable as well.

A new sensation entered Flinx's mind, rising from the snake. It was the first time he had ever experienced a mental purr. He sensed no intelligence in the creature, but there *was* something else. In its own way, the empathic communication was as clear as speech, the emotional equivalent of an ancient Chinese ideograph—a whole series of complex thoughts expressed as a single projection. Simple, yet efficient.

The small arrowhead-shaped head lifted from Flinx's shoulder, its bright little eyes regarding him intently. The pleated wings were folded flat against the side of the body, giving the creature a normal snakelike appearance. Flinx stared back, letting his own feelings pour from him.

Slowly, the creature relaxed. The single long coiled muscle of itself, which had been squeezing Flinx's shoulder with instinctive strength, relaxed, too, until it was only maintaining a gentle grip, just enough to hold its position. Pins and needles started to run down Flinx's arm. He ignored them. The animal's head lowered until it moved up against Flinx's neck.

The snake was sound asleep.

Flinx stood there for what felt like an eternity, though surely it was not even half that long. The strange apparition that the night had brought slept on his shoulder, its small head nestled in the hollow of shoulder bone and neck tendon. The animal shivered once. Flinx knew it could not be drawing full warmth from his body because the slickertic formed a layer between them. Better to get the poor thing inside, he thought, suddenly aware of how long he had been standing there in the rain. His new companion needed rest as well as warmth. How he knew that, he could not have explained; but he knew it as clearly as he recognized his own exhaustion.

Flinx did not for a moment debate the snake's future. Its presence on his shoulder as well as in his mind was too natural for him to consider parting with it—unless, of course, some owner appeared to claim it. Clearly, this was no wild animal. Also, Flinx was well-read, and if this creature was native to the Drallarian vicinity, it was news to him. He had never seen or heard of such an animal before. If it was some kind of valuable pet, its owner would surely come looking for it, and soon. For now, though, the snake was clearly as much an orphan as Flinx himself had once been. Flinx had experienced too much suffering in his own life to ignore it in anything else, even in a lowly snake. For a while, it was his charge, much as he was Mother Mastiff's.

She had wanted to know his name on that first day long ago.

"What do I call you?" he wondered aloud. The sleeping snake did not respond.

There were thousands of books available to Flinx via the library chips he rented from Central Education. He had only read a comparative few, but among them was one with which he had particularly identified. It was pre-Commonwealth—precivilization, really—but that hadn't mitigated its impact on him. Those characters with the funny names; one of them was called—what? Pip, he remembered. He glanced back down at the sleeping snake. That'll be your name unless we learn otherwise one day.

As he started back for the shop, he tried to tell himself that he would worry about that proverbial "one day" if and when it presented itself, but he could not. He was already worried about it, because although he had only had contact with the creature for less than an hour, it seemed a part of him. The thought of returning the snake to some indifferent, offworld owner was suddenly more than he could bear. Since he had been an infant, he couldn't recall becoming so deeply attached to another living creature. Not even Mother Mastiff had such a lock on his feelings.

Feelings. This creature, this snake-thing, it *understood* what he was feeling, understood what it meant to have the emotions of strangers flood unbidden into one's mind, interrupting one's life and making every waking moment a potential abnormality. That was what made it special. He knew it, and the snake knew it, too. No longer were they individuals; they had become two components of a larger whole.

I will not give you up, he decided then and there in the cold morning rain. Not even if some wealthy, fatuous offworlder appears to lay claim to you. You belong with me. The snake dozed on, seemingly oblivious to any decisions the human might make.

The street fronting the shop was still deserted. The lock yielded to his palm, and he slipped inside, glad to be out of the weather. Carefully, he relocked the door. Then he was back in the dining area where the glow light still shone softly. Using both hands, he unraveled the snake. It did not resist as he slid the coils from his shoulder. From the bedroom to his right came Mother Mastiff's steady snores, a drone that matched the patter of rain on the roof.

Gently, he set the snake down on the single table. In the glow lamp's brighter light he could see its true colors for the first time. A bright pink and blue diamondback pattern ran the length of the snake's body, matching the pleated wings. The belly was a dull golden hue and the head emerald green.

"Exquisite," he murmured to the snake. "You're exquisite."

The creature's eyes—no, he corrected himself, Pip's eyes—opened in lazy half sleep. It seemed to smile at him. Mental projection, Flinx thought as he slipped out of the slickertic and hung it on its hook.

"Now where can I keep you?" he whispered to himself as he glanced around the small living area. The stall out front was out of the question. Mother Mastiff surely had customers suffering from snake phobias, and they might not take kindly to Pip's presence—besides, the stall was unheated. By the same token, he didn't think Mother Mastiff would react with understanding if the snake playfully sprang out at her from one of the kitchen storage cabinets while she was trying to prepare a meal.

His own room was spartan: There was only the small computer terminal and chip readout, the single clothes closet he had rigged himself, and the bed. The closet would have to do. Carrying the snake into his room, Flinx set it down on the foot of the bed. Then he made a pile of some dirty clothes on the closet floor. Pip looked clean enough; most scaled creatures were dirt-shedders, not collectors. He lifted the snake and set it down gently in the clothes, careful not to bruise the delicate wings. It recoiled itself there, seemingly content. Flinx smiled at it. He didn't smile often.

"Now you stay there, Pip," he whispered, "and in the morning we'll see about scrounging something for you to eat." He watched the snake for several minutes before fatigue returned with a rush. Yawning, he pushed his own clothes off the bed, set his boots on the drypad, and climbed back into bed. A few droplets of water had crawled under the edge of the slickertic. He brushed them from his hair, sighed deeply, and lapsed into a rich, undisturbed sleep.

Once the flow of mental energy from the human in the bed had smoothed out and the snake was certain its new symbiote was not about to enter a disturbing REM period, it quietly uncoiled itself and slithered out of the closet. Silently, it worked its way up one of the bed legs, emerging next to the single battered pillow.

The animal rested there for a long moment, gazing through double lidded eyes at the unconscious biped. Inside itself, the snake was warm and comfortable. The hunger was still there, but it had received an indication of sorts that it would soon be fed.

The bed was very warm, both the thermal blanket and the symbiote's mass exuding comfortable, dry heat. The snake slithered across the pillow until it was resting against the back of the human's head. It stretched itself once, the wings flexing and retracting. Then it coiled itself tightly into the convenient pocket formed by the symbiote's neck and shoulder. Soon its own brain waves matched those of the human as it drifted into its own variety of sleep.

5

Mother Mastiff was careful not to wake the boy as she slowly began backing out of his room. Her eyes, alert and fearful, remained fixed on the alien thing curled up against his head. There was no telling what it might do if startled into wakefulness.

How the invader had penetrated her tight little home, she had no idea. No time to worry about that now. Her thoughts went to the little gun, the delicate, ladylike needler she kept under her pillow. No, too chancy—the snake was much too close to the boy's head, and she was not as good a shot as she had been twenty years ago.

There was also the possibility the invader might not even be dangerous. She certainly did not recognize it. In the ninety plus years she had spent on Moth, she had seen nothing like it. For one thing, there was no hint of fur anywhere on its body. Only scales. That immediately identified it as a non-native. Well, maybe. Moth was home to a few creatures—deep-digging burrowers—that did not sport fur. This didn't look like a burrower to her, but she was no zoologist, nor had she ever traveled far outside the city limits.

Yet she felt certain it came from offworld. Something she couldn't put a mental finger on marked the beast as alien, but that didn't matter. What did was that it had somehow penetrated to the boy's room, and she had better do something about it before it woke up and decided the matter for her.

Get it away from him, she told herself. Away from his head, at least. Get it away, keep it occupied, then wake the boy and have him make a run for the gun under her pillow.

The broom she hefted had a light metal handle and wire bristles. Taking it out of storage, she re-entered Flinx's room and reached past his head with the broom's business end. The metal bristles prodded the invader.

The snake stirred at the touch, opened its eyes, and stared at her. She jabbed at it again, harder this time, trying to work the bristles between the snake's head and the boy's exposed neck. It opened its mouth, and she instinctively jerked back, but it was only a yawn. Still sleepy, then, she thought. Good, its reactions would be slowed. Leaning forward again, she reached down and shoved hard on the broom. Several of the snake's coils went rolling over to the side of the bed, and for the first time she had a glimpse of its brilliant coloring.

Again, she shoved with the broom, but the snake was no longer on the bed. It hovered in midair, its wings moving so rapidly they were no more than a blue-pink blur. They generated a rich, vibrant humming sound in the small room. Aghast and uncertain how to attack this new threat, Mother Mastiff backed away, holding the broom defensively in front of her. Awakened by the last shove of the broom, the boy blinked sleepily at her. "Mother? What is it?"

"Hush, be quiet!" she warned him. "I don't know how this thing got into your room, but—"

Flinx sat up quickly. He glanced up at the hovering snake, admiring it for the first time in daylight, and bestowed a reassuring grin on Mother Mastiff.

"Oh, that. That's just Pip."

The broom dipped slightly, and she stared narrowly at her charge. "Ye mean, ye know what it be?"

"Sure," he said cheerfully. "I, uh, heard something last night, so I went outside to investigate." He gestured with a thumb at the snake. "It was back in the garbage, cold and hungry. Hey, I bet he's still hungry, and—"

"I'll bet it is, too," she snapped, "and I'll not have some scaly, gluttonous carrion eater crawling about my house. Get out!" she yelled at it. "Shoo!" She swung the broom at the snake once, twice, a third time, forcing Flinx to duck the flying bristles. Each time, the snake dodged nimbly in the air, displaying unexpected aerial agility. Once it darted straight to its left, then backward, then toward the ceiling.

"Don't!" Flinx shouted, suddenly alarmed. "It might think you're trying to hurt me."

"A guardian angel with beady eyes and scales? Mock-mush, boy, it knows well what I'm swinging at!"

In fact, the snake was well aware the new human had no intention of harming its symbiote, for it could feel the honest affection and warmth flowing between them. It did not worry on that score. Conversely, no love flowed toward it from the new person, and the shiny thing that was being thrust at it was hard to avoid in the small, enclosed space.

"Please, Mother," Flinx pleaded anxiously, scrambling out of bed and dragging the blanket with him, "stop it. I don't know how it'll react."

"We're going to find out, boy," she told him grimly. The broom struck, missed, bounced off the far wall. She cocked her arms for another swing.

The snake had been patient, very patient. It understood the bond between the two humans. But the broom had backed it into a corner, and the hard bristles promised danger if they connected solidly with the snake's wings. It opened its mouth. There was a barely perceptible squirting sound. A thin, tight stream of clear liquid shot forward. It sparkled in the light and impacted on the broom as it was swinging forward. As Mother Mastiff recovered and brought the broom back for yet another strike, she heard a faint but definite hissing that did not come from the snake. She hesitated, frowning, then realized the noise was coming from the broom. A glance showed that approximately half of the metal bristles had melted away. Something was foaming and sizzling as it methodically ate its way down the broom.

She dropped the weapon as if the metal handle had abruptly become red hot, her expression fearful. The liquid continued to sputter and hiss as it ate away the metal. Soon it had worked its way through the last stubble and was beginning to eat holes in the metal handle itself.

"Boy, get out of the room while ye have the chance," she called huskily, staring wide-eyed at the snake while continuing to back toward her own bedroom. "If it can do that to metal, there's no telling what—"

Flinx laughed, then hurriedly put a hand to his mouth and forced himself to be understanding. "I'm sorry, Mother," he said apologetically. "It's just that Pip would never hurt me. And he's just proved that he wouldn't hurt anyone close to me, either."

"How do ye know that?" she sputtered.

"You *know,*" he replied, sounding puzzled, "I don't know how I know it. But it's true. Here, see?" He extended his left arm.

Still keeping a wary eye on the woman, who continued to block the exit, the snake zipped down to land on the proffered perch. In an instant, it had multiple coils wrapped around the human's shoulder. Then the snake relaxed, the pleated wings folding up to lie flat against the gleaming body.

"See?" Flinx lowered his arm and gently rubbed the back of the snake's head. "He's just naturally friendly."

"Naturally ugly, ye mean," Mother Mastiff snorted. Bending, she picked up the remnant of the broom and inspected it. All the bristles were gone, along with several centimeters of handle. A weak crackling still came from the raw edges of the tube where the metal had dissolved, though the extraordinarily corrosive liquid seemed to have largely spent itself.

She showed the remains of the broom to Flinx, still nervous about getting too near the thing wrapped around his shoulder. "See that? Imagine what it would do to your skin."

"Oh, Mother, can't you see?" Flinx spoke with all the exasperation of the young for the aged. "He was protecting himself, but because he senses that you're important to me, he was careful not to spit any of it on you."

"Lucky thing for it," she said, some of her normal bravado returning. "Well, it can't stay here."

"Yes, it can," Flinx argued.

"No, it can't. I can't have some lethal varmint like that fluttering and crawling all over the place, frightening off the customers."

"He'll stay with me all the time," Flinx assured her soothingly. His hand continued to caress the snake's head. Its eyes closed contentedly. "See? He's just like any other house pet. He responds to warmth and affection." Flinx brought forth his most mournful, pleading expression. It had the intended affect.

"Well, it won't get any warmth or affection from me," Mother Mastiff grumbled, "but if you're determined to keep it . . ."

"I think," Flinx added, throwing fuel on the fire, "he would become very upset if someone tried to separate us."

Mother Mastiff threw up her hands, simultaneously signifying acquiescence and acceptance. "Oh, Deity, why couldn't ye stumble over a normal pet, like a cat or a saniff? What does the little monster eat, anyways?"

"I don't know," Flinx admitted, remembering the hunger he had sensed the night before and resolving to do something about it soon. He had been hungry himself and knew more of the meaning of that word than most people. "Aren't most snakes carnivorous?"

"This one certainly looks like it," she said.

Reaching down, Flinx gently ran a forefinger along the edge of the snake's mouth until he could pry it open. The snake opened one eye and looked at him curiously but did not raise any objection to the intrusion. Mother Mastiff held her breath.

Flinx leaned close, inspecting. "The teeth are so small I can't tell for sure."

"Probably swallows its food whole," Mother Mastiff told him. "I hear that's the way of it with snakes, though this be no normal snake and I wouldn't care to make no predictions about it, much less about its diet."

"I'll find out," Flinx assured her. "If you don't need me to help in the shop today—"

"Help, hah! No, go where ye will. Just make sure that creature goes with ye."

"I'm going to take him around the marketplace," Flinx said excitedly, "and see if anyone recognizes him. There's sure to be someone who will."

"Don't bet your blood on it, boy," she warned him. "It's likely an offworld visitor."

"I thought so, too," he told her. "Wouldn't that be interesting? I wonder how it got here?"

"Someone with a grudge against me brought it, probably," she muttered softly. Then, louder, she said, "There be no telling. If 'tis an escaped pet and a rare one, ye can be sure its owner will be stumbling about here soonest in search of it."

"We'll see." Flinx knew the snake belonged right where it was, riding his shoulder. It felt right. He could all but feel the wave of contentment it was generating.

"And while I'm finding out what he is," he added briskly, "I'll find out what he eats, too."

"Ye do that," she told him. "Fact be, why not spend the night at it? I've some important buyers coming around suppertime. They were referred to me through the Shopkeeper's Association and seem especial interested in some of the larger items we have, like the muriwood table. So ye take that awful whatever-it-be," and she threw a shaky finger in the direction of the snake, "and stay ye out 'til well after tenth hour. Then I'll *think* about letting the both of ye back into my house."

"Yes, Mother, thank you." He ran up to give her a kiss. She backed off.

"Don't come near me, boy. Not with that monster sleeping on your arm."

"He wouldn't hurt you, Mother. Really."

"I'd feel more confident if I had the snake's word on it as well as yours, boy. Now go on, get out, be off with the both of ye. If we're fortunate, perhaps it will have some homing instinct and fly off when you're not looking."

But Pip did not fly off. It gave no sign of wishing to be anywhere in the Commonwealth save on the shoulder of a certain redheaded young man.

As Flinx strolled through the marketplace, he was startled to discover that his ability to receive the emotions and feelings of others had intensified, though none of the isolated bursts of reception matched in fury that first overpowering deluge of the night before. His receptivity had increased in frequency and lucidity, though it still seemed as unpredictable as ever. Flinx suspected that his new pet might have something to do with his intensified abilities, but he had no idea how that worked, anymore than he knew how his Talent operated at the best of times.

If only he could find someone to identify the snake! He could always work through his terminal back home, but requests for information were automatically monitored at Central, and he was afraid that a query for information on so rare a creature might trigger alarm on the part of curious authorities. Flinx preferred not to go through official channels. He had acquired Mother Mastiff's opinion of governmental bureaucracy, which placed it somewhere between slime mold and the fleurms that infested the alleys.

By now, he knew a great many inhabitants of the marketplace. Wherever he stopped, he inquired about the identity and origin of his pet. Some regarded the snake with curiosity, some with fear, a few with indifference. But none recognized it.

"Why don't you ask Makepeace?" one of the vendors eventually suggested. "He's traveled offworld. Maybe he'd know."

Flinx found the old soldier sitting on a street corner with several equally ancient cronies. All of them were pensioners. Most were immigrants who had chosen Moth for their final resting place out of love for its moist climate and because it was a comparatively cheap world to live on, not to mention the laxity of its police force. On Moth, no one was likely to question the source of one's pension money. For several of Makepeace's comrades, this was the prime consideration.

The other aged men and women studied the snake with nothing more than casual interest, but Makepeace reacted far more enthusiastically. "Bless my remaining soul," he muttered as he leaned close—but not too close, Flinx noted—for a better look. Pip raised his head curiously, as if sensing something beyond the norm in this withered biped.

"You know what he is?" Flinx asked hopefully.

"Aye, boy. Those are wings bulging its flanks, are they not?"

Flinx nodded. "Then it's surely an Alaspinian miniature dragon."

Flinx grinned at the old man, then down at Pip. "So that's what you are." The snake looked up at him as if to say, I'm well aware of what I am, and do you always find the obvious so remarkable?

"I thought dragons were mythical creatures," he said to Makepeace.

"So they are. It's only a name given from resemblance, Flinx."

"I suppose you know," Flinx went on, "that he spits out a corrosive fluid."

"Corrosive!" The old man leaned back and roared with laughter, slapping his legs and glancing knowingly at his attentive cronies. "Corrosive, he says!" He looked back at Flinx.

"The minidrag's toxin is, my boy, a venomous acid known by a long string of chemical syllables which this old head can't remember. I was a soldier-engineer. Biochemistry was never one of my favorite subjects. I'm more comfortable with mathematical terms than biological ones. But I can tell you this much, though I never visited Alaspin myself." He pointed at the snake, which drew its head back uncertainly. "If that there thing was to spit in your eye, you'd be a kicking, quivering mess on the ground inside a minute—and dead in not much more than that.

"I also remember that there's no known antidote for several of the Alaspinian toxins, of which that minidrag of yours wields the most potent. A corrosive, neurological poison—aye, who wouldn't remember hearing about that? You say you know it's corrosive?"

Flinx had an image of the dissolved end of the broomstick, the metal melted away like cheese before a hot blade. He nodded.

"Just make sure you never get to know of it personally, lad. I've heard tell of such creatures being kept as pets, but it's a rare thing. See, the associational decision's all made by the snake. The would-be owner has no choice in the matter. You can't tame 'em. They pick and choose for themselves." He gestured toward Flinx's shoulder. "Looks like that one's sure settled on you."

"He's more than welcome," Flinx said affectionately. "He feels natural there."

"Each to his own," an elderly woman observed with a slight shudder. Affirmative nods came from others in the group.

"And there's something else, too." The old soldier was frowning, struggling to remember long-dormant knowledge. "What you just said about it feeling 'natural' there reminded me. They say those flying snakes have funny mental quirks all their own. Now me, I wouldn't be able to say for certain if that's so—I'm only relating hearsay, didn't read it off no chip. But the stories persist."

"What kind of stories?" Flinx asked, trying not to appear over-anxious.

"Oh, that the snakes are empathic. You know, telepathic on the emotional level." He scratched his head. "There's more to it than that, but I'm damned if I can remember the rest of it."

"That's certainly interesting," Flinx said evenly, "but pretty unlikely."

"Yeah, I always thought so myself," Makepeace agreed. "You wouldn't have noticed anything like that since being around this one, of course."

"Not a thing." Flinx was an expert at projecting an aura of innocence; in this case, it glowed from his face, not his mind. "Thanks a lot for your time, Mr. Makepeace, sir."

"You're more than welcome to it, boy. Old knowledge dies unless somebody makes use of it. You watch yourself around that thing. It's no saniff, and it might could turn on you."

"I'll be careful," Flinx assured him brightly. He turned and hurried away from the gaggle of attentive oldsters.

Makepeace was rubbing his chin and staring after the youngster as he vanished into the swirling crowd. "Funny. Wonder where the little flying devil came from? This is one hell of a long way from Alaspin. That reminds me of the time . . ."

Flinx glanced down at his shoulder. "So you're poisonous, huh? Well, anyone could have guessed that from the little demonstration you gave with Mother's broom this morning. If you spit in my eye, I'll spit in yours."

The snake did not take him up on the offer. It stared at him a moment, then turned its head away and studied the street ahead, evidently more interested in its surroundings than in its master's indecipherable words.

Maybe miniature dragons don't have much of a sense of humor, Flinx mused. Probably he would have ample opportunity to find out. But at least he knew what his pet was. Glancing up beyond the fringe of the slickertic hood, he wondered where the snake's home world lay. Alaspin, old Makepeace had called it, and said it was far away.

The morning mist moistened his upturned face. The cloud cover seemed lighter than usual. If he was lucky, the gloom would part sometime that night and he would have a view of Moth's fragmented ice rings, of the moon Flame, and beyond that, of the stars.

Someday, he thought, someday I'll travel to far places as Makepeace and the others have. Someday I'll get off this minor wet world and go vagabonding. I'll be a free adult, with nothing to tie me down and no responsibilities. I'll lead a relaxed, uncompli- cated life of simple pleasures. He glanced down at his new-found companion. Maybe someday they would even travel to the snake's home world of Alaspin, wherever it might be.

Sure you will, he thought bitterly. Better be realistic, like Mother Mastiff says. You're stuck here forever. Moth's your home, and Moth's where you'll spend the rest of your days. Count yourself fortunate. You've a concerned mother, a warm home, food. . . .

Food. Surely the flying snake was hungrier than ever. "We'd bet- ter get you something to eat," he told Pip, who gazed up at him with fresh interest.

He checked his credcard. Not much money there. Not that there ever was. Well, he could manage. Trouble was, he had no idea what Alaspinian minidrags liked to eat. "I wonder what you'd settle for," he murmured. The snake did not respond. "If it's live food only, then I don't think there's much I can do to help you. Not on a reg- ular basis, anyway. Let's try here, first."

They entered a stall well known to Flinx. Most of the booths and tables were unoccupied, since it was between mealtimes. As it de- veloped, finding suitable food for the minidrag turned out to be less of a problem than he had feared. Much to Flinx's surprise, the flying snake was omnivorous. It would eat almost anything he set in front of it, but raw meat seemed to be a special favorite. Flinx cut the meat into small chunks, which the snake gulped down whole. Flinx helped himself to an occasional bite. When times were bad, he and Mother Mastiff had existed on far less savory items.

Pip was fond of any kind of fruit or berry, though it shied away from vegetables. Something else they had in common, Flinx thought. Oddly enough, the snake would even lap up milk. Flinx was sure he could supply enough variety to keep his pet both happy and alive. Maybe it would even eat table scraps. Perhaps *that* would weaken Mother Mastiff's antagonism. As he experi- mented further, he discovered that the snake was particularly fond of anything with a high iron content, such as raisins or flakes of guarfish. Had he been a biochemist equipped with a field labora- tory, he might have learned that the minidrag's blood contained an extraordinary amount of hemoglobin, vital to transport the oxygen necessary to sustain the snake's hummingbirdlike flight.

When Pip had swollen to twice his normal diameter, Flinx stopped trying new foods on his pet. He relaxed in the booth, sipping mulled wine and watching the lights of the city wink to life. It wouldn't be too bad to live out his life on Moth, he admitted to himself. Drallar was never dull, and now he had a special companion with whom to share its excitement.

Yes, the flying snake had filled a definite void in his life as well as in some mysterious, deeper part of himself. But he still longed for the stars and the magical, unvisited worlds that circled them.

Be realistic, he ordered himself.

He waved to some acquaintances as they strolled past the restaurant. Older men and women. Sometimes Mother Mastiff worried that he preferred the company of adults to youngsters his own age. He couldn't help it. It wasn't that he was antisocial, merely that he chose his friends carefully. It was the immaturity of those his own age that drove him into the company of adults.

A fleeting emotion from one of those to whom he had waved reached back to him as the group rounded a corner, laughing and joking in easy camaraderie. Flinx snatched at it, but it was gone. He sat back in his booth, the wine making him moody. Better to have no Talent at all, he thought, than an unmanageable one that only teases.

He paid the modest bill, slipping his card into the table's central pylon. Outside, the evening rain had begun. Pip rode comfortably on his shoulder beneath the slickertic, only its head exposed. It was sated, content. Ought to be after all you ate, Flinx thought as he gazed fondly down at his pet.

Rain transformed the brilliant scales of the snake's head into tiny jewels. The moisture did not seem to bother the snake. I wonder, Flinx thought. Is Alaspin a wet world, also? I should have asked old Makepeace. He'd probably have known. People lucky enough to travel learn everything sooner or later.

Suddenly a stinging, serrated burst of emotion—hammer blow, unexpected, raw—doubled him over with its force. It was like a soundless screaming inside his head. Flinx was feeling the naked emotion behind a scream instead of hearing the scream itself. He had never experienced anything like it before, and despite that, it felt sickeningly familiar.

A bundled-up passer-by halted and bent solicitously over the crumpled youngster. "Are you all right, son? You—" He noticed something and quickly backed off.

"I—I'm okay, I think," Flinx managed to gasp. He saw what had made the man flinch. Pip had been all but asleep on his master's shoulder only a moment before. Now the snake was wide awake, head and neck protruding like a scaly periscope as it seemed to search the night air for something unseen.

Then the last vestiges of that desperate, wailing cry vanished, leaving Flinx's head aching and infuriatingly empty. Yet it had lingered long enough for him to sort it out, to identify it.

"Listen, son, if you need help, I can—" the stranger started to say, but Flinx did not wait to listen to the kind offer. He was already halfway down the street, running at full speed over the pavement. His slickertic fanned out like a cape behind him, and his boots sent water flying over shop fronts and pedestrians alike. He did not pause to apologize, the curses sliding off him as unnoticed as the rain.

Then he was skidding into a familiar side street. His heart pounded, and his lungs heaved. The street appeared untouched, unaltered, yet something here had been violated, and the moment of it had touched Flinx's mind. Most of the shops were already shuttered against the night. There was no sign of human beings in that damp stone canyon.

"Mother!" he shouted. "Mother Mastiff!" He pounded on the lock plate with his palm. The door hummed but did not open—it was locked from inside.

"Mother Mastiff, open up. It's me, Flinx!" No reply from the other side.

Pip danced on his shoulder, half airborne and half coiled tight to its master. Flinx moved a dozen steps away from the door, then charged it, throwing himself into the air sideways and kicking with one leg as Makepeace had once shown him. The door gave, flying inward. It had only been bolted, not locksealed.

He crouched there, his eyes darting quickly around the stall. Pip settled back onto his shoulder, but its head moved agitatedly from side to side, as if it shared its master's nervousness and concern.

The stall looked undisturbed. Flinx moved forward and tried the inner door. It opened at a touch. The interior of the living area was a shambles. Pots and pans and food had been overturned in the kitchen. Clothing and other personal articles lay strewn across floor and furniture. He moved from the kitchen-dining area to his own room, lastly to Mother Mastiff's, knowing but dreading what he would find.

The destruction was worse in her room. The bed looked as if it had been the scene of attempted murder or an uncontrolled orgy. Across the bed, hidden from casual view, a small curved door blended neatly into the wall paneling. Few visitors would be sharp-eyed enough to notice it. It was just wide enough for a man to crawl through.

It stood ajar. A cold breeze drifted in from outside.

Flinx dropped to his knees and started through, not caring what he might encounter on the other side. He emerged from the slip-me-out into the alley and climbed to his feet. The rain had turned to mist. There was no hint that anything unusual had occurred here. All the chaos was behind him, inside.

Turning, he ran two or three steps to the north, then stopped himself. He stood there, panting. He had run long and hard from the street where the scream had struck him, but he was too late. There was no sign that anyone had even been in the alley.

Slowly, dejectedly, he returned to the shop. Why? he cried to himself. Why has this happened to me? Who would want to kidnap a harmless old woman like Mother Mastiff? The longer he thought about it, the less sense it made.

He forced himself to take an inventory out front. There was no sign of anything missing. The shop's stock seemed to be intact. Not thieves, then, surprised in the act of burglary. Then what? If not for the ample evidence that there had been a struggle, he would not even have suspected that anything was amiss.

No, he reminded himself, not quite true. The lockseal on the front door was dead. It would have taken half the thieves in Drallar to drag Mother Mastiff from her shop while it stood unsealed. He thought of thieves a second time, knowing he would not be staying here long. His mind full of dark and conflicting thoughts, he set about repairing the lock.

6

"*Pssst!* Boy! Flinx-boy!"

Flinx moved the door aside slightly and gazed out into the darkness. The man speaking from the shadows operated a little shop two stalls up the side street from Mother Mastiff's, where he made household items from the hardwoods that Moth grew in abundance. Flinx knew him well, and stepped out to confront him.

"Hello, Arrapkha." He tried to search the man's face, but it was mostly hidden by the overhanging rim of his slickertic. He could feel nothing from the other man's mind. A fine and wondrous Talent, he thought sarcastically to himself.

"What happened here? Did you see anything?"

"I shouldn't be out like this." Arrapkha turned to glance worriedly up the street to where it intersected the busy main avenue. "You know what people say in Drallar, Flinx-boy. The best business is minding one's own."

"No homilies now, friend," Flinx said impatiently. "You've been neighbor to my mother for many years, and you've watched me grow up. Where is she?"

"I don't know." Arrapkha paused to gather his thoughts. Flinx held back his anxiety and tried to be patient with the man— Arrapkha was a little slow upstairs but a good soul.

"I was working at my lathe, feeling good with myself. I'd only just sold a pair of stools to a programmer from the Welter Inurb and was counting my good fortune when I thought I heard noises from your house." He smiled faintly. "At first, I thought nothing of it. You know your mother. She can fly into a rage at any time over nothing in particular and make enough noise to bring complaints from the avenue stores.

"Anyhow, I finished turning a broya post—it will be a fine one, Flinx-boy, fashioned of number-six harpberry wood—"

"Yes, I'm sure," Flinx said impatiently. "I'm sure it will be a fine display stand, as all your work is, but what about Mother Mastiff?"

"I'm getting to that, Flinx-boy," Arrapkha said petulantly. "As I said, I finished the post, and since the noise continued, I grew curious. It seemed to be going on a long time even for your mother. So I put down my work for a moment and thought to come see what was going on. I mediate for your mother sometimes.

"When I was about halfway from my shop to yours, the noise stopped almost entirely. I was about to return home when I saw something. At least, I think I did." He gestured toward the narrow gap that separated Mother Mastiff's shop from the vacant shop adjoining hers.

"Through there I thought I saw figures moving quickly up the alley behind your home. I couldn't be certain. The opening is small, it was raining at the time, and it's dark back there. But I'm pretty sure I saw several figures."

"How many?" Flinx demanded. "Two, three?"

"For sure, I couldn't say," Arrapkha confessed sadly. "I couldn't even for certain tell if they were human or not. More than two, surely. Yet not a great number, though I could have missed seeing them all.

"Well, I came up to the door quickly then and buzzed. There was no answer, and it was quiet inside, and the door was locked, so I thought little more of it. There was no reason to connect shapes in the alleyway with your mother's arguing. Remember, I only heard noise from the shop.

"As it grew dark I started to worry, and still the shop stayed closed. It's not like Mother Mastiff to stay closed up all day. Still, her digestion is not what it used to be, and sometimes her liver gives her trouble. Too much bile. She could have been cursing her own insides."

"I know," Flinx said. "I've had to listen to her complaints lots of times."

"So I thought best not to interfere. But I *have* known both of you for a long time, Flinx-boy, just as you say, so I thought, when I saw you moving about, that I ought to come and tell you what I'd seen. It's clear to me now that I should have probed deeper." He struck his own head. "I'm sorry. You know that I'm not the cleverest man in the marketplace."

"It's all right, Arrapkha. There's no blame for you in this matter." Flinx stood there in the mist for a long moment, silent and thinking hard.

Arrapkha hesitantly broke in on his contemplation. "So sorry I am, Flinx-boy. If there's anything I can do to help, if you need a place to sleep tonight, ay, even with the devil thing on your shoulder, you are welcome to share my home."

"I've spent many a night out on my own, sir," Flinx told him, "but the offer's appreciated. Thank you for your help. At least now I have a better idea of what happened, though not for the life of me *why*. Could you see if Mother Mastiff was among those running down the alley? She's not here."

"So I guessed from your look and words. No, I cannot say she was one of them. I saw only shapes that seemed to be human, or at least upright. But they seemed to run with difficulty."

"Maybe they were carrying her."

"It may be, Flinx-boy, it may be. Surely she would not go off on her own with strangers without leaving you so much as a message."

"No, she wouldn't," Flinx agreed, "and if she went with the people you saw, it wasn't because they were her friends. The inside of the house is all torn up. She didn't go with them quietly."

"Then surely for some reason she's been kidnapped," Arrapkha concurred. "Fifty years ago, I might could give a reason for such a thing. She was a beauty then, Mother Mastiff, though she has not aged gracefully. Grace was not a part of her, not even then. A hard woman always, but attractive. But for this to happen now—" He shook his head. "A true puzzle. Did she have access to much money?"

Flinx shook his head rapidly.

"Um. I thought not. Well, then, did she owe anyone any dangerous amounts?"

"She owed a lot of people, but no great sums," Flinx replied. "At least, nothing that she ever spoke to me about and nothing I ever overheard talk of."

"I do not understand it, then," Arrapkha said solemnly.

"Nor do I, friend."

"Perhaps," Arrapkha suggested, "someone wished a private conversation with her and will bring her back in the morning?"

Flinx shook his head a second time. "I think that since she didn't go with them voluntarily, she won't be allowed to come back voluntarily. Regardless, one thing she always told me was not to sit around and stare blankly at the inexplicable but always to try and find answers. If she does come walking freely home tomorrow, then I can at least try to meet her coming."

"Then you're determined to go out after her?" Arrapkha lifted bushy black eyebrows.

"What else can I do?"

"You could wait. You're a nice young fellow, Flinx-boy." He waved toward the distant avenue. "Most everyone in the marketplace who knows you thinks so, also. You won't lack for a place to stay or food to eat if you decide to wait for her. Your problem is that you're too young, and the young are always overanxious."

"Sorry, Arrapkha. I know you mean well for me, but I just can't sit around here and wait. I think I'd be wasting my time and, worse, maybe hers as well. Mother Mastiff doesn't have much time left to her."

"And what if her time, excuse me, has already fled?" Arrapkha asked forcefully. Subtlety was not a strong trait of the marketplace's inhabitants. "Will you involve yourself then in something dangerous which has chosen to spare you?"

"I have to know. I have to go after her and see if I can help."

"I don't understand," Arrapkha said sadly. "You're a smart young man, much smarter than I. Why risk yourself? She wouldn't want you to, you know. She's not really your mother."

"Mother or mother-not," Flinx replied, "she's the only mother I've ever known. There's more to it than simple biology, Arrapkha. The years have taught me that much."

The older man nodded. "I thought you might say something like that, Flinx-boy. Well, I can at least wish you luck. It's all I have to give you. Do you have credit?"

"A little, on my card."

"If you need more, I can transfer." Arrapkha started to pull out his own card.

"No, not now, anyway. I may need such help later." He broke into a broad smile. "You're a good friend, Arrapkha. Your friendship is as solid as your woodwork." He turned. "Did you see which direction these figures took?"

"That's little to start on." He pointed to the north. "That way, up the alley. They could have turned off any time. And in the weather"—he indicated the clouds hanging limply overhead—"they'll have left no trail for you to follow."

"Perhaps not," Flinx admitted. "We'll see."

"I expect you will, Flinx-boy, since you feel so strongly about this. All I can do, then, is wish luck to you." He turned and strode back up the street toward his shop, keeping the slickertic tight around his head and neck.

Flinx waited until the rain had swallowed up the older man before going back inside and closing the door behind him. He wandered morosely around the living area, salvaging this or that from the mess and returning things to their proper places. Before long, he found himself in Mother Mastiff's room. He sat down on the bed and stared at the ajar slip-me-out that led to the alley.

"What do you think, Pip? Where did she go, and who took her, and why? And how am I going to find her? I don't even know how to start."

He shut his eyes, strained, tried to sense the kinds of emotions he knew she must be generating, wherever she had been taken. There was nothing. Nothing from Mother Mastiff, nothing from anyone else. His Talent mocked him. He started fixing up the bedroom, hoping that contact with familiar objects might trigger some kind of reaction in his mind. Something, anything, that would give him a start on tracking her down. Pip slipped off his shoulder and slithered across the bed, playing with covers and pillows.

There were gaps—missing clothing—in the single closet, Flinx noted. Whoever had abducted her evidently intended to keep her for a while. The sight cheered him because they would not have troubled to take along clothing for someone they intended to kill immediately.

Pip had worked its way across the bed to the night table and was winding its sinuous way among the bottles and containers there. "Back off that, Pip, before you break something. There's been enough damage done here today." The irritation in his voice arose more out of personal upset than any real concern. The minidrag had yet to knock over anything.

Pip reacted, though not to his master's admonition. The snake spread luminous wings and fluttered from the tabletop to the slip-me-out. It hovered there, watching him. While Flinx gaped at his pet, it flew back to the night table, hummed over a bottle, then darted back to the opening.

Flinx's momentary paralysis left him, and he rushed to the end table. The thin plasticine bottle that had attracted Pip was uncapped. It normally held a tenth liter of a particularly powerful cheap perfume of which Mother Mastiff was inordinately fond. Now he saw that the bottle was empty.

If Mother Mastiff had retained enough presence of mind to remember that the Drallarian gendarmery occasionally employed the services of tracking animals—for the first time hope crowded despair from Flinx's thoughts. Those animals could track odors even through Moth's perpetual dampness.

If an Alaspinian minidrag possessed the same ability . . . Was he completely misinterpreting the flying snake's actions? "Pip?"

The flying snake seemed to accept the mention of its name as significant, for it promptly spun in midair and darted through the slip-me-out. Flinx dropped to his hands and knees and crawled after. In seconds, he was in the alley again. As he climbed to his feet, he searched for his pet. It was moving eastward, almost out of sight.

"Pip, wait!" The snake obediently halted, hovering in place until its master had caught up. Then it took off up the alley again.

Flinx settled into a steady run. He was an excellent runner and in superb condition, on which he had always prided himself. He resolved to follow the flying snake until one or the other of them dropped.

Any moment he expected the snake to pause outside one of the innumerable faceless structures that peppered the commercial sections of Drallar. But while the minidrag twisted and whirled down alleys and up streets, not once did it hesitate in its steady flight. Soon Flinx found his wind beginning to fail him. Each time he stopped, the snake would wait impatiently until its master caught up again.

Drallar was the largest city on Moth, but it was a village compared to the great cities of Terra or the underground complexes of Hivehom and Evoria, so Flinx was not surprised that when Pip finally began to slow, they had reached the northwestern outskirts of the metropolis. Here the buildings no longer had to be built close to one another. Small storage structures were scattered about, and individual homes of blocked wood and plastic began to blend into the first phalanx of evergreen forest. Pip hesitated before the trees, zooming in anxious circles, soaring to scan the treetops. It ignored Flinx's entreaties and calls until finally satisfied, whereupon the snake turned and dropped down to settle once again on the familiar perch of his master's shoulder.

Turning a slow circle, Flinx fought to pick up even a fragment of lingering emotion. Once again, his efforts met with failure. It seemed clear that whoever had carried off Mother Mastiff had taken her into the forest and that the olfactory trail that had led Pip so far had finally dissipated in the steady onslaught of mist and rain. On a drier world or in one of Moth's few deserts, things might have been different, but here Pip had come to a dead end.

After a moment's thought, Flinx started away from the trees. In addition to the storage buildings and homes, several small indus-

trial complexes were visible nearby, including two of the ubiqui-
tous sawmills that ringed the city and processed Moth's most
prolific crop. Flinx wandered among them until he located a public com station on a service street. He stepped inside and slid the
spanda-wood door shut behind him. Even after curing, spanda retained a significant coefficient of expansion. When he closed the
door, it sealed itself against the elements, and only the ventilation
membranes would keep him from suffocating. He took out his battered credcard and slid it into the receptacle on the unit, then
punched the keyboard. A pleasant-looking middle-aged woman
appeared on the small viewscreen. "Yes, sir. What can I do for
you?"

"Is there a Missing Persons Bureau in the Drallar Municipal
Strata?"

"Just a moment, please." There was a pause while she glanced at
something out of range of the pickup. "Human or alien?"

"Human, please."

"Native or visitor?"

"Native."

"You wish connection?"

"Thank you, yes." The woman continued to stare at him for a
moment, and Flinx decided she was fascinated by the coiled shape
riding his shoulder. The screen finally flashed once and then
cleared.

This time, the individual staring back at him was male, bald, and
bored. His age was indeterminate, his attitude barely civil. Flinx
had never liked bureaucrats. "Yes, what is it?"

"Last night," he declared, "or early this morning"—in his rush
through the city streets he'd completely lost track of the time—
"I—my mother disappeared. A neighbor saw some people running
away down an alley, and our house was all torn apart. I don't know
how to start looking for her. I think she's been taken out of the city
via the northwest quadrant, but I can't be sure."

The man perked up slightly, though his voice sounded doubtful.
"I see. This sounds more like a matter for the police than for
Missing Persons."

"Not necessarily," Flinx said, "if you follow my meaning."

"Oh." The man smiled understandingly. "Just a moment. I'll
check for you." He worked a keyboard out of Flinx's view. "Yes,
there were a number of arrests made last night, several of them including women. How old is your mother?"

"Close to a hundred," Flinx said, "but quite lively."

"Not lively enough to be in with the group I was thinking of," the clerk responded. "Name?"

Flinx hesitated. "I always just called her Mother Mastiff."

The man frowned, then studied his unseen readout. "Is Mastiff a first name or last name? I'm assuming the 'Mother' is an honorific."

Flinx found himself staring dumbly at the clerk. Suddenly, he was aware of the enormous gaps that made up much of his life. "I—I don't know, for sure."

The bureaucrat's attitude turned stony. "Is this some kind of joke, young man?"

"No, sir," Flinx hastened to assure him, "it's no joke. I'm telling you the truth when I say that I don't know. See, she's not my natural mother."

"Ah," the clerk murmured discreetly. "Well, then, what's your last name?"

"I—" To his great amazement, Flinx discovered that he was starting to cry. It was a unique phenomenon that he had avoided for some time; now, when he least needed it, it afflicted him.

The tears did have an effect on the clerk, though. "Look, young man, I didn't mean to upset you. All I can tell you is that no woman of that advanced an age is on last night's arrest recording. For that matter, no one that old has been reported in custody by any other official source. Does that help you at all?"

Flinx nodded slowly. It helped, but not in the way he'd hoped. "Th-thank you very much, sir."

"Wait, young man! If you'll give me your name, maybe I can have a gendarme sent out with—" The image died as Flinx flicked the disconnect button. His credcard popped from its slot. Slowly, wiping at his eyes, he put it back inside his shirt. Would the clerk bother to trace the call? Flinx decided not. For an instant, the bureaucrat had thought the call was from some kid pulling a joke on him. After a moment's reflection, he would probably think so again.

No one of Mother Mastiff's age arrested or reported in. Not at Missing Persons, which was bad, but also not at the morgue, which was good because that reinforced his first thoughts: Mother Mastiff had been carried off by unknown persons whose motives remained as mysterious as did their identity. He gazed out the little booth's window at the looming, alien forest into which it seemed she and her captors had vanished, and exhaustion washed over him. It was toasty warm in the com booth.

The booth's chair was purposely uncomfortable, but the floor was heated and no harder. For a change, he relished his modest size as he worked himself into a halfway comfortable position on the floor. There was little room for Pip in the cramped space, so the flying snake reluctantly found itself a perch on the com unit. Anyone entering the booth to make a call would be in for a nasty shock.

It was well into morning when Flinx finally awoke, stiff and cramped but mentally rested. Rising and stretching, he pushed aside the door and left the com booth. To the north lay the first ranks of the seemingly endless forest, which ran from Moth's lower temperate zone to its arctic. To the south lay the city, friendly, familiar. It would be hard to turn his back on it.

Pip fluttered above him, did a slow circle in the air, then rose and started northwestward. In minutes, the minidrag was back. In its wordless way, it was reaffirming its feelings of the night before: Mother Mastiff had passed that way. Flinx thought a moment. Perhaps her captors, in order to confuse even the most unlikely pursuit, had carried her out into the forest, only to circle back into the city again.

How was he to know for certain? The government couldn't help him further. All right, then. He had always been good at prying information from strangers. They seemed to trust him instinctively, seeing in him a physically unimposing, seemingly not-too-bright youngster. He could probe as facilely here as in the marketplace.

Leaving the booth and the sawmill block, he began his investigation by questioning the occupants of the smaller businesses and homes. He found most houses deserted, their inhabitants having long since gone off to work, but the industrial sites and businesses were coming alive as the city's commercial bloodstream began to circulate. Flinx confronted the workers as they entered through doors and gates, as they parked their occasional individual transports, and as they stepped off public vehicles.

Outside the entrance to a small firm that manufactured wooden fittings for kitchen units, he encountered someone not going to work but leaving. "Excuse me, sir," he said for what seemed like the hundred thousandth time, "did you by any chance see a group of people pass through this part of town last night? They would have had an upset old lady with them, perhaps restrained somehow."

"Now that's funny of you to mention," the man said unexpectedly. "See, I'm the night guard at Koyunlu over there." He gestured at the small building that was filling up with workers. "I didn't see no old woman, but there was something of a commotion late last night over that way." He pointed at the road which came to a dead end against the nearby trees.

"There was a lot of shouting and yelling and cursing. I took a look with my nightsight—that's my job, you know—and I saw a bunch of people getting out of a rented city transport. They were switching over to a mudder."

The watchman appeared sympathetic. "They weren't potential thieves or young vandals, so I didn't watch them for long. I don't know if they were the people you're looking for."

Flinx thought a moment, then asked, "You say that you heard cursing. Could you tell if any of it was from a woman?"

The man grinned. "I see what you're thinking, son. No, they were too far away. But I tell you this: someone in that bunch could swear like any dozen sewer riders."

Flinx could barely contain his excitement. "That's them; that's her! That's *got* to be her!"

"In fact," the watchman continued, "that's really what made it stick in my mind. Not that you don't see people switching transports at night—you do, even way out here. It's just a bad time to go mudding into the woods, and when it is done, it's usually done quietly. No need that I can see for all that yelling and shouting."

"It was them, all right," Flinx murmured decisively. "It was her swearing—or her kidnappers swearing at her."

"Kidnap—" The man seemed to notice Flinx's youth for the first time. "Say, son, maybe you'd better come along with me."

"No, I can't." Flinx started to back up, smiling apologetically. "I have to go after them. I have to find her."

"Just hold on a second there, son," the watchman said. "I'll give a call to the police. We can use the company coms. You want to do this right and proper so's—"

"They won't do anything," Flinx said angrily. "I know them." On an intimate basis, he could have added, since he'd been arrested for petty theft on more than one occasion. He was probably on their question-list right now. They would hold him and keep him from going after Mother Mastiff.

"You wait, son," the watchman insisted. "I'm not going to be part of something—" As he spoke, he reached out a big hand. Something bright blue-green-pink hissed threateningly. A triangular head darted menacingly at the clutching hand. The man hastily drew it back.

"Damn," he said, "that's alive!"

"Very alive," Flinx said, continuing to back away. "Thanks for your help, sir." He turned and dashed toward the city.

"Boy, just a minute!" The watchman stared after the retreating figure. Then he shrugged. He was tired. It had been a long, dull night save for that one noisy bunch he'd seen, and he was anxious to be home and asleep. He sure as hell didn't need trouble himself with the antics of some kid. Pushing the entire incident from his thoughts, he headed toward the company transport stop.

Once he was sure he was out of sight of the watchman, Flinx paused to catch his breath. At least he knew with some certainty that Mother Mastiff had been kidnapped and taken out of the city. Why she had been carried off into the great northern forest he could not imagine.

In addition to the hurt at the back of his mind, a new ache had begun to make itself felt. He had had nothing to eat since the previous night. He could hardly go charging off into Moth's vast evergreen wilderness on an empty stomach.

Prepare yourself properly, then proceed. That's what Mother Mastiff had always taught him. I'll go home, he told himself. Back to the shop, back to the marketplace. The kidnappers had switched to a mudder. Such a vehicle was out of Flinx's financial reach, but he knew where he could rent a stupava running bird. That would give him flexibility as well as speed.

His legs still throbbed from the seemingly endless run across the city the previous day, so he used public transport to return home. Time was more important than credits. The transport chose a main spoke avenue and in minutes deposited him in the marketplace.

From the drop-off, it was but a short sprint to the shop. He found himself half expecting to see Mother Mastiff standing in the entrance, mopping the stoop and waiting to bawl him out for being gone for so long. But the shop was quiet, the living space still disarranged and forlorn. Nonetheless, Flinx checked it carefully. There were several items whose positions he had memorized before leaving; they were undisturbed.

He began to collect a small pile of things to take with him. Some hasty trading in the market produced a small backpack and as much concentrated food as he could cram into it. Despite the speed of his bargaining, he received full value for those items he traded off from Mother Mastiff's stock. With Pip riding his shoulder, few thought to cheat him. When anyone tried, the minidrag's reactions

instantly alerted its master and Flinx simply took his trade elsewhere.

Flinx switched his city boots for less gaudy but more durable
forest models. His slickertic would serve just as well among the
trees as among the city's towers. The outright sale of several items
gave his credcard balance a healthy boost. Then it was back to the
shop for a last look around. Empty. So empty without her. He
made certain the shutters were locked, then did the same to the
front door. Before leaving, he stopped at a stall up the street.

"You're out of your mind, Flinx-boy," Arrapkha said from the entrance to his stall, shaking his head dolefully. The shop smelled of
wood dust and varnish. "Do you know what the forest is like? It
runs from here to the North Pole. Three thousand, four thousand
kilometers as the tarpac flies and not a decent-sized city to be
found.

"There's mud up there so deep it could swallow all of Drallar,
not to mention things that eat and things that poison. Nobody goes
into the north forest except explorers and herders, hunters and
sportsmen—crazy folk from offworld who like that sort of
nowhere land. Biologists and botanists—not normal folk like you
and me."

"Normal folk didn't carry off my mother," Flinx replied.

Since he couldn't discourage the youngster, Arrapkha tried to
make light of the situation. "Worse for them that they did. I don't
think they know what they've gotten themselves into."

Flinx smiled politely. "Thanks, Arrapkha. If it wasn't for your
help, I wouldn't have known where to begin."

"Almost I wish I'd said nothing last night," he muttered sadly.
"Well, luck to you, Flinx-boy. I'll remember you."

"You'll see me again," Flinx assured him with more confidence
than he truly felt. "Both of us."

"I hope so. Without your Mother Mastiff, the marketplace will
be a duller place."

"Duller and emptier," Flinx agreed. "I have to go after her, friend
Arrapkha. I really have no choice."

"If you insist. Go, then."

Flinx favored the woodworker with a last smile, then spun and
marched rapidly toward the main avenue. Arrapkha watched until
the youngster was swallowed up by the crowd, then retreated to his
own stall. He had business to attend to, and that, after all, was the
first rule of life in the marketplace.

Flinx hadn't gone far before the smells of the market were replaced by the odors, heavy and musky, of locally popular native transport animals. They were usually slower and less efficient than mechanized transport, but they had other advantages: they could not be traced via their emissions, and they were cheap to rent and to use.

In a licensed barn, Flinx picked out a healthy-looking stupava. The tall running bird was a good forager and could live off the land. It stood two and a half meters at its bright orange crest and closely resembled its far more intelligent cousins, the ornithorpes, who did not object to the use of ignorant relatives as beasts of burden. Flinx haggled with the barn manager for a while, finally settling on a fair price. The woman brought the bird out of its stall and saddled it for the youngster. "You're not going to do anything funny with this bird, now?"

"Just going for a little vacation," Flinx answered her blithely. "I've finished my studies for the year and owe myself the time off."

"Well, Garuyle here will take you anywhere you might want to go. He's a fine, strong bird." She stroked the tall bird's feathers.

"I know." Flinx put his right foot in the first stirrup, his left in the second, and threw his body into the saddle. "I can see that from his legs."

The woman nodded, feeling a little more relaxed. Evidently, her youthful customer knew what he was doing. She handed him the reins.

"All right, then. Have a pleasant journey."

Flinx had indeed ridden such birds before, but only within the city limits and not for any length of time. He snapped the reins, then gave the bird a serious whistle. It hooted back and started off, its long legs moving easily. Guiding it with gentle tugs of the reins and sharp whistles, Flinx soon had the stupava moving at a respectable rate up the first spoke avenue, jostling aside irritated pedestrians and avoiding faster public vehicles. The stupava seemed undisturbed by Pip's presence, a good sign. It would not do to head into the great forest on an easily spooked mount.

In a gratifyingly short time, Flinx found they had retraced his frenzied marathon of the night before. A sawmill passed by on his left, the com booth that had sheltered him somewhere behind it. Then only the forest loomed ahead. Trees, a hundred meters tall and higher soared above scattered smaller trees and bushes. Where the pavement vanished there was only a muddy trail. The stupava wouldn't mind that—its splayed, partially webbed feet would carry them over the bogs and sumps with ease.

"Heigh there!" he shouted softly at the bird, following the command with a crisp whistle. The stupava cawed once, jerked its head sharply against the bridle, and dashed off into the woods. The regular *flap-flap* from beneath its feet gave way to an irregular *whacking* sound broken by occasional splashes as it spanned a deeper puddle. Sometimes they touched thick moss or fungi and there was no sound at all. In no time, the immense trees formed a solid wall of bark and green behind Flinx, and the city that was his home was for the first time completely out of his sight.

7

Joppe the Thief thought for sure he had found himself a couple of fleurms. The man and woman he was stalking so intently looked to be in their midthirties. Their dress was casual, so casual that one not interested in it might not have identified them as offworlders. Their presence in that part of Drallar's marketplace late at night proved one of two things to Joppe: either they had a great deal of confidence in their ability to pass unnoticed, or they were simply ignorant. Joppe guessed they were searching for a little excitement.

That was fine with Joppe. He would happily provide them with some excitement, something really memorable to relate to the neighbors back home on some softer world like Terra or New Riviera. They did not look like the kind who would be awkward about it. If they were, then they might have more than merely an interesting encounter to talk about.

Joppe was hungry. He had not made a strike in over a week. He regarded the strolling, chatting couple with the eye of a covetous farmer examining a pair of his prize meat animals.

As it was still comparatively early, not all the lights had been extinguished in that part of the marketplace, but enough of the shops had closed to give Joppe hope. The nature of his work required privacy. He did not rush himself. Joppe had an instinctive feel for his work. He had to balance waiting for more shopkeepers to retire against the possibility of the couple's realizing their error and turning back toward the more brightly lit sections of the market.

The couple did not seem inclined to do that. Joppe's hopes continued to rise. He could hear them clearly, talking about some sight seen earlier in the day. Joppe's hand closed around the handle of the little needler in his pocket, and he started forward, closing the distance between himself and his prey.

By now the couple had reached the end of the cul-de-sac and had stopped in front of the last shop, which was shuttered and dark. They seemed to be debating something. Then the man bent to the shop's door and took several objects from his pockets. He started manipulating something out of Joppe's view.

The thief slowed, the needler only halfway out of his holster pocket, and stared in confusion. What were they up to? He moved a little nearer, still clinging to the shadows. He was close enough to see that the door was sealed with a palm lock, which required the imprint of all five of the shop owner's fingers, in proper sequence, to release. The little black disk that the tourist had attached to the palm lock was a very expensive, sophisticated device for decoding and solving such locks. The man's fingers roved over the keys, and he examined the readout with the attitude of someone who not only knew exactly what he was doing but who had done it frequently.

While the man worked at the door, his companion stood watching him, hands on hips, obviously intent on what he was doing. Abruptly, she glanced away from her husband, and Joppe found himself staring straight at her.

The matronly giggle she had affected all evening was abruptly gone from her voice. Suddenly, nothing about her seemed soft. The unexpected transformation, accomplished solely by a change in posture and tone, was shocking. "I'm sorry we had to waste your evening, friend, but we needed a good screen to keep away the rest of the rabble. Thanks for that. Now turn around, call it a bad day, and look elsewhere. We don't have time for you right now. Oh, and leave that gun where it won't do you or anyone else any harm, okay?" Then she smiled pleasantly.

Too startled to react, Joppe just stood there, his hand still clutching the needler. He could take this one, he thought momentarily. However, something in her stance held him back. The proximity of a weapon was clearly implied, as was the intent to use it. Her companion had paused in his work and crouched before the doorway in a waiting position.

This was all very wrong, Joppe thought. He was not an especially imaginative individual, but he was an intent observer, and he was good at putting things together.

Here stood an offworld couple dressed for an evening out, calmly working a lock decoder on an unprepossessing stall doorway at the end of a side street on a dark and damp night. That, plus the way the woman had spoken to him, did not add up.

Joppe let go of the needler and took his hand from his pocket. Slowly, his fingers spread so that they could see he held nothing in them. He nodded once, smiled a twisted, fleeting smile at the woman, and backed away. She returned his smile. He backed away until the shadows engulfed him once again and he stood behind a protective stone wall. He sucked in a deep breath and let it out. His pulse was racing. Unable to restrain his curiosity, he turned and just peeked around the edge of the wall. The woman had not budged, and was still staring after him. The man had returned to his work.

Joppe was well out of his depth, and he knew it. Without another backward glance, he turned and jogged off toward the main avenue, disappointed with his luck and still hungry for a strike. As to the purpose of the peculiar couple, he gave it not another thought. Such folk operated on a level far above that of Joppe and his ilk and were better forgotten.

"Sensible, that one," the woman said thoughtfully. She turned her attention from the distant street to her companion's work. "I thought he might give us trouble."

"Better that he didn't," her companion agreed. "We don't need to fool with such silliness. Not now." His fingertips danced lightly over the keys set into the black disk.

"How you coming?" the woman asked, peering over his shoulder.

"How does it look like I'm coming?"

"No need to be sarcastic," she said easily.

"It's an updated twenty-six," he informed her. "I didn't expect anyone in this slum would take the trouble and expense to keep updating something like this. Someone sure likes his privacy."

"Don't you?"

"Very funny." Suddenly, the disk emitted a soft beep, and the numbers on the readout froze. "That's got it." The man's tone was relaxed, methodical. There was no pleasure in his announcement, only a cool, professional satisfaction. He touched buttons set at five points spaced evenly around the black disk. It beeped again, twice. The illuminated numbers vanished from the readout. Unsealing the disk, he slid it back inside his coat. There were a number of pockets inside that coat, all filled with the kinds of things that would raise the hackles of any police chief. The man put a hand on the door and pushed. It moved aside easily. After a last, cursory glance up the narrow street, the two of them stepped inside.

The center section of the man's ornate belt buckle promptly came to life, throwing a narrow but powerful beam of light. It was matched a moment later by a similar beam projected from his companion's brooch. They wandered around the stall, noting the goods on display and occasionally sniffing disdainfully at various overpriced items. Inspection led them to an inner door and its simpler locking mechanism.

Both stood just inside the second doorway and gazed around the living area. "Someone put up a hell of a fight," the man commented softly.

"The boy—or his adoptive mother, do you think?" The woman moved in, stooping to examine an overturned end table and the little silver vase that had tumbled from it. The vase was empty. She carefully replaced it where it had fallen.

"Maybe both of them." Her companion was already inspecting the larger of the two bedrooms. They went through the area methodically: kitchen, bedrooms, even the hygiene facilities.

When they had finished—and it did not take them very long—and when fingerprinted samples of air and dust and tiny bits of hopefully significant detritus had been relegated to the safety of tiny storage vials, the man asked his companion, "What do you think? Wait for them here?"

The woman shook her head as she glanced around the kitchen-dining area. "They obviously left under duress—and you know what that suggests."

"Sure, that's occurred to me. No way it couldn't. But there's no guarantee."

She laughed, once. "Yeah, there's no guarantee, but what do you *think*?"

"The same as you. I'm just saying we shouldn't jump to conclusions."

"I know, I know. Isn't it odd, though, that both of them are missing? That surely suggests something other than a common break-in."

"I said I concurred." The man's tone was a mite testy. "What now?"

"The shopkeeper up the street who watched us break in," she said. He nodded agreement.

They retraced their steps, leaving nothing disturbed save the air and the dust. The palm lock snapped tight behind them as they stepped back out into the street, giving no hint that it had been foiled. The couple strolled back up the little side street until they stood before Arrapkha's doorway. They thumbed the buzzer several times.

After the third try, the man leaned close to the little speaker set above the buzzer. "It's been a long, hard day for us, sir, and we're both very tired. We mean you no harm, but we are empowered to take whatever steps we think advisable to carry out our assignment. Those steps will include making our own entrance if you don't let us in.

"We saw you watching us as we let ourselves into the old woman's shop. I promise you we can let ourselves into your place just as easily. You might also like to know that we have an automon trained on the alley behind your shop. If you have a slip-me-out in your back wall, it won't do you a bit of good. So why not be pleasant about this"—he smiled in case the shopkeeper had a video pickup hidden somewhere—"and come on out? If you prefer, we can chat here on the street, in full view of your other neighbors."

They waited a suitable time. The woman looked at her companion, shrugged, and withdrew a small, thimble-shaped object from an inside breast pocket. The door opened immediately. The man nodded, then smiled. The woman put the thimble-thing away and moved back.

Arrapkha stepped outside, closing the door behind him, and looked hesitantly from one visitor to the other. "What can I do for you, lady and sir, this night? Your insistence moved me to concern despite the fact that I am closed now for more than—"

"Skip the banter," the man said crisply. "We know you were watching us. You know that we're not here to buy"—he glanced at the sign above the doorway—"woodwork. Or do you deny having watched us?"

"Well, no," Arrapkha began, "but I—"

"And you didn't call the police," the man continued easily, "because the police often ask questions you'd rather not answer, right?"

"Sir, I assure you that I—"

"We're looking for the old woman and the boy who live in that shop." The man glanced briefly back toward Mother Mastiff's stall. "You wouldn't happen to know where they are, would you?"

Arrapkha shook his head, his expression blank. "No, sir, I would not."

"There are signs of a struggle inside. This is a small street. You didn't hear anything, see anything?"

"A struggle? Dear me," Arrapkha muttered, showing signs of distress. "Well, you know, even though this is a small street, it can still be very noisy here, even at night. We don't always pay close attention."

"I'll bet," the woman muttered. "Just like you didn't pay attention to all the noise we weren't making while we were letting ourselves into your neighbor's shop?"

Arrapkha favored her with a wan smile.

"We haven't time for these games," the man said impatiently, reaching into his pants pocket.

"Please, sir and lady." A look of genuine concern came over Arrapkha's face. "You said that you wouldn't do anything—"

"We won't." The man's hand paused a moment as he saw the shopkeeper's nervous stare. "Even if we have to, we probably won't." He slowly withdrew his hand to bring out a small folder. Arrapkha let out a relieved sigh, and studied the contents of the folder. His eyes widened.

The visitor slipped the little case back into his pocket. "Now, then," he said pleasantly, "I tell you again that we mean you no harm, nor have we any intention of harming the old woman and her boy. Quite the contrary. If they've been the victims of violence, as seems probable, we need to know everything you know, so that if they're still alive, we can help them. Regardless of what you may think of *us* personally and what we stand for, you must realize that if they've met with ill fortune, they're bound to be better off in our care than in the hands of whoever carried them away. You can see that, surely."

"Besides," his companion added matter-of-factly, "if you don't tell us what you know, we'll escort you to a place in city center where you'll be strapped into a machine, and you'll end up telling us, anyway. It won't hurt you, but it will waste our time. I don't like wasted time." She stared into his eyes. "Understand?"

Arrapkha nodded slowly.

"The old woman you seek—Mother Mastiff?" The man nodded encouragingly. "I think I saw her carried off by several figures. I couldn't even tell you if they were human or alien. It was dark and misty."

"Isn't it always here?" the man muttered. "Go on."

"That's all I know, all I saw." Arrapkha shrugged. "Truly." He pointed down the street toward the gap that separated Mother Mastiff's shop from the one next to hers. "Through there I saw struggling shapes in the alley. It still confuses me. She is a very old woman, quite harmless."

"How long ago was this?" the man asked him. Arrapkha told him. "And the boy? What of the boy?"

"He returned home that same night. He often goes off by himself until quite late. At least he's been doing so for as long as I've known him, which is most of his life."

"Long solo walks through this city? At his age?" the woman asked. Arrapkha tried not to show his surprise at the woman's seemingly casual remark. These people knew a great deal in spite of how far they had come from.

"He's not your average youth," Arrapkha informed them, seeing no harm in doing so. "He's grown up largely on his own here." He waved toward the brighter lights and the noise that drifted in from the main avenue. "If you let it, Drallar will mature you quickly."

"I'm sure." The man nodded. "You were saying about the boy?"

"He came back that night, saw what had happened, and was very upset. He's an emotional type, though he fights not to show it, I think. Mother Mastiff is all he has."

Still the couple did not respond, remaining maddeningly uninformative. Arrapkha went on. "He vowed to find her. I don't think he has much chance."

"He went after her, then?" the woman asked eagerly. "How long ago?"

Arrapkha told her. She muttered in some language that Arrapkha did not recognize, then added in the more familiar Commonwealth lingua franca to her companion, "Only a couple of days. We missed them by a lousy couple of days."

"It's happened before," the man reminded her, seeming unperturbed. His attention returned to Arrapkha. "Which way did the boy intend to go?"

"I have no idea," the shopkeeper said.

"You know," the man said pleasantly, "maybe we just ought to all take that little jaunt downtown and visit the machine."

"Please, sir, I tell you truly everything. You have believed my words until now. Why should it be different because the facts no longer please you? That is not my fault. What reason would I have for suddenly lying to you?"

"I don't know," the man said in a more conversational tone. "What reason would you?"

"No reason." Arrapkha felt his few wits deserting him. "Please, I don't understand what's happening here. It's all very confusing to me. What is all this interest suddenly in poor old Mother Mastiff and this Flinx-boy?"

"We'd only confuse you further by telling you, wouldn't we?" the man said. "So you have no idea how the boy intended to begin his search?"

"None at all because that is all that he told me," Arrapkha confessed. "He said only that he was determined to find her. Then he left."

"Well, that's wonderful. That's just wonderful," the man declared sardonically. "All that work, all that research, and we get them narrowed down to one modest-sized city. Now we get to start all over again with a whole damn world to cover."

"It's not that bad," the woman soothed. "The native population is thin outside the city."

"It's not that which worries me." The man sounded tired. "It's our happy competitors."

"I think we'll run into them simultaneously." The woman gestured at Arrapkha as if he weren't there. "We've learned all we can from this one."

"Yes. One more thing, though." He turned to Arrapkha and handed him a small blue metal box. A single button marred its otherwise smooth, vitreous surface. "This is a sealed-beam, high-intensity, low-power transmitter," he explained to the shopkeeper. "If either the woman or the boy should return here, all you have to do is push that button once. That will summon help, both for them and for you. Do you understand?"

"Yes," Arrapkha said slowly. He accepted the metal box, then turned it over in his hand and inspected it.

"There is a reward—a considerable reward," the woman added, "for anyone who assists us in bringing this matter to a speedy and successful resolution." She looked past him, into the little woodworking shop. "I don't know what kind of a life you make for yourself here, but it can't be much. This isn't exactly the high-rent district. The reward would amount to more, much more, than you're likely to clear in an entire year."

"It sounds nice," Arrapkha admitted slowly. "It would be very nice to make a lot of money."

"All right, then," the man said. "Remember, the people who'll show up here in response to a signal from the cube won't necessarily include us, but they'll be people familiar with our mission. We'll follow as quickly as we're able. You're certain you understand all this, now?"

"I understand."

"Fine." The man did not offer to shake Arrapkha's hand. "Your help is appreciated, and I'm sorry if we upset you."

Arrapkha shrugged. "Life is full of tiny upsets."

"So it is," the man agreed. He turned to his companion. "Let's go." They ran back toward the main avenue, leaving Arrapkha standing in front of his shop.

After several hours, Arrapkha put away his woodworking tools, cleaned himself, and prepared to retire. The blue metal cube sat on the stand next to his bed. Arrapkha studied it for a moment. Then he picked it up and walked into the bathroom. Without ceremony or hesitation, he dropped it into the waste-disposal unit and thumbed the "flush" control. He wondered how it would affect the cube, if it would send any kind of signal, and if those on the receiving end of such a signal would interpret it properly.

Feeling much better, he slipped into bed and went to sleep.

8

The forest was full of revelations for the thoroughly urbanized Flinx. The first few nights were hard. The silence hit him with unexpected force, and he found sleeping difficult. Pip spent those nights in uneasy rest, sensing its master's discomfort. Only the stupava, its head bobbing methodically with its soft snores, was content.

By the fourth night, Flinx slept soundly, and by the fifth, he was actually enjoying the silence. I've been deceived by circumstances and fate, he thought. This is much better than city life. True, he missed the color, the excitement, the ever-shifting landscape of beings from dozens of worlds parading through the marketplace and the wealthy inurbs, the smells of different foods and the sounds of sinister bargains being consummated. Nor did the forest offer him any opportunity to practice his skills: there wasn't anything to steal. The woods gave freely of their bounty. It was all too easy, somehow.

He had almost relaxed when the squook surprised him. It shot out of its hole in the ground, startling the stupava and nearly causing it to buck Flinx off. The squook was, like its near-relative the canish, a hyperactive ground-dwelling carnivore. It was somewhat larger, boasting claws the length of Flinx's own fingers. The slim, brown-and-black-striped body was built low to the ground. It spent the majority of its life burrowing, searching out other, herbivorous burrowers, but it occasionally would erupt from its hole in an attempt to snag and drag down some larger prey.

The critter had evidently mistaken the comparatively light footsteps of the stupava for those of a much smaller animal. The bird squawked and wrenched at its reins while Flinx fought to bring it under control. At its master's surge of alarm, Pip had instantly leaped clear and now hovered menacingly over the occupied burrow.

The squook favored the minidrag with an impressive snarl but could only glare at its airborne nemesis. Though the riding bird was clearly afraid of it, the squook still had a healthy respect for the bird's long, powerfully muscled legs. Still, if it could just get its teeth around one of those legs, it could bring the large meal to the ground.

But it wasn't so sure about the human perched on the bird's back. Though uncommon thereabouts, humans were not unknown to the inhabitants of that part of the great forest. A squook could kill a human, but the reverse was also true. And then there was that peculiar and utterly unfamiliar humming thing that darted through the air overhead. That made three opponents, one alien and unpredictable, the other two potentially dangerous. Letting out a last, disgruntled snarl, the squook backed into its burrow and expanded to fill the opening. With only its muzzle showing, it sat there and set up a steady warning bark.

Flinx finally got the stupava back under control and urged it forward. The angry calls of the squook receded slowly behind him.

There had been no real danger, he thought. On the other hand, if he had lost his saddle and fallen off—he recalled clearly the long, toothy snout of the carnivore and watched the forest with more respect.

Nothing else emerged to menace them. They encountered nothing larger than the many soaring rodents which inhabited that part of the forest. Pip amused itself by flying circles around them, for they were natural gliders rather than true fliers. They could do nothing but squeak angrily at the intruder as it executed intricate aerial maneuvers in their midst. Those that chattered and complained the loudest, the flying snake selected for lunch.

"That's enough, Pip," Flinx called out to the gallivanting minidrag one day. "Leave them alone and get down here." Responding to the urgency of its master's mind, the flying snake stopped tormenting the flying rodents and zipped down to wrap itself gently around Flinx's neck.

The inn they were approaching was one of hundreds that formed an informal backwoods network in the uninhabited parts of the vast forests. Such establishments provided temporary home to hardwood merchants and cutters, sightseers, fishermen and hunters, prospectors, and other nomadic types. There were more inns than a casual observer might expect to find because there were more nomads. They liked the endless forest. The trees concealed many people and a comparable quantity of sin.

Flinx tethered the stupava in the animal compound, next to a pair of muccax. The inn door sensed his presence and slid aside, admitting him. Smoke rose from a central chimney, but the stone fireplace was more for atmosphere than for heating. The latter was handled by thermal coils running beneath the inn floors. Many of the structures dotting the forest were rustic only in appearance, their innards as modern in design and construction as the shuttle-port outside Drallar. The offworlder tourists who came to Moth to sample the delights of its wilderness generally liked their rough accommodations the same as their liquor: neat.

"Hello." The innkeeper was only a few years older than Flinx. "You're out by yourself?" He glanced at Pip. "That's an interesting pet you have."

"Thanks," Flinx said absently, ignoring the first comment. "What time do you serve midday meal?" He looked longingly toward the nearby dining room, calculating what remained on his credcard. At the present rate, he would starve before he could catch up to his quarry.

"You don't want a room, then?"

"No, thanks." He would sleep in a tube tent in the forest, as usual. Exhaustion made him sleep as soundly these days as any soft bed.

"What about your animal?" The innkeeper gestured toward the animal compound outside.

"He'll be all right."

The young innkeeper looked indifferent. A pleasant-enough sort, Flinx thought, but sheltered—like so many of his potential friends back in Drallar.

"You can get a meal here anytime. We're all autoserve here. This isn't a fancy place. We can't afford a live kitchen."

"The machines will be fine for me," Flinx told him. He walked through the entry area and on into the dining room. Other people were already seated about, enjoying their food. There was a young touring couple and one solitary man far back in a corner. After the usual curious glance at Pip, they ignored the newcomer.

Flinx walked over to the autochef, his mouth watering. Living off the land was fine for the stupava, but occasionally he needed something neither stale nor dehydrated. He made his selections from the extensive list, inserted his card, and waited while it processed the request. Two minutes later he picked up his meal, chose a table, and dug into the roast, fried tuber, and crisp green vegetable. Two tall cups of domestic coffee-substitute washed it down.

The innkeeper strolled in. He chatted a moment with the couple, then sauntered over to Flinx's table. Despite his desire for solitude,

Flinx didn't feel much like arguing, so he said nothing when the 'keeper pulled over a chair and sat down nearby.

"Excuse me," the young man said cheerfully. "I don't see many people my own age here, let alone anyone younger traveling on his own—certainly never with so interesting a companion." He pointed to Pip.

The flying snake had slithered down from Flinx's neck and was sprawled across the table, gulping down green seeds. They complemented a steady diet of arboreal rodents. The seeds really weren't necessary, but the minidrag was not one to pass up a meal that couldn't fight back.

"What are you doing out here all by yourself?"

A real diplomat, this one, Flinx thought to himself. "I'm looking for a friend," he explained, chewing another chunk of roast.

"No one's left any messages for you here if that's what you're wondering," the innkeeper said.

"The friends I'm looking for don't like to leave messages," Flinx said between mouthfuls. "Maybe you've seen them," he asked without much hope. "A very old woman is traveling with them."

"We don't get many very old people out this way," the innkeeper confessed. "They stay closer to the city. That's what's so funny." Flinx stopped in midchew. "There was a group in here just recently that might be the friends you're looking for."

Flinx swallowed carefully. "This old woman is short, a good deal shorter than me. She's close to a hundred."

"Except for her mouth, which is a lot younger?"

"You've seen her!" The meal was suddenly forgotten.

"Five days ago," the innkeeper said. Flinx's heart sank. The distance between them was increasing, not growing shorter.

"Did you happen to see which way they went?"

"Their mudder took off almost due north. I thought that was odd, too, because the line of inns most tourists follow runs pretty much northwest from here, not north. There are a few lodges due north, of course, up in the Lakes District, but not many. They were a funny bunch, and not just because the old woman was with them. They didn't look like sightseers or fishermen."

Trying not to show too much anxiety, Flinx forced himself to finish the rest of his meal. It wasn't that he didn't appreciate the help, but the talkative youth seemed just the type to blab to anyone who might be curious about a visiting stranger, including the forest patrol. Flinx did not want anyone slowing his pursuit with awkward questions—especially since he intended to increase his speed as soon as feasible and like as not by methods the police would frown upon. Nor had he forgotten the watchman in Drallar whose helpfulness had nearly turned to interference.

"You've been a big help," he told the other.

"What's all this about?" the innkeeper persisted as Flinx finished the last of his food and let Pip slide up his proffered arm and onto his shoulder. "What's going on?"

Flinx thought frantically. What could he say to keep this loud-mouthed innocent from calling up the patrol? "They're on vacation—my great-grandmother and some other relatives. They argue a lot." The innkeeper nodded knowingly. "I wasn't supposed to be able to go along," Flinx continued with a wink. "But I slipped away from my studies, and I've sort of been playing at trailing them. You know. When they get to the lodge where they'll be spending the rest of the month, I'm going to pop in and surprise them. Once I land in their laps, they can hardly send me home, can they?"

"I get it." The innkeeper smiled. "I won't tell anyone."

"Thanks." Flinx rose. "Food's good." He gathered up Pip and headed for the door.

"Hey," the innkeeper called out at a sudden thought, "what lodge are your relatives headed for?" But Flinx was already gone.

Outside, he hurriedly mounted his stupava and turned it into the woods. Five days, he thought worriedly. Two more at this pace and they would be ten ahead of him. The stupava was doing its best, but that was not going to be good enough. Somehow he had to increase his speed. He reined in and let the bird catch its breath as he extracted a ten-centimeter-square sheet of plastic from his backpack. It was half a centimeter thick and had cost him plenty back in the marketplace, but he could hardly have risked this journey without it. A series of contact switches ran down the left side of the plastic. He touched the uppermost one, and the sheet promptly lit up. Additional manipulation of the controls produced a map of the forest, and further adjustments zoomed in on a blowup of his immediate surroundings.

He entered the name of the inn where he had had his hasty meal. Instantly, the map shifted position. It was as if he were flying above an abstract landscape. When the image settled, he widened the field of view, expanding the map until it included several other inns and a small town that he had unknowingly skirted the previous day. He touched controls, and the map zoomed in on the town. On its fringe was a small wood-processing plant, several minor commercial structures, a forest service station, and a communications supply-and-repair terminal. He thought about trying the forest service station first, then decided that of all the structures it was the one most likely to be manned around the clock. That left the communications depot. He turned off the map, replaced it carefully in his pack, and chucked the reins. The bird whistled and started forward.

Night was falling, and soon the sun would have settled completely behind the shielding clouds. One thing he could count on was the absence of moon—even Flame's maroon glow could not penetrate the cloud cover that night.

Though he had completely missed the town, it was not far off. The buildings were scattered across a little knoll—the driest land around—and remained hidden by trees until he was right on top of them. Most of the homes and apartments were located across the knoll. To his left was a low, rambling structure in which a few lights shone behind double-glazed windows: the forest station. The communications depot was directly ahead of him. He slid easily off the back of the stupava, tied it to a nearby log, and waited for midnight.

A single, three-meter-high fence ran around the depot, enclosing the servicing yard. Flinx could make out the silhouettes of several large vehicles designed for traveling through the dense forest with a full complement of crew and equipment. Flinx wasn't interested in them. They were too big, too awkward for his needs. Surely there had to be something better suited to his purpose parked inside the machine-shed beyond. There had better be. He doubted that the sawmill or smaller commercial buildings would have anything better to offer.

He made certain the stupava's bonds were loose. If he failed, he would need the riding bird in a hurry, and if he succeeded, the stupava would grow restless before too long and would break free to find its way back to Drallar and its barn. That was another reason Flinx had chosen the riding bird over the toadlike muccax: a muccax had no homing instinct.

With Pip coiled firmly around his left shoulder, he made his way down through the night mist. The yard was not paved, but the ground there had been packed to a comparative dryness and he was able to move silently along the fence. He carefully made a complete circuit of both yard and buildings. No lights were visible, nor did he see any suggestion of alarm beams. Though he had circumvented antitheft equipment before, this would be the first time he had tried to break into a government-owned facility.

The fence arched outward at the top, a design that would make climbing over it difficult, and he could clearly see transmitter points positioned atop each post, ready to set off the alarm if anything interrupted their circuit. Flinx lowered his gaze to the back gate. The catch there appeared to be purely mechanical, almost too simple. He could open it without any special tools. The catch to the catch was a duplicate of the units that ran along the crest of the fence. He could not open the latch without interrupting the beam and setting off the alarm.

Cutting through the mesh of the fence itself was out of the question. The metal was sensitized: any nonprogrammed disruption of its structure would sound the alarm as surely as if he had tried to knock a section over with a dozer.

Nudging Pip aside, Flinx slipped off his backpack and hunted through it. In addition to the concentrated foods and basic medical supplies, he carried equipment that would have shocked the innkeeper who had chatted with him earlier that day. He didn't need long to find what he was looking for. From the pack he extracted one of several odd lengths of wire. A single contact switch was spliced to its center. Making certain the switch was open, he looped one end of the wire carefully around the tiny transmitter point on the left side of the gate latch. Gently, he formed the wire into an arch and brought it across the long latch to loop it over the transmitter on the opposite side. A minuscule LED on the wire's switch glowed a satisfying green.

Then out of the backpack Flinx took a small, oddly formed piece of dull metal, inserted it into the gate lock, and turned it a couple of times. In the heat from his hand, the metal softened and flowed obediently. The latch *click*ed. Holding the metal tool with only two fingers, Flinx lowered the heat it was absorbing until it resolidified, and then turned it. He heard a second, softer click from the latch. He pulled it free, put a hand on the gate, and pushed. It moved two meters inward, swaying slightly on its supports. He hesitated. No audible alarm ran through the night. He hoped that a rural community would have no need of silent alarms. Still, he gathered up his tools and backpack and retreated hastily to the forest.

He waited until half an hour had passed without anyone's appearing to check the gate or the yard, then he crept back to the fence. The gate still sat ajar. The glass fiber, looped from terminal to terminal, permitted the alarm beam to flow uninterrupted, but there would be a problem when he had to open the gate farther than the length of the wire allowed.

He slipped easily into the maintenance yard. Pip flew over the fence and hovered just above its master's tousled hair.

Flinx searched the yard. There was still no hint that his intrusion had been detected. The machine shed lay directly in front of him, doorless and open to the night. He used the huge repair vehicles for cover as he made his way into the shed. Among the equipment and supplies were a pair of two-passenger mudders. His heart beat a little faster. The compact vehicles had flared undersides and enclosed cabs to protect pilot and passenger in side-by-side comfort.

He tried them both. Jumping the simple electric engines was easy enough. He grew anxious when the fuel gauge on the first machine didn't react, indicating an empty storage cell, but the second mudder showed a ninety-five-percent charge. That was better than good; it was critical, because he doubted he would have access to recharge stations where he was going.

Since the depot remained peaceful, Flinx gambled his success thus far to resolve one additional difficulty: the mudder's government markings. In a storage cabinet, he found dozens of cans of catalytic bonding paint. He chose a couple of cans of brown. After a moment's thought, he went back to the cabinet and selected an additional canister of red. He had never had a personal transport of his own—as long as he was going to add a little art, he might as well put some flash into it. Besides, that would be more in keeping with the character of a sixteen-year-old boy. The trees would still conceal it well.

When he had finished spraying the mudder, he climbed into the pilot's seat. Pip settled into the empty one alongside. The controls were simple and straightforward, as he'd expected. His right hand went to the little steering wheel, his left to the jump he had installed beneath the dash. The engine came to life, its steady hum little louder than Pip's. A nudge on the accelerator sent the mudder forward. The single, wide-beam searchlight mounted on its nose remained dark. It would stay that way until he was sure he was safe.

He drove into the yard, and still there was no sign of concern from the nearby buildings. At the gate, he left the craft on hover and jumped out. Patching his remaining passfibers onto the first, he was able to open the gate wide enough for the mudder to pass through. He was so fearful of being spotted that he nearly forgot to duck as he drove through the gap—the fibers that served to fool the alarm system almost decapitated him.

Then he was out through the gate, on the smooth surface bordering the depot. In moments, he was concealed by the forest. A touch on a dash control locked the transparent plastic dome over his head, shutting out the mist. Another control set the craft's heater to thrumming. For the first time since he had left Drallar, he was warm.

He held the mudder's speed down until he was well away from the town. Then he felt safe in turning on the searchlight. The high-power beam pierced the darkness and revealed paths between the trees. Now he was able to accelerate, and soon the mudder was skipping along over the moist earth. Too fast, perhaps, for night-driving, but Flinx wanted to make up time on his quarry. And he was a little drunk with success.

It wouldn't have been that easy in Drallar, he told himself. Out here, where there wasn't much to steal, he had succeeded because thieves were scarce.

The underside of the mudder was coated with a special hydrophobic polyresin that allowed it to slide across a moist but solid surface with almost no friction, propelled by the single electric jet located in the vehicle's stern. It also made very little noise; not that he could detect any sign of pursuit. The mudder's compass control kept him headed north.

It was midmorning before Flinx finally felt the need to stop. He used daylight and the canister of red paint to decorate the brown vehicle, adding decorative stripes to side and front. It took his mind off his problems for a little while. Then he was traveling again, in a craft no casual observer would ever have mistaken for a sober government vehicle.

The night before there had been a touch of a mental tingle of almost painful familiarity. As usual, it vanished the instant he sought to concentrate on it, but he felt sure that that touch had reached out to him from somewhere to the north.

Confident and comfortable, he soared along with the dome retracted. Suddenly, the air turned gray with thousands of furry bodies no bigger than his little finger. They swarmed about him on tiny membranous wings, and he swatted at them with his free hand as he slowed the car to a crawl. They were so dense he couldn't see clearly.

Pip was delighted, both with the opportunities for play and for dining. Soon the storm of miniature fliers became so thick that

Flinx had to bring the mudder to a complete halt for fear of running into something ahead. At least now he could use both hands to beat at them.

He hesitated to close the protective dome for fear of panicking the dozens that would inevitably be trapped inside. Besides, except for blocking his view, they weren't bothering him. Their square little teeth were designed for cracking the hulls of nuts and seeds, and they showed no interest in live flesh. They had large bright-yellow eyes, and two thin legs suitable for grasping branches. Flinx wondered at them, as well as how long it would be before they moved on and he could resume his journey.

Suddenly, the air was full of *whooshing* sounds. The earth erupted head-sized round shapes. Flinx saw long thin snouts full of needlelike teeth and multiple arms projecting from narrow bodies. The *whooshing* noise was composed of a long series of explosive popping sounds.

He squinted through the mass of fliers and saw one creature after another emerge from vertical burrows. The poppers were black-bodied with yellow and orange variolitic colorings. They became airborne by inflating a pair of sausage-shaped air sacs attached to their spines—by regulating the amount of air in the sacs, the animals could control not only their altitude but their direction. They lit into the swarm of fliers, utilizing long, thin snouts to snatch one after another from the air. Once a popper had made several catches, it would deflate its air sacs and settle parachutelike to the ground. They always seemed to land directly above their respective burrows, down which they would promptly vanish.

When neither the cloud of fliers nor attacking poppers showed any signs of thinning, Flinx made the decision to move forward. He traveled slowly, picking his way through the trees. He had traveled nearly a kilometer before the swarms started to disperse, and eventually he passed into open forest once again. A backward glance showed a solid wall of gray, black, and yellow-orange shifting like smoke among the trees. It took a moment before he realized something was missing from the mudder.

"Pip?" The minidrag was not coiled on the passenger seat, nor was it drifting on the air currents above the mudder.

It took Flinx several worried minutes before he located his pet lying on its belly in the storage compartment behind the seats, swollen to three times its usual diameter. It had thoroughly gorged itself on the tasty little gray fliers. Flinx was convinced that his currently immobile companion did not look at all well.

"That'll teach you to make a durq of yourself," he told his pet. The minidrag moved once, slowly, before giving up totally on the effort. It would be a while before it flew again, even to its master's shoulder.

Flinx continued northward, hardly pausing to sleep. Two days had passed since he had appropriated the mudder. Given the likely laxity of rural bureaucratic types, it might be some time before its absence was remarked upon. By the time someone figured out that a real theft had been pulled off, Flinx would be two hundred kilometers away, and the local authorities would have no way of knowing which direction he had taken. Skimming along just above the surface, a mudder left no trail. Its simple electric jet emitted practically no waste heat to be detected from the air. But Flinx did not expect any kind of elaborate pursuit, not for a single, small, comparatively inexpensive vehicle.

He continued to wonder about all the effort and expense someone was going through to abduct a harmless old woman. The implausibility of the whole situation served only to heighten his anxiety and did nothing to dampen his anger or determination.

Several days went by before he detected the change in the air. It was an alien feeling, something he couldn't place. The omnipresent dampness remained, but it had become sharper, more direct in his nostrils. "Now what do you suppose that is, Pip?" he murmured aloud. The flying snake would not have answered had it been able. All its efforts and energies were still directed to the task of digesting fur, meat, and bone.

The mudder moved up a slight hill. At its crest a gap in the trees revealed a scene that took Flinx's breath away. At first, he thought he had somehow stumbled onto the ocean. No, he knew that couldn't be. No ocean lay north from Drallar, not until one reached the frozen pole or unless one traveled east or west for thousands of kilometers.

Though the body of water looked like an ocean, he recognized it for what it was: a lake, one of the hundreds that occupied the territory from his present position northward to the arctic. No sunlight shone directly on it, for the clouds were as thick here as they were in distant Drallar, but enough light filtered through to create a glare—a glare that exploded off that vast sheet of water to reflect from the cloud cover overhead and bounced again from the water.

The-Blue-That-Blinded, Flinx thought. He knew enough of Moth's geography to recognize the first of the lakes which bore that collective description. The lake itself he could not put a name to, not without his map. It was only one of hundreds of similarly impressive bodies of fresh water whose names he had had no need to memorize during his readings, for he had never expected to visit that part of the world.

The glare imprisoned between surface and clouds brought tears to his eyes as he headed the mudder toward the water's edge. The lake blocked his path northward. He needed to know whether to skirt it to the east or the west or to attempt a crossing. He had no way of figuring out what his quarry had done.

The weather was calm. Only a modest chop broke the otherwise smooth expanse before him. A mudder could travel over water as well as land, provided its charge held out; if not, the vehicle would sink quickly.

Flinx decided that the first thing he needed was some advice. So he turned to his map, which showed a single, isolated lodge just to the east. He headed for it.

The building came into view ten minutes later, a large rambling structure of native stone and wood. Boats were tied up to the single pier out back. Several land vehicles were parked near the front. Flinx tensed momentarily, then relaxed. None of the craft displayed government markings. Surely his theft had been discovered by now, but it was likely that the search would tend more in the direction of populated areas to the south—toward Drallar—rather than into the trackless north.

Nevertheless, he took a moment to inspect the assembled vehicles carefully. All four were deserted. Two of them were tracked—strictly land transportation. The others were mudders, larger and fancier than his own, boasting thickly upholstered lounges and self-darkening protective domes. Private transport, he knew. More comfortable than his own craft but certainly no more durable. There was no sign of riding animals. Probably anyone who could afford to travel this far north could afford mechanized transportation.

Flinx brought the mudder to a stop alongside the other vehicles and took the precaution of disconnecting the ignition jumper. It wouldn't do to have a curious passer-by spy the obviously illegal modification. The mudder settled to the ground, and he stepped out over the mudguard onto the surface.

The parking area had not been pounded hard and smooth, and his boots picked up plenty of muck as he walked up to the wooden steps leading inside. Suction hoses cleaned off most of the mud. The steps led onto a covered porch populated by the kind of rustic wooden furniture so popular with tourists who liked to feel they were roughing it. Beyond was a narrow hall paneled with peeled, glistening tree trunks, stained dark.

Flinx thought the inn a likely place to obtain information about lake conditions, but before that, something equally important demanded his attention. Food. He could smell it somewhere close by, and he owed himself a break from the concentrates that had been fueling him for many days. His credcard still showed a positive balance, and there was no telling when he would be fortunate enough to encounter honest cooking again. Nor would he have to worry about curious stares from other patrons—Pip, still unable to eat, would not be dining with him this time. He inhaled deeply. It almost smelled as if the food were being prepared by a live chef instead of a machine.

Flinx found his way to the broad, exposed-beam dining room. The far wall had a fire blazing in a rock fireplace. To the left lay the source of the wonderful aroma: a real kitchen. A couple of furry shapes snored peacefully nearby. An older couple sat near the entrance. They were absorbed in their meal and didn't even turn to look up at him. Two younger couples ate and chatted close by the fireplace. In the back corner was a group of oldsters, all clad in heavy north-country attire.

He started down the few steps into the dining room, intending to question someone in the kitchen about the possibility of a meal. Suddenly, something hit his mind so hard he had to lean against the nearby wall for support.

Two younger men had entered the dining room from a far, outside door. They were talking to the group of diners in the far corner. No one had looked toward Flinx; no one had said a word to him.

He tottered away from the wall, caught and balanced himself at the old couple's table. The man looked up from his plate at the uninvited visitor and frowned.

"You feeling poorly, son?"

Flinx didn't answer, but continued to stare across the room. Faces—he couldn't make out faces beneath all that heavy clothing. They remained hidden from his sight—but not from something else.

He spoke sharply, unthinkingly.

"Mother?"

9

One of the bundled figures spun in its chair to gape at him. Her eyes were wide with surprise as well as with a warning Flinx ignored. She started to rise from her seat.

The rest of the group gazed at the young man standing across the room. One of the younger men put a hand on Mother Mastiff's shoulder and forced her back into her chair. She promptly bit him. The man's companion pulled something out of a coat pocket and started toward Flinx. The group's stunned expressions, brought on by Flinx's unexpected appearance, had turned grim.

Flinx searched the floor and walls nearby, found the switch he was hunting for, and stabbed at it. The lights in the dining room went out, leaving only the dim daylight from the far windows to illuminate the room.

What a fantastic Talent he possessed, he thought as he dove for cover. It had reacted sharply to Mother Mastiff's presence—after he had all but tripped over her.

The room filled with screams from the regular guests, mixed with the curses of those Flinx had surprised. He did not try to make his way toward the table where Mother Mastiff was being held; he had been through too many street fights for that. Keeping the layout of the dining room in his mind, he retreated and dropped to a crawl, taking the long way around the room toward the table in an attempt to sneak behind her captors. Three had been seated at the table with her, plus the two who had arrived later. Five opponents.

"Where is he—somebody get some lights!" Very helpful of them, Flinx mused, to let him know their location. He would have to make use of the information quickly, he knew. Soon one of the guests, or a lodge employee, would have the lights back on, robbing him of his only advantage.

A sharp crackling richocheted around the room, accompanied by a brief flash of light. One of the other guests screamed a warning. Flinx smiled to himself. With everyone hugging the floor, that ought to keep the lights off a little longer.

A second bolt split the air at table level, passing close enough to set his skin twitching. Paralysis beam. Though Flinx took some comfort from this demonstration of his opponent's intent not to shoot to kill, he did not stop to think why they might take such care. The kidnappers continued to fire blindly through the darkness. With those nerve-petrifying beams filling the room, no employee was likely to take a stab at a light switch.

Grateful once more for his small size, Flinx kept moving on his belly until he reached the far wall. At the same time, the random firing ceased. Imagining one of his opponents feeling along the walls in search of a light switch, Flinx readied himself for a hurried crawl past the glow of the fireplace. Then someone let out a violent curse, and he heard the sound of chair and table going over very close by. Flinx's hand went to his boot. He rose to a crouching position, waiting.

Again, he heard the sound of stumbling, louder and just ahead. He put his hand on a nearby chair and shoved it into the darkness. A man appeared in the glow from the fireplace, and a flash enveloped the chair. Flinx darted in behind the man and used the stiletto as old Makepeace had instructed him. The man was twice Flinx's size, but his flesh was no tougher than anyone else's. He exhaled once, a sharp wheeze, before collapsing in a heap. Flinx darted forward, out of the illuminating glare of the fire.

"Erin," a voice called uncertainly, "you okay?" Several new flashes filled the air, striking the stone around the fireplace where Flinx had stood moments earlier. If the intent of those shots was to catch Flinx unaware, they failed; on the other hand, they did force him to hug the floor again.

Moments later, the lights winked back on, shockingly bright. Flinx tensed beneath the table that sheltered him, but he needn't have worried. The party of travelers had fled, along with the remaining paralysis-beam wielder and Mother Mastiff.

Flinx climbed to his feet. The other guests remained cowering on the floor. There was no hint of what had brought the lights back to life, and he had no time to think about it.

The door at the far end of the room was ajar. It led out onto a curving porch. He hurried to it but paused just inside to throw a chair out ahead of him. When no one fired on it, he took a deep breath and jumped out, rolling across the porch and springing out of the roll into a fighting crouch.

There was no enemy waiting to confront him—the porch was deserted. The beach off to the left was not. Two mudders were parked on the shore. As Flinx watched helplessly, the travelers he had sought for so long piled into the two crafts. Heedless now of his own safety, he charged down the steps onto the slight slope leading toward the lake shore. The first mudder was already cruising across the wave tops. By the time he reached the water's edge and sank exhausted to his knees, the useless knife held limply in his right hand, both craft were already well out on the lake surface itself.

Fighting for breath, Flinx forced himself erect and started back up the slope. He would have to go after them quickly. If he lost sight of them on the vast lake, he would have no way of knowing on which far shore they would emerge. He staggered around the front of the lodge and grabbed at the entrance to his mudder. A supine and unsettled shape stared back at him. Pip looked distinctly unhappy. It flittered once, then collapsed back onto the seat.

"Fine help you were," Flinx snapped at his pet. The minidrag, if possible, managed to look even more miserable. Clearly, it had sensed danger to Flinx and had tried to go to his aid, but simply couldn't manage to get airborne.

Flinx started to climb into the cab when a voice and a hand on his shoulder restrained him. "Just a minute." Flinx tensed, but a glance at Pip showed that the flying snake was not reacting defensively.

"I can't," he started to say as he turned. When he saw who was confronting him, he found himself able only to stare.

She seemed to tower over him, though in reality she was no more than a couple of centimeters taller. Black hair fell in tight ringlets to her shoulders. Her bush jacket was tucked into pants that were tucked into low boots. She was slim but not skinny. The mouth and nose were child-sized, the cheekbones high beneath huge, owl-like brown eyes. Her skin was nearly as dark as Flinx's, but it was a product of the glare from the nearby lake and not heredity. She was the most strikingly beautiful woman he had ever seen.

He tracked down his voice and mumbled, "I have to go after them." The hand remained on his shoulder. He might have thrown it off, and might not.

"My name's Lauren Walder," she said. "I'm the general manager at Granite Shallows." Her voice was full of barely controlled fury as she used her head to gesture toward the lake. Ringlets flew. "What have you to do with those idiots?"

"They've kidnapped my mother, the woman who adopted me,"

he explained. "I don't know why, and I don't much care right now. I just want to get her back."

"You're a little out-numbered, aren't you?"

"I'm used to that." He pointed toward the dining-room windows and the still-open porch doorway. "It's not me lying dead on your floor in there."

She frowned at him, drawing her brows together. "How do you know the man's dead?"

"Because I killed him."

"I see," she said, studying him in a new light. "With what?"

"My stiletto," he said.

"I don't see any stiletto." She looked him up and down.

"You're not supposed to. Look, I've got to go. If I get too far behind them—"

"Take it easy," she said, trying to soothe him. "I've got something I have to show you."

"You don't seem to understand," he said insistently. "I've no way to track them. I won't know where they touch land and—"

"Don't worry about it. You won't lose them."

"How do you know?"

"Because we'll run them down in a little while. Let them relax and think they've escaped." Her fingers tightened on his shoulder. "I promise you we'll catch them."

"Well . . ." He spared another glance for Pip. Maybe in a little while the flying snake would be ready to take to the air. That could make a significant difference in any fight to come. "If you're sure . . ."

She nodded once, appearing as competent as she was beautiful. Lodge manager, he thought. She ought to know what she was talking about. He could trust her for a few minutes, anyway.

"What's so important to show me?" he asked.

"Come with me." Her tone was still soaked with anger.

She led him back into the lodge, across the porch and back into the dining room. Several members of her staff were treating one of the women who had been dining when the lights had gone out and the guns had gone off. Her husband and companions were hovering anxiously over her; and she was panting heavily, holding one hand to her chest.

"Heart condition," Lauren explained tersely.

Flinx looked around. Tables and chairs were still overturned, but there was no other indication that a desperate fight had been fought in the room. Paralysis beams did not damage inanimate objects.

The man he had slain had been moved by lodge personnel. He was glad of that.

Lauren led him toward the kitchen. Lying next to the doorway were the pair of furry shapes he had noticed when he had first entered the room. Up close, he could see their round faces, twisted in agony. The short stubby legs were curled tightly beneath the fuzzy bodies. Their fur was a rust red except for yellow circles around the eyes, which were shut tight. Permanently.

"Sennar and Soba." Lauren spoke while gazing at the dead animals with a mixture of fury and hurt. "They're wervils—or were," she added bitterly. "I raised them from kittens. Found them abandoned in the woods. They liked to sleep here by the kitchen. Everybody liked to feed them. They must have moved at the wrong time. In the dark, one of those"—she used a word Flinx didn't recognize, which was unusual in itself—"must have mistaken them for you. They were firing at anything that moved, I've been told." She paused a moment, then added, "You must have the luck of a pregnant Yax'm. They hit just about everything in the room except you."

"I was down on the floor," Flinx explained. "I only stand up when I have to."

"Yes, as that one found out." She jerked a thumb in the direction of the main hall. Flinx could see attendants wrapping a body in lodge sheets. He was a little startled to see how big his opponent had actually been. In the dark, though, it's only the size of your knife that matters.

"They didn't have to do this," the manager was murmuring, staring at the dead animals. "They didn't have to be so damned indiscriminate. Four years I've coddled those two. Four years. They never showed anything but love to anyone who ever went near them." Flinx waited quietly.

After a while, she gestured for him to follow her. They walked out into the main hall, down a side corridor, and entered a storeroom. Lauren unlocked a transparent wall case and removed a large, complex-looking rifle and a couple of small, wheel-shaped plastic containers. She snapped one of them into the large slot set in the underside of the rifle. The weapon seemed too bulky for her, but she swung it easily across her back and set her right arm through the support strap. She added a pistol to her service belt, then led him back out into the corridor.

"I've never seen a gun like that before." Flinx indicated the rifle. "What do you hunt with it?"

"It's not for hunting," she told him. "Fishing gear. Each of those clips"—and she gestured at the wheel-shapes she had handed over to Flinx—"holds about a thousand darts. Each dart carries a few milliliters of an extremely potent neurotoxin. Prick your finger on one end . . ." She shrugged meaningfully.

"The darts are loaded into the clips at the factory in Drallar, and then the clips are sealed. You can't get a dart out unless you fire it through this." She patted the butt of the rifle, then turned a corner. They were back in the main hallway.

"You use a gun to kill fish?"

She smiled across at him. Not much of a smile but a first, he thought. "You've never been up to The-Blue-That-Blinded before, have you?"

"I've lived my whole life in Drallar," he said, which for all practical purposes was the truth.

"We don't use these to kill the fish," she explained. "Only to slow them up if they get too close to the boat."

Flinx nodded, trying to picture the weapon in use. He knew that the lakes of The-Blue-That-Blinded were home to some big fish, but apparently he had never realized just how big. Of course, if the fish were proportional to the size of the lakes . . . "How big is this lake?"

"Patra? Barely a couple of hundred kilometers across. A pond. The really *big* lakes are farther off to the northwest, like Turquoise and Hanamar. Geographers are always arguing over whether they should be called lakes or inland seas. Geographers are damn fools."

They exited from the lodge. At least it wasn't raining, Flinx thought. That should make tracking the fleeing mudders a little easier.

Flinx jumped slightly when something landed heavily on his shoulder. He stared down at it with a disapproving look. "About time." The flying snake steadied himself on his master but did not meet his eyes.

"Now that's an interesting pet," Lauren Walder commented, not flinching from the minidrag, as most strangers did. Another point in her favor, Flinx thought. "Where on Moth do you find a creature like that?"

"In a garbage heap," Flinx said, "which is what he's turned himself into. He overate a few days ago and still hasn't digested it all."

"I was going to say that he looks more agile than that landing implied." She led him around the side of the main lodge building.

There was a small inlet and a second pier stretching into the lake. Flinx had not been able to see it from where he had parked his mudder.

"I said that we'd catch up to them." She pointed toward the pier.

The boat was a single concave arch, each end of the arch spreading out to form a supportive hull. The cabin was located atop the arch and was excavated into it. Vents lined the flanks of the peculiar catamaran. Flinx wondered at their purpose. Some heavy equipment resembling construction cranes hung from the rear corners of the aft decking. A similar, smaller boat bobbed in the water nearby.

They mounted a curving ladder and Flinx found himself watching as Lauren shrugged off the rifle and settled herself into the pilot's chair. She spoke as she checked readouts and threw switches. "We'll catch them inside an hour," she assured Flinx. "A mudder's fast, but not nearly as fast over water as this." A deep rumble from the boat's stern; air whistled into the multiple intakes lining the side of the craft, and the rumbling intensified.

Lauren touched several additional controls whereupon the magnetic couplers disengaged from the pier. She then moved the switch set into the side of the steering wheel. Thunder filled the air, making Pip twitch slightly. The water astern began to bubble like a geyser as a powerful stream of water spurted from the subsurface nozzles hidden in the twin hulls. The boat leaped forward, cleaving the waves.

Flinx stood next to the pilot's chair and shouted over the roar of the wind assailing the open cabin. "How will we know which way they've gone?"

Lauren leaned to her right and flicked a couple of switches below a circular screen, which promptly came to life. Several bright yellow dots appeared on the transparency. "This shows the whole lake." She touched other controls. All but two dots on the screen turned from yellow to green. "Fishing boats from the other lodges that ring Patra. They have compatible instrumentation." She tapped the screen with a fingernail. "That pair that's stayed yellow? Moving, nonorganic, incompatible transponder. Who do you suppose that might be?"

Flinx said nothing, just stared at the tracking screen. Before long, he found himself staring over the bow that wasn't actually a bow. The twin hulls of the jet catamaran knifed through the surface of the lake as Lauren steadily increased their speed.

She glanced occasionally over at the tracker. "They're moving pretty well—must be pushing their mudders to maximum. Headed due north, probably looking to deplane at Point Horakov. We have to catch them before they cross, of course. This is no mudder. Useless off the water."

"Will we?" Flinx asked anxiously. "Catch them, I mean." His eyes searched the cloud-swept horizon, looking for the telltale glare of diffused sunlight on metal.

"No problem," she assured him. "Not unless they have some special engines in those mudders. I'd think if they did, they'd be using 'em right now."

"What happens when we catch them?"

"I'll try cutting in front of them," she said thoughtfully. "If that doesn't make them stop, well—" she indicated the rifle resting nearby. "We can pick them off one at a time. That rifle's accurate to a kilometer. The darts are gas-propelled, you see, and the gun has a telescopic sight that'll let me put a dart in somebody's ear if I have to."

"What if they shoot back?"

"Not a paralysis pistol made that can outrange that rifle, let alone cover any distance with accuracy. The effect is dispersed. It's only at close range that paralysis is effective on people. Or lethal to small animals," she added bitterly. "If they'll surrender, we'll take them in and turn them over to the game authorities. You can add your own charges at the same time. Wervils are an endangered species on Moth. Of course, I'd much prefer that the scum resist so that we can defend ourselves."

Such bloodthirstiness in so attractive a woman was no surprise to Flinx. He'd encountered it before in the marketplace. It was her motivation that was new to him. He wondered how old she was. Probably twice his own age, he thought, though it was difficult to tell for sure. Time spent in the wilderness had put rough edges on her that even harsh city life would be hard put to equal. It was a different kind of roughness; Flinx thought it very becoming.

"What if they choose to give themselves up?" He knew that was hardly likely, but he was curious to know what her contingency for such a possibility might be.

"Like I said, we take them back with us and turn them over to the game warden in Kalish."

He made a short, stabbing motion with one hand. "That could be awkward for me."

"Don't worry," she told him. "I'll see to it that you're not involved. It's not only the game laws they've violated. Remember that injured guest? Ms. Marteenson's a sick woman. The effect of a paralysis beam on her could be permanent. So it's not just the game authorities who'll be interested in these people.

"As to you and your mother, the two of you can disappear. Why has she been kidnapped? For ransom?"

"She hasn't any money," Flinx replied. "Not enough to bother with, anyway."

"Well, then, why?" Lauren's eyes stayed on the tracker, occasionally drifting to scan the sky for signs of rain. The jet boat had a portable cover that she hoped they wouldn't have to use. It would make aiming more difficult.

"That's what I'd like to know," Flinx told her. "Maybe we'll find out when we catch up with them."

"We should," she agreed, "though that won't do Sennar and Soba any good. You've probably guessed by now that my opinion of human beings is pretty low. Present company excepted. I'm very fond of animals. Much rather associate with them. I never had a wervil betray me, or any other creature of the woods, for that matter. You know where you stand with an animal. That's a major reason why I've chosen the kind of life I have."

"I know a few other people who feel the way you do," Flinx said. "You don't have to apologize for it."

"I wasn't apologizing," she replied matter-of-factly.

"Yet you manage a hunting lodge."

"Not a hunting lodge," she corrected him. "Fishing lodge. Strictly fishing. We don't accommodate hunters here, but I can't stop other lodges from doing so."

"You have no sympathy for the fish, then? It's a question of scales versus fur? The AAnn wouldn't like that."

She smiled. "Who cares what the AAnn think? As for the rest of your argument, it's hard to get cozy with a fish. I've seen the fish of this lake gobble up helpless young wervils and other innocents that make the mistake of straying too far out into the water. Though if it came down to it"—she adjusted a control on the instrument dash, and the jet boat leaped to starboard—"I'm not sure I wouldn't prefer the company of fish to that of people either."

"It's simple, then," Flinx said. "You're a chronic antisocial."

She shrugged indifferently. "I'm me. Lauren Walder. I'm happy with what I am. Are you happy with what you are?"

His smile faded. "I don't know what I am yet." He dropped his gaze and brooded at the tracker, his attention focused on the nearing yellow dot that indicated their quarry.

Odd thing for a young man like that to say, she thought. Most people would've said they didn't know *who* they were yet. Slip of the tongue. She let the remark pass.

The gap between pursued and pursuer shrank rapidly on the tracker. It wasn't long before Flinx was able to gesture excitedly over the bow and shout, "There they are!"

Lauren squinted and saw only water and cloud, then glanced down at the tracker. "You've got mighty sharp eyes, Flinx."

"Prerequisite for survival in Drallar," he explained.

A moment later she saw the mudders also, skittering along just above the waves and still headed for the northern shore. Simultaneously, those in the mudders reacted to the appearance of the boat behind them. They accelerated and for a moment moved out of sight again. Lauren increased the power. This time they didn't pull away from the jet boat.

She nodded slightly. "I thought so. Standard mudder engines, no surprises. I don't think they're hiding anything from us." She glanced at her companion. "Think you can drive this thing for a little while?"

Flinx had spent the past half hour studying the controls as well as the image on the tracker. The instrumentation was no more complex than that of his mudder. On the other hand, he was used to driving over land. "I think so," he said. This was not the time for excessive caution.

"Good." She slid out of the pilot's chair and waited until he slipped in and took control over the wheel. "It's very responsive," she warned him, "and at the speed we're traveling, even a slight turn of the wheel will send us shooting off in another direction. So watch it."

"I'll be okay," he assured her. He could feel the vibration of the engine through the wheel. The sensation was exhilarating.

A flash of light suddenly marked the fleeing mudders, but it dissipated well shy of the jet boat's bow. Flinx maintained the gap between the three craft. The flash was repeated; it did no more damage to the boat or its crew than would a flashlight beam.

"No long-range weapons," Lauren murmured. "If they had 'em, now'd be the time to use 'em." Flinx saw she was hefting the dart rifle. It was nearly as tall as she was. She settled it onto a vacant bracket and bent over to peer through the complex telescopic sight. In that position, it resembled a small cannon more than a rifle.

Two more flares of light shot from the mudders, futile stabs at the pursuing jet boat. "I can see them," Lauren announced as she squinted through the sight. "They look confused. That's sensible. I don't see anything but hand weapons. Two of them seem to be arguing. I don't think they expected this kind of pursuit."

"They didn't expect to see me in the dining room, either," Flinx said confidentially. "I'll *bet* they're confused."

She looked over from the sight. "You're sure they weren't looking for you to follow?"

"I doubt it, or I'd never have come this close to them."

She grunted once and returned her eyes to the sight. "At this range, I can pick their teeth." She moved the rifle slightly. "Hold her steady, please." She pushed the button which took the place of a regular trigger. The gun went *phut!* and something tiny and explosive burst from the muzzle.

"Warning shot," she explained. "There—someone's pulling the dart out. I put it in the back of the pilot's chair. Now they're gathering around and studying it, except the driver, of course. Now they're looking back at us. One of them's keeping two hands on a little old lady. Your mother?"

"I'm sure," Flinx said tightly.

"She's giving the one restraining her fits, trying to bite him, kicking at him even though it looks like her feet are bound at the ankles."

"That's her, all right." Flinx couldn't repress a grin. "What are they doing now?"

Lauren frowned. "Uh oh. Putting up some kind of transparent shield. Now the regular vehicle dome over that. The dome we can penetrate. I don't know about the shield-thing. Well, that's no problem. Go to port."

"Port?" Flinx repeated.

"To your left," she said. "We'll cut around in front of them and block their course. Maybe when they see that we can not only catch them but run circles around them, they'll be willing to listen to reason."

Flinx obediently turned the wheel to his left and felt the catamaran respond instantly.

"Okay, now back to star—to your right, not too sharply." The boat split the water as he turned the wheel.

Suddenly, everything changed. A new sound, a deep humming, became audible.

"Damn," Lauren said in frustration, pointing upward.

Flinx's gaze went toward the clouds. The skimmer that had appeared from out of the northern horizon was of pretty good size. It was certainly more than big enough to hold its own crew in addition to the mudders' occupants. If there was any doubt as to the skimmer's intent, it was quickly eliminated as the versatile craft dipped low, circled once, and then settled toward the first mudder as it strove to match the smaller vehicle's speed.

"If they get aboard, we'll lose them permanently," said a worried Flinx. "Can you pick them off as they try to transfer?" Already the skimmer's crew had matched velocity with the mudder and was dropping a chute ladder toward the water.

Lauren bent over the rifle again. Her finger hesitated over the button; then she unexpectedly pulled back and whacked the butt of the gun angrily. "Lovely people. They're holding your mother next to the base of the chute. I can't get a clear shot."

"What are we going to do? We can't just keep circling them like this!"

"How the hell should I know?" She abandoned the rifle and rushed to a storage locker amidships. "Mudders, paralysis pistols, kidnapping, and now a skimmer sent out from the north. Who are these people, anyway?"

"I don't know," Flinx snapped. "I told you before that I don't understand any of this." He hesitated, trying to watch her and keep the jet boat circling the still-racing mudders and the skimmer hovering above them. "What are you going to do now?"

The device she had extracted from the storage locker was as long as the dart rifle but much narrower. "When I give the word," she said tightly, "I want you to charge them and pull aside at the last moment. I don't think they'll be expecting a rush on our part. They're much too busy transferring to the skimmer."

"What are you going to try and do?" he asked curiously. "Disable the skimmer?"

"With a dart gun? Are you kidding?" she snorted. "Just do as I say."

"So long as what you say continues making sense," he agreed, a bit put off by her tone.

"You're wasting time. Do it!"

He threw the wheel hard over. The catamaran spun on the surface so sharply that the portside hull lifted clear of the water. A high rooster tail obscured them from sight for a moment.

In seconds, they were on top of the mudder and the skimmer drifting steadily above it. Activity on both craft intensified as the jet boat bore down on the mudder. As Lauren suspected, the last thing their opponents were expecting was a broadside charge. A couple of shots passed behind the onrushing boat, hastily dispatched and imperfectly aimed.

"Hard to port!" Lauren shouted above the roar of the engine. Those still on board the mudder had hunched down in anticipation of a collision. Flinx leaned on the wheel. Engine screaming, the catamaran spun to its left, nearly drowning those starting up the chute ladder toward the skimmer.

Lauren must have fired at least once, Flinx thought as the jet boat sped away. He turned the wheel, and they started back toward their quarry in a wide arc. To his surprise, the woman put the peculiar-looking weapon back in the storage locker and returned to the bracket-held dart rifle. "Now let's go back and take our best shots."

"A one-shot gun?" he murmured. "I didn't even hear it go off. What was the purpose of that crazy charge?" He wrestled with the wheel.

"That charge was our insurance, Flinx." She gestured back toward the storage locker where she had repositioned the narrow gun. "That gun was a Marker. We use it to help track injured fish that break their lines." She nodded toward the skimmer. "I think I hit it twice. The gun fires a capsule which holds a specially sensitized gel. Epoxied bonder, sticks to *anything* on contact, and it's not water soluble. As long as they don't think to check the underside of their skimmer for damage, and there's no reason for them to do so since it's operating perfectly, they'll never see the gel. It's transparent, anyway. Now we can track them."

"Not with this boat, surely."

"No. But there's a skimmer back at the lodge. Would've taken too long to ready it or we'd be on it now instead of on this boat. Wish we were. No reason to expect a skimmer to show up suddenly to help them, though." She gestured toward the mudder.

"As long as they don't get too far ahead of us, we'll be able to follow them—just like we did with this boat. But if we can hurt them now . . ." She looked back through the telescopic sight. "Ah, they've taken your mother up on a hoist. Strapped in. I'm sure she didn't make it easy for them."

"She wouldn't," Flinx murmured affectionately.

"Clear shooting now," Lauren said delightedly. A loud beeping sounded from the tracking unit.

"What's that?" Flinx gave the device a puzzled glance.

Lauren uttered a curse and pulled away from the rifle. A quick glance at the screen and Flinx found himself shoved none too gently out of the pilot's chair. He landed on the deck hard.

"Hey, what's—!"

Lauren wasn't listening to him as she wrenched the wheel hard to starboard. Flinx frantically grabbed for some support as the boat heeled over. He could just see the port hull rising clear of the water as something immense and silvery-sided erupted from the lake's surface.

10

Screams and shouts came from the vicinity of the mudders and the skimmer. A violent reactive wave nearly capsized the jet boat; only Lauren's skillful and experienced maneuvering kept them afloat.

Flinx saw a vast argent spine shot through with flecks of gold that shone in the diffused sunlight. It looked like a huge pipe emerging from beneath the waves, and it turned the sunlight to rainbows. Then it was gone, not endless as he first believed. Another wave shook the catamaran as the monster submerged once again. Flinx pulled himself up to where he could peer over the edge of the cabin compartment.

The mudders had vanished completely, sucked down in a single gulp by whatever had materialized from the depths of the lake. The skimmer itself just missed being dragged down by that great gulf of a mouth. It hovered above the disturbed section of lake where its companion craft had been only a moment ago. Then someone on the skimmer apparently made a decision, for it rose another twenty meters toward the clouds and accelerated rapidly northward.

"They're leaving," Flinx shouted. "We have to get back to the lodge, get the skimmer you mentioned, and hurry after them before—"

"We have to get out of here alive first." Lauren followed her announcement with another curse as her hands tore at the wheel. The silver mountain lifted from the lake just starboard of the jet boat. Flinx was gifted with a long, uncomfortable view down a throat wide enough to swallow several mudders intact. Or a jet boat. The jaws slammed shut, sending a heavy spray crashing over the gunwales. The monster was so close Flinx could smell its horrid breath. Then it was sinking back into the waters boiling behind the catamaran.

Something moved on his shoulder, and he reached up to grasp at the muscular form that was uncoiling. "No, Pip! Easy . . . this one's too big even for you." The snake struggled for a moment before relaxing. It bobbed and ducked nervously, however, sensing a threat not only to its master but to itself. Yet it responded to the pressure of Flinx's restraining fingers and held its position.

For a third time, the penestral struck, snapping in frustration at the spot where the jet boat had been only seconds earlier. Thanks to the tracker, which had first warned Lauren of the nightmare's approach, they were able to avoid its upward rush.

"This won't do," she murmured. "It'll keep working us until I make a mistake. Then it'll take us the way it took the poor souls still stuck on those mudders." She studied the tracker intently. "It's circling now. Trying to cut us off from shallow water and the shore. We'll let it think we're headed that way. Then we'll reverse back into deep water."

"Why?"

She ignored the question. "You didn't care for it when I had to shove you away from the wheel a few minutes ago, did you? Here, it's all yours again." She reached down and half pulled, half guided him back into the pilot's chair. "That's enough." She threw the wheel over, and the boat seemed to spin on its axis. Flinx grabbed for the wheel.

"It'll follow us straight now instead of trying to ambush us from below and will try to hit us from astern. Keep us headed out into the lake and let me know when it's tangent to our square." She indicated the red dot on the tracking screen that was closing on them from behind.

"But shouldn't we—?"

She wasn't listening to him as she made her way back to the pair of gantrylike structures protruding from the rear of the boat. She took a seat behind one, stretched it out so the arm hung free over the water, then checked controls.

"When I tell you," she shouted back at him over the roar of the engine and the spray, "go hard a-port. That's left."

"I remember," he snapped back at her. His attention was locked to the tracker. "It's getting awfully close."

"Good." She positioned herself carefully in the seat, touched a switch. Flexible braces snapped shut across her waist, hips, shoulders and legs, pinning her to the seat in a striped cocoon.

"*Awfully* close," Flinx reiterated.

"Not ready yet," she murmured. "A fisherman has to be patient." The water astern began to bubble, a disturbance more widespread than a mere boat engine could produce. "Now!" she shouted.

Flinx wrenched the wheel to his left. Simultaneously, the surface of the lake exploded behind them. With both hands on the wheel, there was nothing Flinx could do except cry out as Pip left its perch and launched itself into the air. A muffled explosion sounded from the stern, and a moment later its echo reached him as the harpoon struck the penestral just beneath one of the winglike fins that shielded its gills.

The soaring monster displaced the lake where the jet boat had been before Flinx had sent it screaming into a tight turn. A distant *crump* reached the surface as the harpoon's delayed charge went off inside the guts of the penestral. Polyline spewed from a drum inside the ship's hull, a gel coating eliminating dangerous heat buildup where line rubbed the deck.

"Cut the engine," came the command from astern.

"But then we won't have any—" he started to protest.

"Do it," she ordered.

Flinx sighed. He was not a good swimmer. He flicked the accelerator until their speed dropped to nothing. The jet engine sank to an idle. Instantly, the catamaran began moving in reverse. The twin hulls were pointed aft as well as forward, and the boat moved neatly through the water as it was towed backward. The retreating polyline slowed from a blur to where Flinx could count space markings as it slid off the boat. Meanwhile, Lauren had reloaded the harpoon gun and was watching the surface carefully.

She called back to him. "Where's the penestral?"

"Still moving ahead of us, but I think it's slowing."

"That's to be expected. Keep your hands on the accelerator and the wheel."

"It's still slowing," he told her. "Slowing, slowing—I can't see it anymore. I think it's under the boat!"

"Go!" she yelled, but at that point he didn't need to be told what to do; he had already jammed the accelerator control forward. The jet boat roared, shot out across the lake. An instant later a geyser erupted behind them as the penestral tried to swallow the sky. Flinx heard the harpoon gun discharge a second time.

This time, the penestral was struck just behind one crystal-like eye the size of a telescope mirror. It collapsed back into the water like a tridee scene running in reverse, sending up huge waves over which the retreating catamaran rode with ease. The waves were matched in frequency if not intensity by the palpitations of Flinx's stomach.

This time, the fish didn't sink back into the depths. It stayed on the surface, thrashing convulsively.

"Bring us back around," Lauren directed Flinx. She was sweating profusely as she reloaded the harpoon cannon for the third time. Only the autoloading equipment made it possible for one person to manipulate the heavy metal shaft and its explosive charge.

This harpoon was slightly smaller and thinner than the two that had preceded it. As the boat swung back toward the penestral, Flinx heard the gun go off again. Several minutes passed. The penestral stopped fighting and began to sink.

Lauren touched another button. There was a hum as a compressor located inside the catamaran started up, pumping air through the plastic line that ran to the hollow shaft of the last harpoon. She unstrapped herself from the chair and began to oversee the reeling in of the colossal catch. "Air'll keep it afloat for days," she said idly, exchanging seats with Flinx once again. "Too big for darts, this one."

"Why bother with it?" Flinx stared as the silver-sided mountain expanded and drew alongside the catamaran.

"You might be right—it's not much of a fish. Bet it doesn't run more than fifteen meters." Flinx gaped at her. "But there are hungry people in Kaslin and the other towns south of the lake, and the penestral's a good food fish—lean and not fatty. They'll make good use of it. What they don't eat they'll process for resale further south. The credit will go to the lodge.

"Besides, we have guests staying with us who come up to Patra regularly, twice a year for many years, and who in all that time have never seen anything bigger than a five-meter minnow. Your first time and you've participated in a catch. You should feel proud."

"I didn't catch it," he corrected her quickly. "You did."

"Sorry, modesty's not permitted on this lake. Catching even a penestral's a cooperative effort. Dodging is just as important as firing the gun. Otherwise, *we* end up on *his* trophy wall." She jabbed a thumb in the direction of the inflated bulk now secured to the side of the catamaran.

A weight settled gently onto Flinx's left shoulder. "I'd hoped you hadn't gone off to try and attack it," he said to the minidrag as it slipped multiple coils around his arm. "It's good to know you have *some* instinct for self-preservation." The flying snake stared quizzically back at him, then closed its eyes and relaxed.

Flinx inspected what he could see of the penestral while the jet boat headed back toward the southern shore. "Those people in the mudders, they didn't stand a chance."

"Never knew what hit them," Lauren agreed. "I'm sure they weren't carrying any kind of tracking equipment. No reason for it. If our tracker had been out of order, we'd have joined the mudders in the penestral's belly."

A quick death at least, Flinx thought. Death was a frequent visitor to the unwary in the Drallarian marketplace, so he was no stranger to it. Thoughts of death reminded him of Mother Mastiff. Would his persistence result in her captors' deciding she wasn't worth the trouble anymore? What might they have in mind for her, now that her presence had caused the death of a number of them? Surely, he decided, they wouldn't kill her out of hand. They had gone to so much trouble already.

But the thought made him worry even more.

Exhilarated by the fight, Lauren's voice was slightly elevated and hurried. She had reason to be short of wind, Flinx thought. "One of these days, Flinx, after we've finished with this business, you'll have to come back up here. I'll take you over to Lake Hozingar or Utuhuku. Now those are respectable-sized lakes and home to some decent-sized fish. Not like poor little Patra, here. At Hozingar, you can see the real meaning of the name The-Blue-That-Blinded."

Flinx regarded the immense carcass slung alongside the jet boat in light of her words. "I know there are bigger lakes than this one, but I didn't know they held bigger penestrals."

"Oh, the penestral's a midrange predator," she told him conversationally. "On Hozingar you don't go fishing for penestral. You fish for oboweir."

"What," Flinx asked, "is an oboweir?"

"A fish that feeds regularly on penestrals."

"Oh," he said quietly, trying to stretch his imagination to handle the picture her words had conjured up.

Quite a crowd was waiting to greet them as they tied up at the lodge pier. Lauren had moored the inflated penestral to a buoy nearby. The carcass drew too much water to be brought right inshore.

Flinx slipped through the *oohing* and *ahhing* guests, leaving Lauren to handle the questions. Several of her employees fought their way to her and added questions of their own. Eventually, the crowd began to break up, some to return to their rooms, others to remain to gawk at the fish bobbing slowly on the surface.

Flinx had collapsed gratefully into a chair on the porch that encircled the main building. "How much do you want for the use of the skimmer and a tracker?" he asked Lauren when she was able to join him. "I'll need you to show me how to use it, of course."

She frowned at him. "I'm not sure I follow you, Flinx."

"I told you, I'm going after them. You've made it possible for me to do that, and I'm very grateful to you."

She looked thoughtful. "Management will scream when they find out I've taken out the skimmer for personal use. They're a lot more expensive than a jet boat or mudder. We'll have to be careful with it."

He still wasn't listening to her, his mind full of plans for pursuing the kidnappers. "I don't know how I'll ever repay you for this, Lauren."

"Don't worry about it. The lodge's share of profit from the disposal of the penestral ought to defray all the operating expenses. Come on, get yourself and your snake out of that chair. We have to gather supplies. The skimmer's usually used for making quick runs between here and Attock. That's where we pick up our guests. We'll need to stock some food, of course, and I want to make sure the engine is fully charged. And if I don't take ten minutes to comb my hair out, I'm going to die." She tugged at the tangles of black ringlets that the action on the lake had produced.

"Just a minute." This time it was Flinx who put out the restraining hand as he bounded out of the chair. "I think I've misunderstood. You don't mean you're coming with me?"

"You don't know how to use the tracking equipment," she pointed out.

"I can figure it out," he assured her confidently. "It didn't take me long to figure out how to handle the boat, did it?"

"You don't know the country."

"I'm not interested in the country," he responded. "I'm not going on a sightseeing trip. That's what the tracker's for, isn't it? Just loan the stuff to me. I'll pay you back somehow. Let me just have the tracker and a charge for my mudder, if you're worried about the skimmer."

"You're forgetting about my wervils. Besides, you can't track a skimmer with a mudder. What if you hit a canyon?"

"Surely you're not giving up your work here," he said, trying another tack, "just so you can seek revenge for the deaths of a couple of pets?"

"I told you, wervils are an endangered species on Moth. And I also told you how I feel about animals."

"I know," he protested, "but that still doesn't—"

He broke off his protest as she reached out to ruffle his hair. "You know, you remind me of another wervil I cared for once, though his fur wasn't quite as bright as yours. Near enough, though." Then she went on more seriously. "Flinx, I don't like these people, whoever they are. I don't like them because of what they've done to you, and I don't like them because of what they've done to me. Because of that, I'm going to help you as well as myself. Because I'd be going out after them whether you were here or not, for the sake of Sennar and Soba.

"Don't try to deny that you couldn't use a little help and don't give me any of that archaic nonsense about your not wanting me along because I'm a woman."

"Oh, don't worry," he told her crisply. "The last thing I'd try to do would be to inflict any archaic nonsense on you."

That caused her to hesitate momentarily, uncertain whether he was joking or not. "Anyway," she added, "if I can't go, not that you can stop me, then you couldn't go, either. Because I'm the only one who has access to the skimmer."

It was not hard for Flinx to give in. "I haven't got time to argue with you."

"And also the sense not to, I suspect. But you're right about the time. The tracker should pick up the gel underneath their skimmer right away, but let's not play our luck to the limit. I don't know what kind of skimmer they were using. I've never seen the like before, so I've no idea if it's faster than usual. We go together, then?"

"Together. On two conditions, Lauren."

Again, she found herself frowning at him. Just when she thought she could predict his actions, he would do something to surprise her again. "Say them, anyway."

"First, that Pip continues to tolerate you." He rubbed the back of the flying snake's head affectionately. It rose delightedly against the pressure. "You see, I have certain feelings toward animals myself."

"And the other condition?" she inquired.

"If you ever touch my hair like that again, you'd better be prepared for me to kick your lovely backside all the way to the Pole.

Old ladies have been doing that to me ever since I can remember, and I've had my fill of it!"

She grinned at him. "It's a deal, then. I'm glad your snake isn't as touchy as you are. Let's go. I have to leave a message for my superiors in case they call in and want to know not only where their skimmer is but their lodge manager as well."

When she informed the assistant manager of the lodge, he was very upset. "But what do I tell Kilkenny if he calls from Attoka? What if he has guests to send up?"

"We're not expecting anyone for another week. You know that, Sal. Tell him anything you want." She was arranging items in a small sack as she spoke. "No, tell him I've gone to the aid of a traveler in distress across the lake. That's an acceptable excuse in any circumstance."

The assistant looked past her to where Flinx stood waiting impatiently, chucking Pip under its jaw and staring in the direction of the lake.

"He doesn't look like he's very distressed to me."

"His distress is well hidden," Lauren informed him, "which is more than I can say for you, Sal. I'm surprised at you. We'll be back real soon."

"Uh-huh. It's just that I'm not a very good liar, Lauren. You know that."

"Do the best you can." She patted his cheek affectionately. "And I'm not lying. He really is in trouble."

"But the *skimmer,* Lauren."

"You still have the lodge mudders and the boats. Short of a major catastrophe of some kind, I can see no reason why you'd need the skimmer. It's really only here to be used in case of emergency. To my mind"—she gestured toward Flinx—"this is an emergency."

The assistant kicked at the dirt. "It's your neck."

"Yes, it's my neck."

"Suppose they ask which way you went?"

"Tell them I've headed—" A cough interrupted her. She looked back at Flinx and nodded once. "Just say that I've had to go across Patra."

"But which way across?"

"Across the lake, Sal."

"Oh. Okay, I understand. You've got your reasons for doing this, I guess."

"I guess I do. And if I'm wrong, well, you always wanted to be manager here, anyway, Sal."

"Now hold on a minute, Lauren. I never said—"

"Do the best you can for me," she gently admonished him. "This means something to me."

"You *really* expect to be back soon?"

"Depends on how things go. See you, Sal."

"Take care of yourself, Lauren." He watched as she turned to rejoin the strange youth, then shrugged and started back up the steps into the lodge.

As Lauren had said, it was her neck.

It didn't take long for the skimmer to be checked out. Flinx climbed aboard and admired the utilitarian vehicle. For almost the first time since he left Drallar, he would be traveling totally clear of such persistent obstacles as mist-shrouded boulders and towering trees. The machine's body was made of black resin. It was large enough to accommodate a dozen passengers and crew. In addition to the standard emergency stores, Lauren provisioned it with additional food and medical supplies. They also took along the dart rifle and several clips and a portable sounding tracker.

Flinx studied the tracking screen and the single moving dot that drifted northwestward across the transparency. A series of concentric gauging rings filled the circular screen. The dot that represented their quarry had already reached the outermost ring.

"They'll move off the screen in a little while," he murmured to Lauren.

"Don't worry. I'm sure they're convinced by now that they've lost us."

"They're zigzagging all over the screen," he noted.

"Taking no chances. Doesn't do any good if you're showing up on a tracker. But you're right. We'd better get moving."

She slid into the pilot's chair and thumbed controls. The whine of the skimmer's engine drowned out the tracker's gentle hum as the craft rose several meters. Lauren held it there as she ran a final instrument check, then pivoted the vehicle on an invisible axis and drove it from the hangar. A nudge of the altitude switch sent them ten, twenty, thirty meters into the air above the lodge. A touch on the accelerator and they were rushing toward the beach.

Despite the warmth of the cabin heater, Flinx still felt cold as he gazed single-mindedly at the screen.

"I told you not to worry," Lauren said with a glance at his expression as they crossed the shoreline. "We'll catch them."

"It's not that." Flinx peered out through the transparent cabin cover. "I was thinking about what might catch us."

"I've yet to see the penestral that can pick out and catch an airborne target moving at our speed thirty meters up. An oboweir might do it, but there aren't any oboweirs in Lake Patra. Leastwise, none that I've ever heard tell of."

Nevertheless, Flinx's attention and thoughts remained evenly divided between the horizon ahead and the potentially lethal waters below.

"I understand you've had some trouble here."

Sal relaxed in the chair in the dining room and sipped at a hot cup of toma as he regarded his visitors. They had arrived in their own mudder, which immediately stamped them as independent as well as wealthy. If he played this right, he might convince them to spend a few days at the lodge. They had several expensive suites vacant, and if he could place this pair in one, it certainly wouldn't do his record any harm. Usually, he could place an offworlder by accent, but not these two. Their words were clear but their phonemes amorphous. It puzzled him.

Routine had returned as soon as Lauren and her charity case had departed. No one had called from down south, not the district manager, not anyone. He was feeling very content. Unless, of course, the company had decided to send its own investigators instead of simply calling in a checkup. That thought made him frown at the woman.

"Say, are you two Company?"

"No," the woman's companion replied, smiling pleasantly. "Goodness no, nothing like that. We just like a little excitement, that's all. If something unusual's going on in the area, it kind of tickles our curiosity, if you know what I mean."

"You had a man killed here, didn't you?" the woman asked.

"Well, yes, it did get pretty lively here for a day." No accounting for taste, Sal mused. "Someone was killed during a fight. A nonguest," he hastened to add. "Right in here. Quite a melee."

"Can you describe any of those involved?" she asked him.

"Not really. I'm not even positive which guests were involved and which day visitors. I didn't witness the argument myself, you see, and by the time I arrived, most of the participants had left."

The woman accepted this admission with a disappointed nod. "Was there a young man involved? Say, of about sixteen?"

"Yes, him I did see. Bright-red hair?"

"That's the one," she admitted.

"Say, is he dangerous or anything?" The assistant manager leaned forward in his chair, suddenly concerned.

"Why do you want to know?" the man asked.

"Well, my superior here, the regular manager—Lauren Walder. She went off with him."

"Went off with him?" The pleasant expression that had dominated the woman's face quickly vanished, to be replaced by something much harder.

"Yes. Three, maybe four days ago now. I'm still not completely sure why. She only told me that the young man had a problem and she was going to try to help him out."

"Which way did their mudder go?" the man asked.

"North, across Lake Patra," Sal informed them. "They're not in a mudder, though. She took the lodge skimmer."

"A skimmer!" The woman threw up her hands in frustration and sat down heavily in a chair opposite the assistant. "We're losing ground," she told her companion, "instead of gaining on him. If he catches up with them before we do, we could lose him *and* the . . ." Her companion cut the air with the edge of his hand, and her words trailed away to an indecipherable mumble. The gesture had been quick and partly concealed, but Sal had noticed it nonetheless.

"Now you've really got me worried," he told the pair. "If Lauren's in some kind of trouble—"

"She could be," the man admitted, pleased that the assistant had changed the subject.

Sal thought a moment. "Would she be in danger from these people who had the fight here, or from the redhead?"

"Conceivably from both." The man was only half lying. "You'd better tell us everything you know."

"I already have," Sal replied.

"You said they went north, across the lake. Can't you be any more specific than that?"

Sal looked helpless. "Lauren wouldn't be any more specific than that."

"They might not continue heading north."

"No, they might not. Do you have a tracker for following other craft?" Sal asked.

The man shook his head. "We didn't think we'd need one. The last we knew, the young man we'd like to talk with was traveling on stupava-back."

"I think he arrived here in a mudder."

The woman looked surprised and grinned ruefully at her companion. "No wonder we fell behind. Resourceful, isn't he?"

"Too resourceful for my liking," the man murmured, "and maybe for his own good if he backs those you-know-whos into a corner."

The woman sighed, then rose from her chair. "Well, we've wasted enough time here. We'll just have to return to Pranbeth for a skimmer and tracking unit. Unless you think we should try to catch up to them in the mudder."

The man let out a short, humorless laugh, then turned back to the assistant manager. "Thanks, son. You've been helpful."

"I wish I could be more so," Sal told him anxiously. "If anything were to happen to Lauren—you'll see that nothing happens to her, won't you?"

"I promise you we'll do our best," the woman assured him. "We don't want to see innocent bystanders hurt. We don't even want to see noninnocents hurt." She favored him with a maternal smile, which for some reason did nothing to make the nervous assistant feel any better about the situation.

11

The tracker hummed quietly, the single glowing dot showing clearly on its screen as the skimmer rushed northward. It was clipping the tops of the tallest trees, more than eighty meters above the bogs and muck that passed for the ground. They had crossed Lake Patra, then an intervening neck of dry land, then the much larger lake known as Tigranocerta and were once more cruising over the forest. A cold rain was falling, spattering off the skimmer's acrylic canopy to form a constantly changing wet topography that obscured much of the view outside. The skimmer's instruments kept its speed responsive, maintaining a predetermined distance between it and its quarry to the north.

Awfully quiet, Lauren Walder thought. He's awfully quiet, and maybe something else.

"No, I'm not too young," he said into the silence that filled the cabin, his tone softly defensive.

Lauren's eyebrows lifted. "You can read minds?"

He responded with a shy smile. "No, not that." Fingers stroked the head of the minidrag sleeping on his shoulder. "I just feel things at times. Not thoughts, nothing that elaborate. Just the way people are feeling." He glanced up at her. "From the way I thought you were feeling just now, I thought you were going to say something along that line."

"Well, you were right," she confessed, wondering what to make of the rest of his declaration.

"I'm not, you know."

"How old are you?" she asked.

"Sixteen. As best I know. I can't be certain."

Sixteen going on sixty, she thought sadly. During her rare visits to Drallar, she had seen his type before. Child of circumstance, raised in the streets and instructed by wrong example and accident, though he seemed to have turned out better than his brethren. His face held the knowledge withheld from his more fortunate contemporaries, but it didn't seem to have made him vicious or bitter.

Still she felt there was something else at work here.

"How old do you think I am?" she asked idly.

Flinx pursed his lips as he stared at her. "Twenty-three," he told her without hesitating.

She laughed softly and clapped both hands together in delight. "So that's what I'm helping, a sixteen-year-old vengeful diplomat!" Her laughter faded. The smile remained. "Tell me about yourself, Flinx."

It was a question that no stranger in Drallar would ever be so brazen as to ask. But this was not Drallar, he reminded himself. Besides, he owed this woman.

So he told her as much as he knew. When he finished his narrative, she continued to stare solemnly at him, nodding her head as if his words had done no more than confirm suspicions already held. She spared a glance to make sure the tracker was still functioning efficiently, then looked back at him. "You haven't exactly had a comfortable childhood, have you?"

"I wouldn't know," he replied, "because I only have hearsay to compare it with."

"Take my word for it, you haven't. You've also managed to get along with the majority of humanity even though they don't seem to want to have anything to do with you. Whereas I've had to avoid the majority of people who seem to want to have a lot to do with me."

Impulsively, she leaned over out of the pilot's chair and kissed him. At the last instant, he flinched, nervous at such unaccustomed proximity to another human being—especially an attractive member of the opposite sex—and the kiss, which was meant for his cheek, landed instead on his lips.

That made her pull back fast. The smile stayed on her face, and she only blinked once in surprise. It had been an accident, after all. "Take my word for something else, Flinx. If you live long enough, life gets better."

"Is that one of the Church's homilies?" He wondered if she wore some caustic substance to protect her lips from burning, because his own were on fire.

"No," she said. "That's a Lauren Walder homily."

"Glad to hear it. I've never had much use for the Church."

"Nor have I. Nor have most people. That's why it's been so successful, I expect." She turned her gaze to the tracker. "They're starting to slow down. We'll do the same."

"Do you think they've seen us?" Suddenly, he didn't really care what the people in the skimmer ahead of them decided to do. The fire spread from his lips to his mouth, ran down his throat, and dispersed across his whole body. It was a sweet, thick fire.

"I doubt it," she replied. "I'll bet they're close to their destination." Her hands manipulated controls.

"How far ahead of us are they?" He walked forward to peer over her shoulder at the screen. He could have stood to her left, but he was suddenly conscious of the warmth of her, the perfume of her hair. He was very careful not to touch her.

She performed some quick calculations, using the tracker's predictor. "Day or so. We don't want to run up their tail. There's nothing up in this part of the country. Odd place to stop, but then this whole business is odd, from what you've told me. Why bring your mother up here?"

He had no answer for her.

They dropped until the skimmer was rising and falling in concert with the treetops. So intent were they on the actions of the dot performing on the tracking screen that neither of them noticed that not only had the rain stopped but the cloud cover had cracked. Overhead, one of the rings of Moth, the interrupted ring which encircled the planet, shimmered golden against the ceiling of night.

"What makes you so sure they're stopping here instead of just slowing down for a while?" he asked Lauren.

"Because a skimmer operates on a stored charge, just like a mudder. Remember, they had to come from here down to Patra. Our own charge is running low, and we're not on the return leg of a round trip. I don't know what model they're flying, but I saw how big it was. It can't possibly retain enough energy to take them much farther than we've gone the past several days. They at least have to be stopping somewhere to recharge, which is good."

"Why is that?" Flinx asked.

"Because we're going to have to recharge, also." She pointed to a readout. "We've used more than half our own power. If we can't recharge somewhere around here, we're going to have some hiking to do on our way out."

Flinx regarded her with new respect, if that was possible; his opinion of her had already reached dizzying heights. "Why didn't you tell me when we reached the turnaround point?"

She shrugged slightly. "Why? We've gone to a lot of trouble to come as far as we have. You might have argued with me about turning back."

"No," Flinx said quietly, "I wouldn't have done that."

"I didn't think so. You're almost as determined to see this through as I am, and at least as crazy."

She stared up at him, and he stared back. Nothing more needed to be said.

"I vote *no*."

Nyassa-lee was firm in her disagreement. She sat on one side of the table and gazed expectantly at her colleagues. Brora was thoughtfully inspecting the fingernails of his left hand, while Haithness toyed with her eyelashes.

"Really," the tall black woman murmured to her compatriot, "to show such reluctance at this stage is most discouraging, Nyassa-lee." Her fingers left her eyes. "We may never have the chance to manipulate another subject as promising as this Twelve. Time and events conspire against us. You know that as well as I."

"I know." The shorter woman leaned forward in the chair and gazed between her legs at the floor. Cracks showed between the panels; the building had been assembled in haste. "I'm just not convinced it's worth the risk."

"What risk?" Haithness demanded to know. "We've still seen nothing like a demonstration of threatening power. Quite the contrary, I'd say. Certainly the subject had the opportunity to display any such abilities. It's evident he does not possess them, or he would doubtless have employed them against us. Instead, what did we see? Knife." She made it sound disgusting as well as primitive.

"She's right, you know." Brora rarely spoke, preferring to let the two senior scientists do most of the arguing. He stepped in only when he was completely confident of his opinion.

"We don't want another repeat of the girl," Nyassa-lee said. "The Society couldn't stand another failure like that."

"Which is precisely why we must pursue this last opportunity to its conclusion," Haithness persisted.

"We don't know that it represents our last opportunity."

"Oh, come on, Nyassa-lee." Haithness pushed back her chair and stood; she began pacing nervously back and forth. Behind her, lights shone cold green and blue from the consoles hastily assembled. "Even if there *are* other subjects of equal potential out there, we've no guarantee that any of us will be around much longer to follow up on them."

"I can't argue with that," Nyassa-lee admitted. "Nor can I argue this Number Twelve's statistical promise. It's just those statistics which frighten me."

"Frighten you?" Haithness stopped pacing and looked over at her companion of many hard years. The tall woman was surprised. She had seen Nyassa-lee wield a gun with the cold-blooded efficiency of a qwarm. Fear seemed foreign to her. "But why? He's done nothing to justify such fear."

"Oh, no?" Nyassa-lee ticked off her points on the fingers of one hand. "One, his statistical potential is alarming. Two, he's sixteen, on the verge of full maturity. Three, he could cross into that at *any* time."

"The girl," Brora pointed out, "was considerably younger."

"Agreed," said Nyassa-lee, "but her abilities were precocious. Her advantage was surprise. This Number Twelve is developing slowly but with greater potential. He may be the kind who responds to pressure by reaching deeper into himself."

"Maybe," Brora said thoughtfully, "but we have no proof of it, nor does his profile predict anything of the sort."

"Then how do you square that," she responded, "with the fact that he has by himself—"

"He's not by himself," Brora interrupted her. "That woman from the lodge was helping him out on the lake."

"*Was* helping him. She didn't help him get to that point. He followed us all the way to that lake on his own, without any kind of external assistance. To me that indicates the accelerated development of a Talent we'd better beware of."

"All the more reason," Haithness said angrily, slapping the table with one palm, "why we must push ahead with our plan!"

"I don't know," Nyassa-lee murmured, unconvinced.

"Do you not agree," Haithness countered, forcing herself to restrain her temper, "that if the operation is a success we stand a good chance of accomplishing our goal as regards outside manipulation of the subject?"

"Possibly," Nyassa-lee conceded.

"Why just 'possibly'? Do you doubt the emotional bond?"

"That's not what concerns me. Suppose, just suppose, that because his potential is still undeveloped, he has no conscious control of it?"

"What are you saying?" Brora asked.

She leaned intently over the table. "With the girl Mahnahmi we knew where we stood, once she'd revealed herself. Unfortunately, that knowledge came as a surprise to us, and too late to counteract. We've no idea where we stand vis-à-vis this subject's Talents. Suppose that, despite the emotional bond, pressure and fear conspire to release his potential regardless of his surface feelings? Statistically, the subject is a walking bomb that may not be capable or mature enough to control itself. *That's* what worries me, Haithness. The emotional bond may be sufficient to control his conscious self. The unpredictable part of him may react violently in spite of it."

"We cannot abandon our hopes and work on so slim a supposition, one that we have no solid facts to support," Haithness insisted. "Besides, the subject is sixteen. If anything, he should have much more control over himself than the girl did."

"I know, I know," Nyassa-lee muttered unhappily. "Everything you say is true, Haithness, yet I can't help worrying. In any case, I'm outvoted."

"That you are," the tall woman said after a questioning glance at Brora. "And if Cruachan were here with us, you know he'd vote to proceed too."

"I suppose." Nyassa-lee smiled thinly. "I worry too much. Brora, are you sure you can handle the implant?"

He nodded. "I haven't done one in some time, but the old skills remain. It requires patience more than anything else. You remember. As to possible unpredictable results, failure, well"—he smiled—"we're all condemned already. One more little outrage perpetrated against society's archaic laws can't harm us one way or the other if we fail here."

Off in a nearby corner, Mother Mastiff sat in a chair, hands clasped in her lap, and listened. She was not bound. There was no reason to tie her, and she knew why as well as her captors. There was nowhere to run. She was in excellent condition for a woman her age, but she had had a good view of the modest complex of deceptive stone and wood structures as the skimmer had landed. Thousands of square kilometers of damp, hostile forest lay between the place she had been brought to and the familiar confines of Drallar. She was no more likely to steal a vehicle than she was to turn twenty again.

She wondered what poor Flinx was going through. That had been him, out on the boat on the lake far to the south. How he had managed to trace her so far she had no idea. At first, her concern had been for herself. Now that she had had ample opportunity to listen to the demonic trio arguing in front of her—for demonic she was certain they were—she found herself as concerned for the fate of her adopted son as for her own. If she was lost, well, she had had a long and eventful life. Better perhaps that her brave Flinx lose track of her than stumble into these monsters again.

One of the trio, the short, toad-faced man, had spoken of "adjusting" her and of "implants." That was enough to convince her to prepare for something worse than death. Many of their words made no sense to her. She still had no idea who the people were, much less where they had come from or the reasons for their actions. They never spoke to her, ignoring her questions as well as her curses.

Actually, they did not treat her as a human being at all, but rather as a delicate piece of furniture. Their current conversation was the most peculiar yet, for one of them was expressing fear of her boy. She could not imagine why. True, Flinx had tamed a dangerous animal, that horrid little flying creature, but that was hardly a feat to inspire fear in such people. They knew he occasionally had the ability to sense what others were feeling. Yet far from fearing such erratic and minor talents, these people discussed them as if they were matters of great importance.

None of which explained why they'd kidnapped her. If their real interest lay with her boy, then why hadn't they kidnapped him? The whole affair was too complicated a puzzle for her to figure out. Mother Mastiff was not a stupid woman, and her deficiency in formal education did not blunt her sharp, inquiring mind; still she could not fathom what was happening to her, or why.

She let her attention drift from the argument raging across the table nearby to study the room to which she had been brought. Most of the illumination came from the impressive array of electronics lining the walls. Everything she could see hinted of portability and hurried installation. She had no idea as to the purpose of the instrumentation, but she had been around enough to know that such devices were expensive. That, and the actions of the people who had abducted her, hinted at an organization well stocked with money as well as malign intentions.

"I'm not even sure," Nyassa-lee was saying, "that the subject realizes how he's managed to follow us this far."

"There is likely nothing mysterious about it," Haithness argued. "Remember that he is a product of an intensely competitive, if primitive, environment. Urban youths grow up fast when left to their own resources. He may not have enjoyed much in the way of a formal education, but he's been schooled in the real world—

something we've had to master ourselves these past years. And he may have had some ordinary, quite natural luck."

"These past years," Brora was mumbling sadly. "Years that should have been spent prying into the great mysteries of the universe instead of learning how to make contacts with and use of the criminal underworld."

"I feel as wasted as you do, Brora," the tall woman said soothingly, "but vindication lies at hand."

"If you're both determined to proceed, then I vote that we begin immediately." Nyassa-lee sighed.

"Immediately with what?" a crotchety voice demanded. For some reason, the question caused the trio to respond, whereas previous attempts to draw their attention had failed miserably.

Nyassa-lee left the table and approached Mother Mastiff. She tried to adopt a kindly, understanding expression, but was only partly successful. "We're scientists embarked on a project of great importance to all mankind. I'm sorry we've been forced to inconvenience you, but this is all necessary. I wish you were of a more educated turn of mind and could understand our point of view. It would make things easier for you."

"Inconvenienced!" Mother Mastiff snorted. "Ye pluck me out of my house and haul me halfway across the planet. That's inconvenience? I call it something else." Her bluster faded as she asked, "What is it you want with my boy Flinx?"

"Your *adopted* boy," Nyassa-lee said. While the small Oriental spoke, Mother Mastiff noted that the other two were studying her the way a collector might watch a bug on a park bench. That made her even madder, and the anger helped to put a damper on her fear. "I wouldn't make things any easier for you people if ye promised me half the wealth of Terra."

"I'm sorry you feel that way, but it's only what we have come to expect," Nyassa-lee said, turning icy once again. "Have you heard of the Meliorare Society?"

Mother Mastiff shook her head, too angry to cry, which is what she really wanted to do. Names, words they threw at her, all meaningless.

"We're part of an experiment," the Oriental explained, "an experiment which began on Terra many years ago. We are not only scientists, we are activists. We believe that the true task of science is not only to study that which exists but to forge onward and bring into existence that which does not exist but eventually will. We determined not to stand still, nor to let nature do so, either."

Mother Mastiff shook her head. "I don't understand."

"Think," Nyassa-lee urged her, warming to her subject, "what is there in Commonwealth society today that could most stand improvement? The government?" A bitter, derogatory laugh sounded behind her, from Haithness. "Not the government, then. What about the ships that carry us from star to star? No? Language, then, an improvement on Terranglo or symbospeech? What about music or architecture?"

Mother Mastiff simply stared at the woman ranting before her. She was quite certain now, quite certain. These three were all as insane as a brain-damaged Yax'm.

"No, none of those things!" Nyassa-lee snapped. It was terrible to see such complete assurance in one so diminutive. "It's us. We." She tapped her sternum. "Humankind. And the means for our improvement lie within." Her hand went to her head. "In here, in abilities and areas of our mind still not properly developed.

"We and the other members of the Society decided many years ago that something could and should be done about that. We formed a cover organization to fool superstitious regulators. In secret, we were able to select certain human ova, certain sperm, and work carefully with them. Our planning was minute, our preparations extensive. Through microsurgical techniques, we were able to alter the genetic code of our humans-to-be prior to womb implantation. The result was to be, *will* be, a better version of mankind."

Mother Mastiff gaped at her. Nyassa-lee sighed and turned to her companions. "As I feared, all this is beyond her meager comprehension."

"Perfectly understandable," Brora said. "What I don't understand is why you trouble to try?"

"It would be easier," Nyassa-lee said.

"Easier for her, or for you?" Haithness wondered. The smaller woman did not reply. "It won't matter after the operation, anyway." At these words, the fine hair on the back of Mother Mastiff's neck began to rise.

"It might," Nyassa-lee insisted. She looked back down at Mother Mastiff, staring hard into those old eyes. "Don't you understand yet, old woman? Your boy, your adopted son: he was one of our subjects."

"No," Mother Mastiff whispered, though even as she mouthed the word, she knew the woman's words must be true. "What—what happened to your experiment?"

"All the children were provided with attention, affection, education, and certain special training. The majority of the subjects displayed nothing unusual in the way of ability or talent. They were quite normal in every way. We proceeded with great care and caution, you see.

"A few of the subjects developed abnormally. That is in the nature of science, unfortunately. We must accept the good together with the bad. However, in light of our imminent success, those failures were quite justified." She sounded as if she were trying to reassure herself as much as Mother Mastiff.

"A few of the children, a very small number, gave indications of developing those abilities which we believe to lie dormant in every human brain. We don't pretend to understand everything about such Talents. We are in the position of mechanics who have a good idea how to repair an imperfect machine without really knowing what the repaired machine is capable of. This naturally resulted in some surprises.

"An ignorant Commonwealth society did not feel as we did about the importance of our activities. As a result, we have undergone many years of persecution. Yet we have persisted. As you can see, all of us who are original members of the Society are nearly as advanced in years as yourself.

"The government has been relentless in its efforts to wipe us out. Over the years, it has whittled away at our number until we have been reduced to a dedicated few. Yet we need but a single success, one incontrovertible proof of the worthiness of our work, to free ourselves from the lies and innuendo with which we have been saddled.

"It was a cruel and uncaring government which caused the dispersal of the children many years ago and which brought us to our current state of scientific exile. Slowly, patiently, we have worked to try and relocate those children, in particular any whose profiles showed real promise. Your Flinx is one of those singled out by statistics as a potential Talent."

"But there's nothing abnormal about him," Mother Mastiff protested. "He's a perfectly average, healthy young man. Quieter than most, perhaps, but that's all. Is that worth all this trouble? Oh, I'll admit he can do some parlor tricks from time to time. But I know a hundred street magicians who can do the same. Why don't you go pick on them?"

Nyassa-lee smiled that humorless, cold smile. "You're lying to us, old woman. We know that he is capable of more than mere tricks and that something far more important than sleight of hand is involved."

"Well, then," she continued, trying a different tack, "why kidnap me? Why pull me away from my home like this? I'm an old woman, just as ye say. I can't stand in your way or do ye any harm. If 'tis Flinx you're so concerned with, why did ye not abduct *him*? I surely could not have prevented ye from doing so."

"Because he may be dangerous."

Yes, they are quite mad, this lot, Mother Mastiff mused. Her boy, Flinx, dangerous? Nonsense! He was a sensitive boy, true; he could sometimes know what others were feeling, but only rarely, and hardly at all when he most wished to do so. And maybe he could push the emotions of others a tiny bit. But dangerous? The danger was to him, from these offworld fools and madmen.

"Also," the little Oriental continued, "we have to proceed very carefully because we cannot risk further harm to the Society. Our numbers have already been drastically reduced, partly by our too-hasty attempt to regain control of one subject child a number of years ago. We cannot risk making the same mistake with this Number Twelve. Most of our colleagues have been killed, imprisoned, or selectively mindwiped."

Mother Mastiff's sense of concern doubled at that almost indifferent admission. She didn't understand all the woman's chatter about genetic alterations and improving mankind, but she understood mindwiping, all right. A criminal had to be found guilty of some especially heinous crime to be condemned to that treatment, which took away forever a section of his memories, of his life, of his very self, and left him to wander for the rest of his days tormented by a dark, empty gap in his mind.

"You leave him alone!" she shouted, surprised at the violence of her reaction. Had she become so attached to the boy? Most of the time she regarded him as a nuisance inflicted on her by an unkind fate—didn't she?

"Don't you hurt him!" She was on her feet and pounding with both fists on the shoulders of the woman called Nyassa-lee.

Though white-haired and no youngster, Nyassa-lee was a good deal younger and stronger than Mother Mastiff. She took the older woman's wrists and gently pushed her back down into the chair.

"Now, we're not going to hurt him. Didn't I just explain his importance to us? Would we want to damage someone like that? Of course not. It's clear how fond you've become of your charge. In our own way, we're equally fond of him."

What soulless people these are, Mother Mastiff thought as she slumped helplessly in her chair. What dead, distant shadows of human beings.

"I promise you that we will not try to force the boy to do anything against his will, nor will we harm him in any way."

"What do ye mean to do with him, then?"

"We need to guide his future maturation," the woman explained, "to ensure that whatever abilities he possesses are developed to their utmost. It's highly unlikely he can do this without proper instruction and training, which is why his abilities have not manifested themselves fully so far. Experience, however, has shown us that when the children reach puberty, they are no longer willing to accept such training and manipulation. We therefore have to guide him without his being aware of it."

"How can ye do this without his knowing what is being done to him?"

"By manipulating him through a third party whose suggestions and directions he will accept freely," the woman said. "That is where you become important."

"So ye wish for me to make him do certain things, to alter his life so that your experiment can be proven a success?"

"That's correct," Nyassa-lee said. "All this must be carried out in such a way that he cannot suspect he is being guided by an outside force." She gestured toward the far end of the room, past transparent doors sealing off a self-contained operating theater. In the dim blue and green light of the instrument readouts, the sterile theater gleamed softly.

"We cannot allow the possibility of interference or misdirection to hamper our efforts, nor can we risk exposure to the Commonwealth agencies which continue to hound us. It is vital that our instructions be carried out quickly and efficiently. Therefore, it will be necessary for us to place certain small devices in your brain, to ensure your complete compliance with our directives."

"Like hell," Mother Mastiff snapped. "I've spent a hundred years filling up this head of mine. I know where everything is stored. I don't want somebody else messing around up there." She did not add, as she glanced surreptitiously toward the operating room, that she had never been under the knife or the laser and that she had a deathly fear of being cut.

"Look," she went on desperately, "I'll be glad to help ye. I'll tell the boy anything ye wish, have him study anything ye want and avoid whatever matters ye wish him to avoid. But leave my poor old head alone. Wouldn't I be much more help to ye if I did what ye require voluntarily instead of like some altered pet?"

Brora folded his hands on the table and regarded her emotionlessly. "That would certainly be true. However, there are factors which unfortunately mitigate against this.

"First, there are mental activities you will be required to carry out which involve complex processes you are not conversant with but which can be stimulated via direct implants. Second, there is no guarantee that at some future time you would not become discouraged or rebellious and tell the subject what you know. That could be a catastrophe for the experiment. Third, though you may direct the boy with surface willingness, his abilities may enable him to see your inner distress and know that something is amiss, whereas I do not think he can detect the implants themselves, as they are wholly mechanical. Lastly, I think you are lying when you say you would be willing to help us."

"But I don't want an operation!" she cried, pounding at the arms of the chair with her fists. "I tell you 'tis not necessary! I'll do anything ye ask of me if you'll but leave the boy alone and instruct me. Why should I lie to ye? You've said yourself that he's not my true child, only an adopted one. I'll be glad to help ye, particularly," she added with a sly smile, "if there be any money involved."

But the man Brora was shaking his head. "You lie forcefully, but not forcefully enough, old woman. We've spent most of our lives having to cope with traitors in our midst. We can't afford another one. I'm sorry." His attention was drawn to the main entrance and to the two men who'd just entered. He nodded toward Mother Mastiff.

"Restrain her. She knows enough now to do something foolish to herself."

One of the new arrivals held Mother Mastiff's right arm and glanced back toward Brora. "Anesthetic, sir?"

"No, not yet." Mother Mastiff stared at the horrid little man and shuddered as he spoke quietly to the black woman. "What do you think, Haithness?"

She examined Mother Mastiff. "Tomorrow is soon enough. I'm tired. Better to begin fresh. We'll all need to be alert."

Brora nodded in agreement, leaving the two younger men to bind the raving Mother Mastiff.

Later that evening, over dinner, Nyassa-lee said to Haithness, "The woman's advanced age still gives me concern."

"She's not that old," the taller woman said, spooning down something artificial but nourishing. "With care, she has another twenty years of good health to look forward to."

"I know, but she hasn't the reserves of a woman of fifty anymore, either. It's just as well we haven't told her how complex tomorrow's operation is or explained that her mind will be permanently altered."

Haithness nodded agreement. "There's hardly any need to upset her any more than she already is. Your excessive concern for her welfare surprises me."

Nyassa-lee picked at her food and did not comment, but Haithness refused to let the matter drop.

"How many of our friends have perished at the hands of the government? How many have been mindwiped? It's true that if this old woman dies, we lose an important element in the experiment, but not necessarily a final one. We've all agreed that implanting her is the best way to proceed."

"I'm not arguing that," Nyassa-lee said, "only reminding you that we should be prepared for failure."

Brora leaned back in his chair and sighed. He was not hungry; he was too excited by the prospects raised by the operation.

"We will not fail, Nyassa-lee. This is the best chance we've had in years to gain control over a really promising subject. We won't fail." He looked over at Haithness. "I checked the implants before dinner."

"Again?"

"Nothing else to do. I couldn't stand just waiting around. The circuitry is complete, cryogenic enervation constant. I anticipate no trouble in making the synaptic connections." He glanced toward Nyassa-lee. "The woman's age notwithstanding.

"As to the part of the old woman that will unavoidably be lost due to the operation"—he shrugged—"I've studied the matter in depth and see no way around it. Not that there seems a great deal worth preserving. She's an ignorant primitive. If anything, the implants and resulting excisions will result in an improved being."

"Her strongest virtues appear to be cantankerousness and obstinacy," Haithness agreed, "coupled to an appalling ignorance of life outside her immediate community."

"Typical specimen," Brora said. "Ironic that such a low example should be the key not only to our greatest success but our eventual vindication."

Nyassa-lee pushed away her food. Her colleague's conversation was upsetting to her. "What time tomorrow?"

"Reasonably early, I should think," Haithness murmured. "It will be the best time for the old woman, and better for us not to linger over philosophy and speculation."

Brora was startled at the latter implication. "Surely you don't expect the boy to show up?"

"You'd best stop thinking of him as a boy."

"He barely qualifies as a young adult."

"Barely is sufficient. Though he's demonstrated nothing in the way of unexpected talent so far, his persistent pursuit of his adopted mother is indication enough to me that he possesses a sharp mind in addition to Talent." She smiled thinly at Nyassa-lee. "You see, my dear, though I do not share your proclivity to panic in this case, I do respect and value your opinion."

"So you *are* expecting him?"

"No, I'm not," Haithness insisted, "but it would be awkward if by some miracle he were to show up here prior to the operation's successful completion. Once that is accomplished, we'll naturally want to make contact with him through his mother. When he finds her unharmed and seemingly untouched, he will relax into our control."

"But what if he does show up prior to our returning the old woman to Drallar?"

"Don't worry," Haithness said. "I have the standard story prepared, and our personnel here have been well coached in the pertinent details."

"You think he'd accept that tale?" Nyassa-lee asked. "That hoary old business of us being an altruistic society of physicians dedicated to helping the old and enfeebled against the indifference of government medical facilities?"

"It's true that we've utilized the story in various guises before, but it will be new to the subject," Haithness reminded her colleague. "Besides, as Brora says, he barely qualifies as an adult, and his background does not suggest sophistication. I think he'll believe us, especially when we restore his mother to him. That should be enough to satisfy him. The operation will, of course, be rendered cosmetically undetectable."

"I do better work on a full night's sleep." Brora abruptly pushed back from the table. "Especially prior to a hard day's work."

They all rose and started toward their quarters, Brora contemplating the operation near at hand, Haithness the chances for success, and only Nyassa-lee the last look in Mother Mastiff's eyes.

12

They had to be close to their destination because their quarry had been motionless for more than an hour. That's when the pain hit Flinx; sharp, hot, and unexpected as always. He winced and shut his eyes tight while Pip stirred nervously on its master's shoulder.

Alarmed, Lauren turned hurriedly to her young companion. "What is it? What's wrong, Flinx?"

"Close. We're very close."

"I can tell that by looking at the tracker," she said.

"It's her, it's Mother Mastiff."

"She's hurt?" Already Lauren was dropping the skimmer into the woods. The minidrag writhed on Flinx's shoulder, hunting for an unseen enemy.

"She's—she's not hurting," Flinx mumbled. "She's—there's worry in her, and fear. Someone's planning to do something terrible to her. She fears for me, too, I think. But I can't understand— I don't know what or wh—"

He blinked. Pip ceased his convulsions. "It's gone. Damn it, it's gone." He kicked at the console in frustration. "Gone and I can't make it come back."

"I thought—"

He interrupted her; his expression was one of resignation. "I have no control over the Talent. No control at all. These feelings hit me when I least expect them, and never, it seems, when I want them to. Sometimes I can't even locate the source. But this time it was Mother Mastiff. I'm sure of it."

"How can you tell that?" Lauren banked the skimmer to port, dodging a massive emergent.

"Because I know how her mind feels."

Lauren threw him an uncertain look, then decided there was no point in trying to comprehend something beyond her ken.

The skimmer slowed to a crawl and quickly settled down among the concealing trees on a comparatively dry knoll. After cutting the power, Lauren moved to the rear of the cabin and began assembling packs and equipment. The night was deep around them, and the sounds of nocturnal forest dwellers began to seep into the skimmer.

"We have to hurry," Flinx said anxiously. He was already unsnapping the door latches. "They're going to hurt her soon!"

"Hold it!" Lauren said sharply. "You don't know what's going to happen to her. More important, you don't know when."

"Soon!" he insisted. The door popped open and slid back into the transparent outer wall. He stared out into the forest in the direction he knew they must take even though he hadn't checked their location on the tracking screen.

"I promise that we'll get to her as fast as is feasible," Lauren assured him as she slipped the sling of the dart rifle over her shoulder, "but we won't do her or ourselves any good at all if we go charging blindly in on those people, whoever they are. Remember, they carried paralysis weapons on their vehicles. They may have more lethal weapons here. They're not going to sit idly by while you march in and demand the return of the woman they've gone to a helluva lot of trouble to haul across a continent. We'll get her back, Flinx, just as quickly as we can, but recklessness won't help us. Surely you know that. You're a city boy."

He winced at the "boy," but otherwise had to agree with her. With considerable effort he kept himself from dashing blindly into the black forest. Instead, he forced himself to the back of the skimmer and checked out the contents of the backpack she had assembled for him. "Don't I get a gun, too?"

"A fishing lodge isn't an armory, you know." She patted the rifle butt. "This is about all we keep around in the way of a portable weapon. Besides, I seem to recall you putting away an opponent bigger than yourself using only your own equipment."

Flinx glanced self-consciously down at his right boot. His prowess with a knife was not something he was particularly proud of, and he didn't like talking about it. "A stiletto's not much good over distance, and we may not have darkness for an ally."

"Have you ever handled a real hand weapon?" she asked him. "A needler? Beam thrower, projectile gun?"

"No, but I've seen them used, and I know how they work. It's not too hard to figure out that you point the business end at the person you're mad at and pull the trigger or depress the firing stud."

"Sometimes it's not quite that simple, Flinx." She tightened the belly strap of her backpack. "In any case, you'll have to make do with just your blade because there isn't anything else. And I'm not going to give you the dart rifle. I'm much more comfortable with it than you'd be. If you're worried about my determination to use it, you should know me better than that by now. I don't feel like being nice to these people. Kidnappers and wervil killers."

She checked their course on the tracker, entered it into her little compass, and led him from the cabin. The ground was comparatively dry, soft and springy underfoot.

As they marched behind twin search beams, Flinx once more found himself considering his companion. They had a number of important things in common besides independence. Love of animals, for example. Lauren's hair masked the side of her face from him but he felt he could see it, anyway.

Pip stirred on its master's shoulder as it sensed strange emotions welling up inside Flinx, emotions that were new to the minidrag and left it feeling not truly upset but decidedly ill at ease. It tried to slip farther beneath the protective jacket.

By the time they reached their destination, it was very near midnight. They hunkered down in a thick copse and stared between the trees. Flinx itched to continue, knowing that Mother Mastiff lay in uneasy sleep somewhere in the complex of buildings not far below. The common sense that had served him so well since infancy did more to hold him back than logic or reason.

To all appearances, the cluster of dimly lit structures resembled nothing so much as another hunting or fishing lodge, though much larger than the one that Lauren managed. In the center were the main lodge buildings, to the left the sleeping quarters for less wealthy guests, to the right the maintenance and storage sheds. Lauren studied the layout through the thumb-sized daynight binoculars. Her experienced eye detected something far more significant than the complex's deceptive layout.

"Those aren't logs," she told Flinx. "They're resinated plastics. Very nicely camouflaged, but there's no more wood in them than in my head. Same thing goes for the masonry and rockwork in the foundations."

"How can you tell?" he asked curiously.

She handed him the tiny viewing device. Flinx put it to his eyes, and it immediately adjusted itself to his different vision, changing light and sharpening focus.

"Look at the corner joints and the lines along the ground and ceilings," she told him. "They're much too regular, too precise. That's usually the result when someone tries to copy nature. The hand of the computer, or just man himself, always shows itself. The protrusions on the logs, the smooth concavities on the 'rocks'—there are too many obvious replications from one to the next.

"Oh, they'd fool anyone not attuned to such stuff, and certainly anyone flying over in an aircraft or skimmer. But the materials in those buildings are fake, which tells us that they were put here recently. Anyone building a lodge for long-term use in the lake country always uses native materials."

Closest to their position on the little hillside was a pair of long, narrow structures. One was dark; the other had several lights showing. Phosphorescent walkways drew narrow glowing lines between buildings.

To the right of the longhouses stood a hexagonal building, some three stories tall, made of plastic rock surmounted with more plastic paneling. Beyond it sprawled a large two-story structure whose purpose Flinx could easily divine from the tall doors fronting it and the single mudder parked outside: a hangar for servicing and protecting vehicles.

Nearby squatted a low edifice crowned with a coiffure of thin silvery cables. The power station wasn't large enough to conceal a fusion system. Probably a fuel cell complex, Flinx decided.

More puzzling was the absence of any kind of fence or other barrier. That was carrying verisimilitude a little too far, he thought. In the absence of any such wall, Flinx's attention, like Lauren's, was drawn to the peculiar central tower, the one structure that clearly had no place in a resort complex.

She examined it closely through the binoculars. "Lights on in there, too," she murmured. "Could be meant to pass as some kind of observation tower, or even a restaurant."

"Seems awfully small at the top for an eating room," he commented.

Searchlights probed the darkness between the buildings as the rest of the internal lights winked out. Another hour's wait in the damp, chilly bushes confirmed Lauren's suspicions about the mysterious tower. "There are six conical objects spaced around the roof," she told Flinx, pointing with a gloved hand. "At first, I thought they were searchlights, but not one of them has shown a light. What the devil could they be?"

Flinx had spotted them, too. "I think I recognize them now. Those are sparksound projectors."

She looked at him in surprise. "What's that? And how can you be sure that's what they are?"

He favored her with a wan smile. "I've had to avoid them before this. Each cone projects a wide, flat beam of high-intensity sound. Immobile objects don't register on the sensors, so it can be used to blanket a large area that includes buildings." He studied the tower intently.

"Just guessing from the angles at which the projectors are set, I'd say that their effective range stops about fifty meters out from the longhouses."

"That's not good," she muttered, trying to make out the invisible barrier though she knew that was impossible.

"It's worse than you think," he told her, "because the computer which monitors the beams is usually programmed automatically to disregard anything that doesn't conform to human proportions. The interruption of the sonic field by anything even faintly human will generate a graphic display on a viewscreen. Any guard watching the screen will be able to tell what's entered the protected area and decide on that basis whether or not to sound further alarm." He added apologetically, "Rich people are very fond of this system."

"When we didn't see a regular fence, I was afraid of something like this. Isn't there any way to circumvent it, Flinx? You said you've avoided such things in the past."

He nodded. "I've avoided them because there's no way to break the system. Not from the outside, anyway. I suppose we might be able to tunnel beneath it."

"How deep into the ground would the sound penetrate?"

"That's a problem," he replied. "Depends entirely on the power being fed to the projectors and the frequencies being generated. Maybe only a meter, or maybe a dozen. We could tunnel inside the camp and strike it without knowing we'd done so until we came up into a circle of guns. Even if we made it, we'd have another problem, because the beams probably cover the entire camp. We'd almost have to come up inside one of the buildings."

"It doesn't matter," she murmured, "because we don't have any tunneling equipment handy. I'm going to hazard a guess that if they have the surface monitored so intently, the sky in the immediate vicinity will be even more carefully covered."

"I'd bet on that, too." Flinx gestured toward the tower. "Of course, we could just run the skimmer in on them. There aren't that many buildings. Maybe we could find Mother Mastiff and get her out before they could react."

Lauren continued to study the complex. "There's nothing more expensive than a temporary facility fixed up to look permanent. I'd guess this setup supports between thirty and a hundred people.

They're not going to make this kind of effort to detect intruders without being damn ready to repel them as well. Remember, there are only two of us."

"Three," Flinx corrected her. A pleased hiss sounded from the vicinity of his shoulder.

"Surprise is worth a lot," Lauren went on. "Maybe ten, but no more than that. We won't do your mother any good as corpses. Keep in mind that no one else knows we're here. If we go down, so do her chances."

"I know the odds aren't good," he said irritably, "but we've got to do something."

"And do something we will. You remember that partially deforested section we flew over earlier today?"

Flinx thought a moment, then nodded.

"That was a trail line."

"Trail line for what?"

"For equalization," she told him. "For evening out the odds. For a better weapon than this." She patted the sling of the dart rifle. "Better even than that snake riding your shoulder. I don't share your confidence in it."

"You haven't seen Pip in action," he reminded her. "What kind of weapon are you talking about?"

She stood and brushed bark and dirt from her coveralls. "You'll see," she assured him, "but we have to be damn careful." She gazed toward the camp below. "I wish I could think of a better way, but I can't. They're sure to have guards posted in addition to monitoring the detection system you described. We don't even know which building your mother is in. If we're going to risk everything on one blind charge, it ought to be one hell of a charge.

"The weapon I have in mind is a volatile one. It can cut both ways, but I'd rather chance a danger I'm familiar with. Let's get back to the skimmer."

She pivoted and headed back through the forest. Flinx rose to join her, forcing himself away from the lights of the camp, which gleamed like so many reptilian eyes in the night, until the trees swallowed them up.

They were halfway back to the little grove where they had parked the skimmer when the sensation swept through him. As usual, it came as a complete surprise, but this time it was very different from his recent receptions. For one thing, no feeling of pain was attached to it, and for another, it did not come from the direction of the camp. It arose from an entirely new source. Oddly, it carried overtones of distress with it, though distress of a confusing kind.

It came from Lauren and was directed at him.

There was no love in it, no grand, heated follow-up to the casual kiss she had given him in the skimmer. Affection, yes, which was not what he had hoped for. Admiration, too, and something more. Something he had not expected from her: a great wave of concern for him, and to a lesser extent, of pity.

Flinx had become more adept at sorting out and identifying the emotions he received, and there was no mistaking those he was feeling now. That kiss, then, had not only carried no true love with it—it held even less than that. She felt sorry for him.

He tried to reject the feelings, not only from disappointment but out of embarrassment. This was worse than looking into someone's mind. He was reading her heart, not her thoughts. Though he tried hard, he could not shut off the flow. He could no more stop the river of emotion than he could willingly turn it on.

He made certain he stayed a step or two behind her so she would not be able to see his face in the darkness, still soaking up the waves of concern and sympathy that poured from her, wishing they might be something else, something more.

They hesitated before approaching the skimmer, circling the landing area once. The quick search revealed that their hiding place had remained inviolate. Once aboard, Lauren took the craft up. She did not head toward the camp; instead, she turned south and began to retrace their course over the treetops. Very soon they encountered the long, open gash in the woods. Lauren hovered above it for several minutes as she studied the ground, then decisively headed west. Flinx kept to himself, trying to shut the memory of that emotional deluge out of his mind. Then, quite unexpectedly, the open space in the trees came to a dead end.

"Damn," Lauren muttered. "Must have picked the wrong direction. I thought sure I read the surface right. Maybe it's the other way."

Flinx did not comment as she wheeled the skimmer around and headed southeast. When the pathway again ended in an unbroken wall of trees, she angrily wrenched the craft around a second time. This time when they encountered the forest wall, she slowed but continued westward, her gaze darting repeatedly from the darkened woods below to the skimmer's instrumentation.

"Maybe if you were a little more specific, I could help you look," he finally said, a touch of frustration in his voice.

"I told you. Weapons. Allies, actually. It comes to the same thing. No sign of them, though. They must have finished eating and entered semidormancy. That's how they live; do nothing but eat for several days in a row, then lie down to sleep it off for a week. The trouble is that once they've finished an eating period, they're apt to wander off in any direction until they find a sleep spot that pleases them. We haven't got the time to search the whole forest for the herd."

"Herd of what?" Flinx asked.

"Didn't I tell you? Devilopes."

Enlightenment came to Flinx. He had heard of Devilopes, even seen a small head or two mounted in large commercial buildings. But he had had no personal experience of them. Few citizens of Drallar did. There was not even one in the city zoo. As Flinx understood it, Devilopes were not zooable.

The Demichin Devilope was the dominant native life form on Moth. It was unusual for a herbivore to be the dominant life form, but excepting man, a fairly recent arrival, they had no natural enemies. They were comparatively scarce, as were the mounted heads Flinx had seen; the excessive cost of the taxidermy involved prevented all but the extremely wealthy from collecting Devilope.

The skimmer prowled the treetops, rising to clear occasional emergents topping ninety meters, dropping lower when the woods scaled more modest heights. Occasionally, Lauren would take them down to ground level, only to lift skyward again in disappointment when the omens proved unhelpful. There was no sign of a Devilope herd.

Meanwhile, another series of sensations swept through Flinx's active mind, and Pip stirred on his shoulder. He had continually tried to find Mother Mastiff's emotions, without success. Instead, his attempts seemed to be attracting the feelings of everyone but his mother-not. He wondered anew at his heightened perception since he had acquired his pet; though it was likely, he reminded himself that here in the vastness of the northern forests where minds were few and scattered, it might be only natural that his receptivity improved.

These latest sensations carried a female signature. They were also new, not of Mother Mastiff or Lauren. Cool and calm, they were vague and hard to define: whoever they belonged to was a particularly unemotional individual. He felt fear, slight but unmistakable, coupled with a formidable resolution that was cold, implacable—so hard and unyielding that it frightened Flinx almost as much as Mother Mastiff's own terror. Save for the slight overtones of fear, they might have been the emotions of a machine.

The feelings came from the camp where Mother Mastiff was being held. Flinx had little doubt that they belonged to one of those mysterious individuals who had abducted her. From the one brief, faint sensation he felt he could understand her fear. Then it was gone, having lasted less than a minute. Yet, in that time, Flinx had received a complete emotional picture of the person whose feelings he had latched onto. Never before had he encountered a mind so intent on a single purpose and so devoid of those usual emotional colorations that comprised common humanity. Pip hissed at the empty air as if ready to strike and defend its master.

"This isn't working," Lauren muttered, trying to see through the trees. "We'll have to—" She paused, frowning at him. "Are you all right? You've got the most peculiar expression on your face."

"I'm okay." The coldness was at last fading from his mind; evidently he hadn't been conscious of how completely it had possessed him. Her query snapped him back to immediacy, and he could feel anew the warmth of the skimmer's cabin, of his own body. Not for the first time did he find himself wondering if his unmanageable Talent might someday do him harm as well as good. "I was just thinking."

"You do a lot of that," she murmured. "Flinx, you're the funniest man I've ever met."

"You're not laughing."

"I didn't mean funny ha ha." She turned back to the controls. "I'm going to set us down. This skimmer really isn't equipped for the kind of night-tracking we're doing. Besides, I don't know about you, but it's late, and I'm worn out."

Flinx was exhausted too, mentally as much as physically. So he did not object as Lauren selected a stand of trees and set the skimmer down in their midst.

"I don't think we need to stand a watch," she said. "We're far enough from the camp so that no one's going to stumble in on us. I haven't seen any sign of aerial patrol." She was at the rear of the skimmer now, fluffing out the sleeping bags they had brought from the lodge.

Flinx sat quietly watching her. He had known a few girls—young women—back in Drallar. Inhabitants of the marketplace, like himself, students in the harsh school of the moment. He could never get interested in any of them, though a few showed more than casual interest in him. They were not, well, not serious. About life, and other matters.

Mother Mastiff repeatedly chided him about his attitude. "There's no reason for ye to be so standoffish, boy. You're no older than them." That was not true, of course, but he could not convince her of that.

Lauren was a citizen of another dimension entirely. She was an attractive, mature woman. A self-confident, thinking adult—which was how Flinx viewed himself, despite his age. She was already out of pants and shirt and slipping into the thin thermal cocoon of the sleeping bag.

"Well?" She blinked at him, pushed her hair away from her face. "Aren't you going to bed? Don't tell me you're not tired."

"I can hardly stand up," he admitted. Discarding his own clothing, he slipped into the sleeping bag next to hers. Lying there listening to the rhythmic patter of rain against the canopy, he strained toward her with his mind, seeking a hint, a suggestion of the emotions he so desperately wanted her to feel. Maddeningly, he could sense nothing at all.

The warmth of the sleeping bag and the cabin enveloped him, and he was acutely aware of the faint musky smell of the woman barely an arm's length away. He wanted to reach out to her; to touch that smooth, sun-darkened flesh; to caress the glistening ringlets of night that tumbled down the side of her head to cover cheek and neck and finally form a dark bulge against the bulwark of the sleeping bag. His hand trembled.

What do I do, he thought furiously. How do I begin this? Is there something special I should say first, or should I reach out now and speak later? How can I tell her what I'm feeling? I can receive. If only I could broadcast!

Pip lay curled into a hard, scaly knot near his feet in the bottom of the sleeping bag. Flinx slumped in on himself, tired and frustrated and helpless. What was there to do now? What could he possibly do except the expected?

A soft whisper reached him from the other sleeping bag. Black hair shuffled against itself. "Good night, Flinx." She turned to smile briefly at him, lighting up the cabin, then turned over and became still.

"Good night," he mumbled. The uncertain hand that was halfway out of his covering withdrew and clenched convulsively on the rim of the material.

Maybe this was best, he tried to tell himself. Adult though he believed himself to be, there were mysteries and passwords he was still unfamiliar with. Besides, there was that surge of pity and compassion he had detected in her. Admiring, reassuring, but not what he was hoping to feel from her. He wanted—had to have— something more than that.

The one thing he didn't need was another mother.

13

He said nothing when they rose the next morning, downed a quick breakfast of concentrates, and lifted once again into the murky sky. The sun was not quite up, though its cloud-diffused light brightened the treetops. They had to find Lauren's herd soon, he knew, because the skimmer's charge was running low and so were their options. He did not know how much time Mother Mastiff had left before the source of fear he had detected in her came to meet her.

Perhaps they had been hindered by the absence of daylight, or perhaps they had simply passed by the place, but this time they found the herd in minutes. Below the hovering skimmer they saw a multitude of small hills the color of obsidian. Black hair rippled in the morning breeze, thick and meter-long. Where one of the hills shifted in deep sleep, there was a flash of red like a ruby lost in a coal heap as an eye momentarily opened and closed.

Flinx counted more than fifty adults. Scattered among them were an equal number of adolescents and infants. All lay sprawled on their sides on the damp ground, shielded somewhat from the rain by the grove they had chosen as a resting place.

So these were the fabled Demichin Devilopes!—awesome and threatening even in their satiated sleep. Flinx's gaze settled on one immense male snoring away between two towering hardwoods. He guessed its length at ten meters, its height when erect at close to six. Had it been standing, a tall man could have walked beneath its belly and barely brushed the lower tips of the shaggy hair.

The downsloping, heavily muscled neck drooped from between a pair of immense humped shoulders to end in a nightmarish skull from which several horns protruded. Some Devilopes had as few as two horns, others as many as nine. The horns twisted and curled, though most ended by pointing forward; no two animals' horns grew in exactly the same way. Bony plates flared slightly outward from the horns to protect the eyes.

The forelegs were longer than the hind—unusual for so massive a mammal. This extreme fore musculature allowed a Devilope to push over a fully grown tree. That explained the devastated trail that marked their eating period. A herd would strip a section of forest bare, pushing down the evergreens to get at the tender branches and needles, even pulling off and consuming the bark of the main boles.

The Devilopes shifted in their sleep, kicking tree-sized legs.

"They'll sleep like this for days," Lauren explained as they circled slowly above the herd. "Until they get hungry again or unless something disturbs them. They don't even bother to post sentries. No predator in its right mind would attack a herd of sleeping Devilopes. There's always the danger they'd wake up."

Flinx stared at the ocean of Devilope. "What do we do with them?" Not to mention how, he thought.

"They can't be tamed, and they can't be driven," Lauren told him, "but sometimes you can draw them. We have to find a young mare in heat. The season's right." Her fingers moved over the controls, and the skimmer started to drop.

"We're going into *that*?" Flinx pointed toward the herd.

"Have to," she said. "There's no other way. It ought to be okay. They're asleep and unafraid."

"That's more than I can say," he muttered as the skimmer dipped into the trees. Lauren maneuvered it carefully, trying to break as few branches and make as little noise as possible. "What do we need with a mare in heat?"

"Musk oil and blood," Lauren explained as the skimmer gently touched down.

Up close, the herd was twice as impressive: a seething, rippling mass of shaggy black hair broken by isolated clumps of twisted, massive horns, it looked more like a landscape of hell than an assembly of temporarily inanimate herbivores. When Lauren killed the engine and popped open the cabin door, Flinx was assailed by a powerful odor and the steady sonority of the herd's breathing. Earth humming, he thought.

Lauren had the dart rifle out and ready as they approached the herd on foot. Flinx followed her and tried to pretend that the black cliffs that towered over them were basalt and not flesh.

"There." She pointed between a pair of slowly heaving bulks at a medium-sized animal. Picking her spot, she sighted the long barrel carefully before putting three darts behind the massive skull. The mare stirred, coughing once. Then the head, which had begun to rise, relaxed, slowly sinking back to the surface. Flinx and

Lauren held their breath, but the slight activity had failed to rouse any of their target's neighbors.

Lauren fearlessly strode between the two hulks that formed a living canyon and unslung her backpack next to the tranquilized mare. Before leaving the skimmer, she had extracted several objects from its stores. These she now methodically laid out in a row on the ground and set to work. Flinx watched with interest as knife and tools he didn't recognize did their work.

One container filled rapidly with blood. A second filled more rapidly with a green crystalline liquid. Lauren's face was screwed up like a knot, and as soon as the aroma of the green fluid reached Flinx, he knew why. The scent was as overpowering as anything his nostrils had ever encountered. Fortunately, the smell was not bad, merely overwhelming.

A loud, sharp grunt sounded from behind him. He turned, to find himself gazing in horrified fascination at a great crimson eye. An absurdly tiny black pupil floated in the center of that blood-red disk. Then the eyelid rolled like a curtain over the apparition. Flinx did not relax.

"Hurry up!" he called softly over his shoulder. "I think this one's waking up."

"We're not finished here yet," Lauren replied, stoppering the second bottle and setting to work with a low-power laser. "I have to close both wounds first."

"Let nature close them," he urged her, keeping an eye on the orb that had fixed blankly on him. The eyelid rippled, and he feared that the next time it opened, it would likely be to full awareness.

"You know me better than that," she said firmly. Flinx waited, screaming silently for her to hurry. Finally, she said, "That's done. We can go."

They hurried back through the bulwark of black hair. Flinx did not allow himself to relax until they sat once more inside the skimmer. He spent much of the time trying to soothe Pip; in response to its master's worry, it had developed a nervous twitch.

Despite the tight seal, the miasma rising from the green bottle nearly choked him. There was no odor from the container of blood.

"The green is the oil," she explained unnecessarily. "It's the rutting season."

"I can see what you have in mind to do with that," Flinx told her, "but why the blood?"

"Released in the open air, the concentrated oil would be enough to interest the males of the herd. We need to do more than just interest them. We need to drive them a little crazy. The only way to do that is to convince them that a ready female is in danger. The herd's females will respond to that, too." She set to work with the skimmer's simple store of chemicals.

"You ought to be around sometime when the males are awake and fighting," she said to him as she mixed oil, blood, and various catalysts in a sealed container. Flinx was watching the herd anxiously. "The whole forest shakes. Even the tallest trees tremble. When two of the big males connect with those skulls and horns, you can hear the sound of the collision echo for kilometers."

Five minutes later, she held a large flask up to the dim early-morning light. "There, that should do it. Pheromones and blood and a few other nose-ticklers. If this doesn't draw them, nothing will."

"They'll set off the alarm when they cross the sonic fence," he reminded her.

"Yes, but by that time they'll be so berserk, nothing will turn them. Then it won't matter what they set off." She smiled nastily, then hesitated at the thought. "My only concern is that we find your mother before they start in on the buildings."

"We'd better," Flinx said.

"There should be enough confusion," she went on, "to distract everyone's attention. Unless they're downright inhuman, the inhabitants of the camp aren't going to be thinking of much of anything beyond saving their own skins.

"As to getting your mother out fast, I think we can assume that she's not in the hangar area or the power station or that central tower. That leaves the two long structures off to the west. If we can get inside and get her out before whoever's in charge comes to his senses, we should be able to get away before anyone realizes what's happening.

"Remember, we'll be the only ones ready for what's going to happen. A lot will depend on how these people react. They're obviously not stupid, but I don't see how anyone could be adaptable enough to react calmly to what we're going to do to them. Besides, I don't have any better ideas."

Flinx shook his head. "Neither do I. I can see one difficulty, though. If we're going to convince this herd that they're chasing after an injured Devilope in heat, we're going to have to stay on the ground. I don't see them following the scent up in the air."

"Quite right, and we have to make our actions as believable as possible. That means hugging the surface. Not only would tree-level flight confuse the herd, air currents would carry the scent upward too quickly and dissipate it too fast."

"Then what happens," Flinx pressed on, "if this idea works and the herd does follow us back toward the camp and we hit a tree or stall or something?"

Lauren shrugged. "Can you climb?"

"There aren't many trees in Drallar free for the climbing," he told her, "but I've done a lot of climbing on the outsides of buildings."

"You'll find little difference," she assured him, "with the kind of motivation you'll have if the skimmer stalls. If something happens, head for the biggest tree you can find. I think they'll avoid the emergents. The smaller stuff they'll just ignore." She hesitated, stared sideways at him. "You want to wait a little while to think it over?"

"We're wasting time talking," he replied, knowing that every minute brought Mother Mastiff closer and closer to whatever fate her abductors had planned for her. "I'm ready if you are."

"I'm not ready," she said, "but I never will be, for this. So we might as well go." She settled into the pilot's chair and thumbed a control. The rear of the cabin's canopy swung upward.

"Climb into the back. When I give the word, you uncap the flask and pour out, oh, maybe a tenth of the contents. Then hold it out back, keep it open, and pour a tenth every time I say so. Got it?"

"Got it," he assured her with more confidence than he felt. "You just drive this thing and make sure we don't get into an argument with a tree."

"Don't worry about that." She gave him a last smile before turning to the control console.

The skimmer rose and turned, heading slowly back toward the somnolent herd. When they were just ten meters from the nearest animal, Lauren pivoted the craft and hovered, studying the scanner's display of the forest ahead.

Violent grunts and an occasional bleating sound began to issue from the herd as Flinx held the still tightly sealed flask over the stern of the skimmer. He looked around until he found a piece of thin cloth and tied it across his nose and mouth.

"I should have thought of that," she murmured, watching him. "Sorry."

"Don't you want one?" he asked.

She shook her head. "I'm up here, and the wind will carry the scent back away from me. I'll be all right. You ready?" Her hands tightened on the wheel.

"Ready," he said. "You ready, Pip?"

The flying snake said nothing; it did not even hiss in response. But Flinx could feel the coils tighten expectantly around his left arm and shoulder.

"Open and pour," she instructed him.

Flinx popped the seal on the flask as Lauren slowly edged the skimmer forward. Even with the improvised mask and a breeze to carry the aroma away from him, the odor was all but overpowering. His eyes watered as his nostrils rebelled. Somehow he kept his attention on the task at hand and slowly measured out a tenth of the liquid.

A violent, querulous bellow rose from several massive throats. As the skimmer slipped past a cathedral-like cluster of hardwoods, Flinx could see one huge male pushing itself erect. It seemed to dominate the forest even though the great trees rose high above. The metallic red eyes were fully open now, the tiny black pupils looking like holes in the crimson.

The Devilope shook its head from side to side, back and forth, and thundered. It took a step forward, then another. Behind it, the rest of the herd was rising, the initial uncertain bellowing turning to roars of desire and rage. A second male started forward in the wake of the first; then a third took up the long, ponderous stride. At this rate, Flinx thought, it would take them days to reach the camp.

But even as he watched and worried, the pace of the awakening herd began to increase. It took time for such massive animals to get going. Once they did, they ate up distance. Not long after, Flinx found himself wishing for the skimmer to accelerate, and accelerate again.

The herd was bearing down on the weaving, dodging craft. Lauren had to avoid even the smaller trees, which the herd ignored in its fury to locate the source of that pungent, electrifying odor. She turned to yell something to him, but he couldn't hear her anymore.

Trees whizzed by as Lauren somehow managed to increase their speed without running into anything. Behind them sounded a rising thunder as the noise of hundreds of hooves pulverizing the earth mixed with the crackle of snapping tree trunks and the moan of larger boles being torn from their roots.

Red eyes and horns were all Flinx could see as he poured another tenth of the herd-maddening liquid from the flask, drawing the thunder down on the fragile skimmer and its even more fragile cargo. . . .

There was nothing in the small operating theater that had not been thoroughly sanitized. Mother Mastiff had no strength left to fight with as they gently but firmly strapped her to the lukewarm table. Her curses and imprecations had been reduced to whimpered pleas, more reflex than anything else, for she had seen by now that nothing would dissuade these crazy people from their intentions. Eventually, she lost even the will to beg and contented herself with glaring tight-lipped at her tormentors.

Bright lights winked to life, blinding her. The tall black woman stood to the right of the table, checking a palm-sized circle of plastic. Mother Mastiff recognized the pressure syringe, and looked away from it.

Like her companions, Haithness wore a pale surgical gown and a mask that left only her eyes showing. Nyassa-lee plugged in the shears that would be used to depilate the subject's skull. Brora, who would execute the actual implantation, stood off to one side examining a readout on the display screen that hung just above and behind Mother Mastiff's head. Occasionally, he would glance down at a small table holding surgical instruments and several square transparent boxes frosted with cold. Inside the boxes were the microelectronic implants that he would place in the subject's skull.

A globular metal mass hung from the ceiling above the operating table, gleaming like a steel jellyfish. Wiry arms and tendrils radiated from its underside. They would supply power to attachments, suction through hosing, and supplementary service to any organs that exhibited signs of failure during the operation. There were microthin filament arms that could substitute for cerebral capillaries, tendrils that could fuse or excavate bone, and devices that could by-pass the lungs and provide oxygen directly to the blood.

"I'm ready to begin." Brora smiled thinly across at Nyassa-lee, who nodded. He looked to his other colleague. "Haithness?" She answered him with her eyes as she readied the syringe.

"A last instrument check, then," he murmured, turning his attention to the raised platform containing the microsurgical instruments. Overhead, the jellyfish hummed expectantly.

"Now that's funny." He paused, frowning. "Look here." Both

women leaned toward him. The instruments, the tiny boxes with their frozen contents, even the platform itself, seemed to be vibrating.

"Trouble over at power?" ventured Nyassa-lee. She glanced upward and saw that the central support globe was swaying slightly.

"I don't know. Surely if it was anything serious, we would have been told by now," Brora muttered. The vibration intensified. One of the probes tumbled from the holding table and clattered across the plastic floor. "It's getting worse, I think." A faint rumble reached them from somewhere outside. Brora thought it arose somewhere off to the west.

"Storm coming?" Nyassa-lee asked, frowning.

Brora shook his head. "Thunder wouldn't make the table shake, and Weather didn't say anything about an early storm watch. No quake, either. This region is seismically stable."

The thunder that continued to grow in their ears did not come down out of a distant sky but up out of the disturbed earth itself. Abruptly, the alarm system came to life all around the camp. The three surgeons stared in confusion at one another as the rumbling shook not only tables and instruments but the whole building.

The warning sirens howled mournfully. There came a ripping, tearing noise as something poured through the far end of the conference room, missing the surgery by an appreciable margin. It was visible only for seconds, though in that time it filled the entire chamber. Then it moved on, trailing sections of false log and plastic stone in its wake, letting in sky and mist and leaving behind a wide depression in the stelacrete foundation beneath the floor. Haithness had the best view as debris fell slowly from the roof to cover the mark: it was a footprint.

Nyassa-lee tore off her surgical mask and raced for the nearest doorway. Brora and Haithness were not far behind. At their departure, Mother Mastiff, who had quietly consigned that portion of herself that was independent to oblivion, suddenly found her voice again and began screaming for help.

Dust and insulation began to sift from the ceiling as the violent shaking and rumbling continued to echo around her. The multi-armed surgical sphere above the operating table was now swinging dangerously back and forth and threatening, with each successive vibration, to tear free of its mounting.

Mother Mastiff did not waste her energy in a futile attempt to break the straps that bound her. She knew her limits. Instead, she devoted her remaining strength to yelling at the top of her lungs.

As soon as they had entered the monitored border surrounding the camp, Lauren had accelerated and charged at dangerously high speed right past the central tower. Someone had had the presence of mind to respond to the frantic alarm siren by reaching for a weapon, but the hastily aimed and fired energy rifle missed well aft of the already fleeing skimmer.

At the same time, the wielder of the rifle had seen something flung from the rear of the intruder. He had flinched, and when no explosion had followed, leaned out of the third-story window to stare curiously at the broken glass and green-red liquid trickling down the side of the structure. He did not puzzle over it for very long because his attention—and that of his companions in the tower—was soon occupied by the black tidal wave that thundered out of the forest.

The frustrated, enraged herd concentrated all its attention on the strongest source of the infuriating odor. The central tower, which contained the main communications and defensive instrumentation for the encampment, was soon reduced to a mound of plastic and metal rubble.

Meanwhile, Lauren brought the skimmer around in a wide circle and set it down between the two long buildings on the west side of the camp. The camp personnel were too busy trying to escape into the forest and dodging massive horns and hoofs to wonder at the presence of the unfamiliar vehicle in their midst.

They had a fifty-fifty chance of picking the right building on the first try. As luck would have it, they chose correctly . . . no thanks, Flinx thought, to his resolutely unhelpful Talent.

The roof was already beginning to cave in on the operating theater when they finally reached that end of the building.

"Flinx, how'd ye—?" Mother Mastiff started to exclaim.

"How did he know how to find you?" Lauren finished for her as she started working on the restraining straps binding the older woman's right arm.

"No," Mother Mastiff corrected her, "I started to ask how he managed to get here without any money, I didn't think ye could go anywhere on Moth without money."

"I had a little, Mother." Flinx smiled down at her. She appeared unhurt, simply worn out from her ordeal of the past hectic, confusing days. "And I have other abilities, you know."

"Ah." She nodded somberly.

"No, not that," he corrected her. "You've forgotten that there are other ways to make use of things besides paying for them."

She laughed at that. The resounding cackle gladdened his heart. For an instant, it dominated the screams and the echoes of destruction that filled the air outside the building. The earth quivered beneath his feet.

"Yes, yes, ye were always good at helping yourself to whatever ye needed. Haven't I warned ye time enough against it? But I don't think now be the time to reprimand ye." She looked up at Lauren, who was having a tough time with the restraining straps.

"Now who," she inquired, her eyebrows rising, "be this one?"

"A friend," Flinx assured her. "Lauren, meet Mother Mastiff."

"Charmed, grandma." Lauren's teeth clenched as she fought with the recalcitrant restraints. "Damn magnetic catches built into the polyethylene." She glanced across to Flinx. "We may have to cut her loose."

"I know you'll handle it." Flinx turned and jogged toward the broken doorway, ducking just in time to avoid a section of roof brace as it crashed to the floor.

"Hey, where the hell do you think you're going?" Lauren shouted at him.

"I want some answers," he yelled back. "I still don't know what this is all about, and I'll be damned if I'm leaving here without trying to find out!"

"'Tis you, boy!" Mother Mastiff yelled after him. "They wanted to use me to influence you!" But he was already out of earshot.

Mother Mastiff laid her head back down and stared worriedly at the groaning ceiling. "That boy," she mumbled, "I don't know that he hasn't been more trouble than he's worth."

The upper restraint suddenly came loose with a click, and Lauren breathed a sigh of relief. She was as conscious as Mother Mastiff of the creaking, unsteady ceiling and the heavy mass of the surgical globe swaying like a pendulum over the operating table.

"I doubt you really mean that, woman," she said evenly, "and you ought to stop thinking of him as a boy." The two women exchanged a glance, old eyes shooting questions, young ones providing an eloquent reply.

Confident that Lauren would soon free Mother Mastiff, Flinx was able to let the rage that had been bottled up inside him for days finally surge to the fore. So powerful was the suddenly freed emotion that an alarmed Pip slid off its master's shoulder and followed anxiously above. The tiny triangular head darted in all directions in an attempt to locate the as-yet-unperceived source of Flinx's hate.

The fury boiling within him was barely under control. "They're not going to get away with what they've done," he told himself repeatedly. "They're not going to get away with it." He did not know what he was going to do if he confronted these still-unknown assailants, only that he had to do *something*. A month ago, he would never have considered going after so dangerous an enemy, but the past weeks had done much for his confidence.

The herd was beginning to lose some of its fury even as its members still hunted for the puzzling source of their discomfort. Females with young were the first to break away, retreating back into the forest. Then there were only the solitary males roaming the encampment, venting their frustration and anger on anything larger than a rock. Occasionally, Flinx passed the remains of those who had not succeeded in fleeing into the trees in time to avoid the rampaging Devilopes. There was rarely more than a red smear staining the ground.

He was heading for the hangar he and Lauren had identified from their hilltop. It was the logical final refuge. It didn't take long for him to reach the building. As he strode single-mindedly across the open grounds, it never occurred to him to wonder why none of the snorting, pawing Devilopes paused to turn and stomp him into the earth.

The large doorway fronting the hangar had been pushed aside. Flinx could see movement and hear faint commands. Without hesitation, he walked inside and saw a large transport skimmer being loaded with crates. The loading crew worked desperately under the direction of a small, elderly Oriental woman. Flinx just stood in the portal, staring. Now that he had located someone in a position of authority, he really didn't know what to do next. Anger and chaos had brought him to the place; there had been no room in his thoughts for reasoned preparation.

A tall black lady standing in the fore section of the skimmer stopped barking orders long enough to glance toward the doorway. Her eyes locked on his. Instead of hatred, Flinx found himself thinking that in her youth this must have been a strikingly beautiful woman. Cold, though. Both women, so cold. Her hair was nearly all gray, and so were her eyes.

"Haithness." A man rushed up behind her. "We haven't got time for daydreaming. We—"

She pointed with a shaky finger. Brora followed her finger and found himself gaping at a slim, youthful figure in the doorway. "That boy," Brora whispered. "Is it him?"

"Yes, but look higher, Brora. Up in the light."

The stocky man's gaze rose, and his air of interested detachment suddenly deserted him. His mouth dropped open. "Oh, my God," he exclaimed, "an Alaspinian minidrag."

"You see," Haithness murmured as she looked down at Flinx, regarding him as she would any other laboratory subject, "it explains so much." Around them, the sounds of the encampment being destroyed continued to dominate everyone else's attention.

Brora regained his composure. "It may, it may, but the boy may not even be aware that—"

Flinx strained to understand their mumblings, but there was too much noise behind him. "Where did you come from?" he shouted toward the skimmer. His new-found maturity quickly deserted him; suddenly, he was only a furious, frustrated adolescent. "Why did you kidnap my mother? I don't like you, you know. I don't like any of you. I want to know why you've done what you've done!"

"Be careful," Nyassa-lee called up to them. "Remember the subject's profile!" She hoped they were getting this upstairs.

"He's not dangerous, I tell you," Haithness insisted. "This demonstrates his harmlessness. If he was in command of himself, he'd be throwing more than childish queries at us by now."

"But the catalyst creature." Brora waved a hand toward the flying snake drifting above Flinx.

"We don't know that it's catalyzing anything," Haithness reminded him, "because we don't know what the boy's abilities are as yet. They are only potentials. The minidrag may be doing nothing for him because it has nothing to work with as yet, other than a damnable persistence and a preternatural talent for following a thin trail." She continued to examine the subject almost within their grasp. "I would give a great deal to learn how he came to be in possession of a minidrag."

Brora found himself licking his lips. "We failed with the mother. Maybe we should try taking the subject directly in spite of our experience with the girl."

"No," she argued. "We don't have the authority to take that kind of risk. Cruachan must be consulted first. It's his decision to make. The important thing is for us to get out of here now with our records and ourselves intact."

"I disagree." Brora continued to study the boy, fascinated by his calm. The subject appeared indifferent to the hoofed death that was devastating the encampment. "Our initial plan has failed. Now is the time for us to improvise. We should seize the opportunity."

"Even if it's our last opportunity?"

Flinx shouted at them. "What are you talking about? Why don't you answer me?"

Haithness turned and seemed about to reply when a vast groaning shook the hangar. Suddenly, its east wall bulged inward. There were screams of despair as the loading crew flung cargo in all directions and scattered, ignoring Nyassa-lee's entreaties.

They didn't scatter fast enough.

Walls and roof came crashing down, burying personnel, containers, and the big cargo skimmer. Three bull Devilopes pushed through the ruined wall as Flinx threw himself backward through the doorway. Metal, plastic, and flesh blended into a chaotic pulp beneath massive hoofs. Fragments of plastic flew through the air around Flinx. One nicked his shoulder.

Red eyes flashing, one of the bulls wheeled toward the single figure sprawled on the ground. The great head lowered.

Coincidence, luck, something more: whatever had protected Flinx from the attention of the herd until now abruptly vanished. The bull looming overhead was half insane with fury. Its intent was evident in its gaze: it planned to make Flinx into still another red stain on the earth.

Something so tiny it was not noticed swooped in front of that lowering skull and spat into one plate-sized red eye. The Devilope bull blinked once, twice against the painful intrusion. That was enough to drive the venom into its bloodstream. The monster opened its mouth and let out a frightening bellow as it pulled away from Flinx. It started to shake its head violently, ignoring the other two bulls, which continued to crush the remains of the hangar underfoot.

Flinx scrambled to his feet and raced from the scene of destruction, heading back toward the building where he had left Lauren and Mother Mastiff. Pip rejoined him, choosing to glide just above its master's head, temporarily disdaining its familiar perch.

Behind them, the Devilope's bellowing turned thick and soft. Then there was a crash as it sat down on its rump. It sat for several moments more before the huge front legs slipped out from under it. Very slowly, like an iceberg calving from a glacier, it fell over on its side. The eye that had taken Pip's venom was gone, leaving behind only an empty socket.

Breathing hard, Flinx rushed back into the building housing the surgery and nearly ran over the fleeing Lauren and Mother Mastiff. He embraced his mother briefly, intensely, then swung her left arm over his shoulder to give her support.

Lauren supported the old woman at her other shoulder and looked curiously at Flinx. "Did you find who you were looking for?"

"I think so," he told her. "Sennar and Soba are properly revenged. The Devilopes did it for them."

Lauren nodded as they emerged from the remains of the building. Outside, the earth-shaking had lessened.

"The herd's dispersing. They'll reform in the forest, wonder what came over them, and likely go back to sleep. As soon as they start doing that, this camp will begin filling up with those who managed to escape. We need to improve our transportation, and fast. Remember, there's nowhere near a full charge in the skimmer. You and I could walk it, but—"

"I can walk anywhere ye can," Mother Mastiff insisted. Her condition belied her bravado—if not for the support of Flinx and Lauren, she would not have been able to stand.

"It's all right, Mother," Flinx told her. "We'll find something."

They boarded their skimmer. Lauren rekeyed the ignition, removed to prevent potential escapees from absconding with their craft, and they cruised around the ruined building back into the heart of the camp.

Their fear of danger from survivors was unfounded. The few men and women who wandered out of their way were too stunned by the catastrophe to offer even a challenging question. The majority of them had been administrative or maintenance personnel, quite unaware of the importance of Flinx or Mother Mastiff.

The Devilopes were gone. The power station was hardly damaged, perhaps because it lay apart from the rest of the encampment, perhaps because it operated on automatic and did not offer the herd any living targets. None of the camp personnel materialized to challenge their use of the station's recharge facility, though Lauren kept a ready finger on the trigger of the dart rifle until a readout showed that the skimmer once again rode on full power.

"I don't think we have to worry about pursuit," she declared. "It doesn't look like there's anyone left to pursue. If the leaders of this bunch got caught in that trampled hangar as you say, Flinx, then we've nothing to worry about."

"I didn't get my answers," he muttered disappointedly. Then, louder, he said, "Let's get out of this place."

"Yes," Mother Mastiff agreed quickly. She looked imploringly at Lauren. "I be a city lady. The country life doesn't agree with me." She grinned her irrepressible grin, and Flinx knew she was going to be all right.

Lauren smiled and nudged the accelerator. The skimmer moved, lifting above the surrounding trees. They cruised over several disoriented, spent Devilopes and sped south as fast as the skimmer's engine could push them.

"I didn't learn what this was all about," Flinx continued to mutter from his seat near the rear of the cabin. "Do you know why they abducted you, Mother? What did they want with you?"

It was on her lips to tell him the tale the Meliorares had told her the previous night—was it only last night? Something made her hesitate. Natural caution, concern for him. A lifetime of experience that taught one not to blunder ahead and blurt out the first thing that comes to mind, no matter how true it might be. There were things she needed to learn, things he needed to learn. There would always be time.

"You've said 'tis a long story as to how ye managed to trace me, boy. My tale's a long one, too. As to what they wanted with me, 'tis enough for ye to know now that it involves an old, old crime I once participated in and a thirst for revenge that never dies. Ye can understand that."

"Yes, yes I can." He knew that Mother Mastiff had enjoyed a diverse and checkered youth. "You can tell me all about it after we're back home."

"Yes," she said, pleased that he had apparently accepted her explanation. "After we're safely back home." She looked toward the pilot's chair and saw Lauren gazing quizzically back at her.

Mother Mastiff put a finger to her lips. The other woman nodded, not fully understanding but sensitive enough to go along with the older woman's wishes.

14

Several hours passed. The air was smooth, the mist thin, the ride comfortable as the skimmer slipped southward. Mother Mastiff looked back toward the rear of the craft to see Flinx sound asleep. His useful if loathsome pet was, as usual, curled up close to the boy's head.

She studied the pilot. Pretty, hard, and self-contained, she decided. Night was beginning to settle over the forest speeding by below. Within the sealed canopy of the skimmer, it was warm and dry. "What be your interest in my boy?" she asked evenly.

"As a friend. I also had a personal debt to pay," Lauren explained. "Those people who abducted you slaughtered a couple of rare animals who were long-time companions of mine. 'Revenge never dies.'" She smiled. "You said that a while ago, remember?"

"How did ye encounter him?"

"He appeared at the lodge I manage on a lake near here."

"Ah! The fight, yes, I remember. So that place was yours."

"I just manage it. That's where I'm heading. I can help you arrange return passage to Drallar from there."

"How do ye know we're from the city?"

Lauren gestured with a thumb back toward the sleeping figure behind them. "He told me. He told me a lot."

"That's odd," Mother Mastiff commented. "He's not the talkative kind, that boy." She went quiet for a while, watching the forest slide past below. Flinx slept on, enjoying his first relaxed sleep in some time.

"'Tis an awful lot of trouble you've gone through on his behalf," she finally declared, "especially for a total stranger. Especially for one so young."

"Youth is relative," Lauren said. "Maybe he brought out the maternal instinct in me."

"Don't get profound with me, child," Mother Mastiff warned her, "nor sassy, either." Ironic, that last comment, though. Hadn't she once felt the same way about the boy many years ago? "I've watched ye, seen the way ye look at him. Do ye love him?"

"Love him?" Lauren's surprise was quite genuine. Then, seeing that Mother Mastiff was serious, she forced herself to respond solemnly. "Certainly not! At least, not in *that* way. I'm fond of him, sure. I respect him immensely for what he's managed to do on his own, and I also feel sorry for him. There is affection, certainly. But the kind of love you're talking about? Not a chance."

"'Youth is relative,'" Mother Mastiff taunted her gently. "One must be certain. I've seen much in my life, child. There's little that can surprise me, or at least so I thought until a few weeks ago." She cackled softly. "I'm glad to hear ye say this. Anything else could do harm to the boy."

"I would never do that," Lauren assured her. She glanced back at Flinx's sleeping form. "I'm going to drop you at the lodge. My assistant's name is Sal. I'll make some pretense of going in to arrange your transportation and talk to him. Then I'll take off across the lake. I think it will be better for him that way. I don't want to hurt him." She hesitated. "You don't think he'll do anything silly, like coming after me?"

Mother Mastiff considered thoughtfully, then shook her head. "He's just a little too sensible. He'll understand, I'm sure. As for me, I don't know what to say, child. You've been so helpful to him and to me."

" 'Revenge,' remember?" She grinned, the lights from the console glinting off her high cheekbones. "He's a funny one, your Flinx. I don't think I'll forget him."

"Ye know, child, 'tis peculiar," Mother Mastiff muttered as she gazed out into the clouds and mist, "but you're not the first person to say that."

"And I expect," Lauren added as she turned her attention back to her driving, "that I won't be the last, either."

The mudder circled the devastated encampment several times before leaving the cover of the forest and cruising among the ruined buildings. Eventually, it settled to ground near the stump of what had been a central tower.

The woman who stepped out was clad in a dark-green and brown camouflage suit, as was the man at the vehicle's controls. He kept the engine running as his companion marched a half-dozen meters toward the tower, stopped, and turned a slow circle, hands on hips. Then they both relaxed, recognizing that whatever had obliterated the installation no longer posed any threat. No discussion was necessary—they had worked together for a long time, and words had become superfluous.

The man killed the mudder's engine and exited to join his associate in surveying the wreckage. A light rain was falling. It did not soak them, for the camouflage suits repelled moisture. The field was temporary, but from what they could see of the encampment, they wouldn't be in the place long enough to have to recharge.

"I'm sick of opening packages, only to find smaller packages inside," the man said ruefully. "I'm sick of having every new avenue we take turn into a dead end." He gestured toward the destruction surrounding them; crumpled buildings, isolated wisps of smoke rising from piles of debris, slag where power had melted metal.

"Dead may be the right description, too, judging by the looks of things."

"Not necessarily." His companion only half heard him. She was staring at a wide depression near her feet. It was pointed at one end. A second, identical mark dented the ground several meters away, another an equal distance beyond. As she traced their progress, she saw that they formed a curving trail. She had not noticed them at first because they were filled with water.

She kicked in the side of the one nearest her boots. "Footprints," she said curtly.

"Hoof prints," the man corrected her. His gaze went to the mist-shrouded woods that surrounded the camp. "I wish I knew more about this backwater world."

"Don't criticize yourself. We didn't plan to spend so much time here. Besides, the urban center is pretty cosmopolitan."

"Yeah, and civilization stops at its outskirts. The rest of the planet's too primitive to rate a class. That's what's slowed us up from the beginning. Too many places to hide."

Her gaze swept the ruins. "Doesn't seem to have done them much good."

"No," he agreed. "I saw the bones on the way in, same as you did. I wonder if the poor monster died here, too?"

"Don't talk like that," she said uneasily. "You know how we're supposed to refer to him. You don't watch yourself, you'll put that in an official communiqué sometime and find yourself up for a formal reprimand."

"Ah, yes, I forgot," he murmured. "The disadvantaged child. Pardon me, Rose, but this whole business has been a lousy job from the beginning. You're right, though. I shouldn't single him out. It's not his fault. The contrary. He isn't responsible for what the Meliorares did to him."

"Right," the woman said. "Well, he'll soon be repaired."

"*If* he got away," her companion reminded her.

"Surely some of them did," the woman said.

The man pointed toward several long walls of rubble that might once have been buildings. "Speak of the devil."

A figure was headed toward them. It took longer than was necessary because it did not travel in a straight line. It attempted to, but every so often would stagger off to its right like a wheel with its bearings out. The man's clothes were filthy, his boots caked with mud. They had not been changed in several days. He waved weakly at the newcomers. Save for the limp with which he walked, he seemed intact. His stringy hair was soaked and plastered like wire to his face and head. He made no effort to brush it from his eyes.

He seemed indifferent to the identity of the new arrivals. His concerns were more prosaic. "Have you any food?"

"What happened here?" the woman asked him as soon as he had limped to within earshot.

"Have you any food? God knows there's plenty of water. That's all this miserable place has to offer is plenty of water. All you want even when you don't want it. I've been living on nuts and berries and what I've been able to salvage from the camp kitchen. Had to fight the scavengers for everything. Miserable, stinking hole."

"What happened here?" the woman repeated calmly. The man appeared to be in his late twenties. Too young, she knew, for him to be a member of the Meliorare's inner circle. Just an unlucky employee.

"Caster," he mumbled. "Name's Caster. Excuse me a minute." He slid down his crude, handmade crutch until he was sprawled on the damp earth. "Broke my ankle, I think. It hasn't healed too well. I need to have it set right." He winced, then looked up at them.

"Damned if I know. What happened here, I mean. One minute I was replacing communications modules, and the next all hell opened up. You should've seen 'em. Goddamn big as the tower, every one of 'em. Seemed like it, anyhow. Worst thing was those dish-sized bloody eyes with tiny little black specks lookin' down at you like a machine. Not decent, them eyes. I don't know what brought 'em down on us like they came, but it sure as hell wasn't a kind providence."

"Are you the only survivor?" the man asked.

"I haven't seen anyone else, if that's what you mean." His voice turned pleading. "Hey, have you got any food?"

"We can feed you," the woman said with a smile. "Listen, who were you working for here?"

"Bunch of scientists. Uppity bunch. Never talked to us ordinary folk." He forced a weak laugh. "Paid well, though. Keep your mouth shut and do your job and see the countryside. Just never expected the countryside to come visiting me. I've had it with this outfit. Ready to go home. They can keep their damn severance fee." A new thought occurred to him, and he squinted up at the couple standing over him.

"Hey, you mean you don't know who they were? Who are you people, anyway?"

They exchanged a glance; then the woman shrugged. "No harm in it. Maybe it'll help his memory."

She pulled a small plastic card from an inside pocket and showed it to the injured man. It was bright red. On it was printed a name, then her world of origin: Terra. The eyes of the man on the ground widened slightly at that. The series of letters which followed added confusion to his astonishment.

FLT-I-PC-MO. The first section he understood. It told him that this visitor was an autonomous agent, rank Inspector, of the Commonwealth law enforcement arm, the Peaceforcers.

"What does 'MO' stand for?" he asked.

"Moral Operations section," she told him, repocketing the ident. "These scientists you worked for—even though you had little or no personal contact with them, you must have seen them from time to time?"

"Sure. They kept pretty well to themselves, but I sometimes saw 'em strolling around."

"They were all quite elderly, weren't they?"

He frowned. "You know, I didn't think much about it, but yeah, I guess they were. Does that mean something?"

"It needn't trouble you," the man said soothingly. "You've said you haven't seen anyone else around since this horde of beasts overwhelmed you. That doesn't necessarily mean you're the only survivor. I assume some form of transportation was maintained for local use here. You didn't see anyone get away in a mudder or skimmer?"

The man on the ground thought a moment, and his face brightened. "Yeah, yeah I did. There was this old lady and a younger one—good-looking, the younger one. There was a kid with 'em. I didn't recognize 'em, but there were always people coming and going here."

"How old was the kid?" the woman asked him.

"Damned if I know. I was running like blazes in one direction, and their skimmer was headed in the other, so I didn't stop to ask questions. Kid had red hair, though. I remember that. Redheads seem scarce on this ball of dirt."

"A charmed life," the older man murmured to his companion. There was admiration as well as frustration in his voice. "The boy leads a charmed life."

"As you well know, there may be a lot more than charm involved," the woman said tersely. "The old woman he refers to is obviously the adopting parent, but who was the other?" She frowned, now worried.

"It doesn't matter," her companion said. He spoke to the injured man. "Look, how well do you remember the attitudes of this trio? I know you didn't have much time. This younger woman, the attractive one. Did she give the appearance of being in control of the other two? Did it seem as if she was holding the boy and old lady under guard?"

"I told you, I didn't get much of a look," Caster replied. "I didn't see any weapons showing, if that's what you're talking about."

"Interesting," the woman murmured. "They may have enlisted an ally. Another complication to contend with." She sighed. "Damn this case, anyway. If it didn't carry such a high priority with HQ I'd ask to be taken off."

"You know how far we'd get with a request like that," her companion snorted. "We'll get 'em. We've come so damn close so many times already. The odds have to catch up with us."

"Maybe. Remember your packages inside packages," she taunted him gently. "Still, it might be easy now." She waved at the ruined camp. "It doesn't look like many, if any, of the Meliorares got away."

"Melio—Meliorares?" The injured man gaped at them. "Hey, I know that name. Weren't they the—?" His eyes widened with realization. "Now wait a second, people, I didn't—"

"Take it easy," the man in the camouflage suit urged him. "Your surprise confirms your innocence. Besides, you're too young. They've taken in smarter folk than you down over the years."

"We shouldn't have that much trouble relocating the boy."

She was feeling confident now. "We should be able to pick them up at our leisure."

"I wish I were as sanguine," her associate murmured, chewing on his lower lip. "There's been nothing leisurely about this business from the start."

"I didn't know," the injured man was babbling. "I didn't know they were Meliorares. None of us did, none of us. I just answered an ad for a technician. No one ever said a word to any of us about—!"

"Take it easy, I told you," the older man snapped, disgusted at the other's reaction. People panic so easily, he thought. "We'll see that your leg is set properly, and there's food in the mudder. One thing, though: you'll have to undergo a truth scan. There's no harm in that, you know. And afterwards, it's likely you'll be released without being charged."

The man struggled to his feet, using his crutch as a prop. He had calmed down somewhat at the other's reassuring words. "They never said a word about anything like that."

"They never do," the woman commented. "That's how they've been able to escape custody for so many years. The gullible never ask questions."

"Meliorares. Hell," the man mumbled. "If I'd known—"

"If you'd known, then you'd never have taken their money and gone to work for them, right?"

"Of course not. I've got my principles."

"Sure you do." He waved a hand, forestalling the other man's imminent protest. "Excuse me, friend. I've developed a rather jaundiced view of humanity during the eight years I've spent in MO. Not your fault. Come on," he said to the woman named Rose, "there's nothing more for us here."

"Me, too? You're sure?" The younger man limped after them.

"Yeah, you, too," the Peaceforcer said. "You're sure you don't mind giving a deposition under scan? It's purely a voluntary procedure."

"Be glad to," the other said, eager to please. "Damn lousy Meliorares, taking in innocent workers like that. Hope you mindwipe every last one of 'em."

"There's food in back," the woman said evenly as they climbed into the mudder.

"It's strange," her companion remarked as they seated themselves, "how the local wildlife overran this place just in time to allow our quarry to flee. The histories of these children are full of such timely coincidences."

"I know," Rose said as the mudder's engine rose to a steady hum and the little vehicle slid forward into the forest. "Take this flying snake we've been told about. It's from where?"

"Alaspin, if the reports are accurate."

"That's right, Alaspin. If I remember my galographics correctly, that world's a fair number of parsecs from here. One hell of a co-incidence."

"But not impossible."

"It seems like nothing's impossible where these children are concerned. The sooner we take this one into custody and turn him over to the psychosurgeons, the better I'll like it. Give me a good clean deviant murder any time. This mutant-hunting gives me the shivers."

"He's not a mutant, Rose," her companion reminded her. "That's as inaccurate as me calling him a monster." He glanced toward the rear of the mudder. Their passenger was gobbling food from their stores and ignoring their conversation. "We don't even know that he possesses any special abilities. The last two we tracked down were insipidly normal."

"The Meliorares must have thought differently," Rose challenged. "They've gone to a lot of trouble to try and catch this one and look what's happened to them."

They were well into the forest now, heading south. The ruined camp was out of sight, swallowed up by trees and rolling terrain behind them.

"Some big native animals did them in," her companion said. "A maddened herd that had nothing whatsoever to do with the boy or any imagined abilities of his. So far, his trail shows only that he's the usual Meliorare disturbed youth. You worry too much, Rose."

"Yeah. I know. It's the nature of the business, Feodor."

But their concerns haunted them as night began to overtake the racing mudder.

The woman manning the communications console was very old, almost as old and shaky as the small starship itself, but her hands played the instrumentation with a confidence born of long experience, and her hearing was sharp enough for her to be certain she had not missed any portion of the broadcast. She looked up from her station into the face of the tall, solemn man standing next to her and shook her head slowly.

"I'm sorry, Dr. Cruachan, sir. They're not responding to any of our call signals. I can't even raise their tight-beam frequency any-more."

The tall man nodded slowly, reluctantly. "You know what this means?"

"Yes," she admitted, sadness tinging her voice. "Nyassalee, Haithness, Brora—all gone now. All those years." Her voice sank to a whisper.

"We can't be sure," Cruachan murmured. "Not one hundred percent. It's only that," he hesitated, "they ought to have responded by now, at least via the emergency unit."

"That stampede was terrible luck, sir."

"If it was bad luck," he said softly. "History shows that where the subject children are concerned, the unknown sometimes gives luck a push—or a violent shove."

"I know that, sir," the communicator said. She was tired, Cruachan knew; but then they were all tired. Time was running out for them and for the Meliorare Society as well as for its noble, much-misunderstood goals. There had been thoughts, years ago, of training new acolytes in the techniques and aims of genetic manipulation pioneered by the Society, but the onus under which they were forced to operate made the cooperation of foolish younger researchers impossible to obtain, thanks to the unrelenting barrage of slanderous propaganda propagated by the Church and the Commonwealth government.

Curse them all for the ignorant primitives they were! The Society was not dead yet!

Haithness, Nyassa-lee, Brora—the names were a dirge in his mind. If they were truly gone now, and it seemed that must be so, that left very few to carry on the Work. The conflict within him was strong. Should he press on or flee to set up operations elsewhere? So many old friends, colleagues, great scientific minds, lost; was this one subject worth it? They still had no proof that he was. Only graphs and figures to which the computers held. But the computers didn't care. Nobody cared.

There was nothing to indicate that the subject had been in any way responsible for the unfortunate stampede that had destroyed the camp together with their hopes. Of course, it was quite possible that the subject had perished along with the others, Cruachan mused. If not, if he decided to pursue this one to a conclusion, then there could be no more external manipulation attempted. They would have to confront the subject directly, as they had years ago tried to do with the girl.

It was a long, roundabout course to their next "safe" station. Cruachan was not at all confident of working through another several years of hiding and seeking out another promising subject. If the long arm of the Peaceforcers had not caught up with him by then, time and old age were liable to do the job for the government. They had come a long way together, he and his associates. A great effort; many lives had been expended to keep the project alive. He and his few remaining colleagues had to follow this case to its conclusion.

"Thank you, Amareth," he told the woman waiting patiently at the console. "Keep the receiver open just in case."

"Of course, Dr. Cruachan, sir."

Turning, he headed slowly toward Conference. Halfway there, his step picked up, his stride became more brisk. This won't do, he told himself. As president of the Society, it was incumbent upon him to set an example for the others, now more than ever. By the time he reached the meeting room and strode inside, his initial despair at the reports from below had been replaced by icy determination.

Half a dozen elderly men and women sat waiting for him. So few, he thought, so few left. The last of the Society, the last supporters of a great idea. Their upturned faces all silently asked the same question.

"Still no word," he said firmly. "We must therefore assume that doctors Brora, Haithness, and Nyassa-lee have been lost." There were no outward expressions of grief, no wails or cries. They waited expectantly for him to continue, and their quiet vote of confidence redoubled his resolve.

"I recommend that we proceed with the attempt to regain control of Number Twelve."

"We have reason to believe that MO operatives are now working in this region," an old woman said from the far side of the comfortable room.

"What of it?" another woman asked sharply. "They've always been two steps behind us, and they always will be."

"I wish I was as positive of that as you, Hanson," the first woman said. "The longevity of the Society is the result of foresight and caution, not contempt for those who hold us in contempt." She looked up at their leader. "You're sure about continuing to operate here, Cruachan?"

"More so than ever," he told her. "We have too much invested in this Number Twelve *not* to continue." He proceeded to recite the long list of factors responsible for his decision.

When he finished, a thin little man seated in the far corner of the room spoke out sharply in an incongruously deep voice. He had an artificial leg and heart, but the look in his eyes was as blindly intense as it had been fifty years earlier.

"I concur! The promise still lies here. If the subject is still accessible—"

"We have no reason to believe he is not," Cruachan half lied.

"—then we have a chance to get to him before the MO insects do. As Cruachan says, we must balance the potential here against our own intensifying infirmities." He kicked the floor with his false leg.

"Very well," said the old lady who had raised the specter of Commonwealth interference. "I see that most of you are of a mind to continue with our work here. I must confess that I cannot muster an argument against Dr. Cruachan's many good points. But we now have a new problem to overcome which will not be solved by a vote.

"Is it true that the last report from the camp places the subject in proximity to an Alaspinian miniature dragon?"

Cruachan nodded slowly. "The presence of the catalyst creature close to the subject was alluded to, yes."

"Then how are we to proceed? Besides acting as a magnifying lens for any latent Talent the subject may possess, this particular animal is deadly in and of itself. If it has formed an emotional bond with the subject, it will be a much more dangerous opponent than any dozen MO officers."

Cruachan waved her worries aside. "I've given the matter proper consideration. The snake will be taken care of, I promise you. If we cannot neutralize a mere reptile, then we have no business pretending to the ideals of our Society."

"It is not a reptile," a man near the back put in. He was glassy-eyed because of the thick contact lenses he was forced to wear. "It is reptilian in appearance, but warm blood flows in its veins, and it should more properly be classified as—"

"I don't give a damn what Order it fits into," Cruachan broke in impatiently. "The beast will be handled." His brows drew together at a sudden thought. "In fact, if such a mental bond now exists, it is likely stronger than that which ties the subject to his adoptive parent."

"Another chance for external control!" a woman exclaimed.

"Yes. Instead of presenting us with a new threat, it's possible this creature may be our key to subject control. So you all see how seeming difficulties may be turned to our advantage."

"Too bad about Haithness and the others," one of the old men murmured. "I'd known Haithness for forty-five years."

"So did I," Cruachan reminded him. "We must not let her and Nyassa-lee and Brora down. If, as now seems likely, they have sacrificed themselves for the cause, they provide us with still another reason to press onward. As we shrink in numbers, so must we grow in determination."

Murmurs of assent rose from around the conference room.

"We will not abandon this subject," Cruachan continued forcefully. "He will be brought under our wing by whatever means is required. I call for a formal vote for proceeding."

Cruachan was gratified to see the decision to continue confirmed unanimously. Such decisions usually were; dissent had no place in an organization bent to such a singular purpose.

"Thank you all," he said when the hands dropped. "Remember, this Number Twelve may hold the key to our vindication. We should proceed with that hope in mind. From this moment on, our entire energy will be devoted to gaining control over him." He turned toward the doorway.

"We have to hurry. If the MOs find him first, they will ruin him for our purposes."

The group dissolved in a rush of activity and fresh resolve that was matched in intensity only by the desperation that gave it life.

15

The city stank of human and other beings, of animals and exotic cooking, of resins and building materials old and new, all affected by the eternal dampness that permeated organic and inorganic materials alike. But it was all flowers and spice to Flinx. The transport car hissed to a halt outside the paneled exterior of the little bar and with the little credit remaining to him, he paid the machine. It responded with a mechanical "Thank you, sir" before drifting off up the street in search of its next fare.

Mother Mastiff leaned heavily against him as they made their way inside. Her ordeal had left her feeling her age, and she was very tired. So tired that she did not pull away from the snake riding high on Flinx's shoulder.

Once inside, Pip uncoiled from its perch beneath the slickertic Lauren Walder had provided and made a snakeline for the bar itself. This place he knew. On the counter ahead sat bowls of pretzels, tarmac nuts, and other interesting salty delicacies that were almost as much fun to play with as to eat.

Flinx had deliberately brought them back to the marketplace via a zigzag, roundabout course, changing transports frequently, trying until the last moment to travel with other citizens. Try as he might, he had been unable to see any indication that they had been followed, nor had the minidrag reacted negatively to any of the travelers who had looked askance at the exhausted youth and the old woman with him. Still, it was this caution that prompted them to visit this bar before returning to the shop. It would be wise not to go home alone, and Small Symm, the bar owner, would be good company to have around when they again set palm print to the front-door lock. To some degree his physical talents matched those of Flinx's mind.

As giants go, Small Symm was about average. He had been a friend of Flinx since the day of the boy's adoption. He often bought interesting utensils from Mother Mastiff for use in his establishment.

An enormous hand appeared and all but swept the two travelers into a booth. At the long metal bar, patrons nervously moved aside to allow the acrobatic flying snake plenty of access to the pretzels.

"I've heard," the young giant said by way of greeting, his voice an echo from deep within a cavernous chest, "that you were back. Word travels fast in the market."

"We're okay, Symm." Flinx favored his friend with a tired smile. "I feel like I could sleep for a year, but other than that, we're all right."

The giant pulled a table close to the booth and used it for a chair. "What can I get for the two of you? Something nice and hot to drink?"

"Not now, boy," Mother Mastiff said with a desultory wave of one wrinkled hand. "We're anxious to be home. 'Tis your good company we'd make use of, not your beverages." She turned quiet and let Flinx do the majority of the explaining.

Small Symm frowned, his brows coming together like clouds in the sky. "You think these people might still be after you?"

She almost started to say, "'Tis not me they're after," and just did manage to hold her tongue. She still believed it was too soon to reveal to Flinx everything she had learned. Much too soon. "Unlikely but possible, and I'm not the type to tempt fate, the unkind bastard."

"I understand." Symm stood, his head just clearing the ceiling. "You would like some friendly companionship on your way home."

"If you could spare the time," Flinx said gratefully. "I really believe that we're finished with these people." He did not explain that he thought they were all dead. No need to complicate matters. "But we'd sure be a lot more comfortable if you'd come with us while we checked out the shop."

"I'll be just a moment," Symm assured him. "Wait here." He vanished into a back room. When he returned, it was in the company of a tall young woman. He spoke softly to her for a minute, she nodding in response, then rejoined his visitors. He was wearing a slickertic not quite large enough to protect a medium-sized building.

"I'm ready," he told them. "Nakina will watch business until I return. Unless you'd rather rest a while longer."

"No, no." Mother Mastiff struggled to her feet. "I'll rest when I'm back home in my shop."

It was not far from Small Symm's place to the side street where

Mother Mastiff's stall was located. With Symm carrying her, they made good time.

"Seems empty," the giant commented as he gently set the old woman on her feet. It was evening. Most of the shops were already shuttered, perhaps because the rain was falling harder than usual. In the marketplace, weather was often the most profound of economic arbiters.

"I guess it's all right." Mother Mastiff stepped toward the front door.

"Wait a minute." Flinx put out an arm to hold her back. "Over there, to the left of the shop."

Symm and Mother Mastiff stared in the indicated direction. "I don't see anything," the giant said.

"I thought I saw movement." Flinx glanced down at Pip. The flying snake dozed peacefully beneath the cover of the slickertic. Of course, the snake's moods were often unpredictable, but his continued calm was a good sign. Flinx gestured to his right. The giant nodded and moved off like a huge shadow to conceal himself in the darkness next to the vacant shop off to the left. Flinx went to his right—to starboard, as Lauren might have said. It had taken him awhile to forgive her for leaving—and Mother Mastiff for letting her leave—while he was still sound asleep. He wondered what she was doing, yet the memory of her was already beginning to fade. It would take somewhat longer to escape his emotions.

Mother Mastiff waited and watched as friend and son moved off in opposite directions. She did not mind standing in the rain. It was Drallarian rain, which was different somehow from the rain that fell anywhere else in the universe.

Flinx crept warily along the damp plastic walls of the shop fronts, making his way toward the alley that meandered behind their home. If the movement he thought he had spied signified the presence of some scout awaiting their return, he did not want that individual reporting back to his superiors until Flinx had drained him of information.

There—movement again, and no mistaking it this time! It was moving away from him. He increased his pace, keeping to the darkest shadows. The stiletto that slept in his boot was in his right hand now, cold and familiar.

Then a cry in the darkness ahead and a looming, massive shape. Flinx rushed forward, ready to help even though it was unlikely the giant would need any assistance. Then something new, something unexpected.

Nervous laughter?

"Hello, Flinx-boy." In the dim light, Flinx made out the friendly face of their neighbor Arrapkha.

"Hello, yourself." Flinx put the stiletto back where it belonged. "You gave me reason to worry. I thought we were finished with shapes in the night."

"I gave *you* reason to worry?" The craftsman indicated the bulk of Small Symm standing behind him.

"I'm sorry," Symm said apologetically. "We couldn't see who you were."

"You know now." He looked back toward Flinx. "I've been watching your shop for you." Symm went to reassure Mother Mastiff. "You know, making sure no one broke in and tried to steal anything."

"That was good of you," Flinx said as they started back toward the street.

"It's good to see you back, Flinx-boy. I'd given you up not long after you left."

"Then why have you kept watching the shop?"

The older man grinned. "Couldn't stop hoping, I guess. What was it all about, anyway?"

"Something illegal that Mother Mastiff was involved in many years back," Flinx explained. "She didn't go into the details. Just told me that revenge was involved."

"Some people have long memories," Arrapkha said, nodding knowingly. "Since you have returned well and safe, I presume that you made a peace with the people who kidnapped your mother?"

"We concluded the business," Flinx said tersely.

They returned to the street, where Small Symm and Mother Mastiff waited to greet them.

"So it was you, Arrapkha. Ye ignorant fleurm, worrying us like that." She smiled. "Never thought I'd be glad to see ye, though."

"Nor I you," the woodworker confessed. He gestured toward Flinx. "That boy of yours is as persistent as he is foolhardy. I did my best to try and convince him not to go rushing off after you."

"I would have told him the same," she said, "and he would have ignored me, too. Headstrong, he be." She allowed herself a look of pardonable pride. Flinx was simply embarrassed. "And fortunate it is for me."

"Old acquaintances and bad business." Arrapkha waggled an admonishing finger at her. "Beware of old acquaintances and bad business and deeds left unresolved."

"Ah, yes." She changed the subject. "Been watching the old place for me, eh? Then I'd best check the stock carefully as soon as we're inside." They both laughed.

"If you think it's all right for me to leave," Small Symm murmured. "Nakina has a bad temper, and that's not good for business."

Mother Mastiff looked thoughtful. "If our friend here insists he's kept a close eye on the shop . . ."

"I've watched and watched," Arrapkha insisted. "Unless they've tunneled in, no one's gone inside since your boy left to look for you."

"No tunneling under these streets," she observed with a grin. "They'd hit the sewers." She looked back up at their escort. "Thank ye, Symm. Ye can run back to your lovely den of iniquity."

"It's hardly that," he replied modestly. "Someday if I work hard, perhaps."

Flinx extended a hand, which vanished in the giant's grasp. "My thanks, also, Symm."

"No trouble. Glad to help." The giant turned and lumbered away into the night.

The three friends moved to the front door. Mother Mastiff placed her right palm against the lock plate. It clicked immediately, and the door slid aside, admitting them. Flinx activated the lights, enabling them to see clearly that the stall area was apparently untouched. Stock remained where they had left it, gleaming and reassuringly familiar in the light.

"Looks to be the same as when I left," Mother Mastiff observed gratefully.

"Looks to be the same as it did ten years ago." Arrapkha shook his head slowly. "You don't change much, Mother Mastiff, and neither does some of your stock. I think you're too fond of certain pieces to sell them."

"There be nothing I'm too fond of not to sell," she shot back, "and my stock changes twice as fast as that pile of beetle-eaten garbage ye try to pass off on unsuspecting customers as handicrafts."

"Please, no fighting," Flinx implored them. "I'm tired of fighting."

"Fighting?" Arrapkha said, looking surprised.

"We're not fighting, boy," Mother Mastiff told him. "Don't ye know by now how old friends greet one another? By seeing who can top the other's insults." To show him that she meant what she said, she smiled fondly at Arrapkha. The woodworker wasn't a bad sort at all. Only a little slow.

The living quarters they found likewise untouched: in total chaos, exactly as Flinx had last seen it.

"Housekeeping," Mother Mastiff grumbled. "I've always hated housekeeping. Still, someone has to get this place cleaned up, and better me than ye, boy. Ye have no touch for domesticity, I fear."

"Not tonight, Mother." Flinx yawned. His initial sight of his own bed had expanded until it filled the whole room.

"No, not tonight, boy. I must confess to being just the slightest bit tired." Flinx smiled to himself. She was on the verge of physical collapse, quite ready to go to sleep wherever her body might fall, but she was damned if she would show weakness in front of Arrapkha lest it damage her image of invincibility.

"Tomorrow we'll put things to rights. I work better in the daytime, anyway." She tried not to look toward her own bedroom, waiting on Arrapkha.

"Well, then, I will leave you," the craftsman said. "Again, it's good to see you back and healthy. The street wasn't the same without you."

"We monuments are hard to get rid of," Mother Mastiff said. "Perhaps we'll see ye tomorrow."

"Perhaps," Arrapkha agreed. He turned and left them, making certain that the front door locked behind him.

Once outside, Arrapkha drew his slickertic tight around his head and shoulders as he hurried back to his own shop. He had no more intention of turning his friends over to the authorities, as he had been instructed, than he did of cutting the price of his stock fifty percent for some rich merchant. He would not hinder the police, but he would do nothing to assist them, either. He could always plead ignorance, for which he was famed in this part of the marketplace.

So tired; they looked so tired, he thought. It was the first time he could remember Mother Mastiff looking her age. Even the boy, who, though slight of build, had never before seemed exhausted by any labor, appeared completely worn out. Even that lethal pet that always rode his shoulder had looked tired.

Well, he would give them a few days to get their house in order and regain their strength. Then he would surprise them by taking them to Magrim's for some tea and tall sandwiches and would tell them of the mysterious visit of the two Peaceforcers to their little street. It would be interesting to see what Mother Mastiff would make of that. She might welcome the interest of the authorities in her case—and then again, she might not. Not knowing the details of her history, Arrapkha could not be sure, which was why he had elected not to help those offworld visitors.

Yes, he decided firmly. Wait a few days and let them rest up before springing that new information on them. No harm in that, surely. He opened the door to his own shop and shut it against the night and the rain.

One day passed, then another, and gradually the shop again assumed the appearance of home as the mess the kidnappers had made was cleaned up. Comfortable in such familiar surroundings, Mother Mastiff regained her strength rapidly. She was such a resilient old woman, Flinx thought with admiration. For his part, by the second day he was once again venturing out into his familiar haunts, greeting old friends, some of whom had heard of the incident and some of whom had not, but never straying far from the shop lest even at this late date and in spite of his beliefs some surviving members of the organization that had abducted Mother Mastiff return, still seeking their revenge.

Nothing materialized, however, to give any credence to such anxieties. By the third day, he had begun to relax mentally as well as physically. It was amazing, he thought, as he settled in that night, the things that one misses the most during a long absence. Odd how familiar and friendly one's own bed becomes when one has had to sleep elsewhere. . . .

It was the hate that woke Pip. Cold and harsh as the most brutal day winter could muster on the ice world of Tran-ky-ky, it shook the flying snake from a sound sleep. It was directed not at the minidrag but at its master.

Pink and blue coils slid soundlessly clear of the thermal blanket. Flinx slept on, unaware of his pet's activity. Several hours remained until sunrise.

Pip rested and analyzed. Examining the minidrag lying at the foot of the bed, an observer might have believed it to be a reasoning being. It was not, of course, but neither was its mental capacity inconsequential. Actually, no one was quite sure how the mind of the Alaspinian miniature dragon worked or what profound cogitations it might be capable of, since no xenobiologist dared get close enough to study it.

Blue and pink wings opened, pleats expanding, and with a gentle whirr the snake took to the air. It hovered high over its master's head, worried, searching, trying to pinpoint the source of the unre-

lenting malignancy that was poisoning its thoughts. The hate was
very near. Worse, it was familiar.

There was a curved roof vent that Pip had appropriated for its
own private comings and goings. The snake darted toward it, the
wings folding up at the last second to allow the slim body to slip
through the curving tube. Nothing much bigger than a mouse
could have slipped through that vent. With wings folded flat
against its muscular sides, the minidrag made the passage easily.

Pip emerged atop the roof into the light, early-morning rain. Up
that way the hate lay, to the north, up the alley. Wings unfolded and
fanned the air. The minidrag circled once above the shop, paused
to orient itself, then buzzed determinedly into the opening nearby
where the alley emerged into cloud-light.

It braked to a halt and hovered, hissing at the mental snarl that
had drawn it.

"Over here pretty, pretty," coaxed a voice. "You know who hates
your master, don't you? And you know what we'll do to him if we
get the chance."

The flying snake shot through the partly open doorway into the
hate-filled room beyond. Two humans awaited it with deadly calm.
Never would they have the chance to harm the minidrag's master.
Never!

A thin stream of venom spewed from the roof of the flying
snake's upper jaw and struck toward the nearest of the vicious
bipeds. It never reached the man. Something was between him and
Pip, something hard and transparent. The venom contacted it,
hissed in the still air as it started to eat at the transparent shield.
Startled, the two monsters seated behind the shield flinched and
began to rise.

But the door opening on the alley had already slammed shut behind the minidrag. Suddenly, a strange, sweet smell filled the
room. Wingbeats slackened and grew weak. Twin eyelids fluttered
and closed. The flying snake flopped about on the floor like a fish
out of water, wings beating futilely against the plastic as it gasped
for breath.

"Be careful," a distant voice warned. "We don't want to overdose
it. It's no good to us dead."

"I'd sooner see it dead and take our chances with the subject,"
another said.

"We need every hold we can manage, including the possibility
raised by this little devil."

The voices faded. Soon the flying snake had stopped moving.

Long minutes passed before a man dared to enter the sealed room. He was dressed head to toe in a protective suit. His eyes were anxious behind the transparent visor. With the long metal prod he carried he poked once, twice at the comatose minidrag. It jerked convulsively in response to the touches, but otherwise displayed no sign of life.

The man took a deep breath and set the long prod aside as he bent to pick up the thin body. It hung limply in his gloved hands as he inspected it.

"Still breathing," he declared to the people pressed close to the transparent wall.

"Good. Get it in the cage quick," said the shorter of the two observers. Her companion was studying the hole where the venom had finally eaten through the protective shield.

"I'd like to see a molecular breakdown on this stuff," he murmured, careful to keep his fingers clear of the still-sizzling edges of the ragged gap. "Anything that can eat through pancrylic this fast . . ." He shook his head in disbelief. "I don't see how the venom sacs can contain the stuff without dissolving right through the creature's jaw."

"You'd need a toxicologist and biochemist to explain it, if they could," said the woman standing next to him, likewise taking a moment to examine the hole. "Perhaps there's more to it than just a straightforward poison. The snake's mouth may hold several separate sacs whose contents mix only when it's spraying someone."

"Makes sense." The man turned away from the shield that had nearly failed them. "We better get moving. The subject may awaken any minute now. Be sure you keep the monster thoroughly narcotized."

"Is that necessary?" She frowned. "Surely the cage will hold it."

"That's what we thought about the wall. The cage is tougher, but we don't want to take any chances. I don't want our guest spitting his way free while we're asleep in our beds."

"No, we sure as hell don't." The woman shuddered slightly. "I'll take charge of it myself."

"I was hoping you'd say that." Cruachan smiled to himself. He was intimately familiar with the theories that attempted to explain the special bonds that could spring into being between a catalyst creature such as the minidrag and one of the Talented. Certainly the link that existed between this creature and the boy known as Number Twelve was as powerful as any of the imperfectly recorded cases he had studied. It was not unreasonable to suppose that it could be stronger than the affection bond between the boy and his adoptive mother.

They came at him without warning during his final period of REM sleep, when he was defenseless. They sprang into existence out of emptiness, laughing at him, tormenting him with feelings and sensations he could not define or understand.

Nightmares.

Someone was twisting a wire around his brain, compressing it tighter and tighter until it seemed certain that his eyes would explode out of his head and fly across the room. He lay in his bed, twitching slightly, his eyelids quivering, as they did their work on him and took advantage of his helpless, unconscious mind.

This batch was worse than most; twisting, abstract forms, dark swirling colors, and himself somehow in the middle of them all, racing down a long, ominous corridor. At the end of that corridor lay his salvation, he knew, and almost as important, answers. Understanding and safety.

But the faster he ran, the slower he advanced. The floor that was not a floor dissolved beneath his feet, dropping him like some relativistic Alice down a rabbit hole of space-time distortions, while the far end of the corridor and its promises of light and comprehension receded into the wastes overhead.

He woke up with a silent start and glanced rapidly around the room. Only after he convinced himself of its reality did he begin to relax.

It was the right room, his room, the one he had lived in most of his life: tiny, spartan, comfortable. The patter of morning rain was music on the roof, and faint daylight filtered through the window above his bed. He swung his legs out clear of the blanket and rubbed both throbbing eyes with his fingers.

The fingers abruptly ceased their ministrations, and he looked back to the bed. Something was wrong.

"Pip?" The flying snake was not coiled in its familiar position at the top of the pillow, nor was it underneath. Flinx pulled back the blanket, then bent to peer under the bed. "C'mon boy, don't hide from me this morning. I'm worn out, and my head is killing me."

There was no familiar hissing response to his confession. He prowled the room's meager confines, at first puzzled, then concerned. At last, he stood on the bed and shouted toward the air vent overhead.

"Pip, breakfast!"

No comforting hum of brightly hued wings reached him from beyond. He found a piece of wire and used it to probe the vent. It was clear to the outside.

He left his room and frantically started an inspection of the rest of the living quarters. Mother Mastiff stood by the convection stove, cooking something redolent of pepper and less exotic spices. "Something the matter, boy?"

"It's Pip." Flinx peered beneath recently righted furniture, moved bowls, and dropcloths.

"I gathered as much from the hollering ye were doing in your bedroom," she said sardonically. "Disappeared again, has he?"

"He never stays out through morning when he takes a solo night flight. Never."

"Always a first time, even for monsters," Mother Mastiff said, shrugging and concentrating on her cooking. "Wouldn't upset me if the little nastiness never did come back."

"Shame on you, Mother!" Flinx said, his tone agonized. "He saved my life, and probably yours, too."

"So I'm an ungrateful old Yax'm," she snorted. "Ye know my feelings toward your beast."

Flinx finished inspecting her room, then resolutely stormed back to his own and began dressing. "I'm going out to look for him."

Mother Mastiff frowned. "Breakfast ready soon. Why bother yourself, boy? Likely it'll be back soon enough, more's the pity. Besides, if it has got its slimy little self stuck someplace, you're not likely to find him."

"He could just be in the alley behind the shop," Flinx argued, "and I can hear him even when I can't see him."

"Suit yourself, boy."

"And don't wait breakfast on me."

"Think I'll starve meself on your account? Much less on account of some devil-wing." She had long ago given up arguing with him. When he made up his mind about something—well, one might as well wish for the planet's rings to be completed. He was a dutiful-enough son in most ways, but he simply refused to be restricted.

"It'll be here when ye get back," she said softly, checking the containers and lowering their ambient temperatures fifty degrees. "Ye can warm it up for your shiftless self."

"Thanks, Mother." Despite her contorting attempt to avoid him, he managed to plant a hurried kiss on one leathery cheek. She wiped at it, but not hard, as she watched him dash from the shop.

For an instant, she thought of telling him about what she had learned days ago up in the forest. About those strange Meliorare people and their intentions toward him. Then she shrugged the idea off. No, they were well clear of the horrid folk, and from the glimpse she had of their camp, they would not be bothering her boy ever again.

As to what she had learned of his history, it would be better to keep that secret for a few years yet. Knowing his stubborn impulsiveness, such information might send him running off in all sorts of dangerous directions. Much better not to say anything for a while. When he reached a reasonable age, twenty-three or so, she could let on what she had learned about his background. By then, he would have taken over management of the shop, perhaps married. Settled down some to a nice, sensible, quiet life.

She tasted the large pot, winced. Too little saxifrage. She reached for a small shaker.

"Pip! To me, boy!" Still no blue and pink flash enlivening the sky, still no rising hum. Now where would he get to? Flinx mused. He knew the minidrag was fond of the alley behind the shop. That was where he had first encountered the flying snake, after all, and to a snake's way of thinking, the alley was usually full of interesting things to eat. For all the minidrag's aerial agility, a box tumbling from the crest of a garbage heap or a rolling container could easily pin it to the ground. Flinx knew that no stranger was likely to get within ten meters of a trapped snake.

Might as well try the first, he decided. Slipping down the narrow space separating Mother Mastiff's shop from the vacant structure next to it, he soon found himself in the alleyway. It was damp and dark, its overall aspect dismal as usual.

He cupped his hands to his mouth, called out, "Pip?"

"Over here, boy," said a soft voice.

Flinx tensed, but his hand did not grab for the knife concealed in his boot. Too early. A glance showed that his retreat streetward was still unblocked, as was the section of alley behind him. Nor did the individual standing motionless beneath the archway in front of him look particularly threatening.

Flinx stood his ground and debated with himself, then finally asked, "If you know where my pet is, you can tell me just as easily from where you're standing, and I can hear you plainly from where *I'm* standing."

"I know where your pet is," the man admitted. His hair was entirely gray, Flinx noted. "I'll take you to it right now, if you wish."

Flinx stalled. "Is he all right? He hasn't gotten himself into some kind of trouble?"

The little man shook his head and smiled pleasantly. "No, he isn't in trouble, and he's just fine. He's sleeping, in fact."

"Then why can't you bring him out?" Flinx inquired. He continued to hold his position, ready to charge the man or race for the street as the situation dictated.

"Because I can't," the man said. "Really, I can't. I'm just following orders, you know."

"Whose orders?" Flinx asked suspiciously. Suddenly, events were becoming complicated again. The speaker's age and attitude abruptly impacted on him. "Are you with the people who abducted my mother? Because if you're trying to get revenge on her for whatever she was involved in years ago by harming me, it's not going to work."

"Take it easy, now," the man said. A voice Flinx could not hear whispered to the speaker from behind the door.

"For heaven's sake, Anders, don't get him excited!"

"I'm trying not to," the elderly speaker replied through clenched teeth. To Flinx he said more loudly, "No one wants to harm you or your pet, boy. You can have my word on that even if you don't think it's worth anything. My friends and I mean you and your pet only well." He did not respond to Flinx's brief allusion to his adoptive mother's past.

"Then if you mean us only well," Flinx said, "you won't object if I take a minute to go and reassure—"

The speaker took a step forward. "There's no need to disturb your parent, boy. In a moment she'll have her shop open and the crowd will ensure her safety, if that's what you're concerned about. Why alarm her needlessly? We just want to talk to you. Besides," he added darkly, taking a calculated risk, "you don't have any choice but to listen to me. Not if you want to see your pet alive again."

"It's only a pet snake." Flinx affected an air of indifference he didn't feel. "What if I refuse to go with you? There are plenty of other pets to be had."

The speaker shook his head slowly, his tone maddeningly knowledgeable. "Not like this one. That flying snake's a part of you, isn't it?"

"How do you know that?" Flinx asked. "How do you know how I feel about him?"

"Because despite what you may think of me right now," the

speaker said, feeling a little more confident, "I am wise in the ways of certain things. If you'll let me, I'll share that knowledge with you."

Flinx hesitated, torn between concern for Pip and a sense of foreboding that had nothing to do with his peculiar Talents. But the man was right: there was no choice. He wouldn't chance Pip's coming to harm even though he couldn't have said why.

"All right." He started toward the speaker. "I'll go with you. You'd better be telling the truth."

"About not wishing to harm you or your pet?" The smile grew wider. "I promise you that I am."

Try as he might, Flinx couldn't sense any inimical feelings emanating from the little man. Given the erratic nature of his abilities, that proved nothing—for all Flinx could tell, the man might be planning murder even as he stood there smiling. Up close, the speaker looked even less formidable. He was barely Flinx's height, and though not as ancient as Mother Mastiff, it was doubtful he would be much opposition in a hand-to-hand fight.

"This is my friend and associate Stanzel," the man said. An equally elderly woman stepped out of the shadows. She seemed tired but forced herself to stand straight and look determined.

"I don't want to hurt you, either, boy." She studied him with unabashed curiosity. "None of us do."

"So there are still more of you," Flinx murmured in confusion. "I don't *understand* all this. Why do you have to keep persecuting Mother Mastiff and me? And now Pip, too? Why?"

"Everything will be explained to you," the woman assured him, "if you'll just come with us." She gestured up the alley.

Flinx strode along between them, noting as he did so that neither of them appeared to be armed. That was a good sign but a puzzling one. His stiletto felt cold against his calf. He looked longingly back toward the shop. If only he could have told Mother Mastiff! But, he reminded himself, as long as he returned by bedtime, she wouldn't worry herself. She was used to his taking off on unannounced explorations.

"Mark me words," she would declaim repeatedly, "that curiosity of yours will be the death of ye!"

If it didn't involve striking against Mother Mastiff, though, then what did these people want with him? It was important to them, very important. If not, they wouldn't have risked an encounter with his deadly pet. Despite their age, he still feared them, if only for the fact that they had apparently managed to capture Pip, a feat beyond the capabilities of most.

But something, an attitude perhaps, marked these people as different from the usual run-of-the-mill marketplace cutthroats. They were different from any people he had ever encountered. Their coolness and indifference combined with their calm professionalism to frighten him.

The alley opened onto a side street, where an aircar waited. The old man unlocked it and gestured for him to enter. As Flinx started to step into the little cab, he experienced one of those mysterious, unannounced bursts of emotional insight. It was brief, so brief he was unsure he had actually felt it. It wiped out his own fear, leaving him more confused and uncertain than ever.

He might be afraid for Pip and perhaps even a little for himself, but for some unknown reason, these two outwardly relaxed, supremely confident individuals were utterly terrified of him!

16

Cruachan studied the readouts carefully. The section of the old warehouse in which they had established themselves was a poor substitute for the expensively outfitted installation they had laboriously constructed far to the north. He did not dwell on the loss. Years of disappointment had inured him to such setbacks. The machines surrounding him had been hastily assembled and linked together. Wiring was exposed everywhere, further evidence of haste and lack of time to install equipment properly. It would have to do, however.

He was not disappointed. In spite of all their problems, they appeared on the verge of accomplishing what they had intended to do on this world, albeit not in the manner originally planned. It seemed that the presence of the Alaspinian immigrant was going to turn to their advantage. For the first time since they had placed themselves in orbit around the world, he felt more than merely hopeful. His confidence came from Anders' and Stanzel's last report. The subject, accompanying them quietly, seemed reluctantly willing to cooperate, but had thus far displayed no sign of unexpected threatening abilities.

While a potentially lethal act, the taking of the subject's pet had turned out far more successful than the attempted adjustment of the subject's adoptive parent. Cruachan now conceded that that had been a mistake. If only their information had included mention of the catalyst creature in the first place! He did not blame the informant, though. It was likely that the minidrag came into the subject's possession subsequent to the filing of the informant's report.

He felt like an old tooth, cracked and worn down by overuse and age. But with the semisymbiotic pet now under their control, the subject would have to accede to their wishes. There could no longer be any consideration of attempting to influence the boy externally. They would have to implant the electronic synapses intended for his parent in the lad's own brain. Direct control posed some risks, but as far as Cruachan and his associates could see, they had no other choice. Cruachan was glad the case was nearing conclusion. He was very tired.

It was raining harder than usual for the season when the little air-car pulled up outside the warehouse. Flinx regarded the place with distaste. The section of Drallar out toward the shuttleport was bloated with stark, blocky monuments to bad business and over-consumption, peopled mostly with machines—dark, uninviting, and alien.

He had no thought of changing his mind, of making a break for the nearest side street or half-open doorway. Whoever these people were, they were not ignorant. They had correctly surmised the intensity of his feelings for Pip, which was why they had not bound him and carried no arms.

He still couldn't figure out what they wanted with him. If they were not lying to him and truly meant him no harm, then of what use could he be to them? If there was one thing he couldn't stand, it was unanswered questions. He wanted explanations almost as badly as he wanted to see Pip.

They seemed very sure of themselves. Of course, that no weapons were in evidence did not mean no weapons were around. He could not square their fear of him with the absence of arma-ment. Perhaps, he mused, they were afraid of him because they feared he might reveal what he knew of the kidnapping to the lo-cal authorities. Maybe that was what they wanted from him: a promise to remain silent.

But somehow that didn't make much sense, either.

"I wish you'd tell me what you want with me," he said aloud, "and what's going on."

"It's not our place to explain." The man glanced at his compan-ion and then said, as if unable to suppress his own curiosity, "Have you ever heard of the Meliorare Society?"

Flinx shook his head. "No. I know what the word means, though. What's it got to do with me?"

"Everything." He seemed on the verge of saying more, but the old woman shushed him.

The building they entered was surrounded by similarly nonde-script edifices. They were off the main shuttleport accessway. Flinx had seen only a few people about from the time they had entered the area. No one was in the dingy hallway.

They rode an elevator to the third floor. His escorts led him through broad, empty corridors, past high-ceilinged storage rooms filled with plasticine crates and drums. Finally, they halted before a small speaker set into the plastic of an unmarked door. Words were exchanged between Flinx's escort and someone on the other side, and the door opened to admit them.

He found himself in still another room crammed full of bundles and boxes. What set it apart from a dozen similar rooms was the right-hand wall. Stacked against it was an impressive array of electronics. Empty crates nearby hinted at recent and hasty unpacking and setup. The consoles were powered-up and manned. Their operators spared curious glances for the new arrivals before returning their attention to their equipment. Save for their uniformly grim expressions, they looked like retirees on a holiday outing.

Two people emerged from a door at the rear of the room. They were soon joined by a third—a tall, silver-haired, ruggedly handsome man. He carried himself like a born leader, and Flinx concentrated on him immediately. The man smiled down at Flinx. Even though he was close to Mother Mastiff's age, the man held himself straight. If he was subject to the infirmities of old age, he did a masterful job of concealing them. Vanity or will? Flinx wondered. He sought the man's emotions and drew the usual blank. Nor could he feel anything of Pip's presence in the room or nearby.

Even as the tall senior was shaking his hand and mouthing platitudes, Flinx was searching for the most likely escape route. There seemed to be only one exit: the door through which he had entered. He had no idea where the door at the far end of the room led, but suspected that freedom was not one of the possibilities.

"What a great pleasure to finally meet you, my boy," the old man was saying. His grip was firm. "We've gone to a great deal of trouble to arrive at this meeting. I would rather not have had to proceed in this fashion, but circumstances conspired to force my hand."

"It *was* you, then"—Flinx gestured at the others—"who were responsible for abducting my mother?"

Cruachan relaxed. There was no danger in this skinny, innocent boy. Whatever abilities he might possess remained dormant, awaiting proper instruction and development. Certainly his attitude was anything but threatening.

"I asked him," the man who had brought Flinx from the marketplace reported, "if he'd heard of the Society. He said no."

"No reason for him to," Cruachan observed. "His life has been restricted, his horizons limited."

Flinx ignored that appraisal of his limitations. "Where's Pip?"

"Your pet, I assume? Yes." The tall man turned and called out toward the rear doorway. The section of wall containing the door creaked as hidden winches pulled it aside. Beyond lay still another of the endless series of storage chambers, packed with the usual containers and drums and crates. On a table in the forefront stood a transparent cube, perhaps a meter square, topped with several small metal tanks. Hoses ran from the tanks into the cube.

To the left of the table stood a nervous-looking old man holding a small, flat control box. His thumb was pressed hard against one of the buttons set in the box. His eyes shifted regularly from the cube to Flinx and back to the cube.

Pip lay in the bottom of the cube, coiled into itself apparently deep in sleep. Flinx took a step forward. Cruachan put out a hand to hold him back.

"Your pet is resting comfortably. The air in the cage has been mixed with a mild soporific. Westhoff is regulating the mixture and flow of gases even as we speak. If you were to try anything foolish, he would increase the flow from the tanks before you could possibly free your pet. You see, the cage has been weld-sealed. There is no latch.

"The adjusted normal atmosphere inside the cube will be completely replaced by the narcoleptic gas, and your pet will be asphyxiated. It would not take long. All Westhoff has to do is press violently on the button his thumb is caressing. If necessary, he will throw his body across it. So you see, there is nothing you could do to prevent him from carrying out his assignment."

Flinx listened quietly even as he was gauging the distance between himself and the cage. The elderly man holding the control box gazed grimly back at him. Even if he could somehow avoid the hands that would surely reach out to restrain him, he did not see how he could open the cage and free Pip. His stiletto would be useless against the thick pancrylic.

"You've made your point," he said finally. "What do you want from me?"

"Redemption," Cruachan told him softly.

"I don't understand."

"You will eventually, I hope. For now, suffice for you to know that we are interested in your erratic but unarguable abilities: your Talent."

All Flinx's preconceived ideas collapsed like sand castles in a typhoon. "You mean you've gone through all this, kidnapping Mother Mastiff and now Pip, just because you're curious about *my* abilities?" He shook his head in disbelief. "I would have done my best to satisfy you without your having to go through all this trouble."

"It's not quite that simple. You might say one thing, even believe it, and then your mind might react otherwise."

Crazier and crazier, Flinx thought dazedly. "I don't know what the hell you're talking about."

"Just as well," Cruachan murmured. "You are an emotional telepath, is that not correct?"

"I'm sensitive sometimes to what other people are feeling, if that's what you mean," Flinx replied belligerently.

"Nothing else? No precognitive abilities? Telekinesis? True telepathy? Pyrokinesis? Dimensional perceptivity?"

Flinx laughed at him, the sound sharpened by the tension that filled the room. "I don't even know what those words mean except for telepathy. If by that you mean can I read other people's minds, no. Only sometimes their feelings. That other stuff, that's all fantasy, isn't it?"

"Not entirely," Cruachan replied softly, "not entirely. The potentials lie within every human mind, or so we of the Society believe. When awakened, further stimuli, provided through training and other means, can bring such abilities to full life. That was the—" He paused, his smile returning.

"As I said, someday you will understand everything, I hope. For now, it will be sufficient if you will permit us to run some tests on you. We wish to measure the probable limits of your Talent and test for other possible hidden abilities as yet undeveloped."

"What kinds of tests?" Flinx regarded the tall man warily.

"Nothing elaborate. Measurements, electroencephalotopography."

"That sounds elaborate to me."

"I assure you, there will be no discomfort. If you'll just come with me . . ." He put a fatherly hand on Flinx's shoulder. Flinx flinched. There should have been a snake there, not an unfamiliar hand.

Cruachan guided him toward the instruments. "I promise you, give us twenty-four hours and you'll have your pet restored to you unharmed, and you'll never have to go through this again."

"I don't know," Flinx told him. "I'm still not sure of what you want from me." It seemed to him that there was an awful lot of instrumentation around for just a few simple tests, and some of it looked almost familiar. Where had he seen that tendriled globe before?

Over a table in a room far to the north, he realized suddenly.

What do I do? he thought frantically. He could not lie down on that table, beneath those waiting tentacles. But if he hesitated, what might they do to Pip out of impatience and anger?

Unexpectedly, as his thoughts were tied in knots and he tried to decide what to do next, a sudden surge of emotion burst into his brain. There was hate and a little fear and a self-righteous anger that bordered on the paranoiac. He looked up at Cruachan. The older man smiled pleasantly down at him, then frowned as he saw the expression that had come over the subject's face. "Is something wrong?"

Flinx did not reply, methodically searching every face in the room. None of them seemed to be the source of the feelings he was receiving. And they were getting steadily stronger, more intense. They came—they came from—

He looked sharply toward the main entrance.

"Nobody move!" snapped a determined voice. The couple who burst through the door, having quietly circumvented the lock, were complete strangers to Flinx. A middle-aged pair dressed like off-world tourists, each holding a gun bigger than a pistol and longer than a rifle carefully balanced in both hands, they surveyed the startled occupants of the storage chamber.

Flinx did not recognize their weapons. That was unusual. His learning expeditions through the marketplace had made him familiar with most personal armament. But these were new to him. As new as this couple. They looked unrelentingly average. There was nothing average about the way they moved, however, or gave commands or held those peculiar guns. The Meliorares certainly seemed familiar with them.

"MO Section, Commonwealth Peaceforce," the man barked. "All of you are under government detention as of this moment." He grinned crookedly, almost savagely. "The charges against you, the specifics of which I'm sure you're all quite familiar with, are many and varied. I don't think I have to go into details."

Flinx started gratefully toward them. "I don't know how you people found me, but I'm sure glad to see you."

"Hold it right there." The woman shifted her weapon toward him. The expression on her face assured Flinx she was ready to shoot him if he took so much as another half step toward her. He froze, hurt and confused.

There was something new there, partly in her eyes but also in her mind: not so much fear as a kind of twisted hatred, a loathing. The emotion was directed squarely at him. It was so new, so alien and sickening, that he didn't know how to react. He knew only that his would-be saviors held no more affection for him, and perhaps even less in the way of good intentions, than this insane society of Meliorare people.

His confusion was being replaced by anger, a frantic fury born of frustration and despair, compounded by helplessness and desperation. Through no fault of his own, desiring only to be left alone, he had become the focal point of forces beyond his control, forces that extended even beyond his world. And he didn't know how, couldn't begin to think how to deal with them.

Through all the confusion came one lucid realization: he wasn't as grown-up as he had thought.

Near the back room the man named Westhoff had gone unnoticed by the Peaceforcers. He did not linger. Putting aside the control box he commenced a cautious retreat, utilizing crates and containers to make good his escape.

Pressure removed, the button he had been holding down rebounded.

"Over against that empty packing and away from the consoles. All of you," the woman commanded them, gesturing meaningfully with her gun. Rising from their seats and showing empty hands, the Meliorares hurried to comply with her order.

"Anybody touches a switch," the other Peaceforcer warned them, "it'll be the last thing he ever touches."

The woman threw Flinx a hard look. "Hey, you too. Move it." Revulsion emanated from her. Disgust and pity washed over Flinx in waves. She was broadcasting them all. Flinx tried to squeeze the degrading emotions out of his mind.

"I'm not with them," he protested. "I'm not part of this."

"I'm afraid that you are, boy, whether you like it or not," she told him. "You've caused a lot of trouble. But don't worry." She tried to smile. The result was a discomfiting parody. "Everything's going to be all right. You're going to be fixed up so you can live a normal life."

A buzzer suddenly roared to life on one of the unattended consoles, filling the room with insistent discordance. Cruachan stared dumbly at it, then at Flinx, then at the Peaceforcers.

"For heaven's sake, don't threaten him!"

"Threaten me?" Flinx was almost crying now, ignoring Cruachan's sudden terror, the buzzing, everything, as he spoke to the female Peaceforcer. "What does he mean, threaten me? What did you mean when you said you're going to have me fixed up? I'm *fine.*"

"Maybe you are, and maybe you aren't," she replied, "but these *Meliorares,*" she spat the word out, "seem to think otherwise. That's good enough for me. I'm no specialist. They're the ones who'll decide what's to be done with you."

"And the sooner the better," her companion added. "Did you call for backup?"

"As soon as we were sure." She nodded. "It'll take them a few minutes to get here. This isn't Brizzy, you know."

Flinx felt unsteady on his feet as well as in his mind. Where he had expected rescue, there was only new hurt, fresh indifference. No, worse than indifference, for these people saw him only as some kind of deformed, unhealthy creature. There was no understanding for him here in this room, not from his ancient persecutors or these new arrivals. The universe, as represented by organizations illegal and legitimate, seemed wholly against him.

Fixed, the woman had said. He was going to be *fixed.* But there was nothing wrong with him. Nothing! Why do they want to do these unnameable things to me? he thought angrily.

The pain and confusion produced results unnoticed by the anxious antagonists facing each other across the floor. Prodded by the powerful emotions emanating from his master, half-awakened by the thinning quantity of soporific gas entering its cage, the flying snake awoke. It did not need to search visually for Flinx—his outburst of hurt was a screaming beacon marking his location.

The snake's wings remained folded as it quickly examined its prison. Then it rose up and spat. In the confused babble that filled the opposite end of the room, the quiet hissing of dissolving pancrylic went unnoticed.

"Let's get them outside." The male Peaceforcer moved to his right, separating from his companion to stand to one side of the entrance while she moved to get behind the shifting group gathered in the middle of the room.

"Single file now," she ordered them, gesturing with her gun. "All of you. And please keep your hands in the air. No dramatic last-minute gestures, please. I don't like a mess."

Cruachan pleaded with her. "Please, we're just a bunch of harmless old scholars. This is our last chance. This boy"—and he indicated Flinx—"may be our last opportunity to prove—"

"I've studied your history, read the reports." The woman's voice was icy. "What you did is beyond redemption or forgiving. You'll get just what you deserve, and it won't be a chance to experiment further on this poor, malformed child."

"Please, somebody," Flinx said desperately, "I don't know what you're talking about! Won't somebody tell me—?"

"Somebody probably will," she told him. "I'm not privy to the details, and explanations aren't my department." She shuddered visibly. "Fortunately."

"Rose, look out!" At the warning cry from her companion, the woman whirled. There was something in the air, humming like a giant bumblebee, moving rapidly from place to place: a pink and blue blur against the ceiling.

"What the hell's that?" she blurted.

Flinx started to answer, but Cruachan spoke first, taking a step out of the line and toward the Peaceforcer. "That's the boy's pet. I don't know how it got out. It's dangerous."

"Oh, it is, is it?" The muzzle of the short rifle came up.

"No!" Cruachan rushed toward her, the console buzzer screaming in his ears. "Don't!"

The Peaceforcer reacted instinctively to the unexpected charge. A brief burst of high-intensity sound struck the leader of the Meliorares. His stomach exploded through his spine. No sound had come from the gun. There had been only a slight punching noise when the burst had struck home.

One of the elderly women screamed. The Peaceforcer cursed her overanxiousness and took aim at the source of her embarrassment. As she pointed her weapon at Pip, all the fury and pain and anguish crashed together inside Flinx's head.

"Pip! No!" he yelled, rushing the woman. The other Peaceforcer moved to cover his companion. Pip darted toward the rear of the storage room. The woman's gun tracked the minidrag as her finger started to tighten on the trigger.

Something happened. Cruachan's eyes were still open. A smile of satisfaction appeared on his face. Then he died.

Night descended unexpectedly.

Flinx was floating inside a giant bass drum. Someone was pounding on it from both sides. The rhythm was erratic, the sound soul-deafening. It hurt.

Something was resting on his chest. I am lying on my back, he thought. He raised his head to look down at himself. Pip lay on the slickertic, bruised but alive. The flying snake looked dazed. As consciousness returned with a vengeance, the narrow tongue darted out repeatedly to touch Flinx's lips and nose. Content, the minidrag ceased its examination and crawled from chest to shoulder. Flinx fought to sit up.

There was something wrong with his balance. It made the simple act of changing from a prone to a sitting position into a major operation. Two things he noted immediately; it was cold, and rain was soaking his face. Then his vision cleared and he saw the old man bending over him.

For an instant the fear returned, but this was no Meliorare. It was a kindly, unfamiliar face. The oldster was dressed very differently from the Society members. There hadn't been anything shabby about their attire. This stranger was a refugee from a simpler life.

"Are you all right, boy?" He looked over his shoulder. "I think he's all right."

Flinx looked past the old man. Several other strangers were gathered behind him. It occurred to Flinx that he was the center of their concerned curiosity. Strong arms reached toward him and helped him to his feet. There were comments about the flying snake riding his shoulder.

A younger man stepped forward. "You okay?" He searched Flinx's face. "I've had a little medical training."

"I'm not—I think—" Funny, his mouth wasn't working right. He swallowed. "What happened?"

"You tell me," said the unsmiling young man. He was dressed neatly, much more so than the oldster who had first examined Flinx. A yellow-and-green-striped slickertic covered what Flinx could see of a brightly colored business suit.

"I'm a factotum for the Subhouse of Grandier. I was just coming down to check on the arrival of a recent shipment from Evoria." He turned and pointed. "That's our warehouse over there. I nearly tripped over you."

"Me, too," the oldster said, "though I'm no factotum for anybody 'cept my own house." He grinned, showing missing teeth.

Flinx brushed wet strands of hair from his eyes and forehead. How had he gotten so wet? He couldn't remember lying down in the street. He couldn't remember lying down at all.

Now that those around him had quieted, the roar that had filled his ears since he had regained consciousness assumed deafening proportions. Sirens sounded in counterpart.

A couple of blocks away, flames shot skyward from the top of a warehouse in defiance of the steady, light rain. A fire-control skimmer hovered off to one side, its crew spraying the flames with fire-retardant chemical foam. It combined with the rain to knock the blaze back into itself.

"Anyway," the younger man next to Flinx continued as they both watched the dying inferno, "I was just entering our office over there when that building"—he nodded toward the flames—"blew up. If I remember aright, it was four or five stories tall. There are only two left, as you can see. Top three must've been incinerated in the first seconds. There's charred debris all over the streets. Knocked me right off my feet, just like you." Flinx's gaze roved over the crowd that had gathered to watch the unusual sight. Large fires were rare in Drallar.

"Somebody's let themselves in for a nest o' trouble," the oldster muttered. "Storing explosives or volatiles inside the city limits. Bad business. Bad."

"Someone told me they felt it all the way to the inurbs," the younger man said conversationally. "I wonder what the devil was stored in there to cause an explosion like that? Piece of building went past me like a shot. It's stuck in our front door, no less, if you want to see it. As I was getting up, I saw you lying there in the street. Either something mercifully small hit you or else you got knocked out when your head hit the pavement."

"I didn't see him get hit," the oldster said.

"Doesn't mean anything, as fast as stuff was flying." The executive looked at Flinx. "I'll bet you never even felt it."

"No," Flinx admitted, still terribly confused. "I didn't. But I'm okay now."

"You're sure?" The man looked him over. "Funny. Whatever it was that knocked you down must have whizzed right past. I don't see any bruises or cuts, though it looks like your pet got a little banged up."

"Can do you like that," the oldster said. " 'Nother centimeter and maybe you'd have a piece of metal sticking out of your head. Conversation piece." He chuckled.

Flinx managed a weak grin. "I feel all right now." He swayed a moment, then held steady.

The executive was still studying the minidrag coiled around Flinx's left shoulder. "That's an interesting pet, all right."

"Everybody thinks so. Thanks for your concern, both of you." He staggered forward and joined the ring of spectators gawking at the obliterated building.

Slowly, reluctantly, his brain filled in the blank spaces pockmarking his memory. Third floor, he'd been up there, and the

Meliorares . . . Yes, the Meliorares—that was their name—were getting ready to run some tests on him. Then the Peaceforcers had broken in, and Pip had gotten loose, and one of them had been ready to shoot it, and the head Meliorare—Flinx couldn't remember his name, only his eyes—had panicked and rushed the Peaceforcer, and Flinx remembered screaming desperately for the woman not to fire, not to hurt Pip, not to, not to—!

Then he had awakened, soaked and stunned in the street, an old man bending solicitously over him and Pip licking his mouth.

His hand went to the back of his head, which throbbed like the drum he had dreamed of being imprisoned inside. There was no lump there, no blood, but it sure felt like something had whacked him good, just as the executive had surmised. Only the pain seemed concentrated *inside* his head.

People were emerging from the burning warehouse: medical personnel in white slickertics. They were escorting someone between them. The woman's clothes were shredded, and blood filled the gaps. Though she walked under her own power, it took two medics to guide her.

Suddenly, Flinx could feel her, for just an instant. But there was no emotion there, no emotion or feelings of any kind. Then he noticed her eyes. Her stare was vacant, blank, without motivation. Probably the explosion had stunned her, he thought. She was the Peaceforcer who had been about to shoot Pip.

In a hospital that blankness would doubtless wear off, he thought. Though it was almost as if she had been mindwiped, and not selectively, either. She looked like a walking husk of a human being. Flinx turned away from her, uncomfortable without really knowing why, as she was put in a hospital skimmer. The vehicle rose above the crowd and headed downtown, siren screaming.

Still he fought to reconstruct those last seconds in the warehouse. What *had* happened? That unfortunate woman had been about to kill Pip. Flinx had started toward her, protesting frantically, and her companion had started to aim his own weapon at him. The weapons themselves functioned noiselessly. Had the woman fired? Had the man?

The instrumentation that had filled the storage chamber required a lot of power. If the Peaceforcer had missed Flinx, perhaps deliberately firing a warning shot, the bolt might have struck something equally sensitive but far more volatile than human flesh. As a rule, warehouses did not draw much power. There might have been delicately attuned fuel cells in the room. The shot might have set them off.

Or had one of the Meliorares—perhaps the one who had fled from Pip's cage—set off some kind of suicide device to keep his colleagues from the disgrace of an official trial? He felt much better as he considered both reasonable explanations. They fit what had happened, were very plausible.

The only thing they failed to explain was how he had landed two blocks away, apparently unhurt except for a raging headache.

Well, he *had* been moving toward the door, and explosions could do funny things. The streets of the industrial district were notorious for their potholes, which were usually full of rain water. And he was soaked. Could the force of the explosion have thrown him into one deep enough to cushion his fall and cause him to skip out again like a stone on a pond? Obviously, that was what had happened. There was no other possible explanation.

His head hurt.

Local gendarmes were finally beginning to show up. At their arrival Flinx instinctively turned away, leaving the crowd behind and cradling Pip beneath his slickertic. He was glad that he hadn't been forced to use his own knife, felt lucky to be alive. Maybe now, at last, external forces would leave him and Mother Mastiff and Pip in peace.

He thought back a last time to that final instant in the warehouse. The rage and desperation had built up in him until he had been unable to stand it any longer and had charged blindly at the Peaceforcer about to kill Pip. He hoped he would never be that angry again in his life.

The crowd ignored the boy as he fled the scene; he vanished into the comforting shadows and narrow alleys that filtered back toward the central city. There was nothing remarkable about him and no reason for the gendarmes to stop and question him. The old man and the executive who had found him lying in the street had already forgotten him, engrossed in the unusual sight of a major fire in perpetually damp Drallar.

Flinx made his way back toward the more animated sections of the city, toward the arguing and shouting and smells and sights of the marketplace and Mother Mastiff's warm, familiar little shop. He was sorry. Sorry for all the trouble he seemed to have caused. Sorry for the funny old Meliorares who were no more. Sorry for the overzealous Peaceforcers.

Mother Mastiff wouldn't be sorry, he knew. She could be as vindictive as an AAnn, especially if anything close to her had been threatened.

For himself, however, he regretted the deaths of so many. All for nothing, all because of some erratic, harmless, usually useless emotion-reading ability he possessed. Their own fault, though. Everything that happened was their own fault, Meliorares and Peaceforcers alike. He tried to warn them. Never try to come between a boy and his snake.

The damp trek homeward exhausted his remaining strength. Never before had the city seemed so immense, its byways and side streets so convoluted and tortuous. He was completely worn out.

Mother Mastiff was manning the shop, waiting for him as anxiously as she awaited customers. Her thin, aged arm was strong as she slipped it around his back and helped him the last agonizing steps into the store.

"I've been worried like to death over ye, boy! Damn ye for causing a poor old woman such distress." Her fingers touched his bruised cheeks, his forehead, as her eyes searched for serious damage. "And you're all cut up and bleeding. What's to become of ye, Flinx? Ye have got to learn to stay out of trouble."

He summoned up a grin, glad to be home. "It seems to come looking for me, Mother."

"Hmpnh! Excuses. The boy's wit is chock full of excuses. What happened to ye?"

He tried to marshal his thoughts as he slid Pip out from beneath the slickertic. Mother Mastiff backed away. The minidrag was as limp as a piece of rope. It lay curled up in its master's lap, if not asleep then giving a fine scaly imitation of some similar state.

"Some people kidnapped Pip. They called themselves Meliorares. But they really wanted me. They—" His expression screwed tight as he remembered, "One of them said something about wanting to fix me. Fix what? What did they want with me?"

She considered a long moment, studying the boy. Truly, it appeared that he was telling the truth, that he had learned no more than what he said. Ignoring the proximity of the hated flying snake, she sat down and put an arm around his shoulders.

"Now mark me well, boy, because this is vital to ye. I don't have to tell ye that you're different. You've always been different. Ye have to hide that as best ye can, and we'll have to hide ourselves. Drallar's a big place. We can move the shop if need be. But you're going to have to learn to live quietly, and you're going to have to keep your differences to yourself, or we'll be plagued with more of this unwelcome and unwholesome attention."

"It's all so silly, Mother. Just because I can sometimes sense what other people are feeling?"

"That. And maybe more."

"There isn't anything more. That's all I can do."

"Is it, boy? How did ye get away from these people." She looked past him toward the street, suddenly concerned. "Will they be coming after ye again?"

"I don't think so. Most of them were kind of dead when I left. I don't know how I got away from them. I think one of them shot at something explosive and it blew up. I was blown clear out of a building and into the street."

"Lucky to be alive ye are, it seems, though by what providence I wonder. Maybe 'tis best this way. Maybe 'tis best ye don't know too much about yourself just yet. Your mind always was advanced of your body, and maybe there's something more that's advanced even of that."

"But I don't *want* to be different," he insisted, almost crying. "I just want to be like everyone else."

"I know ye do, boy," she said gently, "but each of us must play the cards fate deals us, and if you've been stuck with the joker, you'll just have to learn to cope with it, turn it to your advantage somehow."

"I don't want any advantage! Not if it's going to cause us this kind of trouble."

"I'll have none of that, boy! A difference can always be to one's advantage. 'Tis time ye chose a profession. I know you've no like for running a shop like this one. What is it ye like to do?"

He mulled it over a while before replying. "All I enjoy doing is making other people happy."

She shook her head sadly. "Sometimes I think you've not enough self-interest to keep yourself alive. However, if that's what ye like, then you'll have to find some way to earn a living at it."

"Sometimes I dream of becoming a doctor and healing people."

"I'd advise ye to set your sights a bit lower, boy."

"All right. An actor, then."

"Nay, not that low. Be sensible. Set yourself to something ye can do *now*, without years of study."

"I could perform right here in the marketplace," he said thoughtfully. "I can juggle pretty good. You've seen me."

"Aye, and yelled at ye often enough for practicing with my expensive baubles. But 'tis a sound thought. We must find ye a good street corner. Surely ye can't get into trouble performing before these simple locals."

"Sure! I'll go and practice right now."

"Easy, boy, easy. You're nearly asleep on your feet, and I'll not have ye breaking either my goods or yourself. Go inside and lie down. I'll be in soon to fix ye something to eat. Go on now, boy, and be sure and take your monster with ye."

Cradling the exhausted Pip in his hands, Flinx rose and made his way through the displays to the section of the shop that served as their home. Mother Mastiff's eyes followed him.

What *was* to become of the boy? Somehow he had come to the attention of powerful, dangerous people. At least there was a good chance they wouldn't be bothered for a while. Not if he had left them "kind of dead."

How had he escaped? Sometimes he still frightened her. Oh, not because he would ever harm a hair of her old head. Quite the contrary, as his dogged pursuit and rescue of her these past days had proven. But there were forces at work within that adolescent body, forces beyond the comprehension of a simple shopkeeper, forces he might not be able to control. And there was more to it than reading the emotions of others. Of that she was certain. How much more she could only suspect, for it was clear enough the boy had little awareness of them himself.

Well, let him play at the trade of jongleur for a while. Surely that was harmless. Surely he could not find much trouble plying so simple an occupation.

She told herself that repeatedly all the rest of the afternoon and on into evening as she sat watching him sleep. When she finally slipped into her own bed, she thought she had put such imaginary fears beyond her, but such was not the case.

She sensed that the boy lying content and peaceful in the room opposite hers was destined for more than an idle life of entertaining on street corners. Much more. She knew somehow that a damnable universe, which was always sticking its cosmic nose into the destinies of innocent citizens, would never let anyone as unique as Flinx alone.

THE TAR-AIYM
KRANG

To
Larry Thor
and
John W. Campbell, Jr.
Mentors

1

The Flinx was an ethical thief in that he stole only from the crooked. And at that, only when it was absolutely necessary. Well, perhaps not absolutely. But he tried to. Due to his environment his morals were of necessity of a highly adaptable nature. And when one is living alone and has not yet reached one's seventeenth summer, certain allowances in such matters must be made.

It could be argued, if the Flinx were willing to listen (a most unlikely happenstance), that the ultimate decision as to who qualified as crooked and who did not was an awfully totalitarian one to have to make. A philosopher would nod knowingly in agreement. Flinx could not afford that luxury. His ethics were dictated by survival and not abstracts. It was to his great credit that he had managed to remain on the accepted side of current temporal morality as much as he had so far. Then again, chance was also due a fair share of the credit.

As a rule, though, he came by his modest income mostly honestly. This was made necessary as much by reason of common sense as by choice. A too-successful thief always attracts unwanted attention. Eventually, a criminal "law of diminishing returns" takes over.

And anyway, the jails of Drallar were notoriously inhospitable.

Good locations in the city for traveling jongleurs, minstrels, and such to display their talents were limited. Some were far better than others. That he at his comparatively slight age had managed to secure one of the best was a tribute to luck and the tenacity of old Mother Mastiff. She had reserved the small raised platform next to her shop for him, driving off other entrepreneurs with shout or shot, as the occasion and vehemence of the interloper required. Mother Mastiff was not her real name, of course, but that was what everyone called her. Flinx included. Real names were of little use in Drallar's marketplaces. They served poorly for identification and too well for the tax-gatherers. So more appropriate ones were rapidly bestowed upon each new inhabitant. Mother Mastiff, for example, bore a striking resemblance to the Terran canine of the same name. It was given in humor and accepted with poor grace, but accepted, nevertheless. Her caustic personality only tended to compliment the physical similarity.

The man-child had been an orphan. Probably involuntary, as most of his ilk were. Still, who could tell? Had she not been passing the slave coops at that time and glanced casually in a certain direction, she would never have noticed it. For reasons she had never fully understood she had bought it, raised it, and set it to learning a trade as soon as it was old enough. Fortunately his theatrical proclivities had manifested themselves at quite an early stage, along with his peculiar talents. So the problem of choosing a trade solved itself. He proved to be a keen if somewhat solemn observer, and so his own best apprentice. Fine and well, because the older performers always became more nervous in his presence than they cared to admit. Rather than admit it, they pronounced him unteachable, and left him to his own devices.

She had also taught him as early as was practical that in Drallar independence was ever so much more than an intangible thought. It was a possession, even if it would not fit into one's pocket or pouch, and to be valued as such. Still, when he had taken to her word and moved out to live on his own, the sadness lingered with her as a new coat of paint. But she never revealed it to him for fear of communicating weakness. Not in her words nor in her face. Urged on affectionately but firmly he was, much as the young birds of the Poles. Also she knew that for her the Moment might come at any time, and she wanted it to brush *his* life as lightly as possible.

Flinx felt the cottony pain of a sugar-coated probe again in his mind; the knowledge that Mother Mastiff was his mother by dint of sympathy and not birth. Coincidence was his father and luck his inheritance. Of his true parents he knew nothing, nor had the auctioneer. His card had been even more than usually blank, carrying not even the most elementary pedigree. A mongrel. It showed in his long orange-red hair and olive complexion. The reason for his orphanhood would remain forever as obscure as their faces. He let the life flood of the city enter his mind and submerge the unpleasant thoughts.

A tourist with more insight than most had once remarked that strolling through the great central marketplace of Drallar was like standing in a low surf and letting the geometrically patient waves lap unceasingly against one. Flinx had never seen the sea, so the reference remained obscure. There were few seas on Moth anyway, and no oceans. Only the uncounted, innumerable lakes of The-Blue-That-Blinded and shamed azure as a pale intonation.

The planet had moved with unusual rapidity out of its last ice age. The fast-dwindling ice sheets had left its surface pockmarked with a glittering lapis-lazuli embroidery of lakes, tarns, and great ponds. An almost daily rainfall maintained the water levels initially set by the retreating glaciers. Drallar happened to be situated in an exceptionally dry valley, good drainage and the lack of rainfall (more specifically, of mud) being one of the principal reasons for the city's growth. Here merchants could come to trade their goods and craftsmen to set up shop without fear of being washed out every third-month.

The evaporation-precipitation water cycle on Moth also differed from that of many otherwise similar humanx-type planets. Deserts were precluded by the lack of any real mountain ranges to block off moisture-laden air. The corresponding lack of oceanic basins and the general unevenness of the terrain never gave a major drainage system a chance to get started. The rivers of Moth were as uncountable as the lakes, but for the most part small in both length and volume. So the water of the planet was distributed fairly evenly over its surface, with the exception of the two great ice caps at the poles and the hemispheric remnants of the great glacial systems. Moth was the Terran Great Plains with conifers instead of corn.

The polyrhythmic chanting of barkers hawking the goods of a thousand worlds formed a nervous and jarring counterpoint to the comparatively even susurrations and murmurings of the crowd. Flinx passed a haberdashery he knew and in passing exchanged a brief, secret smile with its owner. That worthy, a husky blond middle-aged human, had just finished selling a pair of *durfarq*-skin coats to two outlandishly clad outworlders . . . for three times what they were worth. Another saying trickled lazily through his mind.

"Those who come unprepared to Drallar to buy skin, inevitably get."

It did not offend Flinx's well-considered set of ethics. This was not stealing. *Caveat emptor.* Fur and fibers, wood and water, *were* Moth. Can one steal seeds from a tomato? The seller was happy with his sale, the purchasers were pleased with their purchase, and the difference would go to support the city in the form of welfares and grafts anyway. Besides, any outworlder who could afford to come to Moth could damn well afford to pay its prices. The merchants of Drallar were not to any extent rapacious. Only devious.

It was a fairly open planet, mostwise. The government was a monarchy, a throwback to the planet's earlier days. Historians found it quaint and studied it, tourists found it picturesque and frozepixed it, and it was only nominally terrifying to its citizens. Moth had been yanked abruptly and unprepared into the vortex of interstellar life and had taken the difficult transition rather well. As would-be planetbaggers rapidly found out. But on a planet where the bulk of the native population was composed of nomadic tribes following equally nomadic fur-bearing animals who exhibited unwonted bellicosity toward the losing of said furs, a representative government would have proved awkward in the extreme. And naturally the Church would not interfere. The Counselors did not even think of themselves as constituting a government, therefore they could not think of imposing one on others. Democracy on Moth would have to wait until the nomads would let themselves be counted, indexed, labeled, and cross-filed, and that seemed a long, long way off. It was well known that the Bureau of the King's Census annually published figures more complementary than accurate.

Wood products, furs, and tourism were the planet's principal industries. Those and trade. Fur-bearing creatures of every conceivable type (and a few inconceivable ones) abounded in the planet's endless forests. Even the insects wore fur, to shed the omnipresent water. Most known varieties of hard and soft woods thrived in the Barklands, including a number of unique and unclassifiable types, such as a certain deciduous fungus. When one referred to "grain" on Moth, it had nothing to do with flour. The giant lakes harbored fish that had to be caught from modified barges equipped with cyborg-backed fishing lines. It was widely quoted that of all the planets in the galaxy, only on Moth did an honest-to-goodness *pisces* have an even chance of going home with the fisherman, instead of vice-versa. And hunters were only beginning to tap *that* aspect of the planet's potentialities . . . mostly because those who went into the great forests unprepared kept a disquieting silence.

Drallar was its capital and largest city. Thanks to fortuitous galactic coordinates and the enlightened tax policies of a succession of kings it was now also an interstellar clearing-house for trade goods and commercial transactions. All of the great financial houses had at least branch headquarters here, reserving their showier offices for the more "civilized" planets. The monarch and his civil service were no more than nominally corrupt, and the king saw to it that the people were not swamped by repressive rules and regulations. Not that this was done out of love for the common man. It was simply good business. And if there were no business, there would be no taxes. No taxes would mean no government. And no government would mean no king, a state of affairs which the current monarch, his Driest Majesty King Dewe Nog Na XXIV, was at constant pains to avoid.

Then too, Drallar could be smelled.

In addition to the indigenous humans, the business of Drallar was conducted by half a hundred intelligent races. To keep this conglomeration of commerce pulsing smoothly, a fantastic diversity of organic fuels was demanded. So the central market place itself was encircled by a seemingly infinite series of serving stands, auto-chefs, and restaurants that formed in actuality one great, uninterrupted kitchen. The resulting combination of aromas generated by these establishments mingled to form an atmosphere unduplicated anywhere else in the known galaxy. On more refined trade stops such exotic miasmas were kept decently locked away. In Drallar there was no ozone to contaminate. One man's bread was another man's narcotic. And one man's narcotic could conceivably make another being nauseous.

But by some chance of chemistry, or chemistry of chance, the fumes blended so well in the naturally moist air that any potentially harmful effects were canceled out. Left only was an everswirling thick perfume that tickled one's throat and left unexpecting mouths in a state of perpetual salivation. One could get a deceptively full and satisfying meal simply by sitting down in the center of the markets and inhaling for an hour. Few other places in the Arm had acquired what might best be described as an olfactory reputation. It was a truth that gourmets came from as far away as Terra and Procyon merely to sit on the outskirts of the marketplace and hold long and spirited competitions in which the participants would attempt to identify only the wisps of flavor that were wafted outward on the damp breeze.

The reason for the circular arrangement was simple. A businessman could fortify himself on the outskirts and then plunge into the whirl of commerce without having to worry about being cut down in the midst of an important transaction by a sudden gust of, say, pungent *prego*-smoke from the bahnwood fires. Most of the day the vast circle served admirably well, but during the prime meal hours it made the marketplace resemble more than ever that per-spicacious tourist's analogy of the ebb and flow of a sea.

Flinx paused at the stand of old Kiki, a vendor of sweets, and bought a small *thisk*-cake. This was a concoction made from a base of a tough local hybrid wheat. Inside, it was filled with fruit-pieces and berries and small, meaty *parma*-nuts, recently ripened. The finished product was then dipped in a vat of warmish honey-gold and allowed to harden. It was rough on the teeth, but, oh, what it did for the palate! It had one drawback: consistency. Biting into *thisk* was like chewing old spacesuit insulation. But it had a high energy content, the *parma*-nuts were mildly narcotic, and Flinx felt the need of some sort of mild stimulant before performing.

Above the voices and the smells, above all, Drallar could be viewed.

The edifices of the marketplace were fairly low, but outside the food crescents one could see ancient walls, remnants of Old City. Scattered behind and among were the buildings where the more important commerce took place. The lifeblood of Moth was here, not in the spectacular stalls below. Every day the economies of a dozen worlds were traded away in the dingy back rooms and of-fices of those old-new structures. There the gourmet restaurants catered to the rich sportsmen returning from the lakes, and turned up their noses and shut their windows against the plebeian effluvia assailing them from the food stalls below. There the taxidermists plied their noisome arts, stuffing downy Yax'm pelts and mounting the ebony nightmare heads of the horned Demmichin Devilope.

Beyond rose the apartment houses where the middle and lower classes lived, those of the poorer characterized by few windows and cracking plaster, and those of the better-off by the wonderful multistoried murals painted by the gypsy artists, and by the bril-liant azurine tiles which kept the houses warm in winter and cool in summer. Still farther off rose the isolated tower groupings of the rich inurbs, with their hanging gardens and reinforced crystal ter-races. These soared loftily above the noise and clamor of the com-monplace, sparkling as jeweled giraffes amid each morning fog.

Rising from the center of the city to dominate all was the great palace of the rulers of Drallar. Generations of kings had added to it, each stamping a section here, a wing there, with his own per-sonality. Therein dwelt King Dewe Nog Na and his court. Sometimes he would take a lift to the topmost minaret, and there, seated comfortably on its slowly revolving platform, leisurely sur-vey the impossible anthill that constituted his domain.

But the most beautiful thing about Moth was not Drallar, with its jeweled towers and chromatic citizenry, nor the innumerable lakes and forests, nor the splendid and variegated things that dwelt therein. It was the planet itself. It was that which had given to it a name and made it unique in the Arm. That which had first attracted men to the system. Ringed planets were rare enough.

Moth was a winged planet.

The "wings" of Moth doubtless at one time had been a perfect broad ring of the Saturn type. But at some time in the far past it had been broken in two places—possibly the result of a gravitational stress, or a change in the magnetic poles. No one could be certain. The result was an incomplete ring consisting of two great crescents of pulverized stone and gas which encircled the planet with two great gaps separating them. The crescents were narrower near the planet, but out in space they spread out to a natural fan shape due to the decreasing gravity, thus forming the famed "wing" effect. They were also a good deal thicker than the ancient Saturnian rings, and contained a higher proportion of fluorescent gases. The result was two gigantic triangular shapes of a lambent butter-yellow springing out from either side of the planet.

Inevitably, perhaps, the largest moon of Moth was designated Flame. Some thought it a trite appellation, but none could deny its aptness. It was about a third again smaller than Terra's Luna, and nearly twice as far away. It had one peculiar characteristic. It didn't "burn" as the name would seem to suggest, although it was bright enough. In fact, some felt the label "moon" to be altogether inappropriate, as Flame didn't revolve around its parent planet at all, but instead preceded it around the sun in approximately the same orbit. So the two names stuck. The carrot leading a bejeweled ass, with eternity forever preventing satisfaction to the latter. Fortunately the system's discoverers had resisted the impulse to name the two spheres after the latter saying. As were so many of nature's freaks, the two were too uncommonly gorgeous to be so ridiculed.

The wing on Drallar's side was visible to Flinx only as a thin, glowing line, but he had seen pictures of it taken from space. He had never been in space himself, at least, only vicariously, but had visited many of the ships that landed at the Port. There at the feet of the older crewmen he listened intently while they spun tales of the great KK ships that plied the dark and empty places of the firmament. Since those monster interstellar craft never touched soil, of course, he had never seen one in person. Such a landing would never be made except in a dire emergency, and then never on an inhabited planet. A Doublekay carried the gravity well of a small sun on its nose, like a bee carrying pollen. Even shrunk to the tiny size necessary to make a simple landing, that field would protect the great bulk of the ship. It would also gouge out a considerable chunk of the planetary crust and set off all sorts of undesirable natural phenomena, like tsunamis and hurricanes and such. So the smaller shuttle ships darted yoyolike between traveler and ground, carrying down people and their goods, while the giant transports themselves remained in Polyphemian exile in the vastnesses of black and cold.

He had wanted to space, but had not yet found a valid reason to, and could not leave Mother Mastiff without anyone. Despite unceasing bellows asserting to her good health she *was* a hundred and something. To leave her alone simply for a pleasure trip was not a thought that appealed to him.

He tugged his cloak tighter around his shoulders, half-burying Pip in the folds of thick fur. As human-inhabited worlds go, Moth was not an exceptionally cold planet, but it was far from tropical. He could not remember the time when he had not been greeted upon awakening by a wet and clammy fog. It was a dependable but dampish companion. Here furs were used more to shed water than to protect from bitter chill. It was cold, yes, but not freezing. At least, it snowed only in winter.

Pip hissed softly and Flinx absently began feeding him the raisins he'd plucked from the *thisk*-cake. The reptile gulped them down whole, eagerly. It would have smacked its lips, if it'd had any. As it was, the long tongue shot out and caressed Flinx's cheek with the delicate touch of a diamond cutter. The minidrag's iridescent scales seemed to shine even brighter than usual. For some reason it was especially fond of raisins. Maybe it relished their iron content.

He glanced down at the plus window of his personal cardmeter. They weren't broke, but neither were they swimming in luxury. Oh, yes, it was definitely time to go to work!

From a counter of her variegated display booth, Mother Mastiff was pleading amiably with a pair of small, jeweled thranx *touristas*. Her technique was admirable and competent. It ought to be, he reflected. She'd had plenty of time in which to perfect it. He was only mildly surprised at the insectoids' presence. *Where humans go, thranx also, and vicey-versy, don't you know?* So went the children's rhyme. But they did look a bit uncomfortable. Thranx loved the rain and the damp, and in this respect Moth was perfect, but they also preferred a good deal less cold and more humidity. Paradoxically, the air could be wet and to them still too dry. Every time a new hothouse planet turned up they got ecstatic, despite the fact that such places invariably possessed the most objectionable and bellicose environments. Like any human youngster, he'd seen countless pictures of thranx planets: Hivehom, their counterpart of Terra, and also the famous thranx colonies in the Amazon and Congo basins on Terra itself. Why should humans wear themselves out in an unfriendly climate when the thranx could thrive there? They had put those inhospitable regions to far better use than man ever could or would have—as had humans the Mediterranean Plateau on Hivehom.

Indeed, the Amalgamation had worked out very well all around.

From the cut of their necklaces these two were probably from Evoria. Anyhow the female's tiara and ovipositor glaze were dead giveaways. Probably a hunting couple, here for some excitement. There wasn't much to attract thranx to Moth, other than recreation, politics, and the light metals trade. Moth was rich in light metals, but deficient in many of the heavier ones. Little gold, lead, uranium, and the like. But silver and magnesium and copper in abundance. According to rumor, the giant thranx Elecseed complex had plans to turn Moth into a leading producer of electrical and thinkmachine components, much as they had Amropolous. But so far it had remained only rumor. Anyway, inducing skilled thranx workers to migrate to Moth would necessitate the company's best psychopublicists working day and night, plus megacredits in hardship pay. Even off-world human workers would find the living conditions unpalatable at best. He didn't think it likely. And without native atomics there'd be a big power problem. Hydroelectricity was a limited servant due to the lack of white water. It formed an intriguing problem. How to generate enough electricity to run the plant to produce electrical products?

All this musing put not credit in one's account nor bread in one's mouth.

"Sir and madame, what think ye on my wares? No better of the type to be found this side of Shorttree, and damn little there." She fumbled, seemingly aimless, about her samples. "Now here's an item that might appeal to ye. What of these matched copper drink-jugs, eh? One for he and one for she." She held up two tall, thin, burnished copper thranx drinking implements. Their sides were elaborately engraved and their spouts worked into intricate spirals.

"Notice the execution, the fine scroll work, sir," she urged, tracing the delicate patterns with a wrinkled forefinger. "I defy ye to find better, yea, anywheres!"

The male turned to his mate. "What do you say, my dear?" They spoke symbospeech, that peculiar mixture of Terran basic and thranx click-hiss which had become the dominant language of commerce throughout the Humanx Commonwealth and much of the rest of the civilized galaxy besides.

The female extended a handfoot and grasped the utensil firmly by one of its double handles. Her small, valentine-shaped head inclined slightly at an angle in an oddly human gesture of appraisal as she ran both truehands over the deeply etched surface. She said nothing, but instead looked directly into her mate's eyes.

Flinx remained where he was and nodded knowingly at the innocent smile on Mother Mastiff's face. He'd seen that predatory grin before. The taste of her mind furnished him with further information as to what would inevitably follow. Despite a century of intimate familiarity and association with the thranx there still remained some humans who were unable to interpret even the commoner nuances of thranx gesture and gaze. Mother Mastiff was an expert and knew them all. Her eyes were bright enough to read the capital letters flashing there: SALE.

The husband commenced negotiations in an admirably offhand manner. "Well . . . perhaps something might be engendered . . . we already have a number of such baubles . . . exorbitant prices . . . a reasonable level. . . ."

"Level! You speak of *levels?*" Mother Mastiff's gasp of outrage was sufficiently violent to carry the odor of garlic all the way to where Flinx stood. The thranx, remarkably, ignored it. "Good sir, I survive at but a subsistence level now! The government takes all my money, and I have left but a pittance, a pittance, sir, for my three sons and two daughters!"

Flinx shook his head in admiration of Mother Mastiff's unmatched style. Thranx offspring always came in multiples of two, an inbred survival trait. With most things terrene and human there had been little or no conflict, but due to a quirk of psychology the thranx could not help but regard human odd-numbered births as both pathetic and not a little obscene.

"Thirty credits," she finally sighed.

"Blasphemous!" the husband cried, his antennae quivering violently. "They are worth perhaps ten, and at that I flatter the craftsman unmercifully."

"Ten!" moaned Mother Mastiff, feigning a swoon. "Ten, the creature says, and boasts of it! Surely . . . surely, sir, you do not expect me to consider such an offer *seriously!* 'Tis not even successful as a jest."

"Fifteen, then, and I should report you to the local magistrate. Even common thieves have the decency to work incognito."

"Twenty-five. Sir, you, a cultured and wealthy being, surely you can do better than taunt and make sport of an old female. One who has doubtless fertilized as many eggs as you . . ." The female had the grace to lower her head and blush. The thranx were quite open about sex . . . theirs or anyone else's . . . but still, Flinx thought, there *were* lines over which it was improper to step.

Good manners it might not have been, but in this case at least it appeared to be good business. The male harrumphed awkwardly, a deep, vibrant hum. "Twenty, then."

"Twenty-three five, and a tenth credit less I will not say!" intoned Mother Mastiff. She folded her arms in a recognizable gesture of finality.

"Twenty-one," countered the male.

Mother Mastiff shook her head obstinately, immovable as a Treewall. She looked ready to wait out entropy.

"Twenty-three five, not a tenth credit less. My last and final offer, good sir. This pair will find its own market. I must survive, and I fear I may have allowed you to sway me too far already."

The male would have argued further, on principle if for nothing else, but at that point the female put a truehand on his b-thorax, just below the ear, and stroked lightly. That ending the bargaining.

"Ahhh, Dark Centers! Twenty-five . . . no, twenty-three five, then! Thief! Assaulter of reason! It is well known that a human would cheat its own female-parent to make a half-credit!"

"And it is well known also," replied Mother Mastiff smoothly as she processed the sale, "that the thranx are the most astute bargainers in the galaxy. You have gotten yourself a steal, sir, and so 'tis you and not I the thief!"

As soon as the exchange of credit had been finalized, Flinx left his resting place by the old wall and strolled over to the combination booth and home. The thranx had departed happily, antennae entwined. On their mating flight? The male, at least, had seemed too old for that. His chiton had been shading ever so slightly into deep blue, despite the obvious use of cosmetics, while the female had been a much younger aquamarine. The thranx too took mistresses. In the moist air, their delicate perfume lingered.

"Well, mother," he began. He was not indicating parentage—she had insisted on that years ago—but using the title bestowed on her by the folk of the markets. Everyone called her mother. "Business seems good."

She apparently had not noticed his approach and was momentarily flustered. "What? What? Oh, 'tis you, cub! Pah!" She gestured in the direction taken by the departed thranx. "Thieves the bugs are, to steal from me so! But have I a choice?" She did not wait for an answer. "I am an old woman and must sell occasionally to support myself, even at such prices, for who in this city would feed me?"

"More likely, mother, it would be you who would feed the city. I saw you purchase those same mugspirals from Olin the Coppersmith not six days ago . . . for eleven credits."

"Ay? Harrumph," she coughed. "You must be mistaken, boy. Even you can make a mistake now and then, you know. Um, have you eaten yet today?"

"A *thisk*-cake only."

"Is that the way I raised ye, to live on sweets?" In her gratefulness for a change of subject she feigned anger. "And I'll wager ye gave half of it to that damned snake of yours, anyway!"

Pip raised his dozing head at that and let out a mild hiss. Mother Mastiff did not like the minidrag and never had. Few people did. Some might profess friendship, and after coaxing a few could even be persuaded to pet it. But none could forget that its kind's poison could lay a man dead in sixty seconds, and the antidote was rare. Flinx was never cheated in business or pleasure when the snake lay curled about his shoulder.

"Gentle, mother. He understands what you say, you know. Not so much what as why, really."

"Oh surely, surely! Now claim intelligence for the monster! Bewitched it is, perhaps. I believe it that latter, at least, for I can't deny I've seen the thing react oddly, yes. But it does no work, sleeps constantly, and eats prodigiously. You'd be far better off without it, lad."

He scratched the minidrag absently behind the flat, scaly head. "Your suggestion is not humorful, mother. Besides, it *does* work in the act. . . ."

"Gimmick," she snorted, but not loudly.

"And as to its sleeping and eating habits, it is an alien thing and has metabolic requirements we cannot question. Most importantly, I like it and . . . and it likes me."

Mother Mastiff would have argued further except that they had gone through uncounted variations of this very argument over the years. No doubt a dog or one of the local domesticated running-birds would have made a more efficacious pet for a small boy, but when she'd taken in the maltreated youngster Mother Mastiff'd had no credits for dogs or birds. Flinx had stumbled on the minidrag himself in the alley behind their first shack, rooting in a garbage heap for meats and sugars. Being ignorant of its identity, he'd approached it openly and unfearing. She'd found the two huddled together in the boy's bed the following morning. She had hefted a broom and tried to shoo it off, but instead of being frightened the thing had opened its mouth and hissed threateningly at her. That initial attempt constituted her first and last physical effort at separating the two.

The relationship was an unusual one and much commented upon, the more so since Alaspin was many parsecs away and none could recall having heard of a minidrag living unconfined off its native world before. It was widely surmised that it had been the pet of some space trader and had gotten loose at the shuttleport and escaped. Since the importation of poisonous animals was a felony on most planets, Moth included, few were surprised that the original owner had not made noisy efforts to reclaim his property. In any case it had harmed no one (Flinx knew otherwise, and better than to boast the fact) and so none in the marketplace protested its presence to the authorities, although all wished with a passion it would go elsewhere.

He moved to change the subject.

"How are you equipped for credit, mother?"

"Fah! Poorly, as always. But," and this with a sly, small grin, "I should be able to manage for a while off that last transaction."

"I'd wager," he chuckled. He turned to survey the chromatically colored crowd which flowed unceasingly around and in front of the little shop, trying to gauge the proportion of wealthy tourists among the everyday populace. The effort, as usual, made his head ache.

"A normal day's passings or not, mother?"

"Oh, there's money out there now, all right! I can smell it. But it declines to come into my shop. Better luck to you, perhaps, lad."

"Perhaps." He walked out from under the awning and mounted the raised dais to the left of the shop. Carefully he set about rearranging the larger pots and pans which formed the bulk of Mother

Mastiff's cheaper inventory to give himself sufficient room to work.

His method of enticing an audience was simple and timeworn. He took four small *brana* balls from a pocket and began to juggle them. These were formed from the sap of a tree that grew only in Moth's equatorial belt. Under the sun's diffused UV they pulsed with a faint yellow light. They were perfect for his needs, being solid and of a uniform consistency. A small crowd began to gather. He added a fifth ball now, and began to vary the routine by tossing them behind his back without breaking rhythm. The word was passed outward like invisible tentacles, occasionally snatching another person here, another there, from the fringes of the shuffling mob. Soon he had acquired his own substantial little island of watchful beings. He whispered softly to the minidrag, almost buried in the soft fur.

"Up, boy."

Pip uncurled himself from Flinx's shoulder, unfurling his leathery wings to their fullest extent. In spite of its rarity the crowd recognized the lethal shape and drew back. The snake soared into the air and performed a delicate, spiraling descent, to settle like a crown around the boy's head. It then proceeded to catch each ball and toss it high into the air, changing the shape but not the rhythm of the act. The unbroken fluorescent trail took on a more intricate weave. A mild pattering of applause greeted this innovation. Jugglers were more than common in Drallar, but a young one who worked so deftly with a poisonous reptile was not. A few coins landed on the platform, occasionally bouncing metallically of the big pans. More applause and more coins when the snake flipped all five balls, one after another, into a small basket at the rear of the dais.

"Thank you, thank you, gentlebeings!" said Flinx, bowing theatrically, thinking, now for the real part of the act. "And now, for your information, mystification, and elucidation . . . and a small fee" (mild laughter), "I will endeavor to answer any question, *any* question, that anyone in the audience, regardless of his race or planet of origin, would care to tempt me with."

There was the usual skeptical murmuring from the assembly, and not a few sighs of boredom.

"All the change in my pocket," blurted a merchant in the first row, "if you can tell me how much there is!" He grinned amid some nervous giggling from within the crowd.

Flinx ignored the sarcasm in the man's voice and stood quietly,

eyes tightly shut. Not that they had to be. He could "work" equally
as well with them wide open. It was a piece of pure showmanship
which the crowds always seemed to expect. Why they expected
him to look inward when he had to look outward remained ever-
puzzling to him. He had no real idea how his answers came to him.
One minute his mind was empty, fuzzy, and the next . . . sometimes . . . an answer would appear. Although "appear" wasn't quite
right either. Many times he didn't even understand the questions,
especially in the case of alien questioners. Or the answers.
Fortunately that made no difference to the audience. He could not
have promised interpretations. There!

"Good sir, you have in your pocket four tenth pieces, two hun-
dredth pieces . . . and a key admitting you to a certain club
that. . . ."

"Stop, stop!" The man was waving his gnarled hands frantically
and glancing awkwardly at those in the crowd nearest him. "That
will do! I am convinced." He dug into his pocket, came out with a
handful of change, thrust the troublesome key back out of sight of
the curious who leaned close for a look. He started to hand over
the coins, then paused almost absently, a look of perplexity on his
face. It changed slowly to one of surprise.

"By Pali's tide-bore, the whelp is right! Forty-two hundredths.
He's right!" He handed over the coins and left, mumbling to himself.

Flying coins punctuated the crowd's somewhat nervous applause. Flinx judged their mood expertly. Belief had about pulled
even with derision. There were naturally those who suspected the
merchant of being a plant. They granted he was a very convincing
one.

"Come, come, gentlebeings! What we have here is larvae play.
Surely there are those among you with questions worth tempting
my simple skill?"

A being at the back of the crowd, a Quillp in full post-mating
plumage, craned its thin ostrichlike neck forward and asked in a
high, squeaky voice, "In what summer-month my hatchlings come
about will?"

"I am truly sorry, sir, but that is a question that involves the future, and I am not a clairvoyant." The creature sighed unhappily
and prepared to leave the gathering. At this sign of mortality on
Flinx's part a number of others seemed inclined to go with the tall
Ornithorpe. Flinx said hurriedly, "But I hope fervent all *five* of
your hatchlings successful are!"

The Quillp whirled in surprise and turned goggling eyes on the small stage. "How did you know that number my circle had?" In its excitement it spoke in its native tongue and had to be reminded by a neighbor to shift to symbospeech.

"I make it a policy not to reveal professional secrets." Flinx yawned with calculated elaboration. "Come, a real question, gentlebeings. I bore quickly. Miracles I cannot produce, though, and they usually bore anyway."

Two humans, big, muscular fellows, were pushing their way ungently to the stage. The one on Flinx's left wore glasses—not for their antique therapeutic value, but because in some current fashion circles it was considered something of a fad. He extended a credcard.

"Can you accept this, boy?"

Flinx bridled at the "boy," but extracted his cardmeter. "Indeed I can, sir. Ask your question."

The man opened his mouth, paused. "How do I know what to pay you?"

"I can't set value on my answers, only on your question. Whatever you deem it worth, sir. If I give no answer I will refund your credits." He gestured to where the minidrag rested alertly on his shoulder. "My pet here seems to have a feel for the emotional states of others which is quite sensitive. Even more so than myself. A swindler, for example, exudes something that he is especially sensitive to. I am rarely swindled."

The man smiled without mirth. "I wonder why?" He dialed a setting on the card, extended it again. "Will a hundred credits do?"

Flinx was quick to stifle his reaction. A hundred credits! That was more than he sometimes made in a month! For a moment he was tempted to lower the figure, mindful of the laugh Mother Mastiff might have if she found out. Especially after his comments on *her* pricings this morning. Then he reminded himself that, after all, the man had set the price and surely would not cheat himself. He tried but could detect no trace of humor about the man. Nor his companion. Quite the contrary. And he hadn't heard the question yet. What if he couldn't answer it?

"A . . . a hundred credits would be most satisfactory, sir."

The man nodded and stuck his card in the little black meter. The compact machine hummed softly and the amount, one-oh-oh-zero-zero, clicked into place on its tiny dial. There was a brief pause and then it buzzed once, the red light on its top glowing brightly. It noted that the amount of so-and-so, card number such-

and-such, was good for the amount dialed, and that credits num-
bering one hundred (100) had been transferred to the account of
one Philip Lynx (his given name in the city records) in the Royal
Depository of the sovereign Republic of Moth. Flinx returned the
box to its place in his pouch and looked back to the two expectant
men.

"Ask your question, sirs."

"My companion and I are searching for a man . . . a friend . . .
whom we know to be somewhere in this part of the city, but whom
we have been unable as yet to contact."

"What is there distinctive about him?" Flinx asked from under
closed eyes.

The other man spoke for the first time. His voice revealed an impatience that his mind confirmed. It was brusque and low-pitched.
"He is not tall . . . thin, has red hair like yourself, only darker and
tightly curled. Also his skin is not so dark as yours. It is mottled,
and he has wet eyes."

That helped. Redheads were not plentiful in Drallar, and the reference to "wet eyes" indicated a man with a high sexual potential.
The combination ought to be easy to locate. Flinx began to feel
more confident. Still, Drallar was large. And there was the shuttleport to consider, too.

"Not enough. What else?"

The two looked at each other. Then the bigger one spoke again.
"This man is dressed in navigator's clothes. He has with him . . .
probably on his person . . . a small map. A star map. It is hand-
drawn and very unprofessional looking. He usually keeps it in his
blouse, which bulges slightly in consequence."

Flinx concentrated harder. So, a shift in the internal abstract, an
angle resolved. . . . He opened his eyes, looked up in surprise. His
gaze roved over the rear of the silent crowd and came to rest on an
individual at the back. A redheaded man, not tall, with mottled
skin, wet eyes, and a slight bulge over his heart. Not surprisingly,
Flinx sensed paper therein. As soon as their eyes met the man's
went wide. He broke and plunged into the market mob. At the en-
suing commotion the big man turned his head and strained to see
through the mass. He clasped a hand on his companion's shoulder
and pointed urgently. They started off in the direction of the disturbance, forcing the other members of the assembly out of their way
with far more strength than tact.

Flinx almost called to them, but the action turned to a shrug instead. If this form of an answer satisfied the two, he certainly

wasn't going to argue the matter. A hundred credits! Without even committing himself. And the loose coin on the dais for Mother Mastiff. He waved an impulsive hand at the crowd.

"Thank you ever so for your attention, gentlebeings. For today, at least, the show is over."

The assemblage began to melt back into the flow of traffic, accompanied by not a few groans of disappointment from would-be questioners. With the unexpected dramatic build-up he had been given by the two strangers he probably could have milked the remainder for a pile, but his gift was capricious and possessed of a tendency to tire him quickly. Best to halt with an unchallenged success. This windfall entitled him to a serious celebration, and he was already impatient to get on with it.

"Pip, if we could take in what we took today on a regular basis, the king would make me royal treasurer and you his official guardian." The snake hissed noncommittally, the jet-black eyes staring up at him. Ink boiled in those tiny poolings. Apparently government work didn't have much appeal.

"And you are no doubt hungry again." This produced a more positive hiss, and Flinx chuckled, scratching the minidrag under its leather-soft snout. "That's what I thought. However, I feel that something of a more liquid nature is in order for myself. So we will make our way over to Small Symm's, and I will guzzle spiced beer, and you may have all the pretzels your venomous little carcass will hold!" The snake wagged its tail at this, which involved its quivering all over, since it was mostly tail in the first place.

As they made their way over the cobblestone back street he began mentally to reproach himself for not playing the crowd longer. He still felt that to overuse his talent would be to burn it out. But there were times when one had to be businesslike as well as cautious, a point Mother Mastiff had made to him many times. Still, he had slept late today and gotten started later than was usual. It would probably have proved difficult to hold the crowd much longer anyway. In Drallar darkness had a tendency to disperse people rapidly, and it was even now quite black out. Besides, he had a hundred credits in his pocket! Effectively, not actually, since it was in his account at the depository. So why worry? Did the sun fight to gather new hydrogen?

He had almost reached the dimly lit bar when he tasted the sounds. They came filtering out of the alleyway to his left, a hole dark as the gullet of a giant pseudo-sturgeon from one of the Great

Northern Lakes. It sounded very much like a fight. A questing probe brought back overtones of fear/anger/terror/greed/bloodlust. Fighting in fun was accompanied by much cursing and shouting. None were uttered in a battle to the death since the participants were too busy and too intent of purpose to waste the breath. Only humans fought quite that silently, so he knew they were not a part of the city's alien populace. There was that peculiar muteness of thought . . .

Flinx did not mix in such conflicts. In a city like Drallar where fat bellies and empty purses coexisted in abundance, one's own business remained healthy so long as one minded it. He had taken one step toward the peace of the bar when Pip uncoiled himself from his shoulder and streaked into the alley.

Even at his comparatively young age, Flinx could curse fluently in fourteen languages. He had time for only five before he was hurtling into the blackness after his pet. It was only in precaution that he drew the thin stiletto from its boot sheath without breaking stride.

Now he could perceive three forms in the dim light from the cloud-masked stars and the city-glow. Two were large and stood upright. The other was slight of build and lay with a recognizable stillness on the ground. One of the others bent over the prostrate body. Before it could carry out its unknown purpose, it jerked and roared loudly in the quiet.

"GODDAMN!"

The man began flailing wildly at a thin, leathery shape which dived and swooped at his head. The other pulled the wicked shape of a neuronic pistol from a shoulder cup and tried to sight on the rapidly moving object. Flinx had no time to think. With vague thoughts of forcing the man to the ground and knocking him out, he leaped onto the man's back. The thick ropes of broad muscle he felt beneath the man's blouse rapidly squelched that idea. The man lurched. In another second he'd be smashed against the wall of the nearest building. The thin blade plunged once, instinctively. The big man buckled horribly and crashed to the ground like a great tree. Flinx had already left the dead hulk before it reached the pavement.

The other whirled to meet this new menace as his companion pitched forward onto his face. Cursing, he fired in Flinx's direction. Rolling like mad, the youth had made the cover of a broken metal crate. Fortunately the man's night vision didn't seem as good as his own. Even so, the near miss sent a painful tingle up his leg.

An almost-hit with the ugly weapon would cause a man literally to shake himself to death in a series of uncontrollable muscular spasms. A direct hit to the heart or brain would kill instantly. Supposedly such weapons were outlawed on Moth. Obviously the law could be circumvented. The man rayed the area to his left. It was a mistake. Unhampered, Pip had the time he needed. The minidrag spat once.

It was not a gesture of defiance, but of death. The flying snakes or "miniature dragons" of Alaspin are akin to a few other carnivorous creatures. Among these is the *Hemachacus*, or spitting cobra, of Terra. The latter has forward-facing fangs, and instead of injecting its venom via a bite, can spit it to a surprising distance with remarkable accuracy. The Alaspinian minidrags, however, have no fangs. Only small cutting teeth for biting. Little work has actually been done on them on their seldom visited planet, but they apparently eject their poison through a narrowing tube of cartilaginous material running along the roof of the mouth. Muscles running the length of the jaw and along the neck force the venom even farther than the Terran types, and with greater accuracy. Fortunately the minidrag has a relatively mild disposition and attacks only when threatened. Pip's actions were therefore unusual but not incomprehensible.

The man gave vent to a shockingly shrill, soul-tearing scream and sank to his knees, clawing at his eyes. The venom was corrosive as well as killing. It was not fatal unless it got into the bloodstream, and so by rubbing at his eyes the man effectively killed himself. In thirty seconds he had become incapable of even that.

In another thirty he was incapable of doing anything at all.

Pip returned to his familiar resting place. As he settled his coils around Flinx's shoulder, the boy could feel the unnatural tension in the reptile's muscles. There was a brief urge to bawl the minidrag out good and proper, but his narrow escape and the fact that the snake had once again saved his life put it off. Time pressed. Still shaking slightly from muscular reaction of his own, he crept from his hiding place to the results of an undesired action.

The only sounds in the alley were the ruffling whispers made by the always moist air flowing over the silk-cool stones and the steady plop, plop, plop of blood flowing from the wound in the back of the man the stiletto had finished. There remained the third body. In spite of everything, he had been too late to help the small man. His neck had been broken cleanly. Unmoving, the sightless eyes reflected the silent stars.

There was just sufficient light for him to make out the man's brilliant red hair.

A crumpled piece of plastic lay clutched in a spasmodically frozen hand. Flinx pried it from his grasp, bending open the lifeless but still stubborn fingers. Above him lights began to come on as the cautious inhabitants of the alleyway decided it was safe to trust their precious selves to the quiet uncertainty of the night. Prudence had been served and now curiosity had taken over. It was time for him to leave. Now that the locals had bestirred themselves and the action had been resolved the local constabulary would be arriving. Although they would take their time, they would get here nonetheless. It would not do to be found standing over three lifeless bodies, all of them blatantly outworld. Especially when one of them had registered a hundred credits to his account only this afternoon.

He didn't like stealing from the dead, but anything that small that could cause the death of three men in one night was too important to leave to the discretion of the police. Without more than a casual glance at it, he shoved the rumpled sheet into his pouch.

The police arrived shortly after he had exited the mouth of the alley. A sudden increase in the babble of thoughts and voices told him that the bodies had been discovered. For locals action was time-defined and pedantic. When the police discovered that the three corpses were outworlders, a search pattern would be put into effect with small delay. Murder was not conducive to increased tourism. He hurried a mite faster toward the bar.

Small Symm's establishment was notable not so much for its food and drink, but rather for the reputation it enjoyed as being one of the few places in Drallar where a being could go at night, get comfortably drunk, and still be assured of retaining the same amount of body fluid that he had commenced the evening with. Small Symm himself was well aware of the business this favorable standing attracted to his place and so labored mightily to maintain it. He did not know it, but if his business had been a country on Terra several odd centuries ago, it would have been called Switzerland.

As Small Symm stood well over two meters tall and weighed in the neighborhood of a hundred and fifty kilos, few felt inclined to dispute his neutrality. Those who had yearnings to contented themselves with imbibing elsewhere and commenting on the inordinate size of the barkeep's ears.

There were no drinking laws on Moth. Only sober ones, as the saying went. As far as the judges were concerned one could proceed directly from the mother's breast to a bottle of Old Yeast-Bubble's best mash brew liquor. The end result of this oft-commented upon degenerate policy was a thriving local industry and a surprisingly small number of alcoholics.

However, there had been a few who had commented at times on Flinx's comparative youth and thereby questioned his right to imbibe fermented spirits. One particular person, a traveling sinspinner from Puritan, had been especially obnoxious in this respect. Small Symm had lumbered over and politely advised the fellow to mind his own business. Holding fast to the tenets of his faith (and being a bit tipsy himself), the man had told Symm in no uncertain terms what he could do with his suggestions. The next thing he knew, his right arm had been neatly broken in two places. As gently as possible. The outworlder had gone straight to the police and the police had objected . . . after all, an outworlder, respected . . . but not too vigorously. Especially after Symm had picked up their paddycraft and jammed it immovably into a sewer opening. After that Flinx and Symm both found themselves little troubled by minions of either God or Cop.

The giant was pleased to see him. Not the least of the things they had in common was the fact that both were technically orphans.

"A dry hearth, young master! And how does the world find you tonight?"

Flinx took the seat at the end of the bar. "It finds me well enough, enormous one. Well enough so that I will have a bottle of your very finest Burrberry beer, and a cauldron of pretzels for my friend."

He rubbed the snake under the jaw and Pip's eyes slitted in appreciation. There were times when he would swear he could hear the thing purr. But since no one else could, he never made it a point of discussion.

Symm's eyebrows went up slightly. Burrberry was expensive, and potent. He was far more concerned about the youth's ability to handle the former, however. The red ale was imported all the way from Crnkk, a thranx planet, and packed quite a kick for even a full-grown human. But he fetched it, and the pretzels for the minidrag.

When he returned, the snake did not wait for an invitation, but dived immediately into the bowl and began wallowing around in the salty twists, its tongue darting and flicking with machine-like rapidity at the big halite crystals. Like many things in Drallar,

even the pretzels disdained subtlety. Flinx reflected again that
for an undeniably carnivorous animal, his pet was notoriously
fond of grain products. The minidrag's culinary adaptability had
been one reason why it had been able to thrive so well in the city.
There had been times when meat had been scarce, and vermin as
well, and he and Mother Mastiff had watched in wonderment as
the reptile happily downed large portions of salted bread or *pime*,
the cheap cornlike growths that infested many of Moth's soft-
woods.

Flinx hefted the delicately formed bottle and poured the cherry-
red brew, watching it foam pinkly over the lip of the mug. Brew-
ing was one of the thranx's most polished abilities. It was too late
for the few perpetual drunkards and too early for most night
crawlers. Small Symm satisfied himself that his other customers
were taken care of and hunkered himself over the bar, leaning
on crossed arms like hirsute trees. He watched silently as the boy
downed a long draught of the effervescent liquid, then began
on the remainder with short, caressing sips. Now and then a satisfied hiss would come from the region to their right, among the
pretzels.

The barkeep's eyebrows jumped again when Flinx elected to pay
for the nourishments in coin. "Business has been so good, then?"

"It has, it has. Believe it or not, old friend, I made a hundred
credits today. Honestly, too!" The recent memory of three bodies
in an alley came back to him. "Although now I am not so glad I
did, maybe."

"That is a strange thing to say." The giant poured himself a tiny
yttrium cognac. "I am happy for you, but somewhat disappointed
also, for it will mean that you will not need the job I've lined up
for you."

"Oh? Don't be in such a hurry, massive one. And don't try to
psych me, either. I am solvent at the moment, true, but money has
a tendency to slip unnoticed from my fingers. I give too much
away, also. And I have the old woman to think of, although by now
she might own the city fountains, despite her protestations of
poverty."

"Ah. Mother Mastiff, of course. Well, possibly you would be interested, then. I can at least promise you some intriguing company." He gestured behind Flinx. "The third booth. Two most extraordinary personages."

Flinx turned to look at the small, cloth-covered booths which
lined the back of the establishment. Business and pleasure, some-

times mixed, were often conducted in those shrouded enclaves. He peered harder in the fuzzy light. Most people could not have discerned anything at even that short distance, but Flinx did not look with his eyes alone. Yes, there were indeed two figures in the indicated booth. And yes, from what he could see of them they did form an odd pair.

One was a very tall human. His face was not sallow, but composed mostly of acute angles, like knife blades protruding out from under the skin. His hair seemed to be graying at the temples and back, a natural turning of color, and one streak of pure white ran all the way from front to back. The eyes were sharply slanted, almost mongoloid, and as black as most of his hair. They were made to appear mildly incongruous by the bushy eyebrows which met over the bridge of the nose. The mouth was small and thin-lipped, and the body, while not skinny, had the slenderness of careful diet more than vigorous exercise. He was heavily tanned on the visible portions of his body, the tan that Flinx had come to recognize as belonging to men who had been long in space and exposed to greater amounts of naked ultraviolet than most.

If the man was unusual, his companion was twice so. Although Flinx had not seen so very many thranx, for they did not congregate in Drallar, he had seen enough to know that the one lounging across from the man was by far the oldest he'd ever come across. Its chiton had faded from a normal healthy pale blue to a deep purple that was almost black. The antennae drooped to the sides and were scaly at the base. Even at this distance he could perceive how the shell below the wing cases (both sets were present: unmated, then) was exfoliating. Only the glowing, jewellike compound eyes glittered with a gold that signified youth and vigor. A pity that he could not perceive even deeper.

The cloth effectively cut off their conversation at this distance, but now and then the insect would make a gesture with a truehand and the human would nod solemnly in response. Flinx found the liquor hampering him. Almost angrily, he turned back to his friend.

"You were right, Symm. An odd coupling to find here."

"They've been in every night for four nights running now, and they drink steadily, although it seems to have about as much effect on them as water. But to the point. As is plain to a *Mottl*-bird, they are strangers here. Yesterday they first began inquiring after a guide, saying that they wish to see more of the city. I was at a loss to help them until I thought of you. But now, since you are grown as rich as the king. . . ."

"No, no. Wait." Flinx was feeling expansive. Perhaps it was the beer. "They should be good for a few stories, if nothing else. Yes, I'll assume the conveyance."

Symm grinned and ruffled the boy's hair roughly. "Good! I thought a glimpse of them might persuade you, as your interest in things off-world is notorious. Why it should be, though, the Tree knows! Wait here, I'll go tell them."

He went out from behind the bar and over to the booth. Through the faintly puce haze induced by the beer he could see the giant part the curtain and murmur to the two beings within.

"Well," he muttered to himself. "One thing's helping, anyways. At least they're not common tourists. Perhaps I'll be spared the agony of watching them chortle over buying shiploads of junk at three times the honest price." He made a sound that was a long hiss ending in a popped bubble. A scaly, smug head popped up from the bowl of demolished pretzels, which had shrunken considerably in volume. The minidrag slid out onto the table and up the proffered arm, curling into its familiar position on Flinx's shoulder. It burped once, sheepishly.

Symm returned with the two off-worlders in tow. "This youth is called Flinx, sirs, and offers to be your guide. A finer or more knowledgeable one cannot be found in the city. Do not be misled by his comparative youth, for he has already acquired more information than is good for him."

Here at close range Flinx was able to study his two charges better. He did so, intently. The tall human was a fair sixth meter shorter than the huge Symm, but the thranx was truly a giant of its kind. With its upper body raised as it was now, its eyes were almost on a level with Flinx's own. The entire insect was a full 2 meters long. One and a half was normal for a male of the species. That their eyes were busy in their own scrutiny of him he did not mind. As a performer he was more than used to that. But he found himself looking away from those great golden orbs. Meeting them was too much like staring into an ocean of shattered prisms. He wondered what it was like to view life that way, through a thousand tiny eyes instead of merely two large ones.

When the man spoke, it was with a surprisingly melodious voice. "How do you do, youngster. Our good dispenser of spirits here informs us that you are practically indispensable to one who wishes to see something of your city."

He extended a hand and Flinx shook it, surprised at the calluses there. As the effects of the mildly hallucinogenic brew wore off, he became increasingly aware of the uniqueness of the two beings he was going to be associating with. Each exuded an aura of something he'd not encountered before, even in his wanderings among the denizens of the shuttleport.

"My name is Tse-Mallory . . . Bran. And this, my companion, is the Eint Truzenzuzex."

The insect bowed from the "waist" at the introduction, a swooping, flowing motion not unlike that of a lake-skimmer diving for a surface swimming fish. Another surprise: it spoke Terranglo, instead of symbospeech. Here was a learned and very polite bug indeed! Few thranx had the ability to master more than a few elementary phrases of Terranglo. Its inherent logical inconsistencies tended to give them headaches. The insect's pronunciation, however, was as good as his own. The rasping quality of it was made unavoidable by the different arrangement of vocal cords.

"High metamorphosis to you, youth. We've been in need of a guide to this confusing city of yours for several days, actually. We're very glad you've agreed to help us out of our difficulty."

"I'll do what I can, gentlesirs." This flattery was embarrassing.

"We would prefer to start at dawn tomorrow," said Tse-Mallory. "We're here on business, you see, and a more intimate acquaintance with the city is a prerequisite which we have put off too long already. We were expecting a guide to meet us, actually, but since he has apparently changed his mind, you will have the commission."

"We are staying at a small inn a short distance down this same street," added Truzenzuzex. "Its sign is three fishes and . . ."

". . . a starship. I know the place, sir. I'll meet you at first-fog— seven hours—tomorrow, in the lobby."

The two shook hands with him once again and made as if to take their leave. Flinx coughed delicately but insistently. "Uh, a small detail, sirs."

Tse-Mallory paused. "Yes?"

"There is the matter of payment."

The thranx made the series of rapid clicking sounds with its mandibles which passed for laughter among its kind. The insects had a highly developed, sometimes mischievous sense of humor.

"So! Our guide is a plutocrat as well! No doubt as a larva you were a hopeless sugar-hoarder. How about this, then? At the conclusion of our tour tomorrow—I daresay one day will be sufficient for our purposes—we will treat you to a meal at the finest comestabulary in the food crescent."

Well! Let's see now, twelve courses at Portio's would come to . . . well! His mouth was watering already.

"That'll be great . . . sufficient, I mean, sirs." Indeed, it would!

2

Flinx was of course not a guide by profession, but he knew ten times as much about the real Drallar as the bored government hirelings who conducted the official tours of the city's high spots for bemused off-worlders. He'd performed this function for other guests of Small Symm more than once in the past.

These, however, had proved themselves rather outré *touristas*. He showed them the great central marketplace, where goods from halfway across the Arm could be found. They did not buy. He took them to the great gate of Old Drallar, a monumental arch carved from water-pure silicon dioxide by native craftsmen, and so old it was not recorded in the palace chronicles. They did not comment. He took them also to the red towers where the fantastic flora of Moth grew lush in greenhouses under the tender ministrations of dedicated royal botanists. Then to the tiny, out-of-the-way places, where could be bought the unusual, the rare, and the outlawed. Jeweled dishware, artwork, weaponry, utensils, gems, rare earths and rare clothings, tickets to anywhere. Scientific instruments, scientists, females or other sexes of any species. Drugs: medicinal, hallucinogenic, deadly, preservative. Thoughts and palm-readings. Only rarely did either of them say this or that small thing about their surroundings. One might almost have thought them bored.

Once it was at an antique cartographer's, and then in a language incomprehensible to the multilinguistic Flinx.

Yes, for two who had seemed so needful of a guide, they had thus far shown remarkably little interest in their surroundings. They seemed far more interested in Flinx and Pip than in the city he was showing them. As late afternoon rolled around he was startled to realize how much they had learned about him through the most innocent and indirect questioning. Once, when Truzenzuzex had leaned forward to observe the minidrag more closely, it had drawn back warily and curled its head out of sight behind Flinx's neck. That itself was an oddity. The snake's normal reaction was usually either passivity or belligerence. This was the first time Flinx could recall its displaying uncertainty. Apparently Truzenzuzex made little of the incident, but he never tried to approach the reptile closely again.

"You are an outstanding guide and a cheerful companion," the thranx said, "and I for one count myself fortunate to have you with us." They had moved along until they were now quite a distance from the city's center. Truzenzuzex gestured ahead to where the tower homes of the very wealthy stretched away in landscaped splendor. "Now we would wish to see the manicured grounds and hanging gardens of Drallar's inurbs, of which we have both heard so much."

"I'm afraid I cannot manage that, sir. The grounds of Braav inurb are closed to such as I, and there are groundkeepers—with guns—who are posted by the walls to keep the common folk from infesting the greens."

"But you *do* know the ways within?" prodded Tse-Mallory.

"Well," Flinx began hesitantly. After all, what did he really know of these two? "At night I have sometimes found it necessary to . . . but it is not night now, and we would surely be seen going over the walls."

"Then we shall go through the gate. Take us," he said firmly, shutting off Flinx's incipient protests, "and we will worry about getting past the guards."

Flinx shrugged, irritated by the man's stubbornness. Let them learn their own way, then. But he mentally added an expensive dessert to the evening's meal. He led them to the first gateway and stood in the background while the large, overbearing man who lounged in the little building there came over toward them, grumbling noticeably.

It was now that the most extraordinary event of the day took place. Before the obviously antagonistic fellow could so much as utter a word, Truzenzuzex put a truehand into a pouch and thrust under the man's eyes a card taken from somewhere inside. The man's eyes widened and he all but saluted, the belligerence melting from his attitude like wax. Flinx had never, never seen an inurb guard, a man widely noted for his cultivated rudeness and suspicious mannerisms, react so helplessly to anyone, not even the residents of the inurbs themselves. He grew even more curious as to the nature of his friends. But they remained basically unreadable. *Damn* that beer! It seemed to him that he had heard the name Tse-Mallory somewhere before, but he couldn't be certain. And he would have given much for a glimpse of the card Truzenzuzex had so negligently flashed before the guard.

The way was now quite unopposed. He would at least have the opportunity of seeing some familiar things for the first time in the light of day. At leisure, too, without having to glance continually over his shoulder.

They strolled silently amid the emerald parklike grounds and tinkling waterfalls, occasionally passing some richly dressed inhabitant or sweating underling, sometimes startling a deer or phylope among the bushes.

"I understand," said Tse-Mallory, breaking the silence, "that each tower belongs to one family, and is named thusly."

"That's true enough," replied Flinx.

"And are you familiar with them?"

"Most, not all. Since you are curious, I'll name the ones I do know as we pass them."

"Do that."

It seemed silly, but they were paying, so who was he to argue the practicality? A fine wine joined the dinner menu. . . .

". . . and this," he said as they drew abreast of a tall black-glazed tower, "is the House of Malaika. A misnomer, sir. As I understand, it means 'angel' in a dead Terran language."

"No Terran language is 'dead,' " said Tse-Mallory cryptically. Then, "He who is named Maxim?"

"Why, yes. I know because I've performed here for parties, several times past. This next, the yellow. . . ."

But they weren't listening, he saw. Both had halted by the black tower and were staring upward to where the rose-tinted crystal proto-porches encircled the upper stories and overhung the lush greenery of the hanging vines and air-shrubs.

"It is fortuitous," he heard Truzenzuzex remark, "that you know each other. It might or might not facilitate certain matters. Come, we shall pay a call on your Mister Malaika."

Flinx was completely taken aback. Was this why they had hired him in the first place? To come this far to an impossibility? Next to the king and his ministers, the trader families of Drallar, nomads who had taken their talents off-planet, were the wealthiest and most powerful individuals on the planet. And some might possibly be wealthier, for the extent of the great fortunes was not a subject into which even the monarch could inquire with impunity.

"It is a slight acquaintance only, sirs! What makes you believe he will do anything but kick us out? What makes you believe he'll even see us?"

"What makes you think we can enter an oh-so-restricted inurb?" replied Truzenzuzex confidently. "He will see us."

The two began to head up the paved walkway toward the great arch of the tower entrance and Flinx, exasperated and puzzled, had little choice but to follow.

The double doorway of simple carved crystal led to a domed hallway that was lined with statuary and paintings and mindgrams which even Flinx's untrained eye could recognize as being of great value. There, at the far end, was a single elevator.

They halted before the platinum-inlaid wood. A woman's voice greeted them mechanically from a grid set off to one side.

"Good afternoon, gentlebeings, and welcome to the House of Malaika. Please to state your business."

Now they would finish this foolishness! The message was all very nicely put, the surroundings pleasant. Out of the corner of an eye he could see a screen, delicately painted, ruffling in the slight breeze of the chamber's ventilators. Beyond which no doubt the muzzle of a laser-cannon or other inhospitable device was already trained on them. It was comfortably cool in the hall, but he felt himself nonetheless beginning to sweat.

"Ex-chancellor second sociologist Bran Tse-Mallory and first philosoph the Eint Truzenzuzex present their compliments to Maxim of the House of Malaika and would have converse with him if he is at home and so disposed."

Flinx's mind parted abruptly from thoughts of making a run for the entrance. No wonder they'd gotten past the gate guard so easily! A churchman and a pure scientist. High-ranked at that, although Tse-Mallory had said "ex." Chancellor second—that was planetary level, at least. He was less sure of Truzenzuzex's importance, but he knew that the thranx held their philosophs, or theoreticians, in an esteem matched only by that of the honorary Hive-Mothers and the Chancellor Firsts of the Church themselves. His mind was deluged with questions, all tinged by uncertainty as much as curiosity. What were two such eminences doing slumming in a place like Small Symm's? Why had they picked him for a guide—a youth, a nothing—when they could have had a royal escort by a king's minister? That answer he could read clearly. Incognito; the one word said much and implied more. At the moment, what dealings did two such sophisticated minds have with a solid, earthy merchant like Maxim Malaika?

While he had been dazedly forming questions without answer, a mind somewhere had been coming to a decision. The grid spoke again.

"Maxim of the House of Malaika extends greetings, albeit astonished, and will have converse immediately with the two honorsirs. He wishes the both of you . . ." there was a pause while a hidden eye somewhere scanned, ". . . the three of you to come up. He is now in the southwest porchroom and would greet you there soonest."

The grid voice clicked off and immediately the rich-grained doors slid back. Man and thranx stepped unbidden into the dark-pile interior. Flinx debated a second whether to follow them or run like hell, but Tse-Mallory decided for him.

"Don't stand there gawking, youth. Didn't you hear it say he wished to see the *three* of us?"

Flinx could nowhere detect malignance. He stepped in. The elevator held them all more than comfortably. He'd been in this house before, but if there was one thing he was certain of it was that he was not now being summoned to provide entertainment. And this was not the servants' entrance he'd used before. The soft *fsssh* of air as the doors closed sounded explosively loud in his ears.

They were met at the end of their ride by a tall skeleton of a man dressed in the black and crimson of the Malaika family colors. He said nothing as he conducted them to a room Flinx had not seen before.

The far end of the room looked open to the sky. Actually it was one of the great crystal proto-porches which made this section of Drallar resemble so well a bejeweled forest. He quivered momentarily as he stepped out onto what appeared to be slick nothingness. The two scientists seemed unaffected. He had been on one of these before, when performing, but it had been opaque. This one was perfectly transparent, with just a hint of rose coloring, all the way to the ground. He looked up and the vertigo passed.

The furnishings were all in red and black, with here and there an occasional bright color in some imported article or work of art. Incense hung cloyingly in the air. In the distance the sun of Moth had begun to set, diffused by the perpetual thin fog. It got dark early on Moth.

On one of the numerous big fluffy couches sat two figures. One he immediately recognized: Malaika. The other was smaller, blond, and quite differently formed. The majority of her covering was formed by her waist-length hair.

The voice that rumbled out of the thick-muscled neck was like a dormant volcano stirring to life. "*Je*? Our visitors are here. You run along, Sissiph, dear, and make yourself more pretty, *ndiyo*?"

He gave her a crushing peck on the cheek and sent her from the room with a resounding swat on the most prominent portion of her anatomy. He's got a new one, thought Flinx. This one was blonde and a bit more ripely curved than the last. Apparently the trader's tastes were expanding along with his belly. In truth, though, it showed only slightly as yet.

"Well! Well," boomed Malaika. His teeth flashed whitely in the ebony face, sparkling amidst wisps of curly beard. He was up to them and shaking hands in two steps. "Bran Tse-Mallory and the Eint Truzenzuzex. *Usitawi. The* Truzenzuzex?"

The insect performed another of its slow, graceful bows. "I plead guilty of necessity to the accusation." Flinx took the time to admire the insect's abilities. Due to the nature of their physiology the thranx were usually extremely stiff in their movements. To see one bow as did Truzenzuzex was exceptional.

When the Humanx Commonwealth was in the process of being formed, humans had marveled at the scintillating blue and blue-green iridescence of the thranx body coloring and swooned at the natural perfume they exuded. They had wondered miserably what the thranx would see in their own dun-colored, stinky soft selves. What the thranx had seen was a flexibility coupled with firmness which no thranx could ever hope to match. Soon traveling dance companies from humanoid planets had become among the most popular forms of live entertainment on the thranx colonies and homeworlds.

But from the thorax up, at least, Truzenzuzex gave the impression of being made of rubber.

Malaika finished shaking hands with both and then gave Flinx another little surprise. The merchant extended his head and touched nose to antenna with the insect. It was the nearest a human could come to the traditional thranx greeting of intertwining antennae. But then, he reminded himself, a man who did business with as many races as had Malaika would know every gesture as a matter of course . . . and commerce.

"Sit down, sit down!" he roared in what he undoubtedly thought to be a gentle tone of voice. "What do you think of my little *mwen-zangu* there, eh? Companion," he added, seeing the puzzlement on their faces. He jerked his head in the direction taken by the departed girl.

Tse-Mallory said nothing, the twinkle in his eyes being sufficient. Truzenzuzex went further. "If I read current human values aright, I should venture to say that such a proportion of marmoreal flesh to the width of the pelvic region would be viewed as more than usually aesthetic."

Malaika roared. "Stars, you *are* a scientist, sir! Powers of observation, indeed! What can I give you both to drink?"

"Ginger ale for me, if you have a good year."

"Fagh! I do, but 'pon my word, sir, you've mellowed if you're the same Tse-Mallory I've heard tell of. And you, sir?"

"Would you by any chance have some apricot brandy?"

"Oh ho! A gourmet, as well as a man of science! I believe we can accommodate you, good philosoph. But it will necessitate a trip to the cellars. I don't often receive such a discerning guest." The shadow which had conducted them from the elevator still stood wraithlike at the back of the room. Malaika waved to it. "See to it, Wolf." The sentinel bowed imperceptibly and shuffled from the room, taking something in the atmosphere with him. More sensitive to it than the others, Flinx was relieved when the man's presence had gone.

Now, for the first time, that hearty voice lost some of its bantering tone. "*Je*? What brings you two here, to Drallar? And so very quietly, too." He glanced keenly from one imperturbable face to the other, stroking that rich Assyrian beard slowly. "Much as my ego would be flattered, I cannot believe that such a stealthy entrance to our fair city has been effected purely for the pleasure of making my company." He leaned forward expectantly in a manner that suggested he could smell money at least as well as Mother Mastiff.

Malaika was not as tall as Tse-Mallory, but he was at least twice as broad and had the build of an over-age wrestler. Shockingly white teeth gleamed in the dusky face which bore the stamp of the kings of ancient Monomotapa and Zimbabwe. Massive, hairy arms protruded from the sleeves of the one-piece semisilk dressing gown he wore casually belted at the waist. Legs to match, as solid looking as a Mothian ironwood tree, thrust out from the pleated folds at the knees. The short, knobby toes on the splayed feet bore a close resemblance to the woody parasites that often infested such growths. At least, they did on one foot. The other, Flinx knew, ended at the knee. Fueled by credits, the prosthetic surgeons had labored their best to make the left match its natural counterpart on the right. The match was not quite perfect.

The real one, Flinx had learned from a talkative young woman at one of Malaika's parties, had been lost in the man's youth. He had been on a fur-gathering expedition to the planet of a minor sun in Draco when his party had been attacked by an ice-lizard. Being rather stupidly caught away from their weapons, they had watched helplessly as the carnivore instinctively sought out the weakest member of their party, the youthful female accountant. Malaika alone had intervened. Lacking a suitable weapon, he had choked the beast to death by the simple expedient of jamming his left leg down its throat. It was the sort of extreme stunt that one wouldn't expect of the pragmatic merchant. Unfortunately, by the time they could get him to sufficient hospital facilities the limb had been torn and frozen beyond repair.

"We neither intended nor expected to deceive you, friend Malaika. We happen in fact to be on the trail of something we have good reason to think you would find of value, yes. To us, however, it means much more than a paltry few hundred million credits."

Flinx swallowed.

"But," Tse-Mallory continued, "our personal resources are limited, and so we are forced, however reluctantly, to seek an outside source of aid. One with an open credit slip and a closed mouth."

"And so you've wound your way to me. Well, well, well! It seems I'm to be flattered after all. I wouldn't be truthful if I said I were not. Nonetheless, you must of course prove that what you wish me to provide credit for is going to be profitable to me . . . in hard credit, not philosophical intangibles . . . your pardon, friends. Tell me more about this thing which is worth much more than a mere few millions of credit."

"We assumed that would be your reaction. Any other, to tell the truth, would have made us suspicious. It is one of the reasons why we feel we can deal openly with your type of person."

"How comforting to know that you regard me as so obviously predictable," Malaika said drily. "Do go on."

"We could have gone to a government organization. The best are all too often corrupt, despite Church pronouncements. We could have gone to a large philanthropic organization. They are too prone to shock. In the end we decided it would be best to go where the promise of much credit would insure the exclusivity of our enterprise."

"And supposing that I do agree to put up the *fedha* for this venture, what guarantee have you that I will not kill you outright if it proves successful and return with the object of search and two canceled checks?"

"Very simple. First, odd as it may sound, we know you to be both reliable and reasonably honest in your business dealings. This has proved among the best of your wares in the past and should again, despite the bloodthirsty image your publicists enjoy presenting to the gullible public. Second, we don't know what we're looking for, but we will know it when we find it. And there is an excellent possibility that we will find nothing at all. Or worse, something will be found which will still remain worthless to us because of its incomprehensibility."

"Good! Any other thoughts and *I* would have become suspicious! I become more and more curious. Elucidate for the benefit of my poor, ignorant trader's mind. Why me, *por favor*?"

Truzenzuzex ignored the pun and made the thranx equivalent of a shrug. "Someone was necessary. As already mentioned, your reputation in a business noted for its back-stabbing made my ship-brother select you." Another revelation, thought Flinx. "And Moth itself is close to our objective . . . in a relative sense only, so it would do you little good and much expense to try to find it on your own. Also, another vessel departing Moth would mean nothing, with its constant flux of star travel. Our course would not be suspect from here, whereas elsewhere it might engender unwanted cogitation. Traders, however, often fly peculiar tangents to throw off competitors."

At this point the drinks arrived. Conversation was suspended by mutual consent as the debaters sipped at their refreshments. Flinx sampled Tse-Mallory's mug of ginger ale and found it delicious, if mild. Malaika drained at least half the contents of a huge tankard in one gulp. He rubbed his foamy lips with the sleeve of an immaculate gown, staining it irreparably. Knowing the fabric's worth in the marketplace, Flinx couldn't help but wince.

"I again apologize for my denseness, sirs, but I would have whatever it is the competition is to be thrown off of spelled out to me." He turned to face Tse-Mallory directly. "And although you are apparently no longer associated with the Church in an official capacity, sociologist, I confess I am curious to know why you did not approach them seeking aid."

"My dealings with the United Church, Malaika, have not been overclose for a number of years now. My parting was amicable enough, but there was a certain amount of unavoidable bitterness in certain quarters over my leaving that . . . matters would be complicated, shall we say, should I reveal our knowledge to them at this time. Such would be necessary to secure their aid."

"Um. Well, that's blunt enough. I won't prod a sore. Maybe we should get on to. . . ." He paused and looked to his right. Tse-Mallory and Truzenzuzex followed his gaze with their own.

Flinx shifted his position on the floor uncomfortably. He had managed to hear as much as he had by remaining utterly inconspicuous while in plain sight, an art he had learned from a certain patient and very sneaky old man. Aided by his own odd abilities, it had served him importantly more than once. These three, however, were far more observant than the folk one encountered in the marketplace. He could see clearly that he would have to leave. Why not voluntarily?

"Uh, sirs, I could do with some . . . if you, honored host, would point me in the direction of a pantry, I will endeavor to make myself instantly and painlessly nonpresent."

Malaika chuckled deafeningly. "Astuteness is laudable, youth. So instead of sending you home . . . I could wonder where *that* might be . . . you go back to the hall, to your right, second door. You should find in there enough nourishment to keep even you busy for a few minutes!"

Flinx uncurled from his lotus position on the floor and departed in the indicated direction. He felt their eyes and minds on him until he was out of view, at which point the pressure relaxed. Malaika's conviviality did not fool him. He might already have heard more than would prove healthy. He was intensely interested in the answers to a good many questions that Malaika was now undoubtedly putting to his guests, and entertained thoughts of locating a good listening place at a thin section of wall. However, the death's head had reappeared and stationed himself by the entrance to the porch-room. The blue eyes had passed over him once, as though he were not worthy of a second glance. Flinx bridled, then sighed. He would have to make do with what he could pick up without visual contact. Might as well enjoy the other opportunity while he had it. He walked on.

The pantry was all of fantastic. He almost forgot the unusual progression of incidents that had brought him here while he gorged himself and the minidrag on the store of luxuries. He had gotten as far as debating between Terran champagne and pine mint from Barrabas when a short series of extremely odd thoughts drifted across his open mind. He turned and noticed that the door to the room on his right was slightly open. The teasing subvocalizations came from beyond there. He did not for a moment doubt that that door should be securely locked. Cautiously, with a quick glance at the kitchen entrance, he made his way over to the door and slid it back another inch.

The room next to the kitchen was narrow but long. It probably ran the whole length of this radius of the tower. Its function, at least, was unmistakable. It was a bar. With an eye towards locating an even more palatable drink and his curiosity piqued he prepared to enter, only to catch himself quickly.

The room was already occupied.

A figure was hunched over by the opposite wall, its head pressed tightly against it. He could make out the outlines of a ventilating grid or something similar on the other side of the head. The face was turned away from him and so hidden. The metal and wood he could see there was thin and light. The voices from the next room sounded clearly to him even from where he stood in the kitchen.

He eased the door back as slowly and easily as possible. Apparently totally engrossed in the conversation taking place on the other side of the wall, the figure did not notice his quiet approach. The grid itself could now be seen to be much larger than would be required for ventilating purposes. It looked loose and was probably hinged. Garbage could be passed through it from the other room, and thence shifted to nearby disposal units. He had a hunk of spiced Bice cheese in one hand and a pheasant leg between his teeth. His free hand started down for the stiletto hidden in his boot, then paused. The thoughts of the figure did not have the coldness nor the death-clear logic of the professional spy or assassin. Quite the contrary. Deaf killers were also rare, and this one had *still* refused cognizance of his presence.

He made a rapid decision and brought back a foot, delivering a solid blow to the upthrust portion of the unbalanced figure below. It uttered a single screech and shot through the grill into the room beyond. In a split second he had regretfully discarded both pheasant and cheese and rolled through after it, coming up on his feet on the other side. The startled faces of Malaika, Tse-Mallory, and Truzenzuzex were already gazing in astonishment at the scene. The figure stood opposite him, rubbing the injured portion. It cursed him steadily and fluently. He noticed absently as he dodged the fingers which drove for his larynx that the figure was very much that of a woman. It matched the thoughts he had picked up. Reluctantly he assumed a defensive pose, legs apart, knees slightly bent, arms out and forward. Pip fluttered nervously on his shoulder, the pleated wings unfurling preparatory to the minidrag's taking flight.

The woman made another motion as if to attack again, but was frozen by the bellow which came from Malaika's direction.

"ATHA!" She turned to face him.

The big merchant strode over to stand between them. His eyes went from one to the other, finally settling hard on Flinx.

"Well, *kijana*? I suggest something profound, and quickly!"

Flinx tried to keep his voice as even as possible, despite the adrenalin pumping through his system.

"I was in the pantry and happened to notice the door to the room next to it was open" (never mind why he had noticed it). "Looking in, I saw a figure . . . that figure . . . hunched over next to a grill. The room most certainly ought to have been locked. I assumed that this was not part of your normal method of conducting private business talks and so I decided to force the issue—and the person—into the open, where the air is clearer. I'm sorry if I've broken a fetish or taboo of yours."

"What!" Then he caught the humor of it and grinned. "Think I'm a weirdie, eh, *kijana*?"

"It was a thought, sir."

"*Adabu*! No, you did right, Flinx." He turned a furious gaze on the girl. She shrank back slightly under that withering visage but the obstinate glare never left her face. Somehow she found the where-withal to look righteous.

"Goddamn you, girl, double-damn and collapsed drives, I've told you about this, before!" He shook his head in exasperation. "Again, *kwa ajili ya adabu*, for the sake of manners, I forgive it. Get out to the port and check out the shuttle."

"It was checked again only last week and nothing was wrong with. . . ."

"Agggh!" He raised a hand the size of a ham. "I . . . strongly . . . suggest . . . that you . . . !" She skittered by the descending hand and sped for the exit. The look she sent Flinx on the way out was brief, but hot enough to melt duralloy. Malaika caught his breath and seemed to calm himself somewhat.

"How much of what she heard did you hear?"

Flinx lied. In the situation he considered it more than ethical. "Enough."

"So, so!" The merchant considered. "Well, perhaps it will work out for the better. You'll probably turn out to be the sharpest one aboard, lad, but I'd stay clear of Atha for a while. I'm afraid your method of making first greetings will never replace shaking hands!" He shook with laughter at his own witticism. He put out

an arm as if to embrace Flinx's shoulders, drew it back hastily at a
warning gesture from Pip.

"She works for you?" It was a rhetorical question. But Flinx was
curious to know what position the girl held that could inspire such
trust on Malaika's part that he could treat her as he had without
fear of reprisal.

"Atha? Oh yes." He looked in the direction taken by the girl.
"You wouldn't think a *mwanamke* that ferocious would have the
patience to make starship copilot at her age, would you? She's
been with me in that capacity for six years now."

Flinx resumed his former position on the floor. In reply to Tse-
Mallory's inquiring gaze, Malaika said, "I've decided that our
young friend will accompany us on the journey. I know what I'm
doing, gentlesirs. If the trip is long and tedious he will provide relief for us, and he's sharp as a whip besides. He also has some peculiar abilities which might prove useful to us, despite their capriciousness. It is a subject to which I have meant to give more
attention in the past, but have never found the time." Flinx glanced
up interestedly, but could detect nothing beyond the merchant's ve-
neer of surface geniality. "In any case, he is too poor and not rich
enough to pose a threat to us. And I believe him to be disgustingly
honest. Although he has had ample opportunity to steal from my
house he has never done so . . . as far as I know."

"His honesty was never in question," said Truzenzuzex. "I've no
objection to the lad's presence."

"Nor I," added Tse-Mallory.

"Then, sociologist, if you would continue with your narrative?"

"Actually, there is not much that is new to tell. Would that there
were. As you might know my companion and I gave up our respective careers and regular pursuits some twelve odd years ago to research jointly the history and civilization of the Tar-Aiym."

"Some talk of your work has filtered down to my level, yes. Do
continue. Naturally I am interested in anything that has to do with
the Tar-Aiym . . . or their works."

"So much we—naturally—supposed."

"Pardon, sir," interrupted Flinx. "I know of the Tar-Aiym, of
course, but only by rumor and book. Could you maybe tell me
more, please?" He looked properly apologetic.

Since Malaika offered no objection, perhaps himself not considering such information redundant, Tse-Mallory agreed.

"All right then, lad." He took another long swig of his drink. "As
near as we have been able to determine, some 500,000 Terran-

standard years ago this area of the galaxy was, as it is now, occupied by a large number of diverse and highly intelligent races. The Tar-Aiym were by far the strongest of these. Most of their time and effort was apparently absorbed in warring with their less powerful neighbors, as much for the pleasure of it, it seems, as for the wealth it brought them. At one time the Tar-Aiym empire covered this section of space to a depth of four quadrants and a width of at least two. Maybe more.

"Any reason we could put forth to explain the total disappearance of the Tar-Aiym and most of their subject races would be mostly conjecture. But working painstakingly with bits and pieces of myth and rumor, and a very few solidly documented facts, researchers have put together one explanation that seems to offer more than most.

"At the height of their power the Tar-Aiym came across a more primitive race far in toward the galactic center. This race was not quite the intellectual equal of the Tar-Aiym, and they'd had star travel for only a short time. But they were tremendously tenacious and multiplied at an extraordinary rate. They resisted, successfully, every effort to be forced into the Tar-Aiym hegemony. In fact, under the impetus provided by Tar-Aiym pressures, they began to make giant strides forward and to spread rapidly to other systems.

"Apparently the Tar-Aiym leadership did a most uncharacteristic thing. It panicked. They directed their war scientists to develop new and even more radical types of weaponry to combat this supposed new menace from the center. True to form, their great laboratories soon came up with several offerings. The one that was finally implemented was a form of mutated bacterium. It multiplied at a phenomenal rate, living off itself if no other host was available. To any creature with a nervous system more complex than that of the higher invertebrates it was completely and irrevocably lethal.

"The story from there," continued Truzenzuzex, "is a simple and straightforward one. The plague worked as the leadership had hoped, to the extent of utterly wiping out the Tar-Aiym enemies. It also set about totally eliminating the Tar-Aiym themselves and most of the intelligent and semi-intelligent life in that huge sector of space we know today as the Blight. You know it, Flinx?"

"Sure. It's a big section between here and the center. Hundreds of worlds on which nothing intelligent lives. They'll be filled again someday."

"No doubt. For now, though, they are filled only with the lower animals and the wreckage of past civilizations. Fortunately the surviving space-traversing worlds were informed of the nature of the plague by the last remnants of the dying Tar-Aiym. A strict quarantine must have been put into effect, because for centuries it appears that nothing was permitted in or out of the Blight. Otherwise it is probable that none of us would be sitting here now. It is only in recent times that the systems of the Blight have been rediscovered and somewhat hesitantly explored."

"The taboo lingers even if the reason behind it has gone," said Malaika quietly.

"Yes. Well, some of the quarantined races on the fringe of the epidemic died out rather slowly. By means of interspace relay or some similar device they managed to pass out some threads of fact describing the Armageddon. Innocent and guilty alike died as the plague burned itself out. Thank Hive that all traces of the germ have long since departed the cycle of things!"

"Amen," murmured Malaika surprisingly. Then, louder, "But please, gentlesirs, to the point. And the point is—credit."

Tse-Mallory took over again. "Malaika, have you ever heard of the Krang?"

"*Nini*? No, I . . . no, wait a minute." The trader's thick brows furrowed in thought. "Yes. Yes, I believe I have. It forms part of the mythology of the, uh, the Branner folk, doesn't it?"

Tse-Mallory nodded approval. "That's right. The Branner, as you may or may not recall, occupy three star systems on the periphery of the Blight, facing Moth. According to a folk-legend of theirs passed down from the cataclysm, even though the Tar-Aiym were hard pressed to find a solution to the threat from the center, they had not yet given up all forms of nonmilitary development and experimentation. As we now know for a fact, the Tar-Aiym were inordinately fond of music."

"Marches, no doubt," murmured Truzenzuzex.

"Perhaps. Anyway, one of the last great works of artistic merit that their culture was supposed to have produced was a great musical instrument called the Krang. It was theoretically completed in the waning days of the Empire, just as the plague was beginning to make itself known on Empire planets as well as those of the enemy."

"*Ili*?" said Malaika. "So?"

"On the side of the Blight almost one hundred and fifty parsecs from Branner lies the home world of a primitive race of hominids, little visited by the rest of the galaxy. They are far off the main trade routes and have little to offer in the way of value, either in produce or culture. They are pleasant, pastoral, and nonaggressive. Seemingly they once possessed star travel, but sank back into a preatomic civilization and are only just now beginning to show signs of a scientific renaissance. Interestingly enough, they also have a legend concerning something called the Krang. Only in their version it is not an artistic device, but a weapon of war. One which the Tar-Aiym scientists were developing parallel with the plague, before the latter was put into widespread use. According to the legend it was intended to be primarily a defensive and not an offensive weapon. If so, it would be the first time in the literature that the Tar-Aiym had been reduced to building a device for defensive purposes. This runs contrary to all we know of Tar-Aiym psychology and shows how severely they believed themselves pressed by their new enemy."

"Fascinating dichotomy," said Malaika. "And you have some indication as to where this weapon or lute or whatever might be? If either, it would be very valuable in Commonwealth markets."

"True, though we are only interested in its scientific and cultural properties."

"Of course, of course! While my accountants are estimating its net worth, you can draw theoretical rationalizations from its guts to your heart's content . . . provided that you remember how to put its pieces back together again. Now just where is this enigmatic little treasure trove, eh?" He leaned forward eagerly.

"Well, we know exactly, almost," said Tse-Mallory.

"Exactly? Almost? My weak mind again, gentlesirs. Forgive me, but I profess lack of comprehension."

Truzenzuzex made a very human-sounding sigh. Air made a soft *whoosh!* as it was forced out the breathing spicules of his b-thorax.

"The planet on which the Krang is supposedly located was discovered accidentally nearly a t-year ago by a prospector working independently in the Blight. He was hunting for heavy metals, and he found them. Only they weren't arranged in the ground the way he'd expected."

"This fellow, he must have had sponsors," said Malaika. "Why didn't he take this information to them?"

"The man owed a very great debt to my ship-brother. He knew of his interest in Tar-Aiym relics. Supplying Bran with this information was his way of paying off the debt. It was of a personal nature and going into it here can serve no purpose. It would have been a more than equitable reimbursement."

"Would have been?" Malaika's humor was degenerating visibly

into irritation. "Come, come, gentlesirs, all this subtle evasion makes my mind sleepy and shortens my patience."

"No evasion intended, merchant. The man was to have met us in our rooms in the market section of the city, bringing with him a star map listing complete coordinates for the planet. As we had previously agreed on you as a likely sponsor, the three of us were then to proceed on to this house. When he did not arrive as scheduled we decided after some deliberation to seek you out anyway, in the hope that with your resources you might discover some hint as to his whereabouts. In any case, it would have been difficult to maintain our independence much longer. Despite our best efforts, we do not look like tourists. Enterprising persons had already begun asking awkward questions."

"I will—" began Malaika, but Flinx interrupted.

"Did your friend by any chance have red hair?"

Tse-Mallory jerked around violently. For a second Flinx had a glimpse into something terrifying and bloody, which until now the sociologist had kept well buried beneath a placid exterior. It faded as rapidly as it had appeared, but a hint of it persisted in the crisp, military tones of the sociologist's voice.

"How did you know that?"

Flinx pulled the crumpled piece of plastic from his pocket and handed it to an astounded Truzenzuzex. Tse-Mallory recovered himself and glanced at the unfolded sheet. Flinx continued unperturbed.

"I have a hunch that's your star map. I was on my way to Small Symm's establishment when my attention was caught by a commotion in an alleyway. Ordinarily I would have ignored it. That is the way one lives in Drallar, if one wishes to live long. But for reasons unknown and thrice cursed my pet," he gestured at Pip, "got curious, and took it into his head to investigate. The occupants of the alley took exception to his presence. An unfunny fight was in progress, and in the situation which developed the only argument I had was my knife.

"Your friend had been attacked by two men. Professionals by their looks and actions. They weren't very good ones. I killed one, and Pip finished the other. Your friend was already dead. I'm sorry." He did not mention his earlier encounter with the three.

Tse-Mallory was looking from the map to Flinx. "Well, it was said before that it was a fortuitous circumstance that brought you to our notice. Now it appears to have been doubly so."

He was interrupted by an intent Malaika, who snatched up the map and moved over to where a flexilamp was poised. Positioning the powerful beam he began to study the lines and symbols on the plastic with great deliberation. Dust motes danced drunken spirals in the subdued light.

"A most unusual and versatile pet," commented Truzenzuzex idly. "I've heard of them. The mortality rate from their venom is notoriously high, giving them a reputation all out of proportion to their numbers and disposition. Fortunately, as I understand it, they do not seem to attack without due provocation."

"That's right, sir," said Flinx, scratching the object under discussion on the side of its narrow head. "A ship's physician at the shuttleport once told me he'd met a scientist who'd actually been to Alaspin. The minidrag is native to there, you know. In his spare time, the man had done some limited research on them.

"He said they seemed standoffish, which struck me as kind of a funny way to describe a poisonous reptile. But harmless unless, as you said, provoked. Pip was already pretty tame when I found him. At least, I've never had any trouble with him. The people in my area have learned to tolerate him, mostly because they haven't any choice."

"Understandable attitude," murmured the philosoph.

"This doctor's friend was with an expedition to Alaspin to study the ruins of the ancient civilization there. He hypotha . . . hypothesized that the minidrag's ancestors might have been raised as pets by whoever had produced that culture. Selective breeding could account for some of their peculiar characteristics. Like, they have no natural enemies on the planet. Fortunately their birthrate is very low. And they are omnivorous as well as carnivorous. I found out early what that meant, when Pip started eating bread when he couldn't find meat. Oh yes, he also said they were suspected of being empathetic telepaths. You know, telepathic on the emotional but not the mental level. That's why I'm never cheated in the marketplace or at business or gambling. Pip's sensitive to such things."

"A fascinating creature, I say again," Truzenzuzex continued. "A subject I would like to pursue further. However as I am not an exoherpetologist, I don't think it would be worthwhile just now. Too many other things on my mind." The confession did not entirely ring true, as Flinx could read it. Not entirely.

Malaika was craning his neck over the map, tracing out lines in the plastic with his fingers and nodding occasionally to himself. "*Ndiyo, ndiyo* . . . yes." He looked up finally.

"The planet in question circles a GO, sol-type star. Four-fifths of the way toward GalCenter, straight through the Blight. Quite a trip, gentlesirs. He doesn't supply much information on the planet itself, no, not by an *ndege*-depositing, but it might be enough. Terratype, slightly smaller, marginally thinner atmosphere, higher proportion of certain gases . . . helium, for example. Also eighty-one point two percent water, so we should have little trouble finding the thing."

"Unless it happens to be submerged," said Truzenzuzex.

"So. I prefer not to consider possibilities upsetting to the liver. Besides, if that were the case I don't think your prospector friend would have found it. We'll have the same kind of heavy-metal detection instruments with us anyway, but I'd wager on its being above the water-line. If I recall, the information we do have on the Tar-Aiym suggests they were anything but aquatic in build."

"That's true," admitted the philosoph.

"We'll travel most of the way through unspaced areas, but then, one section of nothing is very much like any other, *kweli?* I foresee no problems. Which probably means a *mavuno* of them. At least we will be comfortable. The *Gloryhole* will not be crowded with all of us."

Flinx smiled but was careful to hide it from the merchant. The origin of the name of Malaika's private cargo-racer was a well-known joke among those in the know. Most thought it an ancient Terran word meaning a rich mineral strike. . . .

"Unless, of course, this gun or giant harp or whatever is going to crowd us. How big did you say it was?"

"I didn't," said Tse-Mallory. "We've no better idea than you. Only that it's . . . large."

"Hmph! Well, if it's too big to go up on the shuttle, we'll just have to send back for a regular transport. I'd rather sit on it once we've found it, but there are no relay stations in that area. If it's been there untouched for a few millennia it will wait a few days." He rolled up the map. "So then, sirs. If there are no objections, I see no reason why we cannot leave *kesho*, tomorrow."

There were none.

"*Ema*! A toast, then. To success and profit, not necessarily in that order! *Nazdrovia*!" He raised his tankard.

"Church and Commonwealth," murmured man and thranx together, softly. They sipped down the remainder of their drinks.

Malaika burped once, glanced out through the crystal wall where the sun of Moth was sinking rapidly behind the fog-squalls.

"It is late. Tomorrow then, at the port. The dock stewards will direct you to my pit. The shuttle will take us all in one trip and I need little time to set my affairs in order."

Tse-Mallory rose and stretched. "If I may ask, who are 'us all'?"

"Those four of us here now, Wolf and Atha to run the ship, and, of course, Sissiph."

"Who?" asked Tse-Mallory.

"The Lynx, the Lynx," whispered Truzenzuzex, grinning and nudging his ship-brother in the ribs. "Have your eyes aged as much as your brain? The girl!" They were strolling to the hallway now.

"Ah yes." They paused by the shadowlike Wolf, who held the door open for them. The man grinned in what was obviously supposed to be a friendly gesture. It did not come off that way. "Yes, a very, ah, interesting and amusing personage."

"*Ndiyo*," said Malaika amiably. "She does have quite a pair, doesn't she?"

As the others bid the spectral doorman goodeve, a hand came down on Flinx's shoulder. The merchant whispered. "Not you, *kijana*. I've a question for you yet. Stay a moment."

He shook hands with Tse-Mallory and touched olfactory organs with Truzenzuzex, waving them toward the elevator.

"Good rest to you, sirs, and tomorrow at first fog!"

Wolf closed the door, cutting off Flinx's view of the scientists, and Malaika immediately bent to face him intently.

"Now, lad, that our ethical friends have left, a point of, um, business. The two hired corpses you left rotting so properly in that alley. Did they have any special insignia or marks on them or their clothing? *Think*, youth!"

Flinx tried to recall. "It was awfully dark . . . I'm not sure. . . ."

"And when did that ever bother you? Don't hedge with me, *kijana*. This is too important. Think . . . or whatever it is you do."

"All right. Yes. When I was trying to pry that map away from the dead man, I did notice the feet of the man Pip had killed. He'd fallen close by. The metal of his boots had a definite design etched on them. It looked to be some kind of bird . . . an abstract representation, I think."

"With teeth?" prompted Malaika.

"Yes . . . no . . . I don't know for sure. The questions you ask,

merchant! It could have been. And for some reason, during the
fight I got this picture of a woman, an old-young woman."

Malaika straightened and patted the boy on the back. His expression was jovial but his thoughts were grim—grim. Ordinarily
Flinx would have resented the patronizing gesture, but this time,
coming from the merchant, it seemed only complimentary.

"Thank the Mti of Miti for your powers of observation, lad. And
for a good memory." Flinx saw another word: *uchawi*, witchcraft,
but did not press the point. The big man changed the subject
abruptly. "I'll see you *kesho*, on ship, then?"

"I would not miss it. Sir, may I ask the why of your question?"

"You may not. The ship tomorrow, then. Good rest." He ushered
a puzzled Flinx to the elevator.

The merchant stood pondering silently awhile, curses bubbling like froth from the cauldron of his mouth. They constituted
the only sounds in the now deserted room. He turned and walked
over to an apparently blank section of wall. Striking a hidden
switch he sent the deep-grained paneling sliding up into the ceiling to reveal a complex desk. The slim bulk of an interstellar transceiver dominated the other apparatus. Buttons were pushed, dials
turned, meters adjusted. The screen lit up suddenly in a glorious
fireball of chromatic static. Satisfied, he grunted and hefted a small
mike.

"Channel six, please. Priority. I wish to speak straight-line direct
person, to Madame Rashalleila Nuaman, on Nineveh, in the Sirius
system."

A small voice floated out of a tiny speaker set to one side of the
rainbow flux rippling on the screen. "Call is being placed, sir. One
moment, please."

Despite the incredible distances involved, the slight delay was
occasioned by the need to boost the call through half a hundred relay stations. Time of transit, due to the less-than-space concepts in
use, was almost instantaneous.

The screen began to clear, and in a short while he was facing one
of the ten wealthiest humanoid females in the universe.

She was lounging on some sort of couch. To one side he could
easily make out the muscled, naked leg of whoever was holding
the portable transceiver hookup for her. In the background he
could see lush greenery, growing to fantastic size and shapes without the restraints of heavy gravity. Beyond that, he knew, was the
dome which shut out the airless void that was the normal atmosphere of Nineveh.

Nature battled surgery as the woman pulled her face into a tooth-some, slinky smile. This time, surgery won. It was intended to be sexy, but to one who knew, it only came out vicious.

"Why Maxy, darling! What a delightful surprise! It's always so delicious to hear from you. That lovely body of yours is well, I trust, and business equally?"

"I'm only well *when* business is good. At the moment it is pass-able, Rasha, just passable. However I have hopes it will take a sud-den jump for the better very shortly. You see, I've just had a most interesting chat with two gentlemen . . . three, if you count the red-head."

Nuaman tried to project an aura of disinterest, but surgery couldn't hide the way the tendons tautened in her neck. "How in-teresting, I'm sure. I do hope it proves profitable for you. But your tone seems to imply that you believe I am somehow involved."

"It did? I don't recall saying anything that might lead you to that conclusion . . . darling. Oh, it isn't the redhead you're thinking of. Your bully-boys did get to that one . . . as per instructions, no doubt."

"Why Maxy, whatever are you thinking of? Why should any of my assistants be on Moth? My dealings on the planet are small, as you well know. You're the one who keeps blocking all my at-tempts to expand my interests there. Anyhow, I don't know many redheads altogether . . . certainly can't recall any I'd want killed. Messed up a little, perhaps, but not killed. No, darling, you're mis-taken. What an odd conversation! There's nothing on that pitifully damp ball of dirt of yours, redheaded or otherwise, that I'd risk a murder for."

"Ummm. Not even this, *hasa*?" He held up the map. Folded, so that the interior would not show.

It didn't matter. She recognized it, all right! She sat bolt upright and leaned forward so that her face, witchlike, seemed to fill the whole screen.

"Where did you get that? That belongs to me!"

"Oh now Rasha, *bibi*, I do doubt that. And do sit back a little. Closeups are not your forte, you know." He made a pretense of ex-amining it. "No name, I'm afraid. And besides, I got it from a *live* redhead. A boy, really. He happened along just as your 'assistants' happened to be performing acts of doubtful legality against the original owner. Either the youth is an extraordinary chap . . . which I am inclined to believe . . . or else the two assistants you as-signed to this job were very low-grade morons . . . which, come to think of it, I am also inclined to believe. They *were* yours, I see. It had your typically brazen touch about it. I merely wanted to make certain. I've done that. Thank you, Rasha dear. *Sikuzuri*, now."

He cut her off in midcurse and went off to find Sissiph.

All in all, it had been rather a good day.

3

On Nineveh, Rashalleila Nuaman, matriarch and head of one of the largest private concerns in the Commonwealth and one of the ten richest humanoid females in the known firmament, was howling mad. She booted the nearly nude male servant who held the portable transceiver in an indelicate place. The unfortunate machine fell into a pool of mutated goldfish. Startled, they scrambled for cover amidst pastel lily pads. A number of very rare and expensive opaline glasses were shattered on the stone pathway.

Her anger momentarily assuaged, she sat back down on the lounge and spent five minutes rearranging her hair. It was olive this week. At that point she felt sufficiently in control of herself to get up and walk to the main house.

How had that utter bastard Malaika found out about the map? And how had it found its way into his hands? Or possibly . . . possibly it had been the other way around? The two gentlemen he had so snidely referred to were undoubtedly that Tse-Mallory person and his pet bug. But who was this new "redhead"? Who had so rapidly and shockingly managed to wreck what had until a few minutes ago been a comparatively smooth, routine operation? And all this now, with Nikosos only two days out of Moth! It was insufferable! She took a clawed swipe in passing at a stand of priceless Yyrbittium trumpet-blooms, shredding the carmine leaves. The delicate tube-shaped petals sifted brokenly to the floor. Someone was definitely, yes definitely, going to be flayed!

She stomped into the lounge-room that doubled as her office and collapsed disconsolately in the white fur mouldchair. Her head dropped onto her right hand while the left made nervous clicking sounds on the pure corundum table. The brilliant quicksilver flickering was the only movement in the wave-proofed room.

It *was* insufferable! He would not get away with it. It would be on his head, yes, on his, if a single killing operation devolved into a multiple one. It might even extend itself to his own exquisite carcass, and wouldn't that be sad. He *would* make a lovely corpse.

Don't just sit there, you slobbering bitch. Get cracking! She leaned over the desk and jabbed a button. A thin, weary face formed on the screen in front of her.

"Dryden, contact Nikosos and tell him that he is not to land at Drallar. He is instead to monitor all starships that are in parking orbit around the planet and stand off. Any which depart in the direction of the Blight he is to follow as closely as possible while at all times staying out of immediate detector range. If he complains, tell him I realize it's a difficult proposition and he's simply to do his best." I can always fire him later, she thought grimly. "If he presses you for an explanation, tell him plans have been changed due to unforeseen and unpreventable circumstances. He is to follow that ship! I guarantee there will be one, and probably shortly. It will be headed for the planet he was originally to have proceeded to by map. For now he'll have to do without his own set of coordinates. Is that all clear?"

"Yes, Madame."

She had cut him off before he reached the second "m." Well, she'd done what she could, but it seemed so goddamn *little*! Her feeling of comparative impotence magnified her rage and the corresponding desire to take out her frustration on someone else. Let's see. Who was handy? And deserving? Um. The idiot who had bungled with those two assassins? A fine choice! Her niece? That bubble-head. And to think, to think that one day she might have to take over the firm. When she couldn't even oversee a simple extraction. She pressed another button.

"Have Teleen auz Rudenuaman report to my office at, oh, five hours tomorrow morning."

"Yes Madame," the grid replied.

Now if there were only someone else. A budding career to squelch, perhaps. But in good faith there was no one else she could rake over the coals. Not that that should prove a consideration if she felt especially bitchy, but a loyal staff could be assured only through an equal mixture of fear and reward. No point in overdoing the former. No, face to it, what she really needed was relaxing. Hopefully that fop van Cleef would be in decent shape tonight. A smile suddenly sickled across her face. The unlucky button got jabbed again.

"Cancel that last. Have my niece report at five hours tomorrow . . . but to my sleeping quarters, not the office."

"Noted," said the grid compactly.

Rashalleila leaned back and stretched luxuriously. Definitely she felt better. She knew her niece was hopelessly in love with her current gigolo. Why, she couldn't for the life of her see, but it was a fact. It would be interesting to see if the girl could keep a straight face tomorrow as she was bawled out in front of him. While he stirred groggily in her aunt's bed. It would fortify her character, it would. She giggled at the thought and even in the empty room it was not a pleasant sound.

4

Bran Tse-Mallory and Truzenzuzex were making their way casually back to their rooms via the routes of the marketplace. It was twice as noisy and confusing at night as it was during the day. The flashing lights of motorized handcarts and fluorescent vendors added much to the atmosphere of controlled anarchy. Still, they did not need the Flinx. No matter how tortuous or confused the route, a thranx could always retrace it once traveled.

"Well, brother," said Truzenzuzex, dodging a mobile seller of novelties, "what do you think of our friend the merchant?"

"I would feel much better if our friend the unusual youth were twenty years older and in his place. A partial telepath, for sure. I could sense it. But such wishes are useless. Chaos. Up the universe!" he muttered.

"Up the universe!" replied Truzenzuzex. Both smiled at the private joke, which had a deeper meaning than the surface humor implied. "The man seems as trustworthy a member of his type as we are likely to find, and he has the ship we need. I cannot be positive yet, of course, but under the circumstances I think we have done quite well. And the boy's presence on the vessel should serve as a moderating factor. He seems to trust the trader, too."

"Agreed. The lad's presence will inject an uncertainty element, if nothing else."

"A certain uncertainty factor. How apropos of this venture so far!" The insect shook its head in deliberate aping of the human gesture. "This has caused three deaths so far. I would hope there will be no more."

"So would I, brother, so would I. The two of us have seen too much death already." Truzenzuzex did not reply, as he was concentrating on a difficult forking of their path.

Tse-Mallory followed mechanically. The noise and lights had a tendency to hypnotize, he allowed his mind to drift. . . .

5

The picture they were seeing in the viewscreen of the stingship was identical to the one being flashed to every member of the task force. It showed a tall, thin Ornithorpe with primarily black and yellow plumage. The being was possessed of a large amount of natural dignity, which it was at present being hard-pressed to retain. It is not easy to be dignified when one is begging.

Ensign Bran Tse-Mallory, aged twenty-six years, Fourth Battle Group, Sixth Corps of the Enforcement Arm of the United Church, watched the military governor of the blue planet below them crumble mentally as he pleaded with their own commander for aid. Anger and embarrassment mingled in his own throat, which was unaccountably dry, as he followed the conversation.

"Major Gonzalez," the Ornithorpe intoned, "I will ask you for a final time, and then I must go and do what I can to aid my people, even if it is only to die with them. *Will* you use the forces at your command to intercede and prevent a massacre?"

The voice of Task Force Commander Major Julio Gonzalez filtered through the small grid used for interfleet frequencies. It was cool and controlled. Bran wanted to smash the grid and the sickly smug face that sat behind it.

"And I am forced to remind you once again, Governor Bolo, that much as I sympathize with your plight there is nothing I can do. It is, after all, only by pure coincidence that my force is here at all. We are on a peaceful patrol and stopped by your planet only to pay the customary courtesy call. Had we been a week earlier or later we would not even be witness to this unfortunate situation."

"But you *are* here and you *are* witness, Jaor," began the governor for the seventeenth time, "and. . . ."

"Please, sir, I've listened quite too long as it is. The Church and the Commonwealth have been at peace with the AAnn Empire for years now. . . ."

"Some peace!" muttered an indiscreet voice elsewhere on the network. If Gonzalez heard it, he gave no sign.

". . . and I refuse to jeopardize that peace by interceding in an affair that is none of my business. To intervene on either side would be tantamount to an act of war. Also, I should be acting directly contrary to my orders and to the purpose of this patrol. I must refuse to do so, sir. I hope you can understand my position."

"Your *position!*" the governor gasped. His voice was breaking noticeably under the strain of the last few days and he had to fight to keep his thoughts framed in symbospeech. "What of those AAnn-*ghijipps* out there? An open attack on a helpless colony. 'Act of war' you say! Isn't that a direct violation of your precious Convention? The one that 'your' patrol is supposed to be upholding?"

"If your claim is just, I am sure the Convention arbiters will decide in your favor."

"*Whose* favor!" roared the Governor. "Surely you know what the AAnn do to subject planets! Especially those who have the impertinence to resist. If there are none of us left alive to accept the favorable decision of the arbiting board, what use your damned Convention! Will our memories receive pensions?"

"I *am* sorry, governor. I wish I could help you, but. . . ."

"Send just *one* of your ships, a token showing," he cried. "They might hesitate. . . ."

"I said I was sorry, governor. I am distraught. Goodbye, sir." Gonzalez had broken the connection.

From above and behind him, Bran heard the voice of his young ship-brother. The insect's deep blue-green chiton was rendered even more resplendent by the silver battle harness that enclosed its cylindrical body.

"That," said Truzenzuzex in cool, even tones, "was just possibly the most nauseating bit of rhetorical doggerel it has ever been my misfortune to overhear."

Bran agreed. He was finding it more and more difficult to restrain himself. Even without the heightened-instinct-perception drugs, the killing urge was beginning to steal warmly over him. It had the powerful push of righteous indignation behind it.

"Isn't it possible that maybe the locals . . . ?"

". . . haven't got a chance," finished Truzenzuzex. "They're outnumbered and outgunned, and not a regular armed force among them in the first place. As the AAnn doubtlessly surmised well in advance. I doubt if their ships even have doublekay drives. Theirs is only a colony and they wouldn't have need of many."

"Typical AAnn maneuver. Damn those anthropomorphic bastards! Always sniping and chipping at edges. I wish they'd come right out and say they're going to contest us for this part of the galaxy. Let 'em stand up and fight like men!"

"No can do, brother, because they obviously aren't. And I refer not to their physiologies alone. According to the AAnn standards set down by their philosophy of 'perpetual warfare as the natural state of things,' any advantage you can get over your opponent is by definition of success ethical. They're not immoral, just amoral. Sneak attacks are like sugar—pardon, like bread—to them."

"If the major agreed to step in I'm sure headquarters would give retroactive approval to the action," Bran said. "They'd offer obeisance in public, sure, but privately I'll bet Marshal N'Gara would approve."

"He might. Might not. As soldiers grow older and more powerful their personalities tend more and more to the mercurial. I can't see dear sweet Gonzalez risking a chance to help a bunch of aliens, especially non-Commonwealth. He's far too fond of his scotch and imported Terran cigars. Besides, to undertake such an action would require at least a modicum of imagination, a commodity in which our commander is sadly deficient. Look. It's starting already."

Bran glanced up above the communications equipment to the huge battle screen. Out in the void a number of ships represented only by ghostly dots were maneuvering across thousands of kilometers for position in a battle which would prove notable only for its brevity. Somehow the locals had mustered six spaceworthy ships. He'd bet a year's credit not one of them was a regular warship. Police launches, most likely. Opposite, the well-drilled, superbly disciplined AAnn force was forming one of its characteristic tetrahedrons. Fifteen or so attack ships, a couple of destroyers, and two bloated pips that in a normal battle situation he would have interpreted as dreadnoughts. The finer instruments on the big board told the true story: same mass, small gravity wells. Troop carriers, nursing dozens of small, heavily screened troop shuttles.

He'd observed AAnn occupation forces in action before. No doubt by now the members of the first assault wave were resting comfortably in their respective holds, humming softly to themselves and waiting for the "battle" to begin, making sure their armor was highly polished, their nerve-prods fully charged. . . .

He slammed a fist down on the duralloy board, scraping the skin on the soft underside of his wrist. There were ten stingers and a cruiser in the humanx force . . . more than a match for the AAnn, even without the dubious "help" of the locals. But he knew even before the pathetic debate of a few moments ago that Major Gonzalez would never stir from his wood-paneled cabin on the *Altair* to intervene in any conflict where humanx interests weren't directly threatened. He paused at a sudden thought. Of course, if a confrontation could be forced to the point that such a threat occurred . . . still no certain guarantee . . . definite court-martial . . . dismissal from the Corps . . . 300,000 sentient beings . . . processing camps. . . . He suddenly wasn't so sure that he wanted to make captain after all. Still, he'd need the concurrence of. . . .

"Bran, our drive appears to be malfunctioning."

"Wha? I don't. . . ."

"Yes, there is no question about it. We appear to be drifting unavoidably into the area of incipient combat. At top speed, no less. A most unusual awkwardness, wouldn't you agree?"

"Oh. Oh, yes." A pseudo-smile sharp as a scimitar cut his face. "I can see that we're helpless to prevent it. Goddamn unfortunate situation. Naturally we'll have to make emergency preparations to defend ourselves. I don't think the AAnn computers will be overly discerning about ships which float into their target area."

"Correct. I was just about to commence my own injections."

"Myself also." He snuggled back into the reaction seat, felt the field that enabled them to maneuver at high speed and still live take hold gently. "Best hurry about it."

He followed accepted procedure and did his best to ignore the barely perceptible pressures of the needles as they slipped efficiently into the veins on his legs. The special drugs that heightened his perceptions and released the artificial inhibitions his mind raised to constrain the killer instinct immediately began to take effect. A beautiful rose-tinted glow of freedom slipped over his thoughts. This was proper. This was *right*! This was what he'd been created for. Above and behind him he knew that Truzenzuzex was undergoing a similar treatment, with different drugs. They would stimulate his natural ability to make split-second decisions and logical evaluations without regard to such distractions as Hive rulings and elaborate moral considerations.

Shortly after the Amalgamation, when human and thranx scientists were discovering one surprising thing after another about each other, thranx psychologists unearthed what some humans had long suspected. The mind of *Homo sapiens* was in a perpetual state of uneasy balance between total emotionalism and computerlike control. When the vestiges of the latter, both natural and artificial, were removed, man reverted to a kind of controlled animalism. He became the universe's most astute and efficient killing machine. If the reverse was induced he turned into a vegetable. No use had been found for that state, but for the former. . . .

It was kept fairly quiet. After a number of gruesome but honest demonstrations put on by the thranx and their human aides, mankind acknowledged the truth of the discovery, with not a small sigh of relief. But they didn't like to be reminded of it. Of course a certain segment of humanity had known it all along and wasn't affected by the news. Others began to read the works of ancients like Donatien Francois de Sade with a different eye. For their part human psychologists brought into clearer light the marvelous thranx ability to make rapid and correct decisions with an utter lack of emotional distraction and a high level of practicality. Only, the thranx didn't think it so marvelous. Their Hive rulings and complicated systems of ethics had long kept that very same ability tied down in the same ways humanity had its killer desires.

The end result of all the research and experimentation was this: in combination with a ballistics computer to select and gauge targets, a thranx-human-machine triumvirate was an unbeatable combination in space warfare. Thranx acted as a check on human and human as a goad to thranx. It was efficient and ruthless. Human notions of a "gentleman's" war disappeared forever. Only the AAnn had ever dared to challenge the system more than once, and they were tough enough and smart enough to do it sporadically and only when they felt the odds to be highly in their favor.

It was fortunate that thranx and human proved even more compatible than the designers of the system had dared hope—because the nature of the drug-machine tie-up resulted in a merging of the two minds on a conscious level. It was as if the two lobes of a brain were to fight out a decision between themselves, with the compromise then being passed on to the spinal cord and the rest of the body for actual implementation. Some stingship pilots likened it more closely to two twins in the womb. It was that intimate a relationship. Only in that way would the resultant fighting machine operate at 100 percent effectiveness. A man's partner was his shipbrother. Few stinger operators stayed married long, except those who were able to find highly understanding wives.

The tingling mist flowed over his eyes, dimming and yet enhancing his vision. The tiniest things became obvious to his perception. Specks of dust in the cabin atmosphere became clear as boulders. His eyes fastened on the white diamonds on the battle screen with all the concentration of a starving cobra. All stinger pilots admitted to a slight but comforting sense of euphoria when under battle drugs. Bran was experiencing it now. For public relations purposes the enforcement posters insisted it was a beneficial by-product of the HIP drugs. The pilots knew it for what it was: the natural excitement that overtakes most completely uninhibited humans as they anticipate the thrill of the kill. His feelings whirled within, but his thoughts stayed focused.

"Up the universe, oh squishy bug!" he yelled drunkenly. Off from never-never land Truzenzuzex's voice floated down to him.

"Up the universe, oh smelly primate!"

The ship plunged toward one corner of the AAnn tetrahedron.

The enemy force stood it as long as possible. Then three ships broke out to intercept their reckless charge. The rest of the formation continued to form, undaunted. Undoubtedly no one in a position of command had yet noticed that this suicidal charge did not come from the region of the pitiful planetary defense force circling below. And having all heard the interfleet broadcast they *knew* it couldn't possibly be a Commonwealth vessel. Bran centered their one medium SCCAM on the nearest of the three attackers, the pointer. Dimly, through the now solid perfumed fog, he could make out the outraged voice of Major Gonzalez on intership frequency. It impinged irritatingly on his wholly occupied conscious. Obviously Command hadn't bought their coded message of engine trouble.

"You there, what do you think you're doing! Get back in formation! Ship number . . . ship number twenty-five return to formation! Acknowledge, uh . . . by heaven! Braunschweiger, whose ship is that? Someone get me some information, there!"

It was decidedly too noisy in the pod. He shut off the grid and they drove on in comparative silence. He conjured up a picture of the AAnn admiral. Comfortably seated in his cabin on one of the troop carriers, chewing lightly on a narco-stick . . . one eye cocked on the Commonwealth force floating nearby. Undoubtedly he'd also been monitoring the conversation between the planetary governor and Major Gonzalez. Had a good laugh, no doubt. Expecting a nice, routine massacre. His thoughts must now be fuzzing a bit, especially if he'd noticed the single stinger blasting crazily toward the center of his formation. Bran hoped he'd split an ear-sac listening to his trackers.

His hand drifted down to the firing studs. The calm voice of Truzenzuzex insinuated itself maddeningly in his mind. No, it was already *in* his mind.

"Hold. Not yet." Pause. "Probability."

He tried angrily to force the thought out and away. It wouldn't go. It was too much like trying to cut away part of one's own ego. His hand stayed off the firing stud as the cream-colored dot grew maddeningly large in the screen.

Again the calm, infuriating voice. "Changing course ten degrees minus y, plus x two degrees achieve optimum intercept tangent."

Bran knew they were going to die, but in his detached haze of consciousness it seemed an item of only peripheral importance. The problem at hand and the sole reason for existence was to kill as many of *them* as possible. That their own selves would also be destroyed was a certainty, given the numbers arrayed against them, but they might at least blunt the effect of the AAnn invasion. A tiny portion of him offered thanks for Truzenzuzex's quiet presence. He'd once seen films of a force of stingships in action with only human operators. It had resembled very much a tridee pix he'd seen on Terra showing sharks in a feeding frenzy.

The moment notified him of itself. "Firing one!" There were no conflicting suggestions from the insectoid half of his mind. He felt the gentle lurch of his body field as the ship immediately executed an intricate, alloy-tearing maneuver that would confuse any return fire and at the same time allow them to take the remaining two enemy vessels between them. Without the field he would have been jellied.

The disappearance of a gravity well from the screen told him that the SCCAM projectile had taken the AAnn ship, piercing its defenses. A violent explosion flared silently in space. A SCCAM was incapable of a "near-miss."

The SCCAM system itself was a modification of the doublekay drive that powered the ships of most space-going races. When human and thranx met it was found that the human version was more powerful and efficient than the thranx posigravity drive. It also possessed a higher power-conservation ratio, which made it more reasonable to operate. Working with their human counterparts after the Amalgamation, thranx scientists soon developed a number of improvements in the already remarkable system. This modified propulsive drive was immediately installed in all humanx ships, and other races began to order the components which would enable them to make their own modifications.

A wholly thranx innovation, however, had been the adaptation of the gravity drive as a weapon of irresistible power. The SCCAM projectiles were in actuality thermonuclear devices mounted on small ship drives, with the exception that all their parts other than those requiring melting points over 2400 degrees were made of alloyed osmium. Using the launching vessel's own gravity well as the initial propelling force, the projectile would be dispatched toward a target. At a predetermined safe distance from the ship, the shell's own drive would kick in. Instantly the drive would go into deliberate overload. Impossible to dodge, the overloaded field would be attracted to the nearest large gravity well—in this case, the drive system of an enemy ship. Coupled with the uncontrolled energy of a fusion reaction, the two intersecting drive fields would irrevocably eliminate any trace of the target. And it would be useless for an enemy vessel to try to escape by turning off its own field, for while it might survive impact with the small projectile field, the ship had not yet been constructed that could take the force of a fusion explosion unscreened. And as the defensive screens were powered by the posigravity drives. . . .

He felt the ship lurch again, not as violently this time. Another target swung into effective range. He fired again. Truzenzuzex had offered a level-four objection and Bran had countered with a level-two objective veto. The computer agreed with Bran and released the shell. Both halves of the ship-mind had been partially correct. The result was another hit . . . but just barely.

The AAnn formation seemed to waver. Then the left half of the Tetrahedron collapsed as the ships on that side sought to counter this alarming attack on their flank. More likely than not the AAnn commander had ordered the dissolution. Penned up in a slow, clumsy troop carrier he was by now likely becoming alarmed for his own precious skin. Heartened by this unstrategic move on the part of their opponents the native defensive force was diving on the broken formation from the front, magnifying the confusion if not the destruction and trying to avert the attention of the AAnn warships from their unexpected ally.

Bran had just gotten off a third shot—a miss—when a violent concussion rocked the stinger. Even in his protective field he was jerked violently forward. The lights flickered, dimmed, and went off, to be replaced a moment later by the eerie blue of the emergency system. He checked his instruments and made a matter-of-course report upward.

"Tru, this time the drive is off for real. We're going to go into loosedrift only" . . . he paused. A typically ironic reply was not forthcoming.

"Tru? How are things at your end?" The speaker gave back only

a muted hiss. He jiggled the knob several times. It seemed operative. "Tru? Say something, you slug! Old snail, termite, boozer . . .
goddamn it, say *some*thing!"

With the cessation of the ship's capacity for battle the HIP anti-
dotes had automatically been shot into his system. Thank Limbo
the automedics were still intact! He felt the killing urge flow out of
him, heavily, to be replaced by the dull aftertaste and temporary
lethargy that inevitably followed battle action.

Cursing and crying all at once he began fighting with his harness. He turned off the body field, not caring if the ship suddenly
decided to leap into wardrive and spatter him all over the bulk-
head. Redfaced, he started scrambling over broken tubing and
sparkling short-circuits up to where Truzenzuzex lay in his own
battle couch. His own muscles refused to respond and he damned
his arms which persisted in slipping off grips like damp hemp. He
hadn't realized, in the comfort of HIPnosis, how badly the little
vessel had been damaged. Torn sheeting and wavering filaments
floated everywhere, indicating a loss of shipboard gravity. But the
pod had remained intact and he could breathe without his hoses.

The thranx's position was longer and lower than his own, since
the insect's working posture was lying prone and facing forward.
Therefore the first portion of his fellow ensign's body that Bran encountered was the valentine-shaped head with its brilliant, multifaceted compound eyes. The familiar glow in them had dimmed
but not disappeared. Furiously he began to massage the b-thorax
above the neck joint in an operation designed to stimulate the
thranx's open circulatory system. He kept at it despite the cloying
wetness that insisted on floating into his eyes. Throwing his head
back at least made the blood from the gash on his forehead drift
temporarily backwards.

"Tru! C'mon, mate! Move, curse you! Throw up, do something,
dammit!" The irony of trying to rouse his companion so that he
could then be conscious when the AAnn disruption beams scattered their component parts over the cosmos did not interrupt his
movements.

Truzenzuzex began to stir feebly, the hissing from the breathing
spicules below Bran's ministering hands pulsing raggedly and unevenly.

"Mmmfff! Ooooo! My friend, I hereby inform all and sundry
that a blow on the cranium is decidedly not conducive to literate
cogitation! A little lower and to the right, please, is where it itches.
Alas, I fear I am in for a touch of the headache."

He raised a truehand slowly to his head and Bran could see where a loose bar of something had struck hard after the body-field had lapsed. There was an ugly dark streak in the insect's azure exoskeleton. The thranx organism was exceptionally tough, but very vulnerable to deep cuts and punctures because of their open circulatory system. When their armor remained intact they were well-nigh invulnerable. Much more so than their human counter-parts. The same blow probably would have crushed Bran's skull like eggshell. The great eyes turned to face him.

"Ship-brother, I notice mild precipitation at the corners of your oculars, differing in composition from the fluid which even yet is leaking from your head. I know the meaning of such a production and assure you it is not necessary. Other than injury to my immac-ulate and irresistible beauty, I am quite all right . . . I think.

"Incidentally, it occurs to me that we both have been alive en-tirely too long. As I appear to be at least momentarily incapacitated I would appreciate it if you would cease your face-raining, get back to your position, and find out just what the hell is going on."

Bran wiped the tears from the corners of his eyes. What Tru said was perfectly correct. He had been so absorbed in reviving the in-sect he had failed to notice that by all reasonable standards of war-fare they should both have been dead several minutes now. The AAnn might be unimaginative fighters, but they were efficient. He scrambled back to his seat and flipped emergency power to the bat-tle screen. What he saw there stunned his mind if not his voice.

"Oooo-wowwww! Fibbixxx! Go get 'em Sixth, bay-bee!"

"Will you cease making incomprehensible mouth-noises and tell me what's taking place? My eyes are not fully focused yet, but I can see that you are bouncing around in your seat in a manner that is in no way related to ship actions."

Bran was too far gone to hear. The scene on the screen was cor-respondingly weak, but fully visible nonetheless. It resembled a ping-pong game being played in zero gravity by two high-speed computers. The AAnn force was in full retreat, or rather, the re-mainder of it was. The bright darts of Commonwealth stingships were weaving in and out of the retreating pattern with characteris-tic unpredictability. Occasionally a brief, terse flare would denote the spot where another ship had departed the plane of material ex-istence. And a voice drifted somehow over the roaring, screaming babble on the communicator, a voice that could belong to no one but Major Gonzalez. Over and over and over it repeated the same essential fact in differing words.

"What happened what happened what happened what . . . ?"

Bran at this time suffered his second injury of the action. He sprained a lattisimus, laughing.

It was all made very clear later, at the court martial. The other members of the Task Force had seen one of their members break position and dive on the AAnn formation. Their pilot-pairings had stood the resultant engagement as long as possible. Then they began to peel off and follow. Only the cruiser *Altair* had taken no part in the battle. Her crew had a hard time living it down, even though it wasn't their fault.

Not so much as a tree on the planet had been scorched.

The presiding officer at the trial was an elderly thranx general officer from the Hiveworld itself. His ramrod stiffness combined with fading exoskeleton and an acid voice to make him a formidable figure indeed. As for the majority of the Task Force, its members were exonerated of wrongdoing. It was ruled that they had acted within Commonwealth dictates in acting "under a justifiable circumstance where an act of violence against Commonwealth or Church property or persons shall be met with all force necessary to negate the effects of such violence." This provision was ruled to have taken effect when the AAnn ships had engaged stingship number twenty-five in combat. That ship number twenty-five had provoked the encounter was a point that the court would "take under careful study . . . at length."

Ensigns Bran Tse-Mallory and Truzenzu of the Zex were ordered stripped of all rank and dismissed from the service. As a preliminary, however, they were to be awarded the Church Order of Merit, one star cluster. This was done. Unofficially, each was also presented with a scroll on which those citizens of the colony-planet known as Goodhunting had inscribed their names and thanks . . . all two hundred and ninety-five thousand of them.

Major Julio Gonzalez was promoted to commander and transferred immediately to a quiet desk post in an obscure system populated by semi-intelligent amphibians.

After first being formally inducted into his ship-brother's Hive, the Zex, Bran had entered the Church and had become deeply absorbed in the Chancellory of Alien Sociology, winning degrees and honors there. Truzenzuzex remained on his home planet of Willow-Wane and resumed his preservice studies in psychology and theoretical history. The title of Eint was granted shortly after. Their interests converged independently until both were immersed in the study of the ancient Tar-Aiym civilization-empire. Ten years had passed before they had remet, and they had been together ever since, an arrangement which neither had had cause to regret.

"Buy a winter suit, sir? The season is fast nearing, and the astrologers forecast cold and sleet. The finest *Pyrrm* pelts, good sir!"

"*Pas*? No. No thank you, vendor." The turnout to their little inn loomed just ahead, by the seller of prayer-bells.

Bran felt an uncommonly strong need of sleep.

6

Flinx returned to his apartment to set himself in order for the trip. On the way back from the inurb he had stopped at a shop he knew well and purchased a small ship-bag. It was of a type he'd often seen carried by crewmen at the port and would do equally as well for him. It was light, had a built-in sensor lock on the seal, and was well-nigh indestructible. They haggled formally over the price, finally settling on the sum of nine-six point twenty credits. He could probably have cut the price another credit, but was too occupied by thoughts of the trip, so much so that the vendor inquired as to his health.

At the apartment he wasn't too surprised to find that all his possessions of value or usefulness fit easily into the one bag. He felt only a slight twinge of regret. He looked around for something else to take, but the bed wouldn't fit, nor would the portikitchen, and he doubted there'd be a shortage of either on the ship anyway. Memories were stored comfortably elsewhere. He shouldered the bag and left the empty room.

The concierge looked at him warily as he prepared to leave her the keys. She was generally a good woman, but inordinately suspicious. In reply to her persistent questioning he said only that he was departing on a journey of some length and had no idea when he would return. No, he wasn't "running from the law." He could see that the woman was suffering from a malady known as tri-dee addiction, and her imagination had been drugged in proportion. Would she hold the room for his return? She would . . . for four months' rent, in advance if you please. He paid it rather than stand and argue. It took a large slice out of the hundred credits he'd made so recently, but he found that he was in a hurry to spend the money as quickly as possible.

He strolled out into the night. His mind considered sleep but his body, tense with the speed at which events had been moving around him, vehemently disagreed. Sleep was impossible. And it was pleasant out. He moved out into the lights and noise, submerging himself in the familiar frenzy of the marketplace. He savored the night-smells of the food crescent, the raucous hooting of the barkers and sellers and vendors, greeting those he knew and smiling wistfully at an occasional delicate face peeping out from the pastel-lit windows of the less reputable saloons.

Sometimes he would spot an especially familiar face. Then he would saunter over and the two would chat amiably for a while, swapping the stories and gossip of which Flinx always had a plentiful supply. Then the rich trader or poor beggar would rub his red hair for luck and they'd part—this time, at least, for longer than the night.

If a jungle could be organized and taxed, it would be called Drallar.

He had walked nearly a mile when he noticed the slight lightening of the western sky that signified the approach of first-fog (there being no true dawn on Moth). The time had run faster than expected. He should be at the port shortly, but there remained one last thing to do.

He turned sharply to his right and hurried down several alleys and backways he knew well. Nearer the center of the marketplace, which was quieter at night than the outskirts, he came on a sturdy if small frame building. It advertised on its walls metal products of all kinds for sale. There was a combination lock, a relic, on the inside of the door, but he knew how to circumvent that. He was careful to close it quietly behind him.

It was dark in the little building but light seeped in around the open edges of the roof, admitting air but not thieves. He stole softly to a back room, not needing even the dim light. An old woman lay there, snoring softly on a simple but luxuriously blanketed bed. Her breathing was shallow but steady, and there was what might have been a knowing smile on the ancient face. That was nonsense, of course. He stood staring silently at the wrinkled parchment visage for several long moments. Then he bent. Gently shifting the well-combed white hair to one side he planted a single kiss on the bony cheek. The woman stirred but did not awaken. He backed out of the room as quietly as he had entered, remembering to lock the main door behind him.

Then he turned and set off at a brisk jog in the direction of the shuttleport, Pip dozing stonelike on one shoulder.

7

The great port lay a considerable distance from the city, so that its noise, fumes, and bustling commerce would not interfere with the business of the people or the sleep of the king. It was too far to walk. He hailed a *Meepah*-beast rickshaw and the driver sent the fleet-footed creature racing for the port. The *Meepahs* were fast and could dodge jams of more modern traffic. It was a sporting way to travel, and the moist wind whistling past his face wiped away the slight vestiges of sleepiness which had begun to overtake him. As the animals were pure sprinters and good for only one long run an hour they were also expensive. They flew past slower vehicles and great hoverloaders bringing tons of goods to and from the port. As they had for centuries and doubtless would for centuries to come, the poor of Moth walked along the sides of the highway. There were none of the public moving walkways on Moth that could be found in profusion in the capitals of more civilized planets. Besides being expensive, the nomad populace tended to cut them up for the metal.

When he reached an area away from the bustling commercial pits that he thought would be close to the private docks, he paid off the driver, debarked, and hurried off into the great tubular buildings. He knew more than a little of the layout of the great port from his numerous trips here as a child. Where his interest in the place had sprung from he couldn't guess. Certainly not from Mother Mastiff! But ever since an early age he'd been fascinated by the port for the link it provided with other worlds and races. When he had been able to steal away from that watchful parental eye he'd come here, often walking the entire distance. He'd sit for hours at the feet of grizzled old crewmen who chuckled at his interest and spun their even older tales of the void and the pinpricks of life and consciousness scattered through it for his eager mind and the fawning attention he gave freely. There were times when he'd stay till after dark. Then he'd sneak ever so carefully home, always into the waiting, scolding arms of Mother Mastiff. But at the port he was all but mesmerized. His favorites had been the stories of the interstellar freighters, those huge, balloonlike vessels that plied the distances between the inhabited worlds, transporting strange cargoes and stranger passengers. Why sonny, they'd tell him, if'n it weren't fer the freighters, the hull damn uneeverse 'ud collapse, 'an Chaos himself 'ud return t' rule!

Now maybe he'd have a chance to see one of those fabulous vessels in person.

A muted growl went audible behind him and he turned to see the bulky shape of a cargo shuttle leap spaceward, trailing its familiar tail of cream and crimson. The sound-absorbing material in its pit was further abetted by the layered glass of the building itself in muffling the scream of the rockets and ramjets. It was a sight he'd seen many times before, but a little piece of him still seemed to go spaceward with each flight. He hurried on, searching for a dock steward.

· Approximately every fifteen minutes a shuttle landed or took off from Drallar port. And it was by no means the only one on the planet. Some of the private ports managed by the lumbering companies were almost as big. The shuttles took out woods, wood products, furs, light metals, foodstuffs; brought in machinery, luxury goods, traders, and *touristas*. There! Checking bales of plastic panels was the white and black checkered uniform of a steward. He hurried over.

The man took in Flinx's clothing, age, and ship-bag and balanced these factors against the obviously dangerous reptile coiled alertly now about the boy's shoulder. He debated whether or not to answer the brief question Flinx put to him. Another, senior steward pulled up on a scoot, slowed and stopped.

"Trouble, Prin?"

The steward looked gratefully to his superior. "This . . . person . . . wishes directions to the House of Malaika's private docks."

"Um." The older man considered Flinx, who waited patiently. He'd expected something of this sort, but read only good intentions on the elder's part. "Tell him, then. 'Twill do no harm to let him have a gander at the ships, and mayhap he has real reason for being there. I've seen queerer board Malaika's craft." The man revved his scoot and darted off down the vaulting hallway.

"Pit five, second transverse tube on your left," the man said reluctantly. "And mind you go nowhere else!"

But Flinx had already started off in the indicated direction.

It wasn't hard to find, but the telescoping rampway seemed endless. It was a relief to see the tall figure of the merchant waiting for him.

"Glad to see you show, *kijana*!" he bellowed, slapping Flinx on the back. Fortunately, he managed to avoid most of the blow. Pip stirred slightly, startled. "You're the last to arrive. Everyone else is already aboard and safely tucked away. Give your pack to the steward and strap in. We're just ready to cut."

Malaika disappeared forward and Flinx gave his bag to the officious-looking young fellow who wore the House of Malaika arms (crossed starship and credit slip) on his cap and jacket. The man ducked into a low door to the rear, leaving Flinx alone in the small lock. Rather than stand by himself until the man returned to check him off, he moved forward to the passenger cabin and found himself an empty seat.

Since this was a private and not a commercial shuttle, it was smaller than most. There were only ten seats in the low, slim compartment. The craft was obviously not designed for extended journeys. The decoration verged on the baroque. He peered down the narrow aisle.

The first two seats were occupied by Malaika and his Lynx, Sissiph. She was clad in a bulky jumpsuit for a change, but it served only to emphasize the beauty of her face. In the second row Bran Tse-Mallory and Truzenzuzex were leaning into the aisle, arguing animatedly but amiably on some subject which remained incomprehensible to Flinx on every level of perception. Then came their two starship pilots, Atha Moon and the shadow man, Wolf. Both were staring intently, but at different things. Atha was gazing out the port, observing what she could of their normal preparations for lift. The man's eyes were focused unwaveringly on an invisible point six inches in front of his nose. His face was, as usual, utterly devoid of expression. He remained unreadable.

Atha's attention seemed to vary awkwardly between the outside of their tiny vessel and the front of the cabin. She was continually darting her head into the aisle or poking it above the back of the seat in front of her. Especially whenever an unusually loud giggle or chuckle came from that vicinity. Probably she thought herself inconspicuous. Perhaps she hadn't noticed him come aboard behind her. In any event she seemed unconcerned about Wolf's presence. Even from here he could see the way the muscles in her neck and cheeks tightened, the way her blood pressure changed and her breathing increased, in response to the by-play from up front. It was mild, but still. . . . He shook his head. They hadn't even reached their ship yet and already an explosive situation was building. He could not tell how long it had been forming, but he did know one thing. He personally had no wish to be around when it finally came to a head.

He wondered if Malaika had the slightest inkling that his personal pilot of six years was hopelessly in love with him.

There were several empty seats, so he chose the one behind Atha. Not that he preferred it so much to any other, but he preferred to stay as far away as possible from the enigmatic Wolf. He couldn't read the man, so he was still unsure of him. As he had on numerous other occasions, he wished his peculiar talents wouldn't be so capricious in their operation. But when he directed his attention to Wolf there was only an oddly diffuse blank. It was like trying to fathom a heavy mist. Dew did not hold the symbols well.

A brief admonition came over the cabin speaker and Flinx felt the ship tilt under him. It was being raised hydraulically. Shortly it had settled steady at its liftoff angle of seventy degrees.

Another problem brought itself to his notice as he was strapping himself in. Pip was still coiled comfortably about his left shoulder. This definitely was not going to work! How were they going to handle the minidrag? He motioned the steward over. The man struggled up the aisle by means of handles set into the sides of the chairs. He eyed the snake warily and became a bit more polite.

"Well, sir, it seems to be capable of keeping a pretty firm grip with that tail. It can't stay like it is, though, because on lift it'd be crushed between your shoulder and the chair." The way he said it made it plain that he wouldn't mind observing that eventuality. He went back down the aisle.

Flinx looked around and finally managed to urge the snake onto the thick arm of the seat opposite his. Since Pip was an arboreal creature, Flinx was much more concerned about how it would react to the pressure of liftoff than to the condition of weightlessness. Not to mention how he'd manage himself.

He needn't have worried. The luxurious little craft lifted so smoothly that pressure was practically nonexistent, even when the rockets took over from the ramjets. It was no worse than a heavy blanket on his chest, pressing him gently back into the padded seat. The muted hum of the rockets barely penetrated the well-shielded cabin. Overall, he felt only a mild sense of disorientation. By contrast, Pip appeared positively ecstatic. Then he remembered that Pip had been brought to Moth by spaceship and had therefore undergone this same experience at least twice before. His apprehensions had been groundless. But they had served to take his mind off the flight. Another glance at the minidrag showed the narrow head weaving from side to side while the single-tipped tongue darted rapidly to and fro, touching everything within reach. The pleated wings were unfurled and flapping in sheer pleasure.

After the rockets cut off and the little ship drifted weightlessly, Flinx felt acclimated enough to reach over and pick up the snake. He replaced it on its familiar spot on his shoulder. The confident pressure on his arm and back was, as ever, reassuring. Besides, the darn thing was having entirely too much fun. And the one thing they definitely did not need at the outset of their expedition was the venomous reptile flapping crazily in free fall about the confined space of the cabin.

They passed several vessels in parking orbit around the planet, including one of the great fueling stations for the shuttles. Some of the giant craft were in the process of loading or unloading, and men in suits floated about them sparkling like diamond dust. The boy's eyes drank in everything and hungered for more. Once, when the shuttle turned ninety degrees on its side and moved to line up for conjunction with their starship, the planet itself rolled majestically into view beneath them.

From this angle the famous ring-wings were clearly visible. The radiant butter-gold layers of rock and gas combined with the lakes which glistened sapphirelike through breaks in the cloud cover to make the planet more than ever resemble the Terran insect for which it had been named.

He got only the slightest glimpse of their ship, the *Gloryhole*. That was enough. Sandwiched in among bloated freighters and pudgy transports she looked like a thoroughbred in a barnyard. She still had the inevitable shape of a doublekay drive ship, a balloon stuck onto the end of a plumber's helper, but the lines were different from most. The balloon at one end was the passenger and cargo space, and the plunger at the other the generating fan for the posigravity field. Instead of being wide and shallow, like a plate, the *Gloryhole*'s generating fan was narrower and deep, chalicelike. The passenger-cargo area was still balloon-shaped, but it was a streamlined, tapered balloon. Simply on looks alone one could tell that the *Gloryhole* was faster than any regular freighter or liner aspace. It was one of the most beautiful things he'd ever seen.

He felt a slight jolt through his harness as the shuttle clicked into the transfer lock of the big ship. Following the steward's instructions he released himself from the restraining straps and drifted after the others into the umbilical tube, pulling himself hand over hand along the portable pullway. The luxury of the *Gloryhole* in comparison to the freighters he'd had described to him made itself quickly apparent. The starship's airlock was furlined.

The steward and Malaika exchanged brief orders and the uniformed young man drifted out of the tube, pulling in the line behind him. After a bit the door whirred shut, and they were effectively separated from the shuttle.

"*Je*? If you'll all follow me—use the handholds—we'll adjourn to the salon." Malaika started off through the lock exit. "Atha, you and Wolf get up to Control and start up the drive. Let's have some decent gravity around here. A *buibui* I'm not, to spin my own web! The two of you know where your cabins are." Atha and the skull-face moved off through a side passage. Malaika swiveled to face them. "The rest of you I'll show to your rooms myself."

The salon was a fairyland of glass, wood, and plastics. Bubbles of crystal containing brilliantly colored forms of aquatic life were suspended throughout the big room by a thin but unbreakable network of plastic webbing. Real trees grew through the green-fur floor, each representing a different species native to Moth. Metal sculptures layered with gem dust hung cloud-like from the ceiling, which was a tri-dee soloid depicting an open sky complete to clouds and sun. It began to darken, effectively simulating the sunset taking place on the planet's side below. It was an odd simile to come to mind, but for some reason Flinx could best liken the sensation to walking through an especially fine beer.

The ship shuddered once, twice, ever so imperceptibly, and he could feel the weight beginning to return to his body. He started to float toward a side door and then began flailing frantically so that he would land on his feet and not his head. A glance showed that none of the other passengers were experiencing similar difficulties. Sissiph was being steadied by Malaika, and Tse-Mallory and Truzenzuzex hadn't even bothered to pause in their argument. Angrily he got his errant legs under him. No one commented on his obvious difficulty, for which he was grateful. Full gravity returned after a very short interval.

Malaika walked over to what looked like a cactus but was actually a bar. "We'll remain at point nine five gravity for the duration of the trip. Possibly most of you aren't used to keeping up muscle tone in space" (Flinx took a quick sensing of the two scientists' compositions and doubted the accuracy of Malaika's remark) "and so I'd hesitate to set it lower than that. The slight difference should be just enough to be exhilarating, and it approximates what we'll encounter on our objective planetfall.

"This will serve as a regular gathering place. Meals will be served here by the autochef, unless you prefer to eat in your cabin. *Njoo*, I will show you your own. . . ."

Flinx spent three days just examining his "own." It was packed with fantastic devices that sprang at you out of floor, ceiling, and walls. You had to watch your step. Press the wrong switch and you were liable to be doused with warm water . . . irrespective of your attire of the moment. That had been a disheartening experience, especially as he had been trying for a haircut. Fortunately no one but Pip had been around to witness it.

He had been concerned to see how his pet would take to the confinements of shipboard life. Everyone else, excepting possibly Sissiph, had adjusted to the reptile's presence. So that didn't give him cause for worry. As it happened, there were no others. The minidrag would go swooping in and out among the pylons and plastic tapestries of the salon as if he owned them, frightening the devil out of the inhabitants of the glass bubbles. Occasionally it would hang batlike from a particularly inviting artificial branch or real one. When it was discovered that the food selector in their cabin could deliver fresh bits of raw *Wiodor* meat, the snake's contentment was assured.

They had been moving out of Moth's system at a slow but continually building speed for several days now. Malaika was in an expansive mood, and so when Flinx requested permission to stand by in Control during changeover, the merchant acceded gracefully. Once they made the initial jump past lightspeed at changeover their rate of acceleration would go up tremendously.

Apparently no one else shared his curiosity. Malaika remained secluded in his cabin with his Lynx. Tse-Mallory and Truzenzuzex spent most of their time in the salon, playing personality chess and conversing in languages and on subjects Flinx could grasp only an occasional bit of. Once more he reflected on their complete ease and familiarity with starship travel.

Malaika had half-promised to come up to Control for changeover to explain the workings to Flinx. But when the time came, Sissiph was pouting over some incomprehensible slighting and the merchant was compelled to remain in the cabin with her. In his place he instructed Atha to answer any questions Flinx might have regarding the workings of the ship or drive. She had acknowledged the order with obvious distaste.

Flinx had come to the conclusion that he was going to have to be the one to break the silence that their unceremonious first meeting had produced. Otherwise they might not exchange a word the entire trip, and even a large spaceship is too small an area in which to retain animosities.

He entered Control and strolled up behind her seat. Wolf was off on the opposite side of the room. She said nothing, but he knew she had noticed his entrance.

He read directness and decided to counter with same.

"Look, I didn't mean to kick you back there in the tower, that time." She swiveled to eye him questioningly. "That is, I didn't mean to kick *you*, I meant to kick . . . oh, hell!" The explanation hadn't seemed this complicated when he'd rehearsed it in his mind. Of course, then, he hadn't had to contend with the rich red-brown in those eyes. "I thought you were a spy . . . or an assassin, or something. You certainly didn't look as though you belonged where you were, so I took the least bloody route I could think of at the time of forcing you into the open. It worked, you turned out to be not what I expected, and I apologize. There! Truce?"

She hesitated, and then her face softened into an abashed grin. She put out a hand. "Truce!" He kissed it instead of shaking it, and she turned, pleased, back to her instruments. "You know, you were right, actually. I had no business at all being where I was. Nor doing what I was doing. Do I look that much like an assassin from the back?"

"The contrary, the contrary." Then, abruptly, "You're quite attracted to your boss, aren't you?"

Her face jerked up, surprised. One would have thought he'd just revealed one of the great secrets of the universe. He had to work to keep from grinning. Tree, was she that naive?

"Why . . . why, what a thing to say! What a perfectly *absurd* thought! Maxim Malaika is my employer, and a good one. Nothing more. What makes . . . ? Uh, do you have any questions about the ship? If not, I *am* bus. . . ."

Hastily, he said, "Why is it that while this ship is infinitely more complicated than the shuttle, both require the same crew of two?" He knew the answer, but wanted to keep her talking.

"That's the reason, right there." She indicated the panoply of ranked lights and instruments around them. "Because it is so complex, it requires a lot more automation just to operate. Actually, the

Gloryhole pretty well runs herself most of the time. Except for providing instructions and handling decisions, we're here just in case of the unforeseen situation. Interstellar navigation, for example, is much too complex for human or thranx minds to manage on any really practical level. Starships *have* to be run by machines or they'd be impossible altogether."

"I see. By minor situations and unforeseen things, do you mean like at changeover?"

"Oh, there's no real danger from changeover. The companies like to make a big thing of it to give their passengers a slight thrill. Sure, once in a while you'll hear about something happening. A meteor will make a millions-to-one infringement on the gravity well of a ship at the moment of shift and the ship will turn inside out, or something equally weird. Those are real exceptions. The tri-dee and faxcax blow those incidents all out of proportion for their ratings value. Usually it's no more trouble than stepping from land onto a floating boat."

"Glad to hear it. I don't think I'd enjoy being turned inside out. That was the old *Curryon*, wasn't it?"

"Why, yes. It was twenty-four thirty-three, old calendar. Actually, we have to worry only about keeping the center of the field positioned constant with respect to the fan and generator. The computers take care of most of that. Once it falls too far ahead or drops too close, you have to stop the ship, then start up all over again. That takes a lot of time, for deceleration and acceleration, and it's expensive as well as tricky. If the field should start to oscillate, the ship could be shaken to pieces. But as I said, the computers handle all that worry for us. Barring those unforeseen circumstances, of course."

"I've never been on a doublekay drive ship before. I'm no physicist, but could you maybe give me a quickee explanation of how the thing works? One that even my simple mind could understand?"

She sighed. "Okay. What the Caplis generator does . . . that's what we hold in the 'fan' up ahead . . . is in effect produce a powerful but concentrated gravitational field at the nose of the ship. As soon as the field exceeds the natural one of the ship, the ship moves toward it, naturally attracted by a 'body' of greater 'mass' than itself. Being part of the ship, the doublekay drive unit naturally goes along with it. But the unit, having moved forward, is set to keep the field at a constant distance from the hull of the craft. Therefore the field is moved forward also. The ship will try to catch up to it again, and so on, ad infinitum. The field is in effect pulling the ship instead of pushing it, as the shuttle rockets do. Doublekay vessels actually move in a series of continuous jerks, so rapid and close together that they seem to be one smooth, unbroken pull. The increase or decrease in the size of the field determines the speed of the ship.

"Being a wave and not a particle form of energy, gravity isn't affected in the same way that mass is on approaching the speed of light. The doublekay field creates a cone-shaped zone of stress behind it, in which mass acts differently than it does under normal circumstances. That's why when we exceed the speed of light I don't see through you, or something. Once we've made that initial breakthrough, or 'changeover,' our rate of travel goes up enormously. It's something like riding the back of a very tame SCCAM shell.

"Our initial power comes from a small hydrogen 'sparkplug' . . . I wonder sometimes where that word came from . . . up near the generator housing in the tube section of the ship. Once started up, the field can be 'channeled' to a certain extent. That's where we get our gravity for the ship and power to run the lights and autobar and things.

"In the event of a drive failure there are provisions for converting the fan to an old ion-type drive, powered by the hydrogen plug. It would take twelve years at its best speed to get from Moth to Powerline, the nearest inhabited planet. Farther out where the stars are more scattered it's even worse. But twelve years or so is better than never. Stranded ships *have* been saved that way . . . those that managed to overcome problems like lack of food and insanity. But the rate of failure for doublekay drives is minuscule. Only rarely can a mere human manage to screw one up."

"Thanks," said Flinx. "That helps . . . sort of." He glanced over at Wolf and saw that the man was totally immersed in his work. He lowered his voice. "Incidentally, I think maybe you've got the wrong idea of what a Lynx is."

"A prostitute," she replied automatically.

"Uh-uh. The Lynx are a group of very beautiful and ambitious women who don't regard lifemating as the end-all of civilization. They prefer to move from one fascinating man to another."

"So I've been told. And seen. That's still a matter of opinion." She sniffed calculatingly.

He started for the exit. "So I don't think you need worry about

Sissiph or any of the others settling down with your merchant, permanent-like."

"Listen!" she shouted, "For the last time, I . . . !" She dropped her voice as Wolf looked over curiously. "I am *not* in love with Maxim Malaika!"

"Sure, sure," said Flinx from the doorway. "I can see that."

It was only a short while later, while watching a viewtape in his cabin, that he realized he'd missed changeover.

8

Teleen auz Rudenuaman was resting easily in her rooms on the great estate complex of her aunt. She was scantily clad. That is, she wore at least as little as the huge male form which stood admiring the play of its muscles in the wall-length mirror across from the bed-desk.

"Rory," she said to the ceiling, "you do love me, don't you?"

"Um-hmm," said the figure, bending on one knee and flexing a forearm.

"And you'd do anything for me, wouldn't you?"

"Um-hmm."

"Then why," she said, sitting up abruptly and shouting, "the hell didn't you do anything when the old witch started in on me this morning?"

The figure sighed and turned regretfully from the mirror to face her. Its body was hard, but the face was curiously soft, almost childlike. Beautiful and soft. The expression it wore was amiable and best described as intensely vacuous.

"I *could* have said something, Teleen, dear, but what would it have accomplished? Besides making her even more suspicious of *us*. She had it in for you anyway, and nothing I could have said would likely have turned her off. Besides, she was right, you know. You *did* foul up that. . . ."

"I'm not interested. I had enough of that from *her* this morning. Surely she can't reasonably expect me to be responsible for the ineptitude of men *her* people hired in the first place?"

Rory Mallap van Cleef sighed again and began pulling on a gold dressing gown. "I suppose not, dear. But then when has she ever been reasonable about anything? I really don't understand the intricacies of such dealings. She was awfully bitchy, wasn't she?"

Teleen slid out of the bed and moved to sit next to him. She put her arms possessively around the massive shoulders, resting her head against one bulging dorsal.

"Look, Rory, I've told you before. The only way we're ever going to have any happiness is to eliminate the old bag once and for all."

Rory grinned. He was not without a sense of humor, even if it did tend more than a bit to the primitive.

"Now is that any way to talk about your beloved aunt?"

"No. It's the *only* way to talk about her! And at that I'm flattering her. Every time we discuss her elimination my charitable instincts get the better of me. But to be specific. . . ."

"Please, darling, I'm not in the mood now."

"Rory," she said, sitting back, "are you in love with me . . . or with her?"

"Don't be obscene, dear! You have no idea, no *idea*, what a task it is constantly to have to feign interest in that sack of surgical miracles. Especially," and he drew her onto his lap and kissed her, "after you."

"Mmmmm. That's the way I like to hear you talk!" He had her purring again. "You'll go along with me, then?"

"As I've said before, if you come up with a reasonably sensible plan. Love or not, I'm not going to take a chance on spending the rest of my life on some prison moon because some scheme is only half worked out. I'm no genius, but I'm smart enough to know it. So you manage the brains for both of us. I'll supply any needed muscle. Of which," he added, flexing a tricep lovingly, "I have more than sufficient."

She slipped out of his grasp and stamped angrily on the deep fur floor. It did interesting things to the rest of her body. "Stop admiring yourself for a minute and try to be serious. Murder is not a funny business!"

"It is when it involves your aunt."

"Oh, you're impossible! All right; look, you know how fond she is of bathing in that pool, the little one with all those lovely fish and snails and things?" Her eyes were slitted. "How she never misses a daily swim?"

"Yes, I know the place. So?"

"Would it be a simple matter to wire the thing, do you think?"

He shook his head, doubtfully. "Her people would notice that sort of thing. You know how careful she is."

"Not if we disguised it as one of those censored frogs, or something!" She glowed. "Yes, a frog. I'm sure such a device could be made. Waterproof, small, but still capable of delivering a lethal charge, yes. And you could, um, put the guard 'to sleep' for the minute necessary to slip the thing into the water."

"That does sound good, darling. Yes, Teleen, I do think so too!" He lifted her off the floor and kissed her gently. "One thing, though. Why haven't you thought of something like this before?"

Her mouth twisted in a feral smile that, had she known it, was almost a carbon copy of her aunt's. "Oh, I have, I have, sort of. But until this morning, I really hadn't been sufficiently inspired! Today I was finally convinced she is quite mad. It will be only a kindness to gift her with a long sleep."

Rashalleila Nuaman switched off the spy-screen and smiled kittenishly to herself. Her niece's generosity and concern was . . . well, appalling. So she had finally dug up enough courage to actually plan the thing! About time, yes. But to trust that side of beef van Cleef with such knowledge! Tsk. Poor judgment, poor. How anyone could actually fall in *love* with an automaton, an utter nonentity, like that! Oh sure, he was great between the sheets. But beyond that he was a nothing, a void, a null factor. Well-meaning and affectionate, to be sure. Like a large puppy-dog. Ah, well. Let them enjoy their private games. It would be good practice for Teleen. Buoy her self-confidence, and all that. Eventually, though, the poor thing would have to be jolted back to her senses. She giggled at the small witticism. Such folderol was fine, but not on company time. Which reminds. Must have the ground keeper get rid of all those nice froggies. Temporarily, at least. No use wasting. Dinner tomorrow, perhaps.

She had turned off the spy-screen a few moments too early. Downstairs, her niece's stimulated mind had come up with another thought.

"We also ought to keep the old bitch off balance, Rory. While we're trying to hammer this thing out. She's not a complete idiot, you know."

"I suppose that's a good idea," said van Cleef, flexing his quadriceps. "You'll think of something."

Her face was alight. "I have. Oh, *have* I!" She turned away and walked over to the china desk. A hidden switch revealed a comm-screen she *knew* wasn't being tapped by any of her dear auntie's automatic spy monitors. It was the one machine on the estate whose circuitry she'd checked over herself. She tapped out a rapid, high-speed series of numbers that sped her call over a very special and very secret relay system to a little-contacted section of space.

Eventually the screen cleared and a face began to take shape.

"Well, good light to you, Amuven DE, and may your house always be filled with dust."

The face of the AAnn businessman crinkled in a toothy smile. "As always, as always. So good to hear from you again, Mistress Rude!"

9

Flinx had been staring silently out through the main viewport of the salon for some time, well aware that there was someone behind him. But to have turned immediately would have engendered unnecessary awkwardness. Now he turned to see the two scientists and became aware that he needn't have been concerned. Neither was paying the slightest attention to him. They had drawn over lounges and were staring out at the magnificent chaos of the drive-distorted heavens. Taking no notice of their scrutiny, the prismatic panoply flowed on unchanged.

"Don't mind us, Flinx. We're here for the same thing. To enjoy the view." The philosoph returned his attention to the great port and the doppler-distorted suns which glowed far more sharply than they ever could in their natural state.

But Flinx's concentration and mood had been broken. He continued facing the two scientists.

"Sirs, doesn't it strike you as odd that in a time when so many folk have so much trouble getting along with one another, you two, of two utterly different races, manage to get along so well?"

"Your questions, I fear, will never carry the burden of subtlety, lad." Tse-Mallory turned to the thranx. "At times in the past my friend and I existed in a rather close—one could say intimate—association. Our work necessitated it. And we are not so very different as you might think."

"I remember your calling each other ship-brother several times."

"Yes? I suppose we did. We've never gotten used to the idea that other people might find it unusual. It's so very natural to us."

"You were a gunnery team?"

"No," said Truzenzuzex. "We flew a stingship. Small, fast, a single medium SCCAM projector."

"As to our relationship irrespective of ship life, Flinx, I'm not sure Tru and I could give you an objective answer. Our personalities just seem to compliment one another. Always have. The attraction between human and thranx is something that psychologists of both races have sweated over for years, without ever coming up with a satisfactory explanation. There are even some pairs and groupings that become physically ill if one is separated long from its alien counterpart. And it seems to work on both sides. A kind of mental symbiosis. Subjectively, we just feel supremely comfortable with each other.

"You know the events leading up to the Amalgamation, the Pitar-humanx war, and such?"

"Only bits and pieces, I'm afraid. Regular schooling is something that eluded me early."

"Umm. Or vice versa, I suspect. Tru?"

"You tell the lad. I'm certain he'd find the human version of the story more palatable."

"All right.

"Human and thranx have known each other for a comparatively short period of time. Hard to believe today, but true. A little over two t-centuries ago, scoutships of both races first encountered each other's civilizations. By that time, mankind had been in space for several previous t-centuries. In that time, while engaged in exploration and colonization, he had encountered many other alien lifeforms. Intelligent and otherwise. This was also true of the thranx, who had been in space even longer than humanity.

"There was an indefinable attraction between the two races from the very outset. The favorable reactions on both sides far outweighed the expected prejudice and aversions."

"Such existed on the thranx planets as well," put in Truzenzuzex.

"I thought I was going to tell this?"

"Apologies, oh omnipotent one!"

Tse-Mallory grinned, and continued. "The thranx were as alien as any race man had yet encountered. A hundred-percent insectoid, hard-shelled, open circulatory system, compound eyes, rigid, inflexible joints . . . and eight limbs. *And* they were egg-layers. As a news commentator of the time put it, 'they were completely and delightfully weird.' "

"If I recall aright, your people laid a few eggs at that time too," piped the philosoph. Tse-Mallory shut him up with an exasperated glance.

"From past experiences one would have expected the human reaction to the discovery of a race of giant sentient insects to be hostile or at least mildly paranoid. That had proved the pattern in too many previous contacts. And man had been fighting smaller and much more primitive cousins of the thranx for thousands of years on the home planet. In fact, if you can believe it, the term 'bug' originally had a derogatory connotation.

"But by now mankind had learned it was going to have to live in peace and harmony with beings whose appearance might be personally repulsive. It didn't help things to know that many of those same beings considered man at least as repulsive-looking as he considered them." He glanced expectantly at Truzenzuzex, but that worthy was at least temporarily subdued. "So the actual reaction between human and thranx was doubly unexpected. The two races took to each other like a pair of long-separated twins. The thranx traits of calmness, cool decision-making ability, politeness, and wry humor were admired tremendously by humans who'd sought such qualities in themselves. By the same token there was a recklessness combined with brains, an impossible self-confidence, and a sensitivity to surroundings that thranx found appealing in man.

"Once it had been voted on by both races and approved by considerable margins despite the expected opposition from moneyed chauvinists, Amalgamation proved to be even less trouble than the optimists had anticipated. Thranx click-speech, with its attendant whistling, actually had a reasonable phonetic counterpart among the thousands of Terran languages and dialects."

"African sub-divisions," mused Truzenzuzex. "Xhosa."

"Yes. For their part thranx could, with difficulty, manage the major human language system of Terranglo. The eventual outgrowth of much work by phoneticists, semanticists, and linguists on both sides was a language that hopefully combined the better aspects of both. The clicks and whistles and some of the rough rasps of Hive-speech major were kept in, intact, along with most of the smoother sounds and vowels of Terranglo. The result was probably the closest thing to a universal language, barring telepathy, we'll ever have: symbospeech. Fortunately for business purposes, most other races with vocal apparatus can also manhandle at least enough of it to get by with. Even the AAnn, who turned out to be better at it than most.

"The mutual admiration society was off and winging. Pretty soon it had extended itself to other aspects of the new humanx life-system. Our politicians, judges, and law-makers couldn't help but admire the beauty and simplicity with which thranx law and government had been put together. It was practically an art-form, built up as it had been from the old Hive structure itself. Not that it was that different from the oldest human municipalities and nation-states. Just much more sensible. Thranx lawyers and magistrates soon cleared away a lot of the backlog that had been clogging human courts. Besides their superlative natural sense of jurisprudence, they could not possibly be accused by anyone of partiality.

"Terran-derived sports, on the other hand, completely revolutionized the thranx's biggest problem—that of leisure. They simply hadn't realized that there were so many organized ways of having fun. When they discovered chess and judo, it was all over with flip-the-rock and that ilk."

"Third-degree black belt," noted Truzenzuzex proudly. "Although I'm getting a bit creaky for such activity."

"So I've noticed. I could go on and on, lad. Human planets were deluged with exquisite examples of thranx workmanship. Machinery, handicrafts, personal gadgetry, delicate electrical products, and so on. Even the body coloring of each was pleasing to the other, although thranx odor had a decided advantage over the human."

"No argument there," puffed the philosoph. That earned him another sharp glance.

"When the thranx got hold of Terran literature, paintings, sculpture, and such seemingly unrelated things as ice-cream and children's toys . . . in short, the two races just seemed to merge amazingly well. And the greatest of humanx achievements, the modified doublekay drive, you must know about.

"But by far the greatest impetus toward amalgamation—along with the Pitar-humanx war—was the formation of the United Church. Powerful, relatively new groups existed among both races with similar beliefs. When they learned of one another's existence, an alien organization with practically identical theologies and desires, they soon had formed a combine which rapidly overwhelmed all but the most die-hard members of the older established churches. Not the least of its strengths was that it insisted on being called a nonreligious organization. For the first time, people could get top-level spiritual guidance without having to profess a belief in God. Back when, it was a real revolution."

"As near as we can tell," put in Truzenzuzex, "it is still unique in being the only multiracial spiritual institution in the galaxy. And other races have members."

"I'm afraid I don't belong," said Flinx.

"Doesn't bother me. The Church really couldn't care less. They don't proselytize, you know. They're much too busy with the important things. Sure, they'd be glad to have you or anyone else as a new member, but you have to go to them. The mountain will have to go to Mohammed, because Mohammed is busy enough in *his* neighborhood!"

"What?" said Flinx.

"Forget it. Archaic reference. Even our materialistic captain is a member."

"I guessed that. Does he believe in God, too?"

"Difficult to tell," said Tse-Mallory thoughtfully. "That's only incidental, anyway. I'm more concerned about whether or not God believes in him, because I've a hunch we're going to need any outside help we can get before this trip is over."

"How about the Pitar-humanx war?" Flinx prompted.

"Oh that. Tomorrow, hmm? I could use a drink right now. Haven't done that much lecturing since . . . a long time."

True to his word he picked up the narrative the following morning, over tea and sweetcakes. Besides, one gets bored quickly in space. His audience had grown, however, since everyone was now in the salon except Wolf. It was his turn on duty watch.

"I too am familiar with the details," put in Malaika, an arm curled possessively around Sissiph's waist. "But I think I'd enjoy hearing you tell it, *juu ya*. I *know* my versions are wrong!" He laughed uproariously.

"So," said Tse-Mallory, unconsciously aping their host. "Some five t-decades after the initial Terran-thranx contact, relations between the two civilizations were growing at a geometric pace. Both sides, however, were still wary of each other. Contact between the two religious groups was still in a formative stage, and amalgamation was a dream in the minds of a few outstanding visionaries of both races. These were still greatly outnumbered by the 'patriots' on both sides.

"Then came the first Terran contact with the Pitar. That race occupied two densely populated planets in the Orion sector. They were a totally unexpected factor, an alien race human to point nine six three places. Really a remarkable and as yet unequaled coincidence of form. Externally they were for all practical purposes identical with humankind. In looks, as a race, they came pretty close to the Terran ideal. The males were tall, muscular, handsome, and exceptionally structured. The women were one hundred percent feminine and at least as attractive as the men. Humanity went through a brief, hysterical phase in which anything even remotely Pitarian was the subject of slavish imitation. The Pitar themselves seemed cordial enough, if a bit nervous and self-centered.

Limitless professions of mutual aid and undying friendship were exchanged between the two races.

"The Pitar were highly scientific, and in a few phases of research came surprisingly close to matching Terra. Weaponry, for example. The reasons for this obvious dichotomy in their seemingly peace-loving civilization became apparent later. Too much later. It also appeared to have a disproportionate influence in their social setup.

"Human-Pitar friendship was progressing at a rate comparable to human-thranx. Several years after first contact, a tramp freighter happened to put in at a large but out-of-the-way humanoid colony. Treetrunk, or Argus V, as it's better known now. Apparently the entire colony, some six hundred thousand souls, had been utterly and ruthlessly wiped out by an unknown lifeform. Not a man, woman, or child had been left alive on the entire planet. Corpses of women seemed to be especially lacking. The reason for this was discovered later also. Well, expressions of sympathy poured in from the other intelligent races, including the Pitar. They were at least as outraged as any of the others. Most races then sent out scouts to try to locate this new and virulent alien race before they themselves could become the victims of a similar atrocity.

"Two months later a man was found orbiting one of the devastated planet's two moons in an antique, jury-rigged lifeboat. A cruiser of the *Unop-Patha*—you know that race?—was on courtesy patrol at the time and happened to drift within range of the boat's feeble transmitter. They had never encountered an insane human before and were pretty much at a loss as to what to do with him until they could finally turn him over to the nearest human authorities. That happened to be the big research group which was sifting Treetrunk for clues. A month of intensive treatment succeeded in restoring the fellow to partial coherency.

"It took them some time to make sense of his story. His mind had been badly unhinged by months of helpless drifting in space, fears of meeting an enemy ship—and, after a while, of not meeting one—and by what he had seen on the planet itself. It was fortunate that he didn't have the courage to commit suicide. The ugly story he told has been documented many times over and I find it personally distasteful, so I will skip over the gory parts.

"The enemy had struck without warning, raining death on the unprepared populace. Being without a regular military force—or need of one—the planet was quite helpless. The police skiffs tried and, as might have been expected, proved useless. All appeals for mercy, negotiations, or surrender were met with the same response as ferocious resistance. When all opposition had been crushed and all interstellar communications completely destroyed or blanketed out, the invaders came down in ships of vaguely familiar design to inspect what remained of the battered colony.

"Our single survivor had been as surprised as anyone when the sneak tri-dee screens had focused on the locks of the landing shuttles and armed Pitarian troops had come pouring out. They were remorseless in their destruction of the surviving human population, treating it as if they were the lowest, filthiest organisms in the universe. They helped themselves to a few valuables and such, but for the most part they seemed to enjoy killing for the love of it. Like weasels on Terra. At this point the man's mind started to shrink away again. The psychiatrists who attended him felt that if he'd remained sane he never would have been able to cope with the other stresses that his escape put on his mind. Like not eating for four days, and such. The Pitar were thorough. They carried life detectors to search out survivors no matter how well they were hidden.

"Our informant had lived in a small town near the planet's equator. He had once been a ship's engineer and had bought a small, obsolete lifeboat which he enjoyed tinkering with in his spare time. Again, it took a madman to suppose that that wreck could ever make it to the nearest moon. Before the enemy troops had reached his area he had managed to provision the tiny ship and perform a successful liftoff. Obviously the orbiting warships were no longer expecting a vessel from the planet's surface. All spaceports had been destroyed, and all the commercial doublekay drive ships in parking orbit had been vaporized while trying to escape or taken over by Pitarian prize crews. No one thought of an attempt to escape simply to space. The moons are uninhabitable and there are no other planets in the system capable of supporting human life. Or possibly they weren't geared to the detection of a propulsive system as tiny and outmoded as his. Anyway, he made it safely through their outward-turned screens and into a closed orbit around the first moon. He never really expected to be picked up. All his addled mind could think of was getting away from the abomination below. It was pure chance that he was rescued.

"That was the gist of his story. Among the nauseating details the probes pumped out of him was what the Pitar did with the bodies of all those missing women. That was so disgusting the authorities tried to keep it from the general public, but as usually happens in such cases, the word got out. The resultant uproar was violent and widespread. War was never even formally declared because most of the members of the Terran Congress held reserve commissions and rushed to get aboard their ships.

"The gigantic armada that was assembled hurled itself into the Pitarian system. Much to everyone's surprise, the Pitarians held their own from their planetary and satellite bases. In space their ships were no match for the human fleet, in addition to being heavily outnumbered, but the possibility of such an eventuality had been considered by the Pitarians and their scientists had put up an offensive-defensive network which the starship weaponry was unable to batter through. It settled down to a war of attrition which the Pitarians hoped to win by making it too expensive to bear. As a result they were effectively blockaded from the rest of the universe, or, as the more polite were wont to put it, were placed in a state of 'enforced quarantine.'

"It appeared as though the situation might stay that way indefinitely. That is, until the thranx stepped in. Like most of the rest of the intelligent races the thranx had heard the details of the Argus V massacre. Unlike most of them, however, they were determined to do something more effective than blockading. As far as the thranx were concerned the final straw was the use to which the Pitar had put human females. The female is considered even more an object of veneration and helplessness on thranx worlds than on the most gallant of humanoid ones. This is a legacy from their early ancestors, when there was one egg-laying queen to protect and nurture. When this hereditary attitude was translated into manners, it was one reason why Terran and other humanoid females who had had contact with the thranx were among the first vociferous boosters of the idea of amalgamation.

"So the thranx added their fleets to the human. At first this had no effect other than to intensify an already near-perfect blockade. Then the human-thranx teams made their first big breakthroughs on the doublekay drive systems, the SCCAM weapons complex, and more. A device had finally been found which could successfully penetrate the Pitarian battle network. It was used. There was at this time some desire among humanx scientists to make an attempt to preserve at least a portion of Pitarian civilization intact, for study. They hoped to find an explanation for their extreme racial paranoia. Sentiment being what it was on the human planets, however, this proved impossible. There is also some reason to believe that the Pitarians themselves would not have permitted this. Their affliction was that strong. Anyway, they fought to the last city.

"The three planets remain, blasted and empty. One human, two Pitarian. They are not often visited, except by the curious and the morbid.

"The scientific teams that worked on the ruins of the Pitarian civilization came to the conclusion that the race was totally unable to accept or understand terms like mercy, compassion, openness, and equality, and similar abstract concepts. They believed themselves to be the only race worthy of existence in the universe. Once they had managed to steal all the knowledge they would stoop to borrow from the barbaric humans, they set out to destroy them. The other intelligent races of the galaxy would have been next on their program of extermination, including the thranx. Compared to them our erstwhile modern competitors, the AAnn, are positively pacific.

"Fortunately, in most respects the Pitarians were nowhere near as sharp as the AAnn. Their weapons development far exceeded their racial maturity, and their conceit their cleverness. I've often wondered whether the Pitar-humanx war was a single boost to amalgamation or a multiple one. There was mutual hatred of the Pitarians, the gratitude mankind felt for the thranx aid, and the fear that somewhere out among the stars there might exist another bunch of psychopathic killers like the Pitar."

It was very quiet in the elegant room when Tse-Mallory had finished.

"Well," said Atha finally, breaking the thought-heavy silence, "it's my turn up front. I'd better go and relieve Wolf." She uncurled herself from the lounge and departed forward.

"*Ndiye, ndiye*." The merchant leaned over and leered at Sissiph. "Come, my *pakadoge*, little pussy. We are only halfway through that delightful book of yours, and I can't wait to see how it turns out. Even if it is mostly pictures. You'll excuse us, gentlesirs?"

Giggling, the girl led him out of the salon.

Tse-Mallory began setting up the levels for the personality-chess board, while Truzenzuzex began shuffling the cards and lining up the blue and red and black pieces.

Flinx looked up at the sociologist. "Sir, *you* didn't participate in the Pitar-humanx war, did you?"

"Pure Flux, youth, no! I'll admit to being aged, and rarely even to old, but archaic—never! I did have a grandfather who participated, though. As I suppose all of our ancestors of that time did, one way or another. Didn't yours?"

Flinx rose and idly brushed off his pants. The fur from the carpet had a tendency to cling. "Excuse me, please, sirs. I recall that I haven't fed Pip his evening meal, and I wouldn't want him to get irritated and start nibbling on my arm."

He turned and headed for the passageway. Tse-Mallory looked after him curiously, then shrugged and turned back to the game. It was his move.

10

Thus far there had been no trouble. The first sign of it came three ship-days later.

Malaika was in Control, checking out coordinates with Wolf. In his cabin Truzenzuzex was rigid in a meditation trance. He utilized that technique whenever he wished to consider a problem involving extreme concentration. And sometimes just to relax. In that state he required less body energy. In the salon, Tse-Mallory was trying to explain the workings of a semantic puzzle to Flinx. Atha was nearby, attempting somewhat boredly to beat herself at the ancient and timeworn game of Mono-Poly. She moved the obscure little idols and symbols in ways that Flinx had always found dully repetitive. Everything continued normally until Sissiph, bored and ejected from Control by the busy Malaika, stomped crankily into the room, a trail of translucent pseudolace flowing behind her.

"This is a *dull* place! Dull, dull, *dull!* Like—like living in a coffin!" She fumed quietly for a few minutes. As no one deigned to notice her, she moved to a more central location. "What a collection! Two pilots, two braincases, and a kid with a poisonous worm for a pet!"

Pip's head lifted abruptly and the minidrag made an unfriendly motion in the girl's direction. Flinx stroked the back of its head until it had relaxed sufficiently for some of the tightness to leave the long muscles. His own response was mild as he considered the self-uncertainty/anger/confusion in the girl's mind.

"It is a reptile, and bears no relation to . . ."

"Reptile! *Worm!* What difference does it make?" She pouted. "And Maxy won't even let me *watch* while he plays with all those *darling* coordinates and standards and things! He says I 'distract' him. Can you imagine? *Distract* him?"

"I can't imagine why it should either, my dear," murmured Atha without looking up from her game.

Ordinarily Sissiph probably wouldn't have made anything of it. Back in Drallar she'd had more than ample opportunity to inure herself to Atha's sarcasm. But the combination of the long flight

and her frustrations of the moment combined to make her turn.
Her voice was tight.

"Is that supposed to be some kind of crack?"

Still Atha did not look up from her game. No doubt she expected
Sissiph to brush off the remark as she usually did and go flounc-
ing from the room in a dignified huff. She returned with a slang
phrase.

" 'Tis truth, forsooth."

"And your mouth," rejoined Sissiph, parodying the words terribly, "is a bit too 'looth'!" She gave the game table a quick shove
with a knee. Being portable and not bolted to the fabric of the ship,
it toppled easily. Small metal objects and plastic cards sailed in all
directions.

Atha closed her eyes tightly, not moving, and then slowly opened
them again. She turned easily to stare at the Lynx, her eyes even
with the other girl's knees.

"I think, honey, that if we're going to pursue this conversation,
we'd do it better on a more equal level."

Her forearm shot out and caught the surprised Sissiph behind
the knees. She let out a startled squeak and sat down hard.

From there on, their bodies seemed to merge so closely that
Flinx was hard put to tell them apart. Their thoughts were indecipherable. Scientific combat went out the port, so to speak. Tse-
Mallory left his puzzle and made a laudable, if foolhardy, attempt
to stop it. All he received for his efforts was a long scratch on one
cheek. At that moment Malaika, summoned hastily by Flinx with
a gentle probe, appeared in the fore doorway. He took in the whole
scene at a half-glance.

*"What in the name of the obscenity seven bells is going on
here?"*

Even his familiar bellow had no effect on the two combatants,
who were by now too deeply engrossed in their work to notice
mere mortal entreaties. The merchant moved forward and made an
attempt to separate the two. Several, in fact. It was like dipping
one's hands into a whirlwind. Frustrated, he backed off.

The longer one lived in the lower levels of Drallar, the greater
one's acquired knowledge of elementary human psychology. Flinx
said loudly but evenly, putting as much disgust into his voice as he
could muster, "My, if you two only knew how funny you look!" He
also risked a brief mental projection of the two combatants, suitably embellished.

There was immediate peace in the room. The cloud of hair, teeth,

nails, and shredded clothing ground to an abrupt halt, resolving itself into two distinct bodies. Both stared blankly at Flinx, then uncertainly at each other.

"Thanks, *kijana*. I'd thought you might help out here and there,
but apparently there's no end to your talents." Malaika reached
down and grasped each girl by the remaining material at the scruff
of her neck, lifting them much as one would a pair of obstinate kittens. The two glared silently at one another and seemed more than
willing to start in all over again. Perceiving this, he shook them so
hard that their teeth rattled and their slippers fell off.

"We're on a billion-credit hunt in rarely spaced territory after
something which any other company in the galaxy would gladly
slit my throat for an inkling of, and you two *mwanamkewivu*,
cretins, idiots, can't live in peace for a month!" He shook them
again, although not as furiously. Neither of them looked in the
mood for fighting now. "If this happens again, and I'll warn you
only once, I will cheerfully chuck the both of you, biting and
scratching if that's the way you want it, out the nearest airlock! *Is
that understood?*"

The two women stared silently at the floor.

"*Au ndiyo au la!* Tell me now!" The voice reverberated around
the salon.

Finally Sissiph murmured, almost inaudibly, "Yes, Maxy." He
turned to glare murderously at Atha.

"Yes, sir," she said meekly.

Malaika would have continued, but Wolf chose that moment to
peer into the room.

"Captain, I think you'd better come take a look at this. There is
an object or objects on the screens which I would say is a ship, or
ships. I'd like your opinion."

"*Nini*?" Malaika roared, whirling. "What!" He let go of the two
women. Both stood quietly, trying to create order out of the chaos
of their clothing. Occasionally one would glance up at the other,
but for now, at least, both were thoroughly abashed.

"It appears to be closing on us, sir. I do wish you'd come take a
look . . . now."

Malaika turned to face the erstwhile fighters. "Atha, you get
fixed up and up front . . . *upesi*! Sissiph, you go back to our cabin
and stay there." Both nodded soberly and departed in different directions.

"Sociologist, you go and get your friend out of that semi-sleep,
or whatever he calls it. I want you at full consciousness in case

anything untoward happens. I have a hunch both of you have had at least a modicum of experience with deep-space ship maneuvers?"

Tse-Mallory had started off toward Truzenzuzex's cabin. Now he paused to smile back at the big trader. "Something of the sort," he said quietly.

"Fine. Oh, *kijana*?" Flinx looked up. "You keep a close eye on that pet of yours. Things might get a little bouncy around here. I don't know how excitable that little devil is, but I wouldn't want him underfoot and nervous around busy people."

"Yes sir. Have you any idea what it is?"

"Yes and no. And I'm afraid it's liable to be the former. And that's bad." He paused, thoughtful. "You can come up front, if you like, so long as you watch that snake. Tell our learned passengers they can too, if they so desire. There's enough room. I just don't want Sissiph around. The darling *pakadogo* has a tendency to get hysterical when things aren't where she can put a finger . . . and other delightful things . . . on them. But I think perhaps the others would like to be around when we find out what is what. And they might have hunches to contribute. I value hunches highly. By the way, I don't suppose you can answer that question for me?"

Flinx concentrated, hard. It was a long way off, but there was nothing else around for light-years, so it came in strong, strong. "It" was malignant/strange/picture of dry air, sun, blood/taste of salt/relief/all wrapped in cold, clear thoughts like snow-melt fitted in only one type. . . .

He looked up, blinked. The merchant was watching him intently, with not a little hint of concern. He became aware then of the beads of sweat on his brow. He said one word, because it was sufficient.

"AAnn."

The merchant nodded thoughtfully and turned for the door.

11

The dot that indicated the presence of an operating posigravity drive field was clear now and far off to their "right"—about ninety degrees or so to the present x-plane. It was moving on a definite convergence course. They still could not be sure what it was, other than that at least one mind occupied a similar area of space.

An ancient aphorism someone had once recited to Flinx came back to him. As he recalled it, there had been two men involved, one old and one young. The younger had said, "No news is good news," and the other, a Terran holy man, had wisely replied, "That's not necessarily true, my young friend. A fisherman doesn't think he's lucky if he doesn't get a bite." He wasn't positive that the story was an appropriate analogy for the moment, because he found himself disagreeing with the holy man.

"Two of them, Captain," said Wolf. "See. . . ."

It was true. Even Flinx could see that as the large dot came closer it was separating into two distinct points. At the same time he sensed a multiplicity of similar minds to the one he'd first noticed although much weaker.

"*Two* ships," said Malaika. "Then my one guess is in error after all. Before shadows. Now, everything in the dark. *Usiku*. Still, it might be. . . ."

"What *was* your guess, Maxim?" asked Truzenzuzex.

"I thought perhaps a competitor of mine—a certain competitor—had gotten drift of your discovery to a greater extent than I originally thought. Or that certain information had leaked. If the latter case, then I should suspect that someone on this ship is a spy." There were some fast, uneasy glances around the cabin. "That is still a possibility, but I am now less inclined to suspect it. I don't know of any combine in the Arm, neither the one I had in mind nor even General Industries, that could afford or would be inclined to put out two ships on what has a very good chance of being a profitless venture on merely spurious, secondhand information. Not even an AAnn Nest-Corporation."

"In which case," said Tse-Mallory, "who are our two visitors?"

"I don't know, sociologist, *hata kidogo*. Not at all. But we will no doubt find out shortly. They should be in reception distance momentarily, if they aren't already. If there were a relay station in this area we might have found out sooner . . . assuming of course that they wished us to know of their presence, and knew closely enough where we were. I think that I doubt that. . . ."

Atha was efficiently manipulating dials and switches. "I've got everything wide open, sir, and if they're beaming us, we'll pick it up, all right!"

They did.

The face that appeared on the screen was not shocking, thanks to Flinx's advance warning, but the garb it wore was because it was so totally unexpected.

"Good-morning to you, *Gloryhole*," said the sallow-faced AAnn officer-noble who looked out at them. "Or whatever day-period you are experiencing at the moment. The illustrious and renowned Maxim Malaika captaining, I assume?"

"The puzzled and curious Maxim Malaika is here, if that's what you mean." He moved into the center of the transceiver's pickup. "You're one up on me."

"Apologies," said the figure. "I am named Riidi WW, Baron Second of Tyrton Six, Officer in the Emperor Maahn the Fourth's Circumspatial Defense Forces. My ship is named *Arr*, and we are accompanied in travel by her sister-ship, the *Unn*."

Malaika spoke in the direction of the omnipickup mike. "All that. Your mother must have been long-winded. You boys are a bit off your usual tracks, aren't you?"

The Baron's face reflected mild surprise. As Flinx suspected, it was mock. "Why, captain! The Blight is unclaimed space and open to all. There are many fine, colonizable, unclaimed planets here, free to any spacegoing race. While it is true that in the past His Majesty's government has been more involved in outward expansion, an occasional search for planets of exceptional promise does sometimes penetrate this far."

"A very concise and seemingly plausible explanation," whispered Truzenzuzex to Malaika from out of range of the audiovisual pickups.

"Yes," the merchant whispered back. "I don't believe a word of it either. Wolf, change course forty-five degrees x-plus."

"Done, Captain."

"Well, Baron, it's always nice to hear from someone away out in the middle of nowhere, and I am sure that two of his Majesty's destroyers will be more than a match for any planet of 'exceptional promise' you may happen to find. I wish you luck in your prospecting."

"Your offers of good fortune are accepted in the spirit in which they are given, Captain Malaika. In return I should like to extend the hospitality of my ship and crew, most especially of our galley. I am fortunate enough to have on board a chef who works wonders with the cuisine of thirty-two different systems. The fellow is a wizard, and would be proud to have the opportunity to display his talents before such discerning gourmets as yourselves."

Wolf's low whisper cut across the cabin. "They've changed course to match our new one, sir. And accelerated, too."

"Keep on course. And pick it up enough to match their increase. But do it subtly, *mwanamume*, subtly!" He turned back to the screen.

"Truly a gracious offer, Baron, and ordinarily I would consider it an honor and a delight to accept. However, I am afraid that circumstances warrant we decline this particular invitation. You see, we had fish for supper last evening, and I am certain it was not prepared half so well as your chef could manage, because we have all been suffering from severe pains of the lower intestinal tract today. If we may, I'll put off your kind offer till a later date."

Away from the mike he whispered, "The rest of you get back to your cabins and strap down. I'll try to keep you up on what happens through your intership viewers. But if we have to bump around a bit, I don't want you all bouncing off the woodwork and messing up my carpets!"

Flinx. Tse-Mallory. and Truzenzuzex made a scramble for the exitway, being careful to stay out of range of the tri-dee video pickup. But apparently Truzenzuzex couldn't resist a dig at a persistent and long-time enemy. The thranx had had dealings with the AAnn long before mankind.

He stuck his head into range of the pickups and yelled, "Know, O sand-eater, that I have sampled AAnn cuisine before, and that my gizzard has found it to be gritty to the palate. Those who dine upon rocks rapidly assume the disposition and mental capacity of the same!"

The AAnn bristled, the scales along its neck-ridge rising. "Listen, dirt-dweller, I'll inform you that . . . !" He caught it in mid-curse and recomposed himself with an effort. Feigning a sigh where he no doubt would have preferred a threat, he said, "I retain the courtesies while it is evident they have departed your ship,

Captain. Have it your way. You cannot outrun us, you know. Now that we are within easy range, my detector operators will be most careful not to lose you. It will be only a matter of time before we come within filial distance of you. At that moment I would hope that you would have reconsidered my really exceptionally polite and generous invitation, and will lower your field. Otherwise," he said grimly, "I am very much afraid we shall be forced to open you up like a can of *zith*-paste."

The screen abruptly went blank.

In his cabin, Flinx lay down on his bed and began to strap into the emergency harness that was affixed permanently to its sides. He had Pip next to his left hand, curled around a bar on that side of the bed. He admonished it to be quiet. The snake, sensing that important things were happening, did as it was told with a minimum of fuss and bother.

When he had finished and settled himself into the closest thing to a comfortable position he could manage in the awkward harness, he turned on the little screen which hung suspended from the roof of the cabin. It cleared instantly to reveal Malaika, Atha, and Wolf busy in Control. Unwillingly, he began to recall more familiar sights and smells. It embarrassed him, but at that moment he wished fervently he were back home in Drallar, juggling before an appreciative crowd and making small boys laugh by telling them the names of their secret loves. What he could interpret of the mind/thoughts of the AAnn commander was not pleasant. The feeling passed abruptly as though a cool rag had been drawn across his mind, and he settled himself grimly to wait.

In the huge, exotically furnished cabin which formed her quarters, Sissiph lay alone on the big bed, curled in her harness. Her knees nearly touched her chest. She felt very alone. The order to don harness had been delivered in a tough, no-nonsense tone that Maxy had never used with her before, and she was frightened. The luxurious accoutrements, the intricately carved furniture and sensuous cantilevered lighting, the king's ransom in clothing scattered about the room, all suddenly seemed as frivolous and flighty as the toys of a child. She had known, she had simply *known*, when she had chosen to try to replace that other little witch—what had been her name?—as Malaika's steady Lynx, that something terrible like this was going to happen. She had *known* it!

Merchants were so *damned* unpredictable!

She did not throw the switch which would lower the screen and put her in communication with Control and the rest of the ship. Let him survive without her for a while! Instead she buried herself as deeply as she could in the purrsilk pillows and promised herself that if she survived this awful, horrible journey into no place, she was going to find some nice hundred-and-fifty-year-old man . . . on the verge of death. A senile, wealthy one, with whom she could look forward to a nice, quiet, comfortable, short, married life . . . and a long, wealthy widowhood.

Bran Tse-Mallory was lying in his bed quietly reviewing the hundred and five maxims of the state of Indifferent Contentment. It was originally invented by a brilliant graduate student to help nervous students relax for examinations. It would do duty in other situations. The current one, for example. But no matter how hard he tried, he couldn't get past twenty-one. It kept repeating itself over and over in his mind every time he tried to concentrate on twenty-two.

"Mankind must without a doubt be the most conceited race in the universe, for who else believes that God has nothing better to do than sit around all day and help him out of tight spots?"

It was an unworthy thought for one who supposedly had mellowed so over the years, but how, oh, how he wished for the comforting grip of a gun—*any* kind of gun—under his fingers. They tightened and relaxed reflexively, making deep furrows in the softness of the blankets.

The Eint Truzenzuzex was lying quietly on his modified lounge, legs fully extended, foothands and truehands crossed on his chest in the proper *Oo* position. He tried to keep one half of his mind focused on the ship viewer, while the other half droned through the ritual.

"I, Tru, of the family Zen, clan zu, the Hive Zex, do hereforth pray that I shall not bring disgrace on my-our ancestors. I, Tru, of the family Zen, clan zu, the Hive Zex, do hereforth pray that in the coming Time of Trouble I may reflect credit on my first-mother, clan mother, and Hive mother. I, Tru, of the family Zen, clan. . . ."

Atha Moon and the man called Wolf thought otherwise. They were much too busy for anything else. And Maxim Malaika, the man who was responsible for them all, did likewise. Also, he was too scared to have time for trivialities like worry. Wolf broke into his nonthoughts.

"They've closed to within five miles, sir. At this rate they'll be within particle-beam range in five, ten minutes."

"*Choovy*! And other unmentionables! Damn!"

Atha looked back at him worriedly. "Couldn't we try to dodge them, Maxim? I mean, captain?"

"*La, hasha*, Atha. No way. Those are AAnn destroyers out there. They're built to chase down and slice up ships much faster than we are. The *Gloryhole* is a rich man's whim, not a navy ship. But it *is* something of a speedster, *sharti*. Of necessity. With any kind of distance between us at initial contact we might have slipped out of detector range and lost them, but they were on top of us before we even knew who they were. Anyway, there are two of them. One, *labda*, we might still slip, but never two. Not at this range."

Atha thought. "Couldn't we just, well, surrender and take our chances? I mean, everything considered, that Baron didn't seem all that awful. Just impatient. And we aren't at war or anything with his people."

"*Ndoto*. A dream. The AAnn don't operate that way, Atha." His lips were firmed, tight. "At best they are . . . intolerant . . . with folk who cooperate with them. With those who don't. . . . If you're curious about details, ask Wolf. He was in an AAnn prison camp for five years, during the last real humanx-AAnn conflict. There may be others who survived that long in one of those hell-pits and lived to tell of it. If so, I haven't met him."

"The captain is right, Miss Moon. I would much rather throw myself into space to blow up like a deep-sea fish than be captured by those again." He nodded at the screen, where the white dots continued their inexorable approach. "Among their other affectations, they are very adept at the more refined forms of torture. Very. It is something of an art form with them, you see. Most of my scars don't show. They're up here, you see." He tapped the side of his head. "If you wish some detailed descriptions. . . ."

Atha shuddered. "Never mind."

"This Riidi fellow seems fairly decent . . . for an AAnn, but to take the chance. . . . If I could spare Wolf from plotting, or myself from the computer . . . *tandunono*! No, wait!" He leaned over the mike pickup. "*Ninyi nyote*! Tse-Mallory, sociologist. And you, bug! Have either of you ever handled a spatial weapon before? Even in simulation?"

In his cabin Tse-Mallory nearly broke a finger struggling with his harness. And Truzenzuzex broke off his ritual in a place and manner that would have earned him the condemnation of every member of his clan, had they known of it.

"You mean you've got a *gun* on this tub?" shouted Tse-Mallory. "What kind? Where? Speak up, mercantilist! Implosion weapons,

particle guns, missile tubes, explosive projectiles, rocks . . . Tru
and I will handle it!"

"*Je*? I hope so. Listen to me. Behind your cabins, *naam*, storage
compartment. There's a walkway, it opens into the cargo balloon.
Then a pullway. Go to the end of the main pullway, you can't get
lost. You'll find branches there. Be careful, there's no gravity in
that part of the ship. Take the one that goes ninety degrees north of
your horizontal. At the top you'll find a medium charge interstice
laser, mounted on a universal belt encircling the ship. I'm power-
ing it now." He paused momentarily while his hands did things below the range of the camera's pickup.

"It is a single-person mounting. Sorry, philosoph. But you could
help him with the computer. If he doesn't have to watch the
imageouts and battlescreen at the same time. . . ."

The two men of peace were already on their way.

Malaika uttered a silent prayer in the hopes that the two scientists wouldn't cut up the ship and turned back to his tables.

"How are we doing, Wolf?"

"They're still closing, sir. Not as rapidly now that we've picked
up our own speed, but still closing. You want to go on maximum?"

"No. No, not yet. That's strictly our last gasp, if we need it. Let
them continue to think the *Glory*'s just another freighter for a
while. First I want to see what our braincases can do with the pop-
gun."

The braincases in question were making their way along the
pullway at breakneck speed. Fortunately, there was no drifting
cargo to impede their progress. The great metal-fabric enclosure
was almost completely empty. A few cases drifted lazily in their
spiderweb enclosures, giving the pale green cavern and its ghostly
atmosphere a tinge of perspective. The feeling was enhanced by
the lighting, or lack of it. Since this area of the ship, although by
far the largest, was rarely visited except upon arriving or departing
a cargo stop, the lighting was kept to a minimum. Even so it would
have been lost in the cargo compartment of one of the great
"Soaring Sun" class freighters.

They had no trouble locating the correct branch-way at the end
nexus of the main one. It was the only strand headed remotely in
the required direction. Tse-Mallory launched himself upward and
began to float up to the rope. He reached out and began to pull
himself rapidly upward, hand over hand. Truzenzuzex, he knew,
would be right behind him. With its four hands the insect could go

faster than he, but there was no reason for him to pass Bran since he couldn't operate the human-contoured gun nearly as well.

They reached the gun housing, a sphere of thick metal like a blister in the skin of the ship. It had its own emergency power and air supply. Far off to both sides he could see where the mounting's powered belt encircled the skin of the vessel. Moving along that belt the gun could cover an approaching threat from any angle. He had only a second to wonder what it was doing on a private yacht before he was inside the shell and buckling himself into the gun-seat. Truzenzuzex secured the hatch behind them, moving to the computer imageouts to Bran's left. A more modern weapon would have had both combined in a single helmet-set that would fit down over the gunner's head. The insect began to cannibalize braces, locks, and belts from the emergency compartments, until he had built himself a reasonably solid harness opposite the 'puter.

Bran wrapped his right hand around the pressure trigger with all the fondness of a proud father caressing his newborn. His left went into the battlescreen sensory pickup. He let go of the trigger for a moment, reluctantly, to tighten the nerve sensors around his spread left hand. He flexed it once to make sure the pickups didn't pinch and then returned the right to the trigger grip. Next began a careful examination of the screen and dial scopes. It was definitely an early model, but then laser weapons hadn't changed much in their basic design for several centuries, and probably wouldn't in several more. The base design was too cheap and efficient. He had no doubt that he could operate this one effectively on the first try. Come to that, he'd damn well have to! Their pursuers weren't likely to give them a practice shot.

Under impulses from his left hand the battlescreen lit. He was gratified to see that his combat reflexes, at least, were still operative. On the screens were two dots the size of his thumbnail. For a moment he almost panicked, thinking he was back on the old Twenty-Five. If an opposing ship had managed to approach this close in a war situation they'd have been vaporized by now. But then, this wasn't a war situation. At least not yet. He put that unpleasant line of thought out of his mind. Something for the diplomats to sharpen their tongues on. Obviously neither of the approaching ships had expectations of meeting even token resistance. It was simply a game of catch-up. They came on openly and without caution. Possibly, hopefully, they also had their screens down or at least underpowered.

From his left Truzenzuzex began rattling off a stream of figures and coordinates. One of the destroyers was slightly nearer than the other. The sloppy formation was the inevitable result of overconfidence on the enemy's part. Bran began lining up a center shot. His finger hesitated over the trigger, and he spoke into the intership mike.

"Look, Malaika. These people are here after something, and since we've only got one something worth risking an interstellar incident over, they're going to want us in one piece. I don't expect them to start any reckless shooting. They're coming in as if all they expect to have to do is net us like a clipped *Geech* bird. I've played with the AAnn before. They're not overimaginative, but they think damn fast. That means one good shot and one only, and then we'd better run like hell. How close can you let them get while still giving us an outside chance to break their detection? Assuming they'll be sufficiently confused to let us."

Malaika calculated rapidly in his head. "Um . . . um . . . *mara kwa mara* . . . that Riidi fellow will have to decide whether to blow us to atoms or make another try . . . the latter, I don't doubt . . . *has* to take us alive, or not at all . . . I can give you another two mils distance. La, one and a half, now."

"Good enough," said Tse-Mallory, concentrating on the screen. It would have to be, he thought. "We'll know it back here when the 'puter hits it." Malaika didn't reply.

"That will bring us down almost to . . . to three," said Truzenzuzex.

"I supposed. Let me know when we reach three point one."

"Time enough?"

Tse-Mallory grinned. "Ole bug-wug, me friend, my reflexes have slowed down through the years, but dead yet they ain't! It'll be enough. Up the universe!"

"Up the universe!" came the even reply.

In Control, Malaika turned to Wolf, his face thoughtful.

"You heard?"

The shadow-man nodded.

"All right then. Start slowing down. Yes, slowing down! If he says he's going to get only one shot, he's probably going to get only one shot, and I want him to have as good a line as possible. So let's make it look nearly as we can as though we're giving up the chase."

Obediently, Wolf began cutting their speed. Slowly, but the AAnn computers would notice it.

"Three point seven . . . three point six . . ." Truzenzuzex's voice recited the figures with machinelike precision and clarity.

Bran's body was steady, but he was trembling ever so slightly inside. He *was* older.

"Tru, uh, did you spot any HIP drugs in that emergency locker?"

"Heightened IP? Three point five . . . you know that stuff's almost as carefully watched as the SCCAM circuitry. Oh, there's some of the bastard stuff back there, the kind that's available on any black market. All that will do, my friend, to borrow a saying, is 'screw up your bod' . . . three point four . . . not to mention your reflexes . . . screw it down, more likely. Relax."

"I know, I know!" His eyes never left the screen. "But, vertebrae, I wish I had some now!"

"Obscenity is better . . . three point three . . . pretend you're back at the University working over old man Novy's thesis. That ought to generate enough anger for you to take those ships apart with your bare hands. . . ."

Bran smiled, and the tenseness left him. Back at the University old professor Novy had been one of their pet animosities.

". . . three point two. . . ."

He could see the bastard's ugly face now. He wondered what had finally happened to the old boy after. . . . His finger tightened on the trigger.

". . . three poi. . . ."

Already the pressure-stud was being depressed.

In the nothingness of nowhere a lancet of emerald green brighter than a sun leaped from the *Gloryhole* across a second of infinity. A milli-instant later it impinged on the drive fan of the nearest AAnn warship, which happened to be the *Unn*. There was a soundless flash of impossible scintillating gold flame, like the waves of tortured hydrogen that march across the skin of stars. It was followed by an explosion of vaporized solids and an expanding, rapidly diffusing cloud of ionized gas.

The battlescreen showed one white dot and one tiny nebula.

In the gun housing, Bran was frantically trying to reline the laser for a shot at the second ship, but he never got a real chance.

At the instant of silent destruction, Malaika had permitted himself one violent cry of "*Oseee-yeee!*"

Then, "Wolf, Atha, get us *moving, watu!*" Atha slammed over a connection and the *Gloryhole* leaped forward at her maximum acceleration.

On the still existing AAnn ship, the *Arr*, panic reigned only in those areas of the vessel where Baron Riidi WW's control was peripheral. Around him the crew only reflected fatal resignation. The one pleasant thought in all their minds was what they would do to the people on their quarry once the commander and the techs had extracted whatever it was they wanted from them. None glanced at the Baron's face for fear of meeting his eyes.

The Baron's polished claws scraped idly at the scales on his left arm. There was a voipickup set by the right one.

"Enginemaster," he said calmly into the grid, "full power, please. Everything you can spare from the screens." He did not bother to inquire if they were now up.

He turned back to the huge battlescreen which dominated the bridge. On it a white dot had shrunk rapidly but had not succeeded in disappearing completely. Now, it could not. Without taking his eyes from the screen he addressed the crew over the comm-system.

"No one is to blame for the loss of the *Unn*. Not expecting interspace weaponry on a private craft of that type, only debris screens were up. That error has since been rectified. The enemy is faster than originally estimated. It apparently hoped to pass out of detector range in the confusion engendered by the loss of our sistership. This has not occured. It *will* not occur. We are through playing polite. Bend your tails to it, gentlemen, we have a ship to catch! And when we have done I can promise you at least some interesting entertainment!"

Inspired, the crew of the *Arr* dipped to their tasks with a will.

Bran cursed once, briefly, as the surviving AAnn ship shrank out of range.

Truzenzuzex was busily disengaging himself from his makeshift harness. "Relax, brother. You did as well as we'd hoped. Better. They had their screens down, all right, or they wouldn't have gone up like that. We must have hit their generator dead on. Metamorphosis, what a show!"

Tse-Mallory took the advice and relaxed as well as he could. "Yes. Yes, you're perfectly correct, Tru. A second time we wouldn't have been so lucky. If we'd had a second time."

"Quite so. I suggest now a return to our cabins. This toy will be of no further use. If we had a *real* gun, now . . . oh, well. After you, Bran."

Truzenzuzex had reopened the hatch and they dived down the pullway. Heading back through the murky green hollows they missed Malaika's congratulations as they poured over the now untended mike in the gunshell.

"Ships and novas, ships and novas! By the tail of the Black Horse nebula! They *did* it! Those effete, simple, peace-loving *nduguzuri did* it! Taking out a warship with one shot from that antique!" He shook his head. "We may not get out of this but, by *mitume*, the prophets, those lizards'll know they've been in a fight!"

Wolf brought the merchant back to reality. Not that his mind had ever really left it, but his spirit had—momentarily. It had been refreshing, anyway.

"They're beginning to pick up on us again, sir. Slower than before. Much slower. But we're running on everything we have and they're still making up distance on us."

Atha nodded concurrence. "The screen may not show it yet, but it's here in the readouts. At this rate we've got maybe three—no, four hours before they're within paralysisbeam range."

"*Je*! That's it, then. *Pepongapi*? How many evil spirits?"

He sat down in his seat. Once they got that close they'd make mummies out of everyone on board and then unwrap their minds at their leisure. The methods might vary, but they would undoubtedly be unique in their unpleasantness. That could not be permitted to happen. As soon as the AAnn got that close he'd see to it that everyone had a sufficiently lethal dose of something from med supply to insure that questioning would remain an impossibility. Or possibly a laser would be better. Burned down to ashes, the AAnn technicians, good as they might be, couldn't reconstruct. Yes, that was a better choice. After he finished with everyone else he'd have to make certain not to miss the brain. He'd have only the one shot. Better start looking for a mirror, Maxim!

If there were only some way they could pick up enough speed to swing out of detector range! Even if only for a few microseconds, it might be enough. Space was vast. Given that one precious interval the *Gloryhole* should easily shake her pursuers. Unconsciously, he put his hand over Atha's.

"There's *got* to be a way to pick up another half multiple!"

He didn't notice the way her hand trembled when his covered it, nor the way she looked down at it. He removed it abruptly without being aware of the effect he'd had on his copilot. It joined the other in digging at their owner's hair.

Flinx was also considering the problem, in his own way. He knew little about stellar navigation, and less about doublekay units . . . but Malaika had forgotten more than he might ever know. He couldn't match the merchant's knowledge, but he could remember for him. The links in the trader's mind branched a million ways. Patiently, he tracked down now this, now that one, bringing long-forgotten studies and applications to the surface where Malaika's own system would pick them up, look them over, and discard them. In a way it was like using the retrieval system at the Royal Library. He kept at it with a steadiness he hadn't known he possessed, until. . . .

"But *akili*! Commonsense . . . !" He paused, and his eyes opened so wide that for a moment Atha was actually alarmed. "*Atha!*" She couldn't prevent herself from jumping a little at the shout.

He had it. Somehow the idea had risen from its hiding place deep in his mind, where it had lain untouched for years.

"Look, when the Blight was first reached, survey ships went through it—some of it—with an eye toward mapping the place, right? The idea was eventually dropped as impractical—meaning expensive—but all the information that had originally been collected was retained. That'd be only proper. Check with memory and find out if there are any neutron stars in our vicinity."

"What?"

"An excellent idea, captain," said Wolf. "I think . . . yes, there is a possibility—outside and difficult, mind—that we may be able to draw them in after us. Far more enjoyable than a simple suicide."

"It would be that, Wolf, except for one thing. I am not thinking of even a complicated suicide. *Mwalizuri*, talk to that machine of yours and find out what it says!"

She punched the required information uncertainly but competently. It took the all-inclusive machine only a moment to image-out a long list of answers.

"Why yes, there is one, Captain. At our present rate of travel, some seventy-two ship-minutes from our current attitude. Co-ordinates are listed, and in this case are recorded as accurate, nine point . . . nine point seven places."

"Start punching them in." He swiveled and bent to the audio mike. "Attention, everybody. Now that you two minions of peace and tranquility have effectively pacified half our pursuit, I've been stimulated enough to come up with an equally insane idea. What I'm . . . what *we're* going to try is theoretically possible. I don't know if it's been done before or not. There wouldn't be any records of an *un*successful attempt. I feel we must take the risk. Any alternative to certain death is a preferable one. Capture is otherwise a certainty."

Truzenzuzex leaned over in harness and spoke into his mike. "May I inquire into what you . . . *we* will attempt to do?"

"Yes," said Wolf. "I admit to curiosity myself, captain."

"*Je*! We are heading for a neutron star in this sector for which we have definite coordinates. At our present rate of speed we should be impinging on its gravity well at the necessary tangent some seventy . . . sixty-nine minutes from now. Atha, Wolf, the computer, and myself are going to work like hell the next few minutes to line up that course. If we can hit that field at a certain point at our speed . . . I am hoping the tremendous pull of the star will throw us out at a speed sufficient to escape the range of the AAnn detector fields. They can hardly be expecting it, and even if they do figure it out, I don't think our friend the Baron would consider doing likewise a worthwhile effort. I almost hope he does. He'd have everything to lose. At the moment, we have very little. Only we humans are crazy enough to try such a stunt anyway, *kweli*?"

"Yes. Second the motion. Agreed," said Truzenzuzex. "If I were in a position to veto this idiotic—which I assure you I would do. However, as I am not . . . let's get on with it, captain."

"Damned with faint praise, eh, philosoph? There are other possibilities, *watu*. Either we shall miss our impact point and go wide, in which case the entire attempt might as well not have been made and we will be captured and poked into, or we will dive too deeply and be trapped by the star's well, pulled in, and broken up into very small pieces. As Captain I am empowered to make this decision by right . . . but this is not quite a normal cruise, so I put it to a vote. Objections?"

The only thing that came over the comm was a slight sniffle, undoubtedly attributable to Sissiph (she had given in to curiosity and flipped on her unit). It could not be construed as an objection.

"*Je*! We will try it, then. I suggest strongly you spend some time checking out your harnesses and spreading yourselves as comfortably as possible. Provided that we strike the star's field at the precise tangent I am almost positive that the *Gloryhole* can stand the forces involved. If it cannot it will not matter, because our bodies will go long before the ship does. *Haidhuru*. It doesn't matter. Physiologically I have no idea what to expect. So prepare your bodies and your spirits as well as possible, because in sixty . . ." he paused to glance at the chronometer, "six minutes, it will be all one way or all the other."

He cut the mike and began furiously feeding instructions and requests into a computer auxiliary.

If they had one consolation, thought Flinx, it was that there would be no horrifyingly slow buildup of gravity within the ship.

They would either fail or succeed at such a supremely high speed that it would be over in an instant . . . as Malaika had said, all one way or all the other. He did not care to imagine what would happen if they missed their contact point and dived too close to the star. Dwell in the well. Not funny. He saw himself and Pip mashed flat, like paper, and that proved unamusing also.

The chronometer, oblivious of mere human concerns, continued to wind down. Sixty minutes left . . . forty . . . twenty to . . . ten tofivetothreetotwo. . . .

And then, unbelievably, there were only sixty seconds left till judgment. Before he had time to muse on this amazing fact, there was a slight jar. A silent screaming from the farthest abyss of time flowed like jelly over the ship. He hung on the lip of a canyon of nothingness, while it tried desperately to ingest him. He refused to be ingested. REFUSED! A pin among other pins in a bowl of milk, while somewhere a million fingernails dug exquisitely scratching on a thousand hysterically howling blackboards-sscRRRREEEEEEEE. . . .

12

On board the destroyer *Arr* the chief navigational officer blinked at his detector screen, then turned to stare up at where the Baron sat in his command chair.

"Sir, the humanx vessel has disappeared from my screens. Also, we are rapidly approaching a neutron star of considerable gravitonic potential. Orders?"

Baron Riidi WW was noted for his persistence. The idea of a trapped quarry escaping him was most unappealing. Neither, however, was he a fool. His eyes closed tiredly.

"Change course thirty degrees, right to our present plane. Cut to cruising speed, normal." He looked up then, eyes open, at the battlescreen. Somewhere out there was a white dot. Out there also, an invisible bottomless pit of unimaginable energy masked an impossible retreat. Or a quick suicide. An inkling of the human's intentions percolated through his cells. He did not feel the least inclined to try to duplicate the event. Whether the idiot was alive or dead, he would not know for many months . . . and that was the most infuriating thing of all.

He flexed his long fingers, staring at the brightly polished claws whose length was suitably trimmed to that for a high member of the aristocracy. Colloid-gems shone lavalike on two of them. He locked them over his chest and pushed outward. Those among the crew who were more familiar with the actions of the nobility recognized the gesture. It indicated Conception of Impractical Power. Under the circumstances it constituted a salute to their departed foe.

"Set a return course for Pregglin Base and signal our industrialist friend the following missive. No, I don't wish an interstar hookup. Just send it. 'Intercepted anticipated vessel and made positive audiovisual identification. Repeat, *positive*. Chased to points' . . . give our current coordinates, shipmaster . . . 'where contact with same was irretrievably lost due to,'" he smiled slightly, "'an unexpected turn of speed on the part of the pursued vessel. In hostile action with same, the destroyer *Unn* was lost with all hands.' Add this note, communicator, and scramble it to my personal code. 'Sir. Your request has proven expensive in the extreme. Contrary to your indications we did not encounter, as you led me to believe, a terrified shipload of frightened moneylenders. As a result of your bungling, I now find myself in the uncomfortable position of having to account for my off-base time to my good friend Lord Kaath, C. How good a friend he is will now be put to a considerable test. As will your ability to place judicious bribes. I hope, for both our sakes, that the latter will be sufficient. Explaining the loss of the *Unn* will be rather more difficult. Should the true circumstances surrounding this idiocy leak out it would be more than enough to condemn us both to death by nth degree torture at the hands of the Masters. Kindly do keep this in mind.'

"Sign it, 'yours affectionately, Riidi WW, Baron, etc., etc.' And get me a drink."

13

It was autumn. Mother Mastiff had closed up the shop, packed a lunch, and taken them both off to the Royal Parks. It was a cloudless day, which was why. Literally cloudless. On Moth this wasn't merely a pleasant exception, it was an event. He could remember staring endlessly at the funny-colored sky. It was blue, so different from the normal light gray. It hurt his eyes. The thoughts of the animals, the birds, were odd and confused. And the hawkers sat listlessly in their respective booths, cursing softly at the sun. It had stolen all their customers. It was a softer sky, and softness of any kind was rare in Drallar. So everyone had taken the day off, including the king.

The Royal Parks were a great, sprawling place. They had originally been created by the builders of the first botanical gardens to use up the space left over from those great constructs. By some monstrous bureaucratic error it had been opened to the general public and had remained so ever since. The great flashing boles of the famous ironwood trees shot straight and proud to impossible heights over his boyish head. They seemed much more permanent than the city itself.

The ironwoods were molting. Every other week the royal gardeners would come and gather up all the fallen leaves and branches. Ironwood was rare, even on Moth, and the scraps were far too valuable to be swept away. The guards in their lemon-green uniforms sauntered easily about the park grounds, there more to protect the trees than the people.

Children were playing on the marvelous gyms and tangles that an earlier king had set up. As long as the people had appropriated the park, he felt that they might as well enjoy it to the fullest. The kings of Drallar had been greedy, yes, but not exceptionally so.

He had been too shy to join the giggling, darting shapes on the funchines. And they had all been frightened of Pip, silly things! There had been one little girl though . . . all curls and blue eyes and flushes. She had shuffled over hesitantly, trying hard to appear disinterested but not succeeding. Her thoughts were nice. For a change, she was fascinated by the minidrag rather than repelled by it.

They had been on the verge of making introductions in the simple but very correct manner that adults lose so quickly, when a great leaf had drifted down unseen and struck him fair between the eyes. Ironwood leaves are heavy, but not enough to produce injury, even to a small boy. Only embarrassment. She had started giggling uncontrollably. Furious, he had stalked off, ears burning with the heat of her laughter, his mind frozen with her picture of him. He had thought momentarily of siccing Pip on her. That was one of the impulses he had learned to control very early, when the snake's abilities had been glass-gruesomely demonstrated on a persistent tormentor, a stray mongrel dog.

Even as he strode farther and farther away, the sounds of her laughter followed, ghostlike. As he walked he took vicious and ineffectual swings at the rust-colored leaves floating down uncaringly about him. And sometimes he didn't even touch them when they dropped brokenly to the ground.

14

Then the sky wasn't blue anymore. Nor light gray. It was pastel green.

He stopped flailing his arms and looked around, moving only his eyes. Pip stopped beating his pleated wings against his master's face and flew off to curl comfortably against the nearest bed-bar, satisfied with the reaction it had produced. The minidrag's tough constitution had apparently suffered few ill effects. Flinx didn't know yet whether to curse it or kiss it.

He tried to sit up but fell back, exhausted by the brief effort. Oddly enough, his bones didn't bother him at all. But his muscles! The tendons and ligaments too, all of the connective web that held the framework together. Felt like they'd been tied end to end, stretched out, rolled together into a ball, and pounded into one of Mother Mastiff's less palatable meatloafs.

It was a trial, but he finally managed to sit up. The events of . . . how long had he been out? . . . came back to him as he rubbed circulation back into benumbed legs. As soon as he felt reasonably humanoid again, he leaned over and spoke into his shipmike. In case the others were in less positive shape than he, he enunciated slowly and clearly so as to be sure to be understood.

"Captain? Captain? Control? Is anyone up there?" He could sense all the other minds but not their condition, as his own was too addled to focus yet.

"*Rahisi, kijana!* Take it easy. Glad to hear you're back too." The trader's voice was a familiar healthy boom but Flinx could read the strain on his mind. In another minute his picture flashed onto the small viewscreen. The blocky face had added another line or two, the beard a few white hairs, but otherwise the craggy visage was unchanged. And although his body and mind looked wearied by the stresses they had undergone, the face reflected old enthusiasms.

"Wolf and I have been up, although not about, by *moyo. Uzito,* what an experience! It seems that our friend the hard-headed philosoph, who wears his bones inside out, stood it better than the

rest of us. He's been up here rubbing us poor softies back into consciousness."

The voice of the insect came over the speaker from somewhere
off-camera, but Flinx could place the thranx from the strength of
its thoughts, which were indeed better organized than those of its
companions.

"If the rest of your body was as hard as your head, captain, you,
at least, would not need my aid."

"*Je*! Well, *kijana*, Tse-Mallory's been up the longest of us poor
humans, and I believe Der Bugg is just now bringing Atha
'round . . . yes, bless her flinty *moyo*. We were going to send him
in to see you next, Flinx, but I see that's not necessary."

"Did we . . . ?" but Malaika seemed not to hear and Flinx was
too tired to probe.

"*Mwanamume* and *mtoto*, what a buggy ride! Sorry, bwana
Truzenzuzex. No offense intended. It's an old Terran saying, meaning 'to go like blazes,' roughly. I know only that it's appropriate to
our present situation. Perhaps it's designed to invoke a friendly
Mungu, *je*? Metamorphosis! Flinx me lad, me *kijana*, me *mtoto*,
we went past that star so fast after hitting that field that our trans-
version 'puter couldn't handle it! The mechanism wasn't built to
program that kind of speed, and I'd hate to tell you where the cut-
off max is! If there were only some way this sort of thing could be
done on a commercial basis . . . owk!"

He winced and gingerly touched a hand to the back of his neck.

"However, I must admit that at the present time there appear to
be certain drawbacks to the system. *Uchawi*! I would have given
much to have seen the face of our friend the Baron when we shot
off his screens, *je*! Unannounced, as it were. I wonder if he . . . but
unwrap yourself from that webbing, *kijana*, and get thee forward.
I've a bit of a surprise for you, and it looks even better from up
front."

Flinx could feel the tone beginning to return to his muscles. He
undid the rest of the harness and slid slowly off the bed. There was
an awkward moment as he had to grab the wall for support, bal-
ancing himself on shaky legs. But things began to normalize themselves quickly now. He walked around the room a few times, experimentally, and then turned and headed for Control, Pip curled
comfortably about his left shoulder.

Malaika swiveled slightly in his seat as Flinx appeared on the
bridge.

"Well? What's the surprise?" He noted that Truzenzuzex had

disappeared, but could feel the insect's presence in another part of the ship.

Apparently Malaika noted his searching gaze. Or possibly he was becoming sensitive. He'd have to be careful around the big trader.

"He's gone to try to help Sissiph. She figured to be the last to return, *rudisha*."

That was undoubtedly true. Atha and Wolf he could clearly see busy at their instruments.

"*Kijana*, that big kick in the . . . boost we got shoved us far ahead of my anticipated schedule . . . on our prearranged path! I planned it that way when we were setting up the interception coordinates. No use wasting a brush with death if it can be utilized to profit also . . . but I honestly didn't think the *Glory*'s field could hold us that steady. However, it did, and here we are."

"Which is where?" asked Flinx.

Malaika was smug. "Not more than ninety minutes ship-*nafasi* from our intended destination!" He turned back to his desk, muttering. "Now if there's only some way to make it commercially feas. . . ."

Flinx put together what he knew of how far they'd come when they were intercepted by the AAnn warship and how far they'd still had to go at that time. The result he came up with was an acceleration he had no wish to dwell on.

"That's great, of course, sir. Still, it would also be nice if. . . ."

"Um? If what?"

"If when we get where we're going we find something worth getting there for."

"Your semantics are scrambled, *kijana*, but I approve the sentiment. *Mbali kodogo*, a little way off, perhaps, but I do indeed approve."

15

The planet itself was a beauty. It would have been ideal for colonization if it hadn't been for the unfortunate dearth of land area. But even the fact that ninety percent of the land was concentrated in one large continent might not make such exploitations prohibitive. Oceans could be farmed and mined, too, as on colony worlds like Dis and Repler. And those of Booster, as they had named it, were green enough to suggest that they fairly seethed with the necessary base-matrix to support humanx-style sea-culture. Fortunately the chlorophyll reaction had proved the norm on most humanx-type planets found to date.

By contrast the single continent appeared to be oddly dry. Especially discouraging to Truzenzuzex, as the thranx would have preferred a wet, tropical climate. He confirmed this opinion by voicing it every chance he got.

As far as they were able to determine from orbit, everything was exactly as it had been described on the star-map. Atmospheric composition, with its unusual proportion of free helium and other rare gases, UV radicount (est. surf./sq.mi./ki.), mean and extreme temperatures, and so forth. There was only one fact their observer had failed to note.

As near as their probes could estimate, at no place on the surface of Booster did the wind ever blow less than 70 kilometers an hour. At certain points over the oceans, especially near the equator, it was remarkably consistent. But it did not appear to drop below that approximated minimum. There was currently one gigantic storm system visible in the southeastern portion of the planet. The meteorology 'puter guessed the winds near its center to be moving in excess of 780 kilometers per hour.

"Impossible!" said Malaika, when he saw the initial imageout. *"Mchawi mchanganyiko!"*

"Quite," said Truzenzuzex. "Definitely. Go fly a kite." The scientist indulged in the whistling laughter of the thranx.

Malaika was confused, by the laughter as well as the referent. "Translation, please?"

"It means," put in Tse-Mallory over the insect's laughter, "that it is more than possible." He was gazing in complete absorption at the sphere turning below. The unusual silver-gold tinge to the atmosphere had aroused interest in his mind. "And there might be places, on the single continent, for example, where canyons and such would channel even higher velocities."

The merchant took a deep breath, whooshed it out, and fingered the small wooden image that hung omnipresent about his neck. "*Namna gani mahaili?* What kind of place? No wonder there's nothing more than one little continent and a few *visiwabovu*. Such winds would cut down high places like chaff!" He shook his head. "Why the Tar-Aiym would pick a place like this to develop their whatever-it-is I'll not guess."

"There is much we don't know of the Tar-Aiym and their motives," said Tse-Mallory. "Far more than we do know. From their point of view it might have been perfect. Maybe they felt that its very unattractiveness would discourage inspection by their enemies. And we have no final evidence as to what they considered a hospitable climate. We don't even know for certain what they looked like, remember. Oh, we've got a vague idea of the basics. The head goes here, the major manipulative limbs there, and so on. But for all we really know they might even have been semiporous. A nice three-hundred-kilo-an-hour hurricane might have been as a refreshing bath to them. In which case I'd expect the Krang to be some sort of resort facility."

"Please!" said Malaika. "No obscenities. If that were true, why haven't we found such winds on any of the other planets we know the Tar-Aiym inhabited?"

Tse-Mallory shrugged, bored with the turn of the conversation. "Perhaps the weather has changed since then. Perhaps they changed it. Perhaps I am wrong. Perhaps I am crazy. In fact, there are times when my suspicions of the latter approach certitude."

"I've noticed," said Truzenzuzex, unable to resist.

"Agh! If I knew all the answers," said the sociologist, "I'd be God. In which circumstance I'd most certainly be outside this ship right now and not cooped up with the rest of you mental cases!" He returned his gaze to the screen, but Flinx could taste the humor in his mind.

"Captain?" broke in Wolf's quiet tone. "Preliminary readout from geosurv probes indicates that the continent has a basaltic base, but is composed on the surface primarily of sedimentary rocks, heavily calcinaceous, and with a high proportion of lime-stones."

"Um-hum. Figures. That would also tend to explain how the wind could knock down any mountains so quickly. In another mil-lion years, barring any rising of the ocean bed, there probably won't be a plot of land sticking above the waters of this planet. Fortunately I do not have to worry about that, too." He turned from the screen. "Atha, go and ready the shuttle. And get set to take us down. It doesn't appear that we're going to need airsuits, thank Mungu, but make damn sure the crawler is in good running condi-tion. And see if you can't turn up something for us to use as eye protection against this infernal wind. So that we won't have to use the suit helmets. *Je?*"

She started to leave, but he halted her at the door, his face thoughtful. "And make sure we have plenty of rope. I've been on planets where the rain would eat right through a suit to your skin, if the fauna didn't get to you first, if the flora didn't beat the fauna out. But this makes the first one I've ever been on where my pri-mary concern will be being blown away."

"Yes, captain." She left then, passing the arriving Sissiph on the way out. The two had recovered enough to glare at each other meaningfully for a moment but, aware that Malaika's eyes were on them, said nothing.

"I don't think we'll have much trouble locating this thing of yours, gentlesirs—providing it does indeed exist. There don't ap-pear to be any canyons or other rugged areas where it could be hid-den, and since your friend found it without seeming difficulty, I see no reason why we, with more sophisticated instrumentation, should not do likewise. Yes, we should get to it quickly, quickly. *Afyaenu*, gentlesirs. Your health!"

He clapped those huge hands together and the report they made in the enclosed space was deafening.

"He looks like a small child in expectation of receiving a new toy," Tse-Mallory whispered to Truzenzuzex.

"Yes. Let us hope that it is indeed of an aesthetic rather than a lethal nature."

The shuttle had its own balloonlike hangar in the bottom of the great cargo section. Sissiph, professing ignorance of maneuvering the pullways, had to be helped down. But the way she snuggled into an obliging Malaika suggested motives other than incompe-tence. The powerful little ship was a complete spacegoing vessel, albeit a far more streamlined and less spacious one than the

Gloryhole. It was powered by rockets of advanced design and, for atmospheric, suborbital flight, by ramjets. Being intended for simple ground-to-space, space-to-ground flights, it had limited cruising range. Fortunately they had only a limited area of probability to search. Conducted from the *Gloryhole* it would have been more leisurely, but Malaika wasn't going to restrain himself any longer than was necessary, despite the attendant inconveniences. He wanted *down*.

The fact that they wouldn't need the flexible but still awkward airsuits would be a great help. Atha had fitted them all with goggles whose original purpose was to protect the wearer from heavy UV. While dark, they would serve equally well to keep dust and airborne particles out of everyone's eyes. For Truzenzuzex she had managed a pair from empty polmer containers.

Off in a corner, Sissiph was arguing petulantly with Malaika. Now that the fun of her escorted trip down the pullway was over. . . .

"But I don't want to go, Maxy. Really I don't."

"But you will, my *mwanakondoowivu*, you will. *Njoo*, come, we all stay together. I don't think our playful AAnn friends will find us. I don't see how they could, but I still fear the possibility. In the event of that obscene happening, I want everyone in one and the same place. And I don't know what we're going to run into downstairs, either. We're going into the ruins of a civilization dead half a million years, more advanced than us, and utterly ruthless. Maybe they have left some uncouth hellos for late drop-ins? So every hand will be along in case it's needed. Even your delicious little ones." He smacked the collection of digits in question with a juicy kiss.

She pulled the hand away and stamped a foot (her favorite non-vocal method of protest, but ineffectual in the zero-gravity). "But Maxy . . . !"

"*Starehe*! Don't 'Maxy' me. A definite no, pet." He put a hand on her shoulder and spun her gently but firmly about, giving her a shove in the direction of the shuttle's personnel port.

"Besides, if I were to leave you on board all by yourself you'd likely as not erase the navigation tapes trying to order dinner from the autochef. No, you come with us, *ndegedogo*, little bird. Also, your hair will look so pretty streaming away in the gentle breezes."

Her caustic voice came faintly as they entered the lock. "Breeze! I heard you talking about the hurric . . . !"

Or, thought Flinx as he struggled with the gun and belt that Atha had given him, it is possible that our Captain hasn't forgotten how neatly the AAnn seemed to find us. Maybe he thinks dear, sweet, helpless Sissiph is not entirely to be trusted. He went quiet, sought within the mind in question for a hint, a relationship that might bear out the merchant's possible suspicion. If anything was there, it was too deeply buried or well-hidden for him to seek out. And there were other things that seeped in around the edges of his probe that embarrassed him, even a sixteen-year-old from Drallar. He withdrew awkwardly. Let Malaika keep the load on his mind.

He was far more interested in admiring the gun. The handle was all filigree and inlay, a good deal fancier than the practical destroyers he'd seen in the barred and shadowed gunshops of Drallar. Unquestionably, it was equally as deadly. He knew what this model could do and how to handle it. In those same shops he had fired this and similar weapons with empty charge chambers while the owners had looked on tolerantly and exchanged patronizing comments with the regular customers.

It was beautiful. Compact and efficient, the laser pistol could cook a man at five hundred meters or a steak at one. It could weld most metals, or burn its way through any form of conventional plastic barrier. All in all, it was a useful and versatile tool as much as a weapon. While he hoped he wouldn't need it down on the surface and still had Pip with him, the streamlined weight felt ever so comfortable hugging his hip.

At Malaika's insistence they had all also been issued a full survival belt. Even Sissiph, who had complained that the negligible weight distorted her figure. This prompted an unflattering comment from Atha which fortunately went unheard by the Lynx, or they might have had another minor cataclysm in the tiny vessel's lock.

The belt was equipped and designed for use on planets which varied no more than ten percent from the humanx norm. Besides hefting the mandatory gun, the belt contained concentrated rations and energy pills, sugarsalt solution, their portable communicator units, a tent for two which was waterproof, conserved body heat, and folded to a package smaller than one's fist, charges for both comm and gun, tools for finding direction, making nails, or planting corn, among other things. There was also a wonderfully compact minimicrofilm reader, with some fifty books on its spool. Among the selections were two staples: the *Universal Verbal Communications Dictionary* (in seven volumes, abridged), and the

Bible of the United Church, *The Holy Book of Universal Truths, and other Humorous Anecdotes.*

If he had had his entire apartment and all its accouterments from Drallar, he would have been less well off than he was with that single fabulous device encircling his waist.

The tremendous winds and jetstreams that flowed unceasingly around the planet should have made their descent difficult. Under Atha's skillful handling, however, it was almost as gentle as it might have been in the *Gloryhole.* The only rough moments came as they passed through the silvery-gold impregnated sections of the atmosphere. The natural layers of airborne metallic particles (there were two) seemed unusually dense to the two scientists, but as long as they remained on rockets, not dangerously so.

Unlike the luxury craft which had lifted them from Moth's surface, this shuttle was equipped more for carrying cargo than folk, and so wasn't provided with as many ports. Despite the smallness of the scattered plexalloy sections, however, Flinx still had some view of the land below. The one continent rambled from the north pole down to a point just below the equator. It was mostly red-yellow at this height, with here and there large splotches of dull green. Small rivers, faint and insignificant in comparison with the coppery blues of the planetary ocean, meandered lazily down among the low hills. Naturally there were no river canyons. Any such would have disappeared millennia ago under the punishing onslaught of the untiring winds.

He had been momentarily worried about Pip, who had adamantly refused to be fitted with a tiny pair of makeshift goggles. Close inspection revealed that the reptile was equipped with transparent nictitating membranes, which slid down to protect the eye. He'd never noticed them before, probably because he'd simply not looked. He berated himself mentally for not realizing that an arboreal animal would naturally come built with some such type of natural protection against wind-carried objects. But then, neither of the two scientists had, either. Actually, Pip was more of a glider than a flyer. If he could master the winds down there he'd no doubt be more at home on Booster's surface than any of them.

A small intercabin comm conveyed the voice of Malaika back to them from Control. The tiny piloting cabin barely had space enough for the two pilots, and the big trader crowded it unmercifully. But he had insisted on remaining "on top of things." It was literally put.

They had been cruising on jets for only a short while when his excited cry broke the cabin's silence.

"*Maisha*, there it is! Check out the ports to your right."

There was a concerted rush to that side of the ship. Even Sissiph, her natural curiosity piqued, joined the movement.

They were still high, but as they banked the ruins of what had been a good-sized city, even by Tar-Aiym standards, came into view. They had built well, as always, but on this planet very little could remain in its original state for long. Still, from here it seemed as well preserved as any of the Tar-Aiym cities Flinx had seen on tape. As they dropped lower the alien city pattern of concentric crescents, radiating out from a fixed point, became as clear as ripples from the shore of a pond.

But even at this height the thing that immediately caught everyone's attention and caused Truzenzuzex to utter a soft curse of undefinable origin was not the city itself, but the building which stood on the bluff above the metropolis's nexus. A single faceless edifice in the shape of a rectangular pyramid, cut off squarely at the top. Both it and the circular base it rose from were a uniform dull yellow-white in color. The very top of the structure appeared to be covered with some kind of glassy material. Unlike the rest of the city it looked to be in a state of perfect preservation. It was also by far the tallest single structure he had ever seen.

"*Baba Giza!*" came Malaika's hushed voice over the speaker. He apparently became aware that his speaker pickup was on. "Take your seats, everybody, and fasten your straps. We are going to land by the base of that bluff. *Rafiki* Tse-Mallory, *rafiki* Truzenzuzex, we will explore the entire city beam by beam if you wish, but I will bet my *majicho* that your Krang is in a certain building at the top of a certain hill!"

Nothing like understatement to heighten anticipation, thought Flinx.

They landed, finally, on the broad stretch of open sandy ground to the left of both city and bluff. Atha had wisely elected to use replaceable landing skids instead of the wheeled gear, being uncertain as to the composition of the land they were going to set down on. There had been no clear, paved stretch of territory nearby. They had had a quick glimpse of the ruins of a monstrous spaceport off to the rear of the city's last crescent. Malaika had vetoed landing there, wishing to land as close as possible to the ziggurat itself. He felt that the less distance they had to travel on the ground and the closer they could remain to the ship itself, the safer he would feel about roaming around the ruined city. The great spaceport had also no doubt served as a military base, and if any unpleasant automatic devices still remained to greet unauthorized visitors, they also would probably be concentrated there. So their landing was a bit rougher than it might have been. But they were down now, in one piece, and had received another benefit none had thought of. It would have been obvious had anyone reflected on it.

The wind came in a constant wall from behind the building and the bluff below which they had landed. While by no means perpendicular, the bluff proved steep enough to cut off a good portion of the perpetual gale. It would mean easier working conditions around the shuttle itself, in addition to eliminating the possible problem of having to tie the ship down. The ship's branch meteorology 'puter registered the outside windage at their resting point at a comfortable forty-five kilometers an hour. Positively sylvan.

"Atha, Wolf, give me a hand getting the crawler out. The rest of you check over your equipment and make sure you've got an extra pair of goggles apiece." He turned to Tse-Mallory. "*Je*! They built their city behind the biggest windbreak they could find. Sort of gives the lie to your 'caressing wind-bath' theory, *kweli*?"

"Do not abuse my guesses, captain, or I'll make no more." His eyes and mind were obviously focused elsewhere.

"Wolf?"

"Here, captain." The skeleton came out of the fore cabin, looking even more outré than usual in his silver belt and goggles. The expression on his face was odd, because *any* expression on his face was an oddity.

"Captain, there's an active thermal power source somewhere under this city."

"Not nuclear?" asked Malaika. A gravitonic power plant was of course impossible on any body with a reasonable field of its own. Still, there were known aspects to Tar-Aiym science that humanx researchers couldn't even begin to explain.

"No, sir. It's definitely thermal. Big, too, according to the sensors, although it was a very fast check-through."

Malaika's eyebrows did flip-flops. "Interesting. Does that suggest any 'guesses' to you, gentlesirs?"

Tse-Mallory and Truzenzuzex pulled themselves away from their rapt contemplation of the monolith above and considered the question.

"Yes, several," began the philosoph. "Among which is the confirmation of a fact we were fairly certain of anyway, that this is a young planet in a fairly young GO system. Tapping the core-power of a planet is difficult enough on the youngest, which this is not. But anyone can *tap*. The problem is to keep it under sufficient control to be able to channel it without causing planetwide earthquakes or volcanoes under major Hive-centers. We're still not so very adept at that ourselves. And only in the most limited sense."

"And," continued Tse-Mallory, "it suggests they needed a hell of a lot of power for something, doesn't it? Now this is a fairly good-sized Tar-Aiym town, but it also seems to be the only one on the planet." He looked at Malaika for confirmation and the trader nodded, slowly. "So for the mind of me I can't see what they had to go to all that trouble for, when their quasinuclear plants would have provided more than enough power for this one city. Especially with all the water that's available."

"Captain," said Truzenzuzex impatiently, "we will be happy to hypothesize for you at length—later. But now I wish you would see about removing our surface transportation from the hold." His head swiveled to a port and the great golden eyes stared outward. "I have little doubt that your unasked questions and, hopefully, most of ours will be answered when we get inside that *Tuarweh* on top of this bluff."

"*If* we get into it," added Tse-Mallory. "It is just possible that the owners locked up when they moved, and left no key behind."

16

The crawler was a low, squat vehicle, running on twin duralloy treads. It also had a universal spherical "wheel" at its center of gravity to facilitate turning. Atha had made a few preliminary safety calculations and had come up with the fact that it would remain relatively stable in winds up to two hundred and fifty kilometers per, at which point things would start to get sticky. Flinx, for one, had no desire to put her calculations to a practical test. Nor did Malaika, apparently. He insisted on filling every empty space on the machine with objects of weight. If the winds got *that* bad, all the paraphernalia they could stuff into it wouldn't help. But it at least provided them with something of a psychological lift.

Not the least of these "objects of weight" was a heavy laser rifle, tripod-mounted.

"Just in case," the merchant had said, "opening the door proves more difficult than it might."

"For a peaceful trader traveling on his private racer you appear to have stocked quite an arsenal," Truzenzuzex murmured.

"Philosoph, I could give you a long, involved argument replete with attractive semantic convolutions, but I will put it, so, and leave it. I am in a very competitive business."

He cocked a challenging eye at the thranx.

"As you say." Truzenzuzex bowed slightly.

They boarded the crawler, which had been maneuvered close to the cargo port to minimize the initial force of the wind. The big land cruiser held all of them comfortably. It had been designed to transport heavy cargo, and even with Malaika's "objects of weight" scattered about there was plenty of room in which to move around. If bored, one might take the ladder up to the driver's compartment, with its two beds and polyplexalloy dome. There was room up there for four, but Malaika, Wolf, and the two scientists occupied it immediately and were disinclined to give it up. So Flinx had to be content with the tiny ports in the main compartment for his view of the outside. He was alone in the quiet spaces with the two women, who sat at extreme opposite ends of the cabin from each other and exchanged deathly thoughts back and forth. A less congenial atmosphere would have been difficult to imagine. Try as he would, they were beginning to give him a headache. He would far rather have been upstairs.

They were making their way up the slope of the bluff now, zigzagging whenever the incline grew too steep for even the crawler's powerful spiked treads to negotiate. Their progress was slow but steady, the machine after all having been designed to get from point A to point B in one piece, and not to race the clock. It did its job effectively.

As might have been predicted, the ground was crumbly and soft. Still, it was more rock than sand. The treads dug in deeply and the engine groaned. It slowed their advance somewhat, but assured them of excellent traction in the teeth of the wind. Still, Flinx would not like to have faced a real blow in the slow device.

They finally topped the last rise. Looking back into the distance Tse-Mallory could make out the crumbled spires and towers of the city, obscured by eternal dust and wind. It was more difficult to see up here. Gravel, dirt, and bits of wood from the hearty ground-hugging plants began to splatter against the front of the dome. For the first time the howl of the wind became audible through the thick shielding, sounding like fabric tearing in an empty room.

Wolf glanced at their anemometer. "A hundred fifteen point five-two kilos an hour . . . sir."

"*Je*! I'd hoped for better, but it could be worse. Much worse. No one is going to be taking long walks. *Upepokuu!* In a gale we can manage. A hurricane would be awkward."

As they moved farther in from the edge of the bluff the air began to clear sufficiently for them to catch sight of their objective. Not that they could have missed it. There wasn't anything else to see, except an occasional clump of what looked like dried sea-weed. They rolled on, the wind dying as they moved farther into the lee of the building. Three pairs of eyes leaned back . . . and back, and back, until it seemed certain it would be simpler to lie down and stare upward. Only Wolf, eyes focused on the instrument board of the massive crawler, failed to succumb to the lure of the monolith.

It towered above them, disappearing skyward in swirls of dust and low clouds, unbroken by ledge or window.

"How *huyukubwa*?" Malaika finally managed to whisper.

"How big do I make it? I couldn't say too well," answered Tse-Mallory. "Tru? You've got the best depth vision among us."

The philosoph was quiet for a long moment. "In human terms?" He lowered his eyes to look at them. If he could have blinked he would, but thranx eye-shields reacted only in the presence of water or strong sunlight, so he could not. His improvised goggles gave his face an unbalanced look.

"Well over a kilo at the base . . . each way. It looked a perfect square from the air, you know. Perhaps . . ." he took another brief glance upward, "three kilometers high."

The slight jolting and bumping they had been experiencing abruptly disappeared. They were now traveling on the smooth yellow-white circle on which the structure was centered.

Malaika peered down at the substance they were traversing, then back at the building. The heavy crawler left no tracks on the solid surface.

"What do you suppose this stuff is, anyway?"

Tse-Mallory had joined him in looking down at the even ground. "I don't know. When I saw it from the air my natural inclination was to think, stone. Just before we grounded I thought it looked rather 'wet,' like certain heavy plastics. Now that we're down on it I'm not sure of anything. Ceramics, maybe?"

"Metal-reinforced, surely," added Truzenzuzex. "But as for the surface, at least, a polymer ceramic would be a good guess, certainly. It's completely different from anything I've ever seen before, even on other Tar-Aiym planets. Or for that matter, from anything I could see of the city as we came in."

"Um. Well, since they built their city in the lee of this bluff, as a windbreak, I don't doubt, I'd expect any *mlango* to be on this side of the structure. *Je?*"

As it turned out shortly enough, there was, and it was.

Unlike the rest of the mysterious building the material used in the construction of the door was readily identifiable. It was metal. It towered a good thirty meters above the cab of the crawler and stretched at least half that distance in either direction. The metal itself was unfamiliar, dull-gray in color, and possessed of an odd glassy luster. Much like the familiar fogs of home, for Flinx. The whole thing was recessed several meters into the body of the building.

"Well, there's your door, captain," said Tse-Mallory. "How do we get in? I confess to a singular lack of inspiration, myself."

Malaika was shaking his head in awe and frustration as he examined the entrance. Nowhere could be seen the sign of a single joint, weld, or seam.

"Drive right up to it, Wolf. The wind is practically dead here. We'll have to get out and look for a doorbuzz or something. If we don't find anything that's recognizably a handle or a keyhole, we'll have to unlimber the rifle and try a less polite entrance." He eyed the massive square dubiously. "Although I hope that alternative doesn't become necessary. I know the stubbornness of Tar-Aiym metals."

As it turned out, the problem was solved for them.

Somewhere in the bowels of the colossal structure, long dormant but undead machinery sensed the approach of an artificial mechanism containing biological entities. It stirred sleepily, prodding resting memory circuits to wakefulness. The design and composition of the approaching vehicle was unfamiliar, but neither was it recognizably hostile. The entities within were likewise unfamiliar, albeit more obviously primitive. And there was an A-class mind among them. Likewise unfamiliar, not hostile. And it had been *such* a long time! The building debated with itself for the eternity of a second.

"Hold it, Wolf!" The merchant had noticed a movement in front of the crawler.

With a smoothness and silence born of eternal lubrication, the great door separated. Slowly, with the ponderousness of tremendous weight, the two halves slid apart just far enough for the crawler to enter comfortably. Then they stopped.

"*Utamu.* We are expected, perhaps?"

"Automatic machinery," mumbled Truzenzuzex, entranced.

"My thoughts also, philosoph. Take us in, Wolf."

The quiet man obediently gunned the engine and the powerful landcraft began to rumble forward. Malaika eyed the sides of the narrow opening warily. The metal was not a reasonably thin sheet. It was not even a moderate one.

"A good nineteen, twenty, meters through," said Tse-Mallory matter-of-factly. "I wonder what it was designed to keep out."

"Not us, apparently," added Truzenzuzex. "You could have played your toy on that for days, Captain, and burned it out before you scratched the entrance. I'd like to try a SCCAM on it, just to see which would come out the winner. I've never heard of any artificial structure resisting a SCCAM projectile, but then I've never seen a twenty-meter-thick Hive-block of solid Aiymetal before, either. The question will undoubtedly remain forever academic."

They had rolled perhaps a few meters beyond the door when it began to slide heavily shut behind them. The silence of it was eerie. Wolf glanced questioningly at Malaika, hand on throttle. The merchant, however, was at least outwardly unconcerned.

"It opened to let us in, Wolf. I think it will do so to let us out." The doors closed. "In any case, *kwa nini* worry? It doesn't matter now."

They got another surprise. Unless they were hollow, which hardly seemed likely with that door, the walls of the pseudoceramic material were a good hundred and fifty meters thick. Far more than was needed merely to support the weight of the building, great as it was. It bespoke much more an attempt at impregnability. Such had been found before in the ruins of Tar-Aiym fortresses, but never approaching this in scale.

Flinx did not know what he expected of the interior. He'd been scanning consistently ever since the great doors had opened, but had not been able to detect anything thinking inside. And he'd lamented his purely sideways view from the crawler. He didn't see how the inside could possibly surprise him any more than that unmatched exterior.

He was wrong.

Whatever it was he had anticipated in his wildest thoughts, it was nothing like the reality. Malaika's voice drifted down to him from above. It was oddly muted.

"*Katika* here, everyone. Atha, open the lock. There's air in here and it's breathable, and light, and no wind, and I don't know whether to believe it myself or not, even though my *majicho* tells me . . . but the sooner you see it. . . ."

They didn't need further urging. Even Sissiph was excited. Atha scrambled to the small personnel lock and they watched while she cracked the triple seal, cutting the flow of liquid at the three prescribed points. The heavy door swung itself outward. The automatic ramp extended itself to touch ground, buzzed once when it had made firm contact, and turned itself off.

Flinx was first out, followed closely by Atha and the two scientists, Malaika and Sissiph, and lastly, Wolf. All stood quite silent under the panorama spread before them.

The interior of the building, at least, was hollow. That was the only way to describe it. Somewhere above Flinx knew those massive walls joined a ceiling, but strain his eyes as he might he couldn't make it out. The building was so huge that despite excellent circulation, clouds had formed inside. The four gigantic slabs pressed heavy on his mind, if not his body. But claustrophobia was impossible in an open space this large. Compared to the perpetual swirl of air and dust outside the utter calm within was cathedral-like. Perhaps, indeed, that was what it was, although he knew the idea to be more the feeling imparted by this first view than the likely truth.

The light, being intended for nonhumanx eyes, was wholly artificial and tinged slightly with blue-green. It was also dimmer than they would have preferred. The philosoph's naturally blue chiton looked good in it, but it made the rest of them appear vaguely fish-like. The dimness did not obstruct their vision as much as it made things seem as though they were being viewed through not-quite-clear glass. The temperature was mild and a bit on the warm side.

The crawler had been halted because it could proceed no farther. Row upon row of what were indisputably seats or lounges of some sort stretched out from where they stood. The place was a colossal amphitheater. The ranks extended onward, unbroken, to the far side of the structure. There they ended at the base of . . . something.

He took a glance and risked a brief probe of the others. Malaika was glancing appraisingly about the limits of the auditorium. Wolf, his permanent nonexpression back on his face, was sampling the air with an instrument on his belt. Sissiph clung tightly to Malaika, staring apprehensively about the disquieting silence. Atha wore much the same look of cautious observation as the big trader.

The two scientists were in a state as close to Nirvana as it was possible for scientists to be. Their thoughts were moving so fast Flinx was hard-pressed even to sample them. They had eyes only for the far end of the great room. For them a search had been vindicated, even if they didn't know what it was they had found. Tse-Mallory chose that moment to step forward, with Truzenzuzex close behind. The rest of them began to file down the central aisle after the scientists, toward the thing at the far side.

It was not an exhausting walk, but Flinx was grateful for the opportunity to rest at the end of it. He sat on the edge of the raised platform. He could have taken one of the seat-lounges below, but they were nowhere near contoured for the human physiology and doubtless were as uncomfortable as they looked.

Large steps led up to the dais he sat on. At its far end a flawless dome of glass or plastic enclosed a single, unadorned couch. A large oval doorway opened in the dome facing the auditorium. It was a good meter higher than their tallest member and far wider than even Malaika's copious frame would require. The bench itself was tilted slightly to face the amphitheater. A smaller dome, shaped like a brandy glass, fitted partway over its raised end. Thick cables and conduits led from it and the bottom of the couch to the machine.

The "machine" itself towered a hundred meters above them and ran the length of the auditorium, melting into the curved corners. While the exterior of the structure was remorselessly acute, the interior was considerably rounded off. Much of the machine was closed off, but Flinx could see dials and switches catching the light from behind half-open plates. Those he could make out had obviously not been designed with humanx manipulative members in mind.

From above the dull metal plating of the machine an uncountable profusion of chromatically colored tubes ran toward the distant roof. Azure, peach, shocking pink, ivory, Tyrolean purple, chartreuse, orange, mutebony, smoke, white-gold, verdanure . . . every imaginable shading and tone, and not a few unimaginable ones. Some were the size of a child's toy, small enough to fit over his little finger. Others looked big enough to swallow the shuttle with ease. In the corners they merged into the fabric of the structure. He turned a slow circle and saw where bulges in the walls, extending even above the entrance way, indicated the presence of more of the colossal pipes. He reminded himself that he had no way of being certain they were even hollow, but somehow the impression of pipes persisted. Sometimes his talents operated independent of his thoughts.

"Well," said Malaika. He said it again. "Well, well!"

He seemed uncertain of himself, a rare state. Flinx smiled at the merchant's thoughts. The big man wasn't sure whether to be pleased or not. He definitely had *something*, all right. But he didn't know what it was, let alone how to market it. He stood while everyone else sat.

"I suggest we obtain whatever supplies we'll need for our investigations." Truzenzuzex and Tse-Mallory were examining everything in minute detail and hardly heard him. "This has passed over my head, and so from my hands. I trust you gentlebeings can find out what this thing does?" He waved a broad hand to encompass what they could see of the machine.

"I do not know," said Truzenzuzex. "Offclaw, I would say that our acquaintances the Branner had the right idea when they spoke of this thing as a musical instrument. It certainly looks like one, and the arrangements in here," he indicated the amphitheater, "would tend to support that assumption. For my wings, though, I can't see as yet how it operates."

"Looks like the ultimate product of a mad organ-builder's worst nightmares," added Tse-Mallory. "I wouldn't say for sure unless we figure out how to operate the thing."

"*Will* you?" asked Malaika.

"Well, it seems to be still partially powered, at least. Wolf recorded the power source, and something operated the doors, turned on the lights . . . and keeps the air fresh, I hope. It wasn't designed according to conceptions we'd find familiar, but that thing," and he gestured at the dome with its enclosed bench, "looks an awful lot like an operator's station. True, it might also be a resting place for their honored dead. We won't know till we dig a lot deeper. I suggest that we move everything we'll need from the shuttle in here. It'll be a lot simpler than running out in this gale every time we need a spanner or a sandwich."

"*Mapatano*! I agree. Wolf, you and I will start transferring things from the shuttle. It will go quickly enough, once we unload some of that junk I piled into the crawler. It appears we are going to be here for a bit, *hata kidogobaya*!"

17

It was an odd feeling to be constantly within the building. Not confining, for the door worked perfectly even for one person—provided he carried with him at least one item of recognizably metallic artificial construction. It was a peculiarly satisfying sensation to approach the great bulks, comm unit or gun extended in front of one, and have a million tons of impregnable metal slide gently aside to reveal a personalized passageway a meter wide and thirty meters high.

It was better outside at night, but not much. In spite of the goggles the dust eventually worked its insistent way into eyes. And it was chilly.

Tse-Mallory and Truzenzuzex had been poring over the immense apparatus, prying behind those panels in the slate-gray wall which would open, ignoring those which would not. There was no point in forcing entry and risking breakage to the intricate device. Not when they could spend years on the unresisting portions. And they didn't have years. So they continued to dig into the exposed guts on the Krang without disturbing a single wire from its proper place, treading with the utmost care lest they nudge some vital circuit from its proper alignment. While the scientists and Malaika labored over the enigma of the machine, Atha and Flinx would sometimes take the crawler into the vast city. Wolf remained behind to help Malaika, and Sissiph to be near him. So Flinx had the crawler's observation dome practically to himself.

He found it hard to believe that structures which even in ruin and under a centuries-old coat of dust could remain beautiful had been raised to house the most warlike race the galaxy had known. The thought cast an unshakable pall over the quiet ruins. Little in the way of decoration was visible on the sandblasted exteriors of the structures, but that didn't necessarily mean much. Anything not integral to the actual support of the edifice would long since have been worn away. And they were cruising far above what had once been a main boulevard. The street itself was somewhere far below, buried under a millennia of shifting sand and soil. They recognized it as such only because of the absence of buildings. Probably this city had been covered and uncovered at least a hundred times, each new cycle grinding away some portion of its original aspect. They had soon discovered that a mild electrostatic field came up regularly every evening and cleared the day's accumulation of dust and debris from the base of the Krang for the width of the yellow-white circle. But no such care was visible in the city. In the evenings, as the sun set, the sands turned blood-red and the hulks of hollowed buildings sparkled like topaz and ruby in a setting of carnelian. The constant, unceasing wind spoiled the illusion of beauty, and its rise-and-fall moan seemed an echoing curse of all the vanished races ever subjugated by the Tar-Aiym.

And they didn't even know what they had looked like.

18

A week later they were all gathered in informal conference on the dais. A small, portable cookstove, powered by an aeternacell, had been set up nearby, giving the place an incongruously domesticated look. Next, thought Flinx, they would be hanging out laundry. It had been found more convenient for the scientists to sleep and eat by their work, instead of making the daily hike to the crawler. They could have brought the cruiser right up to the base of the dais, but for all they knew the seats themselves might play some crucial part in the operation of the Krang. Besides, reducing parts of the place to rubble hardly seemed the proper way to go about resurrecting its secrets. It was just as well that they hadn't, because the sleepy machine would have noted the gesture as hostile and taken immediate and appropriate action.

The odors of frying bacon and eggs, and juquil for Truzenzuzex, added to the homey atmosphere. At the moment, Atha and Sissiph were managing the cooking for the scientists. This was proved a necessity after all the men had demonstrated a monumental ineptitude with the device, which did 90 percent of the work itself. Knowing full well he could operate it better than any of them, Flinx had pleaded ignorance when offered the chance to try it. He had no desire to be tied down with the job of cook, not when he could spend his time watching the two scientists dissect the amazing innards of the machine.

"This thing grows more incredible by the day." Tse-Mallory was talking now. "You know, we found walkways at each corner of the building, where the machine disappears into the walls."

"I'd wondered where you two had disappeared to," said Malaika.

"They extend I don't know how far beneath us. To the center of the planet for all I can tell, although I'd think that the heat would make that a prohibitive development even for the Tar-Aiym. Nor do we have any idea how far it extends on the horizontal level, either. To the ocean? Under it? We didn't have an easy time of it down there, you know. There are steps and ladders and ramps, and none designed for human or thranx hands. But between the two of us, we managed. There must be mechanical lifts somewhere, but we couldn't find them.

"We first went down three days ago . . . apologies for worrying you. I suppose we should have mentioned where we were going, but we didn't really know ourselves, and certainly didn't expect to be gone as long as we were. The excitement of the moment overcame our time-sense.

"We went more or less straight down, pausing only twice, for three hours and sleep-time. These pipes, or whatever," he indicated the rainbow giants ranked above them, "are continuous below this flooring, and descend to levels we didn't reach. Not even at the farthest point of our journey. Most of the machinery was completely unfamiliar to us, and I daresay we two are as familiar with Tar-Aiym design as anyone in the Arm. But the majority of this stuff was way past us."

"Near the surface the machinery is practically solid. Farther down it thins out to a sufficient degree to become recognizable as to its individual components. All of it looked brand-new. In many places the metal was warm, confirming what we've suspected all along. Power is being fed into it continually. And there must be a billion kilometers of wire down there.

"Still, we have no idea what it does, captain. I am sorrier than you could ever be, but you can console yourself in the knowledge that whatever it is, it is far and away the biggest and best of its kind."

This last from a tired-looking Truzenzuzex. The philosoph had been working at an incredible pace the past week, and his age was beginning to show. On the ship he had kept it well masked with his energy and youthful spirits.

"Couldn't you discover *anything* about its function?" pleaded Malaika.

Tse-Mallory sighed. He had been doing a lot of that, lately. "Not really. We both incline to the musical instrument theory, still. There are many arguments against it that bother us, though." He looked at Truzenzuzex, who nodded confirmation.

"*Je?*" Malaika prompted.

"For one thing, we can't quite bring ourselves to believe that in a time of such stress a race as war-oriented as the Tar-Aiym would devote so much effort and material to anything of a nonlethal nature. The metal for that door, for example, must have been required for the construction of warships. Yet it was brought and used here. On the other hand, we know they were artistically inclined in a gruesome sort of way. Their tastes did run strongly to the martial. Possibly they felt the need of a project to stimulate patriotic fervor, and this was their way of doing it. It would also have possible psychological benefits we can't begin to imagine. If that seems unlikely, consider the lack of evidence we have to go on. I'm not ready to believe any of my explanations myself.

"And another thing. Did you happen to notice the unusual silvery-gold tinge to the atmosphere as we were coming down?"

"No . . . yes!" said Malaika. "I've seen it before on other planets, so I didn't think it too out of the ordinary. These . . . there were *mbili* layers, if I remember aright . . . seemed thicker than most. And better defined. But I don't view that as a cause for surprise. I've seen quadruple layers, too. And the unusual thickness of these could easily be accounted for by the scouring effects of these *wachawi upepo*, sorcerer's winds."

"True," Tse-Mallory continued. "Windglitter, I believe they call it. As you say, there could be natural explanations for the odd thickness of the layers. The reason I bring them up at all is because on one of the levels we reached we found what appeared to be at least a portion of a great meteorological monitoring station. Among other things, several of the instruments appeared to be occupied solely with keeping information on those two levels in the atmosphere. We only had time for a fast look at it, as our prime concern was making speed downward. But the only reason we noticed it at all was because the metal was quite warm there, gave off a lot of heat, and seemed to be running at full power. That's something we observed in only a very few other places. We now think that those layers have something to do with the actual function of the Krang. What, I can't imagine."

"To be more specific," said Truzenzuzex, "this thing," and he pointed at the transparent dome and the lounge within, "takes on more and more the aspect of a center control for the operation of the entire apparatus. I know it seems difficult to imagine this monstrosity being operated by a single being lying on that slab, but evidence seems to support it. I am skeptical, myself. There is not a switch, dial, or similar device anywhere near the thing. And yet its location alone, and isolation, seem to support its importance.

"Close examination of that helmet, or headdress, or whatever it is, shows that it's lined with what might be some form of sensory pickups. If the machine is indeed still capable of more than partial activation, then theoretically mere proximity to those pickups ought to do it. Actual physical contact with the operator wouldn't seem to be necessary. So the fact that the size and shape of our heads in no way corresponds to that of the Tar-Aiym . . . in all probability . . . shouldn't hinder us."

"You're thinking of trying it, then," said Malaika.

"We must."

"But suppose it's geared to respond only to the electromagnetic patterns generated by a Tar-Aiym mind?"

"We have no indication that 'electromagnetic patterns' are even the type of whatever is necessary to activate the machine," retorted Tse-Mallory. "But if that does prove to be the case, then unless you can produce a live and cooperative Tar-Aiym, I am very much afraid that we might as well pack and go home." He shrugged. "Tru and I feel we've more or less reached a dead end as far as mere circuit-tracing goes. We could continue to poke around in this pile of complexity for a thousand years—fascinating as that might be—and not come any closer to making it work."

"Trying it . . . couldn't that be awfully dangerous?" asked Atha.

"It could very well be lethal, my dear. We decided that long ago. For instance, there might be a feedback which could . . . for that very reason, and for several others, I shall try it first. If we have still failed to activate it and no obviously harmful results are forthcoming, I see no reason why everyone here should not have an opportunity to try the same."

"Not *me*!" said Sissiph loudly.

"Now wait a minute!" began Malaika, ignoring her.

"Sorry, captain." Truzenzuzex, now. "*Starhe*! Don't bother, as you would say. Bran is correct. Our training may not exactly qualify us as operators of this thing, but our familiarity with the works of the Tar-Aiym and what little we know of their psychologies might help us cope with any unforeseen problems that could develop. Such designs might arise which would overwhelm a complete novice. Sorry, but there is too much involved to permit you to make the initial attempt, at least. We are not on board ship. You are momentarily overruled, captain."

"*Je!*" rumbled Malaika.

Tse-Mallory stepped to the entrance of the dome. "Let's be on with it, then."

"You mean, *sasaa kuume*?" asked Malaika.

Tse-Mallory paused. "I don't see why not." He hesitated again at the entrance, looked back. "I don't expect much to happen, let alone anything dangerous. And if it does I wouldn't expect this to be much protection, but for my own psychological comfort, everyone off the dais, please. It certainly ought to be safe enough in the seats, or lounges, or whatever they are. Obviously the Tar-Aiym used them when this thing was in operation, so they *should* be safe for us as well. Theoretically speaking."

"Sociologist, theoretical injury I don't mind." Malaika smiled in what was intended to be a reassuring manner and joined the others in moving off the raised area into the rows of "seats" below.

Truzenzuzex was the only other one to remain on the platform. Ostensibly he was there to observe, but both he and Tse-Mallory knew that if anything went wrong the insect's aid would not likely be of much use. He took the proverbial and ritual deep breath and entered the dome.

The ceramic-plastic slab was now familiar from days of prolonged and minute inspections. He climbed up onto the smooth, cold surface and turned, facing out and slightly up. From inside the dome the roof of the monolith seemed almost visible. Possibly the transparent material had an actual slight magnifying effect. It did not seem significant.

The slab was much longer than was necessary to hold his lanky frame. It wasn't heated, though. He found himself squirming uncomfortably on the hard, chilly surface and wishing it were a bed. This was too much like the molds in a cryogenic suspension lab. Do it quick, his mind told his body! Digging into the unyielding surface with his heels, he shoved himself upward. In one motion his head was fully within the helmet.

Flinx didn't know what to expect. Explosions, earthquake, a collapsing building, perhaps. In any case the results were disappointing, if safe.

The helmet took on a pale red tinge, shifting to yellow, and thence to a light green. Also, a slight humming sound became audible. Apparently it came from within the slab itself. That was all. No fireworks, not even a few simple flashes of lightning.

Tse-Mallory's face within the dome was twisted, but it was obviously in concentration and not pain. Oddly, his mind was unreachable to Flinx. If nothing else the dome blanketed the thoughts of whoever lay within.

Twenty minutes later he was out of the dome, shaking his head while the others crowded around.

"*Je?*" asked Malaika.

The sociologist looked irritable. "*Je?* Well, we proved one thing.

If this machine is still capable of functioning as it was intended, that helmet is certainly the initiating point."

"I can't believe that this entire insanity was built just to make pretty colored lights in a plastic headdress!"

"No, of course not." Tse-Mallory looked wistfully back at the slab and the once-again transparent helmet. "It seems as though I was able to activate it, but only a very little. Apparently there's a necessary something missing from my mind. Or maybe it merely takes a kind of training we know nothing about. I don't know. I tried everything I could with my mind. Self-hypnosis. Yoga. The Banda exercises. Total objective concentration. An open subconscious. You saw the results. Or rather, the lack of them."

"Could you feel anything, anything at all?" asked Flinx.

"Umm. Yes, it was peculiar. Not painful or threatening. Just peculiar. Like something was trying to get inside my head. A tickling of the outside of the brain, barely noticeable. And when I tried to concentrate on it, it went away and hid. I must say I'm disappointed."

"*Je*? You think perhaps you've got a monopoly on it?" The merchant looked upset, as well he had a right to be. "What now?"

"Now I suggest the rest of the humans give it a try. I believe that I've amply demonstrated its harmlessness, if nothing else. Keeping it attuned to one type of mind might have a beneficial cumulative effect."

One at a time the rest of them took a turn under the innocuous helmet. Excepting of course Sissiph, who refused even to go near it. Malaika managed to generate a strong yellow glow in the transparent material. Flinx did as well (or as poorly, no one could say) as Tse-Mallory, only his coloring also possessed an uneven pulsing. As if to counter Tse-Mallory's claim, he emerged from the domed chamber with a definite headache. Atha and Wolf could each manage a light red, almost rose color. They had better luck when Truzenzuzex at last made his attempt.

The second that aging, iridescent head entered the zone of effectiveness, the soft colors immediately ran from pink up to a deep blue. Tse-Mallory had to remark on it to get everyone's attention. Repeated failure had led to discouraging boredom. But no one was bored now. Even outside the dome the humming from the base of the slab was clearly audible. On one of the open panels of the great gray bulk of the machine, lights were beginning to glow faintly. The helmet had by now turned a deep lavender.

"Look at the dome!" Flinx pointed.

For several inches of its height the dome was glowing a solid and unwavering crimson. Every now and then the cottony light would creep upward a few millimeters, only to sink back and disappear into the floor.

An hour later Truzenzuzex staggered out of the dome. Tse-Mallory had to support the philosoph around the b-thorax, as the old insect's legs proved too shaky to manage on their own. The philosoph was visibly tired. Together they lurched down to the first row of alien benches. Truzenzuzex's visage did not wrinkle as did a primate's, but the usual healthy glow of his eyes was more subdued than before.

"You certainly labeled it correctly, brother," he finally gasped, "when you said there was something trying to get inside your head! I felt like a youth again, trying to break out of my chrysalis. Whew! I could tell it did no good, though."

"Not true," said Flinx. Malaika nodded confirmation. "You had the dome itself glowing red—around the base, anyway."

"I did?" The whistling thranx laughter followed. "I suppose that is an accomplishment of sorts. I could not detect it from the inside. I was concentrating rather deeply, and my optics weren't the nerves I was working with. Does that mean perhaps we are on a proper track?" He turned to face Malaika. The tone was gradually returning to his muscles. "Captain, I retract my earlier statement. Give me another three or four weeks at this and I believe I'll be able to tell you, one way or another, whether this thing can ever be operated by man or thranx. Or whether your investment has proved itself a loss."

Malaika looked resigned rather than frustrated. His own unsuccessful strivings with the Krang had produced a little patience, if no other results.

"*Bado Juzi.* 'Yet the day before yesterday.' An old saying in my family, gentlemen. You've done already much more than I had a right to hope. Take your time, gentlesirs, take your time."

Far below in the secret places of the planet the consciousness of the Krang stirred sluggishly. It considered more fully the impulses which had awakened the Prime Nexus with feeble, childish probings and pressures. Even in its semisomnolent state it was reasonably certain (+prob., 90.97, -prob., 8.03, random factoring, 1.00) that there was an A-class mind present above. One fully capable of arousing the Krang to the state of *Naisma*, or total effectiveness. Apparently it had chosen not to reveal itself yet. The machine considered and allowed the sections of itself which controlled intelligence to lapse back to dormancy, ready.

When the mind was ready, the Krang would be.

After all, it had been built that way.

19

As it developed, Truzenzuzex did not get his month. Nor his three weeks. They had been pouring over the accessible portions of the machine's innards for only three days when Malaika's comm signaled an extra-atmosphere incoming call. As a matter of safety his portable comm was hooked to the big transmitter in the crawler. Flinx was present when the signal came in, helping the two scientists with the more physical aspects of their work. Sissiph, Atha, and Wolf were back in the crawler, rearranging their supplies in its cavernous hold.

In order to facilitate their work, two cots (one modified) had been placed next to the scientists' portastove. The others still found it more comfortable to sleep within the familiar confines of the crawler, despite the attendant daily walk it engendered.

Both scientists paused in their work the moment they spotted the strange expression which had come over Malaika's face. Flinx picked it up from the sudden confusion of the merchant's thoughts. He had been watching them labor over strange markings and unfamiliar alien switching devices all morning. Nine tenths of what they were trying to do mechanically eluded him. He had been able to help them with the more delicate portions of their operations, having, as they put it, a certain "feel" for where things were located. And as always, their conversation on both the vocal and mental level had been fascinating.

"Captain . . ." began Tse-Mallory.

"We're being called," the merchant replied. "Extra-atmospheric."

His thoughts reflected suspicion as much as disbelief. He flipped over the broadcast switch of the tiny communit.

"Wolf, are you monitoring this?"

"Yes, captain," came the unmodulated reply from the distant crawler.

"All right. Send an acknowledgment and put it over. Someone *knows* where we are. Not much use denying it." He turned to the others. "We might be monitored now, although I doubt it's possible through these walls. But then, I also doubt we're receiving a call from another starship, and that is the case. *Haidhuru*. Nothing matters. Leave your comms off and listen on mine, if you wish. No point in broadcasting how many units we have in operation. If they don't know already."

It was the first time Flinx had seen the merchant so downcast. Obviously the strain was taking a bigger toll of his resources than he cared to show. At any rate, all he said into the comm was, "Yes?"

The voice that responded was naturally high. But if the tone was slightly effeminate, the words were not.

"Captain Maxim Malaika, House-Head and Plutocrat? I bring you greetings, sir, from Madame Rashalleila Nuaman and Nuaman Enterprises." Malaika's lips twisted in a subvocal oath which made Flinx blush. "Congratulations!"

That superciliousness was sufficient to stimulate the merchant's tongue.

"Damned decent of you. And who are *ninyi nyote*?"

"Pardon? Oh, *I*. I am of little consequence. But for purposes of facilitating further conversation . . . which, I assure you, *will* be forthcoming . . . you may know me as Able Nikosos."

"*Je*, Mister Nikosos. I agree wholeheartedly that your personage is doubtless of little consequence. I am curious as to how you got here. This planet seems to be acquiring a universal notoriety."

"How so? Umm. As to your question, Captain, why," and the voice reflected mock astonishment, "we followed you. Most of the way from Moth. At a discreet distance, of course. Speaking of which, you certainly changed your course a good deal at the beginning of your journey. Yes you did. But after the first week we had no trouble plotting your approximate course. You know, this is the fourth system in this sector with planets that we've visited. We knew more or less where the one we wanted was, but not its exact coordinates. It made it hard on us, yes hard, when we lost you completely. Those coordinates were on a bit of material which. . . . but never mind that. That's long in the past now, isn't it?"

"You didn't by any chance get some help from a certain AAnn baron?"

"An AAnn baron?" The squeaky voice reflected surprise. Malaika glanced at Flinx.

"He's telling the truth, sir. And they're definitely in a set orbit."

The two scientists looked in surprise at Flinx. Neither said anything, but he could sense a mild resentment of his secrecy in their thoughts. He wanted desperately to tell them of how necessary it was to maintain that secrecy. Even today, psi-sensitives were not universally popular, a fact he had found out early and painfully as a child. Now was not the time, though. The voice on the comm continued.

"What would we have to do with the AAnn? Nasty people, those, nasty! No indeed, sir. We found you all by ourselves, in spite of the difficulties your disappearance occasioned us. But we did find you, didn't we? So no harm done. Besides, no use trying to share the blame, and I refuse to share the credit. Not that it should matter to you in the long run. Or even the short one." A brief giggle broke the commentary. "My ship is parked a couple of field-lengths from your *Gloryhole*. We beamed it first. When we did not receive a reply and when the lock refused us entrance—how clever of you, captain!—we assumed you had already made your drop to the surface. A glance at your shuttlebay confirmed it."

"*Thelathini nguruwe!* Thirty pigs. Which is the ultimate number which can be fitted into a standard captain's cabin, in case you didn't know."

The voice seemed immune to insult as well as to modesty. "Tut, tut, Captain. You'll offend my modest nature."

"Small chance of that."

"Anyway, the emanations from your components would have revealed your location to us even if you had declined to acknowledge our call. As I am sure you were well aware."

"Captain," said Flinx, "I thought you said. . . ."

"Forgot about the relay to the shuttle's comm. That's what they'd pick up. They could hardly miss us anyway." He was already setting up a last-ditch defense in his mind.

"Where are you now, friend Nikosos, other than in orbit?"

"A good guess, Captain. Why, we're drifting over this moisture-poor continent. Rather close to you, I've no doubt. We should be down in a short while, at which time I hope to greet you personally." The voice paused, then resumed again. "Whatever you are hiding in must really be something. We're having no end of trouble picking up your signal."

"You've traveled a long way for a lot of nothing, Nikosos. We've been working on this 'whatever,' as you so accurately say, for weeks now. We haven't been able to figure out what it does, much less how it does it."

"Certainly, captain, certainly!" The voice carried a humoring tone now. "Personally, whenever the cold of space affects me too deeply, I like to fly through the nearest M supergiant to warm my chilly bones. As I said, we'll be seeing you shortly."

"He doesn't believe you," said Flinx.

Malaika nodded. "And then?"

"Well, that does pose a problem, eh? I certainly can't wave you on your happy way home, because then all my hard work would have been for naught, wouldn't it? But then, assassination really isn't my line, either. Perhaps something can be worked. . . ." Malaika cut the comm. He turned to the others.

"*Je*, you heard. Where new planets are concerned, possession is nine tenths of the ancient law. I doubt Rasha will leave me be to call in a Church Evaluation Force." He switched the comm to interpersonnel frequency.

"Wolf, you heard everything?"

"Yes Captain." The shadow-man's reply was even. Flinx wondered if the pilot were capable of an excitement he never showed. "I fear that your pet took it rather hard, though. She's fainted. Miss Moon is caring for her now."

"*Je*! She will be quiet for a while then, anyway. We're going to join you shortly. We'd best all remain *pamoja*." He flipped off the comm again.

"What do you propose?" asked Tse-Mallory.

"Not much I can, sociologist. Even if this Nikosos person should be *mjinga* enough to come down without a portable defensive screen, it would be awkward to attempt to fight our way out. Although we are not," and here he looked directly at Flinx, "without surprises of our own. However, I am certain the men he leaves on his ship—only one this time, for a change—will be monitoring everything that happens. We'd be at their mercy in the shuttle. If this Nikosos doesn't bring a screen, and if we could surprise him and get off a crippling few shots before they had time to warn their starship, and if we could slip up to the *Gloryhole* under their detectors, and if we could get inside and get the generator powered before they noticed—why, we might have a good chance of sneaking off or fighting them."

"Too many 'ifs'," said Truzenzuzex unnecessarily.

"*Kabisa*, quite. Still, we have other weapons. Rest assured I'll try them. Bribery, for one, has often proven more effective in war than nucleonics. But I fear that Rasha wouldn't send a creature that vulnerable on such an important mission. Not one who'd be tempted by total bribery, anyway. Partial, now. . . . There is only one other thing I can think of to do. There's only one *mlango* to this building. Set up the rifle and blast the first being to enter it. As long as he has no certain idea of how we are equipped for supplies and guns he might be impatient enough to dicker with us. Unfortunately we don't have much, even with what we could move in here from the shuttle. *Mibu*, all he has to do is burn the shuttle and take a leisurely safari back to Nineveh with coordinates for the Registry!"

"Why doesn't he do that anyway?" asked Flinx.

"Not his assignment, *kijana*, or he wouldn't even have bothered to call us. Simply disabled the *Glory* and been on his way. Obviously he needs to find out everything he can about the Krang." He gestured at the two scientists. "Rasha knows about you two. I told her myself, *chura* that I am. She could hire experts of her own, but she knows your reputation. Rasha never neglects her homework. So I'm not worried for your lives. Only your reputations. I believe I can also manage something for myself. Too many people would ask awkward questions if I were to disappear suddenly. . . . even on a trip of exploration in an unspaced area. And he *can't* make that much *fedha!* Oh, he still couldn't afford to let any of us go free. Most likely he's been ordered to keep us comfy someplace until Rasha's investment here is tied up six ways in four dimensions. That veiled hint at 'assassination' was probably his way of opening bids."

"A suggestion, captain," said Truzenzuzex.

"Ndiyo?"

"Assuming all you've said to be true, why not simply accede quietly and give him what he wants?"

"What!" Even Flinx was startled.

"I assure you that the Krang will remain useless to both him and his employer. I was pessimistic when I said I would require three weeks to evaluate the machine's potential usefulness. We could learn much about the Tar-Aiym from it, of that I've no doubt. I think that I can also say with a great deal of certitude right now that it will otherwise never be more than an outstanding curiosity for archeologists and *touristas*."

"*Lakini*, but . . . you got it working! Part of it, anyhow."

"What I did was no more than polishing the drive coils of a Caplis generator. I succeeded in warming it up, perhaps, and appearing functional, but I doubt that I could ever, ever bring it to even partial operation. And we still have no more idea of what it's supposed to do than we did before. No being could go further, I think . . . no matter who your Madame Nuaman engages."

"If you're positive—" began Malaika.

Truzenzuzex looked questioningly at Tse-Mallory and both turned back to the merchant. "Nothing is positive, Captain, but I will not bandy Church maxims with you. Without hesitation, I concur with my brother's evaluation."

"*Mbwa ulimwengu!* Very well, then. We will forgo destruction in favor of more subtle maneuvers." He activated the comm for a wide broadcast channel. Now that he was on familiar ground once more, his voice had the old ring back. "Nikosos!"

There was a hiss, sput, pause, and then the mousey voice had returned. "No need to shout, captain. You have thoughts?"

"Look, agent. I will give you the opportunity to gain what you wish and perhaps save a few lives in the process. I have a fully operational six millimeter laser rifle here, and plenty of charges, but I don't see anything worth fighting over. I wish you luck in making it perform if you can, which I doubt. The whole city is yours. I wish only to leave this *nukia* as rapidly as possible. You may have our notes, if you wish. Everything we've found out about the Krang itself . . . which amounts to very little. But I've a boy and two women here, and I want them out of this."

"How touching! I did not expect such admirable altruism from you, captain. Yes, despite my orders I think a financial agreement satisfactory to all concerned can be arranged. Blood tends to upset my liver, anyway. Although I'm sure you'll understand when I say that you and your companions must remain as my guests for a short while. A minimal amount of time, really, but very necessary."

"Naturally, I understand the necessity and will be glad to sign. . . ."

"Oh no, captain, that won't be required. I trust your word. Your reputation precedes you. Personally I find honesty in our profession somewhat nauseating, but in this case it is to my advantage. No, much as you'd like to have such an agreement in words, I'd rather not have such a missive in existence. Such things have a habit of disappearing and turning up later in the most *distressing* places. Shortly, now.

"Our flight has been interesting so far, captain, but I fear I should find this planet boring. If you would be so kind as to leave your transmitter on standby, we will follow its pulse in. This entire distasteful business can be speeded to completion. I am certain you have even less desire than I to prolong it." He clicked off.

"Captain," came Wolf's voice over the comm, "this makes me ill. Is there no other way . . . ?"

"No other way, Wolf. I would rather fight too, but. . . . Leave open the transcomm for them to follow down, as he requested. At least our work here appears to have been fruitless, or I wouldn't consider such an alternative. We can wish them much of the same. Whatever they find in the city they are welcome to. It's been something of a wild *mbizu* chase after all."

"But he as much as threatened murder . . . !"

"Wolf, please, I know. *Jua* is hard. Still, we've little choice. I don't trust him, either. But he *could* simply leave now and return for our emaciated corpses later. No, I'm betting he'd rather pick up the extra credit my offer holds. Why shouldn't he?" He shrugged, despite the fact that Wolf couldn't see it.

"Wolf, if the odds weren't so *nyani*-sided . . . !" He sighed. "House rules."

"I understand, captain."

Malaika switched off and sat down heavily on one of the alien benches, looking suddenly very old and tired.

"Of course, if you gentlesirs had discovered how to make this *mashineuzi* work, I wouldn't even consider. . . ."

"We understand, too, captain," said Tse-Mallory. "A bad choice is no choice. We never worried for ourselves. He must at least display us to Nuaman to convince her of our uselessness. And our abrupt disappearance, too, would cause discussion in certain quarters."

"Nuaman. *Damn* that bitch!" He looked upward. "This day I forget forever that creature is human and *mwanamke*!" He noted Flinx's glance. "She ceased to be a *bibi*, a lady, *kijana*, long before you were born."

20

Kilometers above, a very satisfied Able Nikosos leaned back in his lounge in the plush shuttle cabin and relayed orders to his pilots. He rubbed his hands together. Things had gone nicely, nicely. Almost as nicely as if he had received that map as scheduled, back on Moth. The presence of Malaika already down on the planet made things a mite more complicated, but not overmuch. It appeared that it would make things more profitable. Besides collecting a fat bonus from the old witch for successfully carrying out a mission more difficult than originally assigned, there would be the matter of the wealthy Malaika's ransom . . . payable in advance. As preplanned, the two braincases would be shipped off to Nuaman. As soon as a decent amount of the ransom had been paid—wasn't Malaika's word good now?—the boy could be shunted out the nearest lock. As for the two women, well, the ancestral homestead was in need of a few new toys. The price of healthy young women had gone up insufferably in the past few years. Insufferably! All the fault of those damned priggish Churchmen. "Violence is unsanitary," indeed! At the rate he used them up his hobby was becoming prohibitively expensive. Shameful! The addition of two new, free faces (and bodies, oh yes!) would therefore be a financial as well as an aesthetic bonus. He did not doubt but that they would both prove young and attractive. Otherwise what business would they have with the roguish Malaika?

If they weren't his type, quite, he could still use them. Less artistically, perhaps, but they might still remain serviceable. And he was not known as a connoisseur for nothing.

The shuttle's delta wings began to unfold as it dipped toward atmosphere.

21

Malaika, Tse-Mallory, Truzenzuzex, and Flinx were making their way slowly back to the crawler. No one spoke. Flinx had already determined not to let his gun be taken from him without argument. He could prove equally adept at treachery! He'd read the confusion and little piggish thoughts Nikosos had been having, difficult as it had been with their owner moving so rapidly above the planet's surface. He trusted him now about as far as he could throw the *Gloryhole*. That the two scientists and Malaika would get off safely was a possibility, but from the agent's thoughts the chance that he and the women would do likewise seemed small in the light of what he had read. In the final analysis he would not count—no, not *expect* the merchant to put his life on the line for him, or for the women, or even for the scientists. Survival is an argument that morals do not even belong in the same class with. So he'd best plan on taking some action on his own. It was an unflattering but logical evaluation of their present situation. That scared him almost as much as the reality of it did. He shivered slightly, despite the warmth.

Something had been bothering him for the last few minutes, in addition to the expected quota of fearful anticipation. He shrugged his shoulders despite the lack of an itch there. That was it! Not an itch, but the lack of a persistent and familiar one. The minidrag was elsewhere. In the absorption of the past moments and his concentration on the agent's mind, he'd not noticed that the reptile was missing. He turned abruptly.

"Pip? Where's Pip?"

"Just to be certain," murmured Malaika, not hearing Flinx's low inquiry. He flipped his comm. "Wolf, I don't like to play without at least a few cards. Break out the rifle and set it up facing the entranceway."

"Yes, *captain*!" came the enthusiastic reply.

"If this fellow has us so neatly tied up and packaged," said Tse-Mallory, "why bother with the gun? I thought you'd given up once and for all the idea of our fighting our way out of this?"

Flinx searched the air around them. The snake was still not visible. He felt naked without the familiar reptilian presence.

"So I have, more or less. We know that he has us packaged, and he knows that he has us packaged, but he doesn't know that we know he has us packaged."

"Simplify that, please."

"*Ndiyo*. Sure. Put it this way. A man negotiates with considerably less arrogance than he might when he knows he's sitting under the gun of a man who fears for his life. We've little enough in the way of levers so that we've got to use the slightest we can find."

Despite Flinx's varieties of calls, whistles, and entreaties the minidrag had not shown itself. It was unusual, but not unprecedented. Sometimes the snake had a mind of its own. Truzenzuzex couldn't duplicate the stuttering calls Flinx was using, but the insect was helping with the visual portion of the search. It served to take his mind at least temporarily off their unfortunate circumstances.

"Where would he be likely to hide, lad?" asked the scientist.

"Oh, I'm not sure, sir. Different places." He was becoming honestly concerned now and listened with only one ear to the philosoph's questions. He could not sense the minidrag's presence and that alone worried him. "He doesn't do this sort of thing often. I suppose the depression in the atmosphere got to him. He's sensitive to that, you know. He does prefer cool, closed-in places. Like. . . ."

He broke off in shock. In the distance he could see the minidrag. Even as he watched, it fluttered about the transparent dome. Its natural curiosity got the better of it then, because despite a warning thought from Flinx it poked its head under the attractive shape of the helmet. What happened next surprised both watchers. The minidrag did an awkward turn in the air and seemed to fall in on itself, collapsing into a tight curl at the very highest point of the helmet. It lay still, unmoving, within the structure, which now pulsed an uncertain yellow.

All thoughts of their immediate difficulties were instantly discarded in a paroxysm of fear for his companion. Heedless of Truzenzuzex's cautions he plunged forward at a run for the place they'd just left. Malaika turned and uttered an oath, charging after the boy. His bandy legs were no match for those of the youth but moved at a respectable speed nonetheless.

As he neared the dome Flinx noted a slight but definite tremor underfoot. He paid it no heed.

Truzenzuzex did. He glanced at Tse-Mallory.

"Yes, brother. I felt it too." His voice was reflective. Another tremor, stronger this time.

"What occurs?" said a puzzled Truzenzuzex. "I thought we'd established that this part of the planet, at least, was plutonically secure." He stared uneasily at the vaulting walls, gauging their strength and stability.

The gentle shaking started again, only this time it was somewhat less than gentle. And it didn't stop. It grew progressively louder and more forceful, and although no one noticed it, it did so as Flinx drew closer to the dome.

The steady vibration was felt, no, *sensed*, more than heard. It bespoke power somewhere deep below.

"What *is* going on?" whispered Tse-Mallory.

"*Elitat*! I'm not sure, replied the philosoph in equally subdued tones, "but I think perhaps our puzzle is setting about answering itself."

Flinx had mounted the dais and was moving toward the dome. Pip had still not moved. He barely noticed the tremors which were shaking the structure. As he neared his motionless pet the odd buzzing which had begun in his head began to get worse. He shook his head impatiently to clear it but with no effect. There was an odd feeling of euphoria alternating with the pain.

Don't fight it, something seemed to whisper. He heard waves on a beach, breaking softly. The minidrag's eyes were shut tightly. It appeared to be jerking to the strains of some silent song. His first thought was of convulsions, but the reptile's movements, although irregular, seemed too even for that. He started to reach under the great helmet for his troubled pet. The buzzing increased and he reeled backward under a startling attack of dizziness.

DON'T . . . FIGHT . . . YOU!

Pip's in . . . trouble. Trouble.

He shook his head again and this time it seemed to give him a little relief. Blurred, his thoughts were blurred. He focused watery eyes on the snake and plunged drunkenly under the helmet.

E*P*I*P*H*A*N*Y.

Inside his skull an ancient dam, weakened by chance and evolution, collapsed. The surge of stuff behind it was awesome.

The normally transparent structure of the dome exploded in a mass of scintillating, brilliantine auroras. From crown to base, all the colors of the visible spectrum . . . and probably those of the invisible also. Purples, greens, golds dominated the reds, blues, and other primes. A corruscating maelstrom of angry, almost metallic iridescence wove intricate and indecipherable patterns within the material of the dome itself. Faerie grids of phosphorescence, fox-fire, and ball-lightning etched spiderwebs of light in the air within the building.

On the bench within the dome within the building that was the Krang, Flinx lay stilled in seeming unconsciousness next to his now quiescent pet. The helmet above them pulsed a deep and fiery violet.

"Captain. . . ." Wolf's voice fluttered distorted by waterfalls of static over the crackling communit, but Malaika didn't notice. He had pulled up short in astonishment as soon as the dome had begun its eye-blinding display.

The gigantic pipes of the machine pulsed with anvillike ringings, circlets of lambent electricity crawling up their sides like parasitic haloes. They crackled viciously, much as ripping plastic foil.

". . . interspace call . . . !" Wolf didn't have a chance to pick up Malaika's acknowledgement, for the voice of Nikosos overrode the pilot's on the channel.

"What are you trying down there, merchant? No tricks, I warn you! I will have my men destroy your ship! I wish only a transmitter signal. A whole section of the continent to your east is . . . glowing, yes, glowing, under the surface, it seems. The place looks like it's on fire. I don't know what you're up to, man, but if you so much as. . . ."

The voice disappeared in a Niagara of interference. At that moment the world became filled with H's, U's, N's, and for some reason, especially G's.

Malaika took one step forward and dropped to the floor as if he'd been axed. At least, later, he thought he'd fallen. For all he could actually remember, he might have floated. The air in the ampitheater suddenly seemed to exert its presence, forcing him back and down. He was drowning in it. *Msaada*! Funny, they'd never noticed how dense it was. Dense. His head was imprisoned in a giant vise . . . no, not a vise. A thousand million jackboots drummed alien marches on the sides of his head while a conspiracy of laughing electrons tried to pull his scalp off. He smelled burnt-orange.

As he rolled on the floor trying to keep his head together while it insisted on flying apart, he caught a glimpse of Tse-Mallory. The sociologist was in similar shape. His face was a terrifying sight as he battled the force that was pushing them all toward gentle madness. Deprived of full rational control, the tall body twisted and flopped on the pale white floor like a suffocating *samaki*. Truzenzuzex, on the other hand, was sprawled motionless on his back. His eye membranes were closed for the first time the merchant could recall. Nowhere could he see what might have stimulated the reflex. The philosoph's legs were extended straight out and stiff, but the hands and foothands waved feebly in the electrostatically charged air.

Down below, the trillion kilometers of circuitry (and other things) that was the dormant mind of the Krang stirred, awoke. A-class mind, yes. But *blocked*! *Naturally* blocked! And what's more, unaware of itself! It was unheard of! An A-class mind could be reduced, yes, but only artificially. Blocked? Never! And *naturally*! The situation was . . . unnatural. It conflicted with the Law.

The Krang found itself confronted with a Unique Circumstance. It would be forced to the ultimate mechanical decision. Taking the initiative. But it could not operate itself. The mind above was essential/needed/required. It probed gently. Once the blocks were removed . . . cooperation. . . .

ADJUST YOUR CELLS, ORGANISM . . . SO!

Gently, gently.

Above, the body of Flinx jerked once.

I can't do that!

YOU MUST. IT IS . . . NECESSARY.

It hurts!

IGNORANCE HURTS. TRY.

Flinx's inert body squirmed again. His head throbbed unmercifully, seeming to grow to impossible proportions.

I . . . can't!

The Krang considered. Stronger pulsation could remove the blockage forcefully . . . and possibly destroy the mind forever. Consider alternatives. If blocked, how was the mind able to stimulate initial activation in the first place?

It required the fraction of a nanosecond to locate the answer. There was a catalyst mind nearby. That Explained. In referents the Krang was familiar with. Working swiftly through the moderating channels of the C-mind, the great machine made the necessary adjustments/tunings in the A-class brain. Gratefully, it sensed the barriers go down/dissolve. It was easy, this time. They had been weak and perforated to begin with. ETTA energies started to flow in the waiting floways. Further intervention was no longer required.

E*N*T*R*O*P*Y*R*E*A*L*I*Z*A*T*I*O*N.

In an instant of falling glass shards Flinx perceived the entire universe. It appeared as a very small, opaque ball of crystal. The instant passed, but he saw things clearly for the first time. Yes, much more clearly. He sensed things only half-noticed, suspected, before. And things not noticed at all. He saw the marvelous structure that was the Krang. He perceived the marvelous structure that was himself. Certain energies were required fully to awaken the instrument. Only a tiny part of it pulsed with awareness now. Here, and here, yes.

The Krang awoke. To full awakefulness for the first time in half a million years. Hymn-march. Glorianus! The threnody that flowed from the now attuned activator-mind was an unfamiliar one and crude in technique. But the Krang realized that in five hundred millennia tastes might have changed. The important thing was that the Screen had gone up automatically the instant the tune had supplied the necessary keying impulses.

The Krang's sensors instantly scanned the sky for light-years in all directions. Since the activator had done nothing on an instructional level except to broadcast sensations of danger, the machine instituted a general optimum scan pattern and hoped it would prove sufficient. It recognized the activator now as a novice. He would have to be guided. Somewhere a minor circuit dutifully noted that a single ship of alien construct had been pulverized at the moment of Screen activation, caught as it went up. A close call! Again the Krang regretted it could operate at only partial consciousness until the moment of full stimulation. Fortunately, the vessel had not penetrated. No harm done. The activator was informed and concurred. Another ship—no, two—lurked just outside the Screen. Although it remained stationary and made no hostile gestures, the activating mind directed the Krang to focus on the area of space occupied by the larger of the two vessels. Obediently, the machine complied.

Its field of effective close-range focus was a minimum thousand-kilometer sphere. It would have no trouble impacting the single indicated craft while missing the other. Those incredible sensors could line up the necessary cone of projection within a meter of any desired point. That was far more than necessary. It drew the necessary information as to specifics from a now cooperating A-mind. If the Krang had had feet, it would have been tapping them.

Above, the rhythmic pulsations that were making a pulp of Tse-Mallory's thoughts let up momentarily. They were instantly trans-

formed into an utterly indescribable cross between a modulated
screech and a bellow. The supersonic shriek of a bat amplified a
million times and made audible, backed with electric trumpets and
kettledrums. Even so, it did not press as intolerably onto his skull
as had the other. The sociologist was able to roll onto his back and
lie still, panting and gasping irregularly for the hostile air which
seemed intent on evading his lungs.

Painfully, he turned his head. He fought to keep the skreeling
moan from penetrating too deep, knowing that if he eased up and
allowed it to gain deep purchase, the knife-edge of the sonics
would begin slicing up the nerves and neurons therein. He was
able to stave it off.

Apparently Malaika was stronger in his resistance than any of
them. Somehow he staggered to his feet and began to lurch and
sway in the direction of the platform. He had made half the distance when the building moved.

At the moment of the first thrum, Wolf had gunned the crawler's
engines and made a dash for the door. Fortunately the big cruiser
had been pointing in that direction. When the first full note struck
him he had tumbled from the control seat, clasping his ears. But
the crawler, set on its course, continued on dumbly. As they had
before, the great doors parted. The moment they closed behind the
crawler, the torture stopped.

Wolf pulled himself slowly into the chair and managed to halt
the machine's headlong plunge before it sent them hurling over the
bluff. He didn't know what had happened—too quick! But he did
know that the captain and the others were still inside. He made a
quick check of the cargo area. Both women were sprawled among
the supplies, mercifully unconscious—whether from the effects of
the "thing" or their precipitous exit he couldn't tell.

What to *do*. Sprawled helplessly on the floor of the crawler, beating at the metal in agony, he would be little help to the captain or
anyone. For the moment, returning inside was out of the question.
A try at the communits produced only an ocean of static. Maybe
he could find something in the shuttle that would screen his mind
enough to permit him to re-enter that hell. He wasn't given time to
ponder the problem.

The building, every million-ton of it, was shifting its position. It
leaned backward and for a horrible moment he feared it was going
to topple onto the minuscule crawler. It did not. It hung poised in
the swirling sky for a second and then turned slightly to the south.
It began to hum, deeply. The vibrations could be felt through the

floor of the cab—or in one's teeth. Miles up in the dust-laden air he could see the upper hundred meters or so of the structure begin to glow a rich ebony. He'd never seen anything glow black before and was fascinated by the phenomenon. It continued for some thirty seconds. The circular base on which the building rested also seemed to brighten slightly. The air for some distance around took on a momentary rose color. Then it stopped.

The Krang recorded the dispatch of the second vessel as matter-of-factly as it had the first.

The entire process, from initial activation to now, had taken a little under two minutes.

Impatiently the Krang waited for further orders from the activation Nexus. The directive to destroy the other alien spacecraft did not come. In fact, the mind then and there removed itself from control of the Nexus.

The machine debated with itself. It had been a long, long time since it had existed at full consciousness. It had discovered again that it rather enjoyed the sensation.

But its imprinted instructions were clear and left no room for logical evasions. In the absence of an activating mind it was to return to a state of powered-down dormancy. This meant deactivation of all but the most elementary maintenance functions. The Krang sighed. The purposes of its builders had often seemed at variance with their desires and it had not now been shown reason to change that opinion. But it knew what a Frankenstein was, if it utilized a different reference. The great vanes in the depths of the limestone caverns which channeled the planet's unceasing gales began to shift down. The generators which drew power in countless ergs from the molten core of the planet throttled back, and the bubbling iron-nickel center calmed.

Slowly but efficiently, the Krang went about the necessary task of turning itself off.

22

Flinx rolled over and picked himself up. His head still throbbed but the actual pain had almost disappeared. He'd been drunk only once in his life. The memories of the monstrous hangover he'd suffered as a consequence came back to him now, incongruously. He stared around. After their close swing around the neutron star it had been his muscles which had been beaten and mauled. Controlled by the piano-string tautness of his outraged nervous system, it was now the marrow of his bones which vibrated in remembered sympathy with the ton-tones of the abruptly silent Krang. He looked inward, unconsciously rearranging certain cellular structures, fluids. The pain drifted away, leaving only a lot of light.

Aided by his friend, Truzenzuzex was slowly getting to his feet. Flinx didn't care to imagine what the insect, with its unprotected exoskeleton, had gone through. Malaika had been thwarted in his attempt to reach the dais by the unexpected angling of the building. He was sitting on the edge of a bench now, rubbing a knee and carefully checking the ligaments and tendons to make certain that nothing critical had been damaged. Otherwise he seemed unharmed, for a multiplicity of oaths in a remarkable number of languages flowed in unceasing profusion from his thick lips.

Assured that his humanx companions were all right, Flinx turned his attention to his pet. The small, leathery body was curled tightly under the activation hood. It gave sign of neither motion nor life. Careful not to get his head under that quiet object, he lifted the solid little form from its resting place. Still it did not stir. With his newly stimulated mind he probed gently within the small body. He had been pushed, indeed shoved into a new and unfamiliar universe and was still a little uncertain (honest now, frightened) of his abilities. He probed deeper. The minidrag had served as a conduit for forces beyond its own capacity to handle. Like an overloaded capacitor, certain rearrangements and adjustments were in order.

Flinx set about making them.

The others had gathered together and were standing off to one side, watching silently and having the courtesy not to offer sympathy. With an unoccupied portion of his mind he searched theirs, briefly. All three were still stunned by the events of the past few minutes. Almost as much as he, he reflected wryly. He could feel the empathy radiating outward from them and it made him feel better.

A last readjustment, a stubborn artery . . . no, there! One thin eyelid flickered, raised. An oil-black eye peered out and around. It swiveled up to where it encountered Flinx's own, was joined by its twin. In slow, jerky motions the minidrag began to uncurl. Flinx stuck out his tongue. Pip's darted out to make contact with it in an old gesture of familiarity and affection. He could feel the tension begin to slip from the muscular coils, the life-pulse to strengthen.

He had dropped the habit of crying at about the time he had discovered it did nothing more than clean his pupils. Still, there was a suspicious moisture at the corners of his eyes. He turned away so that the others might not be offended by it. If he had remained facing the other way or had bothered to probe he might have noticed that Truzenzuzex's expression was something more than merely sympathetic.

23

The shuttle had not been harmed and they made the ascent into the upper atmosphere with more ease and certainty than they had managed the trip down. Atha and Wolf were at the controls. The others were in the rear cabin, their minds intent on the present instead of the future for the first time in some while.

"Well, sir," said Truzenzuzex to Malaika, "we apologize. It seems as though your investment has proven singularly unprofitable. I confess that it was not really a concern of ours from the beginning. But after the expense and danger you have been through I do wish you could have realized something in the way of a more substantial increment from it."

"Oh now, you are unnecessarily pessimistic, my hard-shelled *rafiki*." The merchant puffed vigorously on an incredibly foul-smelling pipe. "I have a city that is no doubt filled to overflowing with priceless Tar-Aiym artifacts and inventions . . . if I can ever dig them out of that infernal sand! A fine, inhabitable planet. With a thriving native aqueous ecological system, probably compatible to the humanx norm. I think that this planet might even bring back the sailing ship, *ndiyo!*"

"The reference eludes me," said the philosoph.

"I'll show you trioids when we get back. One of the more poetic bits of man's technological past. No, no, from the *fedha* standpoint I am not ready to count this journey a bust! And there is always the Krang to play with, *je*? Even if our young friend insists it was a freak accident that he had nothing to do with." He looked questioningly at Flinx, who studiously ignored them all. "But for you two, I am afraid, it was a real disappointment. You must be even more frustrated now than when we landed, *je*?"

"It all depends on how you choose to view it," said Tse-Mallory. "When we started on the trail of this thing we really had no idea what we expected to find, other than something big. When we found that, we didn't know what we'd found. And now that we've left it . . . well, when you get ready to come back and dig out those artifacts," he glanced at his ship-brother, "Tru and I will be more than happy to help you with the sorting, if not the excavating. And we still, as you say, have the Krang itself to 'play' with. It will at least form the basis for many a lengthy and infuriating scientific paper." He smiled and shook his head. "The psychological and sociological implications alone . . . eh, Tru?"

"Unquestionably, brother." The thranx tried hard to convey a human attitude of profound reflection, failed, and substituted one of nostalgic unconcern instead. The result did not quite come off.

"It seems as though the legends of both the Branner and our primitive hominids had some validity to them. Who would have suspected it? The Krang is both a weapon *and* a musical instrument."

They had left the atmosphere now and Atha was setting an orbit that would bring them up on the *Gloryhole* from below and behind. The blackness poured in on one side while the sun, filtered down automatically by the photosensitive ports, lit them from the other. Despite the equalizing effects of the cabin lights, it tended to throw facial features into unnaturally sharp relief.

"It tells us a lot about the Tar-Aiym . . . not to mention going a long way toward explaining their interest in two such seemingly divergent fields as war and art. I can't say that I care for their tastes in music, though. Myself, I prefer Debussy and Koretski. No doubt to their ears . . . or whatever they used . . . such sounds were pleasing and exciting, nay, patriotic."

"Subtle sounds of death resound, and lyres smote as children drowned," Tse-Mallory recited.

"Porzakalit, twenty-third sonnet," said Truzenzuzex. "It *would* take a poet."

"I may be overly dense," said Malaika, "but I still don't understand how the *kelelekuu worked*!"

"You are not alone in that respect, captain, but rather the member of a large minority. If you wish, though, I could hypothesize."

"Go ahead and hypothesize, then!"

"Apparently," continued the thranx, discreetly waving away the noxious effluvia produced by the carbonized weed in the merchant's pipe, "the machine generates some form of vibration . . . I confess myself hesitant to label it 'sound waves.' Probably something partaking of those characteristics as well as those of wave forms we could not identify—although their effects were noted! You recall that on our initial passage through the atmosphere I remarked on the unusual density of the double layer of windglitter?" Malaika nodded. "Probably those layers are kept artificially reinforced. The wave forms—let's call them 'k-waves' for want of a better, or more accurate, term—were generated by the Krang. These waves passed through the lower layer of the metallic windglitter but not the higher, denser one. Accordingly, they were then 'bounced' along between the two layers, as they were by now sufficiently weakened to be incapable of breaking back through the lower one. All around the planet, I'd wager. Perhaps more than once, constantly being rejuvenated by the generators of the Krang."

"Oh, now I know they're probably not sound waves," said Malaika, "but planet-wide circulation in the atmosphere? From a single generating source—maintenance of a certain minimal strength—the power requirements. . . . You really think it possible?"

"My dear Malaika, I regard anything as possible unless clearly demonstrated otherwise . . . the more so when *this* machine is involved."

"Even simple sound waves," put in Tse-Mallory. "Back on Terra itself, old calendar eighteen eighty-eight, there was a volcanic explosion in the major ocean. An island called Krakatoa blew up rather violently. The shock waves traveled several times around the globe. The sound of the explosions—simple sound waves, remember—was heard halfway around the globe. Given the Tar-Aiym's abilities and the fact that these were much more than mere sound waves, I should consider the production of such forms an elegant possibility. Besides, I should think you'd need little convincing after that highly spectacular demonstration we had."

"A conclusion after the fact," said Truzenzuzex drily. "Very astute of you, brother. However, as I am only slightly more knowledgeable in this regard than you. . . ."

"Disputed!"

". . . I let the matter drop. The Tar-Aiym were fully capable, as you say, of amplifying on nature—pardon the pun."

"I would suppose that explains what became of our *rafiki* Nikosos, then," murmured Malaika. "Once his shuttle entered the region of effective vibrations. . . ."

"Destructive oscillation?" added Tse-Mallory.

"Shaken to pieces? Possibly," said Truzenzuzex. "Or maybe they cause a breakdown or weakening of the atomic structure. Even in what was probably the safest place on the planet the vibrations—'music' if you must—near to shook my skeleton off. Not an impossible device. Fantastic, yes, but not impossible. Myself, I am much more interested in the method used to eliminate their starship."

"*Ndiyo*," said Malaika. "How about that? It was nowhere near the atmosphere and so could not have been trapped in the windglitter layers."

"In addition to maintaining an impenetrable defensive screen around the planet, the Krang would be no more than a stalemate device if it did not have offensive capabilities as well," continued the thranx. "A device wholly defensive in nature would be contrary to everything we know of Tar-Aiym psychology. And you are all aware of how the quality of vibrations changed ever so significantly toward the end of our ordeal. Now then, Flinx, you say you sensed the destruction of the other starship, yet there was no sign of an explosion? No flare, nothing?"

A safe question, and one he could hardly deny. "That's right, sir. It just . . . vanished."

"Um. A possibility suspected that will probably never be confirmed, but . . . remember that our ship was a very short distance away, yet apparently has not been affected. I suspect gentlesirs, that the Krang is a gravitonic generator—but of power undreamed of even by the ancient Gods." He faced Malaika squarely. "Captain, what would happen if a gravity field approximately one centimeter in diameter with a field equal in strength to the surface of a neutron star impinged on a real mass?"

Malaika's swarthy face reflected puzzlement, revelation, and astonishment in amazingly brief succession. His voice reflected all three.

"*Manisa*! That would trigger a Schwarzchild Discontinuity! But that's . . . !"

"Impossible?" Truzenzuzex smiled. "Pardon, captain, but how else might you explain it? The power necessary to generate such a field would need a planet-sized ship . . . much simpler to use a planet, eh? And remember there was no evidence of an explosion. Of course not. Not even light could escape a field of such strength! And gravity follows an inverse square law, so naturally our ship was not effectively endangered. A more perfectly selective weapon would be hard to imagine. A mere kilometer away and you would not even notice such a field. But touch it and poof! Instant nonexistence! I hope that one might have the sense not to tamper with such a device overmuch, captain." The thranx's voice was steel-solemn. "We do not know anywhere near enough about the operation of such a field. Suppose we did not discover the way to 'uncreate' such a field? The Krang obviously can do that—how, I cannot begin to imagine. But if such a field were to be released, uncontrolled, it would simply wander around the universe gobbling up . . . everything."

It was too quiet in the cabin, now. "But I think there's little chance of that," he continued more spiritedly, "unless our young friend can activate the mechanism once again. Not to mention," he added, "directing it as successfully."

Flinx had read the veiled accusation coming for some time now. He knew it would have to be countered. They must not think him capable of operating such a threatening weapon. Especially, he reminded himself, when he wasn't sure if he could!

"I told you sir, I don't know what happened. The machine controlled *me*, not vice versa!"

"Still," the thranx said significantly.

It would have been easy to rearrange the insect's mind so that he would simply take Flinx's explanation of the occurrence at face value. Too easy. The Krang had not affected his sense of ethics. Besides, the idea of deliberately tampering with another's deepest centers of thought was mildly repulsive, as well as a bit frightening. Especially when the mind in question was recognizably wiser than his own. Power, he reminded himself, is not knowledge. He would need a lot of the latter in the future.

"Look. . . ." He was thinking rapidly. It was easy, now. "As far as 'directing' the device goes, you said yourself that the machine was composed of infinitely sophisticated circuitry. Once started up, it would be fully capable of handling the situation to its own satisfaction. I was merely like the hydrogen 'plug' that starts the KK drive."

"Um. And how do you account for its taking the actions it did?"

"Maybe Nikosos' ship made a movement that the machine interpreted as hostile, and it responded accordingly. Perhaps it was just keyed and ready when I entered it. I'm certainly not that much different from anyone else here." (Lie!) "Probably my gift or talent or whatever you want to call it had something to do with it. Remember, it didn't do anything the first time I entered it."

"I have a hunch your own fears at the moment had a lot to do with it too. Yes, that's plausible."

"Right," Flinx continued, grateful for the opening. "I was scared when I entered it this time . . . really scared." (Truth.) "My emotional strain *had* to be picked up by the machine. It's an artistic device, too! Probably any of us could have stimulated it under those conditions." (Possible, not probable.) "In any case, it's finished now and I've no desire, not the tiniest, to try it again!" (Mixed truth.)

"Enough lad! You are too aggressive for my poor, senile mind." (Baloney!) "I am satisfied, for the nonce." (Flinx read otherwise, but it did not matter.) "You have convinced me in fair and equal oral combat. Try me at personality chess and I'll beat the freckles off you! Yet. . . ." He glanced at the minidrag, then back to Flinx. "You say you feel unchanged? No aftereffects?"

Flinx shook his head with a confidence that would have made Mother Mastiff proud. "No. I really don't know what happened. My mind was. . . ." He broke off as the outside light was abruptly extinguished. The shuttle had slipped into her mooring dock in the cargo hold of the *Gloryhole*.

"And that is that," said Malaika, unnecessarily. To everyone's great satisfaction, his pipe had gone out. "I'd love to discuss this all further with you gentlebeings, but at some future *nafasi, ndiyo*? If I do not get something of a recognizably liquid consistency down my throat very soon, you'll be able to scatter me in orbit with the windglitter, for I shall dry up to dust!"

He moved down the narrow aisle between them and opened the small personnel lock. The pale green light of the cargo balloon sifted inward. A pullway drifted conveniently nearby. Sissiph in hand he began hauling the two of them up its swaying length. Atha went next, followed by the two scientists. Flinx plucked Pip from where the minidrag lay coiled comfortably about a chair arm and placed him on his shoulder. He hurried out of the ship. Even now the figure of Wolf was still one he wished to avoid. He followed the others up the pullway.

On reaching the gravitized section of the ship, everyone went his separate way. Atha and Wolf to Control, Malaika and Sissiph to their cabin. The merchant had not yet had a drop of intoxicant, but he had escaped a ransom and gained a planet. Even if he never realized a cent off his investment, that alone was enough to make him slightly drunk. The two scientists prepared to resume their endless game of personality chess as though they had never been interrupted.

"That was not a legal psychosis," said Tse-Mallory, his voice drifting back to Flinx. "And you are well aware of it!"

"Why, Bran, how can you say that? Surely when I instigated a jump of four places in that secondary childhood fear piece. . . ." Their voices faded as he turned the corner leading to his cabin.

Flinx glanced down at this shoulder. The minidrag, the effects of its ordeal now apparently catching up with it, was fast asleep. He paused after a moment's hesitation for twice that in thought. Then he shrugged, grinned. Whistling a famous and delightfully ribald tune, he sauntered off in expectation of the biggest pseudosteak the ship's autochef could produce. He had much to think about.

And much to do it with.

24

Rashalleila Nuaman lay back in her huge bed and idly examined the bedraggled, seminude figure of her niece. The girl had obviously used more force than good sense in protesting madame's request for her presence.

"Teleen," she said, sighing, "I am awfully disappointed in you, you know. Stupidity I can sometimes understand, but sloppiness is inexcusable. I knew about your amusing plan for doing away with me, of course."

The girl started at this and her eyes darted around the room in search of an escape route. Even assuming she could evade the grasp of the two giants who stood impassively to either side of her, there was nowhere on the airless moon to escape to.

"Oh, don't let it bother you, child. It didn't me. Actually I thought it rather an admirable attempt. Showed some spunk, for a change. But that you should undertake to interfere with *business* . . . that, my dear," and her voice dropped dangerously, "was ill-chosen on your part. I would perhaps have more sympathy for you had you succeeded. And with the AAnn, too. Dear, dear! I suppose you are aware they are the closest thing to a hereditary enemy mankind has?"

Teleen's tone was bitterly sarcastic. "Don't foist patriotic mush on me, you sanctimonious crank! You'd sell babies to the Devil if you thought he was more than a superstition . . . and enough profit."

"You are being absurd, girl. Also impertinent. I certainly would not. At least, certainly not for spite, as you did. Being branded an enemy of the Commonwealth and excommunicated by the Church would require promise of a considerably greater potential return than such pettiness as you aspired to. And on top of everything else, your adolescent ineptitude will force me to tolerate an unbearable amount of ridicule from a very old and dear friend. Who incidentally, I am informed, has long since sewn up the registry of a certain planet by interspace relay, beyond argument of any kind. I will now be forced to fall back on legal means to obtain what was rightfully mine in the first place. As you may know, such procedures are notoriously unfair.

"However, we are not here to discuss that. What we are here to determine, dear niece, is what I am to do with you. I fear that your attitude has taken rather a dangerous turn. I do not fear it, but my men are capable of error too. Accordingly, I am forced to send you on vacation, until such time as you have been persuaded to channel your considerable energies into more productive pursuits. You shall be given ample time to repent and readjust your rebellious attitudes. There is a very excellent and renowned mental institution in the Qatar system. It is operated by a group of exceptional therapists who have aided me often in the past. While their methods have often been questioned, most notably by the Church, their successes cannot be denied. The director is a personal friend of long standing."

"Rory," said Teleen imploringly.

"I am sure they will be more than happy to accommodate you as a guest for a while. Unfortunately, they specialize in childhood neuroses and sexual maniacs of the most extreme kind. Now, which section do you suppose you would find more comfortable for your stay?"

"Rory!" The girl's voice was frightened and shrill, now.

Rory Mallap van Cleef stood quietly by the foot of the bed in silk loincloth and beads.

"Oh, you needn't badger your accomplice and confidant, my dear. Darling Rory knows what side of the bed his butter is on." She smiled sweetly.

His voice was even and mild. Almost neutral, in fact. "I *am* sorry, love." He flexed a bicep. "I still love you, of course, but I don't see why we should both be made to suffer for this unfortunate setback. I'll wait for you." Then, after a thoughtful pause. "I do hope this doesn't complicate our relationship."

Teleen's answer was unprintable.

"Tch! Such language. And after all those expensive schools, too. Yes, I am certain you will be placed in the section most suitable to your attitude, child. I see no reason why you shouldn't take the opportunity to add to your education at the same time as we are about improving your disposition."

She waved a hand negligently and the girl was dragged spitting and squalling from the room.

"Remember now, dear, I am depending on you to show your hosts the true Nuaman spirit! Come back to us in one piece, won't you?" She shook her head mournfully after the closing doors had cut off the sound of the girl's fading shrieks. "Tch. I'm not sure that girl will ever be ready to take over the company reins. Everything devolves upon me, and I am old. But not that old." She extended a hand. "Rory . . . come here. . . ."

They were halfway home and proceeding smoothly for Moth. Flinx looked up from his game of crystal solitaire, now grown childishly simplistic. The sense of thoughts in violent conflict had grown too strong to be ignored. As it was a normal sleep shift he was the only one in the lounge, and the commotion surprised him.

A rather disheveled-looking Atha stepped into the room. She obviously hadn't expected to encounter anyone and was noticeably upset by Flinx's presence.

"Well," she began awkwardly, simultaneously trying to adjust her clothing, "we've, uh, almost finished our journey, Flinx. I imagine you're looking forward to getting home . . . and to that credit slip Malaika's prepared for you!"

"Yes, to both. You're on your way to relieve Wolf at Control, I assume?"

"Hmmm? Oh yes, naturally!" He had to hide his amusement at the way she had pounced on the excuse. "Yes, I've just come from making some alterations, uh, in the arrangement of the ship's supplies. They were becoming unwieldy. I had to . . . work on the problem at some length to get things right."

"And did you?"

Her smile was broad. "Oh, yes. Everything should now be in its proper place." She disappeared forward.

A short while later a much more disheveled Sissiph, clothes and self in nearly equal disarray, staggered into the lounge. The expression on her face was murderous, interrupted only when she grimaced at a particularly painful bruise. She spared him one unfocused glance before weaving off in the direction of the big cabin she shared with Malaika.

Apparently then, everyone had profited from the expedition, with the exception of an attractive and furious minority of one. He sighed and returned to his game, its attraction dimmed. There were many things to do, and he wasn't sure how to go about doing them. If he couldn't have any fun. . . . Malaika, he knew, was preparing great things for him. He could not see himself in the role the merchant had envisioned for him. Dressing up for gala conferences, withering competitors with his astonishing insight. Perhaps a compromise might be arranged. But that might mean leaving the markets, and his friends there. Mother Mastiff would probably have no trouble adapting to such a life. He grinned. Could High Society survive her? More seriously, how would he adapt? With everyone these days convinced of his own righteousness and secure in the knowledge that "his was the proper way of doing things."

He'd also seen what un-nice people could do to the nice, enough to want to modify the situation. Out there were minds which would resist such efforts. And who was he, to arbitrate the lives of others? Did he *want* to play God? He didn't think so. Besides he was only . . . well, he *was* almost seventeen, wasn't he? He had talent, and one innocent man and two probably guilty ones had died because he hadn't used it properly. Now he had Power, and who knew how many had died in space because of it? Power. Fagh! He wasn't one tenth the Man Tse-Mallory was! He'd need men like that to help him or he'd likely make some horrendous mistakes. Now they might prove deadly. Could he handle what he was now? Did he *want* to?

Still, the whole universe was out there and it seemed a shame not to take a look at it.

Now that he could see.

ORPHAN STAR

For Joe and Sherry Hirschhorn, and their
Three Princesses,
Renee, Bonnie, and Janice,
Who would grace any fairy tale,
With love from Alan . . .

1

"Watch where you're going, *qwot!*"

The merchant glared down at the slim, olive-skinned youth and made a show of readjusting his barely rumpled clothing.

"Your pardon, noble sir," the youngster replied politely. "I did not see you in the press of the crowd." This was at once truth and lie. Flinx hadn't *seen* the overbearing entrepreneur, but he had sensed the man's belligerence seconds before the latter had swerved intentionally to cause the collision.

Although his still poorly understood talents had been immensely enriched several months ago by his encounter with the Krang— that awesome semisentient weapon of the now-vanished masters of the galaxy, the Tar-Aiym—they were as inconsistent as ever. The experience of acting as an organic catalyst for the colossal device had almost killed both him and Pip. But they had survived and he, at least, had been changed in ways as yet uncomprehended.

Lately he had found that at one moment he could detect the thoughts of the King himself off in Drallar's palace, while in the next even the minds of those standing in close proximity stayed shut tight as a miser's purse. This made for numerous uncertainties, and oftentimes Flinx found himself cursing the gift, as its capriciousness kept him in a constant state of mental imbalance. He was like a child clinging desperately to the mane of a rampaging devilope, struggling to hang on at the same time he was fighting to master the bucking mount.

He shifted to go around the lavishly clad bulk, but the man moved to block his path. "Children need to learn how to mind their betters," he smirked, obviously unwilling, like Flinx, to let the incident pass.

Flinx could sense the frustration in the man's mind, and sought deeper. He detected fuzzy hints of a large business transaction that had failed just this morning. That would explain the man's frustration, and his apparent desire to find someone to take it out on. As Flinx considered this development, the man was making a great show of rolling up his sleeves to reveal massive arms. His frustration faded beneath the curious stares of the shifting crowd of traders, hawkers, beggars, and craftsmen who were slowing and beginning to form a small eddy of humanity in the round-the-clock hurricane of the Drallarian marketplace.

"I said I was sorry," Flinx repeated tensely.

A blocky fist started to rise.

"Sorry indeed. I think I'm going to have to teach you . . ." The merchant halted in his stride, the threatening fist abruptly frozen in midair. His face rapidly turned pale and his eyes seemed fixed on Flinx's far shoulder.

A head had somehow emerged from beneath the loose folds of the youth's cape. Now it regarded the merchant with a steady, un-blinking gaze that held the quality of otherworld death, the flavor of frozen methane and frostbite. In itself the skull was tiny and unimpressive, scaled and unabashedly reptilian. Then more of the creature emerged, revealing that the head was attached to a long cylindrical body. A set of pleated membranous wings opened, beat lazily at the air.

"Sorry," the merchant found himself mumbling, "it was all a mistake . . . my fault, really." He smiled sickly, looked from left to right. The eyes of the small gathering stared back dispassion-ately.

It was interesting how the man seemed to shrink into the wall of watchers. They swallowed him up as neat and clean as a grouper would an ambling angelfish. That done, the motionless ranks blended back into the moving stream of humanity.

Flinx relaxed and reached up to scratch the flying snake under its leathery snout. "Easy there, Pip," he whispered, thinking warm relaxing thoughts at his pet. "It's nothing, settle down now."

Reassured, the minidrag hissed sibilantly and slid back beneath the cape folds, its pleated wings collapsing flat against its body. The merchant had quickly recognized the reptile. A well-traveled individual, he knew that there was no known antidote for the poi-son of the Alaspin miniature dragon.

"Maybe he learned whatever lesson he had in mind to give us," Flinx said. "What say we go over to Small Symm's for a beer and some pretzels for you. Would you like that, summm?"

The snake summmed back at him.

Nearby buried within the mob, an obese, unlovely gentleman thanked a gratified goldsmith as he pocketed a purchase indiffer-ently made. This transaction had served the purpose of occupying time and covering up his true focus of attention, which had not been the just-bought bauble.

Two men flanked him. One was short and sleek, with an expression like a wet weasel. The other showed a torso like a galvanized boiler, and half a face. His one eye twitched persistently as he stared after the retreating figure of Flinx, while his small companion eagerly addressed the purchaser of the tiny gold-and-pearl piano.

"Did you see the look on that guy's face, Challis?" he asked the plump man. "That snake's a hot death. Nothin' was said to us about anything like that. That big idiot not only saved his own life, but mine and Nanger's, too."

The one-eye nodded.

"Ya, you're goin' to have to find someone else for this bit of dirty stuff." His short companion looked adamant.

The fat merchant remained calm, scratched at one of his many chins. "Have I been ungenerous? Since you both are on permanent retainer to me, I technically owe you nothing for this task." He shrugged. "But if it is a question of more money . . ."

The sleek weasel shook his head. "You can buy my service, Challis, but not my life. Do you know what happens if that snake's venom hits you in the eyes? No antivenom known will keep you alive for more than sixty seconds." He kicked at the gravel and dirt underfoot, still moist from the regular morning rain. "No, this isn't for me and not for Nanger neither."

"Indeed," the man with half a face agreed solemnly. He sniffed and nodded in the direction of the now departed youth. "What's your obsession with the boy, anyway? He's not strong, he's not rich, and he's not particularly pretty."

"It's his head I'm interested in, not his body," sighed Challis, "though this is a matter of my pleasure." Puffing like a leaky pillow, he led them through the bustling, shouting crowd. Humans, thranx, and representatives of a dozen other commercial races slid easily around and past them as though oiled, all intent on errands of importance.

"It's my Janus jewel. It bores me."

The smaller man looked disgusted. "How can anyone rich enough to own a Janus jewel be bored?"

"Oh, but I am, Nolly-dear, I am."

Nanger made a half-smirk. "What's the trouble, Challis? Your imagination failing you?" He laughed, short, stentorian barks.

Challis grinned back at him. "Hardly that, Nanger, but it seems that I have not the right type of mind to produce the kind of fine, detailed resolution the jewel is capable of. I need help for that. So I've been at work these past months looking for a suitable mental adept, trying to find a surrogate mind of the proper type to aid in operating the jewel. I've paid a lot of money for the right information," he finished, nodding at a tall Osirian he knew. The avian clacked its beak back at him and made a gesture with its graceful, ostrichlike neck, its periscope form weaving confidently through the crowd.

Nanger paused to buy a thisk cake, and Challis continued his explanation as they walked on.

"So you see why I need that boy."

Nolly was irritated now. "Why not just hire him? See if he'll participate willingly?"

Challis looked doubtful. "No, I don't think that would work out, Nolly-dear. You're familiar with some of my fantasies and likes?" His voice had turned inhumanly calm and empty. "Would you participate voluntarily?"

Nolly looked away from suddenly frightening pupils. In spite of his background, he shuddered. "No," he barely whispered, "no, I don't guess that I would. . . ."

"Hello, lad," boomed Small Symm—the giant was incapable of conversing in less than a shout. "What of your life and what do you hear from Malaika?"

Flinx sat on one of the stools lined up before the curving bar, ordered spiced beer for himself and a bowl of pretzels for Pip. The flying snake slid gracefully from Flinx's shoulder and worked his way into the wooden bowl of trapezoidal dough. This action was noted by a pair of wide-eyed unsavory types nearby, who promptly vacated their seats and hastily made for the rearmost booths.

"I've had no contact with Malaika for quite a while, Symm. I've heard he's attending to business outsystem."

Flinx's wealthy merchant friend had enabled him to quit performing his personal sideshow, having provided him with a substantial sum for his aid in exploring the Tar-Aiym world of the Krang. Much of the money had gone to set up Flinx's adoptive mother, Mother Mastiff, in a well-stocked shop in one of Drallar's better market districts. Muttering at her capriciousness, the old woman had rescued Flinx as a child from the slave-seller's block, and had raised him. She was the only parent he had ever known. She muttered still, but with affection.

"As a matter of fact," he went on, sipping at the peppery brew, "Malaika wanted me to go with him. But while I respect the old hedonist, he'd eventually get ideas about putting me in a starched suit, slicking my hair back, and teaching me diction." Flinx shuddered visibly. "I couldn't stand that. I'd go back to juggling and audience guessing games first. What about you, father of oafs? I've heard that the municipal troops have been harassing you again."

The owner of the bar leaned his two-and-a-half-meter-tall, one-hundred-seventy-five-kilo frame onto the absorbent wood-plastic counter, which creaked in protest. "Apparently the marketplace commissioner took it as a personal affront when I ejected the first group of officious do-gooders he sent round to close me down. Maybe I shouldn't have broken their vehicle. Now they are trying to be more subtle. I had one in just this week, who claimed to have observed me serving borderline minors certain hallucinogenic liquids."

"Obviously you deserve to be strung up by your extremities," commented Flinx with mock solemnity. He, too, was underage for much of what Symm served him.

"Anyway," the giant went on, "this heckster flies out of a back booth, flashes his municipal peace card, and tries to tell me I'm under arrest. He was going to take me in, and I had best come along quietly." Small Symm shook his massive head mournfully as Flinx downed several swallows.

"What did you do?" He licked liquid from the corners of his mouth.

"I really don't want any more trouble, certainly not another assault charge. I thought an inferential demonstration of a mildly physical nature might be effective in persuading the gentleman to change his opinion. It was, and he left quietly." Symm gestured at Flinx's now empty mug. "Refill?"

"Sure. What did you do?" he repeated.

"I ate his peace card. Here's your beer." He slid a second mug alongside the first.

Flinx understood Small Symm's gratification. He had his reputation to uphold. His was one of the few places in Drallar where a person could go at night with a guarantee of not being assaulted or otherwise set upon by rambunctious rovers. This was because Small Symm dealt impartially with all such disturbers of the peace.

"Be back in a minute," Flinx told his friend. He slid off the stool and headed for the one room whose design and function had changed little in the past several hundred years. As soon as he stepped inside he was overwhelmed by a plethora of rich smells and sensations: stale beer, hard liquor, anxiety, tension, old water, dampness, fearful expectation. The combination of thick thoughts and airborne odors nearly overpowered him.

Looking to his left, where the combination was strongest, he noticed a small twitch of a man watching him anxiously. Flinx observed the man's outward calm and felt his internal panic. He was holding an osmotic syringe in one hand, his finger coiled about it as if it were a weapon. As Flinx started to yell for help, his rising cry was blanketed by the descent of something dark and heavy over his head. A mental cry was aborted by the cool efficiency of the syringe. . . .

He awoke to find himself staring at a jumbled panoply of lights. They were spread out before and below him, viewed as they were through a wall and floor of transparent plastic.

Slowly he struggled to a sitting position, which was accomplished with some difficulty since his wrists were manacled together by two chromed metal cuffs. A long tube of flexible metal ran off from them and disappeared among rich furniture. The chain meandered through the thick transparent carpet like a mirror-backed worm.

Looking out, Flinx could see the lights that were the city-pulse of Drallar, dominated by the glowing spires of the King's palace off to the left. The view enabled him to orient himself. Combining the position of the palace with the pattern of lower lights and the knowledge that he was several stories above ground indicated that he was being held captive in one of the four sealed inurbs of the city. These guarded, restrictive enclaves held the homes of the upper classes, of those native to Drallar and those off-worlders who had commerce here. His assailants, then, were more than gutter thieves.

He was unable to pick up any impressions nearby. At the moment the only alien sensation he could detect was a slight throbbing in the muscles of his upper right arm, where the syringe had struck home. A different kind of sensation was inspired by his own anger, anger directed at himself for not detecting the inimical emanations his attackers must have been putting out before he entered the bathroom.

Suddenly he noticed another sensation missing, too. The comfortable weight of Pip was absent from his shoulders.

"Hello," ventured a tiny, silvery voice.

Spinning, Flinx found himself eye-to-eye with an angel. He relaxed, swung his feet off the couch, and regarded her in surprise. She could not have been more than nine or ten years old, was clad in a powder blue-and-green fringed pantsuit with long sleeves of some transparent lacy material. Long blond hair fell in manicured ripples to the backs of her thighs. Baby-blue eyes looked out at him from the high-boned face of a sophisticated cherub.

"My name's Mahnahmi," she informed him softly, her voice running up and down like a piccolo trill, "what's yours?"

"Everybody calls me Flinx."

"Flinx." She was sucking on the knuckle of her big finger. "That's a funny name, but nice." A smile showed perfect pearly teeth. "Want to see what my daddy brought me?"

"Daddy," Flinx echoed, looking around the room. It was dominated by the great curve of the transparent wall and balcony and the sparkling panorama laid out below. It was night outside . . . but was it that same night? How long had he lain unconscious? No way to tell . . . yet.

The room was furnished in late Siberade: lush cushions, chairs and divan mounted on pencil-thin struts of duralloy, with everything else suspended from the ceiling by duralloy wires so thin that the rest of the furniture appeared to be floating in air. A massive spray of luminescent spodumene and kunzite crystals dominated the domed roof. They were surrounded by circular skylights now open to the star-filled night sky. Climatic adjusters kept the evening rain from falling into the room.

His captor was a very wealthy person.

Petulant-rich with nonattention, the girlish voice interrupted his inspection. "Do you want to see it or not?"

Flinx wished the throb in his upper arm would subside. "Sure," he said absently.

The smile returned as the girl reached into a suit pocket. She moved closer, proudly opened her fist to reveal something in the palm of her hand. Flinx saw that it was a miniature piano, fashioned entirely from filigree gold and real pearls.

"It really plays," she told him excitedly. She touched the tiny keys and Flinx listened to the almost inaudible notes. "It's for my dolly."

"It's very pretty," Flinx complimented, remembering when such a toy would have cost him more credit than he ever thought he would possess. He glanced anxiously past her. "Where is your daddy right now?"

"Over here."

Flinx turned to the source of those simple, yet somehow threatening words.

"No, I already know you're called Flinx," the man said, with a wave of one ring-laden hand. "I already know a good deal about you."

Two men emerged from the globular shadow. One had a sunk-in skull half melted away by some tremendous heat and only crudely reconstructed by medical engineers. His smaller companion exhibited more composure now than he had when he'd held the syringe on Flinx in the bathroom at Symm's.

The merchant was talking again. "My name is Conda Challis. You have perhaps heard of me?"

Flinx nodded slowly. "I know of your company."

"Good," Challis replied. "It's always gratifying to be recognized, and it saves certain explanations." The uncomfortable pulsing in Flinx's shoulder was beginning to subside as the man settled his bulk in a waiting chair. A round, flat table of metal and plastic separated him from Flinx. The half-faced man and his stunted shadow made themselves comfortable—but not too comfortable, Flinx noted—nearby.

"Mahnahmi, I see you've been entertaining our guest," Challis said to the girl. "Now go somewhere and play like a good child."

"No. I want to stay and watch."

"Watch?" Flinx tensed. "Watch what?"

"He's going to use the jewel. I know he is!" She turned to Challis. "Please let me stay and watch, Daddy! I won't say a word, I promise."

"Sorry, child. Not this time."

"Not this time, not this time," she repeated. "You never let me watch. Never, never, never!" As quick as a sun shower turns bright, her face broke into a wide smile. "Oh, all right, but at least let me say good-bye."

When Challis impatiently nodded his approval she all but jumped into Flinx's arms. Much to his distress, she wrapped herself around him, gave him a wet smack on one cheek, and whispered into his right ear in a lilting, immature soprano, "Better do what he tells you to, Flinx, or he'll rip out your guts."

Somehow he managed to keep a neutral expression on his face as she pulled away with a disarmingly innocent smile.

"Bye-bye. Maybe Daddy will let us play later." Turning, she skipped from the room, exiting through a doorway in the far wall.

"An . . . interesting little girl," Flinx commented, swallowing.

"Isn't she charming," Challis agreed. "Her mother was exceptionally beautiful."

"You're married, then? You don't strike me as the type."

The merchant appeared truly shocked. "Me, life-mated? My dear boy! Her mother was purchased right here in Drallar, a number of years ago. Her pedigree claimed she possessed exceptional talents. They turned out to be of a very minor nature, suitable for parlor tricks but little else.

"However, she could perform certain other functions, so I didn't feel the money wholly wasted. The only drawback was the birth of that infant, resulting from my failure to report on time for a standard debiojection. I didn't think the delay would be significant." He shrugged. "But I was wrong. The mother pleased me, so I permitted her to have the child. . . . I tend to be hard on my property, however. The mother did not live long thereafter. At times I feel the child has inherited her mother's minuscule talents, but every attempt to prove so has met with failure."

"Yet despite this, you keep her," Flinx noted curiously. For a second Challis appeared almost confused, a sensation which passed rapidly.

"It is not so puzzling, really. Considering the manner of the mother's death, of which the child is unaware, I feel some small sense of responsibility for her. While I have no particular love for infants, she obeys with an alacrity her older counterparts could emulate." He grinned broadly and Flinx had the impression of a naked white skull filled with broken icicles.

"She's old enough to know that if she doesn't, I'll simply sell her." Challis leaned forward, wheezing with the effort of folding his chest over his protruding belly. "However, you were not brought here to discuss the details of my domestic life."

"Then why was I brought here? I heard something about a jewel. I know a little about good stones, but I'm certainly no expert."

"A jewel, yes." Challis declined further oral explanation; instead, he manipulated several switches concealed by the far overhang of the table between them. The lights dimmed and Challis' pair of ominous attendants disappeared, though Flinx could sense their alert presence nearby. They were between him and the only clearly defined door.

Flinx's attention was quickly diverted by a soft humming. As the top of the table slid to one side, he could see the construction involved. The table was a thick safe. Something rose from the central hollow, a sculpture of glowing components encircled by a spiderweb of thin wiring. At the sculpture's center was a transparent globe of glassalloy. It contained something that looked like a clear natural crystal about the size of a man's head. It glowed with a strange inner light. At first glance it resembled quartz, but longer inspection showed that here was a most unique silicate.

The center of the crystal was hollow and irregular in outline. It was filled with maroon and green particles which drifted with dreamy slowness in a clear viscous fluid. The particles were fine as dust motes. In places they nearly reached to the edges of the crystal walls, though they tended to remain compacted near its middle. Occasionally the velvety motes would jerk and dart about sharply, as if prodded by some unseen force. Flinx stared into its shifting depths as if mesmerized. . . .

On Earth lived a wealthy man named Endrickson, who recently seemed to be walking about in a daze. His family was fond of him and he was well liked by his friends. He also held the grudging admiration of his competitors. Endrickson, though he looked anything but sharp at the moment, was one of those peculiar geniuses who possesses no creative ability of his own, but who instead exhibits the rare power to marshal and direct the talents of those more gifted than himself.

At 5:30 on the evening of the 25th of Fifth Month, Endrickson moved more slowly than usual through the heavily guarded corridors of The Plant. The Plant had no name—a precaution insisted on by nervous men whose occupation it was to worry about such things—and was built into the western slope of the Andes.

As he passed the men and women and insectoid thranx who labored in The Plant, Endrickson nodded his greetings and was always gratified with respectful replies. They were all moving in the opposite direction, since the workday had ended for them. They were on their way—these many, many-talented beings—to their homes in Santiago and Lima and New Delhi and New York, as well as to the Terran thranx colonies in the Amazon basin.

One who was not yet off duty came stiffly to attention as Endrickson turned a corner in a last, shielded passageway. On seeing that the visitor was not his immediate superior—a gentleman who wore irritation, like his underwear, outside his trousers—the well-armed guard relaxed. Endrickson, he knew, was everyone's friend.

"Hello . . . Davis," the boss said slowly.

The man saluted, then studied him intently, disturbed at his appearance.

"Good evening, sir. Are you sure you're all right?"

"Yes, thank you, Davis," Endrickson replied. "I had a last-minute thought . . . won't be long." He seemed to be staring at something irregular and shiny that he held cupped in one palm. "Do you want to see my identity card?"

The guard smiled, processed the necessary slip of treated plastic, and admitted Endrickson to the chamber beyond which contained the shop, a vast cavern made even vaster by precision engineering and necessity. This was the heart of The Plant.

Moving with assurance, Endrickson walked down the ramp to the sealed floor of the enlarged cavern, passing enormous machines, long benches, and great constructs of metal and other materials. The workshop was deserted now. It would remain so until the early-morning shift came on five hours later.

One-third of the way across the floor he halted before an imposing door of dun-colored metal, the only break in a solid wall of the same material that closed off a spacious section of the cavern. Using his free hand while still staring at the thing in his other hand, he pulled out a small ring that held several metal cylinders. He selected a cylinder, pressed his thumb into the recessed area at one end of it, then inserted the other into a small hole in the door and shoved forward. A complex series of radiations was produced and absorbed by the doorway mechanism. These passed judgment on both the cylinder and the person holding it.

Satisfied that the cylinder was coded properly and that its owner was of a stable frame of mind, the door sang soft acquiescence and shrank into the floor. Endrickson passed through and the door noted his passage, then rose to close the gap behind him.

A not quite finished device loomed ahead, nearly filling this part of the cavern. It was surrounded by an attending army of instruments: monitoring devices, tools in repose, checkout panels and endless crates of assorted components.

Endrickson ignored this familiar collage as he headed purposefully for a single black panel. He thoughtfully eyed the switches and controls thereon, then used another of his ring cylinders to bring the board to life. Lights came on obediently and gauges registered for his inspection.

The vast bulk of the unfinished KK-drive starship engine loomed above him. Final completion would and could take place only in free space, since the activated posigravity field of the drive interacting with a planet's gravitational field would produce a series of quakes and tectonic adjustments of cataclysmic proportions.

But that fact didn't concern Endrickson just now. A far more intriguing *thought had overwhelmed him. Was the drive unit complete enough to function? he wondered. Why not observe the interesting possibilities firsthand?*

He glanced at the beauty in his palm, then used a second cylinder to unlock a tightly sealed box at one end of the black board. Beneath the box were several switches, all enameled a bright crimson. Endrickson heard a klaxon yell shrilly somewhere, but he ignored the alarm as he pressed switches in proper order. His anticipation was enormous. With the fluid-state switches activated, instructions began flowing through the glass-plastic-metal monolith. Far off on the other side of the locked door, Endrickson could hear people shouting, running. Meanwhile the drive's thermonuclear spark was activated and Endrickson saw full engagement register on the appropriate monitors.

He nodded with satisfaction. Final relays interlocked, communicated with the computermind built into the engine. For a brief second the Kurita-Kita field was brought into existence. Momentarily the thought flashed through Endrickson's mind that this was something that should never be done except in the deep reaches of free space.

But his last thoughts were reserved for the exquisite loveliness and strange words locked within the object he held in his hand. . . .

Had the unit been finished there might have been a major disaster. But it was not complete, and so the field collapsed quickly, unable to sustain itself and to expand to its full, propulsive diameter.

So, although windows were shattered and a few older buildings toppled and the Church of Santa Avila de Seville's ancient steeple cracked six hundred kilometers away in downtown Valparaiso, only a few things in the immediate vicinity showed any significant alterations.

However, Endrickson, The Plant, and the nearby technologic community of Santa Rosa de Cristóbal (pop. 3,200) vanished. The 13,352-meter-high mountain at whose base the town had risen and in whose bowels The Plant had been carved was replaced by a 1,200-meter-deep crater lined with molten glass.

But since logic insisted the event could have been nothing other than an accident, it was so ruled by the experts called upon to produce an explanation—experts who did not have access to the same beauty which had so totally bedazzled the now-vaporized Endrickson. . . .

Flinx blinked, awakening from the Janus jewel's tantalizing loveliness. It continued to pulse with its steady, natural yellow luminescence.

"Did you ever see one before?" Challis inquired.

"No. I've heard of them, though. I know enough to recognize one."

Challis must have touched another concealed switch because a low-intensity light sprang to life at the table's edge. Fumbling with a drawer built into the table, the merchant then produced a small boxy affair which resembled an abstract carving of a bird in flight, its wings on the downbeat. It was designed to fit on a human head. A few exposed wires and modules broke the device's otherwise smooth lines.

"Do you know what this is?" the merchant asked.

Flinx confessed he did not.

"It's the operator's headset," Challis explained slowly, placing it over his stringy hair. "The headset and the machinery encapsulated in that table transcribe the thoughts of the human mind and convey them to the jewel. The jewel has a certain property."

Challis intoned "property" with the sort of spiritual reverence most men would reserve for describing their gods or mistresses.

The merchant ceased fumbling with unseen controls and with the headset. He folded his hands before his squeezed out paunch and stared at the crystal. "I'm concentrating on something now," he told his absorbed listener softly. "It takes a little training, though some can do without it."

As Flinx watched raptly, the particles in the jewel's center began to rearrange themselves. Their motion was no longer random, and it was clear that Challis' thoughts were directing the realignment. Here was something about which rumor abounded, but which few except the very rich and privileged had actually seen.

"The larger the crystal," Challis continued, obviously straining to produce some as yet unknown result, "the more colors present in the colloid and the more valuable the stone. A single color is the general rule. This stone contains two and is one of the largest and finest in existence, though even small stones are rare.

"There are stones with impurities present which create three- and four-color displays, and one stone of five-color content is known. You would not believe who owns it, or what is done with it."

Flinx watched as the colors within the crystal's center began to assume semisolid shape and form at Challis' direction. "No one," the merchant continued, "has been able to synthesize the oleaginous liquid in which the colored particulate matter drifts suspended. Once a crystal is broken, it is impossible to repair. Nor can the colloid be transferred in whole or in part to a new container. A break in the intricate crystal-liquid formation destroys the stone's individual piezoelectric potential. Fortunately the crystal is as hard as corundum, though nowhere near as strong as artificials like duralloy."

Though the outlines shifted and trembled constantly, never quite firmly fixed, they took on the recognizable shapes of several persons. One appeared to be an exaggeratedly Junoesque woman. Of the others, one was a humanoid male and the third something wholly alien. A two-sided chamber rose around them and was filled with strange objects that never held their form for more than a few seconds. Although their consistency fluctuated, the impression they conveyed did not. Flinx saw quite enough to turn his stomach before everything within the crystal dissolved once again to a cloud of glowing dust.

Looking up and across from the crystal he observed that the merchant had removed the headpiece and was wiping the perspiration from his high forehead with a perfumed cloth. Illuminated by the subdued light concealed in the table edge below, his face became that of an unscrupulous imp.

"Easy to begin," he murmured with exhaustion, "but a devilishly difficult reaction to sustain. When your attention moves from one figure, the others begin to collapse. And when the play involves complex actions performed by several such creations, it is nigh impossible, especially when one tends to become so . . . involved with the action."

"What's all this got to do with me?" Flinx broke in. Although the question was directed at Challis, Flinx's attention was riveted on those two half-sensed figures guarding the exit. Neither Nolly nor Nanger had stirred, but that didn't mean they had relaxed their watch, either. And the door they guarded was hardly likely to be unlocked. Flinx could see several openings in the floor-to-ceiling glass-alloy wall which overlooked the city, but he knew it was a sheer drop of at least fifty meters to the private street below.

"You see," Challis told him, "while I'm not ashamed to admit that I've inherited a most successful family business in the Challis Company, neither do I count myself a dilettante. I have improved the company through the addition of people with many diverse talents." He gestured toward the door. "Nolly-dear and Nanger there are two such examples. I'm hoping that you, dear boy, will be yet another."

"I'm still not sure I understand," Flinx said slowly, stalling.

"That can be easily rectified." Challis steepled his fingers. "To hold the suspended particles of the Janus jewels, to manipulate the particulate clay, requires a special kind of mind. Though my mental scenarios are complex, to enjoy them fully I require a surrogate mind. *Yours!* I shall instruct you in what is desired and you will execute my designs within the jewel."

Flinx thought back to what he had glimpsed a few moments ago in the incomplete playlet, to what Challis had wrought within the tiny god-world of the jewel. In many ways he was mature far beyond his seventeen years, and he had seen a great many things in his time. Though some of them would have sickened the stomach of an experienced soldier, most of them had been harmless perversions. But beneath all the superficial cordiality and the polite requests for cooperation that Challis had expressed, there bubbled a deep lake of untreated sewage, and Flinx was not about to serve as the merchant's pilot across it.

Surviving a childhood in the marketplace of Drallar had made Flinx something of a realist. So he did not reel at the merchant's proposal and say what was on his mind: "You revolt and nauseate me, Conda Challis, and I refuse to have anything to do with you or your sick private fantasies." Instead he said: "I don't know where you got the idea that I could be of such help to you."

"You cannot deny your own history," Challis sniggered. "I have acquired a small but interesting file on you. Most notably, your peculiar talents figured strongly in assisting a competitor of mine named Maxim Malaika. Prior to that incident and subsequent to it you have been observed demonstrating abnormal mental abilities through the medium of cheap sideshow tricks for the receipt of a few credits from passersby. I can offer you considerably more for the use of your talents. Deny that if you can."

"Okay, so I can work a few gimmicks and fool a few tourists," Flinx conceded, while studying the thin silvery bracelets linking his wrists and trying to find a hidden catch. "But what you call my 'talents' are erratic, undisciplined, and beyond my control much of the time. I don't know when they come or why they go."

Challis was nodding in a way Flinx didn't like. "Naturally. I understand. All talents—artistic, athletic, whatever kind—require training and discipline to develop them fully. I intend to help you in mastering yours. By way of example . . ." Challis took out something that looked like an ancient pocket watch but wasn't, pressed a tiny button. Instantly the breath fled from Flinx's lungs, and he arced forward. His hands tightened into fists as he shuddered, and he felt as if someone had taken a file to the bones in his wrists. The pain passed suddenly and he was able to lean limply backward, gasping, trembling. When he found he could open his eyes again, he saw that Challis was staring into them, expectantly interested. His stare was identical to the one a chemist would lavish on a laboratory animal just injected with a possibly fatal substance.

"That . . . wasn't necessary," Flinx managed to whisper.

"Possibly not," a callous Challis agreed, "but it was instructive. I've seen your eyes roving while you've talked. Really, you can't get out of here, you know. Even should you somehow manage to reach the central shaft beyond Nolly and Nanger, there are others waiting." The merchant paused, then asked abruptly, "Now, is what I wish truly so abhorrent to you? You'll be well rewarded. I offer you a secure existence in my company. In return you may relax as you like. You'll be called on only to help operate the jewel."

"It's the ethics of the matter that trouble me, not the salary," Flinx insisted.

"Oh, ethics." Challis was amused, and he didn't try to hide it. "Surely you can overcome that. The alternative is much less subjective." He was tapping two fingers idly on the face of the pseudo-watch.

While pretending to enjoy it all, Flinx was thinking. His wrists were still throbbing, and the ache penetrated all the way to his shoulders. He could stand that pain again, but not often. And anything more intense would surely knock him out. His vision still had an alarming tendency to lose focus.

Yet . . . he *couldn't* do what Challis wanted. Those images—his stomach churned as he remembered—to participate in such obscenities . . . No! Flinx was considering what to say, anything to forestall the pain again, when something dry and slick pressed against his cheek. It was followed by the feathery caress of something unseen but familiar at the back of his neck.

Challis obviously saw nothing in the darkness, since when he spoke again his voice was as controlled as before. His fingers continued to play lazily over the ovoid control box. "Come, dear boy, is there really need to prolong this further? I'm sure you gain less pleasure from it than do I." A finger stopped tapping, edged toward the button.

"HEY!"

The shout came from the vicinity of the door and was followed by muffled curses and dimly perceived movement. Challis' two guards were dancing crazily about, waving and swatting at something unseen.

Challis' voice turned vicious, angry for the first time. "What's the matter with you idiots?"

Nanger replied nervously, "There's something in here with us."

"You are both out of your small minds. We are eight floors from the surface and carefully screened against mechanical intruders. Nothing could possibly—"

Nanger interrupted the merchant's assurance with a scream the likes of which few men ever encounter. Flinx was half expecting it. Even so, the sound sent a chill down his spine. What it did to Nolly, or to Challis, who was suddenly scrambling over the back of the chair and fumbling at his belt, could only be imagined.

Flinx heard a crash, followed by a collision with something heavy and out of control. It was Nanger. The half-face had both hands clamped tight over his eyes and was staggering wildly in all directions.

"The jewel . . . watch the jewel!" a panicky Challis howled. Moving on hands and knees with surprising rapidity, he reached the edge of the table and hit a switch. Instantly the light went out. In the faint illumination from the wall window Flinx could see the merchant disconnect the top of the apparatus, the globe containing the crystal itself, and cradle it protectively in his hands as he removed it.

Suddenly there was another source of light in the room, in the form of sharp intermittent green flares from a needler. Nolly had the weapon out and was sparring desperately with an adversary that swooped and dove at him.

Then something began to buzz for attention within the table, and Challis lifted a receiver and listened. Flinx listened, too, but could hear nothing. Whatever was being said elicited some furious responses from the merchant, whose easygoing manner had by now vanished completely. He mumbled something into the pickup, then let it snap back into the table. The look he threw Flinx in the near blackness was a mixture of fury and curiosity. "I bid you adieu, dear boy. I hope we have the opportunity to meet again. I thought you merely a beggar with talents too big for his head. Apparently you may be something more. I'm sorry you elected not to cooperate. Your maternal line hinted that you might," Challis sneered. "I never repeat mistakes. Be warned." Still scrambling on hands and knees, he made his way to the hidden door. As it opened, Flinx caught a glimpse of a small golden figure standing there.

"Listening again, brat-child?" Challis muttered as he rose to his feet. He slapped the girl, grabbing her by one arm. She started to cry and looked away from Challis as the door cycled shut.

As Flinx turned his attention back to the other door, his mind was already awhirl at an offhand comment of the merchant's. But before he could consider all the implications of the remark, Flinx was hit with a tsunami of maniacal mental energy that nearly knocked him from the couch. It was forceful beyond imagining, powerful past anything he had ever felt from a human mind before. It held screaming images of Conda Challis coming slowly apart, like a toy doll. These visions were mixed haphazardly with other pictures, and several views of Flinx himself drifted among them.

He winced under that cyclonic wail. Some of the fleeting images were far worse than anything Challis had tried to create within the jewel. The merchant's mind may have been one of utter depravity, but the brain behind this mental storm did not stop with anything that petty.

Flinx stared back at the closing door, getting his last view of blue eyes set in an angelic face. In that unformed body, he knew, dwelt a tormented child. Yet even that revelation did not spark the same wild excitement in him that Challis' last casual statement had. "Your maternal line," the merchant had said.

Flinx knew more about the universe than he did about his real parents. If Challis knew even a rumor of Flinx's ancestry . . . the merchant was going to get his wish for another meeting.

2

The door to the tower's central shaft opened as the only other occupant of the room sought escape. Instead of an empty elevator, he found himself confronted by a figure of gargantuan proportions that lifted him squealing from the floor and removed the needler. The new arrival quickly rendered the weapon harmless by crumpling it in a fist that had the force of a mechanical press. Nolly's fingers, which happened to be wrapped around the needler, suffered a similar fate, and a single shriek of pain preceded unconsciousness.

Small Symm ducked to clear the top of the portal, dropping the limp human shape to one side. Simultaneously a long lean shape settled easily about Flinx's shoulders, and a single damp point flickered familiarly at his ear. Reaching back, Flinx scratched under the minidrag's jaw and felt the long muscular form relax. "Thanks, Pip."

Rising from the chair, he moved around the table-safe and played with the controls on the other side. Before very long he succeeded in lighting the entire room.

Where Nanger had crashed and stumbled, the expensive furnishings lay broken and twisted. His body, already growing stiff with venom-inspired death, lay crumpled across one bent chair. The unmoving form of his companion was slumped to one side of the doorway. A mangled hand oozed blood.

"I was wondering," Flinx informed Symm, "when you'd get here."

"It was difficult," the bartender apologized, his voice echoing up from that bottomless pit of a chest. "Your pet was impatient, disappearing and then reappearing when I fell behind. How did he know how to find you?"

Flinx affectionately eyed the now somnolent scaly head. "He smelled my fear. Life-water knows I was broadcasting it loud enough." He held out manacled wrists. "Can you do something about these? I have to go after Challis."

Symm glanced at the cuffs, a look of mild surprise on his face. "I never thought revenge was part of your makeup, Flinx."

Reaching down with a massive thumb and forefinger, Symm carefully pinched one of the narrow confining bands. A moment's pressure caused the metal to snap with an explosive *pop.* Repeating the action freed Flinx's other hand.

Looking at his right wrist as he rubbed it with his left hand, Flinx could detect no mark—nothing to indicate the intense pain that the device had inflicted.

He debated how to respond to his friend's accusation. How could he hope to explain the importance of Challis' remark to this good-natured hulk? "I think Challis may know something of my real parents. I can't simply forget about it."

The unaccustomed bitterness of Symm's answer startled him. "What are they to you? What have they done for you? They have caused you to be treated like chattel, like a piece of property. If not for the intervention of Mother Mastiff you'd be a personal slave now, perhaps to something like Challis. Your real parents—you owe them nothing, least of all the satisfaction of showing them you've survived!"

"I don't know the circumstances of my abandonment, Symm," Flinx finally countered. "I have to find out. I *have* to."

The bartender, an orphan himself, shrugged massively. "You're an idealistic misfit, Flinx."

"And you're an even bigger one," the boy shot back, "which is why you're going to help me."

Symm muttered something unintelligible, which might have been a curse. Then again, it might not. "Where did he get out?"

Flinx indicated the hidden doorway, and Symm walked over to the spot and leaned against the metal panel experimentally. The hinging collapsed inward with surprising ease. Beyond, they discovered a short corridor, which led to a small private lift that conveyed them rapidly to the base of the luxurious tower.

"How did you get in, anyway?" Flinx asked his friend.

Symm twitched. "I told the security people I met that I had an appointments pass, the usual procedure in an inurb like this."

"Didn't anyone demand to see it?"

Symm didn't crack a smile. "Would you? Only one guard did, and I think he'll be all right if he gets proper care. Careful now," the giant warned as the lift came to a stop. Crouching to one side, he sprang out as soon as the door slid open sufficiently to let him pass. But there was no ambush awaiting them. Instead, they found themselves in a groundcar garage, which showed ample sign of having been recently vacated.

"Keep your monumental ears open," Flinx advised quietly. "See if you can find out where Challis has fled. I'm going to work my own sources. . . ."

When they left through the open doorway of the garage, no one challenged their departure, though hidden eyes observed it. But those behind the eyes were grateful to see the pair go.

"You're sure they're not still here?" Symm wondered aloud. "Someone could have taken the car as a diversion."

Flinx replied with the kind of unnerving assurance Symm didn't pretend to understand, but had come to accept. "No, they're no longer in this vicinity."

The pair parted outside the last encircling wall of the inurb. There was no formality, no shaking of hands—nothing of the sort was required between these two.

"If you learn anything get in touch with me at Mother Mastiff's shop," Flinx instructed the giant. "Whatever happens, I'll let you know my plans."

As he made his way back through the market's concentric circles, he clutched his cloak tightly about him. The last drops of the morning rain were falling. In the distance an always hopeful sun showed signs of emerging from the low, water-heavy clouds.

Plenty of activity swirled about him. At this commercial hub of the Commonwealth, business operated round the clock.

Flinx knew a great many inhabitants of this world-within-a-world on sight. Some were wealthy and great, some poor and great. A few were not human and more were less human than others though all claimed membership in the same race.

Passing the stall of the sweets vendor Kiki, he kept his attention resolutely ahead. It was too early and his stomach was too empty for candy. Besides, his innards still rocked slightly from the after-effects of Challis' seemingly harmless jewelry. So, at Chairman Nils he bought a small loaf of bran bread coated with nut butter.

Nils was a fortyish food vendor with an authoritative manner. Everyone called him the Chairman. He ruled his corner of the marketplace with the air of a dictator, never suspecting that he held this power because his fellow sellers and hawkers found it amusing to humor his gentle madness. There were never any delusions in his baked goods, however. Flinx took a ferocious bite out of the triangular loaf, enjoying the occasional crunch of chopped nuts woven into the brown butter.

A glance at the sky still hinted at the possibility of the sun breaking through, a rare occurrence in usually cloud-shrouded Drallar.

His snack finished, Flinx began moving through a section filled with handsome, permanent shopfronts—a section that was considerably different from the region of makeshift shacks and stores in which he had been raised. When he'd first proposed shifting the ancient stall from the noisome depths of the marketplace Mother Mastiff had protested vociferously. "I wouldn't know how to act," she had argued. "What do I know about treating with fancy customers and rich folks?"

"Believe me, Mother"—though they both knew she wasn't his real mother, she acted as one to half the homeless in Drallar— "they're the same as your old customers, only now the idiots will come with bigger bankrolls. Besides, what else would I do with all the money Malaika pressed on me?"

Eventually he had been forced to purchase the shop and thus present her with a *fait accompli*. She railed at him for hours when he told her—until she saw the place. Though she continued muttering dire imprecations about everything he showed her—the high-class inventory, the fancy living quarters upstairs, the automatic cooking devices—her resistance collapsed with unsurprising speed.

But there were two things she still refused to do. One was to change her handmade, homemade attire—as esoteric a collage of beads, bells, and cloth as could be imagined. The other was to use the small elevator that ran between the shop proper and the living quarters above. "The day I can't climb a single flight of stairs," she remonstrated, "is the day you can have me embalmed, stuffed, and put in the window at a curio sale." To demonstrate her determination, she proceeded at once to walk the short stairway on all fours.

No one knew how old Mother Mastiff was and she wasn't telling. Nor would she consent to submit to the extensive cosmetic surgeries Flinx could now afford, or to utilize any other artificial age-reduction device. "I've spent too long and too much effort preparin' for the role of an aged crone, and I'm not about to give up on it now," she told him. "Besides, the more pitiful and decrepit I look, the more polite and sympathetic the suck—the customers are."

Not surprisingly, the shop prospered. For one thing, many of the better craftsmen in Drallar had come from equally humble origins, and they enjoyed selling their better products to her.

As Flinx rounded the corner, he saw she was waiting for him at the rear entrance. "Out all night again. I don't suppose you've been anywhere as healthy as the Pink Palace or Sinnyville. D'you want your throat cut before you make eighteen?" she admonished, wagging a warning finger.

"Not much chance of that, Mother." He brushed past her, but—not to be put off—she followed him into the little storeroom behind the shopfront.

"And that flyin' gargoyle of yours won't save you every time, y' know. Not in a city like this, where everyone has a handshake for you with one palm and a knife for your back in the other. Keep walkin' about at the depths of the night like this, boy, and one day they'll be bringin' you back t' me pale and empty of juice. And I warn you," she continued, her voice rising, "it's a cheap funeral you'll be gettin', because I'm not workin' my fingers to the quick to pay for a fancy send-off for a fool!"

A sharp buzz interrupted the tirade. "So I'll tell you for the last time, boy . . ."

"Didn't you hear the door, Mother?" He grinned. "First customer of the morn."

She peered through the beads in the doorway. "Huh. Tourists, by the look of 'em. You should see the tanzanite on the woman's ring." She hesitated, torn between the need to satisfy affection and avarice simultaneously. "But what's a couple of customers when . . ." another hesitation, "still, that's twelve carats at least in the one stone. Their clothes mark 'em as Terrans maybe, too." She finally threw up her hands in confusion and disgust. "It's my punishment. You're a visitation for the sins of my youth. Get out of my sight, boy. Upstairs and wash yourself, and mind the disinfectant. You smell of the gutter. Dry yourself well, mind . . . you're not too big or old for me to blush your bottom." She slipped through the screen and a radical metamorphosis took place.

"Ah sir, madam," an oily voice cooed soothingly, the voice of everyone's favorite grandmama, "you honor my small shop. I would have been out sooner but I was tending to my poor grandson who is desperately ill and in need of much expensive treatment. The doctors fear that unless the operation is performed soon, he will lose the power of sight, and—"

Her slick spiel was cut off as the elevator door slid shut behind Flinx. Unlike Mother Mastiff, he had no compunction about using modern conveniences—certainly not now, as tired as he was from the experiences of the night before. As he stepped into the upstairs quarters he did wonder how such disparate tones could issue from the same wrinkled throat.

Later, over the evening meal (prepared by him, since Mother

Mastiff had been occupied with customers all day), he began to explain what had happened. For a change, she neither harangued nor chastised him, merely listened politely until he had finished.

"So you're bound to go after him then, boy," she finally said.

"I have to, Mother."

"Why?"

He looked away. "I'd rather not say."

"All right." She mopped up the last of her gravy with a piece of bread. "I've heard much of the man Challis—plenty of rumors about his tastes in certain matters and none of them good. There's less known about his businesses, though word is the Challis Company has prospered since he became the head." She grunted noisily and wiped at her mouth with a corner of her multilayered skirt.

"You sure you got to do this, boy? You've only been off-planet once before, y'know."

"I think I can handle myself, Mother."

"Daresay, daresay," she replied disparagingly. "Though by all the odds you ought to have been dead a dozen times before your fifteenth birthday, and I don't suppose that grinnin' devil could have been responsible for savin' you every time."

She favored a small artificial tree with a poisonous stare. Pip was coiled comfortably around one of its branches. The minidrag did not look up. The relationship between him and Mother Mastiff had always been one of uneasy truce.

"Before you take off, let me make a call," she finished.

While Flinx finished his dessert and fought to pry the last bits of thick gelatin from his back teeth, he listened to her mutter into the pickup of a small communicator at the far end of the room. The machine gave her a mobility she hadn't possessed for decades. It was one of the few conveniences the shop provided that she'd use. It also made her the terror of every city official in any way responsible for the daily operation of the marketplace.

She was back at tableside soon. "Your friend Challis left on the freightliner *Auriga* this morning with his daughter and a covey of servants." Her expression contorted. "From what I was told, he left in a real hurry. You and that great imbecile Symm must have thrown quite a scare into him, but then the giant's enough by himself to frighten the polish off a mirror."

Flinx did not return her inquiring gaze. Instead he played with one edge of the tablecloth. "What's the *Auriga*'s destination?"

"Hivehom," she told him. "The Challis Company has a lot of investments on the Mediterranea Plateau. I expect that's what he'll head for once he sets down."

"I'd better get ready." Flinx rose and started toward his room.

A strong, crinkled hand caught one of his wrists, and a face like a rift valley stared searchingly into his. "Don't do this, boy," she begged, her voice low.

He shook his head. "No choice, Mother. I can't tell you what calls, but call it does. I have to go."

The pressure did not ease on his wrist. "I don't know what dealings you have with this bad man, but I can't believe it's this serious." Flinx said nothing and she finally released him. "If it's in you to go, go then." She looked away. "I don't know how your mind works, boy. Never did, never. But I do know that when you get somethin' like this into it, only you can put it out. Go then, and my blessin's with you. Even," she concluded tightly, "if you won't tell me the why of it."

Bending over, he kissed the gray bun curled at the back of the old woman's head. "Blessings on you, too, Mother," he said as she squirmed violently at the gesture.

It didn't take him long to pack the few possessions he wanted to bring with him. They didn't seem to mean much to him now. As he started to leave the room, he saw that the woman was still sitting alone at the table, a suddenly tiny and frail figure. How could he tell her he had to risk the life she'd coddled in a vain search for the people who had done nothing beyond giving him birth . . . ?

When he arrived at Drallar Port later that day, he found he was only physically tired. His mind was sharp and alert. Over the years he had gradually discovered that he required less and less sleep. Some days he could get by with as little as half an hour. His mind rested when it wasn't being pushed, which was frequently.

He no longer had to worry about how he would travel, for there were sufficient funds registered on his cardmeter to sustain him for some time yet. Malaika had been generous. Not all the determining factors were financial, however. A glance at those waiting to board the first-class section of the shuttlecraft engendered an acute sense of unease in him, so he registered for standard fare.

Traveling so would be more enlightening anyway, for his first journey on a commercial spacecraft and his second time off Moth. As he followed the line into the shuttle, passing under the mildly aristocratic eye of the steward, he was shocked to discover that his about-to-be-realized childhood dream of traveling off-planet in one of the great KK-drive freightliners no longer held any thrill for him. It worried him as he strapped into his couch.

Mother Mastiff could have explained it to him if she were there. It was called growing up.

Though tolerable, the shuttle journey was rougher than his single previous experience with the little surface-to-orbit vessels. Naturally, he told himself, the pokier commercial craft would be nowhere near as luxurious as the shuttle carried by Malaika's yacht, the *Gloryhole*. This one was designed solely to get as many beings and as much cargo as possible from the ground into free fall as economically as possible. There they could be transferred—passengers and cargo alike, with sometimes equivalent handling—into the great globular bulk of the deepspace ship.

Following that transfer Flinx found himself assigned to a small, compactly designed cabin. He barely took the time to inspect it, and he had little to unpack. During the week-long journey he would spend the majority of travel time in the ship's several lounges, meeting fellow travelers—and learning.

The shift from sublight to KK-drive superlight velocity was hardly a surprise. He had already experienced it several times on Malaika's ship.

One part of the liner he especially enjoyed. From a forward observation lounge he could look ahead and see the immense length of the ship's connecting corridor rods stretching outward like a broad narrowing highway to join the back of the colossal curving dish of the KK field projector. It blotted out the stars ahead.

Somewhere in front of that enormous dish, he knew, the drive unit was projecting the gravity well of a small sun. It pulled the ship steadily and, in turn, the drive projector which then projected the field that much further ahead—and so on. Flinx wondered still at the explanation of it and decided that all great inventions were essentially simple.

He was amusing himself in the ship's game lounge on the third day when a neatly painted thranx in the stark brown, yellow, and green of commerce took the couch opposite. Less than a meter high at the b-thorax, he was small for a male. Both sets of wing cases still gleamed on his back, indicating that the traveler was as yet unmated. Brilliant, faceted eyes regarded Flinx through multiple gemlike lenses. The wonderful natural perfume odor of his kind drifted across the game table.

The creature glanced down at the glowing board, then its valentine-shaped head cocked curiously at the young human operating it.

"You play *hibush-hunt*? Most humans find it too complicated. You usually prefer two-dimensional games." The insect's symbospeech was precise and textbook-flat, the variety any good businessthranx would speak.

"I've heard a little about it and I've watched it played," Flinx told his visitor modestly. "I really don't know how to play myself."

Mandibles clacked in a gesture of interest and understanding, since the insect's inflexible chitonous face allowed for nothing as rubbery as a smile. A slight nod of the head was more easily imitated.

Question-response having served for a courteous greeting, the thranx settled himself more firmly on the couch, trulegs doubled up beneath the abdomen, foothands locked to support the thorax and b-thorax, and truhands moving with delicate precision over the board, adjusting the game plan. "My name is Bisondenbit," he declared.

"I'm called Flinx."

"One calling?" The thranx performed an insectoid shrug. "Well, Flinx, if you'd like to learn, I have some small skill at the game. Which is to say I know the rules. I am not a very good player, so I'll probably make a good first opponent for you." Again the mandible clicking, accompanied this time by a whistling sound— thranx laughter.

Flinx smiled back. "I'd like to learn very much."

"Good, good . . . this is a standoffish group and I've been preening antennae till my nerves are beginning to twitch." The head bobbed. "Your biggest mistake," Bisondenbit began in businesslike fashion, "is that you're still neglecting the ability of your pieces to move above ground and downward, as well as through existing tunnels. You've got to keep your antennae to the board and seek to penetrate your opponent's movements."

The thranx touched a silvery figure within the three-dimensional transparent board. "Stay attuned now. This is a *Doan* fighter and can move only laterally and vertically, though it can never appear on the surface. This divisible piece here . . ."

Flinx got to know Bisondenbit fairly well during the remainder of the trip. The alien kept his actual business veiled in vague circumlocutions, but Flinx got the impression he was an antiques dealer. Perhaps there would be a chance to pick up some interesting curios for Mother Mastiff's shop.

Bisondenbit did display in full a trait which had helped endear his kind to humans: the ability to listen attentively no matter how boring the story being told. He seemed to find Flinx's judiciously censored story of his own life up to his present journey fascinating.

"Look," he told Flinx as they shared supper in one of the ship's dining lounges, "you've never been to Hivehom before and you're determined to look up this human what's-his-name—Challis? At least I can help you get oriented. You'll no doubt find him somewhere on the Mediterranea Plateau. That's where most of the human settlers live." The insect quivered. "Though why anyone would choose to set up housekeeping on a chilly tundra like that is beyond my understanding."

Flinx had to smile. The mean temperature on the Mediterranea Plateau, a level area several thousand meters above the steaming, humid swamplands of Hivehom, was a comfortable 22° C. The thranx preferred the high thirties, with humidity as near one hundred percent as possible.

The word colonization was never mentioned in connection with such settlements—on either world. There were several such human regions on Hivehom, of which the Mediterranea Plateau, with a population of nearly three million, was by far the largest. The thranx welcomed such exploitation of the inhospitable regions they had always shunned. Besides, there were some four million thranx living in the Amazon basin on Terra alone—which sort of evened things out.

Most of the large human-dominated concerns, Bisondenbit explained, made their headquarters on the southern edge of the Plateau, near the big shuttleport at Chitteranx. This Challis had no doubt located himself there, too.

"The human city there has a thranx name—Azerick," Bisondenbit went on, whistling softly. "That's High Thranx for 'frozen waste,' which in this case has a double meaning I won't go into, except to say that it's a good thing you humans have a sense of humor approximating our own. After we land, I'll be happy to take you up there myself, though I won't stay long. I'm not equipped for arctic travel. Furthermore, Azerick is not cheap." He hesitated politely. "You look pretty young for a human out traveling on his own. You have funds?"

"I can scrape by," Flinx admitted cautiously. Probably it was his innate distrust of others, though he had to admit that in the past few days Bisondenbit had been not only helpful but downright friendly.

They boarded the shuttle together. Flinx sat near a glassalloy port, where he would have a good view of the principal thranx world, one of the Commonwealth's dual capitals. The planet swung lazily below him as the shuttle separated from the freightliner and commenced its descent. Two large moons glowed whitely above the far horizon, one partly hidden by the planet. Wherever the cloud cover broke, Flinx could see hints of blue from Hivehom's small oceans, rich green from its thick jungles.

Suddenly he felt the force of gravity pressing him back in his seat as the shuttle dropped tail first through the clouds. . . .

3

Chitteranx was impressive. Though a small port for a world as populous and developed as Hivehom, it still dwarfed the shuttle-port of Drallar.

"The city is mostly underground, of course. All thranx cities are, though the surface is well utilized." The jeweled head shook in puzzlement. "Why you humans have always chosen to build up instead of down is something I'll never comprehend."

Flinx's attention was more engaged by the view through the transparent access corridor than by the standard sights of the shuttle terminal. Lush jungle practically overgrew the plastic walls. It was raining outside—steaming, rather. The heat in the terminal was oppressive, despite the fact that it was a compromise between the delightful weather outside—as Bisondenbit called it—and the arctic air atop the nearby plateau.

Rain Flinx had grown up with on Moth, but the humidity was something new and unpleasant. Humans could tolerate a hothouse climate, but not for long without protection, and never comfortably.

Bisondenbit, however, could only grumble about the chill inside the terminal. When Flinx remonstrated, he told him, "This is the principal human port of entry on Hivehom. If we'd landed near the equator, at *Daret* or *Ab-Neub,* you'd be wilting, Flinx." He looked around as they emerged from the terminal proper into a cluster of roofed-over commercial buildings.

"Before I have to accompany you up to the plateau, and struggle into a hotsuit, let me enjoy a rational climate for a while. What about a drink?"

"I'd really like to start looking for Challis as soon as—"

"The plateau shuttles run every ten chronits," Bisondenbit insisted. "Do come. Besides, you still haven't told me: What do you keep in that box?" A truhand gestured at the large square case Flinx lugged with his left hand.

"It must be something exotic and valuable, judging from the care with which you've handled it."

"It's exotic, I suppose," he admitted, "but not particularly valuable."

They found a small eating place just inside the climate-controlled cluster of buildings. Only a few humans were present, though it was crowded with thranx. Flinx was thoroughly enchanted with the thranx resting couches, the subdued lighting which made even midday appear dim, and the ornately carved, communal drinking cannisters suspended from the ceiling above each booth.

Bisondenbit selected an isolated table at the back of the room and made helpful, though unnecessary recommendations. Flinx had no trouble deciphering the menu, which was printed in four languages: High Thranx, Low Thranx, symbospeech and Terranglo.

Bisondenbit ordered after Flinx opted for one of the several thousand liqueurs which the thranx were masters at concocting.

"When do you want to go back to the terminal to pick up the rest of your luggage?" the insect asked casually, after their drinks arrived. He noted with approval that Flinx disdained a glass in favor of one of the weaving-spouted tankards used by the thranx themselves.

"This is it," Flinx told him, indicating his small shoulder bag and the single large perforated case. Bisondenbit didn't try to conceal his surprise.

"That's all you've brought all this way with you, without knowing how long it will take you to find this human, Challis?"

"I've always traveled light," was his companion's explanation. The drink was typically sweet, with a faint flavor of raisin. It went down warm and smooth. The trip, he decided, was beginning to catch up with him. He was more tired than he should be this early in the day. Obviously he wasn't quite the urbane interstellar traveler he pictured himself as.

"Besides, it shouldn't be hard to find Challis. Certainly he'll be staying at his local company headquarters." Flinx let another swallow of the thick, honeylike fluid slide down his throat, then frowned. Despite his age, he considered himself a good judge of intoxicants, but this new brew was apparently more potent than the menu description indicated. He found his vision blurring slightly.

Bisondenbit peered at him solicitously. "Are you all right? If you've never had Sookcha before, it can be a bit overwhelming. Packs quite a concussion?"

"Punch," Flinx corrected thickly.

"Yes, quite a punch. Don't worry . . . the feeling will pass quick enough."

But Flinx felt himself growing steadily groggier. "I think . . . if I could just get outside. A little fresh air . . ." He started to get up, but discovered his legs responded with indifference while his feet moved as if he were walking on an oiled treadmill. It was impossible to get any traction.

Abandoning the effort, he found that his muscular system was entering a state of anarchy. "That's funny," he murmured, "I can't seem to move."

"No need to be concerned," Bisondenbit assured him, leaning across the table and staring at him with an intensity that was new to Flinx. "I'll see that you're properly taken care of."

As all visual images faded, Flinx feared his strange, new acquaintance would do just that. . . .

Flinx awoke to the harmony of destruction, accompanied by curses uttered in several languages. Blinking—his eyelids felt as if they were lined with platinum—he fought unsuccessfully to move his arms and legs. Failing this, he settled for holding his eyes partially open. Dim light from an unseen source illuminated the little room in which he lay. Spartan furnishings of rough-hewn wood were backed by smooth walls of argent gunite. As his perceptions cleared he discovered that metal bands at his wrists and ankles secured him to a crude wooden platform that was neither bed nor table.

He lay quietly. For one thing, his stomach was performing gymnastics and it would be best to keep the surroundings subdued until the internal histrionics ceased. For another, the sensations and sounds surrounding him indicated it would be unwise to call attention to his new consciousness.

The sounds of destruction were being produced by the methodical dissection of his personal effects. Looking slowly to his right, he saw the shredded remains of his shoulder bag and clothing. These were being inspected by three humans and a single thranx. Recognizing the latter as his former games mentor and would-be friend, Bisondenbit, he damned his own naïveté.

Back in Drallar he would never have been so loquacious with a total stranger. But he had been three days isolated and friendless on board ship when the thranx had approached him with his offer of games instruction. Gratitude had shunted aside instinctive caution.

"No weapons, no poison, no beamer, needler—not even a threatening note," complained one of the men in fluent symbospeech.

"What's worse," one of his companions chipped in, "no money. Nothing but a lousy cardmeter." He held up the compact computer unit which registered and transferred credit in unforgeable fashion, and tossed it disgustedly onto a nearby table. It landed among the rest of Flinx's few possessions. Flinx noted that there was one remaining object they had not yet broken into.

"That's not my fault," Bisondenbit complained, glaring with eyes of shattered prism at the three tall humans. "I didn't promise to deliver any fringe benefits. If you don't think I've earned my fee I'll go straight to Challis himself."

One of the men looked resigned. Taking a double handful of small metal rectangles from one pocket, he handed them to Bisondenbit. The thranx counted them carefully.

The human who had paid him looked over at the restraining bonds, and Flinx closed his eyes just in time. "That's a lot of money. I don't know why Challis is so afraid—this is just a kid. But he thinks it's worth the fee you demanded. Don't understand it, though."

The man indicated the biggest of the three. "Charlie, here, could break him in two with one hand." Turning, he tapped the large sealed case. "What's in this?"

"I don't know," the thranx admitted. "He kept it in his cabin all the time."

The third man spoke up. His tone was vaguely contemptuous. "You can all stop worrying about it. I've been examining that container with appropriate instrumentation while the rest of you have been occupying yourselves with a harmless wardrobe." He gave the bag a shove. "There's no indication it contains anything mechanical or explosive. Readings indicated that it's full of shaped organics and organic analogs— probably the rest of his clothing." He sighed. "Might as well check it out. We're paid to be thorough." Taking a pair of thick metal clippers from a neat tool case, he snipped through the squat combination lock. That done, the top of the case opened easily. He peered inside, grunted. "Clothes, all right. Looks like another couple of suits and—" He started to remove the first set of clothing—then screamed and, stumbling backward, clawed at the left side of his face, which was suddenly bubbling like hot mud. A narrow, beltlike shape erupted from the open case.

Bisondenbit chattered something in High Thranx and vanished

out the single door. The one called Charlie fell backward across
Flinx's pinioned form, his beamer firing wildly at the ceiling as he
dug in awful silence at his own eyes. The leader of the little group
of humans was close on Bisondenbit's abdomen when something
hit him at the back of his neck. Howling, he fell back into the room
and started rolling across the floor.

Less than a minute had passed.

Something long and smooth slid onto Flinx's chest.

"That's enough, Pip," he said to his pet. But the minidrag was
beyond persuasion. His inspection over, he took to the air again
and began darting and striking at the man on the floor. Gaping
holes appeared in the supplicant's clothing and skin wherever the
venom struck. Eventually the man stopped rolling.

The first man who had been struck was already dead, while the
second lay moaning against a wall behind Flinx. Pieces of skin
hung loosely from his cheek and neck; and a flash of white showed
where Pip's extremely corrosive poison had exposed the bone.

Meanwhile the minidrag settled gently on Flinx's stomach, slid
upward caressingly. The long tongue darted out again and again to
touch lips and chin. "The right hand, Pip," Flinx instructed, "my
right hand." In the darkness the reptile eyed him questioningly.

Flinx snapped his fingers in a special way and now the minidrag
half crawled, half fluttered over to the hand in question, rested his
head in the open palm. A few scratches and then the hand closed
gently but firmly. The snake offered no resistance.

Adjusting his pet with some difficulty, Flinx aligned Pip's snout
with the place where the metal band was locked to the table. His
fingers moved, massaging various muscles behind the jaw. A few
droplets of poison oozed from the tapered tube which ran through
the minidrag's lower palate.

There was a sizzling sound.

Flinx waited until the noise died away, then pulled hard. A second pull and the rotted metal gave way. Transferring Pip, with
greater control now, he repeated the process on his other bindings,
the snake doing his bidding through each step.

As he was freeing his left leg, Flinx noticed a movement on his
right. So did Pip, and the minidrag took to the air again.

The single survivor shrieked as the dragon shape moved close.
"Get away, get away, don't let it near me!" he gibbered in total terror.

"Pip!" Flinx commanded. A hushed pause. The minidrag continued to hover nervously before the crouching man, its wings a

hummingbird blur, soulless, cold-blooded eyes staring into those of the bleeding human whose clavicle showed pale through dissolved clothing.

Flinx finally ripped clear of the last strap. Getting slowly to his feet, he made his way carefully to the other table. The clothes he'd been wearing were an unsalvageable mess. He began to slip into the second jumpsuit, in whose folds Pip had been so comfortably coiled.

"I'm sorry for your friends, but not too sorry," he murmured. Zipping up the suit, Flinx turned to the shocked creature on the floor. "Tell me the whole story and don't leave out any details. The more questions I have to ask, the more impatient Pip will get."

A stream of information poured from the man's lips. "Your thranx friend is a small-time criminal."

"Antique services," Flinx muttered. "Very funny. Go on."

"It struck him odd that a kid like you, traveling alone, would be so interested in looking up Conda Challis. On a hunch he beamed Challis' offices here and told them about you. Someone high up got upset as hell and told him to deliver you to us, to be checked out."

"Makes sense," Flinx agreed. "What was supposed to happen to me after I was—er—checked out?"

The man huddled into the corner farthest away from the fluttering minidrag, whispered, "Use your head—what do you think?"

"Challis claimed he was the thorough type," Flinx observed. "I could have been an innocent passenger—it wouldn't have mattered." Repacking his few intact belongings in the hand case, Flinx started for the door that Bisondenbit had exited through only moments before.

"What about me?" the man mumbled. "Are you going to kill me?"

Flinx turned in surprise, his eyes narrowing as he regarded the human wreck who had confidently pawed through his luggage just minutes before. "No. What for? Tell me where I can find Conda Challis. Then I'd advise you to get to a hospital."

"He's on the top floor of the executive pylon at the far end of the complex."

"What complex?" Flinx asked, puzzled.

"That's right—you still don't know where you are, do you?" Flinx shook his head. "This is the fourth sublevel of the Challis Hivehom Mining Components plant. The Challis family's very big in mining machinery.

"Go to the corridor outside the door, turn to your left, and keep on until you reach a row of lifts. They all go to the surface. From there anyone can direct you to the executive pylon—the plant grounds are hexagon-shaped and the pylon's at the northeast corner."

"Thanks," said Flinx. "You've been helpful."

"Not helpful, you poisonous little bastard," the unemployed cripple muttered painfully as soon as Flinx had departed, "just pragmatic." He began to crawl slowly toward the open door.

In the corridor, once assured that no one waited in ambush, Flinx snapped his fingers again. "Pip . . . rest now."

The minidrag hissed agreeably and fluttered down into the open case, burying itself quietly within the folded shreds of torn clothing. Flinx snapped the latch shut. At the first opportunity he would have to replace the ruined lock, or else chance some innocent bystander suffering the same fate as his three former captors.

No one challenged him as he continued on toward the lifts. The numbers alongside the doors were labeled 4-B, 3-B and so on to zero, where the count began again in normal fashion. Four levels above ground and four below, Flinx noted. Zero ought to take him to the surface, and that was the button he pressed when a car finally arrived.

The lift deposited him in an efficiently designed four-story glass antechamber. A steady stream of humans and thranx utilized the lifts around him. "Your pardon," a triad of thranx trilled, as they made their way purposefully into the lift he had just vacated.

Although every eye seemed focused on him, in reality no one was paying him the least attention. No reason they should, he thought, relaxing. Only one man and a few of his minions would be hunting him.

A large desk conveniently labeled *Information* was set just inside the transparent façade of the vaulted chamber. A single thranx sat behind it. Flinx strolled over, trying to give the impression that he knew exactly what he was about.

"Excuse me," he began, in fluent High Thranx, "can you tell me how to get to the executive pylon from here?"

The elderly, rather officious-looking insect turned to face him. He was painted black and yellow, Flinx noted, and was utterly devoid of the enamel chiton inlay the thranx were so fond of. A pure business type.

"Northeast quadrant," the thranx said sharply, implying that the asker should know better. "You go out the main door there," he continued, pointing with a truhand as a foothand supported his thorax on the table edge, "and turn left down H portal. The pylon is a full twelve floors with carport on top."

"Blessings of the Hive on you," Flinx said easily. The oldster eyed him sharply.

"Say, what do you want with . . . ?"

But Flinx had already been swallowed up by the bustling crowd. The officer hunted for him a moment longer, then gave up and went back to his job.

Flinx made rapid progress across the factory grounds. A friendly worker gave him ready directions the one time he found himself lost. When he finally spied the unmistakable shape of the executive pylon, he slowed, suddenly aware that from this point on he had no idea how to proceed.

Challis' reaction to his unexpected appearance was going to be something less than loving. And this time he, if not his underlings, would be prepared to deal with Pip. For all his lethal abilities, the minidrag was far from invulnerable.

Somehow, he was going to have to slip inside the tower and find out where Challis was. Even from here he could sense the powerful emanations of a smaller, darker presence. But he had no guarantee that he would find Mahnahmi and Challis together. Did the girl sense his presence as well? It was a sobering thought.

Deciding to move fast and purposefully, he strode boldly through the tower's main entrance. But this was no factory annex. An efficient-looking thranx with three inlaid chevrons on his b-thorax was there to intercept him—politely, of course.

"Swarm be with your business," the insect murmured. "You will state both it and your name, please."

Flinx was about to answer when a door on one side burst open. A squad of heavily armed thranx gushed out, the leader pointing and shouting: "That's the one—restrain him!"

Reacting swiftly, the officer who had confronted Flinx put a truhand on one arm. Flinx brought his leg up and kicked reluctantly. The armorlike chiton was practically invulnerable—except at the joints, where Flinx's foot struck. The joint cracked audibly and the officer let out an agonized chirp as Flinx broke for the rank of lifts directly ahead.

Jumping inside, he swung clear and hit the topmost switch, noticing that it was for the eleventh floor. A key was required to reach the twelfth.

Several beamers pierced the lift doors even as the car began its ascent. Fortunately they didn't strike any vital machinery and his ride wasn't slowed, though the three molten-edged holes bored in the door provided plenty of food for thought.

An angry pounding and banging inside the carrybag attracted his attention. Once the latch was popped a furious Pip rocketed out. After a rapid inspection of the lift's interior the minidrag settled nervously around Flinx's right shoulder. It coiled tightly there, muscles tense with excitement.

There was no point in keeping the reptile concealed any longer, since they clearly knew who he was. But who/what had given him away?

Mahnahmi—it had to be! He almost felt as if he could sense a girlish, mocking laughter. Her capacity for mischief remained an unknown quantity. It was possible that her mental talents exceeded his own, both in strength and lack of discipline. Of course, no one would believe that if he had the chance to tell of it. Mahnahmi had her role of goggle-eyed, innocent infant perfected.

The question, though, was whether her maliciousness was grounded in calculation or merely in a desire for undisciplined destruction. He sensed that she could change from hate to love, each equally intense, at a moment's thought. If only she would realize that he meant her no harm . . . then it came to him that she probably did.

He was a source of potential amusement to her, nothing more.

Some simple manipulations sufficed to jimmy the door mechanism. When the car passed the tenth floor he jumped clear, then turned to watch it continue past him. Frantically, he began to hunt around the room that appeared to be a combination of offices and living quarters, probably belonging to one of Challis' principal assistants. Or maybe the plant manager.

If there were no stairways he would be trapped here. He didn't think Challis' bodyguard was so stupid as to allow him to descend and escape.

At least these quarters were deserted. As he considered his situation, a violent explosion sounded above. Looking up, he saw shredded metal and plastic alloy fall smoking back down the lift shaft.

He suddenly realized that there was only one way to deal with Mahnahmi's mischief. Consciously, he fought to blank his mind, to suppress every consideration of subsequent action, every hint of preconception. The dark cloud which had hovered nearby slowly faded. He could no longer detect Mahnahmi's presence—and she should be equally blind to his whereabouts. There was a chance she, like everyone else, would momentarily think that he had died in the ambush of the lift car.

A quick patrol revealed that these quarters had only one entrance—the single, now useless lift. No other lift opened on this level. That left one way in to the floor above—the roof carport. Gradually his gaze came to rest on the curving window that looked out across the plant and to the Plateau beyond.

Flinx moved to the window, found it opened easily. The side of the pylon was marked with decorative ripples and thranx pebbling. He looked upward, considered one additional possibility.

At least they wouldn't be expecting him anymore.

His mind briefly registered the magnificent panorama of the Mediterranea Plateau, dotted with factories and human settlements. In the distance the mist-filled lowlands stretched to the horizon.

The footing on the rippled metal exterior of the building was not as sure as he would have liked, but he would manage. At least he had to climb only one floor. Moving through the apartment-office, he located the bathroom, opened the window there, and started up.

Unless the floor plan upstairs was radically different, he should encounter another bathroom, perhaps larger but hopefully unoccupied, above the one he had just exited from. That would be the best place from which to make an unobtrusive entrance.

Moving hands and feet methodically, he made slow but steady progress upward, never looking back. In Drallar he had climbed greater heights on wet, less certain surfaces—and at a younger age at that. Still, he moved cautiously here.

The absence of wind was a blessing. In good time he encountered a ledge. There was a window above it. Reaching, he pulled himself up so that he was staring through the transparent pane, and observed with satisfaction that the window was open a few centimeters. Then he noticed the two figures standing at the back of the room. One was fat and sweating, a condition not due to recent exercise. The other was small, blond, and wide-eyed.

Suddenly they saw him.

"Don't let him get me, Daddy," she said in mock-fright. Opening his mind, Flinx sensed the excitement racing through hers and he felt sick.

"I don't know why you persist in tormenting me," Challis said in confusion, his beamer now focused on Flinx's shoulder. "I didn't

hurt you badly. You've turned into something of a pest. Good-bye."
His finger started to tighten on the trigger.

Pip was off Flinx's shoulder instantly. Challis saw the snake
move, shifted his aim, and fired. Remembrance of what the
minidrag was capable of shook the merchant, and his shot went
wild. It struck the wooden molding above the window, missing Pip
and Flinx completely. Whatever the molding was made of, it
burned with a satisfying fury. In seconds the gap between window
and Challis was filled with flame and smoke.

While the smoke chased the merchant from the room and prevented him from getting a clear shot, it also left Flinx pinned outside the window. He started downward as rapidly as he dared, Pip
thrumming angrily around his head and looking for something to
kill. Flinx doubted he could make the ground safely before Challis
got word to the guards below. Slowly he descended past one floor,
a second, a third. On the fourth floor down he noticed that the
reflective one-way paneling had broken and been repaired with
transparent film.

Two sharp kicks enlarged the opening and he jumped through—
to find himself confronting a single startled woman.

She screamed.

"Please," he begged, making calming sounds and moving toward
her. "Don't do that. I don't mean you any harm."

She screamed again.

Flinx made violent shushing motions with his hands. "Be quiet
. . . they'll find me."

She continued to scream.

Flinx halted and thought furiously what to do. Someone was
bound to hear the noise any second.

Pip solved the immediate problem. He lurched speculatively at
the woman. She saw the long, sinuous, quick-moving reptilian
form, mouth agape, rushing toward her on broad membranous
wings.

She fainted.

That stopped the screaming, but Flinx was still trapped in a now
alerted building with next to no prospect of slipping out unseen.
His gaze traveled frantically around the room, searching for a large
carton to hide in or a weapon or . . . anything useful. Eventually
his attention returned to the woman. She had fallen awkwardly and
he moved to shift her into a more natural resting position. As he
propped her up, Flinx noticed a bathroom nearby. His gaze shot
back to the girl. . . .

A minute later several heavily armed guards burst into the unlocked room. It seemed to be deserted. They fanned out, made a quick inspection of every possible hiding place. One guard entered the bathroom, noticed feminine legs beneath the privacy shield, and hastily withdrew, apologizing. With his comrades he left and moved on to inspect the next office.

Three offices later it occurred to him that the woman hadn't responded to his apology—not with a thank-you, not with a frosty acknowledgment, not with a curse. Nothing. That struck him as being strange and he mentioned the fact to his superior.

Together they dashed back to the office in question, entered the bathroom. The legs were still in the same position. Cautiously, the officer knocked on the shield, cleared his throat appraisingly. When there was no response, he directed the other two men to stand back and cover the shield exitway, which he then opened from the outside.

The woman was just opening her eyes. She found herself sitting stark naked on the convenience, staring into the muzzles of two energy weapons held in the steady grip of a pair of resolute-looking, uniformed men.

She fainted again.

By the time the badly shaken woman had been revived once more, Flinx was well clear of the tower. No one had noticed the lithe, short-haired woman leaving the building. Flinx had made excellent use of the cosmetics found in the woman's desk—in Drallar it was useful to have knowledge of abilities others might find absurd or even disreputable. Only one clerk had noticed anything unusual. But he wasn't about to mention to his fellows that the double leather belt encircling the woman's waist had moved independently of her walk.

Finally away from both the tower and the Challis plant, Flinx discarded the woman's clothing and let Pip slip free from around his belly. Disdaining normal transportation channels as too dangerous now, he made his way to the edge of the escarpment.

The two-thousand-meter drop was breathtaking, but he couldn't risk waiting around the Plateau for some of Challis' armed servants to challenge him in the street. Nor did he want to risk awkward questions from the authorities. So he took a deep breath, selected what looked like the least sheer cliff, and began his descent.

The basalt was nearly vertical, but crumbling and weathered, so he encountered an abundance of handholds. Even so, he doubted that Challis would imagine that anyone would consider descending the escarpment by hand and foot.

Flinx came upon some bad places, but the overgrowth of dangling vines and creepers enabled him to bypass these successfully. His arms began to ache, and once, when a foot momentarily became numb, he was left clinging precariously by fingers and one set of toes to tiny cracks in the rock.

At the thousand-meter mark, the cliff started to angle slightly away from him, making climbing much easier. He increased his pace. Finally, bruised, scratched, and utterly exhausted, Flinx reached the jungle at the bottom. Pausing a moment to orient himself, he headed immediately in what he hoped was the direction of the port. He had chosen his place of descent with care, so he didn't have far to go through the dense vegetation.

But he was totally unaware that he was struggling over a region as densely populated as any of Terra's major cities. An entire thranx metropolis lay below him, hewn in traditional fashion, from the earth and rock beneath the sweltering surface. Flinx walked upon a green cloud that hovered over the city.

Totally drained and beginning to wish Challis *had* shot him, he shoved himself through one more stubborn cluster of bushes . . . then stumbled onto the surface of a neatly paved roadway. Two more days, and he had made his way back to Chitteranx Port. Those he met cautiously avoided him. He was quite aware of the sight he must present after his scramble down the cliff wall and his hike through the jungle.

A few thranx did take pity on the poor human, enough to provide him with sufficient food and water to continue on.

The sight of the Port outskirts cheered him immensely. Pip took to the air at Flinx's shout of joy before settling back on his master's shoulder. Flinx glanced up at the minidrag, who looked relaxed and comfortable in the tropical heat so like that of his native world of Alaspin.

"You can afford to look content, spade-face," Flinx addressed his companion enviously. While he had fought his way down the cliff centimeter by centimeter, Pip had fluttered and soared freely nearby, always urging him on faster and faster, when a single misstep could have meant quick death.

The clerk at the overbank counter in the Port terminal was human, but that didn't prevent him from maintaining his composure at the sight of a dirty, ragged youth approaching. A wise man, he had learned early in life a basic dictum: odd appearance may indicate wealth or eccentricity, with the two not necessarily mutually exclusive.

So he treated the ragamuffin as he would have any well-dressed, clearly affluent arrival. "May I be of service, sir?" he inquired politely, unobtrusively turning his head to one side.

Flinx explained his needs. The information he provided was fed to a computer. A short while later the machine insisted that the person standing before the counter—name Flinx, given recorded name Philip Lynx, retina pattern so-and-so, pulse variables such-and-such, heart configuration thus-and-that—was indeed a registered depositor at the King's Bank on Moth, in the city of Drallar, and that his present drawable balance as of this date was . . .

The clerk stood a little straighter, fought to face Flinx. "Now then, sir, how did you happen to lose your registered cardmeter?"

"I had an accident," Flinx explained cryptically, "and it fell out of my pocket."

"Yes." The clerk continued to smile. "No need to worry. As you know, only you can utilize a personal cardmeter. We will note the disappearance of your old cardmeter and within the hour you will have a new one waiting at this desk for you."

"I can wait. However," he indicated his clothing with an eloquent sweep of his hands, "I'd like to buy some new clothes, and get cleaned up a little."

"Naturally," the clerk agreed, reaching professionally into a drawer. "If you'll just sign this slip and permit me to register your eyeprint on it, we can advance you whatever you require."

Flinx applied for a ridiculously modest amount, listened to the clerk's directions as to where he could hire a bath and buy clothing, and left with a grateful handshake.

The jumpsuit he eventually chose was more elaborate than the two Hivehom had already appropriated, but he felt he owed himself a little luxury after what he had been through.

The bath occupied most of the rest of the hour, and when he returned to the overbank desk he once more resembled a human being instead of a denizen of Hivehom's jungles. As promised, his new cardmeter was ready for him.

"Anything else I can do for you, sir?"

"Thanks, you've done more than enough. I . . . ." He paused, looked to his left. "Excuse me, but I see an old friend."

He left the clerk with an open mouth and a tip of ten percent of his total withdrawal.

The central terminal floor was high-domed and filled with the noise of travelers arriving and departing. The smallish thranx Flinx strode up behind was engaged in activity of a different sort.

"I think you'd better give that lady back her abdomen purse," he whispered to the insectoid lightfinger. As he spoke, a lavishly in-laid and chiton-bejeweled thranx matron, her flaking exoskeleton elegantly streaked with silver, turned to stare curiously at him.

At the same time the thranx Flinx had surprised started visibly and whirled to confront his accuser. "Sir, if you think that I have . . ." The voice turned to a clacking gargle. Flinx smiled en-gagingly as Pip stirred on his shoulder.

"Hello, Bisondenbit."

The concept of compound eyes bugging outward was unreason-able from a physiologic standpoint, but that was the impression Flinx received. Bisondenbit's antennae were quivering so violently Flinx thought they might shake free, and the thranx was staring in expectant terror at the lethal length of Pip.

"The abdomen purse," Flinx repeated softly, "and calm down be-fore you crack your braincase."

"Y-ye-yes," Bisondenbit stuttered. Interesting! Flinx had never heard a thranx stutter before. Turning to the old female, Bisondenbit reached into an overly capacious b-thorax pouch and withdrew a small, six-sided bag of woven gold-colored metal.

"You just dropped this, Queen Mother," he muttered reluctantly, using the formalized honorific. "The hooks have come all unbent . . . see?"

The matron was checking her own abdomen with a foothand while reaching for the purse with a truhand.

"I don't understand. I was certain it was secured . . ." She broke off, ducked her head and executed a movement with skull and an-tennae indicative of profound thanks, adding verbally, "Your ser-vice is much appreciated, warsire."

Flinx flinched when she bestowed the undeserved compliment on Bisondenbit.

That worthy's courteous pose lasted until the matron had passed out of hearing range. Then he turned nervous eyes on Flinx. "I didn't want you killed . . . I didn't want anyone killed," he stam-mered rapidly, "they said nothing to me about a killing. I only was to bring you to . . ."

"Settle down," Flinx advised him. "And stop yammering of death. There are already too many deaths in this."

"Oh, on that I concur," the thranx confessed, the tension leaving him slowly. "None of my doing." Abruptly his attitude changed from one of fear to one of intense curiosity.

"How did you manage to escape the tower and leave the Plateau? I am told many were watching for you but none saw you leave."

"I flew down," Flinx said, "after I made myself invisible."

Bisondenbit eyed him uncertainly, started to laugh, stopped, then stared again. "You are a most peculiar fellow, even for a human. I do not know whether to believe you or not." He suddenly looked around the busy terminal, his nervousness returning. "Powerful people around Challis want to know your whereabouts. There is talk of a large reward, to be paid without questions. The only clue anyone has as to your escape, however, resides in a woman who is confined to a hospital. She is hysterical still."

"I'm sorry for that," Flinx murmured honestly.

"It is not good for me to be seen with you—you have become a desired commodity."

"It's always nice to be wanted," Flinx replied, blithely ignoring Bisondenbit's fear for his own safety. "By the way, I didn't know that the thranx counted pickpocketing among their talents."

"From a digital standpoint we've always been adroit. Many humans have acquired equally, ah, useful abilities from us."

"I can imagine," Flinx snorted. "I happen to live in a city overstocked with such abilities. But I haven't time to debate the morality of dubious cultural exchanges. Just tell me where I can find Conda Challis."

Bisondenbit eyed the youth as if he had suddenly sprouted an extra pair of hands. "He almost killed you. It seems he wants another chance. I can't believe you will continue to seek out such a powerful enemy. I consider myself a fair judge of human types. You do not appear revenge-motivated."

"I'm not," Flinx confessed uneasily, aware that Small Symm had assumed he was following Challis for the same reason. People persisted in ascribing to him motives he didn't possess.

"If not revenge, then what is it you follow him for . . . not that it makes me sad to see a being of Challis' reputation squirm a little, even if it be bad for business."

"Just tell me where he is."

"If you'll tell me why you seek him."

Flinx nudged Pip and the flying snake stirred, yawned to show a sac-backed gullet. "I don't think that's necessary," Flinx said softly, meaningfully. A terrified Bisondenbit threw up truhands and foothands in feeble defense.

"Never mind," sighed Flinx, tired of threatening. "If I tell you it might even filter convincingly back to Challis. I just think he holds information on who my real parents are and what happened to them after they . . . abandoned me."

"Parents?" Bisondenbit looked quizzical. "I was told you had threatened Challis."

"Not true. He's paranoid because of an incident in our mutual past. He wanted me to do something and I didn't want to do it."

"For that you've killed several people?"

"I haven't killed anyone," Flinx protested unhappily. "Pip has, and then only to defend me."

"Well, the dead are the dead," Bisondenbit observed profoundly. He gazed in disbelief at Flinx. "I did not believe any being, even a human, could be so obsessed with perverse desire. Does it matter more than your life to know who your parents were?"

"We don't have the tradition of a general hive-mother that I could trace myself to and through," Flinx explained. "Yes, it matters that much to me."

The insect shook his double-lobed head. "Then I wish you musical hunting in your mad quest. In another time, another place, I would maybe be your clanmate." Leaning forward, he extended antennae. After a moment's hesitation, Flinx touched his own forehead to the proffered protrusions. He straightened, gave the slight thranx a warning look.

"Try," he said to Bisondenbit, "to keep your truhands to your own thorax."

"I don't know why my activities should concern you, as long as you are not affected," the thranx protested. He was almost happy, now that it appeared Flinx wasn't going to murder him. "Are you going to report me to the authorities?"

"Only for procrastination," Flinx said impatiently. "You still haven't told me where Challis is."

"Send him a tape of your request," the thranx advised.

"Would you believe it?"

Bisondenbit's mandibles clicked. "I understand. You are a strange individual, man-boy."

"You're no incubator yourself, Bisondenbit. Where?"

Shoulder chiton moved to produce a ruffling sound, like cardboard being scraped across a carpet. Bisondenbit spoke with a modicum of pride.

"I'm not one of Challis' hired grubs—I'll tell you. You drove him from Moth, it seems; and now you've chased him off

Hivehom. The Challis Company's home office is in Terra's capital, and I presume that's where he's fled. No doubt he'll be expecting you, if he hasn't died of fright by now. May you find him before the many-who-pursue find *you.*" He started to leave, then paused curiously.

"Good-bye, Bisondenbit," Flinx said firmly. The thranx started to speak, but spotted the minidrag moving and thought better of it. He walked away, looking back over his shoulder occasionally and muttering to himself, unsatisfied. For his part Flinx felt no guilt in letting the pickpocket go free. It was not for one who had performed his fair share of borderline activities to judge another.

Why wouldn't Challis believe that his purpose in seeking him out was for nothing so useless and primitive as revenge? Challis could understand only his own kind of mind, Flinx decided.

Somehow, he would have to find a way around it.

From Hivehom to the Commonwealth's second capital world of Terra was a considerable journey, even at maximum drive. But eventually Flinx found himself drinking in a view of it from another shuttlecraft port as the little transfer ship dropped free of the freightliner.

This was the green legend, *Terra magnificat,* spawning place of mankind, second capital of the Commonwealth and home of the United Church. This was the world where once a primitive primate had suddenly risen to stand on hind feet to be nearer the sky, never dreaming he would one day step beyond it.

And yet, save for the royal blue of the oceans, the globe itself was unremarkable, mostly swirling white clouds and brown splotches of land.

He hadn't known what to expect . . . golden spires piercing the cloudtops, perhaps, or formed crags of chromium backing against the seas—all that was at once absurd and sublime. Although he couldn't see it, Terra possessed both in munificent quantities, albeit in forms far more muted than his grandiose visions.

Surely, Flinx thought as the shuttle dropped into the outer atmosphere, the omnipresent emerald of Hivehom was more striking and, for that matter, the lambent yellow ring-wings of Moth were more sheerly spectacular.

But somewhere down there his great to the second or third power grandfather had lived and died. . . .

4

Descending on a west-to-east path, the shuttle passed over the big approach station at Perth before beginning its final powerglide over the endless agricult fields of central Australia. Flinx had passing views of isolated towns and food-processing plants and the shining solar power stations ringing the industrial metropolis of Alice Springs. He patted the shiny new case sitting by his feet, heard the relaxed hiss from within, and strapped himself down for landing.

The shuttle was dropping toward the largest shuttleport on Terra. The port formed the base of an enormous urban T whose cap stretched north and south to embrace the warm Pacific. Brisbane had been Terra's capital city for hundreds of years now, and its port, with long, open approaches over the continental center and the open Pacific, was the planet's busiest. It was also convenient to the large thranx settlements in North Australia and on New Guinea, and to the United Church headquarters at Denpasar.

There was a gentle bump, and he was down.

No one took any notice of him in the terminal, nor later as he walked through the streets of the vast city. He felt very much alone, even more so than he had on Hivehom.

The capital surprised him. There were no soaring towers here. Brisbane had none of the commercial intensity of West North America's city of Lala or of London or Jakutsk, or even of the marketplace in Drallar. The streets were almost quiet, still bearing in places a certain quaintness, with architecture that reached back through to the pre-Amalgamation time.

As for the government buildings, they at least were properly immense. But they were built low to the ground and, because they were landscaped on all sides, seemed to reach outward like verdant ripples in a metal and stone pond.

Locating the headquarters of the Challis Company was a simple matter. Careful research then gave him the location of the family residence. But gaining entrance to that isolated and protected sanctum was another matter.

Bisondenbit's comments came back to him. How could he reach Challis and explain his purpose before the merchant had him killed?

Somehow he must extend the time Challis would grant him before destruction. Somehow . . . he checked his cardmeter. He was not wealthy, but he was certainly far above beggar status. If he could stretch things a bit, he would have a few weeks to find the proper company to implement his plan.

There was one such firm located in the southern manufacturing sector of the capital. A secretary shuffled him to a vice-president, who gazed with a bemused expression at the crude plans Flinx had prepared and passed him on to the company's president.

An engineer, the president had no difficulty with the mechanical aspects of the request. Her concern was with other matters.

"You'll need this many?" she inquired, pursing her lips and idly brushing away a wisp of gray hair.

"Probably, if I know the people involved. I think I do."

She made calculations on a tiny desk computer, looked back at his list again. "We can produce what you want, but the time involved and the degree of precision you desire will require a lot of money."

Flinx gave her the name of a local bank and a number. A short conversation via machine finally caused a smile to crease the older woman's face. "I'm glad that's out of the way. Money matters always make me feel a little dirty, you know? Uh . . . may I ask what you're going to use these for?"

"No," Flinx replied amiably as Pip shifted lazily on his shoulder. "That's why I came to you—a small firm with a big reputation."

"You'll be available for programming?" she asked uncertainly.

"Direct transfer, if need be."

That appeared to settle things in the president's mind. She rose, extended a hand. "Then I think we can help you, Mr. . . . . ?"

He shook her hand, smiled. "Just use the bank number I gave you."

"As you wish," she agreed, openly disappointed.

The contrast between the rich blue of the ocean and the sandy hills of the Gold Coast was soft and striking. One high ridge in particular was dotted with widely spaced, luxurious private residences, each carefully situated to drink in as much of the wide bay as possible—and to provide discreet, patrollable open space between neighbors.

One home was spectacular in its unobtrusiveness. It was set back in the cliffs like a topaz in gold. Devoid of sharp corners, it seemed to be part of the grass-dusted bluff itself. Only the sweeping, free-form glassalloy windows hinted that habitation lay behind.

Nearby, curling breakers assaulted the shore with geometric regularity, small cousins of more mature waves to the south. There, at an ancient village named Surfersparadise, many-toned humans, and not a few adaptive aliens rode the surf, borne landward in the slick wet teeth of suiciding waves.

Flinx was there now, but he was watching, not participating. He sat relaxed on a low hill above the beach, studying the most recent converts to an archaic sport. Nearby rested his rented groundcar.

At the moment Flinx was observing a mixed group of young adults, all of whom were at once older and younger than himself. They were students at one of the many great universities that maintained branches in the capital. This party disdained boards in favor of the briefer, more violent experiences of body surfing. He saw a number of young thranx among them, which was only natural. The deep blue of the males and the rich aquamarine of the females was almost invisible against the water, and showed clearly only when a comber broke into white foam.

Body surfing was hardly an activity native to the thranx, but like many human sports it had been adopted joyfully by them. They brought their own beauty to it. While a thranx in the water could never match the seal-like suppleness of a human, when it came to nakedly riding the waves they were far superior. Flinx saw their buoyant, hard-shelled bodies dancing at the forefront of successive waves, b-thorax pushed forward to permit air to reach breathing spicules.

Occasionally a human would mount the back of a thranx friend for a double ride. It was no inconvenience to the insectoid mount, whose body was harder and nearly as buoyant as the elliptical boards themselves.

Flinx sighed. His adolescence had been filled with less innocent activities. Circumstances had made him grow up too fast.

Looking down at the sand he put out a foot to impede the progress of a perambulating hermit crab. A toe nudged it onto its side. The tiny crustacean flailed furiously at the air with minute hairy legs and hurled motes of indignant anger at its enormous assailant. Regaining its balance, it continued on its undistinguished way, moving just a little faster than normal. A pity, Flinx thought, that humans couldn't be equally self-contained.

Looking up and down the coast, where a citrine house lay concealed by curving cliffs, Flinx reflected that Challis should be arriving there soon from his offices in the capital.

A gull cried wildly above, reminding him that it was time. . . .

Conda Challis had all but forgotten his young pursuer as he stepped from the groundcar. Mahnahmi ran from the house to greet him, and they both saw the solemn figure in the gray jumpsuit moving up the walk at the same time. Somehow he had penetrated the outer defenses.

Mahnahmi drew in her breath, and Challis turned a shade paler than his normal near-albino self. *"Francis . . ."*

Challis' personal bodyguard did not wait for further verbal command. Having observed the reaction of both his employer and his employer's daughter, he immediately deduced that this person approaching was something to be killed and not talked to. Pistol out, he was firing before Challis could conclude his order.

Of course, the person coming up the walk might be harmless. But Challis had forgiven him such oversights in the past, and that reinforced the man's already supreme confidence.

Challis' policy seemed to pay off, for the wildly gesticulating figure of the red-haired youth disintegrated in the awesome blast from the illegally overcharged beamer.

"And that," the shaken merchant muttered with grim satisfaction, "is finally that. I never expected him to get this close. Thank you, Francis."

The guard holstered his weapon, nodded once, and headed in to check the house.

Mahnahmi had her arms around Challis' waist. Normally, the merchant disdained coddling the child, but at the moment he was shaken almost to the point of normalcy, so he didn't shove her away.

"I'm glad you killed him," she sniffed. Challis looked down at her oddly.

"You are? But why? Why should he have frightened you?"

"Well . . ." there was hesitation in the angelic voice, "he was frightening you, and so that frightened me, Daddy."

"Um," Challis grunted. At times the child's comments could be startlingly mature. But then, he reminded himself, smilingly, she was being raised surrounded by adults. In another three or four years, if not sooner, she would be ready for another kind of education.

Mahnahmi shuddered and hid her face, hid it so that Challis could not see that the shudder was of revulsion and not fear. Francis returned and took no notice of her. She had experienced the thoughts Challis was now thinking all her life, knew exactly what they were like. They were always sticky and greasy, like the trail a snail left behind it.

"Welcome home, sir. Dinner will be ready soon," the servant at the interior door said. "There is someone to see you. No weapons, I checked thoroughly. He insists you know him. He is waiting in the front portico."

Challis snorted irritably, pushed Mahnahmi away ungently. It was unusual for anyone to come here to conduct business. The Challis offices in the tritower downtown were perfectly accessible to legitimate clients and he preferred to keep his personal residence as private as possible.

Still, it might be Cartesan with information on that purchase of bulk ore from Santos V, or possibly . . . he strolled toward the portico, Mahnahmi trailing behind him.

A figure seated with its back to him stared out the broad, curving window at the ocean below. Challis frowned as he began, "I don't think . . ."

The figure turned. Having just barely regained his composure, Challis was caught completely unprepared. The organic circuits that controlled the muscles of his artificial left eye twitched, sending it rolling crazily in its socket and further confusing his thoughts.

"Look," the red-haired figure began rapidly, "you've got to listen to me. I don't mean you any harm. I only want . . ."

"Francis!" the terrified merchant shrieked at the sight of the ghost.

"Just give me a minute, one minute to explain," Flinx pressed. "You're only going to ruin your furniture if . . ." He started to rise.

Challis jumped backward, clear of the room, and stabbed frantically at a concealed switch. A duplicate of that switch was set just outside of every room in the house. It was his final security and now it worked with gratifying efficiency.

A network of blue beams shot from concealed lenses in the walls, crisscrossing the room like a cat's cradle of light. Two of them neatly bisected the form standing before him.

He had had to wait until the figure rose or the beams would have passed over it.

Now the merchant let out a nervous little laugh as the figure col-

lapsed, awkwardly falling against the couch and then tumbling to
the floor. Behind him, Mahnahmi stared with wide eyes.

Challis fought to steady his breathing, then walked cautiously
toward the unmoving figure. He kicked at it, gently at first, then
good and hard. It did not give under his boot as it should have.

Leaning over he examined the two punctures the beams had
made in the upper torso. There was no blood, and inside both
holes, he saw something charred that wasn't flesh and bone. The
smell drifting from the figure was a familiar one—but the wrong
one.

"Circuitry and coagulated jellastic!" he muttered. "No wonder
there were two of him. Robots."

"A robot?" a small voice squeaked behind him. "No wonder I
couldn't—" She shut up abruptly. Challis frowned, half turned to
face her.

"What was that, Mahnahmi?"

She put a finger in her mouth, sucked innocently on it as she
gazed at the twisted figure on the floor. "Couldn't see any blood,"
she finished facilely.

"Yes, but . . ." A sudden thought brought concern to his face.
"Where's Francis?"

"Sleeping," a new voice informed him. The merchant's hands
fell helplessly to his side, and Mahnahmi drew away as Flinx
walked into the room, smiling softly. Unlike the previous two, this
youth had a gently stirring reptile coiled about his right shoulder.

"I'm sorry. I'm afraid I had to knock him out—and your
overzealous butler, too. You have a nervous staff, Challis." His
hand came up to touch the wall next to the concealed hallway
switch controlling the multiple beamers. "That's a neat trick."

Challis debated whether he ought to drop to the floor, then
looked from the switch back to Flinx and licked his lips.

"Will you stop with your paranoia?" the youth pleaded. "If I
wanted to kill you I could have hit that control already, couldn't I?"
He tapped the wall next to it.

Challis dropped, relaxing even as he fell below the lethal level of
the beams. But Mahnahmi was running in a crouch toward him,
screaming with child-fury: "Kill him, Daddy, kill him!"

"Get away, child," Challis said abruptly, slapping her aside. He
climbed slowly, carefully, back to his feet and stared at the silent
figure in the hall. "You're right . . . you could have killed me easily just now, and you did not. Why?"

Flinx leaned against the door jamb. "I've been trying to tell you all along. That incident on Moth is past, finished, done with. I haven't been following you to kill you, Challis. Not all the way to Hivehom and certainly not here."

"I can't believe . . . maybe you do mean what you say," the merchant confessed, words coming with difficulty as he fought to readjust his thinking. "Is it the real you, this time?"

"Yes." The youth nodded, indicated his shoulder where Pip yawned impressively. "I'm never without Pip. In addition to being *my* insurance, he's my friend. You should have noticed that the mechanicals appeared without reptilian companionship."

"Kill him!" Mahnahmi screamed again.

Challis turned on her. "Shut up, or I'll let Francis play with you when he comes to. Why this sudden fury, Mahnahmi. He's right . . . I could be dead a couple of times over by now, if he really desired that. I'm beginning to think he's telling the truth. Why are you so—"

"Because he . . ." she started to say, then subsided suddenly and looked quietly at the floor. "Because he frightens me."

"Then go where he won't frighten you. Go to your room. Go on, get out."

The golden-haired child turned and stalked petulantly toward a door at the far end of the chamber, muttering something under her breath that Challis would not have appreciated, had he been able to hear her.

He turned curiously back to Flinx. "If you don't want me dead, then why in Aucreden's name have you chased me halfway across the Commonwealth?" He quickly became a solicitous host. "Come in, have a drink then. You'll stay for the evening meal?"

Flinx shook his head, grinning in a way Challis didn't like. "I don't want your friendship, Challis. Only some information."

"If it's about the Janus jewels or anything related to them, I can't tell you anything."

"It has nothing to do with that, or with your attempt to force me to participate in your private depravities. When you were . . . leaving your house in Drallar, you said something about the characteristics of my maternal line."

Challis looked puzzled. "If you say I did, then I guess I did. What of it?"

"I know nothing whatsoever of my true parents. All my seller could give my adoptive mother was my name. Nothing more." He leaned forward eagerly. "I think you know more."

"Well, I . . . I hadn't given it any thought."

"You said you had a file on me . . . that you had amassed information on my background."

"That's true. To insure that you really possessed the kind of talent I was hunting for, it was necessary to research your personal history as completely as possible."

"Where did you find the information?"

"I see no reason to keep it from you, except that I don't know." Flinx's hand moved a little nearer the fatal switch. "It's true, it's true!" Challis howled, panicky again. "Do you think I keep track of every source of minor information my people unearth?" He drew himself up with exaggerated pride. "I happen to be the head of one of—"

"Yes, yes," Flinx admitted impatiently. "Don't regale me with a list of your titles. Can you locate the information source? Let's see if your retrieval system is as efficient as you claim it is."

"If I do," the merchant said sharply, "will that be the last I see of you?"

"I'll have no further interest in you, Challis."

The merchant came to a decision. "Wait here." Turning, he made his way to the far end of the room. There he rolled back the top of what looked to be an antique wooden desk. Its interior turned out to be filled with no-nonsense components combined in the form of an elaborate console. Challis' fingers moved rapidly on the control keys. This produced several minutes of involved blinking and noises from hidden depths within the desk.

Eventually he was rewarded with a small printout which he inserted into a playback.

"Here it is. Come look for yourself."

"Thanks, but I'll stay here. You read it to me."

Challis shook his head at this unreasonable lack of trust, then turned his attention to the magnified readout. "Male child," he began mechanically, "registered age seven months with Church-sponsored orphanage in Allahabad, Terra, India Province. This information is followed by some staff speculation matching identity points . . . cornea prints, fingerprints, retina prints, skull shape, and so on, with purely physical superficialities such as hair and eye color, finger rings and the like.

"These vital statistics are matched to an orphan aged eight years who was sold under the name Philip Lynx at such-and-such a date in the free body market in Drallar, Moth. My people apparently felt there were sufficient similarities to link the two."

"Is the name . . . does it tell . . . ?" Flinx had to know whether the name Lynx was lineal, or given only because he was the off-spring of a Lynx—that is, a sophisticated, independent woman who was mistress by her choice rather than by the man's, free to come and go as she wished.

Challis was unable to tell him. "It does not. If you want additional information you'll probably have to hunt it out of the original Church records—assuming you'll be allowed access to them. You could begin in Allahabad, of course, but without a look at the original records it would be hard to tell where to start. Besides, Denpasar itself is much closer."

"Then I'll go there."

"You'll never gain access to those records. Do you think, dear boy, anyone who wishes is permitted the use of the original Church files?"

"Just tell me where it is."

Challis grinned. "On an island called Bali, about five thousand kilometers northwest of here in the Indonesian archipelago."

"Thank you, Challis. You won't see me again." He turned, left the hall.

As soon as the youth was out of sight Challis' attention was drawn to several tiny screens set into a console. One showed his visitor about to leave via the front door. Challis touched a switch. The red-haired figure grabbed the door mechanism—and both he and the door dissolved in a blinding flash. The concussion shook the merchant where he stood.

"I don't make it easy for unwanted guests to get in," he told the console grimly. "But once in, I see to it they don't get out."

Challis had not become what he was by leaving anything to chance. Perhaps the boy's absurd tale was true—and then, perhaps it was only a device to lure Challis into some unimaginable, fiendish trap. That the lad was cunning he had amply demonstrated. In any case, it cost nothing to make sure.

Only his life.

Shutting down the console, he walked leisurely toward the front of the house. He was surprised to see Mahnahmi standing in the hallway. Behind her, smoke still drifted from the blackened metal frame of the doorway, which now bordered a roughly rectangular crater. The depression extended the length of the hall and well out into the ferrocrete walk leading to the entrance.

The girl was holding something. It was a piece of arm. Variously colored fluids dripped from it and tiny threads of material hung loosely from both torn ends.

Challis was struck with a mixture of fear and admiration as he stared at the section of limb Mahnahmi was examining so intently. For the first time he began to wonder just what sort of creature he had selected for an enemy. That it was more than an unusually clever seventeen-year-old boy he had suspected ever since that incredible escape on Hivehom. Now he was certain of it.

The arm, of course, was mechanical. The Flinx he thought to be real had been but a more convincing automaton, as Mahnahmi could have told him. Now Challis had gone and spoiled her game. But the leftover pieces were interesting. She studied the armature in seemingly casual fashion, compared it to a nearby fragment of mechanical flying snake.

It just wasn't fair! Since Challis had told the machine what it wanted to know, against her advice, she would never see the real Flinx again. And he had been so much fun.

She would have to find someone else's mind to play with. . . .

Flinx watched the hermit crab, its terrestrial explorations concluded, disappear in an obliging wavelet. At the same time he flicked off the recorder at his belt. The tape had recorded nothing since the third simulacrum of himself had been destroyed by the merchant.

Rising, Flinx brushed the sand from the bottom of his jumpsuit and thought sorrowful thoughts about the unfounded paranoia of Conda Challis. Everything he could learn from the fat trader he had finally learned, and the information was carefully stored in the little belt recorder, which functioned over surprising distances. The simulacrums had been an expensive gamble that had worked.

Flinx returned to the rented groundcar. A special console had been rigged on one seat with five telltales at its center. Three were dark, while two still winked a steady green. Challis might have been interested to know that had he destroyed his third visitor before answering its questions, there were two additional elaborate Flinxes in waiting.

For a delicious moment Flinx savored the thought of sending both of them into the merchant's bedroom tonight. But . . . no. That would place him in the position of rendering a judgment of sorts on another.

Instead he gave the two remaining simulacrums the return-to-base signal. The two remaining lights began to blink steadily, indicating they were operating properly and were in motion. They were on their way back to the fabrication plant from which Flinx had ordered them. There, their intricate innards would be salvaged, along with a concomitant part of Flinx's badly depleted bank account.

Starting up the powerful little car, he set it for a formal flight pattern leading to the atmospheric shuttleport. That strictly planetary terminal lay far to the south of the capital, nearer the suburban industrial city of Sydney.

Challis had hinted it would be difficult for a stranger to gain admittance to the United Church headquarters. Well, he would know soon enough. There was an obscure genealogy there that he wanted very much to trace.

5

Suborbital flights to and from every major city and province on Terra were regularly scheduled at the huge port. The clerk Flinx encountered was straight of body but mentally geniculate from a quarter century of answering the same inane questions. Not only could he expect no promotion, but he suspected that his youngest daughter was dating two old men and a young woman simultaneously. As Flinx drew near, the man was reflecting that in his day, children had behaved differently.

"I just tried to buy a ticket to a city called Denpasar," Flinx explained, "and the light on the dispenser flashed *No Such Destination*. Why?"

"Where are you from, young sir?" the clerk inquired politely.

Flinx was startled. He hadn't been called "sir" but a few times in his whole life. He started to reply "Drallar, Moth," but suddenly recalled an early dictum of Mother Mastiff's.

"Always answer a question as concise as you can, boy," she had instructed him. "It makes folks think of you as intelligent and nonborin', while givin' 'em as little information about yourself as possible."

So he said simply, "Off-planet."

"Far off-planet, I'll venture," the clerk added. "Didn't you know, young sir, that Bali is a closed island? Only three classes of people are allowed to travel there." He ticked them off on his fingers as he spoke. "Balinese and their relatives, Church personnel, and government officials with special clearance."

He studied Flinx carefully. "You could pass for Balinese, excepting that carrot top of yours, so you're obviously not a native. You don't claim to be an official of the Church and—" he couldn't repress a little smile "—I don't think you're a special government representative. Why did you want to go there, anyway?"

Flinx shrugged elaborately. "I'd heard it was the seat of the United Church. I thought it would be an interesting place to visit while I'm touring Terra, that's all."

Ah, a standard query. Any incipient suspicions the old man

might have had died aborning. "That's understandable. If you're interested in the same kind of countryside as Bali, though, you can get as close as . . ." he paused to check a thick tape playing on the screen before him, ". . . the eastern tip of the island of Java. I've been there myself. You can see the island from Banjuwangi and Surabaja's a fine old city, very picturesque. You might even take a day-flyer over to Komodo, where the dinosaur-rebreeding station is. But Bali itself," the man shook his head regretfully, "might as well try landing on the Imperial Home world as get into Denpasar. Oh, if you could slip onto a shuttle going in you might get into the city. But you'd never get *off* the island without having to answer some hard questions."

"I see," Flinx replied, smiling gratefully. "I didn't know. You've been very helpful."

"That's all right, sir. Enjoy the rest of your stay on Terra."

Flinx left in a pensive mood. So there was a chance he could get onto the island, somehow. But did he want to have to answer those hard questions on his departure? He did not.

That left him with the problem of gaining admittance to a place no one was allowed into. No, he reminded himself, whispering to the case and its leathery contents, that wasn't entirely true. Three classes of people were permitted onto the island.

He didn't think it would be easy to forge government identification, and he was too young to claim to be anything worth-while. There did exist the possibility of palming himself off as an acolyte of the Church. But what about . . . ? Hadn't the old man said that save for his red hair he could pass for Balinese?

Passing a three-story-high interior panel of polished metal, Flinx caught sight of his reflection. A little hair dye, a crash course in the local dialect, a small boat—surely it couldn't be that easy!

But there was the chance this plan was so simple that he might be overlooked by those on the watch for more sophisticated infiltrators. And Flinx had often seen how possession of a certain amount of brass—nonmetallic variety—could be more useful in fooling bureaucracy than all the formal identification in the Arm.

Turning, he retraced his path to the ticket dispensers. A punched demand and the subsequent insertion of his cardmeter produced a one-way shuttle ticket for Surabaja. . . .

The ancient market town had preserved much of its seventeenth-century flavor. Flinx felt right at home, learning something he had long suspected: one crowded marketplace is much like any other, no matter where one travels.

Everyone spoke Terranglo and symbospeech in addition to the old local dialect known as Bahasa Indonesia. Flinx easily secured black dye, and with his hair color changed he quickly became one of the locals. A stay of several weeks was sufficient to provide him, a natural linguist, with an efficient smattering of the language.

Procuring a small boat was simple enough. If the ploy failed he could always fall back on the story that he was a simple fisherman whose automatic pilot had failed, causing him to be blown off course. Besides, for any off-world spy the really hard part would be passing customs at a Terra port-of-entry, and Flinx had already accomplished that.

So it was that after several days of calm, automatic sailing he found himself in sight of the towering peaks of Mounts Agung and Batur, the two volcanoes that dominated the island.

Under cover of a moonless night, he made his approach at the northernmost tip of the magnificent empty beach called Kuta, on the western side of the island. No patrol appeared to challenge him as he drew his small boat up on the sand. No automated beamers popped from concealed pits to incinerate him where he stood.

So far he had been completely successful. That didn't lessen his sense of unease, however. It was one thing to stand on an empty beach, quite another to penetrate the recesses of the Church itself.

Making his way inland with his single bit of baggage—the perforated case holding a few clothes, and Pip—it wasn't long before he encountered a small, unpaved road through the jungle that fringed the beach. After a walk of several hours he was able to hail a groundcar cultivator. The farmer driving it provided him with a ride into Bena and from there it was easy to hire an automatic bekak into Denpasar proper.

Everything went as well as he dared hope. The farmer had assumed he was a stranger visiting relatives in the city, and Flinx saw no reason to argue with a story so conveniently provided. Nor had the young farmer shown any desire to switch from Terranglo to Bahasa Indonesia, so Flinx's hastily acquired vocabulary was not put to the test.

The innkeeper made Flinx welcome, though she insisted on seeing the animal in the bag. Flinx showed her, hoping that the woman wasn't the garrulous sort. If word got around to representatives of the Church, someone might grow curious about the presence here of such an exotic and dangerous off-world species as the minidrag.

But Flinx refused to worry. After all, he was ensconced in a comfortable room in the city he had been told he would have trouble reaching. Tomorrow he would set about the business of penetrating the Church system.

The first thing he had to find out was where on the island the genealogical records were stored, then what procedures one was required to go through to gain access to them. He might yet have to resort to forgery. More likely he would end up stealing a Church uniform and brazening his way into the facility.

Flinx the priest—he went to sleep smiling at the thought, and at Mother Mastiff's reaction to him in Church garb. . . .

The next morning, he began his private assault on the inner sanctums of the most powerful single organization in the Commonwealth.

The first step was to select a car with a talkative driver. Flinx chose the oldest one he could find, operating on the theory that older men engaged in such professions were more inclined to gabble excessively and otherwise mind their own business. Flinx's driver was a white-maned patriarch with a large drooping mustache. He was slight and wiry, as were most of the locals. The women had a uniform doll-like beauty and appeared to age in jumps, from fourteen to eighty with no in-between.

A few of them had already regarded Flinx somewhat less than casually, something he was becoming used to as he grew older. There was no time for that now, however.

"What did you have in mind for today's journey, sir?"

"I'm just a visitor, here to see my cousins in Singaradja. Before I'm swamped with uncles and aunts, I'd like to see the island unencumbered by family talk. The old temples . . . and the new."

The oldster didn't bat an eye, merely nodded and started his engine. The tour was as thorough as the old man was loquacious. He showed Flinx the grand beaches at Kuta where the huge breakers of the Sunda Bali rolled in, unaware that Flinx had negotiated those same waves the night before. He took him to the great oceanographic research station at Sanur, and to the sprawling grounds of the Church University on Denpasar's outskirts.

He showed him various branches of Church research facilities, all built in the old Balinese style replete with ferrocrete sculptures lining every lintel and wall. He drove him over the ancient rice paddies that terraced the toy mountains—the most beautiful on all Terra, the old man insisted, even if the farmers in their wide hats now rode small mechanical cultivators instead of water buffalo.

Half a day passed before Flinx was moved to comment, "It's not at all like what I expected the headquarters of the United Church to be."

"Well, what did you expect?" asked the old man. "A reproduction on a grander scale of the Commonwealth Enclave in Brisbane? Black- and bronze-mirrored domes and kilo-high spires done in mosaic?"

Flinx leaned back in the worn old seat next to the driver and looked sheepish. "I have never been to the capital, of course, but I have seen pictures. I guess I expected something similar, yes." The old man smiled warmly.

"I am no expert on the mind of the Church, son, but it seems to my farmer's soul to be a collection of uncomplicated, gentle folk. The University is the largest Church building on the island, the astrophysics laboratory, at four stories, its tallest." He became silent for a while as they cruised above a river gorge.

"Why do you suppose," he asked finally, "the United Church decided centuries ago to locate its headquarters on this island?"

"I don't know," Flinx replied honestly. "I hadn't thought about it. To be nearer the capital, I suppose."

The old driver shook his head. "The Church was here long before Brisbane was made Terra's capital city. For someone who travels about with a Garuda spirit for a companion, you seem rather ignorant, son."

"Garuda spirit?" Flinx saw the driver looking back at the somnolent reptilian head that had peeked out from inside his jumpsuit. He thought frantically, then relaxed.

"But the Garuda is a bird, not a snake."

"It is the spirit I see in your pet, not the shape," the driver explained.

"That's good then," Flinx acknowledged, remembering that the monstrous Garuda bird was a good creature, despite its fearsome appearance. "What is the reason for the Church's presence here, if not to be near the capital?"

"I believe it is because the values of the Church and of the Balinese people are so very similar. Both stress creativity and gentleness. All of our own arrogance and animosity is subsumed in our ancient mythology."

Flinx regarded the old man with new respect and new curiosity. At the moment he sounded like something more than merely an old groundcar driver—but that was Flinx's overly suspicious mind looking to create trouble again.

"Our most aggressive movement is a shrug," the old man contin- ued, staring lovingly at the surrounding landscape. "It is the result of living in one of the galaxy's most beautiful places."

A light rain had begun to fall. The old man closed the car's open top and switched on the air-conditioning. Flinx, who prided him- self on his adaptability in strange environments and who until now had been forced to play the role of near-native, let out a mental sigh of relief at the first cooling caress of the air-conditioner.

The humidity in one of the galaxy's most beautiful places could be stifling. No wonder the thranx members of the Church had agreed to build its headquarters here, those many centuries ago.

They paused in Ubud, and Flinx made a show of looking at the famous wood carvings in the shops the old man had recom- mended. This was not an exclusively Balinese custom. Mother Mastiff had her arrangements with guides in Drallar, too.

The tour continued, and the need to show interest became more and more of a burden. Flinx yawned through the elephant cave, blinked at the sacred springs, and saw temples built on tem- ples.

An appropriate location for the home of the Church, Flinx thought, as the clouds cleared and a double rainbow appeared be- hind the smoking cone of 15,000-meter-high Mount Agung. The aquamarine robes and jumpsuits of passing Church personnel blended as naturally with the still flourishing jungle vegetation as the fruit trees which stood stolid watch over roadways and fields and rice terraces.

"It's all very beautiful," Flinx finally told the old driver, "though I'd still like to see the Church headquarters."

"Church headquarters?" the old man looked uncertain, pulled at his mustache. "But the entire island is the headquarters of the United Church."

"Yes, I know," Flinx said, trying not to seem impatient. "I mean the headquarters of the headquarters."

"Well," the old man looked up and left off pulling his mustache, "the nearest thing to that would be the Administration Depot, but why anyone would want to see that I don't know." Surprisingly, he smiled, showing white teeth beneath his wrinkled upper lip.

"Still expecting towers of precious metal and amethyst arches, eh son?" Flinx looked embarrassed. "I'll tell you, though the Depot is nothing to waste one's time with, it's in a setting the Buddha himself would envy."

The driver made up his mind. "Come then, I'll take you there, if you've set your mind on it."

They continued north out of Ubud, passing steeper and steeper terraces as they mounted an old roadway. It showed no evidence of the heavy traffic Flinx would expect to be en route to and from the headquarters of the headquarters. Maybe the old man was right. Maybe the facility he sought didn't exist.

Maybe he was wasting his time.

He leaned out the window, saw that his initial estimate of the road condition still held. The grass covering the path was several centimeters tall. Thick and healthy, it showed none of the characteristic bends the steady passage of groundcars over it would have produced.

Eventually the car sighed to a stop. The oldster motioned for Flinx to get out and he did so, whereupon the driver guided him to the edge of a steep precipice.

Flinx peered cautiously over the side. At the bottom of a valley several thousand meters below lay a broad, shallow lake. Irrigated fields and scattered farmers' homes dotted the greenery.

At the far end of the lake, near the base of smouldering Mount Agung, sprawled a tight group of modest boxlike two-story structures enameled a bright aquamarine. They were strictly utilitarian in appearance if not downright ugly. There wasn't an arch or tower among them.

A few antennae sprouted flowers of abstract metal mesh at one end of the complex, and there was a small clearing nearby that was barely large enough to accommodate a small atmospheric shuttle.

Was that all?

Flinx stared at it disbelievingly. "Are you sure that's it?"

"That is the Administration Depot, yes. I have never been there myself, but I am told it is mostly used for storing old records."

"But the Church Chancellory . . . ?" Flinx started to protest.

"Ah, you mean the place where the Counselors meet? It's the low clamshell-like building that I showed you in Denpasar itself, the one next to the solar research station. Remember it?" Flinx searched his memory, found that he did. It had been only slightly more impressive in appearance than the disappointing cluster of small buildings below.

"The Council of the Church meets there once a year, and that is where their decisions are made. I can take you back there, if you wish?"

Flinx shook his head, unable to hide his disappointment. But . . . if this was a warehouse for old records, it might contain what he'd come to see. If not—well, he could set about solving the problem of leaving this island without incurring unwanted questions. Perhaps in India province, in Allahabad . . .

"You said you've never been inside," he turned to the old man. "Does the Church forbid visitors there?"

His driver looked amused. "Not that I ever heard of. There is no reason to go there. But if you wish . . ."

Flinx started back toward the car. "Let's go. You can leave me there."

"Are you certain, son?" the old man asked with concern, eying the sun in its low-hanging position in the damp sky. "It will grow dark soon. You may have trouble finding a ride back to the city."

"But I thought . . ." Flinx began.

The old man shook his head slowly, spoke with patience. "You still do not listen. Did I not say it was merely a place of storage? There is no traffic down there, in the valley. It is a place of slow-growing things, dull and far from any town. Were I a Churchman, I would far rather be stationed in Benoa or Denpasar. It is lonely here. But," he shrugged at last, "it is your money. At least it will be a warm night."

They climbed back into the car and he started down a winding narrow path Flinx hadn't seen before. "If you do not get a ride back you might try sleeping on the ground. Mind the centipedes, though; they have a nasty bite. I am sure some farmer will give you a ride back to the city in the morning—if you rise early enough to catch him."

"Thanks," Flinx said, his gaze fixed on the valley below. With its shining lake snug against the base of the great volcano, it was attractive indeed, though his attention was still drawn to the prosaic architecture of the Depot. It became even less impressive as they drew nearer. The aquamarine enamel seemed stark against the rich natural browns and greens of the vegetation ringing the mountain. As they reached the valley floor Flinx saw that the structures were devoid of windows. Befitting, he thought grimly, a facility devoted to things and not people.

The car pulled up before what must have been the main entrance, since it was the only entrance. No massive sculptures depicting the brotherhood of the humanx, no playing fountains flanked the simple double-glass door. A few undistinguished-looking groundcars were parked in the small open hangar to one side.

Flinx opened the door, climbed out. Pip stirred within the loose folds of the jumpsuit and Flinx hushed his restless pet as he handed the old driver his cardmeter.

The driver slipped it into a large slot in his dash, waited until the compact instrument ceased humming. The transfer of funds completed, he handed the cardmeter back to Flinx.

"Good luck to you, son. I hope your visit proves worth all your trouble to come here." He waved from the car as it started back toward the mountain road.

"Trouble" is an inadequate word, old man, Flinx thought as he called a farewell to him. *"Selamat seang!"*

Flinx stood alone before the Depot for a moment, listening to the soft trickle of water dropping from terrace to terrace. The soft *phutt-putt* of a mechanical cultivator guided by the hand of a farmer drifted across the fields to him. According to the old guide, the people were in the process of harvesting their fifth rice crop of the year and had begun sowing the sixth.

By now, Flinx was sick of agriculture, temples—and the island itself. He would inspect what this unprepossessing structure had to offer, try the city records in Allahabad, and be on his way home to Moth in a few days, with or without information.

He berated himself for not taking the shuttleport clerk's indirect suggestion and contriving to come here via the diplomatic atmospheric shuttle from South Brisbane. Instead he had wasted weeks on learning the local language and piloting the small boat.

He expected an armed fortress with walls half a kilometer thick and bristling with beamers and SCCAM projectors. Instead he found himself stalking an island of rice farmers and students. Even the Chancellory was out of session.

Flinx mounted the few steps and pushed through the double doors, noting with disgust that they opened manually and without challenge. A short hallway opened into a small circular high-domed chamber. His gaze was drawn upward—where it froze. The dome was filled with a tridee projection of the entire inhabited galaxy. Each Commonwealth world was plainly marked by color and minute block letters in symbospeech.

Flinx studied it, picking out Terra and Hivehom first because of their brighter colors, then moving on to Evoria, Amropolous, Calm Nursery—thranx worlds all. Then on to the human planets of Repler, Moth, Cachalot, and Centaurus III and V. Half-lights indicated the outposts of humanx exploration, fringe worlds like Burley with its vast store of metals, Rhyinpine of the troglodytes and endless caverns, and the frigid globe of far distant Tran-ky-ky.

His eyes lowered to the curving floor of the chamber, and at last he found his mosaic, though the motif in the floor was simple. It consisted of four circles, two representing Terra's hemispheres and the other two Hivehom's. They formed a box with a single smaller sphere at their center, tangent to all four circular maps. The central sphere contained a vertical hourglass of blue, representing Terra, crossed by a horizontal hourglass of green, standing for Hivehom. Where they met the colors merged to form aquamarine—the signet color of the United Church.

Three halls broke the walls around him, one vanishing into the distance ahead, the others to left and right. Each wall between was filled with engravings of impressive figures from the history of the Church—thranx and human both—in modest pose. Most impressive was a scene picturing the signing of the Amalgamation that formally united thranx and mankind. The Fourth Last Resort, David Malkezinski, touched forehead to antennae with the tri-eint Arlenduva, while the insect's truhand was locked in the human's right palm.

To the right of this relief were engraved some of the basic maxims of the Church: Man is animal; thranx is insect—both are of the species Brother. . . . Advise not civilization; physical force reciprocates mentally. . . . If God wished man and thranx to devote themselves to Him, He would not have made the worlds so complicated. . . . Self-righteousness is the key to destruction—the list went on and on.

Opposite that wall was an engraved list of recent philosophical pronouncements, which Flinx read with interest. He had just finished the one about hedonism violating the Prime Edict and was on to the admonition to distrust anything that smacks of absolute right when his attention was broken by a voice.

"Can I help you, sir?"

"What?"

Flinx turned, startled, to see a young woman in aquamarine robes staring quizzically back at him. She was seated near the corridor at the far left, behind a sparsely covered desk. He hadn't even noticed her until she spoke.

"I said, may I help you." She walked over to stand next to him, stared into his eyes. That alone was unusual. Most new acquaintances found their first gaze going somewhat lower, to the scaly shape wrapped around Flinx's shoulder or, in this instance, peeping out of his suit front.

But this slim girl ignored the flying snake. That smacked of poor vision or great self-confidence, Flinx thought. Her indifference to the snake was the first impressive thing he had encountered on this island.

"Sorry," he lied easily, "I was just about to come over and talk to you. Did I keep you waiting?"

"Oh no . . . I just thought you might be getting tired. You've been studying the maps and inscriptions for over an hour now."

His gaze went instantly to the glass doors, and he saw that she was telling the truth. A tropical night black as a gambler's conscience had settled outside.

He was uneasy and upset. It felt as if he had been eying the engravings in the little domed alcove for only a few minutes. His gaze traveled again over the three-dimensional map overhead, to the inlaid pictorials and the subtly inscribed sayings. Did those carefully raised colors and words and reliefs conceal some kind of mnemonic device, something to capture an observer into absorbing them despite himself?

His speculation was abruptly cut off by the girl's soft voice: "Please come over to the desk. I can help you better from there."

Still dazed, Flinx followed her without protest. A few papers and several small screens rested on the desktop, and he saw switches set in ranks of panels at the far side.

"I've been studying," she explained apologetically, "or I would have come over sooner. Besides, you seemed to be enjoying yourself. Nonetheless, I thought I'd better find out if you needed anything since I go off shift soon and my replacement would start ignoring you all over again."

If that was a lie, Flinx thought, it was a smooth one. "What are you studying?"

"Spiritual assignation and philosophical equations as they relate to high-order demographic fluxation."

"I beg your pardon?"

"Diplomatic corps. Now," she continued brightly, "what can I help you with?"

Flinx found himself staring at the unlocked glass doors, the tridee map overhead, the words and pictures engraved on the encircling walls. In his thoughts he matched them with the simple exte-

rior of this structure, compared that to his vaunted imaginary pictures of what it ought to look like.

Everything he'd encountered on this island, from the unpreten-
tiousness of this Depot to the language of his driver, was a mixture
of the simple and the sophisticated. A dangerously uncertain mixture. For a moment he seriously considered forgetting the whole
thing, including his purpose in traveling across half the Commonwealth, and turning to walk out those unguarded doors. He
had spent much of his frenetic young life trying to avoid attention,
but whatever he told this girl now promised to deliver him to questioners.

Instead of leaving, he said, "I was raised by a foster parent who
had no idea who my parents were. I still don't know. I don't know
for certain who I am or where I come from, and it may not matter
much to anyone else, but it matters to me."

"It would matter to me, also," the girl replied seriously. "But
what makes you think we can help you find out?"

"An acquaintance indicated he had found some information on
my parentage, some hints that physically I could match up with a
child born here on Terra, in the city of Allahabad. I do know my
real name as it read on the . . . on the slaver's records, but I don't
know if it's a family name or one given me well after my birth.

"It's Philip Lynx." He pronounced it carefully, distinctly, but it
still wasn't his name. It belonged to an alien; it was a stranger's
name. He was just Flinx.

"I was told that this was a storage facility for Church records, although," he indicated the little chamber with its three connecting
halls, "these buildings hardly look big enough to hold even a portion of those records."

"We're very space-efficient," she told him, as if that should explain it. "The records for Allahabad are kept here, as are the
records of every being registered with the Church." Her eyes
shifted, but not to look at Pip.

Flinx turned, thinking she was staring at something behind him.
When he saw nothing and turned back, he saw she was smiling at
him.

"It's your hair," she said easily. "The dye is beginning to come
off." His hand went instinctively to his scalp, felt of the dampness
there. When he brought it down, it was stained black.

"You've been out in the city too long. Whoever sold you that
dye cheated you. Why dye it, anyway—the red is attractive
enough."

"A friend thought otherwise." He couldn't tell from her thoughts if she believed him; but she chose not to press the matter, touching instead a switch on her desk.

"Allahabad, you said?" He nodded. She bent over the desk, addressed a speaker. "Check for records on a Philip Lynx," she told it, "Allahabad-born." She looked up at him. "Spelling?"

Flinx spread his hands. "L-y-n-x, P-h-i-l-i-p was the way it was listed on the slaver's sheet, but that could be a misspelling."

"Or a corruption," she added, turning to the speaker again. "Check also variational spellings. Also all inquiries into said records for the past . . . five years." Then she clicked off.

"Why that last?" he inquired. Her expression was grim.

"Your acquaintance should not have had access to your records. Those are between you and the Church. Yet it seems someone managed to gain permission to see them. You're going to be asked some hard questions later, if you are this Philip Lynx."

"And if I'm not?"

"You'll be asked questions anyway—only you won't be looking at anyone's files." She smiled pleasantly. "It's not your wrongdoing, it seems . . . though someone is going to lose his robes. The lower grades are always vulnerable to bribery, especially when the request is for seemingly harmless information."

"No need to worry about that," Flinx told her. "About the only thing I'm sure of in this galaxy is that I'm me." He grinned. "Whoever that is."

She did not return the smile. "That's what we're going to find out."

Once Flinx's identity was established, through various checks, the girl became friendly once more. "It's late," she observed when the identification procedures had concluded. "Why don't you wait and begin your retrieval in the morning? There's a dormitory for visitors and you can share cafeteria food with the staff, if you have the money. If not, you can claim charity, though the Church frowns on direct handouts."

"I can pay," Flinx insisted.

"All right." She pointed to the far corridor. "Follow the yellow strip on the floor. It'll take you to the visitors' bureau. They'll handle things from there."

Flinx started toward the hallway, looked back. "What about the retrieval? How do I begin?"

"Come back to this desk tomorrow. I'm on duty ten to six all week. After that you'd have to hunt to find me again. I have to transfer to another manual task, but for the rest of this week, I can help you. My name's Mona Tantivy." She paused, watched Flinx's retreating form, then called to him as he entered the corridor. "What if the name Philip Lynx doesn't match up with the child born in Allahabad?"

"Then," Flinx shouted back to her, "you can call me anything you want. . . ."

6

The cubicle they assigned him was small and simply furnished. He spent an hour washing off the dust of days, and a pleasant surprise awaited him when he exited the shower—his jumpsuit had been taken away and cleaned. It was a good thing he had taken Pip into the bath with him.

Feeling uncomfortably clean, he was directed to the nearest food service facility and soon found himself mingling with a crush of aquamarine robes and suits.

The facility itself was a surprise, decorated with local shrubs and fountains, its lushness in stark contrast to the spartan exterior of the building. It was divided into three sections by semipermeable paneling.

One section was adjusted to the midtemperate zone climate most favored by humans, while the area farthest from the door was almost misted over from the heat and humidity favored by the thranx. The eating area in between was by far the largest. Here the two environments blended imperfectly, to form a climate a touch warm and damp for humans, slightly dry and cool to the thranx, yet suitable to both. All three areas were crowded.

He was thankful for the presence of several humans and thranx who wore something other than the Church color; it made him feel considerably less conspicuous.

The smells of recently prepared food were everywhere. While a few of the aromas were exotic, they couldn't compete with the incredible variety of odors always present in the marketplace in Drallar. Even so, he found himself salivating. He had had nothing to eat since his brief breakfast in the city early that morning.

A short time after placing his order with the auto-chef he was rewarded with a flavorful steak of uncertain origin and an assortment of breads and vegetables. But when he inquired again about the rest of his order, a small screen lit up: *No intoxicants of any sort, however mild, are permitted in Depot commissaries.*

Flinx swallowed his disappointment—a poor substitute for the beer he had ordered—and settled for iced shaka.

Pip was curled about his shoulder once again. The flying snake had aroused a few comments but not fear. The creatures in the facility—they ranged in age from less than his own to elders well over a hundred—were peculiarly indifferent to the possibility of the minidrag suddenly spewing corrosive death.

Flinx took a seat by himself. His ears were no larger than normal, and his talent no sharper than usual, but his hearing was well trained. To survive in Drallar, one had to utilize all one's senses to the utmost. Listening to the conversation around him in the food service facility, they served to satiate his curiosity.

To his left a pair of elderly thranx were arguing over the validity of performing genetic manipulation with unhatched eggs. It had something to do with the scorm process as opposed to the oppordian method, and there was much talk of the morality of inducing mutation by prenatal suggestion in unformed pupae.

Hunting for something less incomprehensible, he overheard an old woman with two cream-colored stripes on her suit sleeve lecturing a group of acolytes: two human, two thranx. A hydrogen atom was emblazoned above the stripes.

"So you see, if you check the research which has been performed on Pluto, Gorisa, and Tipendemos over the last eight years, you'll find that any additional modifications to the SCCAM weapons system must take into account the stress limitations of the osmiridium casing itself."

A bite of bread and yet another wisp of conversation, this from a middle-aged man behind him with a lush white beard: "Production levels on Kansastan and Inter-Kansastan in the Bryan Sector suggest that with proper preatmospheric seeding, food grain production can be increased as much as twenty percent over the next three planting years."

Flinx frowned as he considered this intense babble, but it wasn't the absence of theology in the discussions that troubled him. He really couldn't judge, but even to his untrained ears it seemed that a lot of very sensitive matters were being freely discussed in the presence of non-Church personnel. Whether that proved the Church was inefficient or only typically humanx he could not decide. Though security wasn't his problem, it troubled him nonetheless as he finished his meal.

He was still troubled the following morning, as he made his way back to the desk in the entrance chamber. Mona Tantivy was on duty, and she smiled when she saw him approach. Traffic was moving briskly through the chamber now as Church personnel bustled from one corridor to another and through the double-glass entranceway.

"Ready?" she asked.

"I'd like to get this over with as soon as possible," he said, in a sharper tone than he intended. Flinx, aware he was trembling slightly, resolutely calmed himself.

The woman pursed her lips reprovingly. "Don't act as if you're going to be inoculated or something."

"In a sense that's just how I feel," he replied grimly.

And it was. Flinx had grown up with a deficient image of self. If he found no remedy here, he would likely carry that cross with him forever.

The woman nodded slowly, pressed a switch. A few minutes later a fortyish human with a build like a wrestler came out of the near corridor. His smile was identical to Tantivy's, and he projected the same desire to aid and be helpful. Flinx wondered if this attitude was natural or if that, too, was part of the Church course of instruction: Advanced Personality Manipulation through Traditional Facial Gesticulation—or something similar.

Angrily Flinx thrust his instinctive sarcasm aside. All that mattered was seeing what he had come for.

"My name's Namoto," the blocky oriental said, introducing himself with a smile and handshake. "I'm pleased to meet you, Mr. Lynx."

Flinx put up a restraining hand. "Let's not call me that until we prove it. Just Flinx, please."

The smile didn't fade. "All right, whoever you be. Come with me and we'll see if we can find out who you are."

After what seemed like twenty minutes of walking through hallways and featureless corridors, Flinx was thoroughly disoriented. "It's hard to believe that the Church records of every human being in the Commonwealth . . ."

". . . and of every thranx," Namoto finished for him, "are all stored in this small building, but it is true. Information storage is a thousand-year-old science, Flinx. The art of document reduction has been developed to a high degree. Most of the records in this building would be invisible under a standard microscope. Our scanners and imprinters work with much finer resolutions." He paused before a door that looked no different from a hundred already passed.

"We're here."

The single word engraved in the translucent door said simply,

Genealogy. Behind this door were the early histories of billions of humanx lives—though not all of them. There were still those who did not wish to be documented by anything other than their own epitaph, and a few of them achieved this.

On the other hand, Flinx had been undocumented his whole life, and he was tired of it.

"There could be a large number of Philip Lynxes still alive," Namoto suggested as he keyed the door, "although because of certain colloquial sociological connotations, it is a less common name than many."

"I know what it means," Flinx snapped. Pip shifted uneasily on his master's shoulder at the sudden flare of mental violence.

The room was enormous. Mostly it consisted of seemingly endless aisles alternating with rows of enclosed metal that stretched from floor to ceiling. No row appeared different from its neighbor.

Flinx was led to a row of ten booths. Two were occupied by researchers, the rest were empty. Namoto sat down before the single large screen in the walled booth and gestured for Flinx to sit next to him. Then he pressed both thumbs to a pair of hollows set in the screen's side.

A light winked on beneath them and the screen lit up. Namoto leaned forward, said, "My name is Shigeta Namoto." He relaxed. There was a pause; the machine hummed, and a green light winked on above the screen's center.

"You are recognized, Padre Namoto," the machine intoned. "Awaiting requests."

"Report results of previous night's search on one human male named Lynx, Philip. Hold alternate spellings till directed." He turned, whispered to Flinx, "For a start we'll assume the name on the slaver's record was correct."

"Possible place of origin," he told the machine, "Allahabad, India Province, Terra." The Padre looked over at his anxious companion. "How old are you . . . or do you know?"

"Mother Mastiff tells me I should be about seventeen, though she can't be sure. Sometimes I feel like I'm seven hundred."

"And sometimes I feel like I'm seven," the massive Churchman countered pleasantly, returning his attention to the machine.

"Age approximation noted," the device stated. "Results of search appear."

Namoto studied the list. "I was right . . . it's not a common name. There are records of only three Philip Lynxes having been born and registered at Allahabad within the last half century. Only one of them fits your age bracket." He addressed the machine once more.

"Further information desired."

There was a brief hum, then the screen lit brightly with the legend: TRANSFERRING ALLAHABAD TERMINAL. Then a moment later: TRANSFER COMPLETED . . . CODE LENGTH.

Namoto gazed at the numbers following. "Doesn't seem to be much information at all. I hope it's worth . . ." He paused, suddenly concerned. "Are you all right, Flinx? You're shivering."

"I'm fine . . . it's a lot cooler in here than outside, that's all. Hurry up."

Namoto nodded. "Decode transfer."

Flinx's hands tightened convulsively on his thighs as each word was printed out. . . .

LYNX, PHILIP . . . TRUE NAME . . . BORN 533 A.A., 2933 OLD CALENDAR IN THE SUBURB OF SARNATH, GREATER URBAN ALLAHABAD, INDIA PROVINCE, TERRA.

There was a pause during which nothing further appeared on the screen. Flinx turned to Namoto, almost shouting.

"Is that all?"

"Gentle, Flinx . . . see, more comes." And the printout continued again.

NOTES ADDITIONAL: RECORDS OF ASSISTING SEMI-PHYSICIAN AND MONITORING MEDITECH INDICATE PRESENCE OF UNUSUALLY HIGH BIRTH AURA IN R-WAVE MATERNITY CHAMBER READINGS . . . NO UNUSUAL OR ADVERSE REACTION FROM MOTHER . . . R-WAVE READOUTS INDICATE POTENTIAL OF POSSIBLE ABNORMAL TALENTS, CLASS ONE . . .

DELIVERY NORMAL . . . NO R-WAVE REACTION ASCRIBABLE TO TRAUMA . . . MONITORS POSTOPERATIVE CHECK NORMAL . . . INFANT OTHERWISE NORMAL AND HEALTHY. . . .

MOTHER AGED TWENTY-TWO . . . NAME: ANASAGE . . . GRANDPARENTS UNKNOWN. . . .

Namoto did not look at Flinx as the readout concluded: FATHER UNKNOWN, NOT PRESENT AT BIRTHING. . . .

Flinx fought to relax. Now that this ordeal was over he wondered at his tension. What information there was told him little—and as for the last, well, he had been called a bastard before and far worse than that. But all this new information still did not tell him if Lynx was a lineal name, or one applied solely to him at birth. Without that—or additional information—he might as well not have bothered.

"Any information," he asked in a soft monotone, "on the post-delivery status of the . . ." the word came surprisingly easy now, "mother?"

Namoto requested it of the machine. The reply was short, eloquent.

MOTHER DECEASED . . . OFF-PLANET, 537 A.A. . . . ADDITIONAL DETAIL AVAILABLE . . .

"Explain the . . ." Flinx began, but Namoto hushed him.

"Just a minute, Philip."

Pip stirred nervously as his master bristled in reaction.

"Don't call me that. It's Flinx, just *Flinx*."

"Grant me the minute anyhow." Namoto used a small keyboard to instruct the machine manually. There was a low whine from sealed depths. A tiny wheel of millimeter-wide tape, so narrow as to be almost invisible, was ejected from an almost invisible slot. At the same time the screen lit for the last time.

PRINTOUT OF DELIVERED INFORMATION ACCOMPLISHED . . . SECONDARY INFORMATION WITHDRAWN TEN STANDARD MONTHS TWO WEEKS FOUR DAYS PRIOR THIS DATE . . .

Namoto's gaze narrowed. "Someone's been tampering with your file, all right." To the machine, "Identify withdrawing authority."

UNABLE TO COMPLY . . . AUTHORITY WITHDRAWN IMMEDIATELY SUBSEQUENT TO INFORMATION WITHDRAWAL. . . .

"Neat," was all Namoto said. "Your acquaintance wanted to make certain no one else had access to whatever information he stole."

A red-tinged image grew in his mind—Challis! The merchant had fooled him even at the point of imagined death. He had confessed to the Flinx simulacrum where he had obtained his information on Flinx, without finding it necessary to add that the critical information was no longer there.

What he had left in the Church archives was just enough to satisfy any casual inspector and to prevent any cancellation alarms from being activated.

And Flinx doubted that Challis was awaiting his return back in the capital. So he would have to start his hunt all over again—with no hint of where the merchant had fled to this time. A quiet voice nearby was speaking to him.

Namoto had keyed the machine release and was offering him the tape. "Here's a copy of what the thief left in the archive." Flinx took it, his movements slow and stunned. "I'm sorry about the rest, whatever it consists of. I suspect if you want to know the contents you're going to have to find your acquaintance again and ask him some direct questions. And when you do, I'd appreciate it if you'd contact the nearest Church authorities." The padre was not smiling. "Theft of Church records is a rather serious offense.

"This tape—and the one that was stolen—is a many-times-enlarged duplicate of the archive original. Any microscopic scanner will play it back." He rose. "If you want to see it again use the machine in the booth two alcoves over. I'll be at the monitor's desk if you want me for anything."

Flinx nodded slowly as the padre turned, walked away.

Challis! Thief, would-be murderer, casual destroyer of others' lives—next time he might let Pip kill him. The Commonwealth would be a little cleaner for the absence of . . . Something burned his shoulder and nearly yanked him from the chair.

Pip had all but exploded from his shoulder perch, fast enough to mark the skin beneath Flinx's jumpsuit. Fumbling the cassette into a pocket, he scrambled to his feet and raced down the aisle after his panicked pet.

"Pip . . . wait . . . there's nothing wrong . . . !"

The minidrag had already reached the entrance. Both Namoto and the monitor on duty had moved away from the desk. They were watching the snake warily while backing slowly away. The minidrag beat at the translucent plexite for a moment as Flinx rushed from the booth aisle. He was calling to the reptile verbally and mentally, praying that the snake would relax before someone, gentle and understanding or not, took a shot at him.

The minidrag backed off, fluttering and twisting in the air, and spat once. A loud hissing sound, and a large irregular hole appeared in the door. Flinx made a desperate grab for the receding tail, but too late—the elusive reptile had already squeezed through the aperture.

"Open the door," he yelled, "I've got to go after him!"

The attendant stood paralyzed until Namoto murmured tensely, "Open the door, Yena."

Yena moved rapidly then. "Yes, sir—should I sound an alarm?"

Namoto looked to Flinx, who was ready to rip the door from its glide. "Pip wouldn't hurt anyone unless he sensed a threat to me."

"Then what's the matter with him?" the padre asked as the door slid back. Flinx plunged through, the padre close behind.

"I don't know . . . there he goes! Pip . . . !"

The curling tail was just vanishing around a bend in the corridor. Flinx plunged after.

In the twists and turns of the labyrinthine building, Flinx occasionally lost sight of his pet. But ashen-faced human personnel and thranx with uncontrollably shivering antennae marked the mini-drag's path as clearly as a trail of crimson lacquer. Despite his bulk, Padre Namoto remained close behind Flinx.

It felt as if they had run around kilometers of corners before they finally caught up with the minidrag. Pip was beating leathery wings against another doorway, much larger than any Flinx had seen so far.

Only this time there was more than a single studious monitor in attendance. Two men wearing aquamarine uniforms were crouched behind a flanking tubular barrier. Each had a small beamer trained on the fluttering minidrag. Flinx could see a small knot of Church personnel huddled expectantly at the far end of the corridor.

"Don't shoot!" he howled frantically. "He won't hurt anyone!" Slowing, he moved closer to his pet. But Pip refused every summons, remaining resolutely out of grabbing range as he continued to beat at the doors.

"Whatever's berserked him is on the other side." He called to the two armed men. "Let him through."

"That's a restricted area, boy," one of them said, trying to divide his attention between the flying snake and this new arrival.

"Let us through," a slightly winded Namoto ordered, moving out where he could be seen clearly. The guard's voice turned respectful.

"Sorry, Padre, we didn't know you were in charge of this."

"I'm not, the snake is. But open the doors anyway. My authority."

Flinx had barely a minute to wonder exactly how important his helpful guide was before the surprisingly thick double doors started to separate. Pip squeezed through the minimal opening and an impatient Flinx had to wait another moment before the gap was wide enough to admit him.

Then he was on the other side, which proved to be a corridor no different from any of the many he had already traversed.

Except . . .

Except for the bank of six lifts before him. Two padre-elects were waiting in front of the lift at far left. One was a very old, tall, and oddly deformed human. He stood next to a young female thranx.

Pip was hovering in midair as Flinx and Namoto slipped into the corridor. Then he suddenly dived at the couple, completely ignoring the other Church personnel who were beginning to notice the presence of the venomous reptile in their midst.

"Call him off, Flinx," Namoto ordered. There was no hint of obsequiousness in his voice now. He had his beamer out and aimed.

Flinx suddenly sensed what had pulled so strongly at his pet. As Pip dove, the bent old man ducked and dodged with shocking agility, fairly throwing his young companion against the lift door. She twisted herself as she was shoved. It was sufficient to prevent a nasty break, but too weak to keep her from slamming hard into the unyielding metal. Shiny blue-green legs collapsed and she folded up against the door.

The old cleric's extraordinary suppleness caused Namoto and the others to delay intervening. Producing a beamer of his own from within the folds of his robes, the man—who had yet to utter a word, even a simple cry for help—took a wild shot at Pip. The minidrag spat, and inhuman reflexes enabled his target to just avoid the corrosive venom. It scorched the finish on the wall behind him.

"Pip, that's enough!" Something in his master's voice apparently satisfied the minidrag. Hesitating briefly, the reptile pivoted in midair and raced back to Flinx. But the flying snake still felt uncomfortable enough to disdain his normal shoulder perch, opting instead to remain hovering warily near Flinx's right ear.

For several silent seconds a mass of people were momentarily unified by the paralysis of uncertainty. Then Namoto broke the spell. "What branch are you working with, sir?" he inquired of the object of Pip's assault. "I don't believe I recognize . . ."

The padre became silent as the beamer recently directed against the snake shifted to cover him. Trying to look in every direction at once, the man moved a shifting, glacial glare over the small crowd which had gathered. No one challenged him, electing instead to wait and watch.

"Keep back, all of you," he finally warned. His accent was one Flinx did not recognize, the words almost more whistled than articulated.

As the man began backing toward the portal Flinx and Namoto had just passed through, Flinx cautiously edged around to where he could aid the injured young thranx. She was just regaining consciousness when he came near her. Getting both hands around her thorax, he lifted steadily. "He . . . threatened to kill me," she was murmuring groggily, still none too steady on trulegs and foothands. He could feel her b-thorax pulsing with uneven breathing.

Abruptly in control of herself again, the thranx looked accusingly across at her attacker. "He said if I didn't take him down to command level he'd kill me!"

"You can't get out of this building, sir," Namoto informed the man whom the girl had just accused. "I'm going to have to ask you to put down that beamer and come with me." The beamer waved at him and the padre ceased his approach after a single step.

"To be rational is to live," the man whistle-talked.

Without releasing his grip on the beamer, the man reached into the folds of his robes—exceptionally voluminous they were, Flinx noted. A moment's search produced a small brown cube sporting wires and several awkwardly installed knobs.

"This is a hundred-gram casing of kelite—enough to kill everyone in this corridor." His explanation was enough to send the younger of the watching acolytes scurrying in retreat.

Namoto didn't budge. "No volume of explosives could get you out of this complex," he informed the nervous man, his voice steady now. "Furthermore, although that cube looks like a kelite casing, I find that most unlikely, since no volume of explosives can get *into* this complex without being detected. Furthermore, I don't think you're an authorized member of the Church. If that's true, then you can't be in possession of an activated beamer."

The padre took another step forward.

"Keep away, or you'll find out whether it's activated or not!" the man shouted shrilly.

Every eye in the corridor was locked on the two principals in the threatening standoff—every intelligent eye.

Flinx thought he saw something move close to the ceiling, suddenly glanced to his right. Pip was no longer there.

There was no way of telling whether the same thought occurred simultaneously to the old man, or whether he simply detected motion overhead. Whatever the cause, he was ducking and firing before Flinx could shout to his pet.

Namoto had been right and wrong. The tiny weapon looked like a beamer but wasn't. Instead it fired a tiny projectile that just passed under the minidrag's writhing body. The projectile hit the far wall and bounced to the floor. Whatever it was was nonexplosive, all right; but Flinx doubted its harmlessness.

This time, Pip was too close to dodge. Powerful muscles in jaws and neck forced the poison out through the hypodermal tube in the

minidrag's mouth. The poison missed the eyes, but despite his un-
canny agility, the old man couldn't avoid the attack completely.
The venom grazed head and neck. A sizzling sound came from
dissolving flesh, and the man emitted an unexpected piercing hiss,
sounding like an ancient steam engine blowing its safety valve.

It was not a sound the human throat could manufacture.

Namoto and Flinx rushed the falling figure. But even as he was
collapsing he was fumbling with the cube of "kelite."

The confidence of a dying man was reason enough for Namoto
to fall to the floor and yell a warning to everyone else. Suddenly
there was a muffled explosion—but one far smaller than kelite
would have produced, and it did not come from the brownish cube.
A few screams from the crowd, and the threat was past.

As Flinx climbed back to his feet, he realized that Namoto's observations were once again confused. First, the beamer had turned
out to be a weapon, but not a beamer. And now it seemed this intruder had succeeded in smuggling a minimal amount of explosive
into the complex, but not enough to hurt anyone else. If it was indeed kelite, it was a minute amount; but nonetheless, it made an
impressive mess of the man's middle. His internals were scattered
all over this end of the corridor.

Flinx was still panting when Pip settled around his shoulder
once again. Moving forward, he joined Namoto in examining the
wreckage of what minutes before had been a living creature.

With death imminent, the creature's mind had cleared, his
thoughts strengthened multifold. Flinx suddenly found his head
assailed with a swirl of unexpected images and world-pictures, but
it was the familiarity of one which shocked him so badly that he
stumbled.

Flinx could sense the ghostly rippling picture of a fat man he desired strongly to see again, the man he had given up hope of ever
relocating: Conda Challis. This vision was mixed with a world-
picture and the picture-world had the name Ulru-Ujurr. Many
other images competed for his attention, but the unexpected sight
of Challis in the dying intruder's mind overwhelmed them beyond
identification.

Pip had sensed his master's fury at that very individual long minutes ago, back in the archives. Then this wretched person suddenly—undoubtedly—pictured the very same merchant, in terms
unfavorable to Flinx. So Pip had reacted in proportion to Flinx's
emotional state. Whether the minidrag would still have attacked

the stranger had he not drawn a weapon was something Flinx
would never know.

Namoto was studying the corpse. The explosion had been contained but intense. Little was left to connect the head and upper
torso with the legs. Most of the body between had been destroyed.

Reaching down, the padre felt what appeared to be a piece of
loose skin. He tugged . . . and the skin came away, revealing a second epidermis beneath. It was shiny, pebbled, and scaly—as inhuman as that final cry had been.

As inhuman as the thoughts Flinx had entered.

A low murmur of astonishment began to rise in the crowd, continuing as Namoto, kneeling, pulled and tore away the intricate
molding which formed the false facial structure. When the entire
skull had been exposed, Namoto rose, his gaze moving to the sample of forged flesh he held in one hand. "A nye," he observed
matter-of-factly. He dropped the shard of skin, wiped his hands on
his lower robe.

"An adult AAnn," someone in the crowd muttered.

"In *here*!"

"But why? What did he hope to accomplish with so small an explosive?"

Someone called for attention from the back of the crowd, held
up a tiny shape. "Crystal syringe-dart," she explained. "That's how
he got past the detectors—no beamer, no explosive-shell weapon."

"Surely," someone approached Namoto, "he didn't come all this
way with all this elaborate preparation, just to kill someone with a
little dart gun?"

"I don't think so, either," the padre commented, gazing down at
the body. "That explosive—that was a suicide charge, designed to
kill him in the event of discovery. But perhaps it was also there to
destroy something else."

"What kind of something else?" the same person wondered.

"I don't know. But we're going to analyze this corpse before we
dispose of it." Kneeling again, Namoto pawed slowly through the
cauterized meat. "He was well armed as far as it went—his insides
are full of pulverized crystal. Must have been carrying several
dozen of those syringe-darts."

Flinx jerked at the observation, started to say something—then
turned his budding comment into a yawn. He couldn't prove a
thing, and it was an insane supposition anyway. Besides, if by
some miracle he were half right, he would certainly be subjected
to a year of questioning by Church investigators. He might never

find Conda Challis then. Worse, by that time the indifferent merchant might have destroyed the missing record he had stolen, that remaining piece in the puzzle of Flinx's life.

So he could not afford to venture a childish opinion on what those fragments might be of.

A full crew of uniformed personnel entered the corridor. Some began dispersing the still buzzing crowd while others commenced an intensive examination of the corpse.

One small, very dark human glanced casually at the organic debris, then walked briskly over to confront the padre.

"Hello, Namoto."

"Sir," the padre acknowledged, with so much respect in his voice that Flinx was drawn from his own personal thoughts to consideration of the new arrival. "He was well disguised."

"An AAnn," the short package of mental energy noted. "They're feeling awfully bold when they try to slip one of their own in *here*. I wonder what his purpose was?"

Flinx had an idea, but it formed part of the information he had chosen not to disclose. Let these brilliant Churchmen figure it out for themselves. After he recovered the lost piece of himself from Challis, then he would tell them what he had guessed. Not before.

While the new man talked with Namoto, Flinx turned his attention back to the swarm of specialists studying the corpse. This was not the first time he had encountered the reptilian AAnn, though it was the first time in the flesh.

An uneasy truce existed between the Humanx Commonwealth and the extensive stellar empire of the AAnn. But that didn't keep the reptilians from probing for weak spots within the humanthranx alliance at every opportunity.

"Who penetrated its disguise?"

"I did, sir," Flinx informed him, "or rather, my pet did, Pip." He fondled the smooth triangular head and the minidrag's eyes closed with pleasure.

"How," Namoto asked pointedly, "did the snake know?" He turned to his superior, added for his benefit, "We were in genealogy at the time, sir, halfway around the complex."

Flinx's reply walked a fine line between truth and prevarication. What he left out was more important, however, than what he said.

"The minidrag can sense danger, sir," he explained smoothly. "Pip's an empathic telepath and we've been together long enough to develop a special rapport. He obviously felt the AAnn posed a threat, however distant, to me and he reacted accordingly."

"Obviously," murmured the smaller man noncommittally. He turned to face the young thranx. "How are you involved in this, Padre-elect?"

She stopped preening her antennae, snapped to a pose of semi-attention. "I was on monitor duty at the lift station, sir. I thought it was a human. He approached me and said he had to go down to command level."

Down to—Flinx's mind started envisioning what wasn't visible.

"I wondered why he didn't simply use his own lift pass. No one without a pass should be allowed this far. He had one, and showed it to me. He insisted that either it didn't work or else that the lift receptor was out of order."

She looked downward. "I suppose I ought to have sensed something then, but I did not."

Namoto spoke comfortingly. "How could you know? As you say, he got this far. His forgery wasn't good enough to fool the lift security 'puter, though."

"Anyway," she continued, "I tried my own pass on Lift One, and it responded perfectly. Then I tried his and it didn't even key the *Acknowledge* light. So he asked me to call a lift for him. I told him it would be better to have his pass checked for malfunction, first. He said he didn't have time, but I was obstinate. That's when he pulled the weapon and told me to call him a lift or he'd kill me."

Flinx noted that she was still unsteady despite the support of four limbs.

"Then these two gentlemen arrived, just as I was about to call the lift." She indicated Flinx and Namoto.

"You couldn't sound an alarm?" the smaller man wondered gruffly.

She made an elaborate thranx gesture of helplessness with her truhands.

"When he pulled the weapon I was away from the silent alarm at the desk, sir. I couldn't think of a reason to get back to it . . . and, I was frightened, sir. I'm sorry. It was so unexpected. . . ." She shivered again. "I had no reason to suspect it was an AAnn."

"He looked human to everybody else," Flinx said comfortingly. The valentine-shaped head looked gratefully across at him. Though that face was incapable of a smile, she clicked her mandibles at him in thanks.

"Every experience that doesn't end in death is valuable," the short man pontificated. That appeared to end her involvement as far as he was concerned. His attention was directed again to the people working with the body.

"Get this cleaned up and report to me as soon as preliminary analysis is completed," he snapped. His motions, Flinx noted, were quick, sharp, as if he moved as well as thought faster than the average being. One of those movements fixed Flinx under a penetrating stare. "That's an interesting pet you have, son. An empathic telepath, you say?"

"From a world called Alaspin, sir," Flinx supplied helpfully.

The man nodded. "I know of them, but I never expected to see one. Certainly not a tame one. He senses danger to you, *hmmm?*"

Flinx smiled slightly. "He makes a very good bodyguard."

"I dare say." He extended a hand too big for his body. "I'm Counselor Second Joshua Jiwe."

Flinx now understood the deference which had been shown this man. He shook his hand slowly. "I never expected to meet anyone so high in the Church hierarchy, sir." Though he didn't add that in Bran Tse-Mallory and Truzenzuzex, who had been with him in the hunt for the Tar-Aiym Krang, he had met two who had at one time ranked even higher.

"I'm in charge of Depot security." Again that head whipped around, instead of turning normally, to face Namoto. "What do you know about this young man?"

"He's come a long way in search of his natural parents. I've been doing my best to help him locate traces of them."

"I see." Jiwe spun on Flinx again. "No doubt you're anxious to leave?"

"I've done everything here I can," Flinx admitted. Jiwe could be the man to ask the awkward questions Flinx always feared.

The Counselor Second reminded him of a *Canish,* a small, superactive little carnivore that haunted the chill forests of Moth. It was a quick, sharp-eyed killer whose movements were as hard to pin down as a muffled curse in a crowd, and a threat to creatures many times its size.

Like this Jiwe, Flinx suspected. The man was too interested in Pip and in the minidrag's relationship to Flinx. It was difficult to concentrate on Jiwe, however, when Flinx's mind was still astorm with the knowledge that Conda Challis had appeared in the thoughts of the dying AAnn. What had a human merchant to do with the lizards?

"Are you all right, Flinx?" Namoto was eying him concernedly. "You looked dazed."

"I was. I was drifting home in my mind . . . where my body ought to be headed."

"And where is that?" Jiwe inquired interestedly.

Damn the man! "A central trading world, name of Moth, city of Drallar."

The Counselor looked thoughtful. "I know the world. Interesting, a lightly populated planet with a long history of settlement. Very independent-minded people. The local government's a benevolent monarchy, I believe."

Flinx nodded.

"An indifferent monarchy would be more accurate, I think," ventured Namoto.

The Counselor smiled. "It all amounts to the same thing as far as the locals are concerned." He even grinned like a *Canish,* Flinx mused.

"And you say you can occasionally sense his thoughts and he yours, son?"

"Feelings, not thoughts, sir," Flinx corrected hastily.

The Counselor seemed to consider for a moment before asking, "I wonder if you'd have a minute or two to spare? We won't delay your departure very long. If you'll just accompany us downstairs . . ."

"Sir . . ." Namoto started to interrupt, but the Counselor waved his objection away.

"It doesn't matter. This is a perceptive young man and he's heard more than enough to know by now that there are levels to the Depot below what is visible on the surface. I think he's sufficiently mature to know when to keep his mouth shut and what not to talk loosely about." He stared piercingly at Flinx. "Aren't you, son?"

Flinx nodded vigorously, and the Counselor rewarded him with another quasi-carnivorous smile. "Good . . . I like a free spirit. Now then, we have a small problem we've been unable to solve. You might be able to approach it differently than anyone else. All I ask is that you make an effort for us. Afterward, regardless of the results, we'll put you on an atmospheric shuttle free to anywhere on Terra. What do you say?"

Since he couldn't very well refuse the offer without making the Counselor twice as suspicious of his peculiar abilities as he already was, Flinx smiled cheerfully and replied with a marvelous imitation of innocent enthusiasm.

"I'll be happy to do anything I can, of course!"

"I thought you might say that. I hoped so. Padre Namoto, you might as well join us—this could be instructive. Someone else can temporarily cover your normal duties." He gestured at the reptilian corpse. "Security will be working with this mess for quite a while yet."

Then he turned to face the young thranx. "Padre-elect Syl-zenzuzex, you were about to call a lift. Do so now."

"Yes, sir." She appeared to have recovered completely from the shock of her near-abduction. Returning the Counselor's request with a poised salute of truhand and left antenna, she moved to the nearest lift door and inserted a complex three-pronged card into a slot on its right.

Following an intricate push-and-twist of the card, the slot immediately lit with a soft green glow. A matching telltale winked on above the doorway, *beeped* three times. Sliding silently aside, the door revealed an elevator car of surprising size.

Flinx entered after the padre-elect. Something . . . something about her was nudging a familiar memory. The thought faded as his attention was caught by the rank of numbers set just inside the door.

In descending order the panel read: 2-1-0-1-2-3—and so on down to twelve. Twelve stories below ground level and only three above. Mentally, he smiled, remembering. Now he was certain that his groundcar driver had been something more than a talkative oldster. But he hadn't lied to Flinx—he had simply described the Depot only as it was, without bothering to mention what couldn't be seen.

The thranx inserted the card into a slot below the panel of numbers. Flinx saw there were no switches, buttons, or other controls. Someone without a card might force the doorway into a lift, but without that intricate triangle-shape it could not be activated.

She cocked her head toward Jiwe. "Sir?"

"Seventh level," the Counselor directed her, "quadrant thirty-three."

"That's the hospital, isn't it, sir? I don't get out that way very often."

"That's right, Padre-elect."

Inserting the card into the slot, she made another complex turn with it. The number seven lit on the panel, and a long series of tiny numbers appeared within the material of the card itself. Holding it firmly in place, she slipped one digit over the number 33. As soon as the light was covered, the door slid shut.

Flinx felt the lift move downward, accelerate, and shift in directions he could not follow. Several minutes later it stopped. Combining changes of direction with an approximation of their steady, smooth speed, he decided rapidly that they were no longer beneath the visible structure of the Depot.

When the door finally slid aside Flinx stepped out into a crowd of humans and thranx that was startling in its density. Here white was the predominant color of clothing, though every uniform, robe, or jumpsuit was touched at some spot or another with the identifying aquamarine.

Jiwe and Namoto led while Flinx lagged behind, keeping pace with the young thranx. His nagging supposition concerning her had blossomed impossibly.

She spoke first, however, reaching up to put a delicate truhand on his free shoulder. "I did not have a chance to thank you and your pet for saving my life. My delay shames me. Accept those thanks now."

He inhaled deeply of her natural fragrance. "All the thanks belong to Pip, not me," he mumbled, embarrassed. "Listen, what did the Counselor call you?"

"Padre-elect. The rank is approximately—"

"Not that," he corrected curiously. "Your name."

"Oh . . . Sylzenzuzex."

"That would break down as Syl, of the Hive Zen, family Zu, the Clan Zex?"

"That's right," she acknowledged, unsurprised. Any human could break down a thranx name. "What's yours?"

"Flinx . . . yes, one calling. But I've another reason for making certain of yours, one that goes beyond exchanging identification." They rounded a bend in the pastel-walled corridor.

"You see, I think I know your uncle. . . ."

7

Thranx are stiff-jointed but extremely sure of foot. Nevertheless, Flinx's pronouncement caused his insectoid companion to stumble. Multiple-lensed eyes regarded him with astonishment.

"My . . . *what?*"

Flinx hesitated as they turned still another corner. How far did this underground world extend laterally, he wondered. Perhaps for the length and breadth of the whole island?

"I might not have the pronunciation correct," he said awkwardly. "But aren't you related to an old philosoph named Truzenzuzex?"

"Say that one more time," she coaxed him. He did so. "You're sure of that stress on the family syllable?" A positive nod. "I'm not sure 'uncle' would be a proper Terranglo analog, but yes, we are closely related. I haven't seen Tru in several years, not since my adolescence began."

"You know him well?"

"Not really. He was one of those childish gods—you understand, an adult whom other adults idolized? How do you happen to know him?"

"We were companions on a journey not long ago," Flinx explained.

"He was an Eint, you know," she went on thoughtfully. "Very famous, very controversial in his beliefs. Too controversial, many in the Clan thought. Then when I heard he had left the Church . . ."

The sentence died quickly. "It is not discussed in the Clan. I've heard practically nothing of him since he vanished many years ago to engage in private research with a human sting-ship partner of his youth."

"Bran Tse-Mallory," Flinx supplied, reminiscing.

The girl nearly stumbled again. "I've never known a human so full of the nectar of the unexpected. You are a strange being, Flinx-man."

When the question of his strangeness came up it was always a good time to change the subject.

He gestured upward. "So the Records Depot aboveground isn't much more than camouflage for the *real* Church center."

"I . . ." She looked ahead and Flinx noted that the Counselor hadn't missed a word of their conversation, judging from the speed with which he replied.

"Go ahead and tell him, padre-elect. If we don't he'll probably divine it anyway. How about it, son—are you clairvoyant?"

"If I was, I wouldn't be asking, would I?" Flinx shot back nervously, trying to conceal his increasing unease at the Counselor's pointed comments. He had to get out of here. If he was still present when word of his extraordinary escape on Hivehom trickled down to Jiwe's level, they might never let him go. He would become something he had always fought to avoid—a curiosity, to be studied and examined like a pinned butterfly under glass.

But he couldn't turn and run. He would have to wait this out.

Now that she'd been granted permission, Sylzenzuzex explained enthusiastically, "The aboveground Depot is fully utilized, but the majority of the installation extends under much of Bali, in many directions. There are only two ways in and out. Through the records center, above and behind us now, and through the under-sea shuttleport facing Lombok." Her eyes glistened.

"It's a wonderful place. So much to study. So much to learn here, Flinx!"

Flinx's reaction so far had been something less than boundless enthusiasm. He suspected Sylzenzuzex came from a rather cod-dled family. His own blithe trust of honored people and institutions had died somewhere between the ages of eight and nine.

He noticed how the overhead fluorescents filled her enormous eyes with ever-changing rainbows. "The active volcanic throat of Mount Agung is channeled and controlled. It supplies all the power the Church complex requires. The entire island is com-pletely self-contained and self-sustaining. It . . ."

She broke off as Namoto and Jiwe stopped in front of a door flanked by two Church guards wearing aquamarine uniforms. Their apparent relaxation, Flinx sensed, was deceptive, as was the casual way they seemed to hold their beamers.

Proper identification was exchanged, and they were admitted to a much smaller corridor. Two additional screenings by six more armed men and thranx finally gained them entrance to a modest chamber. In the center of this room was a narrow bed. It sat like a spider in its web at the center of a gleaming mass of highly sophis-ticated medical machinery.

As they moved toward the bed Flinx saw it contained a single immobile man. His eyes were open, staring at nothing. Indirect, carefully aligned lighting insured that his vacant eyes would not be damaged and a tiny device regularly moistened his frozen-open orbs. Awake but unaware, conscious but not cognizant, the man floated nude save for wires and tubes on a bed of clear medical gelatin.

Flinx tried to follow the maze of lines and cables and circuitry that stopped just short of metallic mummification, decided that more than anything else the immobile man resembled an over-utilized power terminal.

Jiwe glanced once at the sleeper. "This is Mordecai Povalo." He turned to Flinx. "Ever hear of him?"

Flinx hadn't.

The Counselor leaned over the motionless figure. "He's been hovering between life and death for weeks now. On certain days he'll show some slight improvement. Other days will require the efforts of a dozen physicians to keep him living. Whether he has any will to live left no one can tell.

"The technicians insist his mind is still active, still functioning. His body tolerates the machines that keep it running. Although his eyes are open we can't tell if they're registering images. Just because his visual centers continue to operate doesn't mean he's seeing anything."

Flinx found himself drawn to the frozen figure. "Will he ever come out of his coma?"

"According to the doctors it's not properly a coma. They don't have a term for it yet. Whatever it is . . . no. They expect him to stay like this until his mind quits or his body finally rejects the life-sustaining equipment."

"Then why," Flinx wanted to know, "keep him alive?"

On Evoria there dwelt a thranx Di-eint called Tintonurac, who was universally famed for his brilliance—though at present, he wore the look of a happy idiot.

Of course, his insectoid face could not produce a human expression, but in the years since the Amalgamation humans had learned to read thranx expressions with the same facility their quasi-symbiotic insect associates had learned to interpret mankind's.

No human or thranx noticed his expression at the moment, an expression alien to the face of the most acclaimed member of his Hive.

Head of his clan, he was a credit to his aunts and uncles, to his hive-mother and to his real parents. Tintonurac's particular wizardry lay in the ability to translate the concepts and schemes of others into reality—for he was a Master Fabricator, or precision engineer. Not only did his mechanical creations improve upon their originator's initial drawings, they were as attractive to look upon as they were supremely functional. Debate raged among his admirers as to whether their idol should more properly be considered a sculptor than an engineer.

Among his many products were a device which neatly dispatched a virulent human disease, an energy multiplex system for the hydroelectric plants so prevalent on thranx worlds, and an improved fire-control system for the sometimes wild yet irresistible SCCAM weapons system that was the mainstay of the combined human-thranx peace-forcer fleet. There were still others, some more esoteric than believable, which only his magic could transform into working devices.

But none of his inventions was the cause of his giddily pleased expression in this eighth month of the tail end of the Season of High Pollen on Evoria. The source of his pleasure was a glistening object that he kept concealed in a drawer of his workbench. He was staring at it now, reveling in its message and its glory as he sat at work in the laboratory, his six assistants attending to business around him. All were respected scientists and engineers in their own right. Of the group, four were thranx and two human. It was a measure of the admiration accorded Tintonurac that such people would volunteer to serve as his assistants, when they could easily have had laboratories and staffs of their own.

The Di-eint's mandibles moved in thranx laughter as he chuckled at a new thought. How curious a thing to occur to him! What might it be like to combine the two liquid metals in the flasks on his truhand's left with the catalyst solvent locked in its container across the room?

Acting as if half asleep, Tintonurac walked to the cabinet and removed the solvent. Turning back to his lounge-seat, he discovered that the pleasure grew deeper and more profound as he pursued this course of action.

Dridenvopa was working with the human Cassidy, but not so intensely that he failed to notice the Di-eint's actions. Distracted, he left his work to stare as Tintonurac poured the syrupy contents of one flask into a second. Bejeweled compound eyes glittered uncertainly when the contents of the overfull flask gushed the new mixture onto the bench, then to the floor. The Di-eint was as clean in his physical manipulations as in his mental, and this was not like him. Nor was the mask of pure, unthinking delight on his face.

Dridenvopa started to comment, then held himself back. Surely the Dieint knew what he was doing. That reassuring thought sent him back to his own task, until he and Cassidy both noticed the brightly labeled container the Di-eint was transferring from a foothand to a truhand.

"Isn't that . . . ?" the human Cassidy began in puzzled symbospeech, the all-purpose galactic patois, as the Di-eint unlocked the container. Instead of finishing the question he let out a strange human yowl and tried to cross meters of intervening benches and equipment before the inevitable occurred. But he was unable to get there in time to prevent a small portion of the harmless liquid in the container from entering the flask of the harmless, mixed liquid metal. Together, these harmless substances formed a rapidly expanding ball so hot and intense as to make white phosphorus seem arctic cold.

Despite the increasing incandescence, Tintonurac concentrated on the pleasing beauty within the object. . . .

The always efficient fire-fighting arm of the local thranx municipality arrived with its usual speed. All that remained for them to lavish their attention on was a scorched region between two buildings. The incredible heat had incinerated the metal walls of the laboratory. Its organic inhabitants had perished.

The investigators decided that someone had made an unusual yet possible mistake. Even the most brilliant scientist could make a fatal slip, even a thranx could lethally err, when hypnotized by a magnificence that the investigators might have understood, had it not been cremated along with the rest of the laboratory's contents—as had been intended.

Jiwe reflected on Flinx's question. "Because he's symptomatic of something which has been happening with distressing frequency lately throughout the Commonwealth. Most people refuse to see any pattern to it, any connection between incidents. A very few, myself among them, aren't so certain these events are unrelated.

"Over the past several years, important people with unique talents have exhibited an unnerving tendency to blow themselves to bits, along with a sometimes equally unique apparatus. Taken individually, these incidents affect only the immolated. Taken collectively, they constitute something potentially dangerous to a great many others."

The silence in the chamber was punctuated only by the efficient hum of life-sustaining equipment, the eerie wheeze of a mechanical zombie.

"Out of dozens, Povalo here is the only one who wasn't quite thorough enough in doing away with himself. Though for all the difference, he might as well be dead. He's certainly no good to himself anymore."

"You say some of you believe these suicides are all linked," Flinx ventured. "Have you discovered anything to connect them?"

"Nothing positive," Jiwe admitted, "which is why there are so few of us. All of them did have *one* thing in common, though. Not one appeared to have any reason for wanting to kill himself. I happen to think that's mighty significant. But the Council doesn't agree."

Flinx showed little interest. Now was the time to quash personal curiosity and get about the business of getting out. "What do you want of me?"

Jiwe moved to a nearby chair, threw himself into it. "Povalo was a wealthy, intelligent, wholly self-possessed engineer doing important research. Now he's a vegetable. I want to know why a man like that—why many humans and thranx like that—seem to find it suddenly necessary to murder themselves. Yes, self-murder . . . I can't call it suicide when I truly believe it's something else."

"What am I supposed to do?" Flinx asked warily.

"You detected that AAnn infiltrator when no one else suspected his presence."

"That was just an accident," Flinx explained. He scratched Pip's jaw. "It happens only when Pip gets excited, when he perceives a possible threat to me." He indicated Povalo. "Your subject is hardly a threat."

"I'm not expecting a thing," Jiwe calmed him, "I'm just asking you to try. I'll try tarot readers and tea leaves after you've failed."

Flinx sighed elaborately. "If you insist . . ."

"Ask," the Counselor reminded him gently, "not insist."

Semantics, Flinx thought sardonically; but he dutifully turned to face the bed and concentrated on its limp occupant. He struggled to reach past those sightless eyes, more afraid of what he might discover than what he might not.

Pip tightened reflexively on his shoulder, sensing his master's effort. Flinx hoped without much confidence that Jiwe hadn't noticed the minidrag's reaction. What he had failed to consider was that his very unease as he concentrated on Povalo was enough to stimulate Pip. There *was* a threat present, even if only in his own mind.

No faint haze obscured his vision. There was no lilting music in his ears to distract him. The bed, its cocoon of circuitry, the shining equipment, and the translucent gelatin suspension—all were clear as ever to his eyes. And yet . . . there was something in his mind that he saw without those eyes, something that hadn't been there a moment ago. It was part of the creature on the bed.

A young man in the fullness of youth—an idealized distortion of Mordecai Povalo—was courting a woman of supernal beauty. Together they floated in thick cumulus clouds engorged with moist love. Side by side they dove ecstatically to the glassy green depths of a shallow ocean. From time to time the figures changed slightly, in build, in coloring, but the subject was ever the same.

Without warning the woman disappeared—swam off, flew off, ran away, depending on the terrain of the moment. Distraught beyond hope, the man walked to a workbench, depressed a switch on a tiny instrument board which would make everything well again.

In the magnificence of youth, Povalo-plus courted a woman of supple grace, swirling and spinning in love-turns about her as they floated among pink clouds. . . .

Flinx blinked once, looked away from the bed. Jiwe was watching him intently. "I'm sorry," he said softly.

"I couldn't detect a thing."

The Counselor held his stare a moment longer, then slumped back into the chair. He appeared to age ten years.

"I got what I expected. I thank you for trying, Flinx."

"May I leave, now?"

"Hm? Oh, yes, of course. Padre-elect," he directed Sylzenzuzex, "you'd better go with our young friend and show him his way out." Then he looked again at Flinx. "I'll authorize a blank voucher for travel anywhere on Terra. You can pick it up on your way out."

"If it's all right with you, sir," Flinx declared, "I'd like to make one more trip to Records. I think I might find some related information on my parents. And I'd like to replay the copy of the information I already have."

Jiwe looked blankly at Namoto, who reminded him: "The boy's parents, remember?"

"Yes. Naturally any help we can give you we will gladly provide.

Padre-elect, you can assist our friend Flinx in finding any information he requires. One last thing, son," Jiwe finished, managing to
smile slightly again, "if you run into any more visitors who smell
like an old jacket instead of a human or thranx, please speak up before your pet assassinates them?"

"I'll do that, sir," Flinx agreed, smiling back. His relief as they
left the room was considerable.

"Where do you want to go?" Sylzenzuzex inquired as they reen-
tered the main hospital corridor. "Back to Genealogy?"

"No . . . I think I've gotten all I can from there. Let's try your
Galographics Department. I think I may have located the world my
parents moved to." This was a lie.

"No problem," Sylzenzuzex assured him, her mandibles clacking politely.

As they continued down the corridor, Flinx mulled over what he
had seen in Povalo's mind. The idealized vision of himself, the
woman, the clouds, seas, and rolling hills—all gentle, simple images of an uncomplicated paradise.

Except for the console. Everything had been all golden and red
and green. He had not seen reality, of course, but merely a simulation of it which the comatose engineer had thought was reality.

Those simple colors. The shifting body outlines. Flinx had seen
them before.

Just prior to his death, the engineer Mordecai Povalo had owned
and played with a Janus jewel.

Povalo's jewel naturally led Flinx to think of Conda Challis and
his own little crystal playhouse. Conda Challis had been in the
mind of the infiltrating AAnn, along with the unknown world
Ulru-Ujurr.

A bizarre series of coincidences which undoubtedly led
nowhere. Never mind the AAnn and to perdition with poor
Mordecai Povalo! Flinx had no room in his mind for anything now
save Challis and the information he had removed from the Church
archive.

That was why he was going to Galographics. His parents . . .
they could quite easily have died right here on Terra. To find out
for certain he had to find Challis; and the merchant might well
have fled to an unfamiliar globe like this Ulru-Ujurr—if indeed
such a world existed and was not merely some aspect of the
AAnn's mind that Flinx had misinterpreted.

It felt as if they had walked for hours before they reached the bank of lifts again. Once more Sylzenzuzex employed the complex card key, once more they traveled an angular pathway.

The level they eventually stepped onto was deserted, a far cry from the bustle of the hospital section. She led him past doors with long compound names engraved in them until they entered the one they sought.

Physically, Galographics looked like a duplicate of the Genealogy Archives, with one exception. This room was smaller and it contained more booths. Furthermore, the monitoring attendant here was much younger than the one he had encountered before.

"I'd like some help hunting up an obscure world."

The attendant drew herself up proudly. "Information retrieval eliminates obscurity. It is the natural building block of the Church, on which all other studies must be based. For without access to knowledge, how can one learn about learning?"

"Please," Flinx said, "no more than two maxims per speech." Behind him, Sylzenzuzex's mandibles clicked in barely stifled amusement.

The attendant's professional smile froze. "You can use the catalog spools, three aisles down." She pointed.

Flinx and Sylzenzuzex walked toward the indicated row. "The world I want to check on is called Ulru-Ujurr."

"Ujurr," she echoed in symbospeech, the odd word sounding more natural when spoken in her consonant-oriented voice. Flinx watched her closely, but she gave no sign that she had ever heard the name before.

He couldn't immediately decide whether that was good or bad.

"Is that symbospeech spelling?" she asked after he made a show of blocking it out. "The tape doesn't say for sure. There may be variables. Let's try phonetic first, though." The attendant appeared to hesitate slightly, wondering if perhaps a Church tape would be so unspecific. But there were variable spellings of far better known worlds, she reminded herself.

They walked down an aisle lined by the vast, nearly featureless walls of the information storage banks. In those metal ramparts, Flinx knew, were stored trillions of bits of information on every known world within and without the Commonwealth.

These records probably had an annex buried somewhere beneath them in the true labyrinth of the Depot complex, an annex closed to casual inspection. For that reason, if Flinx's globular quarry happened to be of some secretive, restricted nature, it might not appear in the spools here.

He was somewhat surprised when they found what appeared to be the proper compartment. Sylzenzuzex pressed a switch nearby and the metal wall responded with oral confirmation.

"It could be a different Ulru-Ujurr," she warned him, as she studied the labels and minute inscriptions identifying the spool case. "But there don't appear to be any cross-references to another world with a similar name."

"Let's try it," Flinx instructed impatiently.

She inserted a card key into the appropriate slot. It was a far simpler device than the one used to operate the multilevel lifts. They were rewarded with a tiny spool of thread-thin tape. She squinted at it—though that was merely an impression Flinx interpreted by her movements, rather than by a physical gesture, since she had no eyelids to narrow.

"It's so hard to tell, but it seems as if there's very little on this tape," she finally told him. "Sometimes, though, you can find a spool that looks like it contains two hundred words and in actuality it holds two million. They could make this system more efficient."

Flinx marveled at anyone who could call such a system inefficient. But, he reminded himself, even the lowliest members of the Church hierarchy were constantly exhorted to find ways to improve the organization. Spiritual methodology, they called it.

Only a few of the booths were occupied. They found one at the end of a row, isolated from the other users.

Flinx took the chair provided for humans, while Sylzenzuzex folded herself into the narrow bench designed for thranx and inserted the fragment of sealed plastic into the playback receptor. Then she activated the viewscreen, using the same procedure Namoto had employed earlier. The screen lit up immediately.

Displayed was the expected statistical profile: Ulru-Ujurr was approximately 20 percent larger than Terra or Hivehom, though its composition produced a gravity only minimally stronger. Its atmosphere was breathable and uncomplicated and it contained plenty of water. There were extensive ice caps at both poles. Further indicative of the planet's cool climate was the extent of apparent glaciation. It was a mountainous world, its temperate zone boasting intemperate weather, and primarily ice north of that.

"It's not a true iceworld," Flinx commented, "but it's cooler than many which are suited to humanx habitation." He examined the extensive list closely, then frowned. "A little cold weather shouldn't discourage all humanx settlement on an otherwise favorable world, but I don't see any indication of even a scientific monitoring post. Every inhabitable world has at least that. Moth supports a good-sized population, and there are humanx settlements of size on far less hospitable planets. I don't understand, Sylzenzuzex."

His companion was all but quivering with imagined cold. " 'Cool,' he calls it. 'Habitable.' For you humans, perhaps, Flinx. For a thranx it's a frozen hell."

"I admit it's far from your conception of the ideal." He turned back to the readout. "Apparently there's both animal and vegetable native life, but no descriptions or details. I can see how the terrain would restrict such studies, but not eliminate them totally the way they seem to have been." He was growing more and more puzzled.

"There aren't any significant deposits of heavy metals or radioactives."

In short, although people *could* live on Ulru-Ujurr—there just wasn't anything to entice them there. The planet lay on the fringe of the Commonwealth, barely within its spatial borders, and it was comparatively distant from the nearest settled world. Not an attractive place to settle.

But dammit, there ought to be some sort of outpost!

That was the end of the tape except for one barely legible addendum: THOSE DESIROUS OF OBTAINING ADDITIONAL STATISTICAL DETAIL CONSULT APPENDIX 4325 SECTION BMQ. . . .

"I presume you're as tired of reading statistics as I am," Sylzenzuzex said as she set the tiny tape to rewind. "As far as your parents are concerned, this world certainly looks like a dead end. What do you wish to see now?"

Trying to keep his tone casual, he said, "Let's go ahead and finish with this one first."

"But that means digging through the sub-indexes," she protested. "Surely you . . ."

"Let's make sure of this," he interrupted patiently.

She made a thranx sound indicating moderate resignation coupled with overtones of amusement, but she didn't argue further.

After nearly an hour of cross-checking they hunted down Appendix 4325, Section BMQ; obtained the necessary sub-index, and prodded the somehow reluctant machine to produce the requested tape sub-subheading. Someone, Flinx thought, had gone to a lot of trouble to conceal this particular bit of information without being obvious about it.

This time his suspicions were confirmed. Slipped into the viewer and activated, the screen displayed glaring red letters which read: ULRU-UJURR . . . HABITABLE WORLD . . . THIS PLANET AND SYSTEM ARE UNDER EDICT. . . .

The date of the first and only survey of the planet was listed, together with the date on which it was placed under Church Edict by the Grand Council.

That was the end of it, as far as Sylzenzuzex was concerned. "You've reached the Hive wall. I can't imagine what led you to think your parents could be on this world. You must have made a mistake, Flinx. That world is Under Edict. That means that nothing and no one is permitted to travel within shuttle distance of its surface. There will be at least one automated peaceforcer in orbit around it, programmed to intercept and challenge anything that tries to reach the planet. Anyone ignoring the Edict . . . well," she paused significantly, "you can't outrun or outmaneuver a peaceforcer." Her eyes glistened. "Why are you looking at me like that?"

"Because I'm going there. To Ulru-Ujurr," he added, at her expression of disbelief.

"I retract my first evaluation," she said sharply. "You are more than strange, Flinx—or perhaps your mind is becoming unhinged by the traumatic events of today."

"My mind's hinges are fastened down and working smoothly, thanks. You want to hear something really absurd?"

She eyed him warily. "I'm not sure."

"I think all these suicides of important people that Jiwe is so worried about have something to do with the Janus jewel."

"The Janus—I've heard of them, but how . . . ?"

He rushed on recklessly. "I saw powder that might have come from a disintegrated jewel on the body of the infiltrator."

"I thought that was from destroyed crystal syringe-darts."

"It could also have been from a whole jewel."

"So what?"

"So . . . I don't know what; but I just have a feeling everything ties together somehow: the jewels, the suicides, this world—and the AAnn."

She looked at him somberly. "If you feel so strongly about this, then for the Hive's sake why did you not tell the Counselor?"

"Because . . . because . . ." his thoughts slowed, ran into that ever-present warning wall, "I can't, that's all. Besides, who'd listen to a crazy theory like that when it comes from . . ." then he smiled suddenly, "an unhinged youngster like myself."

"I don't think you're that young," she countered, pointedly ignoring the comment about him being unhinged. "Then why tell anyone . . . why tell me?"

"I . . . wanted another opinion, to see if my theory sounded as crazy out loud as it does in my head."

Her mandibles clicked nervously. "All right, I think it sounds crazy. Now can we forget all this and go on to the next world your research turned up?"

"My research didn't turn up any other worlds. It didn't turn up Ulru-Ujurr, either."

She looked exasperated. "Then where did you find the name?"

"In the . . ." He barely caught himself. He had almost confessed that he'd plucked it out of the mind of the dying AAnn. "I can't tell you that, either."

"How am I supposed to help you, Flinx, if you refuse to let me?"

"By coming along with me."

She stood there dumbstruck.

"I need someone who can override a peaceforcer command. You're a padre-elect in Security or you wouldn't have been monitoring a station as sensitive as the surface lift corridor. You could do it." He stared anxiously at her.

"You had better go talk to Counselor Jiwe," she told him, speaking very slowly. "Even assuming I could do such a thing, I would never consider challenging a Church Edict."

"Listen," Flinx said quickly, "a higher-ranking Church member wouldn't consider it, and would be followed, if only for protective reasons. Not even a Commonwealth military craft would. But you're not so high up in the hierarchy that it would cause alarm if you suddenly deviated from your planned activities. I'm also betting that you've something of your uncle in you, and he's the most brilliant individual I ever met."

Sylzenzuzex was looking around with the expression of one who suddenly awakens to find herself in a locked room with a starving meat-eater.

"I am not hearing any of this," she muttered frantically. "I am not. It . . . it's blasphemous, and . . . idiotic." Never taking her eyes off him, she started to slide from the bench. "How did I get involved with you, anyway?"

"Please don't scream," Flinx admonished her gently. "As to your question, if you'll think a minute . . . I saved your life. . . ."

8

She paused, all four running limbs cocked beneath her in preparation for a quick sprint toward the monitor's desk. Flinx's words rolled about in her head.

"Yes," she finally admitted, "you saved my life. I'd forgotten, for a moment."

"Then by the Hive, the Mother-Queen and the miracle of metamorphosis," he intoned solemnly, "I now call that debt due."

She tried to sound amused, but he could see she was shaken. "That's a funny oath. Is it designed to tease children?"

For emphasis he repeated it again . . . this time in High Thranx. It was difficult and he stumbled over the clicks and hard glottal stops.

"So you know it," she murmured, slumping visibly, then glancing at the monitor sitting quietly at the distant desk. Flinx knew that a single shout could bring a multitude of armed personnel—and angry questions. He was gambling everything that she wouldn't, that the ancient and powerful life-debt sworn on that high oath would restrain her.

It did. She looked at him pleadingly. "I'm barely adult, Flinx. I still have all my wingcases and I shed my adolescent chiton only a year ago. I've never been wed. I don't want to die, Flinx, for your unexplained obsession. I love my studies and the Church and my potential future. Don't shame me before my family and my Clan. Don't . . . make me do this.

"I'd like to help you . . . truly I would. You've apparently had more than your share of unhappiness and indifference. But please try to understand—"

"I haven't got time to understand," he snapped, shutting her up before she weakened his resolve. He *had* to get to Ulru-Ujurr, if there was even a chance Challis had fled there. "If I'd taken time to understand, I'd be dead half a dozen times already. I call on that oath for you to pay your debt to me."

"I agree then," she replied in a dull voice. "I must. You drown me in your dream." And she added something indicative of hopelessness mixed with contempt.

For a brief moment, for a second, he was ready to tell her to disappear, to leave the room, to run away. The moment passed. He needed her.

If he went directly to someone like Jiwe and told him he had to go to Ulru-Ujurr the Counselor would smile and shrug his shoulders. If he told him about his theory concerning the Janus jewels, Jiwe would demand details, reasons, source of suspicions. That would mean owning up to his talents, something he simply couldn't do.

The Church, for all its goodwill and good works, was still a massive bureaucracy. It would put its own concerns above his. "Sure," they would tell him, "we'll help you find your real parents. But first . . ."

That "first" could last forever, he knew, or at least until a bored Challis had destroyed the last link between Flinx and his heritage. Nor was he convinced they would help him even if he did reveal himself fully—he wasn't certain the Church's adaptability extended to breaking its own Edict.

He was going to Ulru-Ujurr, no matter what, though he couldn't tell anyone the real reason why. Not even the silently waiting Sylzenzuzex, who stared at the floor with the look of the living dead. Surely, though, she would be fully reinstated when it became known she had accompanied him under duress.

Surely . . .

After Sylzenzuzex had applied for and, as a matter of course, received her accumulated leave of several Terran weeks, they took an atmospheric shuttle back to Brisbane Shuttleport. To the questioning machine she had explained that it was time for her to visit her parents on Hivehom. Throughout it all, Flinx never wavered in his determination to take her with him. This couldn't be helped. She was frigidly polite in response to his questions. By mutual agreement they did not engage in casual small talk.

They were held up in Brisbane for over a week while Flinx concluded the complex arrangements required for renting a small, auto-piloted KK-drive ship. Private vessels capable of interstellar travel were not commonly available.

Malaika had been very generous, but the three-day rental fee exhausted the remainder of Flinx's credit account. That didn't trouble him, since he was already guilty of kidnapping. It would hardly matter when the ship broker sent collectors to stalk him after three days had elapsed without his return. He would worry about repaying the astronomical debt he was about to incur another time. If he returned, he reminded himself. The Church had not slapped an Edict on Ulru-Ujurr out of bored perversity. There was a reason . . . and there was always Challis.

Sylzenzuzex knew less about astrogation than he did. If the broker had lied to him about the little ship's self-sufficiency, they would never get to Ulru-Ujurr—or anywhere else.

As a matter of fact, she explained, her chosen field was archeology. Security was only her student specialty. Hivehom's early primitive insectoid societies had always fascinated her. She had dreamed of studying them for the rest of her life, once she graduated and returned home as a full padre—something that would never happen now, she reminded him bitterly.

He ignored her. He had to, or his resolve would crack. Once more he wondered at why an apparently innocuous, inhabitable planet like Ulru-Ujurr should have been placed Under Edict. The information they had studied in Galographics, the long lists of cold statistics that had led him in short order to abduction and fraud and debt, neglected to elaborate on that small matter.

At least one worry was quickly allayed when the powerful little vessel made the supralight jump that took them out of immediate pursuit range. According to simplified readouts, the ship was proceeding at maximum cruising speed on course for the coordinates Flinx had provided it.

Flinx wasn't really concerned that he was worse than broke once again. In a way he was almost relieved. He had spent his entire life in an impecunious state. The abrupt resumption of that familiar condition was like exchanging an expensive dress suit for a favorite pair of old, worn work pants.

The time they spent traveling wasn't wasted. Flinx constantly consulted and questioned the ship's computer, improving his rudimentary knowledge of navigation and ship operation while staying a respectful distance from the autopilot override. He was not ashamed of his ignorance. All KK-drive ships were essentially computer-run. Stellar distances and velocities were far too overwhelming for simple organic minds to manipulate. The humanx crew present on the large KK freightliners was there merely to serve the needs of passengers and cargo, and as a precaution. They constituted the flexible fail-safe, ready to take over in the event the ship's machine mind malfunctioned.

It was fortunate that he was so interested in the ship, because Sylzenzuzex proved to be anything but a lively companion. She preferred instead to remain in her cabin, emerging only to pick up her meals from the autochef. Gradually, however, even the patience of one accustomed to underground living began to wear thin, and she spent more and more time on the falsely luxurious bridge of the ship. Still, when she deigned to say anything at all, her conversation was confined to monosyllabic comments of utter despondency.

Such willing submission to reality grated against Flinx's nature even more than her silence. "I don't understand you, Sylzenzuzex. You're like a person attending her own wake. I told you I'll confirm that I kidnaped you against your will. Surely everyone will have to admit you're blameless for anything that happens?"

"You just don't understand," she muttered sibilantly. "I could not lie like that. Not to my superiors in the Church, or to my family or hive-mother. Certainly not to my parents. I went with you willingly." Her exquisite head, shining like the sea in the overhead lighting, dipped disconsolately.

"You're not making sense," Flinx argued vehemently. "You had no choice! I called on you to fulfill a hereditary debt. How can anyone blame you for that? As for our forbidden destination—that was wholly my choice. You had nothing to say about my decision and you have voiced plenty of objections to it." As he talked, his preprepared meal lay cooling in its container nearby. Meanwhile Pip's jet eyes stared pensively up at his troubled master.

Sylzenzuzex stared across at him. "There are still some things humans do not understand about us," and she turned away as if those were to be her last words on the subject.

Always the convenient phrase, Flinx thought furiously. Whether human or thranx, it mattered not—always the ready willingness to seek refuge in absolutes. Why were supposedly intelligent beings so terrified of reason? He stared out the foreport, frustrated beyond measure. The universe did not run on emotional principles. He had never been able to understand how people could.

"Have it your way," Flinx grumbled. "We'll stick to more immediate concerns. Tell me about this peaceforcer station that's supposed to prevent us from landing on this world."

There was a whistling sound as a large dollop of air was forced out through breathing spicules—a thranx sigh. "Peaceforcers, more likely. There should be anywhere from one to four of them in synchronous orbit around the planet. I'm not certain because so few worlds are Under Edict that the subject is rarely brought up for discussion. So, of course there is no information whatsoever on the worlds themselves. Being Under Edict, as they say, is a situation discussed more as a possibility than a fact.

"I would imagine," she concluded, walking over to a console and gazing idly at the instrumentation, "that we will be signaled or intercepted in some fashion and ordered to leave."

"What if we ignore any such warning?"

She made a thranx shrug. "Then we're likely to have our wing-cases blown off."

Flinx's tone turned sarcastic. "I thought the Church was an inter-species purveyor of gentleness and understanding."

"That's right," she shot back, "and it provides a lot of comfort and assurance to everyone to know that the Church's decrees are enforced." Her voice rose. "Do you think that the Church puts a whole world Under Edict because of some counselor's whim?"

"I don't know," he replied, unperturbed. "Probably we'll get the chance to find out. . . ."

Without warning a flying fortress appeared out of nowhere. One minute they were alone in free-space, cycling in toward the fourth planet of an undistinguished sun, and the next a craft with six points projecting from its principal axes had matched their speed and was cruising alongside. This ship was many times the size of their small vessel.

"Automated peaceforce station twenty-four," a mechanical voice said pleasantly over the speakers. The tridee screen could not pick up any picture.

"To undeclared vessel class sixteen-R. In the name of the Church and the Commonwealth you are hereby notified that the world you approach is Under Edict. You are directed to reverse your present course and re-engage your double-K drive. No vessel is permitted to make shuttlefall on the fourth planet, nor to remain in the vicinity of this sun.

"You have thirty standard minutes from the conclusion of this notification to reprogram your navigational computer. Do not, repeat, do not attempt to approach within scanner range of the fourth world. Do not attempt to move closer than five planetary diameters. Failure to comply with the aforementioned regulations will be dealt with appropriately."

"A polite way of saying it'll blow us to small pieces," Sylzenzuzex commented dryly. "Now can we go back?"

Flinx didn't reply. He was busy studying the mass of metal drifting next to them. That it was supremely fast, far faster than this small craft, had already been demonstrated. Without question, several weapons of various destructive capabilities were trained on the bridge even as he wondered what to do next. They could no more make a desperate dash for the planet's surface than he could outrun a devilope on the plains bordering the Gelerian Swamp, back home.

"This is why I've brought you," he told the waiting thranx. "It sure wasn't for the pleasure of your company." Flinx moved aside, revealing activated instrumentation. "Here's the tridee. Give it your name, Church identity number, Security code—whatever it takes to gain clearance to land."

She didn't budge, her legs seemingly rooted in the metal floor. "But it won't listen to me."

"Try."

"I . . . I won't do it."

"You're under life-oath, you've sworn on your Hive," he reminded her between clenched teeth, hating himself more with every word.

Again the symmetrical head drooped; again the hollow, defeated voice. "Very well." She shuffled over to the console.

"I'm telling you for the last time," she told him, "that if you make me do this, it's as if you've banished me from the Church yourself, Flinx."

"I happen to have more confidence in your own organization than you apparently do. Besides, if after a full explanation of the circumstances they actually do kick you out, then I don't think the organization's worthy of you."

"How sure you are," she said calmly, concluding with a sound so harsh it made Flinx flinch.

"Go ahead," he ordered.

She tested the broadcast, then rattled off a series of superfast words and numbers. Flinx could barely identify them, much less make any sense of the steady stream of hybrid babble. It occurred to him that she might just as well have given the fortress the command to destroy them. That unpleasant thought passed when nothing happened. After all, survival was as strong a thranx drive as it was a human one.

Instead, the announcement brought the hoped-for result. "Emergency temporary cancellation received and understood," came the stiff voice. "Processing."

Two minutes stretched long as two years while Flinx waited for the final reply.

Then: "Other stations notified. You may proceed."

There was no time to waste on giving thanks. Flinx rushed to the navigation input and verbally instructed the ship to take up a low orbit around the temperate equatorial zone, above the largest continent. The detector devices on the ship were then to begin a search for any sign of surface communications facilities—anything that would indicate the presence of humanx settlement.

Anywhere someone like Challis could exist.

"What if there isn't anything like that," Sylzenzuzex asked, her face paling as the ship pulled away from the orbiting fortress. "There's a whole world down there, bigger than Hivehom, bigger than Terra."

"There'll be someplace developed," he assured her. His confident tone belied the uncertainty in his mind.

There was. Only they didn't locate it—it found them.

"What ship . . . what ship . . . ?" the speakers crackled as soon as they entered parking orbit. The query came in perfect symbospeech, though whether from thranx or human throat he couldn't tell.

Flinx moved to the pickup. "Who's calling?" he asked, a mite inanely.

"What ship?" the voice demanded.

This could go on for hours. He responded with the first thing that sounded halfway plausible. "This is the private research vessel *Chamooth* on Church-related business, out from Terra."

There, that wasn't a complete lie. His abduction of Sylzenzuzex certainly constituted Church-related business, and he had been led here by information in Church files.

A long pause followed while unseen beings at the other end of the transmission digested this. Finally: "Shuttleport coordinates for you are as follows."

Flinx scrambled to record the information. His ruse had gotten them that much. After they landed . . . well, he would proceed from there. The numbers translated into a position on a fairly small plateau in the mountains of the southern continent. According to the information, the landing strip bordered an enormous lake at the 14,000-meter-level.

Sweating, muttering at his own awkwardness, Flinx succeeded in positioning the ship over the indicated landing spot with a minimum of corrections to the autopilot. From there it was a rocky, bouncing descent by means of autoprogrammed shuttlecraft to the surface.

Sylzenzuzex was talking constantly now, mostly to herself. "I just don't understand," she kept murmuring over and over, "there shouldn't be anything down there. Not on an edicted world. Not even a Church outpost. This just doesn't make any sense."

"Why shouldn't it make sense?" Flinx asked her, fighting to keep his seat as the tiny shuttle battled powerful crosswinds. "Why shouldn't the Church have business on a world it wants to keep everyone else off of?"

"But only an extreme threat to the good of humanx kind is reason enough for placing a world Under Edict," she protested, her tone one of disbelief. "I've never heard of an exception."

"Naturally not," Flinx agreed, with the surety of one who had experienced many perversities of human and thranx nature. "Because no information is available on worlds which are Under Edict. How very convenient."

The shuttle was banking now, dipping down between vast forested mountain slopes. A denser atmosphere here raised the tree line well above what existed on Moth or Terra. Tarns and alpine lakes were everywhere. At the higher elevations, baby glaciers carved tentative paths downward—even here, near the planet's equator.

"Commencing landing approach," the shuttle computer informed them. Flinx stared ahead, saw that the plateau the ground-based voice had mentioned was far smaller than he had hoped. This was not a true plateau, but instead a broad glacial plain ice-quarried from the mountains. One side of the plateau-plain was filled with a narrow lake that glistened like an elongated sapphire.

As the shuttle straightened out they rushed past a sheer waterfall at least a thousand meters high, falling to the canyon below in a single unbroken plunge like white steel. This, he decided, was a magnificent world.

If only the shuttle would set them down on it in one piece.

His acceleration couch trembled as the ship fired braking jets. Ahead he could now make out the landing strip that ran parallel to the deep lake. At the far end, a tiny cluster of buildings poked above the alluvial gravel and low scrub.

At least the installation here—whoever was manning it—was advanced enough to include automatic landing lock-ons. Built into the fabric of the landing strip itself, they hooked into the corresponding linkups in the belly of the shuttle. The completion of this maneuver was signaled by a violent lurch. Then the landing computer, somewhere below them, took over and brought the shuttle in for a smooth, safe setdown.

Sylzenzuzex stared out the side port on the left even as she was undoing her straps. "This is insane," she muttered, gazing at the considerable complex of structures nearby, "there can't be a base here. There shouldn't be anything."

"Some anythings," he commented, gesturing toward the pair of large groundcars which were now moving onto the field toward them, "are coming to pay their greetings. Remember now," he reminded her as he calmed a nervous Pip and headed for the access corridor leading to the hatch, "you're here because I forced you to come."

"But not physically," she countered. "I told you before, I can't lie."

"The Horse Head," he murmured, looking skyward. "Be evasive then. Ah, do what you think best. I'm no more going to convert you to reason than you're going to convince me to enter your Church."

Flinx activated the automatic lock, and it began to cycle open. If the atmosphere outside had been unbreathable, despite the information in the Galographics records, the lock would not have opened. As the door plug drew aside, a rippled ramp extended itself, sensors at its far end halting it as soon as it touched solid ground.

Pip was stirring violently, but Flinx kept a firm hand on his pet. Apparently the minidrag perceived some threat again, which would be natural if, say, this was indeed a Church installation. In any case they couldn't take on an entire party which was presumably armed. It took several minutes before he succeeded in convincing his pet to relax, regardless of what happened next.

Flinx took a deep breath as he started down the ramp. Sylzenzuzex trooped morosely behind, lost in morose thought. Despite the altitude, the air here was thick and rich in oxygen. It more than counteracted the slightly stronger gravity.

Snow-crowned crags rose around the valley on three sides. Except for the glacial plain they now stood on, the valley and mountain slopes were furred with a thick coat of great trees. Green was still the predominant color but there was a substantial amount of yellow-hued vegetation. Their branches rose stiffly skyward, no doubt to be fully spread by the winter snowfall.

The temperature was perfect—about 20°C. At least, it was as far as Flinx was concerned. Sylzenzuzex was already cold, and the dry air did nothing to help the flexibility of her exoskeletal joints.

"Don't worry," he said, trying to cheer her as the groundcars drew near, "there must be quarters provided for thranx personnel. You can warm up soon."

And explain your story to the local authority in private if you wish, he added silently.

His thoughts were broken as the first big car pulled to a halt before them. As he waited Flinx kept a tight grip on Pip, holding the tense minidrag at the wing joints to prevent any sudden flight. Yet despite the minutes he had already spent calming his pet, Pip still struggled. When he finally settled down, he coiled painfully tight around Flinx's shoulder.

People began to emerge from the groundcar. They did not wear aquamarine robes of the Church, nor the crimson of the Commonwealth. They did not look like Commonwealth-registered operatives, either, and they were carrying ready beamers.

Seven armed men and women spread out in a half-circle which covered the two arrivals. They moved with an efficiency Flinx did not like. As the second car arrived and began to disgorge its passengers, several members of the first group broke off to run up the ramp and disappear into the shuttle.

"Now listen . . ." Flinx began easily. One of the men in the group waved his beamer threateningly.

"I don't know who you are, but for now, shut up."

Flinx complied readily, as Sylzenzuzex—frozen now with more than the cold—stood behind him and studied their captors.

Several minutes passed before the pair who had entered the shuttle re-emerged and shouted down to their companions: "There's no one else aboard, and no weapons."

"Good. Resume your positions."

Flinx turned to the squat, middle-aged woman who had spoken. She was standing directly opposite him. She had the face of one who had seen too many things too soon and whose youth had been a time of blasted hopes and unfulfilled dreams. A vivid scar ran back from a corner of one eye in a jagged curve to her ear, then down the side of her neck to disappear beneath her high collar. Its livid whiteness was shocking against her dusky skin. She flaunted the scar like a favorite necklace. He noticed that her simple garb of work pants, boots, and high-necked overblouse had seen plenty of use.

Taking out a pocket communicator, she spoke into it: "Javits says there's no one else on board and no weapons." A mumble too soft and distant for Flinx to understand issued from the compact unit's speaker.

"No, instruments don't show any automatic senders aboard, either. Has the ship in orbit responded again?" Another pause, then, "It looks like there's only the two of them."

She flipped off the unit, stuck it back in her utility belt and regarded Flinx and Sylzenzuzex. "Does anyone know you've come here?"

"You don't expect me to make it easy for you, do you?" Flinx responded, to divert attention from Sylzenzuzex as well as to answer the query.

"Funny boy." The woman took a deliberate step forward, raised the beamer back over her left shoulder. Pip stirred and she suddenly became aware that the minidrag was not a decoration.

"I wouldn't do that," Flinx told her softly. She eyed the snake.

"Toxic?"

"Very."

She didn't smile back. "We can kill it and the both of you, you know."

"Sure," agreed Flinx pleasantly. "But if you swing that beamer at me, then both Pip and I are going to go for your throat. If he doesn't kill you I probably will, no matter how fast this ring of happy faces moves. On the off chance we don't, then I'll be dead and your superior will be damned displeased at not having the chance to question me. Either way, you lose."

Fortunately the woman wasn't the type to act without thinking. She stepped back, still keeping her beamer trained on him. "Very funny boy," she commented tightly. "Maybe the Madam will let me have you after she's finished asking her questions. Act as smart as you like. You've got a short future." She gestured sharply with the beamer. "Both of you—into the first car."

They walked between the beamers. Flinx tensed in readiness as he entered the large compartment, saw to his disappointment that two armed and equally tense people were awaiting him inside. No chance of jumping for the controls, then. He climbed in resignedly.

Sylzenzuzex followed him, having to squat uncomfortably on the bare floor because the car was equipped only with human seating, which would not accommodate her frame. Several of the armed guards followed. To Flinx's relief, the squat woman was not among them.

A low hum rose to a whine as the groundcar lifted. Staying a meter above ground, it moved toward the nearby buildings, the second car following close behind. As they came nearer, Flinx could see that the complex was built at the edge of the forest. In the distance he could just make out several additional structures hugging the mountainside, high up among the trees.

The cars pulled up before a steeply gabled five-story building. They were escorted inside.

"The buildings here are all slants and angles," Flinx commented to Sylzenzuzex as they made the short walk from car to entrance-way. "The trees already show that the snowfall here must be tremendous in winter. And this is the local equivalent of the tropics."

"Tropics," she snorted, her mandibles clacking angrily. "I'm freezing already." Her voice dropped. "It probably doesn't make any difference, since we're likely to be killed soon. Or hasn't it dawned on you that we've stumbled onto a very large illegal installation of some kind?"

"The thought occurred to me," he replied easily.

Taking a lift to the top floor, they came out into a corridor along which a few preoccupied men and women moved on various errands. They were not so absorbed that they failed to look startled at the appearance of Flinx and Sylzenzuzex.

The group made one turn to the left, continued almost to the end of a branch corridor, then stopped. Addressing the door pickup, the squat woman requested and received permission to enter. She disappeared inside, leaving the heavily guarded twosome to wait and think, before the door slid aside once again.

"Send 'em in."

Someone gave Flinx a hard shove that sent him stumbling forward. Sylzenzuzex was introduced into the room with equal roughness.

They stood in a luxurious chamber. Pink-tinted panels revealed a rosy vista of lake and mountains, landing field and—Flinx noted with longing—their parked shuttlecraft. It seemed very far away now.

A small waterfall danced at one end of the room, surrounded by carpets that were more fur than fabric. Thick perfume scented the air, clutched cloyingly at his senses. Behind them the door slid silently shut.

There was another person in the room.

She was seated in a lounge chair near the transparent panels, and was clad in a light gown. Her long blond hair was done up in a triple whirl, the three braids coiled one above each ear and the last at the back of her head. At the moment she was drinking something steaming from a taganou mug.

Scarface addressed her with deference. "They're here, Madam Rudenuaman."

"Thank you, Linda." The woman turned to face them. Flinx sensed Sylzenzuzex's surprise.

"She's barely older than you or I," she whispered.

Flinx said nothing, merely waited impassively and gazed back into olivine eyes. No, olivine wasn't right—gangrenous would be more appropriate. There was an icy murderousness behind those eyes which he sensed more strongly than the drifting perfume.

"Before I have you killed," the young woman began in a pleasant liquid voice, "I require answers to a few questions. Please keep in mind that you have no hope. The only thing you have any control over whatsoever is the manner of your death. It can be quick and efficient, depending on your willingness to answer my questions, or slow and tedious if you prove reluctant. Though not boring, I assure you. . . ."

9

Flinx continued to study her as she took another sip of her steaming drink. She was almost beautiful, he couldn't help but notice—though any trace of softness was absent from her face.

Reaching to one side, she picked up an intricately carved cane. With this she was able to rise and limp over to examine them more closely. She favored her left leg.

"I am Teleen auz Rudenuaman. You are . . . ?"

"My name's Flinx," he responded readily, seeing no profit in angering this crippled bomb of a woman.

"Sylzenzuzex," his companion added.

The woman nodded, turned and walked back to resume her seat, instructing them both to sit also. Flinx took a chair, noticing out of the corner of an eye that the scarred woman called Linda was watching his—and Pip's—every move from her position by the door. Sylzenzuzex folded herself on the fur floor nearby.

"Next question," the woman Rudenuaman said. "How did you get past the Church peaceforcer?"

"We . . ." he started to say, but stopped as he felt a delicate yet firm grip on his arm. Looking past the truhand, he saw Sylzenzuzex eying him imploringly.

"I'm sorry, Syl, but I've got an aversion to torture. We're not going anywhere and for the moment, at least, I'd like to . . ." The truhand pulled away. He did not miss the look of utter contempt she threw him.

"Sensible as well as sassy," Rudenuaman commented approvingly. "I've been listening to you ever since you landed." The brief flicker of a grin vanished and she repeated impatiently, "The fortresses, how did you get past?"

Flinx indicated Sylzenzuzex. "My friend," he explained, ignoring the hollow mandibular laugh that flowed from her, "is a padre-elect currently working in Church security. She talked the peaceforcer into letting us pass."

Rudenuaman looked thoughtful. "The circumvention was accomplished verbally, then?" Flinx nodded. "We'll have to see if we can do something about that."

"About a peaceforcer fortress?" Sylzenzuzex blurted. "How can you modify—in fact, how did *you* succeed in passing them? What are you doing here, with this illegal installation? This is an edicted world. No one but the Church or those in the highest echelons of the Commonwealth government have the codes necessary to pass a peaceforcer station; certainly no private concern has that ability."

The woman smiled. "This private concern does."

"Which concern is that?" Flinx asked. She turned her unfunny grin on him.

"For a condemned man you ask a lot of questions. However, I don't have the chance to brag very often. It's Nuaman Enterprises. Ever hear of it?"

"I have," Flinx told her, thinking that this search for his parentage was making him a lot of rotten business contacts. "It was founded by . . ."

"By my aunt's relatives," she finished for him, "and then further developed by my Aunt Rashalleila, may a foulness become her soul." The smile widened. "But I am in charge now. I felt a change of personnel at the uppermost executive position was in order.

"Unfortunately, the first time I tried replacing her I chose for my cohort a man of muscle and no brains. No, that's not accurate. Muscle and no loyalty. It cost me," and she frowned in reminiscence, "a bad time. But I managed to escape from the medical hell my aunt had me committed to. My second attempt was better planned—and successful.

"It is now Rudenuaman Enterprises, you see. Me."

"No private concern has the wherewithal to circumvent a Church peaceforcer," Sylzenzuzex insisted.

"Despite your security clearance, stiff one, you seem to cherish all kinds of foolish notions. Not only have we, with some help, I admit, circumvented them; but they remain in operation to warn off or destroy any visitors we do not clear.

"You can see why your sudden appearance caused me considerable initial worry. But I'm not worried anymore—not since you proved so cooperative in following our landing instructions. Of course, you had no reason to expect a greeting from anyone other than a bunch of surprised Churchmen."

"You have no right . . ." Sylzenzuzex began.

"Oh, please," a disgusted Rudenuaman muttered. "Linda . . ."

Scarface left her place at the door. Flinx held on tightly to Pip; this was no time or place to force a final confrontation. Not yet.

The squat woman kicked suddenly and Flinx heard the crack of chiton. Sylzenzuzex let out a high, shrill whistle as one foothand collapsed at the main joint. Reddish-green blood began to leak steadily as she fell on her side, clutching with truhands and her other foothand at the injured member.

Linda turned and resumed her position at the door as if nothing had happened.

"You know she has an open circulatory system," Flinx muttered carefully. "She'll bleed to death."

"She would," Rudenuaman corrected him, "if Linda had cracked the leg itself instead of just breaking the joint. A thranx joint will coagulate. Her leg will heal, which is more than you can say for what mine did after my aunt's medical experimenters finished with it." She tapped her own left leg with the cane. It rang hollowly. "Other parts of me also had to be replaced, but they left the most important thing," she indicated her head, "intact. That was my aunt's last mistake.

"I've only one more question for you." She leaned forward, and for the first time since the interrogation began seemed genuinely interested. "What on Terra possessed you to come here, to a world Under Edict, in the first place? And only two of you, unarmed."

"It's funny," Flinx told her, "but . . . I also have a question that needs to be answered."

Seeing that he was serious, she sat back in her chair. "You're a peculiar individual. Almost as peculiar as you are stupid. What question?"

He was suddenly overwhelmed by a multitude of conflicting possibilities. One fact was clear—whether or not she could tell him what he wished to know, he and Sylzenzuzex would die. As the silence lengthened, even Sylzenzuzex became curious enough to forget the pain in her foothand momentarily.

"I can't tell you that," he finally answered.

Rudenuaman looked at him askance. "Now that's strange. You've told me everything else. Why hesitate at this?"

"I could tell you, but you'd never believe me."

"I'm pretty credulous at times," she countered. "Try me, and if I find it intriguing, maybe I won't kill you after all." The thought seemed to amuse her. "Yes, tell me and I'll let you both live. We can always use unskilled labor here. And I am not surrounded by

clever types. I may keep you around for novelty, for when I'm visiting here."

"All right," he decided, electing to accept her offer as the best
they could hope for, "I came hoping to find the truth of my
birthright."

Her amused expression vanished. "You're right . . . I don't believe you. Unless you can do better than that . . ."

She was interrupted by a chime and looked irritably to the door.
"Linda . . ." There was a wait while the squat woman slid the door
back and silently conversed with someone outside. Simultaneously
something almost forgotten suddenly howled in Flinx's mind.

That was matched by a scream which everyone could hear.

"Challis," an angry Rudenuaman yelled, "can't you keep that
brat quiet? Why you continue to drag her around with you is something I never . . ." She broke off, looking from the merchant who
was standing in the half-open doorway goggling at Flinx, to the
red-haired youth, and then back at the merchant again.

"Gu . . . wha . . . *you*!" Conda Challis finally managed to blurt,
like a man clearing his throat of a choking bone.

"You know this man?" Rudenuaman asked Challis. A terrible
fury was building in her, as it slowly became clear how Flinx had
found this world. She was only partially correct, but it was the part
she could believe. "You *know* each other! Explain yourself,
Challis!"

The merchant was completely out of control. "He knows about
the jewels," he babbled. "I wanted him to help me play with a jewel
and he . . ."

Unwittingly, the merchant had revealed something Flinx half
suspected. "So, the Janus jewels come from here. That's very interesting, and it explains a great deal." He looked down at
Sylzenzuzex.

"Most obviously, Syl, it explains why anyone would go to the incredible expense and chance the enormous penalty involved in ignoring a Church edict."

A miniature, silvery voice exploded. "You colossal, obese idiot!" it half screamed, half bawled.

The already battered Challis looked down, shocked to see the
ever-compliant Mahnahmi making horrible faces up at him. Flinx
watched with interest. The merchant had finally done something
dangerous enough to cause her to break her carefully maintained
shell of innocence.

Rudenuaman looked on with equal curiosity, though her real attention and anger were still reserved for Challis. She was eying him almost pityingly.

"You are becoming a liability, Conda. I don't know why this man has come here, but I don't think it involves the jewels. Nor does it matter anymore that you've just given away the best-kept secret in the entire Commonwealth, because it will never leave this world—certainly not with either of these two." She indicated Flinx and Sylzenzuzex.

"But he's been following me, haunting me!" Challis protested frantically. "It has to have something to do with the jewels."

Rudenuaman turned to Flinx. "You've been following Challis? But why?"

The merchant yammered on, unaware he was providing confirmation of Flinx's earlier reply. "Oh, some blithering insanity about his ancestry!" He didn't add, much to Flinx's dismay, whether he possessed any further information on that particular obsession.

"Maybe I do believe you," Rudenuaman said cautiously to Flinx. "If it's an excuse, it's certainly a consistent one."

Better get her off the subject of himself, Flinx decided. "Where are the jewels mined? Up at that big complex on the mountainside?"

"You are amusing," she said noncommittally. "Yes, I may keep you alive for a while. It would be a change to have some mental stimulation." She turned sternly to face the merchant. "As for you, Conda, you have finally allowed your private perversions to interfere with business once too often. I had hoped . . ." She shrugged. "The fewer who know about the jewels and where they originate, the better. But considering what is at stake here I think I have to risk finding another outside distributor."

"Teleen, no," Challis muttered, shaking his head violently. From an immensely wealthy, powerful merchant he had suddenly been reduced to a frightened, fat old man.

"And we'll have to do something about the whining brat-child, too," she added, turning a venomous stare on the silently watching Mahnahmi. "Linda . . . take them over to Riles. He can do what he wants with Challis, as long as it's reasonably quick. After all," she added magnanimously, "he was an associate of ours for a while. As for the little whiner, save her for after-dinner entertainment. We ought to be able to make her last a few days."

"No!"

Flinx felt himself lifted in the grip of a mental shriek of outrage.

A tremendous force ripped through the room, tearing rugs and furniture and people from their moorings and hurling them away from the doorway. Several of the thick pink polyplexalloy panels were blown out.

Flinx fought for control of his body, managed to come to a halt against a couch firmly anchored in the floor. Pip fluttered uneasily above his head, hissing angrily but unable to do more than hold his air in the face of the gale.

Hair flying, Flinx shielded his face with one hand and squinted into the hurricane.

Sylzenzuzex had been rolled skittering into a far corner. The guard, Linda, was lying unconscious nearby. She had been standing closest to the immense blast. Teleen auz Rudenuaman lay buried in a mass of thick fur rugs and broken fixtures, while the considerable bulk of Conda Challis hugged the fixed fur near the doorway and hung on for dear life as the wind pulled and tore at him.

"You fat imbecile!" the source of that pocket typhoon was screaming at him, stamping childishly at the floor. "You pig's ass, you jelloid moron . . . you've gone and spoiled *everything*! Why couldn't you keep your dumb mouth shut? For years I've kept you from tripping over your own tongue, for years I've made the right decisions for you when you gleefully thought it was your doing! Now you've thrown it all away, all away!" She was crying, girlish tears running down her cheeks.

"Child of my own," Challis gasped into the wind, "get us out of this and—"

"Child of my own!" she spat down at him. "I don't know the words yet to describe what you've thought of doing to me, or what you have done—not that it would matter to you. I can't save you anymore, Daddy Challis." She glared around the room.

"You can all go to your respective hells! I'm not afraid of any of you. But I need time to grow into myself. I don't know what I am, yet."

She glared contemptuously back at Challis. "You've ruined my chance to grow up rich and powerful. The Devil take you."

Turning, she disappeared, running down the corridor. "Someday," a mental shout stabbed fadingly at Flinx, "I'll even be strong enough to come back for *you*."

The wind died slowly, in increments. Flinx was able to roll over in the falling breeze and feel his bruises. He saw that Sylzenzuzex had succeeded in protecting her broken foothand. Her hard exoskeleton had saved her from any additional injury, so that while the first wounded, she actually was the least battered of anyone in the room. Except for Pip, of course, who settled unhurt but disturbed on Flinx's shoulder. Only the force of the wind had prevented him from killing Mahnahmi.

Teleen auz Rudenuaman was more shaken than she cared to admit. "Linda . . . Linda!" The guard was just regaining consciousness. "Alert the base, everyone. That child is to be killed instantly. She's an Adept."

"Yes . . . Madam," the woman replied thickly. Her right cheek was bleeding and discolored, and she was wincing painfully as she touched her left elbow.

Rudenuaman tried to sound confident. "I don't care what kind of magic tricks she can pull. She's only a child and she can't go anywhere."

As if in reply, minutes later a dull rumble reached them through the broken window panels. Rudenuaman limped hurriedly to the transparent wall. Flinx was also there, in time to see something that he, alone of those in the room, wasn't surprised at.

Their shuttlecraft—and all remaining hope of escape—was shrinking rapidly into the sky at the end of the landing strip, a vanishing dot between the mountaintops.

"She . . . she can pilot a shuttle," a dazed Challis was mumbling to himself.

"Quiet, Conda. Anyone can direct a craft attuned to accept verbal commands. Still, alone, at her age . . ."

"She's been using me. Her, using *me,*" Challis continued, oblivious to everything around him. His eyes were glazed. "All these years I thought she was such a charming, pretty little . . . and she's been using me!" The laughter began to fall.

"Will you *shut up!*" Rudenuaman finally had to scream. But the merchant ignored her, continued to roll around on the floor roaring hysterically at the wonderful, marvelous joke that had been played on him. He was still chuckling, albeit more unevenly, when two guards arrived to escort him out.

Flinx envied him. Now he would never feel the beamer when they executed him. Shake a man's world badly enough and the man comes apart, not the world. First the sudden sight of Flinx, here, and then Mahnahmi. No, not even all the King's horses and all the King's men could put Conda Challis together again.

Rudenuaman watched until the door closed and then collapsed, exhausted, on a battered couch—one of the few left undestroyed by Mahnahmi's uncontrolled infantile violence. She debated with herself, then finally said, "It has to be done. Call Riles."

"Yes, Madam," Linda acknowledged.

Momentarily forgotten, Flinx and Sylzenzuzex rested and treated each other's wounds as best they could. Before long a tall, muscular man entered the room.

"I've been briefed," he said sharply. "How could this happen, Rudenuaman?"

Pip bridled and Flinx put a tight restraining grip on his pet. His own senses were quivering. Something he had sensed the moment they'd left the shuttle was intensified in this newcomer's presence.

"It could not be prevented," Rudenuaman told him, her tone surprisingly meek. "The child is apparently a psionic of unknown potentialities. She had fooled even her own father."

"Not a difficult task, from what I am told of how Challis behaved. He will be more useful to us dead," the tall figure said, swinging around to face Flinx and Sylzenzuzex. "These are the two captives who penetrated the defenses?"

"Yes."

"See that they do not also escape, if you can," the figure snapped. "Though if the child escapes to tell of what she knows of this place, it will not matter what is done with these two. This entire deception is beginning to weary me. . . ."

Then he reached up, grabbed his chin, and pulled his face off.

A gargled clicking came from Sylzenzuzex as the irritated notman turned to leave the room. Flinx was shaken, too. He knew now what had been troubling him and his pet, since they had landed on this world. It wasn't just that the man turned out to be an AAnn—for that was a possibility he had suspected ever since he'd fished the image of Conda Challis and Ulru-Ujurr out of the reptilian infiltrator's mind back on Terra.

It was because he knew this particular AAnn.

But the Baron Riidi WW had never set eyes on Flinx, who had never strayed within range of the tridee pickup when the Baron had pursued him and the others on board Maxim Malaika's ship, so many months ago. Flinx, however, had seen all too much of that frigid, utterly self-possessed face, had heard too many threats pronounced by that smooth voice.

Riidi WW turned at the door, and for a moment Flinx feared the AAnn aristocrat had recognized him after all. But he'd paused only to speak to Rudenuaman again.

"You had best hope that the child does not escape, Teleen."

Though no longer conveying the impression of total omnipotence, the merchantwoman was far from being cowed. "Don't threaten me, Baron. I have resources of my own. I could make it difficult for you if I were suddenly missed."

"My dear Rudenuaman," he objected, "I was not threatening you. I would not . . . you have been too valuable to us—both you and your aunt before you. I would not have any other human holding the Commonwealth end of this relationship. But if the child gets away, then by the-sand-that-shelters-life this entire operation will have to be closed down. If a follow-up party from the Church were to discover this base and find that it is being partially funded and operated by the imperial race, that could serve as a pretext for war. While not afraid, the Empire would prefer not to engage in hostilities just now. We would be forced to destroy the mine and obliterate all trace of this installation."

"But it would take years to replace this," she pointed out.

"Several, at least," the Baron concurred. "And that is but an optimistic estimate. Suppose the Church should elect to patrol this system with crewed fortresses instead of gullible automatons? We could never come back."

"I was right," Sylzenzuzex declared with satisfaction. "No private concern *does* have sufficient resources to bypass a Church peaceforcer station. Only another spatial government like the Empire could manage it."

The Baron gave her an AAnn salute that suggested she had just won a Pyrrhic victory. "That is quite so, young lady. Neither would the Empire be concerned, as a private corporation might be, that your Church has placed this world Under Edict. What does concern us is that it lies within Commonwealth territory. Our danger in discovery lies in the diplomatic consequences, not in some imaginary devil someone in your hierarchy places here."

"You haven't found anything on this world to justify its quarantine?" Flinx asked, curiosity drowning his caution.

"Nothing, my young friend," the tall AAnn replied. "It is wet and cold, but otherwise most hospitable."

Flinx eyed the Baron closely, trying to penetrate that calculating mind, without success. His erratic talent refused to cooperate. "You're chancing an interstellar war just to make some credit?"

"What's wrong with money? The Empire thrives on it, as does your Commonwealth. Who knows," the Baron said, smiling, "it may be that my hand in this is concealed from my own government. What the *arkazy* does not see in the sand will not bite him, *vya-nar*?

"Now you must excuse me, for we have a runaway infant who requires scolding." He vanished through the doorway.

Flinx had dozens of questions he could have thrown at the AAnn aristocrat. However, while the Baron had not given any sign of recognition when replying to the single question, the danger remained that in an extended conversation Flinx might let some unthinking familiarity slip. If the AAnn ever suspected that Flinx had been among those who had cheated him and the Empire of the Krang, those several months ago, he would vivisect the youth with infinite slowness. Better not take a chance.

They stayed there waiting while Teleen recomposed herself from both the ordeal of Mahnahmi's escape and from the trauma of confronting the angry Baron. Flinx watched from a broken window as a distant, concealed elevator lifted two big military shuttles from the ground beneath the landing strip. A single groundcar, no doubt containing Riidi WW, pulled up alongside one of the shuttles and several figures hurried from it to the waiting ships.

Once the groundcar had moved out of the way, the two shuttles thundered into the heavens, where they would likely rendezvous with at least one waiting AAnn naval vessel. Mahnahmi had had a good start, but Flinx knew his rented craft could never outrun even a small military ship. However, the girl's mind was like a runaway reactor: there was no telling what she was capable of under sufficient stress. The Baron, he decided, had better watch out for himself.

Turning from the window, Flinx conversed in low tones with Sylzenzuzex. Both tried to come up with reasons for the AAnn's presence here. She no more believed the Baron's casual disclaimer that he was on this world for mere profit than he did. The AAnn had been the Commonwealth's prime enemies since its inception. They never ceased searching, guardedly yet relentlessly, for a new way to hasten its destruction and hurry what they believed was their destiny to rule the cosmos and its "lesser" races.

There had to be a deeper reason involving those unique Janus jewels, though neither of them could think of a viable theory.

On Tharce IV lived a woman called Amasar, who was widely celebrated for her wisdom. At the moment, however, she adopted an air of drunken ecstasy as she reveled in the beauty of the object she held.

Adored by her constituents and respected by opponents, she had been the permanent representative from the Northern Hemisphere of Tharce IV to the Commonwealth Council for two decades. Her mind never rested in its search for solutions to problems or answers to questions, and she worked hours that embarrassed colleagues and assistants half her age. Currently she held the post of Counselor Second in charge of Diplomatic Theory on the Council itself. As such she was in a position to influence strongly the direction of Commonwealth foreign policy.

She should have been studying the transcript of the upcoming agenda, but her mind was occupied instead with the magnificence dwelling in the object in her hand. Besides, on the majority of questions that would come to a vote in the Council her mind was already made up. As a respected counselor, her advice would be a powerful influence.

Yes on this issue, nay on that one, leaning so and so on this proposal, not to withdraw on this matter, not to yield on that particular point—it was a long list.

Her mind focused elsewhere, Amasar switched off the viewer, which had been running blankly for several moments. Leaning back in her chair, she continued to stare raptly at the shining irregularity of the object on her desk.

Tomorrow she would board ship for the annual Council meeting. The gathering place varied between the dual Commonwealth capitals of Terra and Hivehom. This year the thranx capital world was to be the site. This promised to be an absorbing, stimulating session, one she was looking forward to. Several issues of vital importance were due to come to a vote, including measures involving those sly murderers, the AAnn. The Council had some who believed in moderation and appeasement of the reptiles, but not her!

But why worry about such things now? Moving as if in a dream, she opened the center drawer of her desk to perform a final check. Everything was there: diplomatic credentials, reservation confirmations, documentation and information tapes. Yes, it should be an interesting session this year.

She was still aglow with pleasure as she reached into the lowermost drawer on her right, took out the small, lightweight needler, and fried that insidiously seductive thing before blowing out her brains!

The apparent suicide was recorded by the local coroner and confirmed by Commonwealth officials as another of those inexplicable occurrences that periodically afflict even the stablest of hu-

*man beings. Anything could have been the cause. Too little
confidence, too little money, too little affection . . .
Or too much of an especially lethal kind of beauty.*

"A remarkable infant," Teleen auz Rudenuaman finally said, interrupting their talk. She eyed them, and commented, "This appears
to be a day for unusual infants." When her captives remained sul-
lenly silent, she shrugged and looked out the panels again. "I knew
there was a reason for hating that brat so strongly. I admit, though,
that she had me completely fooled. I wonder how long she'd been
manipulating Challis to suit her own ends?"

"According to what she said, all her conscious life." Flinx
thought it a good idea to keep the merchantwoman's attention focused elsewhere. "Are you going to kill us now?" he asked with
disarming matter-of-factness, "or have you decided to believe
me?"

"My having you killed has nothing to do with your story, Flinx,"
she explained, "though Challis seems to have confirmed it. I have
plenty of time to get rid of you. I still find you a novelty." She
gazed appraisingly at him. "You're a bundle of interesting contradictions, and hard to pin down. I'm not sure I like that. I tend to
get frustrated with something I don't understand. That's dangerous, because I might end up killing you on a whim, and that would
only frustrate me more, since you'd die with all the answers.

"No, I think I'll wait for the Baron to return before doing anything irreversible with you two." She showed white teeth. "The
AAnn are very adept at clearing up contradictions."

Sylzenzuzex climbed to her trulegs and tested her injured limb.
She would be forced to limp along on three supports until it
healed. She glared at the merchantwoman—compound eyes being
especially good for glaring.

"To work so with the sworn enemies of humanx-kind."

Rudenuaman was not impressed. "So much outrage over a little
money." She looked reprovingly at the thranx. "The AAnn have
given me exclusive rights to distribute the Janus jewel within the
Commonwealth. In return I permit them to take a certain percent-
age of the production here. I supply much of the means for the
mining, and they neutralized the peaceforcers.

"I've made Nuaman, now Rudenuaman, Enterprises stronger
than it has ever been, stronger than it was under my aunt. We have
discovered only the one pocket of jewels, which appear to be an
isolated mineralogical mutation. In five to ten years we will have

taken the last jewel out of that mountain. Then we will depart from here voluntarily, with the Church none the wiser and the Commonwealth hurt not at all. By that time Rudenuaman Enterprises will be in an invincible financial position. And my aunt, may she rot in limbo, would have approved. I think—"

"*I* think you're blinding yourself," Flinx put in, "voluntarily. There's a great deal more in this as far as the Empire is concerned than a little petty cash."

Rudenuaman eyed him curiously. "What gives you the right to say something like that?"

"I was at the Church administrative headquarters before we came here. During that time an AAnn in surgical disguise—similar to but rather more elaborate than what the Baron was wearing—tried to sneak into the command center there. After he killed himself I found crystalline dust scattered all over his middle. It could have come from a pulverized Janus jewel."

"But the crystal syringe-darts he was carrying . . ." Sylzenzuzex started to remind him.

". . . could have been manufactured from flawed Janus jewels themselves," he told her. "Did you stop to think of that? Wouldn't it make a marvelous cover?" He turned to look at her. "I don't think that infiltrator killed himself to keep from being questioned. You can't break an AAnn. I think the explosion was to destroy what he was carrying—a Janus jewel."

"But what for?" she wondered. "To bribe someone?"

"I don't think so . . . but I'm not sure. Not yet."

"As if I cared what happens to the Church," Rudenuaman added in disgust.

Sylzenzuzex responded with great dignity, "The Church is all that stands between civilization and barbarism."

"Now would the Commonwealth representatives like that, my dear? They appear to consider themselves the guardians of humanx accomplishment."

"The Commonwealth stands only because it's backed by the incorruptible standards of the United Church."

"There is someone I'd like to meet," the merchantwoman quipped, shifting on her couch. "An incorruptible."

"Me, too," admitted Flinx.

Sylzenzuzex spun on him. "Whose side are you on, anyway, Flinx?" The fine hairs rose on the back of her b-thorax.

"I don't know," he replied feelingly. "I haven't studied all the sides carefully enough yet."

"Would you like to see the mine?" Teleen asked suddenly.

"Very much," he admitted. Sylzenzuzex looked indifferent, but he could sense her interest.

"Very well," the merchantwoman decided, apparently on impulse. "Linda . . ."

"Groundcar, Madam—and guards?"

"Just a driver and one other."

The squat bodyguard looked uncertain. "Madam, do you think that . . . ?"

Rudenuaman waved her objections aside. She was in the mood to wipe away the distressing events of the afternoon. Boasting and showing off would be excellent therapy. "You worry too much, Linda. Where can they go? Their shuttle has been stolen, the Baron has taken our craft, and this world grows progressively more inhospitable no matter which way one travels. They're not about to run away."

"Right," Flinx agreed. "Besides, my companion has an injured limb."

"Why should that matter to you?" Sylzenzuzex sneered.

He turned on her angrily. "Because despite everything that's happened, and I regret much of it, I do care what happens to you— whether you want to believe it or not!"

Sylzenzuzex stared at his back as he spun away from her, jamming his hands into his jumpsuit pockets. Security schematics, archeologic chronophysics—all appeared simple alongside this impenetrable young human. It would not have comforted her, perhaps, to know that her opinion of him was shared in varying degrees by the other two women in the room.

No doubt Flinx would have been easier to understand if he had understood himself. . . .

10

The groundcar whined smoothly, well tuned as it was, as it climbed a sloping path covered with a low growth resembling heather. Flinx leaned back and stared through the transparent roof. Just beyond the mine buildings, the mountain became nearly vertical, soaring another 2,500 meters above the lake.

At the moment neither the incredible scenery, nor their present dim prospects, nor Sylzenzuzex's occasional whistling moans of pain held his attention. Instead, his mind was on that stolen tape which might contain the early part of his life. And in his mind, the tape was still inextricably linked with Conda Challis, who would run from him no longer.

Flinx had already seen the sumptuous living quarters/office occupied by Teleen auz Rudenuaman. No doubt Challis possessed a similar if less extensive chamber somewhere in the complex behind them . . . probably in the very same building. Eventually Challis' rooms would be cleaned out, his effects disposed of so that the space could be put to new uses. But for now it was doubtless sealed and undisturbed—including that tape, so tantalizingly near.

If this unpredictable young woman could be persuaded to keep them alive awhile yet, he might still have the chance to see what was on that stolen spool. Though if she knew how desperately he wanted it, she might just slowly unwind it in a dish of acid before his eyes.

It was a measure of her megalomania, or confidence, that she had ordered Challis killed. Someone would have to go to considerable lengths to cover up his disappearance—not that his company subordinates would object. Rudenuaman's agents should have no trouble locating several survivors who would be eager to take over the reins of power unquestioningly. Besides, Challis' private activities were of such a nature as to discourage close investigation. A man engaged in such distasteful hobbies could come to any number of sudden, unexpected ends.

Flinx wondered if the merchant's mind were still functional enough for him to regret the simple manner of his passing. No

doubt he had conceived an eventual demise of grandiose depravity
for himself.

The groundcar came to a halt level with the lowest part of the
sheer-sided, gleaming metal buildings. These were constructed on
a more or less flat area that had been gouged in the flank of the
mountain. Suspended at a higher elevation, a series of square
metal arches punctured the rock walls like silvery hypodermics
sucking blood from a whale. From within the structure, clear
mountain air carried to the arrivals the steady *ca-rank, ca-rank* of
tireless machinery.

A guard who may or may not have been as human as he looked
saluted casually as they entered the structure. "The exterior building we are now in," Rudenuaman was explaining, "houses all our
milling and processing facilities." She waved constantly as they
made their way through the building. "This installation has cost an
incredible amount of credit . . . a tiny drop when compared to the
profit which we will eventually realize."

"I still don't see why the AAnn need you so badly," Flinx told
her, his eyes taking in everything on the principle that knowledge
is freedom. "Particularly since they're the ones responsible for
negating the peaceforcer fortresses."

"I thought I'd already made that clear," she said. "First, the
Commonwealth is a far larger market for the gems than the
Empire. They have no way to market their share except through a
human agent . . . me. But more important, as the Baron explained,
this world lies within Commonwealth boundaries. Though comparatively isolated, there are a number of other busy, inhabited
Commonwealth planets plus numerous automatic monitoring stations between here and the nearest populated Empire world. AAnn
technicians require safe conduct, which Rudenuaman company
ships provide."

Flinx, thinking suddenly of the Baron's pursuit of Mahnahmi, asked, "Then there are no Imperial military vessels in this
region?"

Rudenuaman looked surprised at Flinx's naïveté. "Do you take
the Baron for a fool? It would only take the discovery of one such
ship and this quadrant of space would be swarming with
Commonwealth warships. The Baron," she informed them smugly,
"is far more subtle than the AAnn are normally given credit for."

So subtle, Flinx thought with mixed feelings, that he might have
outfoxed himself. If he were chasing Mahnahmi in a freighter instead of in a destroyer or frigate, she might elude him after all. Not

that he was certain he wanted that precocious talent to escape; but at least a merry chase might prolong the Baron's absence from Ulru-Ujurr for some time.

They had to resolve the situation before that happened and the Baron returned. Novelty value or no, Flinx did not think the AAnn aristocrat would tolerate his and Sylzenzuzex's continued existence. If it came to a confrontation between Flinx and Rudenuaman, she would have him and Sylzenzuzex executed without a thought in order to keep her associate placated.

Though Rudenuaman might be swayed by flattery and amusement, Flinx had no illusions about his ability to so manipulate the Baron. "Teleen," he began absently, "have you ever . . ."

She turned angrily on him, voice chill and expression dark. "Don't ever call me that or you'll die a lot quicker than otherwise. You will address me as Madam or Madam Rudenuaman, or the next way you will amuse me is with your noise as I have the skin stripped from your back."

"Sorry . . . Madam," he apologized carefully. "You still insist that the AAnn's only interest in the Janus jewels is financial?" He was aware of Sylzenzuzex watching him.

"You continue to bring that up. Yes, of course I do."

"Tell me—have you ever seen an AAnn, the Baron, for example, utilize a headset linkage to create particle-plays within one of the crystals?"

"No." She didn't appear to be disturbed by the thought. "This is a mining outpost. There are no hedonists or idlers here."

"Do you have a headset link here?"

"Yes."

"And Challis . . . I presume he did, also? Colloid plays seemed to have been one of his favorite obsessions."

"Yes, though not the only one," she said, her mouth wrinkling in distaste.

"What about the Baron? Surely he enjoys the gems?"

"Baron Riidi WW," she announced with confidence, "is all business- and military-minded. I have on occasion seen him relaxing at various AAnn recreations, but never with a Janus jewel."

"What about the other AAnn of importance and rank here?"

"No, they're all fully absorbed in their assignments. Why so curious to know if I've ever seen one of the reptiles using a gem?"

"Because," Flinx said thoughtfully, "I don't think they can. I don't know what the Baron does with the jewels which are consigned for supposed sale within the Empire, but I'm certain they're not provided for the amusement of wealthy AAnn. Possibly for bribery purposes within the Commonwealth—I haven't worked that out yet.

"The AAnn mind is different from that of human or thranx," he went on. "Not necessarily inferior—probably superior in some ways—but different. I've read a little about it, and I don't believe that their brains produce the proper impulses for operating a Janus jewel linkage. They could scramble the colloidal suspension, but never organize it into anything recognizable."

"Really," Rudenuaman murmured at the conclusion of his little lecture. "What makes you an expert on such matters?"

"I have big ears," Flinx replied. Better she continued to consider him a wild guesser than a calculating thinker.

"All right, suppose they can't operate the jewels the way we can." She shrugged indifferently. "The beauty of the gem is still unsurpassed."

"That's so," he conceded, "but to the point of justifying this kind of risky invasion of Commonwealth territory? I'm damned if I think the AAnn love beauty that much. Somehow those jewels are being used against the Commonwealth, against humanxkind."

Rudenuaman didn't reply, choosing to ignore what she couldn't refute. They had walked deep into the higher levels of the building. A tall AAnn approached them, his surgical disguise perfect—except now Flinx knew what it concealed and was able to recognize the reptilian beneath.

"That's Meevo FFGW," Rudenuaman informed them, confirming Flinx's guess. "He is the AAnn second in command and the Baron's assistant. He's also an excellent engineer, in charge of the overall mining operation here." She glared confidently at Flinx. "I've thought a little about your accusations, and you know what I've decided?" She smiled. "I don't give a goddamn what the AAnn do to the Commonwealth with their share of the jewels, as long as it doesn't interfere with my business."

"That's about what I thought you might say." Sylzenzuzex's voice carried contempt in a way only the sharply clipped tones of a thranx can. Flinx thought it idiotic to antagonize their mercurial host, but she appeared unperturbed. If anything, she was pleased to see one of her captives so upset.

"Isn't it nice to have one's thoughts confirmed?" She faced the newcomer. "Greetings, Meevo."

Flinx used the opportunity to study the reptilian's makeup in detail. Were a Rudenuaman ship to be stopped by Commonwealth inspectors, he doubted that any casual observer could penetrate the carefully crafted disguise.

If one knew to look closely, though, the eyes were a dead giveaway. For Meevo FFGW, like the Baron, like all AAnn, had a double eyelid. A blink would reveal the mind behind such eyes as not human.

"These are the ones who succeeded in passing the adjusted fortresses?" the AAnn lieutenant asked, glancing from Sylzenzuzex to Flinx.

"Just the two of them, yes," Rudenuaman told him.

Meevo appeared amiably curious. "Then why are they still alive?"

Sylzenzuzex shivered again, this time at the utterly inhumanx indifference in that voice.

"They keep me amused for now. And when the Baron returns he may have some questions of his own for them. The Baron's a more efficient interrogator than I. I tend to be impatient."

A low reptilian chuckle came from the engineer. "I heard about the child. Most unfortunate, irritating. There is no need to worry, though. The Baron will finish her before she can contact outsiders. His efficiency extends to other areas besides questioning." He grinned, showing false human teeth set into an elongated false human jaw. At the back of the open mouth Flinx could just make out the gleam of real, far sharper teeth.

"You find them amusing . . . curious," the engineer concluded, with a gesture Flinx was unable to interpret. His attitude suggested that casual amusement was as alien to him as bearing living young.

Curiosity, however, was a trait the AAnn did share with their enemies. Meevo tagged along as Rudenuaman led them through the remainder of the complex.

"The milling and separation you saw downstairs. Polishing and removal of surface impurities takes place over there." She indicated a series of doorless chambers from which musical sounds emerged.

"Are they all AAnn here except you and your bodyguard?" Sylzenzuzex wondered sardonically.

"Oh, no. We're about half and half here. There are a surprising number of talented humanx in our loving society for whom the everyday problems of living have proven too much. They've been driven by insensitive authority to seek marginally reputable work.

Existence overrides any qualms they hold about such intangibles as interspecies loyalty."

"I'll venture none of them ever gets off this world alive."

Rudenuaman appeared genuinely surprised. "Ridiculous woman . . . that would be bad for business. Oh, I don't mean *we* inspire their loyalty. For most of those who work here that term no longer has meaning, or they wouldn't be here in the first place. Any of them would gladly sell their knowledge of this illegal installation the moment they were discharged.

"We employ, with their knowledge and consent, a selective mind-wipe which clears their brains of all memories of their stay here. It leaves them with the vaguely uncomfortable feeling that they've undergone a long period of unconsciousness. That and their newly fat bank accounts insure they will not give away our presence here."

"Mind-wipe," a stunned Sylzenzuzex muttered, "is forbidden for use by anyone other than Commonwealth or Church high physicians, and then only in emergency circumstances!"

Rudenuaman grinned. "You must remember to add that to your report."

They entered a large chamber, and the temperature dropped noticeably. "We'll be going into the main shaft," she explained, indicating long racks of bulky overclothing hanging nearby. Sylzenzuzex saw that a number of them were designed for thranx.

"Did you think that your precious cousins were immune to the lure of credit?" Rudenuaman taunted her. "No species has a corner on greed, child."

"Don't call me a child," Sylzenzuzex countered softly.

Rudenuaman's response was not what Flinx expected—the first real laugh they had heard from her. She leaned on her cane, chuckling. Curious workers turned to glance at them as they passed.

"I'll call you dead, if you prefer," the merchantwoman finally declared. She pointed toward the long racks of overclothing. "Now put one of those on—it's quite cold inside the mountain."

After donning the protective outer garments, they followed her and the AAnn engineer down a wide rectangular avenue. Metal soon gave way to bare rock. Evenly spaced single-span duralloy arches helped support the roof.

Flinx's thermal suit was partly open, permitting a small reptilian head to peep out from within, eyes unblinking as it surveyed the chill surroundings. Double rows of brightly glowing light tubes cast a steady radiance throughout the tunnel.

"This section has already been played out," Rudenuaman explained. "The jewels lie in a vein running horizontally into the mountain."

They slowed.

"There are several additional subsidiary shafts, running the length of lesser veins. Some run slightly above, others below our present position. I'm told that the gems formed in occasional pockets in the volcanic rock which were once filled with gas. An unusual combination of pressure and heat produced the Janus jewels.

"The gemstones themselves lie in a different sort of material from the mountain, like diamonds in the kimberlite of Terra and the Bronine rainbow craters which are mined on Evoria. That's what my engineers tell me, anyhow."

Ignoring her possessive reference to him, Meevo made a curt gesture of acknowledgment. "It is so. Similar examples of isolated gem formation lie within the Empire, though nothing so unusual as this."

Something tickled Flinx's brain, and he found himself staring down into the dim recesses of the shaft. "Someone's coming toward us," he announced finally.

Rudenuaman turned to look, commented idly, "Just a few of the natives. They're primitive types, but intelligent enough to make good menial workers. They have no tools, no civilization, and no language beyond a few grunts and imitated human words. They don't even wear minimal clothing. Their sole claim to rudimentary intelligence appears to be in the simple modifications they make in their cave-homes—rolling boulders in front to make a smaller entrance, digging deeper into the hillside, and so on. They do the heavy manual work for us, and they're careful with the jewels they uncover.

"We've simplified the drilling equipment for their use. Their fur is thick enough so that the cold inside the mountain doesn't seem to bother them, which is fortunate for us. Even with thermal suits it would be hard for humans and impossible for AAnn to work the gem deposits anymore, considering how deep the shaft now runs into the mountain. If they mind the cold, they seem willing to risk it for the rewards we give them in return for each stone."

"What do you reward them with?" Flinx wondered curiously. The bulky shapes were still coming slowly toward them. The hair on the back of his neck prickled and Pip stirred violently within the folds of the warm suit.

"Berries," Meevo snapped in disgust. "Berries and fruits, nuts and tubers. Root eaters!" he finished, with the disdain characteristic of all carnivores.

"They're vegetarians, then?"

"Not entirely," Rudenuaman corrected. "They're apparently quite able to digest meat, and they have the teeth and claws necessary for hunting, but they much prefer the fruits and berries our automatic harvester can gather for them."

"Dirt grubbers," the AAnn engineer muttered. He glanced at Rudenuaman. "Excuse me from your play, but I have work to do." He turned and lumbered back up the shaft.

By this time the four natives had come near enough for Flinx to discern individual characteristics. Each was larger than a big man and two or three times as broad—almost fat. How much of that bulk was composed of incredibly dense brown fur marked with black and white splotches he couldn't tell. In build and general appearance they were essentially ursinoid, though sporting a flat muzzle instead of a snout. It ended in a nearly invisible black nose that was almost comical on so massive a creature.

Short thick claws tipped the end of each of four seven-digited members, and the creatures appeared capable of moving on all fours or standing upright with equal ease. There was no tail. Ears were short, rounded, and set on top of the head. By far the most distinctive features were the tarsier-like eyes, large as plates, which glowed amber in the tunnel's fluorescent light. Huge black pupils like obsidian yolks floated in their centers.

"Nocturnal from the look of them, crepuscular at the least," was Sylzenzuzex's intrigued comment.

The natives noticed the new arrivals, and all rose onto their hind legs for a better look. When they stood upright they seemed to fill the whole tunnel. Flinx noted a slight curve at the back of their mouths, which formed a falsely comic, dolphinish grin on each massive face.

He was about to ask another question of Rudenuaman when something stirred violently within his suittop. Flinx's frantic grab was too late to restrain Pip. The flying snake was out and streaking down the shaft toward the natives.

"Pip . . . wait, there's no . . . !"

He had started to say there was no reason to attack the furry giants. Nothing fearful or threatening had scratched his sensitive mind. If the minidrag were to set the group of huge natives on a rampage, it was doubtful any of them would get out of this tunnel alive.

Ignoring his master's call, Pip reached the nearest of the creatures. On its hind legs, the enormous animal was nearly three meters tall and must have weighed at least half a ton. Great glowing eyes regarded the tiny apparition, whose venom was nearly always fatal.

Pip dove straight for the head. At the last second pleated wings beat the air as the minidrag braked—to land and curl lightly about the creature's shoulder. The monster eyed the minidrag dispassionately, then turned its dull gaze on Flinx, who gaped back at the giant in shock.

For the second time in his life, Flinx fainted. . . .

The dream was new and very deep. He was floating in the middle of an endless black lake beneath an oppressively near night sky. So dark was it that he could see nothing, not even his own body . . . which might not have been there.

Against the ebony heavens four bright lights drifted. Tiny, dancing pinpoints of unwinking gold moved in unpredictable yet calculated patterns, like fireflies. They danced and jigged, darted and twitched not far from the eyes he didn't have, yet he saw them plainly.

Sometimes they danced about each other, and once all four of them performed some intricate weaving in and out, as complex and meaningful as it was quickly forgotten.

"He's back now," the first firefly observed.

"Yes, he's back," two of the others agreed simultaneously.

Flinx noted with interest that the last of the four fireflies was not the steady, unwavering light he had first thought. Unlike the others, it winked on and off erratically, like a lamp running on fluctuating current. When it winked off it disappeared completely, and when it was on it blazed brighter than any of the others.

"Did we frighten you?" the winker wondered.

A disembodied voice strangely like his own replied. "I saw Pip . . ." the dream-voice started to say.

"I'm sorry we shouted at you," the first firefly apologized.

"Sorry we shouted," the other two chorused. "We didn't mean to hurt you. We didn't mean to frighten you."

"I saw Pip," Flinx mused, "settle around one of the native's shoulders. I've never ever seen Pip do that to a stranger before. Not to Mother Mastiff, not to Truzenzuzex, not to anyone."

"Pip?" the third voice inquired.

"Oh," the second firefly explained, "he means the little hard mind."

"Hard but tasty," agreed the first one, "like a *chunut.*"

"You thought the little hard mind meant to hurt us?" first voice asked.

"Yes, but instead he responded to you with an openness I've never seen before. So you must also broadcast on the empathic level, only your thoughts are friendly thoughts."

"If you say we must," third firefly elucidated, "then we must."

"But only when we must," fourth voice said sternly, blazing brighter than the other three before vanishing.

"Why does the fourth among you come and go like a fog?" Flinx's dream-voice murmured.

"Fourth? Oh," first voice explained, "that's Maybeso. That's his name—for this weektime, anyway. I am called Fluff." Flinx got the impression the other two lights brightened slightly. "These are Moam and Bluebright." The fourth light blazed momentarily.

"They're mates," it said, and then winked out once more.

"Gone again," Flinx observed with disembodied detachment.

"That's Maybeso, remember?" reminded Fluff-voice. "Sometimes he's not here. The rest of us are always here. We don't change our names, either, but Maybeso comes and goes and changes his name every weektime or so."

"Where does Maybeso go when he goes?"

Bluebright replied openly, "We don't know."

"Where does he come from when he comes back, then?"

"Nobody knows," Moam told him.

"Why does he change his name from weektime to weektime?"

"Ask him," Moam and Bluebright suggested together.

Maybeso came back, his light brighter than any of theirs.

"Why do you change your name from weektime to weektime, and where do you go when you go, and where do you come from when you come back?" Flinx-voice wondered.

"Oh, there's no doubt about it," Maybeso told him in a dream-singsong, and winked away again.

Fluff spoke in a confidential dream-whisper: "Maybeso, we think, is a little mad. But he's a good fellow all the same."

Flinx noted absently that he was beginning to sink beneath the surface of the black lake. Above him the four lights swirled and dipped curiously.

"You're the first who's talked to us," Fluff-voice murmured.

"Come and talk to us more," Moam requested with pleasure. "It's fun to have someone to talk to. The little hard one listens but cannot talk. This is a fun new thing!"

Flinx's dream-voice bubbled up through the deepening oily liquid. "Where should I come and talk to you?"

"At the end of the long water," Moam told him.

"At the end of the long water," confirmed Bluebright.

"At the far end of the long water," added Fluff, who was rather more precise than the others.

"No doubt about it," agreed Maybeso, winking on for barely a second.

About it, about it . . . the words were subsumed in gentle rippling currents produced by Flinx's slowly sinking body. Sinking, sinking, until he touched the bottom of the lake. His legs touched first, then his hips, then back, and finally his head.

There was something peculiar about this place, he thought. The sky had been blacker than the water, and the water grew lighter instead of darker as he sank. At the bottom it was so bright it hurt his eyes.

He opened them.

A glistening, almost metallic blue-green face dominated by two faceted gems was staring down at him with concern. Inhaling, he smelled coconut oil and orchids. Something tickled his left ear.

Looking for the source, he discovered Pip's small reptilian face lying on his chest. A long pointed tongue darted out and hit him several times on the cheek. Apparently satisfied as to his master's condition, the minidrag relaxed and slid off the pillow to coil itself comfortably nearby.

Pillow?

Taking a deep breath, Flinx smiled up at Sylzenzuzex. She backed away and he saw that they were in a small, neatly furnished room. Sunlight poured in through high windows.

"How are you feeling?" she inquired in the sharp clicks and whistles of symbospeech. He nodded and watched her slump gratefully onto a thranx sleeping-sitting platform across the room. "Thank the Hive. I thought you were dead."

Flinx rested his head on a supporting hand. "I didn't think that mattered much to you."

"Oh, shut up!" she snapped with unexpected vehemence. He detected confusion and frustration in her voice as feelings and fact vied within her. "There have been plenty of times when I would have cheerfully cut your throat, if I hadn't been under oath to protect it. Then there have been an equal number of other occasions when I almost wished you didn't wear your skeleton outside in.

"Like the time back on Terra when you saved my life, and the way you've stood up to that barbaric young female." Flinx saw her antennae flicking nervously, the graceful curve of her ovipositors tightening uncertainly. "You are the most maddening being I have ever met, Flinx-man!"

He sat up carefully, found that everything worked inside as well as out. "What happened?" he asked, confused. "No, wait . . . I do remember blacking out, but not why. Did something hit me?"

"Nobody laid a parcel hook on you. You collapsed when your pet charged one of the native workers. Fortunately, that maneuver seems to have been just a bluff. The native didn't know enough to be frightened." Her expression turned puzzled. "But why should that make you faint?"

"I don't know," he answered evasively. "Probably the shock of visualizing the rest of the natives rending us into pieces after Pip killed one of their number. When he didn't, the shock was magnified because Pip just doesn't take to strangers that way." Flinx forced himself to appear indifferent. "So Pip likes natural fur better than a thermal suit, and he snuggled down in one of the natives. That's probably what happened."

"What does that prove?" Sylzenzuzex wondered.

"That I faint too easily." Swinging his legs off the bed, he gave her a grim look. "At least now we know why this world's Under Edict."

"*Shhh!*" She nearly fell off her sleeping platform. "Why . . . no, wait," she admonished him. Several minutes passed during which she made a thorough inspection of the room, checking places Flinx would never have thought to inspect.

"It's clean," she finally announced with satisfaction. "I expect they don't think we have anything to say that's worth listening to."

"You're certain?" Flinx asked, abashed. "I never thought of that."

Sylzenzuzex looked offended. "I told you I was training in Security. No, there is nothing in here to listen to you save me."

"Okay, the reason this world has been placed Under Edict by the Church met us in the tunnel today. It's the natives . . . Rudenuaman's grunting, goblin-eyed manual laborers. They're the reason."

She continued to stare at him for another minute, considered laughing, thought better of it when she saw how serious he was.

"Impossible," she muttered finally. "You have experienced a delusion of some sort. Surely the natives are nothing more than they appear to be—big, amiable, and dumb. They have not yet developed enough for the Church to isolate this world."

"On the contrary," he objected, "they're a great deal more than they appear to be."

She looked querulous. "If that's true, then why do they perform heavy manual labor for long hours in freezing temperatures in exchange for a few miserable nuts and berries?"

Flinx's voice dropped disconsolately. "I don't know that yet." He glanced up. "But I know this—they're natural telepaths."

"A delusion," she repeated firmly, "a hallucination you experienced."

"No." His voice was firm, confident. "I have a few slight talents of my own. I know the difference between a hallucination and mind-to-mind communication."

"Have it your way," Sylzenzuzex declared, sighing. "For the sake of discussion let us temporarily assume it was not an illusion. That is still no reason for the Church to place a world Under Edict. A whole race of telepaths is only theory, but it would not be enough to exclude them from associate membership in the Commonwealth."

"It's not just that," Flinx explained earnestly. "They're . . . well, more intelligent than they appear."

"I doubt that," she snorted, "but even a race of intelligent telepaths would not be considered such a threat."

"*Much* more intelligent."

"I won't believe that until I see evidence to prove it," she objected. "If they represented any kind of serious threat to the Commonwealth . . ."

"Why else would the Church put this world Under Edict?"

"Flinx, they have no tools, no clothing, no spoken language—no civilization. They run around grubbing for roots and fruits, living in caves. If they're potentially as clever as you claim, why do they persist in dwelling in poverty?"

"That," admitted Flinx, "is a very good question."

"Do you have a very good answer?"

"I do not. But I'm convinced I've found the reason for the Church's actions. What is the effect of putting a race Under Edict?"

"No contact with outside parties, space-going peoples," she recited. "Severest penalties for any infraction of the Edict. The race
is free to develop in its own way."

"Or free to stagnate," Flinx muttered. "The Commonwealth and
the Church have aided plenty of primitive peoples, why not the
Ujurrians?"

"You set yourself up as arbiter of high Church policy," she murmured, drawing away from him again.

"Not me!" he half shouted, slamming both hands noisily against
the bedcovers. His hands moved rapidly as he talked. "It's the
Church Council that sets itself up as the manipulator of racial destinies. And if not the Church, then the Commonwealth government does. And if not the Commonwealth, then the great corpora-
tions and family companies. Then there is the AAnn Empire which
sets itself above everything." He was pacing angrily alongside the
bed.

"My God, but I'm sick to death of organizations that think they
have the right to rule on how others ought to develop!"

"What would you have in its place?" she challenged him.
"Anarchy?"

Flinx sat down heavily on the bed again, his head sinking between his hands. He was tired, tired, and much too young. "How
should I know? I only know that I'm getting damned sick of what
passes for intelligence in this corner of creation."

"I can't believe you're so innocent," she said, more gently now.
"What else do you expect from mere mammals and insects? The
Amalgamation was just the beginning of your race's and mine's
emergence from a long dark age. The Commonwealth and the
United Church are only a few of your centuries old. What do you
expect of it so soon—Nirvana? Utopia?" She shook her head, a
gesture the thranx had acquired from mankind.

"Not for me or you to set ourselves up above the Church, which
helped bring us out of those dark times."

"The Church, the Church, your almighty Church!" he shouted.
"Why do you defend it so? You think it's composed of saints?"

"I never claimed it was perfect," she responded, showing some
heat herself. "The Counselors themselves would be the last to
claim so. That's one of its virtues. Naturally it's not perfect—it
would never claim to be."

"That's what Tse-Mallory once said to me," he murmured reflec-
tively.

"What . . . who?"

"Someone I know who also left the Church, for reasons of his own."

"Tse-Mallory, that name again," she replied thoughtfully. "He was that stingship mate of my uncle's you mentioned before. Bran Tse-Mallory?"

"Yes."

"They talk of him as well as of Truzenzuzex at the Clan meetings." She snapped herself back to the present—no use thinking wistfully about things she would probably never be able to experience again. "Now that you've decided the universe is not perfect and that the instrumentalities of intelligence are somewhat less than all-knowing, what do you propose we do about it?"

"Have a talk with our friends-to-be, the Ujurrians."

"And what are they going to do?" she smirked. "Throw rocks at the Baron's shuttles when he returns? Or at the beamers that are surely stocked in plenty here?"

"Possibly," Flinx conceded. "But even if they can do nothing, I think we'll have a far better chance of surviving among them there, than waiting for Rudenuaman to get tired of having us around. When that happens she'll dispose of us as casually as she would an old dress." He let his mind wander, saw no reason to hide himself from Sylzenzuzex anymore. "There's only one guard outside the door."

"How do you know . . . oh, you told me," she answered herself. "How extensive are your talents?"

"I haven't the vaguest notion," he told her honestly. "Sometimes I can't perceive a spider in a room. Other times . . ." He felt it better to keep a few secrets. "Just take my word that there's only one guard outside. I guess our docility has convinced Rudenuaman we don't require close watching. As she said, there's nowhere for us to run to."

"I'm not sure I disagree with her," Sylzenzuzex murmured, her gaze going to the chill mountains outside. "Though I must admit that if we do escape, she *may* leave us alone. We would be no more danger to her in the mountains than we are here."

"I'm hoping she thinks so," he admitted. "The Baron wouldn't agree with her. We have to leave now." Sliding off the bed, he walked to the door and knocked gently. The door slid aside and their guard eyed them carefully—from several paces away, Flinx noted.

He was a tall, thin human with a worn expression and hair turned too white too soon. As near as Flinx could tell, he was not an AAnn in human disguise.

"You interrupted my reading," he informed Flinx sourly, indicating the small tape viewer that rested nearby. This reminded Flinx of another tape he wanted to read himself. Despite the anxiety surging inside him, he would have to wait until much later, if ever, to see that tape.

"What do you want?" It was clear that this man was well informed about their cooperation thus far. Flinx shouted with his mind, conjuring up a sensation of half-fear.

Pip shot out from under the pillows on the bed and was through the door before the man could put his viewer aside. A beamer came up, but instead of firing the man crossed both hands in front of his face. Flinx jumped through the opening and planted a foot in the other's solar plexus. Only closing lids kept his eyes from popping out of his face.

The guard hit the far wall with a loud *whump,* sat down, and leaned like a rag doll against the chair leg. This time the minidrag responded to Flinx's call. He settled tensely back on Flinx's shoulder, glaring down at the unconscious guard.

Sylzenzuzex came up hurriedly behind him. "Why didn't he shoot immediately? As a matter of fact . . ." She hesitated, and Flinx sensed her mind working.

"That's right. No one here recognized Pip as a dangerous animal. The only one I told was Rudenuaman's bodyguard. In all the rush she must have neglected to inform everyone else. We were trapped here without hope of escape, remember? The only others who knew were Challis and Mahnahmi. He's dead, and she's fled."

Flinx gestured behind him. "That's why I called Pip off and knocked him out myself. Everyone's still ignorant of Pip's full capabilities. Sooner or later, Linda will remember to tell her mistress. But by then we should be free. We'd better be—Rudenuaman won't give us a second chance."

"What are we going to do now?"

"No one's seen us except a small corps of armed security personnel and a few people up at the mine. This is a good-sized installation. Act as if you know what you're doing, and we might walk out of here without being challenged."

"You are crazy," she muttered nervously, as they entered the lift. "This may be a large base, but it's still a closed community. Everyone here must know everyone else."

"You participate in a bureaucracy and still you don't understand," Flinx observed sadly. "Everyone in a complicated operation like this tends to stick pretty much to his own specialty. Each one interacts with people within that specialty. This is hardly a homogeneous little society here. Unless we encounter one of the guards who met us on landing, we ought to be able to move about freely."

"Until our guard regains consciousness," she reminded him. "Then they'll come looking for us."

"But not beyond the boundary of the base, I'll bet. Rudenuaman will be more irritated than angry. She'll assume the environment here will take care of us. And it will, if the Ujurrians don't help us."

They entered the lift car, started downward. "What makes you think they will?"

"I got the impression that they're anxious to talk to me. If you have ten marooned thranx speaking only Low Thranx and an eleventh suddenly appears, wouldn't you want to talk to him?"

"Maybe for a while," she conceded. "Of course, after I'd heard everything he had to say I might want to eat him, too."

"I don't think the Ujurrians will do that." The lift reached ground level.

"What makes you so certain? Berries or not, they are omnivorous, remember. Suppose they're simply telepathic morons?"

"If I'm wrong about them, then we'll die a lot cleaner than at Rudenuaman's hands. I'm betting on two things—a dream, and the fact that I never before saw Pip fly at any being he didn't intend to attack." Reaching down, he rubbed the back of Pip's head through the jumpsuit fabric.

"You were right, Syl, when you said he was flying toward greater warmth, but the warmth wasn't in the Ujurrian's fur." The lift door slid aside and they strode boldly out into the deserted hall.

Leaving the structure they started walking between buildings, heading toward the lake. Several people passed them. Flinx didn't recognize any of them, and fortunately none of them recognized the two prisoners.

As they neared the outskirts of the base Flinx slowed, his senses alert for anything like an automatically defended perimeter. Sylzenzuzex searched for concealed alarms. They didn't find so much as a simple fence. Apparently there were no large carnivores in this valley, and the merchantwoman's opinion of the natives they already knew.

Once they reached the concealing trees, they accelerated their pace, moving as fast as Sylzenzuzex's injured leghand would permit. Despite the abnormally long day, the sun was low in the sky before they slowed. When the sun finally moved behind one of the towering snowy peaks, its warmth would dissipate quickly in the mountain air. Sylzenzuzex would be affected first, and most severely; but Flinx didn't doubt that he'd also be dangerously exposed in his thin jumpsuit.

He hoped their furry hosts could do something about that. If no one was waiting for them at the far end of the lake—the "long water" of his dream—he was going to be very embarrassed. And very sorry.

At its lower end the lake narrowed to a small outlet, then tumbled with the bright humor of all mountain streams down a gentle slope, dancing and falling with fluid choreography over rocks and broken logs and branches. Despite the density of the forest overhead, the thick heatherlike ground cover was lush here.

Flinx picked out small flowering plants with odd needlelike leaves and multiple centers. Minute furred creatures dug and twisted and scurried through this low-level jungle.

Sylzenzuzex sniffed disdainfully, her spicules whistling, as they watched a tiny thing with ten furry legs and miniature hooves dart down a hole in the far bank of the stream.

"Primitive world," she commented. "No insects." She was shivering already. "That's not surprising. This world is too cold for them—and me."

Flinx began hunting through the trees and was rubbing his hands together. Occasionally he would reach into his jumpsuit to fondle Pip. The minidrag also came from a hothouse world. It had grown still in an instinctive effort to conserve energy and body heat.

"I'm not exactly at home here either, you know," Flinx told her. Glancing worriedly upward, he saw that the sun had been half swallowed by a mountain with a backbone like a crippled dinosaur.

"We can freeze to death out here tonight, or go back and take our chances with that female," Sylzenzuzex stammered. "A wonderful choice you've given us."

"I don't understand," he muttered puzzledly. "I was so certain. The voices were so clear."

"Everything is clear in a dream," she philosophized. "It's the real world that never makes sense, that's fuzzy at the fringes. I'm still not sure that you're not a little fuzzy at the fringes, Flinx."

"Ho, ho," a voice boomed like a hammer hitting the bottom of a big metal pot. It was a real voice, not a telepathic whisper.

"Joke. I like jokes!"

Flinx's heart settled back to its normal beat as he and Sylzenzuzex whirled, to see an enormous wide shape waddle out from between two trees. There was little to distinguish one native from another physically.

Flinx, however, now knew to hunt for something less obvious. It blinked brightly out at him, a strong, concentrated mental glow— like a firefly, he reminded himself.

"Hello, Fluff. You have a sense of humor, but don't, please, sneak up on us like that again."

"Sense of humor," the giant echoed. "That mean I like to make jokes?" On hind legs he towered above them. "Yes. What is better than making jokes? Except maybe building caves and eating and sleeping and making love."

Flinx noticed that the broadly grinning mouth was moving.

"You're talking," Sylzenzuzex observed simultaneously. She turned to Flinx. "I thought you said they were telepathic?"

"Can do mind-talk, too," something said inside her head, making her jump.

"So that's telepathy," she murmured at the new experience. "It's kind of unnerving."

"Why trouble with talking?" Flinx wondered.

"Is less efficient, but more fun," Fluff husked.

"Lots more fun," two voices mimicked. Moam and Bluebright appeared, shuffling toward the stream. Lowering to all fours, they began lapping the water.

"Why don't you talk like this to the people at the base?"

"Base? Big metal caves?"

Flinx nodded, was rewarded with a mental shrug.

"No one ask us to talk much. We see inside them that they like us to talk like this," and he proceeded to produce a few grunted words and snorted phrases.

"It make them happy. We want everyone to be happy. So we talk like that."

"I'm not sure I understand," Flinx admitted, sitting down on a rock and shivering. A monstrous shape materialized at his shoulder, and Sylzenzuzex jumped half a meter into the air.

"No doubt about it," thundered Maybeso. One paw cuddled two wrinkled objects while the other held a large plastic case. Flinx felt a warm thought flow over him like a bucket of hot water and then Maybeso was gone.

"What was that?" a gaping Sylzenzuzex wanted to know.

"Maybeso," Flinx told her absently, examining what the mercurial Ujurrian had brought. "Thermal suits—one for you and one for me."

After climbing into the self-contained heated overclothing they spent a few luxurious moments defrosting before they began their inspection of the big case's contents.

"Food," Sylzenzuzex noted. "Two beamers . . ."

Flinx reached into the depths of the container, aware he was trembling. "And this . . . even this." He withdrew his hand, holding a small, slightly battered spool.

"How?" he asked Fluff, awed. "How did he know?" Fluff's smile was genuine and went beyond the one frozen into his features.

"Maybeso plays his own games. Everything is a game to Maybeso, and he's very good at games. Better than any of the family. In some ways he's just like an overgrown cub."

"Cub," agreed Moam, "but a big light."

"Very big light," Bluebright agreed, raising his head and licking water from his muzzle with a long tongue.

"It's fun to have someone who can talk back," Fluff observed playfully. Then Flinx had the impression of a hurt frown. "Others came but did not land. Maybeso saw them and says they did some strange things with constructs—with instruments like those at the metal caves. They got very excited, then went away."

"The Church exploration party," Flinx commented unnecessarily.

"We didn't understand why they went away," a troubled Fluff said. "We wished they would have come down and talked. We were sad and wanted to help them, because they were frightened of something." Again the mental shrug. "Though we could have been wrong."

"I don't think you're wrong, Fluff. Something frightened them, all right."

Sylzenzuzex paid no attention to him. She was staring at Fluff, her mandibles hanging limp. Flinx turned to her, asked, "Now do you understand why this world was put Under Edict?"

"Under Edict," Fluff repeated, savoring the sound of the spoken words. "A general admonition embodying philosophical rationalizations which stem—"

"You're a fast learner, Fluff," gulped Flinx.

"Oh sure," the giant agreed with childish enthusiasm. "Is fun. Let's play a game. You think of a concept or new word and we try to learn it, okay?"

"It wasn't a game to the exploration party which took readings here," Sylzenzuzex announced suddenly. She looked over to Flinx. "I see what you were trying to tell me." To the giant: "They didn't land because . . . because they were afraid of you, Fluff."

"Afraid? Why be afraid of me?" He slapped his meters-wide torso with a paw that could have decapitated a man. "We only live, eat, sleep, make love, build caves, and play games . . . and make jokes, of course. What to be afraid of ?"

"Your potential, Fluff," Flinx explained slowly. "And yours, Moam, and Bluebright, and you, too, Maybeso, wherever you are."

"Someplace else," Moam supplied helpfully.

"They saw your potential and ran like hell instead of coming down to help you. Put you Under Edict so no one else would come to help you, either. They hoped to consign you all to ignorance. You have incalculable potential, Fluff, but you don't seem to have much drive. By denying you that the Church saw they could—"

"No!" Sylzenzuzex shouted, agonized. "I can't believe that. The Church wouldn't . . ."

"Why not?" snorted Flinx. "Anyone can be afraid of the big kid down the block."

"Is wrong to fear," Fluff observed mournfully, "and sad."

"Right both times," concurred Flinx. Suddenly aware his stomach demanded attention, he dug a large cube of processed meat and cheese from the plastic container, sat down on a rock. After removing the foil sealer, he took a huge bite out of it, then started searching the container for something suitable for Pip.

Sylzenzuzex joined him, but her inspection of the supplies was halfhearted at best. Her mind was a maelstrom of conflicting, confusing, and destructive thoughts. The knowledge of what the Church had certainly done was shattering beliefs she'd held since pupahood. Each time another idea came crashing down, it sent a painful stab through her.

Flinx had reached a decision. "You wanted to talk, to play a concept and words game?"

"Yes, let's play," Moam snuffled enthusiastically, ambling over.

"Let's talk," agreed Bluebright.

Flinx looked grim, considered what he was about to do, and was gratified to discover that it made him feel more satisfied than any decision he'd made in his entire life.

"You bet we'll talk. . . ."

11

"But not here," Fluff put in.

"Definitely not here," Bluebright echoed. "Let's go to the cave." Turning away from Flinx, he and Moam started off into the trees, matching each other stride for stride. Fluff waddled after them, gesturing for Flinx and Sylzenzuzex to follow.

"*The* cave?" Flinx inquired later as he and the shaking thranx struggled to maintain the blistering pace. "You all share the same cave?"

Fluff seemed surprised. "Everyone shares the same cave."

"You're all part of the same family, then?" Sylzenzuzex panted.

"Everyone same family." The big native was obviously puzzled at these questions.

It occurred to Flinx that Fluff might have something other than immediate blood relationships in mind. A word with multiple meanings could be confusing to a human, to say nothing of an alien with a bare knowledge of the language.

"Are we of the same family, Fluff?" he asked slowly. Heavily furred brows wrinkled ponderously.

"Not sure yet," their unassuming savior finally told him. "Let you know."

Another hour of scrambling hectically over rocks and ditches, and Flinx found himself becoming winded. It was much worse for his companion, who finally settled to an exhausted halt in the middle of a clump of flowering growth.

"I'm sorry," she murmured, "I can't keep up. Tired and—cold."

"Wait," he instructed her. "Fluff, wait for us!" Ahead, the three Ujurrians paused, looked back expectantly.

Flinx knelt and gently examined the broken leghand. Though Sylzenzuzex wasn't putting any pressure on it, the joint didn't seem to be healing properly.

"We're going to have to splint that break," he muttered softly. She nodded agreement.

"Do at the cave," Fluff advised, having retreated to join them.

"I'm sorry, Fluff," Flinx explained, "but she can't go any further unless we fix this break." He considered, suggested, "You three continue on—leave a trail of broken branches and we'll catch up with you later."

"Foolish," the native advised. He moved nearer, his huge bulk dwarfing the slim youth. Flinx noted that Pip hadn't moved. If his pet expressed no concern, then it sensed no threat behind those advancing luminous eyes.

Fluff studied the quaking Sylzenzuzex, asked curiously, "What to do, Flinx-friend?"

"If you think it's foolish of us to follow your trail," he told the Ujurrian carefully, alert for any indication of outraged anger, "you could let us ride."

Bluebright scratched under his chin with a hind foot. "What is ride?" he asked interestedly.

"Means to carry thems instead of gems," a deep voice snorted with mild contempt at Bluebright's slowness. Flinx spun just in time to see the slightly phosphorescent form of Maybeso vanish into someplace else.

"Understand now," Fluff bubbled with satisfaction. "What do we do?"

"Just stand there," Flinx instructed, wondering as he walked up next to that brown wall if this was going to turn out to be such a clever idea after all. The big ursine head swung to watch him. "Now lie down on your stomach."

Fluff promptly collapsed with a pneumatic *whump*. Tentatively placing one foot against his left flank, Flinx reached up and grabbed a double handful of coarse hair and pulled hard. When no protest was forthcoming, he pulled again, hard enough this time to swing himself up on the broad back.

"Okay, you can get on all fours again," he told his jocular mount.

Fluff rose with hydraulic smoothness, his mind smiling. "I see. This is a better idea."

"A new fun thing," Moam agreed. She and Bluebright ambled over to Sylzenzuzex and spent a minute arguing over who should have the privilege of trying this new experience first. Moam won the debate. She moved next to the watching thranx and lay down next to her.

Sylzenzuzex studied that muscular torso apprehensively, glanced across at Flinx. He nodded encouragement, and she climbed carefully onto Moam, dug her claws into the thick fur, and hung on firmly.

They discovered now how patiently the Ujurrians had walked

before, to enable their two pitiful friends to keep up with them. If either Fluff or Moam noticed the weight on their backs it wasn't apparent, and the little group flew through the forest.

They had only one further mishap, when Flinx was nearly thrown. He barely managed to maintain his seat when Fluff rose without warning onto his two hind legs. He ran on like a biped to the manner born, and at a pace which no Terran bear could have duplicated. With seven limbs to hold on with, Sylzenzuzex kept her perch much more securely when Moam likewise rose to match Fluff's long two-legged stride.

It was impossible to tell how long or how far they had traveled when they descended into the last valley. From the beginning of the real run until the end, none of the ursinoids slackened their pace, though by then they were puffing slightly.

This third valley was dominated by the stream they'd run parallel to during their retreat. It broadened into another lake here, though one much smaller than that bordering the mining encampment now far behind them. A new variety of tree grew here among the quasi-evergreens. It had broad, yellow-brown leaves. Certain varieties, Flinx saw in the moonlight, held different kinds of berries, though these were scarce. Others boasted clusters of oval-shelled nuts, some big as coconuts.

"You eat those?" Flinx asked, pointing at the burdened branches.

"Yes," Fluff informed him.

"And you also eat meat?"

"Only in snowtime," his host explained quietly, "when the *baiga* and *maginac* do not bloom. Meat is no fun, and more work. It runs away."

They were moving toward a steep hillside now. In the soft moonlight Flinx saw that it was bare rock, devoid of talus. Several circles made dark stains against the gray granite.

Ujurrians of many sizes, including the first cubs they had seen, gamboled between the dark shoreline and the cave mouths.

"If one doesn't eat meat for variety," Fluff went on, "one begins to feel sick."

"Why don't you like to eat meat?" Sylzenzuzex wondered.

Flinx prayed she wouldn't involve their impressionable hosts in some abstract spiritual dialogue.

Fluff spoke as if to children. "Even the life of the *najac* or the six-legged ugly *coivet* is like a piece of the sun. When smothered, the warmth leaves it."

"We do not like to make bright things dark," Bluebright elaborated. "We would rather make dark things bright. But," he finished mournfully, "we don't know how."

They slowed to a walk, finally came to a complete stop outside the first of the caves. Flinx observed that the exterior of the entrance was composed of neatly piled boulders, chinked together with smaller rocks and pebbles in the absence of ferrocrete. Motioning for Fluff to lie down, he started to slide off the ursinoid's back.

A glance behind him showed a long glass spear of moonlight broken into pieces by the ripples and eddies on the lake. A look into the cave ahead revealed nothing but blackness.

"You said everyone shares the same cave, Fluff, but I see other openings in the mountainside."

"Is all same cave," the native explained.

"You mean they all connect inside the mountain somewhere?"

"Yes, all meet one another." A warm mental smile came to him. "Is all part of the game we play."

"The game?" Sylzenzuzex echoed, chilled despite the fact her thermal suit was set on high. When Fluff didn't comment, she wondered aloud, "Do you think we could build a fire?"

"Sure," Moam said cheerfully. "What is building a fire? Is like building a cave?"

Patiently, Flinx explained what was necessary, confident he would have to do so only once.

"We will go and gather the dead wood," Moam and Bluebright volunteered, when he had finished his explanation.

"What is this game you play, the one involving your warren, Fluff?" Flinx inquired when the other two had departed.

Fluff ignored the question, urged them into the cave where he silently exchanged greetings with another huge native.

"This is Softsmooth, my mate," he informed them in response to the question Flinx phrased in his mind. "You ask about the game, Flinx-friend? . . . Our parents' parents' parents many times over-and-dead worried that one day the cold would stay forever, and many lights among the family would vanish.

"I wouldn't call this a heat wave right now," Sylzenzuzex commented.

"The cold comes when the sun is smothered by the mountains," Fluff explained. "Our many-times parents felt it was becoming colder each year. It seemed to them that each year the sun grew smaller than the year before."

Flinx nodded slowly. "Your world has an elliptical orbit, Fluff, but it's not a regular orbit. According to the statistics I saw, it's swinging farther and farther away from your sun every century—though how your ancestors realized this I can't imagine."

"Many new concepts," a frowning Fluff murmured. "Anyhows, our parents many times dead decided how to fix. Should move closer to sun in certain way."

"They were talking about regularizing Ulru-Ujurr's orbit," Flinx husked. "But how did they *know*?"

"Have to ask ancestors," Fluff shrugged. "Very difficult to do."

"I'll bet," Sylzenzuzex agreed readily.

"Was a new way, though," the big native went on. "Diggers . . ."

"The people at the mine?"

"Yes. They make their own caves very warm. We asked them how we could make warm, too."

"What did they suggest?" Flinx wondered.

Fluff appeared confused. "They told us to dig big hole in the ground and then pull dirt in on top of ourselves. We tried and found it does make warm. But you can't move, and one gets bored that way. Also no light. We did not understand why they told us to do this way. They do not do for themselves. Why they tell us to do that, Flinx-friend?"

"That's the AAnn excuse for humor at work," he replied with quiet fury.

"AAnn?" Fluff queried. Moam and Bluebright returned, each buried under enormous armloads of dead branches.

"Some of the people at the mine," Flinx explained, "the ones with—the ones with the cold minds."

"Ah, the cold minds," Fluff echoed in recognition. "We did not see how such cold ones could give us knowledge on how to become warm. But we tried anyway."

Flinx couldn't look at the amiable native. "How . . . how many of the experimenters died?"

"Experimenters?"

"The ones who tried burying themselves?"

"Oh, Flinx-friend worries wrongly. No one died," Fluff assured him, feeling relaxation in the human's mind at these words.

"You see, we buried Maybeso. . . ."

"Here is wood," Moam said.

"Do you need more?" asked Bluebright.

"I think this is enough to last us at least a week," Flinx told them. As he spoke Sylzenzuzex was arranging some of the broken wood in a triangular stack, delicate truhands making a sculpture out of twigs and thin trunks.

Flinx eased himself up against the wall of the cave, feeling the coolness of the stone through the thermal suit. "How did your parents many times dead think you could regula—move closer to the sun?"

"By playing the game," Fluff told him again. "Game and making cave home is one."

"Digging caves is supposed to bring your world nearer its sun?" Flinx muttered, not sure he had heard correctly.

But Fluff signaled assent. "Is part of pattern of game."

"Pattern? What kind of pattern?"

"Is hard to explain," Fluff conceded languidly.

Flinx hesitated, voiced a sudden thought, "Fluff, how long have your people been playing the game of digging cave patterns?"

"How long?"

"How many of your days?"

"Days." Fluff decided it was time to consult with the others. He called Bluebright over, and Moam came with Bluebright. Softsmooth joined them and for a brief moment Maybeso winked into existence to add his comment.

Eventually Fluff turned back to Flinx, spoke with confidence as he named a figure. A large figure. Exceedingly so.

"Are you certain of your numerology?" Flinx finally asked slowly.

Fluff indicated the affirmative. "Number is correct. Learned counting system at the mine."

Sylzenzuzex eyed Flinx speculatively as he turned away, leaned back against the wall and stared at the dark cold roof above. She paused prior to starting the fire. "How long?"

There was a long pause before he seemed to come back from a far place, to glance across at her. "According to what Fluff says, they've been playing this game of digging interconnecting tunnels for just under fourteen thousand Terran years. This whole section of the continent must be honey combed with them. No telling how deep they run, either."

"What is honey?" wondered Moam.

"What is comb?" Bluebright inquired.

"How far is deep?" Fluff wanted to know.

Flinx replied with another question. "How long before this pattern is supposed to be finished, Fluff?"

The Ujurrian paused, his mind working busily. "Not too long. Twelve thousand more of your years."

"Give or take a few hundred," Flinx gulped dully.

But Fluff eyed him reprovingly. "No . . . exactly." Great glowing guileless eyes stared back into Flinx's own.

"And what's supposed to happen when this pattern is complete, when the game is finished?"

"Two things," explained Fluff pleasantly. "We move a certain ways closer to the warm, and we start looking for a new game."

"I see." He muttered half to himself. "And Rudenuaman thought these people were primitive because they spent all their time digging caves."

Sylzenzuzex hadn't moved to light the fire. Her face was a mask of uncertainty. "But how can digging a few caves change a planet's orbit?"

"A *few* caves? I don't know, Syl," he murmured softly. "I doubt if anyone does. Maybe the completed pattern produces a large enough alteration in the planetary crust to create a catastrophe fold sufficient to stress space the right amount at the right moment. If I knew more catastrophe math—and if we had the use of the biggest Church computer—I could check it.

"Or maybe the tunnels are intended to tap the heat at the planet's core power, or a combination of it and the fold . . . we need some brilliant mathematicians and physicists to answer it."

Sylzenzuzex eyed Fluff warily. "Can you explain what's supposed to happen, Fluff, and how?"

The bulky ursinoid gave her a mournful look, a simple task with those manifold-souled eyes. "Is sad, but do not have the terms for."

It was quiet in the cave then until the pile of dry wood coughed into life. Several small flames appeared at once, and in seconds the fire was blazing enthusiastically. Sylzenzuzex responded with a long, low whistling sigh of appreciation and settled close to the comforting heat.

"Is warm!" Moam uttered in surprise.

Bluebright stuck a paw close to the flames, drew it back hastily. "*Very* warm," he confirmed.

"We can teach you—hell, we've already taught you—how to make all the fires like this you want. I'm not saying you should abandon your game, but if you're interested Sylzenzuzex and I can show you how to insure your warmth during aphelion a lot sooner than twelve thousand years from now."

"Is easier," Fluff conceded, indicating the fire.

"And fun," added Moam.

"Listen, Fluff," Flinx began energetically, "why do your people work so long and hard for the cold minds and the others at the mine?"

"For the berries and nuts they bring us from far places," Softsmooth supplied from a little alcove cut into the cave wall.

"From far places," Bluebright finished.

"Why not travel there and get them for yourselves?"

"Too far," Fluff explained, "and too hard, Maybeso says."

Flinx leaned away from the wall, spoke in earnest tones, "Don't you understand, Fluff? I'm trying to show you that the people at the mine are exploiting you. They're working you as hard as you're willing, at tremendous profit to themselves, and in return they're paying you off with only enough nuts and berries to keep you working for them."

"What is profit?" asked Moam.

"What is paying off?" Bluebright wanted to know.

Flinx started to reply, then realized he didn't have the time. Not for an explanation of modern economics, the ratio of work to value produced, and a hundred other concepts it would be necessary to detail before he could explain those two simple terms to these people.

Leaning back again, he stared out the cave mouth past the flicker of the fire. A smattering of strange stars had risen above the rim of the mountains hugging the far side of the lake. For hours he remained deep in thought, while his hosts relaxed in polite silence and waited for him to speak again. They recognized his concern and concentration and stayed respectfully out of his thoughts.

Once he moved to help Sylzenzuzex resplint her broken joint with a stronger piece of wood. Then he returned to his place and his thoughts. After a while the stars were replaced by others, and they sank in their turn.

He was still sitting there, thinking, when he heard a sound like that made by a warehouse door mounted on old creaky hinges. Fluff yawned a second time and rolled over, opening saucerish eyes at him.

In a little while, the sun was pouring into the cave, and still Flinx hadn't offered so much as a good morning. They were all watching him curiously. Even Sylzenzuzex maintained a respectful silence, sensing that something important was forming beneath that unkempt red hair.

It was Fluff who broke the endless quiet. "Last night, Flinx-friend, your mind a steady noise like much water falling. Today it is like the ground after water has fallen and frozen—a sameness piled high and white and clean."

Sylzenzuzex was sitting on her haunches. With truhands and her one good foothand she was cleaning her abdomen, ovipositors, great compound eyes, and antennae.

"Fluff," Flinx said easily, as if no time had passed since they had last conversed, as if the long night had been but the pause of a minute, "how would you and your people like to start a new game?"

"Start a new game," repeated Fluff solemnly. "This is a big thing, Flinx-friend."

"It is," admitted Flinx. "It's called civilization."

Sylzenzuzex stopped in mid-preen and cocked her head sharply at him, though there was far less certainty in her voice when she spoke her objections: "Flinx, you can't. You know now why the Church placed this world Under Edict. We can't, no matter how we may feel personally about Fluff and Moam and the rest of these people, contravene the decision of the Council."

"Who says so?" Flinx shot back. "Besides, we don't know that the Edict was declared by the Council. A few bureaucrats in the right place could have made their own little godlike decision to consign the Ujurrians to ignorance. I'm sorry, Syl, but while I admit the Church is responsible for some good works, it's still an organization composed of humanx beings. Like all beings, their allegiance is first to themselves and second to everyone else. Would the Church disband if they could be convinced it was in the Commonwealth's best interests? I doubt it."

"Whereas you, Philip Lynx, are concerned first with everyone else," she countered.

Frowning, he started pacing the warming floor of the cave. "I honestly don't know, Syl. I don't even know who I am, much less what I am." His tone strengthened. "But I do know that in these people I see an innocence and kindness that I've never encountered on any humanx world." He stopped abruptly, stared out at the stars the morning sun made on the lake.

"I may be a young fool, a narrow-minded idealist—call it anything you like, but I think I know what I want to be now. If they'll have me, that is. For the first time in my life, I know."

"What's that?" she asked.

"A teacher." He faced the patient Ujurrians. "I want to teach you,

Fluff. And you Moam, and you, Bluebright and Softsmooth, and even Maybeso, wherever you are."

"Here," a voice grumbled from outside. Maybeso was lying on the low heatherlike growth before the cave entrance, rolling and stretching with pleasure.

"I want to teach all of you this new game."

"A big thing," Fluff repeated slowly. "This is not for us alone to decide."

"Others must be told," Bluebright agreed.

It took some time for everyone to be told. To be exact, it took eleven days, four hours, and a small basket of minutes and seconds. Then they had to wait another eleven days, four hours, and some minutes for everyone to answer.

But it took very little time for each individual to decide.

On the twenty-third day after the question was asked, Maybeso appeared outside the cave. Flinx and Sylzenzuzex were sitting by the lakeshore with Fluff, Moam, and Bluebright. They didn't notice the new arrival.

At that moment, Flinx was holding a long tough vine with sharp shards of bone attached to one end. While the others of their small group watched, he was teaching Fluff how to fish. Fluff looked delighted as he brought in the fourth catch of the day, a rounded silvery organism that looked like a cross between a blowfish and a trout.

Swimmers, the Ujurrians explained, had smaller lights than *najacs* and other land prey. Therefore fishing was a smaller evil than hunting.

"This too is part of the new game?" Moam inquired, duplicating the vine and bone hook arrangement perfectly on her first try.

"It is," Flinx admitted.

"That's good," Bluebright observed. "I hope everyone agrees."

Sylzenzuzex downed another clutch of berries. The sugar content was satisfactory, and the freshness enlivened her diet.

Miffed, Maybeso vanished from before the cave and reappeared next to her. She nearly fell off the smooth granite she'd been crouched on.

"Everyone has answered," Maybeso announced. "Most everybody says yes. We play the new game now."

"Fourteen thousand years of digging, down the excretory canal," Sylzenzuzex commented, climbing to her feet again and brushing at her abdomen. "I hope you know what you're doing, Flinx."

"Not to worry," Maybeso snorted at her. "Only here do we play

new game, now. Other places on backsides of the world will continue with old game. If new game is not fun," he paused slightly,
"we go back to old game." He turned a forceful gaze on Flinx.
"Forever," he added.

Flinx shifted uncomfortably as the enigmatic Ujurrian vanished.
Several weeks ago he had been so sure of himself, fired with a
messianic zeal he had never previously experienced. Now the first
real doubts were beginning to gnaw at his confidence. He turned
away from the stares around him—the ursinoids were well
equipped for staring.

"Is good," was all Fluff murmured. "How do we begin the game,
Flinx?"

He indicated the perfect hook-and-line arrangements everyone
had completed. "Fire was a start. This is a start. Now I want everyone who works for the people at the mine to come here to learn
with us—at nighttime, so the cold minds will not become suspicious. That would be," he hesitated only briefly, "bad for the
game."

"But when will we sleep?" Moam wanted to know.

"I won't talk too long," replied Flinx hopefully. "It's necessary.
Maybe," he added without much confidence, "we can accomplish
the first part of the game without making any light places dark.
Ours or anyone else's."

"Is good," declared Fluff. "We will tell the others at the mine."

Sylzenzuzex sidled close to him as the ursinoids dispersed.

"Teach them something basic about civilization while we help
ourselves," he murmured. "Once they get rid of the people at the
mine, they'll have a start at obtaining all the nuts and berries they
want. . . ."

12

"I hope," Teleen auz Rudenuaman ventured, "that the Baron concludes his hunt soon. We're running low on a number of synthetics and supplements for the food synthesizers, and we're nearly out of stock on several other unduplicatable items."

"There is no need to worry about the Baron," Meevo FFGW assured her from beneath his stiff human face.

There really wasn't any reason for concern, she insisted to herself, turning to look out the newly replaced pink window panels. On the mountain above, the miners worked steadily, efficiently as always.

The Baron had made several journeys through Commonwealth territory before. Nevertheless, she couldn't help experiencing a pang of concern every time one of her ships carried any of the disguised reptilians. She might survive, via a web of confusing explanations, if a Commonwealth patrol ship ever intercepted one of those missions and discovered the AAnn on board.

But she would lose an irreplaceable business associate. Not all of the AAnn aristocracy were as understanding of human motivations or as business-minded as Riidi WW.

The office communit buzzed for attention. Meevo rose and answered the call. Turning from the vista of forest and mountain, she saw his flexible humanoid mask twist repeatedly, a sign that incomprehensible reptilian contortions were occurring beneath.

"Said what . . . what happened?" The AAnn's thick voice rose. Teleen leaned closer. "What is going on, Meevo?"

Slowly the AAnn engineer replaced the communit receiver. "That . . . was Chargis at the mine. The escaped human and thranx have returned alive. He reports that there are many natives with them, and that the newcomers have joined with those working the mine in armed revolt."

"No, no . . ." She felt faint as his words overpowered her. "The natives, in arms . . . that's impossible." Her voice rose to a scream as she regained control of herself. "Impossible! They don't know the difference between a power drill and a beamer. Why would they want to revolt, anyway? What do they want . . . more nuts and berries? This is insane!" Her face elongated suddenly, dangerously. "No, wait—you said the human and thranx had returned with them?"

"So Chargis insists."

"But that's impossible, too. They should have died weeks ago from exposure. Somehow," she concluded inescapably, "they must have succeeded in communicating with the natives."

"I would say that is understatement," the engineer declared. "I was told the natives possessed no language, no means of communicating abstract concepts among themselves—let alone with outsiders."

"We have overlooked something, Meevo."

"As a nye, I say that is so," the engineer concurred. "But it will not matter in the end. It is one thing to teach a savage how to fire a weapon and another to explain the tactics of warfare to it."

"Where did they get weapons, anyway?" Teleen wondered, staring up the mountainside once more. The distant structures showed no sign of the conflict evidently taking place within.

"Chargis said that they overwhelmed the guard and broke into the mill armory," Meevo explained. "There was only one guard, as there are none here who would steal weapons. Chargis went on to say that the natives were clumsy and undisciplined in breaking in, and that the human and thranx tried hard to quiet them." He grinned viciously. "They may have unleashed something they cannot control. Chargis said . . ." The engineer hesitated.

"Go on," Teleen prompted, determined to listen to it all, "what else did Chargis say?"

"He said that the natives gave him the impression that they regarded this all as . . . a game."

"A game," she repeated slowly. "Let them continue to think that, even as they are dying. Contact all personnel on base," she ordered. "Have them abandon all buildings except those here, centered around Administration. We have hand beamers and laser cannon big enough to knock a military shuttle out of the sky. We'll just relax here, holding communications, food processing, this structure, and the power station until the Baron returns.

"After we've incinerated some of their number," she continued casually, as though she were speaking of pruning weeds, "the game may lose interest for them. If not, the shuttles will end it quickly enough." She glanced back at him. "Also have Chargis gather some good marksmen into two groups. They can use the

two big groundcars and keep our friendly workers bottled up
where they are. Mind the shooting, though; I don't want anything
damaged within the mine buildings unless it's absolutely unavoidable. That equipment is expensive. Barring that, they can have target practice on any natives they find outside."

She added, in a half-mutter, "But under no circumstances are
they to kill the human youth or the thranx female. I want both of
them healthy and undamaged."

She shook her head, disgusted, as the engineer moved to relay
her orders. "Damned inconvenient. We're going to have to import
and train a whole new clutch of manual laborers. . . ."

Everything, Flinx thought furiously, had gone smoothly and according to plan—at the start. Then he had watched helplessly as
months of planning and instruction were cast aside, submerged in
the uncontrollable pleasure the Ujurrians took in breaking into the
armory to get at the toys which made things vanish. Not even Fluff
could calm them.

"They're enjoying themselves, Flinx," Sylzenzuzex explained,
trying to reassure him. "Can you blame them? This game is much
more exciting than anything they've ever played before."

"I wonder if they'll still think so when some of their lights are
put out," he muttered angrily. "Will they think my game is still fun
after they've seen some of their friends lying on the ground with
their insides burnt out by Rudenuaman's beamers?" He turned
away, speechless with anger at himself and at the Ujurrians.

"I wanted to take over the mine silently, by surprise, without
killing anyone," he finally grumbled. "With all the noise they made
breaking into the armory, I'm sure the remainder of the building
staff heard and reported below. If she's smart, and she is,
Rudenuaman will place her remaining people on round-the-clock
alert and wait for us to come to her."

He grew aware of Fluff standing nearby, looked deep into those
expectant eyes. "I'm afraid your people are going to have to kill
now, Fluff."

The ursinoid looked back at him unwaveringly. "Is understood,
Flinx-friend. Is a serious game we play, this civilization."

"Yes," Flinx murmured, "it always has been. I'd hoped to avoid
old mistakes, but . . ."

His voice died away and he sat on the floor, staring morosely at
the metal surface between his knees. A cool leathery face rubbed
up against his—Pip. What he didn't expect was the gentle pressure

below the back of his neck, where his b-thorax would have been had he been thranx.

Looking back and up he saw faceted eyes gazing into his. "Now you can only do the best you can do," Sylzenzuzex murmured softly. The delicate truhand moved gently, massaging his back. "You have begun this thing. If you don't help finish it, that female down there will."

He felt a little better at that, but only a little.

A sharp crack like tearing metal foil sounded clearly. Flinx was on his feet, running in the direction of the sound, which was followed soon by a second. From a transparent panel running the length of an access corridor they were able to peer out and down the gentle slope on the right side of the large building. It was devoid of growth, which had been cleared off for a distance of twenty meters from the side of the structure.

Across the clearing, near the edge of the forest, they could see the hovering shapes of two groundcars. The same cars, Flinx noted, which had met their shuttle upon its arrival here so many weeks ago.

Each car mounted a small laser cannon near its front. Even as they watched, a thin red beam jumped from the end of one such weapon to the rocky slope ahead and above. There were several small shafts there, sunk into the cliffside.

Soon the clean rock was scarred by three black ellipsoids, modest splotches of destruction where brush had been crisped and the lighter silicate rocks fused to glass.

From somewhere at the upper end of the mine shaft a blue line from a hand beamer flashed down to strike the exterior of the groundcar. The car's screen was more than strong enough to absorb and dissipate such tiny bursts of energy.

Unexpectedly, the two cars turned and moved rapidly back downslope toward the main installation. Their muted hum penetrated into the corridor where Flinx and the others watched silently as the cars, floating smoothly a meter above the surface on thick cushions of air, turned and stopped just out of beamer range.

A moment later the familiar bulk of Bluebright came churning around the corner toward them. Pulling up sharply, he let his words spill out in between steam-engine pants: "They have killed Ay, Bee, and Cee," he gasped, his enormous eyes wider than usual.

"How did it happen?" Flinx asked quietly. "I *told* everyone that they wouldn't fire into these buildings. They won't risk damaging their equipment because they're not yet convinced we pose a serious threat to them."

Fluff took over the explanation, having already communicated silently and rapidly with Bluebright. "Ay, Bee, and Cee went outside the metal caves."

"But *why?*" Flinx half asked, half cried.

"They thought they had created a new idea," Fluff explained slowly. Flinx showed no comprehension, so the ursinoid continued. "These past many days you have told us over and over that this game you call civilization should be played according to common sense, logic, reason. From what Bluebright tells me, Ay, Bee, and Cee decided among themselves that if this was so the cold minds and the others would see that it was reason and logic to cooperate with us, since we have taken their mine from them.

"They went out without weapons to talk logic and reason to those in the machines. But," and Fluff's voice grew hurt at the wonder of it, "those did not even listen to Ay, Bee, and Cee. They killed them without even listening. How can this thing be?" The shaggy head peered puzzledly down at Flinx. "Are not the cold minds and the ones like you down there also civilized? Yet they did this thing without talking. Is this the reason you speak of?"

Flinx and Sylzenzuzex had yet to see one of the jovial ursinoids angry. Fluff appeared close to it, though it really wasn't anger. It was frustration and lack of understanding.

Flinx tried to explain. "There are those who don't play the game fair, Fluff. Those who cheat."

"What is cheating?" wondered Fluff.

Flinx endeavored to explain.

"I see," Fluff announced solemnly when the youth had finished. "This is a remarkable concept. I would not have believed it possible. The others must be told. It explains much of the game."

Turning, he and Bluebright left Flinx and Sylzenzuzex alone in the corridor.

"How long," she asked, staring out the window panel toward the distant complex, "do you think they will sit down there before growing impatient and coming up after us?"

"Probably until the shuttles return. If we haven't resolved this before then—no, we *must* finish this before the Baron comes back. . . . We have nothing but hand beamers here. They have at least two surface-to-space, gimbal-mounted laser cannons down by the landing strip, in addition to the smaller ones mounted on the groundcars. Possibly more. We can't fight that kind of weaponry. I hope Fluff and Bluebright can get that through their family's hairy skulls." He moved up alongside her to stare out the panel.

"I'm sure the two big guns are directed toward us right now. If we tried a mass retreat they'd incinerate the lot of us, just like Ay, Bee, and Cee. We're going to have to—"

A high-pitched scream suddenly floated shockingly down the corridor. It rose from mid-tenor to the high, wavering shriek of the utterly terrified . . . then stopped. It was undeniably human.

The second scream was not. It came from an AAnn. Then came more screams of both varieties.

Pip was fluttering nervously above Flinx's shoulder and cold perspiration had started flowing from beneath the crop of red hair.

"Now what?" he muttered uneasily, as they started off in the direction of the screams. Every so often another scream would be heard, followed at regular intervals by an answering sound from the opposite camp.

In one respect they were all alike—short and intense.

They must have heard two dozen before encountering Moam and Bluebright. "What happened?" he demanded. "What were those screams?"

"Lights," began Moam.

"Going out," Bluebright finished.

Flinx discovered he was trembling. There was blood on Moam's naturally grinning mouth. Both broad, flat muzzles were stained with it. There were small groups of workers and guards who had been unsuccessful in their attempt to flee the captured mine.

"You've killed the prisoners," was all he could stutter.

"Oh yes," Moam admitted with blood-curdling cheerfulness. "We not sure for a while, but Fluff explained to us and family. Cold minds and people down there," then gesturing in the direction of the main base, "cheat. We think we understand now what is to cheat. It means not playing the game by the rules, yes?"

"Yes, but these aren't my rules," he whispered dazedly, "not my rules."

"But is okay with us," Bluebright offered. "We understand these rules not yours, Flinx-friend. Not good rules. But cold minds make up new rules, we play that way okay, too."

The Ujurrians waddled off down the corridor.

Flinx sank to his knees, leaned up against the wall. "Game, it's still all a game to them." Suddenly he looked at Sylzenzuzex and shuddered. "Goddamn it, I didn't want it to happen like this."

"You are he who rides the *grizel*," Sylzenzuzex said without anger. "You have wakened it. Now you must ride it."

"You don't see," he muttered disconsolately. "I wanted Fluff and Moam and Bluebright and all the rest of them to be spared all our mistakes. I want them to become the great thing they can—and not," he finished bitterly, "just a smarter version of us."

Sylzenzuzex moved nearer. "You still hold the *grizel* by its tails, Flinx. You haven't been thrown yet. It is not you who taught them to kill—remember, they do hunt meat."

"Only when they have to," he reminded her. "Still," and he showed signs of relaxing some, "this may be a time when they have to. Yes, a snowtime hunt, to live. The rules have been altered, but we still have rules. They just need to be defined further."

"That's right, Flinx, you tell them when it's all right to kill and when it's not."

He looked at her oddly, but if there was anything hidden beneath the surface of her words he couldn't sense it. "That's the one thing I never wanted to do, even by proxy."

"What made you think you'd ever have the opportunity?"

"Something . . . that happened not so long ago," he said cryptically. "Now it's been forced on me anyway. I've been shoved into the one position I vowed I'd never hold."

"I don't know what you're rambling on about, Flinx," she finally declared, "but either you ride the *grizel* or it tramples you."

Flinx looked up the corridor to where Moam and Bluebright had turned the corner. "I wonder who's going to ride whom?"

The answer came several days later. There had been no assault from below, as he'd guessed, although the two groundcars pranced daily right next to the walls of the mine structures, daring anyone to show a fuzzy head.

Fluff woke them in the small office Flinx and Sylzenzuzex had chosen for sleeping quarters. "We have made a backtrap," he told them brightly, "and we are going to catch the groundcars now."

"Backtrap . . . wait, what . . . ?" Flinx fought for awareness, rubbing frantically at his eyes still rich with sleep. Vaguely he seemed to recall Fluff or Softsmooth or someone telling him about a backtrap, but he couldn't form a picture of it.

"You can't stop a groundcar with a . . ." he started to protest, but Fluff was already urging him to follow.

"Hurry now, Flinx-friend," he insisted, listening to something beyond the range of normal hearing, "is started."

He led them to the mill supervisor's office, a curving transparent dome set in the southernmost end of the building.

"There," Fluff said, pointing.

Flinx saw several of the ursinoids running on all fours over exposed, bare ground. They were racing for the upper slopes, near the place where the main shaft entered the mountain. Still well behind, Flinx could make out the two groundcars following.

"What are they doing out there!" Flinx yelled, leaning against the transparent polyplexalloy. He looked helplessly at Fluff. "I told you no one was to go outside the buildings."

Fluff was unperturbed. "Is part of new game. Watch."

Unable to do anything else, Flinx turned his attention back to the incipient slaughter.

Moving at tremendous speed, the three ursinoids passed the near end of the building, below Flinx's present position. Fast as they were, though, they couldn't outrun the groundcars. First one burst, then another jumped from the muzzles of the laser cannon. One hit just back of the trailing runner, impelling him to even greater speed. The other struck between the front-runners, leaving molten rock behind.

The three runners, Flinx saw, would never make the open doorway at the upper end of the mill. The groundcars suddenly seemed to double their speed. When they fired again, they would be almost on top of the retreating Ujurrians.

He visualized three more of the innocents he had interfered with turned to ash against the gray stone of the mountainside.

At that point the ground vanished beneath the groundcars.

There was a violent crash, the whine of protesting machinery, as the two vehicles were unable to compensate fast enough for the unexpected change in the surface. Still moving forward, both abruptly dipped downward and smashed at high speed into the far wall of the huge pit.

Flinx and Sylzenzuzex gaped silently at the enormous rift which had unexpectedly appeared in the ground.

"Backtrap," Fluff noted with satisfaction. "I remembered what you tell us about how the little machines work, Flinx-friend." Battered humans and AAnn—the latter's surgical disguises now knocked all askew—were fighting to get control of themselves within the wreckage of the two cars.

A mob of furry behemoths was pouring from the mine buildings toward the pits. Flinx could make out the narrow ledges of solid earth and rock that ran like a spiderweb across the rift. They formed safe pathways across which the three decoy runners had retreated. By the same token, they were far too narrow to provide adequate support for the groundcars. The surface against which their air jets pushed had been suddenly pulled away.

Hundreds of thin saplings now lined the edges of the pit. These had been used to support the heavy cover of twigs, leaves, and earth, all carefully prepared to give the appearance of solid ground.

New screams and the flash of blue hand beamers lit the pit as the ursinoids poured in. Flinx saw a three-hundred-kilo adolescent male pick up a squirming AAnn and treat its head like the stopper of a bottle. He turned away from the carnage, sick.

"Why is Flinx-friend troubled?" Fluff wanted to know. "We play game with their rules now. Is fair, is not?"

"Ride the *grizel*," Sylzenzuzex warned him in High Thranx.

By the head, not the tail, something echoed inside him. He forced himself to turn back and watch the end of the brief fight.

As soon as it became clear to the observers down below what had happened, a red beam the thickness of a man's body reached upward from a small tower at the base's far end. It passed unbroken through several sections of forest, cutting down trees like a lineal scythe and leaving the stumps smoking, until it impinged on the mountainside to the left of the pit. A flare of intense light was followed by a dull explosion.

"Get everyone back inside, Fluff," Flinx yelled. But an order wasn't necessary. Their work concluded, the ursinoids who had assaulted the pit were already running, dodging, scampering playfully back into the mine.

Flinx thought he saw movement far below as the top of the tower started to swivel toward him, but apparently calmer heads prevailed. The mills itself was still out of bounds for destructive weaponry. Rudenuaman had no reason yet to raze the mountainside, to turn the complex mine and mill into a larger duplicate of the small slag-lined crater which now bubbled and smoked where the heavy laser had struck. Much as she might regret the loss of the two groundcars and their crews, she was not yet desperate.

So no avenging light came to destroy the building. The simple natives were to be permitted their one useless victory. Undoubtedly, Flinx thought with irony, Rudenuaman would attribute the brilliant tactic to him, never imagining that the huge dull beasts of burden had conceived and executed the rout entirely by themselves.

"I wonder," he said to Sylzenzuzex over a meal of nuts and berries and captured packaged food, "if there's any point to continuing this. I've never really felt as if I were in control of things. Maybe . . . maybe it would be better to run back to the caves. I can still teach from there—we both can—and we have a lot of life left in us."

"You're still in control, Flinx," Sylzenzuzex told him. She tapped one truhand against the table in a pattern few human ears would have recognized. "The Ujurrians want you to be. But you go ahead, Flinx. You tell them all," and she waved a hand to take in the whole mine, "that they should go back to their caves and resume their original game. You tell them that. But they won't forget what they've learned. They never forget."

"O'Morion knows how much knowledge they've acquired from this mine already," Flinx mumbled, picking at his food.

"They'll go back to digging their cave pattern, but they'll retain that knowledge," she went on. "You'll leave them with the game rules Rudenuaman's butchers have set. If they ever *do* show any initiative of their own, after we've gone . . ." She made a thranx shrug. "Don't blame yourself for what's happened. The Ujurrians are no angels." Whistling thranx laughter forced her to pause a moment. "You can't play both God and the Devil to them, Flinx. You didn't introduce these beings to killing, but we'd better make certain we don't teach them to enjoy it.

"Moping and moaning about your own mistakes isn't going to help us or them. You've put your truleg in your masticatory orifice. You can pull it out or suffocate on it, but you can't ignore it." She downed a handful of sweet red-orange berries the size of walnuts.

"We not enjoy killing," a voice boomed. They both jumped. The Ujurrians moved with a stealth and quietness that was startling in creatures so massive. Fluff stood in the doorway on four legs, filling it completely.

"Why not?" Sylzenzuzex asked. "Why shouldn't we worry about it?"

"No fun," explained Fluff concisely, dismissing the entire idea as something too absurd to be worthy of discussion. "Kill meat when necessary. Kill cold minds when necessary. Unless," and beacon-eyes shone on the room's other occupant, "Flinx say otherwise."

Flinx shook his head slowly. "Never, Fluff."

"I think you say that. Is time to finish this part of game." He gestured with a paw. "You come, too?"

"I don't know what you have planned this time, Fluff, but yes," Flinx concurred, "we come, too."

"Fun," the giant Ujurrian thundered, in a fashion indicating something less than general amusement was about to ensue.

"I don't want any of the buildings down there damaged, if it can be avoided," Flinx instructed the ursinoid as he led him and Sylzenzuzex down corridors and stairways. "They're filled with knowledge—game rules. Mechanical training manuals, records, certainly a complete geology library. If we're going to be marooned on this world for the rest of our lives, Fluff, I'm going to need every scrap of that material in order to teach you properly."

"Is understood," Fluff grunted. "Part of game not to damage buildings' insides. Will tell family. Not to worry."

"Not to worry," Flinx mimicked, thinking of the alert and armed personnel awaiting them at the base of the mountain. Thinking also of the two atmosphere-piercing laser cannons set to swivel freely in the small tower.

Fluff led them downward, down through the several floors of mill and mine, down to the single storage level below ground. Down past rooms and chambers and corridors walled with patiently waiting, snoozing, playful Ujurrians. Down to where the lowest floor itself had been ripped up. There they halted.

Moam was waiting for them, and Bluebright and Softsmooth and a dimly glimpsed flickering something that might have been Maybeso, or might have been an illusion caused by a trick of the faint overhead lighting.

Instead of stopping before a solid ferrocrete barrier, they found three enormous tunnels leading off into total darkness.

Light from the room penetrated those down-sloping shafts only slightly, but Flinx thought he could detect additional branch tunnels breaking off from the three principal ones farther on.

"Surprise, yes?" Fluff asked expectantly.

"Yes," was all a bewildered Flinx could reply.

"Each tunnel," the ursinoid continued, "come up under one part of several metal caves below, in quiet place where cold minds are not."

"You can tell where the floors aren't guarded?" Sylzenzuzex murmured in amazement.

"Can sense," Moam explained. "Is easy."

"Is good idea, Flinx-friend?" a worried Fluff wondered. "Is okay part of game, or try something else?"

"No, is okay part of game, Fluff," Flinx admitted finally. He turned to face the endless sea of great-eyed animals. "Pay attention, now."

A massive stirring and roiling shivered through the massed bodies.

"Those who break into the power station must shut everything off. Push every little knob and switch to the—"

"Know what means *off*," Bluebright told him confidently.

"I probably should leave you alone, you've managed fine without my help," Flinx muttered. "Still, it's important. This will darken everything except for the tower housing the two big cannon. They'll be independently powered, as will the shuttlecraft hangar beneath the landing strip. Those of you who get into the cannon tower will have to—"

"Am sorry, Flinx-friend," a doleful Fluff interrupted. "Cannot do."

"Why not?"

"Floors not like this," the ursinoid explained, eyes glowing in the indirect lighting. He indicated the broken ferrocrete lying around. "Are thick metal. Cannot dig through."

Flinx's spirits sank. "Then this whole attack will have to be called off until we can think of something that will eliminate that tower. They can destroy all of us, even if they have to melt the entire remaining installation to do so. If Rudenuaman were to slip away and reach the tower, I don't think she'd hesitate to give the order. At that point she'd have nothing further to lose."

"Not mean to make you worry, Flinx-friend," comforted Bluebright.

"Nothing to worry about," Moam added.

"Have something else to take care of tower," explained Fluff.

"But you . . ." Flinx stopped himself, went on quietly, "no, if you say you do, then you must."

"What about the three who got themselves killed?" Sylzenzuzex whispered. "They thought they had something, too. This time there are many more lives at stake."

Flinx shook his head slowly. "Ay, Bee, and Cee were playing by different rules, Syl. It's time for us to trust our lives to these. They've risked theirs often enough on our say-so. But just in case . . ."

He turned to Fluff. "There is one thing I must do even if this fails and we all end up dead. I want to come up through the floor of the big living house, Fluff. There is something in there that I need the use of."

"In this tunnel," Fluff told him, indicating the shaft at far left. "Are ready, then?"

Flinx nodded. The huge Ujurrian turned and shouted mental instructions. They were accompanied by a nonverbal emotional command.

A soft, threatening rumble responded . . . a hair-curling sound as dozens, hundreds of massive shapes bestirred themselves in long lines reaching back into the far places of the mine.

Then they were moving down the tunnels. Flinx and Sylzenzuzex hugged close to Fluff, each with a hand tight in his fur. Sylzenzuzex's night vision was far better than Flinx's, but the tunnel was too black even for her acute senses.

If the Ujurrians' activities had been detected, Flinx reflected, they might never re-emerge into the light. They could be trapped and killed here with little effort.

"One question," Sylzenzuzex asked.

Flinx's mind was elsewhere when he responded: "What?"

"How did they excavate these tunnels? The ground here is rock-laden and the tunnels seem quite extensive."

"They've been digging tunnels for fourteen thousand years, Syl." Flinx found he was moving with more and more confidence as nothing appeared to deal death from above them. "I imagine they've become pretty good at it. . . ."

Teleen auz Rudenuaman panted desperately, nearly out of breath, as she limped along the floor. The sounds of heavy fighting sounded outside and below her.

A massive brown shape appeared at the top of the stairwell which she had just exited. Turning, she fired her beamer in its direction. It disappeared, though she was unable to tell whether she'd hit it or not.

She had been relaxing in her living quarters when the attack had come—not from the distant mine, but from under her feet. Simultaneously, hundreds of enormous, angry monsters had exploded out of the sublevels of every building. Every building, that is, except for the cannon tower. She'd barely had time to give the order for those powerful weapons to swing around and beam every structure except the one she was in when they had been destroyed.

A peculiar violet beam no thicker than her thumb had jumped the gap between the uppermost floor of the far-off mine and the tower's base. Where it had touched there was now only a deep horizontal scar in the earth. It had been so quick that she'd neither seen nor heard any explosion.

One moment the tower had been there—three stories of armor housing the big guns—and the next she'd heard a loud hissing sound like a hot ember being dropped in water. When she turned to look, the tower was gone.

Now there was no place to run to, nothing left to bargain with. Her badly outmatched personnel—human, thranx and AAnn alike—had been submerged by a brown avalanche.

She'd tried to make for the underground shuttle hangar in hopes of hiding there until the Baron's return, but the lower floors of this building were also blocked by swarms of lemur-lensed behemoths. The ground outside was alive with them.

It made no sense! There had been perhaps half a hundred of the slow-moving natives living in the immediate vicinity of the mine. Surveys had revealed a few hundred more inhabiting caves outside the vicinity.

Now there were thousands of them, of all sizes, overrunning the installation—overrunning her thoughts. The crash of overturned furniture and shattered glassalloy sounded below. There was no way out. She could only retreat upward.

Limping to another stairwell, she started up to her apartment-office on the top floor. The battle was all but over when the cannon tower had been eliminated. Meevo confirmed that when he reported the power station taken. Those were the last words she heard from the reptilian engineer.

With the station, the power to communications and the lifts had gone. It was hard for her to mount the stairwell, with her bad leg. Her jumpsuit was torn, the carefully applied makeup covering her facial scars badly smudged. She would meet death in her own quarters, unpanicked to the end, showing the true self-confidence of a Rudenuaman.

She slowed at the top of the stairs. Her quarters were at the far end of the hall, but there was a light shining from inside the chamber nearest the stairwell. Moving cautiously, she slid the broken door a little farther back, peered inside.

The light was the kind that might come from a small appliance. There were many such self-powered devices on the base—but what would anyone be doing with one here and now, when he should have a beamer in his fist?

Holding her own tightly, she tiptoed into the chamber.

These quarters had not been lived in since the demise of their former occupant. The light was coming from a far corner. It was generated by a portable viewer. A small, slight figure was hunched intently before it, oblivious to all else.

She waited, and in a short while the figure leaned back with a sigh, reaching out to switch the machine off. Fury and despondency alternated in her thoughts, to be replaced at last by a cold, calm sense of resignation.

"I ought to have guessed," she muttered.

The figure jerked in surprise, spun about.

"Why aren't you decently dead, like you're supposed to be?"

Flinx hesitated, replied without the hint of a smile, "It wasn't destined to be part of the game."

"You're joking with me . . . even now. I should have killed you the same time I finished Challis. But no," she said bitterly, "I had to keep you around as an amusement."

"Are you sure that's the only reason?" he inquired, so gently that she was momentarily taken aback.

"You play word games with me, too." She raised the muzzle of the beamer. "I only regret I haven't got time to kill you slowly. You haven't even left me that." She shrugged tiredly. "The price one pays for undersight, as my aunt would say, corruption be on her spirit. I am curious, though—how did you manage to tame and train these creatures?"

Flinx looked at her pityingly. "You still don't understand anything, do you?"

"Only," she replied, her finger tightening on the beamer's trigger, "that this comes several months too late."

"Wait!" he shouted pleadingly, "if you'll give me one min—"

The finger convulsed. At the same time someone doused her eyes with liquid fire. She screamed, and the beam passed just to the right of Flinx to obliterate the viewer nearby.

"Don't rub!" he started to yell, rushing around the chair he'd been sitting in—already too late. At the moment of contact she'd dropped the beamer and begun rubbing instinctively at the awful pain in her face. She was on the floor now, rolling over and over.

The distance between them was no longer great, but by the time he reached her she was unconscious and stiff. Thirty seconds later she was dead.

"You never did take the time to listen, Teleen," he murmured, kneeling numbly by the doubled-over corpse. Nervously flicking his long tongue in and out, Pip settled softly on Flinx's shoulder. The minidrag was taut with anger.

"Your life was too rushed. Mine's been too rushed, also."

Something moved in the doorway. Looking up, Flinx saw a wheezing Sylzenzuzex standing there, favoring her splinted leg-hand. One truhand had a firm grip on a thranx-sized beamer.

"I see you found her," she observed, her breath coming through the spicules of her b-thorax in long whistles. "Softsmooth tells me that the last bits of resistance are almost cleaned out." Her compound eyes regarded him questioningly as he looked back down at the body.

"I didn't find her. She found me. But before I could make her listen, Pip intervened. I suppose he had to; she would have killed me." Unexpectedly, he glanced at her and smiled.

"You should see yourself, Syl. You look like a throwback from Hivehom's pre-tranquility days. Like a warrior who has just concluded a successful brood raid on a neighboring hive. A wonderful advertisement for the compassionate understanding of the Church."

She didn't respond to the jibe. There was something in his voice. . . . "That's not like you, Flinx." She studied him as he turned back to stare at the corpse, trying to remember everything she knew of human emotion. It seemed to her that his interest in this woman, who for a few *tams* of *vackel* had worked willingly with the sworn enemies of humanx kind, was abnormal.

Sylzenzuzex was not her uncle's equal when it came to intuitive deduction, but neither was she stupid. "You know something more about this human female than you have said."

"I must have known her before," he whispered, "though I don't remember her at all. According to the time intervals given on the tape that's not too surprising." He gestured limply at the chamber behind him. "This was Challis' apartment." His hand returned to indicate the corpse. For a moment his eyes seemed nearly as deep as Moam's. "This was my sister."

Not until the following afternoon, after the bodies had been efficiently buried by the Ujurrians, did Sylzenzuzex insist on hearing about everything that had been recorded on the stolen tape.

"I was an orphan, Syl, raised on Moth by a human woman named Mother Mastiff. The information I found said that I'd been born to a professional Lynx named Rud, in Allahabad on Terra. The records also said I was a second child, though they didn't give details. Those facts were to be found on the tape Challis stole, the tape I didn't read until last night.

"My mother also had an elder sister. My mother's husband, who according to the tape was not my father, gave that elder sister a position in his commercial firm. After he died, under still unexplained circumstances, the sister took control of the company and built it into a considerable business empire.

"It seems my mother and her sister were never the best of friends. Some of the details of what amounted to my mother's captivity, and that's what it reads like, are . . ." He had to stop for a moment.

"It's easy to see how a mind like Challis' would be attracted to details like that. My mother died soon after her husband. A number of unexplained incidents followed. No one could be certain, but it was theorized they might be attributable in some way to her male nephew. So . . . I was disposed of. A small sale in so large a commercial concern," he added viciously.

"It amused the elder sister, Rashalleila, to keep the girl niece around. The sister's name was Nuaman. The niece—my sister—was called Teleen. She became a mirror image of her aunt, took the company from her, and merged her mother's name with her aunt's. Symbospeeched it. Teleen of Rud and Nuaman . . . Teleen auz Rudenuaman.

"As for me—I was long forgotten by everyone. Challis' researchers were interested in the part about my causing some 'unexplained incidents,' as they were called. He never troubled to make any other connections from the information."

They walked on in silence, past the long gouge in the earth where the cannon tower had stood. Fluff, Moam, Bluebright, and Softsmooth trailed behind. They came upon a small building set alongside the landing field. Earlier, one of the Ujurrians had discovered that it led down to the extensive shuttlecraft hangar. The hangar held complete repair and construction facilities for shuttlecraft, as would be necessary on an isolated world like this. There was also an extensive machine shop and an enormous technical library on all aspects of Commonwealth KK-ship maintenance. It would make a very useful branch of the Ujurrian school Flinx was planning to set up.

"I didn't have time to ask last night, Fluff," Flinx began, as they passed the end of the scar, "how did you manage that?"

"Was fun," the big ursinoid responded brightly. "Was Moam's idea mostly. Also a young She named Mask. While others dug tunnels, they two read much that was in books at the mine."

"Made some changes in cold minds' cave digger," Moam supplied.

"The press drill," murmured Sylzenzuzex, "they must have modified the press drill. But how?"

"Change here, add this," explained Moam. "Was fun."

"I wonder if *modified* is quite the word for turning a harmless tool into a completely new kind of weapon," Flinx mused. He looked skyward. "Maybe we'll let Moam and Mask and their friends play with the library and machine shop below. But first we have some other modifications that have to be carried out in a hurry. . . ."

The big freighter came out of KK drive just inside the orbit of Ulru-Ujurr's second satellite, moving nearer on short bursts from its immensely powerful space-spanning engine. The freighter entered a low orbit around the vast blue-brown world, remaining directly above the only installation on its surface.

"Honored One, there is no response," the disguised AAnn operating the ship's communicator reported.

"Try again," a deep voice commanded.

The operator did so, finally looked up helplessly. "There is no response on any of the closed-signal frequencies. But there is something else—something very peculiar."

"Explain," the Baron directed curtly. His mind was spinning.

"There is evidence of all kinds of subatmospheric broadcasting, but none on any frequencies I can tap into. And none of it is directed at us, despite my repeated calls."

A man named Josephson, who was a very important executive in Rudenuaman Enterprises, moved next to the Baron. "What's going on down there? This isn't like Madam Rudenuaman."

"It is not like many things," observed the Baron cautiously. He turned his attention to another of the control pod operatives. "What is the cloud cover like above the base?"

"Clear and with little wind, sir," the atmospheric meteorologist reported quickly. "A typical Ujurrian autumn day."

The Baron hissed softly. "Josephson-sir, come with me, please."

"Where are we going?" the confused executive wanted to know, even as he followed the Baron down the corridor leading to the far end of the command blister.

"Here." The Baron hit a switch and the door slid back. "I require maximum resolution," he instructed the on-duty technician.

"At once, Honored One," the disguised reptilian acknowledged as he hurried to make the necessary adjustments to the surface scope. Sitting down alongside the tech, the Baron punched the requisite coordinates into the scope computer himself.

Then he remained motionless for several minutes, staring through the viewer. Eventually he moved aside, gestured that Josephson should take his place. The human did so, adjusting the focus slightly for his eyes. He gave a verbal and physical start.

"What do you see?" the Baron inquired.

"The base is gone, and there's something in its place."

"Then I may not be mad," the Baron observed. "What do you see?"

"Well, the landing strip is still there, but something like a small city is climbing from the lakeshore up into the mountains. Knowing the terrain, I'd say several of the unfinished structures are a couple of hundred meters high." His voice faded with astonishment.

"What does this suggest to you?" the Baron asked.

Josephson looked up from the scope, shaking his head slowly.

"It suggests," the Baron hissed tightly, "that the structures may be built deeply into the mountains. By whom or how deeply we will not know, unless we go down to see for ourselves."

"Wouldn't advise that," a new voice boomed.

Josephson gave a cry and stumbled out of the chair, pressing himself back against the console. The technician and the Baron whirled, both reaching simultaneously for their sidearms.

An apparition stood solidly in the center of the room. It was a good three meters tall, standing on its hind legs, and its bulk nearly dented the deck. Huge yellow eyes glared balefully down at them.

"Wouldn't advise it," the apparition repeated. "Get lost."

The Baron's hand beamer was aimed—but now there was nothing to shoot at.

"Hallucinations," Josephson suggested shakily, after his voice returned.

The Baron said nothing, walked to the place where the creature had stood. He knelt in a way no human could, hunting for something on the floor. "A very hirsute hallucination," he commented, examining several thick, coarse hairs. His mind was churning furiously.

"You know I've never been outside the main installation," Josephson declared. "What was it?"

"An Ujurrian primitive," the Baron explained thoughtfully, rubbing the hairs between false-skinned fingers.

"What . . . what was it talking about?"

Disgust was evident in the Baron's voice. "There are times when I wonder how you humans ever achieved half of what you have."

"Now, look," the executive began angrily, "there's no need to get abusive."

"No," the Baron admitted. After all, they were still within Commonwealth territory. "There is no reason to get abusive. I apologize, Josephson-sir." Turning, they left the room and the wide-eyed technician.

"Where are we going now?"

"To do what the creature said."

"Just a minute." Josephson eyed the unblinking AAnn aristocrat firmly. "If the Madam is in trouble down there . . ."

"*Sssisssttt* . . . use your brain, warm-blood," the Baron snorted. "Where there was a small base there is now a rapidly growing city. Where there used to be a single welcoming signal there is now a multitude of peculiar local communications. From a few clusters of cave-dwelling natives, there comes a teleport who advises us curtly not to land. Who advises us curtly—in your vernacular I might add, Josephson-sir—to make haste elsewhere.

"I think it reasonable, considering the evidence, for us to comply quickly. I act according to realities and not emotions, Josephson-sir. That is why I will always be one who gives orders and you will always be one who takes them." He hurried his pace, pushing past the man and leaving him standing, to gape down the corridor after him.

As directed by the Baron, the freighter left Ulru-Ujurr's vicinity at maximum velocity. Resting in his sumptuous cabin, the Baron pondered what had taken place during his absence. Something of considerable importance, with unknowable implications for the future.

Of one thing he was certain: Madam Rudenuaman and the enterprise they had collaborated on no longer existed. But there could be a host of reasons why.

That the natives were more than ignorant savages now seemed certain . . . but how much more certain he could not say. A single genius among them could have been mnemonically instructed to deliver what had been, after all, an extremely brief message. A new experimental device could have projected him aboard the freighter.

The burgeoning city below could be the product of the Church, the Commonwealth, a business competitor, or an alien interloper. This section of the Arm was still mostly unexplored; anything could be setting itself up on an isolated, unvisited world like Ulru-Ujurr.

He had done well by the venture. There were a number of small stones still in his possession, which he could ration out slowly to the Commonwealth over the years. His status at the Emperor's court had risen considerably, though the Imperial psychotechnicians' scheme of implanting suicidal impulse-plays into the Janus jewels and then selling them to important humans and thranx would now have to be abandoned.

That was too bad, for the program had been very successful. Yet this could have been worse. Whatever had wiped out the installation and Madam Rudenuaman could also have taken him, had he not gone in pursuit of the human child.

A pity the way she happened to encounter that human patrol vessel, forcing him to abandon any hope of eliminating her. Almost as if she'd known what she was doing. But it did not matter much, he knew. Let her rave about Ulru-Ujurr to any who might be credulous enough to listen—for now that world was no concern of his.

In the future, given the inevitable triumph of the Empire, he could return with an Imperial fleet, instead of skulking about in disguise like this and in the forced company of despised mammals and insects. Then he might re-establish control, nay, sovereignty over that enigmatic world, holding all the glory and profits to be gained therefrom for himself and the house of WW.

Maybe so, he mused pleasurably, maybe so.

He did not hear the voice that echoed in response from the depths of Someplace Else. A voice that echoed . . . maybe not!

The day dawned bright and warm. Sylzenzuzex found she could walk about freely with only the flimsiest covering.

She had developed a special rapport with the shy adolescent female called Mask, who had turned out to be a wonderful guide to the history and unexpectedly complex interrelationships of the Ujurrians. So Sylzenzuzex was reveling in her study of a subject dear to her heart.

Perhaps someday it would form the basis for a monograph, or even a full dissertation, one important enough to win reinstatement in the Church for her. Although the discovery that the Church had indeed been responsible for quarantining these people continued to cause her to question that organization's standards, and her own future participation in it.

She left her quarters in the building, intending to mention yesterday's revelations to Flinx. But he did not seem to be anywhere around, nor was he at the landing strip school, nor at any of the factory centers ringing the old mine. One of the ursinoids finally directed her to a place at the far end of the valley, where she had once fled Rudenuaman's grasp. After a fair climb up a steep bluff, she found him sitting cross-legged on a ledge consorting with a local insect no larger than his finger. It was enameled green and ochre, with yellow-spotted wings.

Pip was darting through the nearby bushes, worrying an exasperated, sinuous mammal half his size.

From here one could look back down the full length of the valley, see the azure lake cradled between snowcapped peaks, and watch the steady progress of construction along the south shore.

When Flinx finally turned to her, he wore an expression so sorrowful it shocked her.

"What's the matter . . . why so sad?" she inquired.

"So who's sad?"

She shook her valentine-shaped head slowly. When he didn't respond, she gestured toward the lake valley.

"I don't know what you have to be disappointed about. Your charges seem to have taken to your game of civilization with plenty of enthusiasm. Is it the ship Maybeso boarded? Whatever he told them must have been effective. They haven't come back, and there's been no sign of another ship in the months since."

By way of reply he pointed toward the north shore of the lake. A vast metal superstructure was rising there. It was nearly as long as the lake itself.

"Something about the ship?"

He shook his head. "No . . . about the reason behind it. Syl, I've only accomplished half of what I set out to do. I know that my mother's dead, but I still don't know who my father was or what happened to him." He stared hard at her. "And I want to know, Syl. Maybe he's long dead, too, or alive and even a worse human animal than my sister turned out to be; but *I want to know*. I *will* know!" he finished with sudden vehemence.

"How does that connect with the ship?"

Now he cracked a wan smile. "Why do you think the Ujurrians are building a ship?"

"I don't know . . . for fun, to explore . . . why?"

"It's my present from them—Moam's little surprise. He knows I want to go looking for my father, so they're doing their best to help me look. I told them they couldn't construct a KK-drive ship here

. . . that it had to be done clear of a planet's gravity. You know what he said? 'We fix . . . too much trouble other way.'

"He located an Ujurrian—skinniest one I ever saw—who thinks only in mathematical terms. She's so weird—her name-translation came out as 'Integrator'—she can almost understand Maybeso. Moam set her the problem. Two weeks ago she cracked the problem of landing in a gravity well on KK-drive. Commonwealth scientists have been trying to solve that puzzle for a couple of hundred years."

He sighed. "All to help me find my father. Syl . . . what happens if the Ujurrians don't find the rest of the cosmos, our civilization, to their liking? What if they decide to 'play' with it? *What have we unleashed?*"

She sat back on trulegs and foothands and pondered. Long minutes passed. The gem-encrusted bug flew away.

"If nothing else," she told him finally, staring down at the ship, "a way to go home. You worry overmuch, Flinx. I don't think our civilization will hold much of interest for these creatures. It's *you* they're interested in. Remember what Maybeso said . . . if this new game bores them, they'll go back to their old one."

Flinx considered this, appeared to brighten. Then abruptly he rose, brushed the dust from his legs. "I suppose you're right, Syl. I can't do any good worrying about it. When they finish the ship, it *will* be time to go home. I need Mother Mastiff's acerbity, and I need to lose myself again, for a while." He glanced up at her oddly. "Will you help?"

Sylzenzuzex turned great, glowing multifaceted eyes on Pip, watched as the minidrag folded pleated wings to dive down a burrow after the retreating mammal. Sounds of scuffling came from below.

"It promises to be intriguing . . . from a purely scientific point of view, of course," she murmured.

"Of course," Flinx acknowledged, properly straight-faced.

A narrow reptilian head popped out of the burrow and a pointed tongue flicked rapidly in their direction. Pip stared smugly back at them, a Cheshire cat with scales. . . .

To learn more about the adventures of Flinx and the Universe of the Commonwealth, visit the author's award-winning Web site, www.alandeanfoster.com.

ALAN DEAN FOSTER has written in a variety of genres, including hard science fiction, fantasy, horror, detective, western, historical, and contemporary fiction. He is the author of the *New York Times* bestseller *Star Wars: The Approaching Storm,* as well as novelizations of several films including *Star Wars,* the first three *Alien* films, and *Alien Nation.* His novel *Cyber Way* won the Southwest Book Award for Fiction in 1990, the first science fiction work ever to do so. Foster and his wife, JoAnn Oxley, live in Prescott, Arizona, in a house built of brick that was salvaged from an early-twentieth-century miners' brothel. He is currently at work on several new novels and media projects.